The CLUNY CROSS

A MONK'S TALE

MARK BLACKHAM

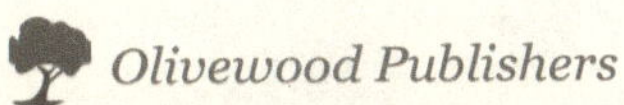

Olivewood Publishers

The Cluny Cross — A Monk's Tale

Previously published as *Cluny Cross — A Mad Medieval Tale* by Mark Blackham (2011). This is a revised edition.

editor@olivewoodpublishers.com

Blackham, Mark

The Cluny Cross — A Monk's Tale

Historical Fiction, Adventure, Crusades, Middle East, Byzantium, Persia,

ISBN: 978-0-9877878-3-5 (Paperback)

ISBN: 978-0-9877878-8-0 (E-book)

Distributed by Ingram

This story is dedicated to the indispensable lessons of history.

CONTENTS

MAPS

N
FLANDERS
EUROPE
NORMANDY
Rhine
HOLY ROMAN EMPIRE
(GERMANY)
KINGDOM OF FRANCE
BURGUNDY
PROVENCE
Corsica
KINGDOM OF LEON
Tyrrhenian
Sardinia
AL-ANDALUS
Sicily
MAGYARS
Danube
PATZINAKS
SERBS AND CROATS
Adriatic
BYZANTIUM
Black Sea
Apulia
Aegean
Crete
TURKS
ASIA
RAMIRO'S JOURNEY
Mediterranean
EGYPT
1. COMPOSTELA
2. LEON
3. SALAMANCA
4. CORDOBA
5. MADRID
6. TOULOUSE
7. LONDON
8. GHENT
9. PARIS
10. CLUNY
11. LYON
12. CHAMBERY
13. TORINO
14. MONFERRATO
15. GENOA
16. PISA
17. ROME
18. TERRACINA
19. NAPLES
20. MELFI
21. BARI
22. BRINDISI
23. DYRRACHIUM
24. OHRID
25. THESSALONICA
26. KOMOTINI
27. ADRIANOPLE
28. ROUSSA
29. CONSTANTINOPLE
30. NICOMEDIA
31. NIKEA
32. GALLIPOLI
33. SMYRNA
34. CAIRO
500 miles
800 km

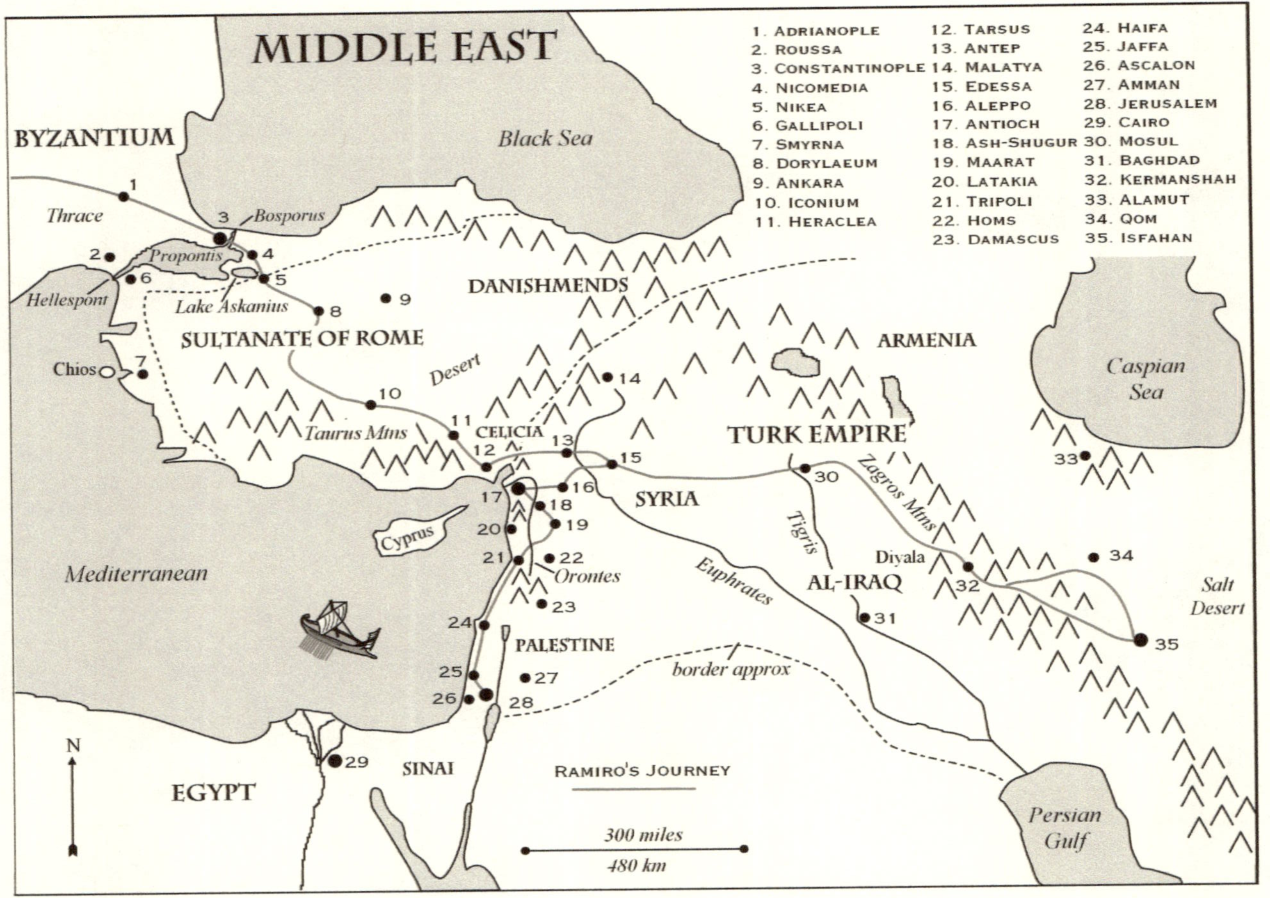

MIDDLE EAST
BYZANTIUM
Thrace
Black Sea
Bosporus
Propontis
Hellespont
Lake Askanius
Chios
SULTANATE OF ROME
DANISHMENDS
Desert
Taurus Mtns
CELICIA
ARMENIA
TURK EMPIRE
Cyprus
Mediterranean
Orontes
SYRIA
Tigris
Euphrates
AL-IRAQ
Zagros Mtns
Diyala
Caspian Sea
Salt Desert
PALESTINE
border approx
EGYPT
SINAI
Persian Gulf
N
RAMIRO'S JOURNEY
300 miles
480 km
1. ADRIANOPLE
2. ROUSSA
3. CONSTANTINOPLE
4. NICOMEDIA
5. NIKEA
6. GALLIPOLI
7. SMYRNA
8. DORYLAEUM
9. ANKARA
10. ICONIUM
11. HERACLEA
12. TARSUS
13. ANTEP
14. MALATYA
15. EDESSA
16. ALEPPO
17. ANTIOCH
18. ASH-SHUGUR
19. MAARAT
20. LATAKIA
21. TRIPOLI
22. HOMS
23. DAMASCUS
24. HAIFA
25. JAFFA
26. ASCALON
27. AMMAN
28. JERUSALEM
29. CAIRO
30. MOSUL
31. BAGHDAD
32. KERMANSHAH
33. ALAMUT
34. QOM
35. ISFAHAN

PROLOGUE

In the seventh century, on the west coast of the Arabian Desert, a man by the name of Muhammad Ibn Abdullah inspired a religious transformation not seen since the days of Christ. Known to his followers as "The Prophet," his teachings ignited flames of holy fervor throughout Arabia, inciting an unprecedented sense of Arab brotherhood and unity. His zealous devotees, convinced they were the chosen of God, stormed out of Mecca to conquer the world in the name of Al-Lah, *The* God.

By the year 1000, Muslim empires had reached their zenith, controlling the whole of the Middle East, North Africa, and Spain. Their ships ruled the Mediterranean, seizing Sicily, Corsica, Sardinia, and southern Italy. And much to the horror of all Christians, Muslim raiders managed to breach the mouth of the Tiber to plunder the outskirts of Rome.

But while the Arabs were busy building their empire, Europe was also undergoing sweeping change. Charlemagne, King of the Franks, created a new European empire, a Christian empire, which he strengthened and solidified by reforming language, religion, money, and government. Over time, the new Europeans forgot their humble past and came to believe they lived in a resurrected Holy Roman Empire. The Pope of Rome was their Supreme Bishop, and they were the chosen of God.

Meanwhile, the remains of the East Roman Empire teetered on the brink of extinction, losing Egypt, Syria, and Anatolia to Muslim armies. This once indomitable empire, now known as Byzantium, was reduced to a stub of its former self, barely hanging on to a shred of the Balkans, Greece, and Thrace. The people of Byzantium followed Roman bureaucracy and law, but in language and culture they were Greek. They believed the Church of Constantinople was the true center of Christianity and their Patriarch was the True Protector of the Faith, and they were the chosen of God.

The two churches, West and East, one Latin, the other Greek, vied for full control of the Mother Church, squabbling endlessly over points of rank and liturgy—even as Muslim armies beat on their doorsteps. But as the eleventh century came to a close, both factions began to realize that the preservation of Christendom, the Domain of Christ, required a new solidarity and a new direction. And so, with a desperate sense of urgency and fear, they began a concerted effort to combat an intelligent and terrifying opponent—Dar Al-Islam—the Domain of Islam.

1 - EUROPE

ABBEY OF CLUNY

June 1089

In 1089, the Abbey of Cluny in western France was a wealthy and power-ful monastic institution, owning and operating over one thousand priories across Europe. It was ruled by the Order of Saint Benedict, a religious brother-hood with deep connections to the popes of Rome. As such, the Benedictines maintained special privileges and sweeping powers, all of which transformed the Order into a government unto itself.

Indeed, four monks from Cluny went on to become popes, including the ven-erable Pope Gregory the Seventh and, in 1088, his successor, Pope Urban the Second, the very man who later rallied a band of fanatical peasants to the First Crusade in 1096.

With such far-reaching powers, the Abbey of Cluny became the undisputed bastion of Christian authority throughout the whole of Europe. And ruling this vast enterprise was Hugh the Great, the Abbot of Cluny, a shrewd man who had assumed a position of unprecedented ecclesiastical power—a maker and shak-er of popes, emperors, and empires.

But not all were pleased with the expansive power of Cluny. King Henry, Em-peror of the Holy Roman Empire, was furious with Pope Gregory's ongoing at-tempts to interfere with his local church affairs, and so he appointed his own pope, Giberto of Ravenna. And by force of arms, he installed Giberto on the Pope's Chair at the Lateran Palace.

But while the kings, popes, and bishops of Europe squabbled over land and power, other troubles brewed afar, ones that were about to shake the very foundation of Christian power. Only Abbot Hugh and a few other prominent individuals, informed as they were of wider political events, perceived the true magnitude of this existential threat.

And such was the state of affairs on this bright Spring day in 1089 when a cou-rier clutching a weathered brown envelope could be seen rushing across the manicured grounds of the abbey.

A LETTER

A loud knock aroused Ramiro from his morning meditations. With a grunt, he rose from his chair to open the door of his small chamber. He was somewhat startled to see the courier and was about to offer greetings, but before he could do so, the man shoved a small package into his hand, telling him it had come all the way from Jerusalem. And without another word, he rushed away.

Ramiro stared at the thick envelope. It was dry and brittle and water stains nearly obliterated the writing. The wax seal was already broken, but that came as no surprise because the Abbot scrutinized all the monk's mail.

"Jerusalem!" he muttered, still standing by the open door. "Who in God's name do I know in Jerusalem?" He immediately groped inside with thick fingers, pulling the folded page out slowly. It was made of fine paper, a paper rarely seen among the rough parchments of Burgundy. Old and yellowed, it crackled when he unfolded it. He straightened it out as carefully as he could, expecting to see Latin or Greek, but it was neither. For a moment, he stared at the odd words, written poorly in a faltering hand. So familiar... "Why... it's Castilian!" he said aloud. He struggled a bit before the tongue of his youth came to his head.

> To my beloved son, Ramiro, son of Sancho of León, blessings and God's love be upon you. From your mother, Isabella Agueda, daughter of Eustace of León.

My mother? He put a hand to the door jamb to steady himself. What cruel farce is this? He slammed the door shut before teetering back to his cluttered desk by the window, gripping the back of his chair to ease himself down. "Impossible!" he shouted to the stark, stone walls of his cubicle.

The bell tower sounded the call to Lauds, but the rich peal failed to reach his ears. He pulled back the sleeves of his black robe, holding the letter up to the waxing light of dawn, straining at the letters.

> I write to you from the Church of the Holy Sepulcher in Jerusalem. To my great happiness, I learned of your whereabouts through a conversation with a fellow monk, Russell of Mainz, who said he met you some years ago while visiting the Abbey.

Russell! I remember him... but this cannot be! He looked at the envelope again, turning it over in his hand. It was old, but it looked authentic, as did the remains of the seal. He looked again at the letter heading, written in Latin and Greek. And my name—my full name—my father's name. Who would know these things? But it cannot be her...

Below his window, fellow monks sauntered along garden pathways, on their way to sing Psalms in praise of Our Lord, but he took no notice. He moved closer to the light of the window and read on.

> With deep sadness, I must tell you that your brothers have all died in war, and your poor sister passed away in childbirth some years ago. After you disappeared, we feared you were dead too and lost all hope. In our grief, your father and I embarked on a pilgrimage to the Holy Land, where we hoped to receive God's forgiveness and the remission of our sins. But, alas, it is to my great sorrow to tell you that your poor father died of a fever in Tripoli. Only by the Grace of God did I manage to arrive in Jerusalem without him. And by His Will, the Church has taken me in as a bride of Christ.
>
> I am pleased, my dear son, that you have dedicated your life to God. The Abbey of Cluny is held in high regard, even in these distant lands. But now I enter the twilight of my life and you must come to me before I take the hand of Jesus. How I long to look once more upon your gentle face. I entreaty you, my dear son. Come, and I will bestow upon you a holy relic, one I have had in my possession for many years. Come to Jerusalem so that I may place this cherished piece in your hands and gaze upon your dear face one last time.
>
> In the year of Our Lord, 1088.

I thought they were all slaughtered by the Moors! I saw the ruins of our home! ... the charred remains ... the devastation. I was told there were no survivors!

He wept again—for his father, his brothers, and my dear sister, oh dear God, she was always so cheerful. But after a moment of sorrow, a glimmer of joy danced amid his gloomy thoughts. He wiped away his tears with a sleeve and smiled a little. My dear mother lives! And she is safe in Jerusalem!

ABBOT HUGH

"Jerusalem? You want to go to Jerusalem?" Abbot Hugh stared in wonder. "That is very curious indeed."

Ramiro tipped his head, candlelight glinting from his dark-brown eyes. "Why is that Reverend Father?" he asked in a rich baritone.

"How did you find out?" asked Hugh. "What do you know?"

"About what, my Lord?"

"About Jerusalem."

"Well... apart from Biblical passages and rumor, I know little indeed, dear Abbot."

Unlike the black habits of the monks, the Abbot's robe was the color of burgundy. It had a peaked hood that wrapped tight around his pale, clean-shaven face, and long bell-sleeves draped from his arms.

With narrowed eyes, Hugh scanned the stout, swarthy monk who stood before him. Perhaps he knows nothing, he thought, but can I trust him?

Hugh had accepted Ramiro to the abbey only because he came from a distinguished family in León, and because he wanted to please Alfonso, the King of León, who petitioned on his behalf. Ramiro was just twenty at the time and now, ten years later, he had become an influential figure in the monastery. Hugh had reluctantly appointed him to the position of dean only because he proved so popular among his fellow monks. But he's too odd, he thought. And too damned dark for my liking—black hair, black eyebrows—even his eyes are as black as ink. His skin... it's as tawny as that stinking German ale.

Whereas Ramiro was considered a foreigner, Hugh was born to nobility in the Kingdom of Burgundy. In his early life, he showed such religious zeal and piety that his father gave him to the priesthood and, by the age of fourteen, he became a novice at Cluny. He was so inspired and devoted to the work of God that he soon rose in the ranks and, by the young age of twenty-five, was unanimously elected Abbot. Now sixty-five, Hugh had become one of the most powerful figures in Western Christendom, a shrewd advisor to popes and kings.

Despite his power, Hugh had trouble meeting Ramiro's intent gaze. The monk's deep, dark stare rattled him, like the baleful, penetrating glare of a... well, of a demon. Alarmed by his thoughts, he dropped his eyes to his desk. "Uh, tell me, Brother Ramiro, why do you have a sudden urge to make a pilgrimage to the Holy Land?"

Ramiro told him about the letter from his mother.

"Oh, yes. I remember that letter. None of the priors could read it."

"It's written in Castilian, Father, the tongue of León."

"No matter, Brother Ramiro. I understand your concerns about your mother," he paused, putting his hands together. "But when you made your vows to the Church, you willingly forsook your earthly family. You should be more concerned with the divine family of God here at the abbey."

"Of course, Reverend Father," he said with a twinge of regret. It had been easy to give up those things he never had... but now it was different, his mother lived. He persisted. "May I suggest, Abbot, that my mother's holy relic would be a wonderful addition to our collection." He opened his big hands in a conciliatory gesture. "We could place it beside the vial of Christ's blood."

"Yes, yes, perhaps, Brother," said Hugh, somewhat ruffled by the suggestion. "And what exactly is the nature of this relic?"

"Alas, my mother did not say, but whatever it is, it must have originated in the Holy Land itself."

Hugh tapped his fingers on the desk, glancing up from time to time. If the relic was real, it might indeed be a powerful one. "But you are one of my deans. And one of our best *medicina*. Who would replace you?"

"Brother Anselm is quite capable, Abbot."

Hugh nodded slowly, his face deadpan. "Perhaps, but nonetheless, I cannot afford to send another monk to Jerusalem."

"Another? What do you mean?"

"If you must know, I'm sending Brother Bernold on a special assignment."

"Brother Bernold? Forgive me again, Father, but why would he want to go to Jerusalem? You know he's more than sixty."

"And so am I, Brother Ramiro."

"Excuse me, Abbot, I meant no offense."

"Never mind. Brother Bernold is in fine health, and he will be safely accompanied by men-at-arms." He rubbed his smooth chin, pausing in thought. "So you know nothing of this?"

"Of what?"

Hugh leaned forward over his desk, studying Ramiro for a time before he finally spoke. "I'll tell you in confidence," he said in a low voice. "We also received a letter from Pope Urban himself, may God protect him, and I was asked to choose one of my monks as an emissary to Jerusalem. His Holiness feels that, on certain matters, he can trust only his brethren here at Cluny."

"It came in the same mailing?" Ramiro blurted with a little too much enthusiasm. "Then perhaps it's a sign, dear Abbot, perhaps it's God's will that I go to Jerusalem!"

Hugh glared. "Hold your tongue, Brother!" He squawked in an aging voice. "And do not presume to lecture me on God's will!"

Ramiro bowed once more. "Forgive me, Father, for my errant ways."

The Abbot waved a hand of finality. "I've already arranged to send Brother Bernold. He knew our blessed Pope when he was the grand prior here. Besides, he's the best qualified."

"But... but Bernold is in poor health, my Abbot. I know, I've treated him many times. His heart is bad. And... and he cannot even speak Greek. And he has no experience with the Muslims as I do."

Hugh leaned back in his velvet chair, brushing the desktop with the wide sleeves of his burgundy robe. The lips of his clean-shaven face curled in a sneer. "What arrogance and pride, Brother Ramiro. Must I remind you of your vow of humility? Must I whip you for your self-obsession?"

Ramiro bowed his head again. "Lord, I am a sinner not worthy to lift his eyes to heaven."

"Not all of us view your experiences as advantageous, Brother." He tapped his fingers in a drum roll. "In fact, they can lead us to view you and your actions with some suspicion. Frankly, I doubt your full commitment to our Holy Cause. Your opinions are much too heretical for my liking, and you spend too much time in the library instead of attending to your duties in the infirmary. The librarian tells me you prefer manuscripts in the heathen tongue."

"That's Arabic, Reverend Father," he said softly. "But I'm only translating the works you suggested—those dealing with science, medicine, and healing, nothing more."

Hugh lowered his wrinkled forehead before raising his eyes skeptically. "And I admire your perseverance in this regard, Brother, but you must not ignore your other duties to the Holy Church."

"Yes, Abbot," Ramiro persisted. "And consider, my Lord, how my talents may assist the Church. I speak several languages and know some customs of the land."

Hugh slammed the desktop with the palm of his hand, the sharp noise echoing from stark, stone walls. "I am well aware of your many talents, Brother Ramiro!" he bellowed with growing annoyance. "And you would do well to remember that it is only by the Grace of God they come to you. He who glories, let him glory in the Lord!"

"Yes, of course, Reverend Father."

"These are difficult times," said Hugh with a scowl. "And I must be cautious. I worry more about your inclinations." He rose from his chair. "Besides, you well know the monastery itself is considered *to be* Jerusalem, do you not?"

"Yes, of course, Father."

"Then you must understand that, in the eyes of God, there is no need for your pilgrimage to the Holy City... and that fact alone should be enough for you!" He shook his head, waving him out. "I deny your request. You may leave."

In a fit of frustration, Ramiro tossed his book across his desk, stacked high with Arabic manuscripts obtained from the Moors in Spain, many of them translations of Greek, Persian, and Hindi, extremely rare in the West. He was always astounded by the science of these people and greatly moved by their literature, arts, and sublime architecture. But the complicated mathematics of

Al-Khwarizmi were beyond him, he simply could not fathom *al-jabra*. Books on medicines and herbs were more to his liking, especially those by Ibn-Sina, an Iranian physician, and those by Ibn-Ishaq, a Christian scholar from Iraq.

But even these compelling subjects no longer caught his interest, he could not concentrate. He closed his eyes and bowed his head, chewing absently on a hairy knuckle as he prayed inwardly. Dear Jesus, help me get to Jerusalem, help me to see my dear mother. I beseech you, my Lord, I will offer many prayers of thanksgiving at the Holy Sepulcher... if only, by your Grace, you grant me this prayer.

STRANGE HORSEMEN

It seemed that everybody came to watch Brother Bernold leave for Jerusalem. They gathered in the courtyard near the gate, praying aloud for his safe journey.

> *The Lord will keep you from all evil*
> *He will keep your life*
> *The Lord will keep your going out*
> *and your coming in*
> *from this time on and forever more*

They were captivated, not just because the Abbot allowed Bernold to ride a horse, which meant it must be a very important journey indeed, but also because of those who waited for him. Just outside the monastery walls, a small army of knights milled about making a tremendous racket. The monks could hear their guttural voices, the constant clack of armor, and the neighs and nickers of many horses.

"Who are they?" Ramiro asked a fellow monk.

"I don't know," he replied. "It seems no one knows."

Ramiro left suddenly, walking fast to the library. He scrambled up three floors with an agility that belied his stocky physique, rushing to a nearby window. There they were, a small but noisy horde, hundreds of armed men and hundreds of horses along with many servants, even women and children. He caught a few words on the breeze, it sounded like a German tongue. Their banner was unfamiliar, but their dress told all—the heavy armor, the flat-topped helmets, the war hammers, the flared axes, the heavy swords, the furs, the stink. They must be Normans—maybe worse. He shuddered as he watched Brother Bernold join them with his novice in tow, and the long procession began to head south, taking the road to Lyon.

"Back to your work!" the Prior shouted from the forecourt. "This is no business of yours! Back to your work!"

A CANTICLE

The stained-glass windows seemed to come alive in the morning light. Biblical scenes, full of brilliant colors, cast a warm kaleidoscope across a long series of white stone columns towering to an ornate roof far overhead. The monks filed in through the main doorway, gathering on the cool wooden benches of the nave and choir. Soon after they took their seats, the presiding monk made the sign of the cross on his forehead before raising his voice from the apse.

> *O God come to my assistance,*
> *O Lord make haste to help me...*

All monks chanted in unison. Ramiro made the motions and mouthed the words, but his thoughts drifted to other things. He looked up to the glistening windows, resting his eyes on a simple scene of color, one depicting the glorious city of Jerusalem bathed in a golden light. Here, in a lull of prayer, he fixed his gaze, staring until his focus blurred, the vibrant colors blending as one.

After a long pause, the presiding monk looked down on the large hymn-book spread open on the lectern before him. Its thick vellum pages, bound between leather-covered boards, were inscribed in a lyrical calligraphy and adorned in the margins with bright illustrations of angels and biblical themes. "The Gloria," he called out, and all monks stood to sing.

A deep chorus reverberated through the enormous church, the sound echoing from its granite walls like the harmony of a second choir. Ramiro moved his lips, but his mind still wandered, preoccupied with rending thoughts. He had given his life to God and the monastery, but now he wanted to leave. He had an overwhelming, defiant urge to head for Jerusalem, with or without the Abbot's consent. His rebellious thoughts made his heart pound. What of my vows of obedience? Could I ever return? He closed his eyes, praying for an answer.

The Gloria ended and they began to chant a Psalm. Ramiro had no need to look at his prayer book, he knew the words by heart. He began to relax and was feeling somewhat soothed by the time they rose again to sing the Canticle of Zechariah.

> *Blessed be the Lord, the God of Israel*
> *He has come to his people and set them free...*

Israel..., he dreamed wistfully. O Jerusalem!

A DEATH

The days passed and Ramiro spent his time making herb potions, tending to the sick, and translating texts for the library. He was on his knees pulling weeds in the garden when a gasping novice ran up to him. The skinny lad stood breathless, quivering with agitation and excitement. But he restrained himself, waiting for permission to speak.

"What is it boy?" Ramiro asked, not looking up. "Can't you see I'm busy here?"

"He's dead, Father!" the novice blurted.

Ramiro looked up. "Who's dead?

"Brother Bernold, Father," the boy choked, sweeping a tear from his cheek.

Ramiro glanced up at the lad, unsure if he had heard correctly. "You say he's dead?"

"Yes, Father Ramiro. Died on the road to Chambéry. In the mountains of Savoy. They say he just collapsed—dead on the ground."

Ramiro paled. "Father of mercies! Dear, oh dear." Still on his knees, he put his hands flat to the ground to steady himself. Guilt gripped his thoughts as he recalled, with growing remorse, his earlier prayers. *I prayed to get to Jerusalem, my Lord—but not this way, not by the death of Brother Bernold!*

A Cross

Abbot Hugh was shocked at the news and began to wonder, with mounting trepidation, if Brother Ramiro was right—*perhaps it is God's will that he goes to Jerusalem.* After all, his letter did arrive the same day as the Pope's—perhaps this really was an omen, a part of Our Lord's Divine Plan. *Could it be so?* These anxious thoughts compelled him, but he had to fight hard to swallow his aversion to this nettlesome monk.

"Well, Brother Ramiro," he said begrudgingly, "you did try to warn me about Brother Bernold's health. I must admit, I never believed it was that serious. A sad business indeed." He glanced down for a moment, trying to appear distressed, but he soon raised his head, changing his tone abruptly. "And now I'm faced with the regrettable and difficult task of choosing another to take his place." He paused, watching Ramiro. "Prior Michael has shown an interest. He speaks Greek, you know."

"Yes, Abbot," Ramiro replied. "But his grammar is poor, and he has been confined within the walls of the monastery since the age of six."

Hugh scowled at the brawny monk. It was all he could do not to belt him across the head as he would a disobedient novice. He well knew Ramiro was the best qualified, but he deeply resented his cocky self-assurance and his light-handed disregard for authority and, because Hugh was a man of letters himself, he also resented Ramiro's gifted erudition. With considerable effort, he quelled his rising ire and spoke again. "And now, with some reluctance, I am forced to consider your request to go to Jerusalem. But tell me, do you know anything at all of current affairs in Italy or among the Greeks?"

Ramiro thought for a moment. "Well, Reverend Father, I know the rightful pope, His Eminence Pope Urban, is kept out of Rome by King Henry's army. And... and that the King has appointed his own pope, a man called Giberto."

Hugh slapped hard on his desk. "The damned anti-pope!" He spat the words. "And he dares to call himself Pope Clement!"

Ramiro's cheeks reddened. He had never heard the Abbot speak so vehemently.

Hugh went on. "And now, our dear Holy Father hides like a thief among the bloody Normans of Italy. He cannot even set foot in Rome!" He fell silent for a moment before jumping up from his chair. "But His Holiness, may God protect him, he's the only one who can continue our reforms." His voice grew louder. "Only he can unite the Church." He clenched a fist. "We must unite! Or the heathen will destroy us!"

Ramiro nodded cautiously. "Yes, yes, Abbot, I agree wholeheartedly."

"Are you aware, Brother Ramiro, that the very existence of Christendom is at stake?"

Ramiro's eyes widened. "Well, I... I know of the battles with the Muslims, Reverend Father. I was once a soldier, as you know. But does it indeed threaten all Christendom?"

"Indeed it does!" Hugh cried, raising thin gray eyebrows. "The infidels hold Hispania as you know. And now, they beat on the shores of southern France. They rule the Middle Sea and the islands within it!" He leaned forward, again slapping his desktop. "Have you forgotten already that one of our very own abbots was abducted by these vile creatures?"

"I remember, my Lord, it was Abbot Maiolus, but that was about a hundred years ago."

"Yes, Maiolus. You see!" He pointed a finger at Ramiro, as if proving a point. "These pagans are a perennial threat. Meanwhile, we squabble among ourselves like children!"

Ramiro fidgeted, not sure how to respond.

Hugh paced. "To start, we must drive that devil Giberto from Rome... him and his German thugs. Once that is done, we can control the West countries." He paused for a moment before shaking his head sadly. "But alas... the Church does not yet have the power to oust them—even with the help of those conniving, bloodthirsty Normans. We need the armies of the Greek King and the support of the Greek Church. We must find a way to convince their chief bishops... you know the ones I mean."

"They are called patriarchs, Abbot."

"Yes, patriarchs, of course. We need to settle our differences and unite under a single banner of Christ. We need someone to confer with them, someone who can reach a compromise on our disagreements."

"It is God's will, my Lord."

"If we can unite forces, we will seize the Holy Land and secure it for the True Faith."

Ramiro raised his thick brow. "That will be a formidable task, Reverend Father."

Hugh sat down again. "There are many dangers on the road to Jerusalem. I need a man who is not afraid to face them—a man who does not fear for his life. Can I rely on you, Brother Ramiro, to complete this assignment?"

Ramiro could barely mask his glee. "Oh yes, very much so!" But then he hesitated, tipping his head. "And uh,... and what would this assignment be, Reverend Father?"

"You will be my legate. You will meet with these bishops... I mean patriarchs... and attempt to resolve our differences. I want you to write down all you see on your journey. I need to know what people think, the social order, the roads, the lay of the land... military capabilities and such."

"Military capabilities?"

"As a precaution, of course. For the safety of Christian pilgrims."

"Yes, of course, Abbot. Uh, do you mean the military of the Greeks?"

"The Greeks, yes... and among the vile heathen, those cursed Muhammadans who corrupt the blessed Holy Land." He leaned forward. "You must send me a full report every three or four months. You may take ample stationary supplies from the *scriptorium*."

"Thank you, Father."

"It is an important journey," said Hugh. "I will give you two horses and a donkey for your gear. First, you must travel to Melfi, south of Rome. There, you will hold council with His Holiness." He picked up an envelope. "You will take this letter to him as a means of identification. You must deliver it personally."

Ramiro nodded, receiving it carefully, as if it were a holy relic, and immediately worried about how he would carry it.

Hugh continued. "The Pope will then give you several letters to deliver—one will be for the King, the others for the patriarchs."

"It is an honor to obey, Father." He smiled, thrilled at the thought of an audience with the Pope himself. "May God bless His Holiness. But uh... which king?"

"The Greek King, of course. In Constantinople... what's his name?"

Ramiro thought for a moment. "Alexios, I believe."

Hugh glanced at him in astonishment. "Yes, Alexios... of course. For years, he has pleaded for Pope Urban's help to defeat the pagans, to drive the devils from the Holy Land! Already this God-forsaken race has destroyed the Holy Sepulcher!"

"Uh, if you would excuse me, Abbot," Ramiro said softly. "But that was many years ago too. The Sepulcher has long since been rebuilt by the Greek King."

Hugh scowled in defiance. "The heathen are still a threat, Brother Ramiro. Do you not agree?"

"Yes, of course, Father." He bowed a little.

"And now for your second objective." Hugh leaned back in his chair. He pulled open a drawer and took out a small package wrapped in oiled linen. He placed it on the desk and opened the wrap slowly. That was when Ramiro first saw it.

It was a simple cross made of polished wood—quite plain except for a small bloodstone embedded at its center and a thin chain of brass looping through a hole drilled into its top.

Hugh pushed it toward him. "This is what I gave to Brother Bernold. By the grace of God, we recovered it. After you complete your business in Constantinople, you must deliver this cross to Jerusalem, where you will present it to the Patriarch along with one of the Pope's letters. The Patriarch's name is... uh..." He picked up a letter from his desktop, straining at the words. "His name is Symeon. He will then give you further instructions."

Ramiro stepped forward. "A cross, Reverend Father? But what is there about this cross that could be so important?"

"Yours is not to question, Brother, but to obey."

Ramiro reached out, picking it up gently, as if it were made of fragile terracotta. He turned it over in his hand, studying it closely. It was not large, neither was it small, fitting nicely across the palm of his thick hand. "It is an artful work, Abbot, although perhaps a little ostentatious for a Benedictine."

"Do not worry about that," Hugh croaked, waving a hand impatiently. "Keep it close to you at all times. And keep it intact. Take off your other cross right now and put this one about your neck."

Ramiro exchanged the crosses, then he glanced down at his new cross to inspect it again. Perhaps it contains a message, he thought. He looked for a plug but saw no seams of any kind.

Hugh leaned forward again. "It is vital that you present this cross to Patriarch Symeon."

"May I ask why, Reverend Father?"

"I will tell you bluntly, Brother Ramiro... it is time to defeat these heathen who threaten the Word of Christ. We can no longer tolerate this wickedness. It is time to put Jerusalem into its rightful hands—the hands of Christians. Only Christians can restore the Mother Church to Jerusalem. Only then can the City of God rule all Christendom!"

Ramiro shook his head. "I'm not sure I understand."

"We need to persuade the Greek Patriarch to join us—to unite the two churches. We need to form an alliance," he declared in a haughty tone. "To do this we need lines of communication, Brother. As my legate, you will report on all you see and hear."

"And delivering this cross will assist the alliance?" he asked skeptically.

"Yes, for reasons you will understand when you reach Jerusalem. In the name of God, do you vow to do so?"

Ramiro balked. "My Lord, I... I will obey you in all things and I vow in the name of God that I will do all in my power to deliver it to Patriarch Symeon."

Hugh nodded. "Very well, I accept your solemn vow. Now remember, there's no need to mention the cross to anyone. Is that understood?"

"Yes, Abbot."

"And you will report to me on all you see and hear."

"Yes, of course," Ramiro replied. The responsibility of this assignment already began to weigh on his thoughts. "Tell me please, Reverend Father. Once I deliver the Pope's letter to the Greek King, how will I get to Jerusalem?"

Hugh strained his thin lips in a weary smile. "Nothing is wanting to those who fear God, Brother Ramiro." He tapped his fingers on the desk. "But I expect the Greek King will put you on a ship sailing to Palestine, or something like that."

"And where shall I stay in Jerusalem?"

"Why, at the monastery, of course." Hugh raised his eyes in thought. "The Monastery of... of Saint Mary, I think it's called. Managed by the Benedictine Order." Once again, he forced a smile. "Do not fret about these things, Brother, and trust our good Lord to guide you."

"Yes, Abbot," Ramiro answered warily.

Hugh took hold of a purse sitting on his desk and pushed it forward. "There should be enough here to fund your journey. If you need more, ask the Patriarch to assist you when you reach Jerusalem."

Ramiro picked it up. It had been a long time since he had used money.

"You must hurry, Brother Ramiro. Count Robert's men will not wait for you much longer. They have already left Lyon and head east again for Chambéry in the mountain passes."

"Count Robert?"

"Yes, Robert of Flanders."

"Is he the one who leads these knights?"

"No, no, but he dispatched these fighting men to serve the Greek King. A promise he made when he last took a pilgrimage to the Holy Land."

Ah! Ramiro thought, then they're Flemings—just as odious as those wretched Normans.

Hugh scribbled out a short note and handed it to him. "This is your letter of commendation for Count Robert's captain. His name escapes me. I do not anticipate trouble, and you should be able to return to us within two years. You will not travel alone. I have assigned two assistants to accompany you—Aldebert the novice and Pepin the groom."

"Aldebert?" Ramiro blurted in dismay. "Please forgive me, Father, but the man is a complete imbecile. Surely, anyone else would be up to the task. And Pepin... well, he's a mere child!"

The Abbot shook his head with a disheartened look, like that of a disappointed father. "They will submit to your orders, Brother," he stressed with frustration. "That is enough. And I command you to review Saint Benedict's Rules before you go. In particular, I want you to give special attention to his advice on humility and obedience."

With a heavy frown, Ramiro bowed. "I will obey, Most Reverend Father."

"Now go," he said with a gesture of impatience. "You must leave at dawn and ride fast to Chambéry."

CHAMBÉRY

Ramiro felt a rush of exhilaration. For so many years, he had worked, prayed, and worshiped within the confines of the abbey, giving his life to the service of God. Now he was, once again, free to roam the compelling, carnal world of men, free to make his own determinations, and free to act. Thoughts of daring adventure raced through his head and aroused in him a long-subdued wanderlust. Jerusalem! I head for the Holy City and the Tomb of Christ! I will see my beloved mother once again! He felt so vibrant, so alive.

His gray mare kept up an ambling gait along the road to Lyon, following the wide, gentle flow of the Saône river. A warm summer breeze whistled past his ears, carrying the sweet scent of lavender from sprawling fields of deep purple.

Behind him, a lanky Brother Aldebert fought awkwardly with his flustered horse as he rushed to keep up. His pale, pockmarked face grimacing in frustration. Young Pepin, a thin, scruffy boy of twelve with long, blonde hair and brown eyes, sat behind him in the saddle, hanging on frantically as the befuddled mare lurched in all directions. A laden donkey trailed behind, secured by a long leash strapped to Aldebert's horse.

Aldebert rode nervously, gripping his reins with white knuckles, pulling hard one way, then the other. Unwittingly, he pulled back and dug in his heels. His mare whinnied, tossing its head, confused by mixed signals. The bewildered creature strayed from side to side as Aldebert over-corrected, first to the left, then to the right, all the while clashing with other travelers on the road. The donkey pulled back, slowing them down, and Pepin jumped off to slap it forward.

Ramiro slowed his horse, waiting for them to catch up. "Brother Aldebert! Must you torture that poor beast? You cannot pull back on the reins and expect it to move forward. Have you never learned to ride?"

"Sorry, Father Ramiro." He loosened the reins and dug in his heels. The mare lurched forward at the signal, snapping the donkey's leash and sending Pepin to the ground.

"Whoa! Whoa!" Ramiro yelled as he bolted past. "Now what are you doing? Rein back!"

"Sorry!" Aldebert yelled as he jerked on the reins. His horse whinnied again, shaking its head madly, as if to rid itself of a giant pest. The donkey brayed in the tumult.

"Really, Brother Aldebert! Perhaps Pepin should take the reins. He could do no worse!"

Aldebert frowned, creasing his pockmarked, white face. He looked askance, sneering at the younger Pepin. "No, no, Father. I'll be fine!" He shouted with chagrin. "It's just that my backside is sore."

"That's because you have yet to learn how to post to the trot, Brother Aldebert. You must move with your mount." He sighed heavily, secretly wishing he was traveling alone. *The man is a complete idiot! May God help me!*

Aldebert looked at him sheepishly with round, pale-blue eyes that seemed too big for his long, drawn face. His nose was almost as long, ending above thin, red lips which he constantly licked. And his large cow-ears hung like wilted flowers, jutting out below his blonde tonsure—the ring of hair left on a monk's shaved head.

Ramiro spurred his mount. "Come on! We must hurry!"

They rushed east, heading to Chambéry, a quaint town nestled in a wide valley among the foothills of the Western Alps. And three days after leaving the abbey, they encountered Count Robert's men just east of the Isère River. The slow-moving line of knights, squires, and servants stretched far ahead.

"There they are!" Ramiro shouted. "Come on!" He spurred his horse forward, soon meeting up with stragglers crossing the bridge. He pushed on to the front, trotting past the long line.

Aldebert and Pepin rushed to follow, but Aldebert, who was unaccustomed to such delicate maneuvers in a large crowd, barged into pedestrians and nearby riders.

"Stupid monk!" someone cried out in an unfamiliar language. "Watch where you're going!"

They sounded angry. "Please excuse me," Aldebert muttered as he struggled with his horse. But a moment later, he rammed into a group of surly, weather-worn knights.

"What the hell?" one shouted. "Get out of the way, monk!"

"Have you got horse-shit for brains?" cursed another. "Move your damned horse!"

Ramiro heard the commotion. He knew some of the tongue, enough to know it was not good. *May God have mercy on us. And the stink! I wonder how long we'll have to tolerate these vulgar brutes.* He reached the front of the line, shouting to one of the knights. "Who leads you?" he yelled in northern French.

The knight looked startled. He studied the black-robed monks. "Who are you? What do you want?" he asked with a Flemish accent.

"I am Ramiro of Cluny. I want to know who commands these men."

"Humph! Of Cluny you say? So you're from the abbey?"

Ramiro scowled. "Is that not obvious, soldier?"

The young knight nodded, somewhat abashed, before pointing to the men at front. "That's the Captain over there—Drugo the Red. The tall one with red hair and shield."

Ramiro left without a word, riding toward the man. But as he neared, two of Drugo's lieutenants, who were riding on either side of the captain, left their positions to stop him. "What do you want, monk?"

"You will address me as Dom Ramiro, soldier!" He looked hard into the man's arrogant, green eyes. "I hail from Cluny and have come to speak with your captain. You will let me pass."

One of them smiled, the one called Otto. "I suppose you've come to replace the old monk who died past Lyon. Maybe you'll last a little longer." The other knight chuckled.

Ramiro glared at the two men, who soon stopped smiling, avoiding his dark glare. "You will let me pass," he repeated with cold authority, and they parted timidly.

Captain Drugo's red hair poked out beneath a domed helmet, draping to his shoulders. A thin beard covered his freckled face. He dressed in expensive mail armor from head to toe and, when he moved, the chain links tinkled like a spring of water. Ramiro thought him no more than twenty-five. But he was older than most of his men—some as young as sixteen.

Drugo rolled his eyes as he watched the monk approach. "Another one?" he posed sarcastically.

Ramiro noted his disdain. "Good day to you too, Sir Drugo. May God bless your journey." He moved alongside. "I am Ramiro of Cluny and you have been selected by the Church to escort me to the Greek Kingdom." He offered him the Abbot's letter of commendation.

Drugo yanked it from his hand without pausing to look at it. He shoved it into his belt. "Let me make this clear, Ramiro of Cluny. I don't want any damn monks on this journey. I'll take you with me only because my Lord Robert ordered me to do so. So keep in mind that you will do as I say, and you will go where I tell you to go. Do you understand?"

Ramiro's eyes flashed. "No, I'm afraid I do not understand, Sir Drugo," he replied with equal strength. "I am a man of God and I follow the orders of my Abbot. I will do as he commands and I will go where he commands. Do *you* understand?"

Drugo glowered, his face reddened and, by force of habit, his hand moved to the hilt of his sword. "Take care with your words, monk, lest no one raise a blade to protect you."

"God will protect me, by his Grace. And you will address me as Dom Ramiro."

Drugo clenched his teeth, returning a silent, hostile glare.

"And I'm sure your heart will rejoice, Sir Drugo, when I tell you I will be conducting prayer services twice a day, at sunrise and sunset. That would be Prime and Vespers, in case you have forgotten. It is an undemanding schedule... but I am impressed with the urgency of this mission and, thus, will forego the other six hours of prayer."

Drugo did not reply, but when Ramiro turned to ride away, he could hear his vile curses.

MONFERRATO

Ramiro nestled into the dry grass to begin his morning meditation. He turned his eyes to the west, looking back toward Torino and the snow-capped Alps they had crossed some days before. Wood warblers whistled in the still of dawn as he sat alone on the rise above the camp—a scattering of tents sprawling among the low, green hills of Monferrato. He pushed back the hood of his black robe, letting the soft glow of dawn warm his face. Taking hold of his new cross, he looked to the thin clouds overhead to begin his morning invocation in silence.

> *Glory be to God who has shown us the light!*
> *Lead me from darkness to light...*

He prayed aloud, "Give me strength, Father, that I may complete the mission before me." But his prayers soon wandered into loving thoughts of his mother, Isabella, always dear to his heart. And, for a while, he dreamed wistfully of Jerusalem and the Holy Sepulcher.

He tried to focus on his prayers, muttering the Pater Noster in a dull monotone as he gazed across the fertile Po Valley, a vast expanse rolling east all the way to Venice on the Adriatic Sea. A blanket of orange haze began to dissipate in the brightening shimmer of a summer sun. He squinted in the growing light. "Kakkak!" a jackdaw sounded, and his concentration faltered.

The spectacular panorama did little to dispel his anxieties. It was a long way to Jerusalem and many, like his father before him, had died on the perilous journey. "Vouchsafe our journey, if it is Your will, my Lord," he prayed as his gaze drifted to the Flemish campsite below, to the hodgepodge of oiled canvas tents and makeshift shelters where a thin grove of chestnut and oak cast long shadows.

In the first rays of morning sun, yellow and purple wildflowers bloomed in greeting. Tents rippled and flapped, and cold ash puffed between the stones of dead campfires. Jackdaws flitted between them, tussling over scraps dropped the night before. Servants began to rise, rekindling their fires with dry twigs collected from the grassy, forest floor. Before long, he caught the aroma of baking bread and roasting boar, a scent broken only by the briny smell of skins and furs stretched out to dry in frames of wood.

Clanging pots and angry bellows soon disturbed the quiet of dawn. He tried to ignore the rising din below him, but before the sun rose a hand above the horizon, a deafening scream for mercy brought the noisy, bustling camp to a silent standstill.

A CARPENTER

A terrified tradesman wrestled in the grip of two soldiers, his voice shaking the cool morning air. "I stole nothing, I swear! Nothing! Let me go!"

Lieutenant Otto pulled out his long knife, putting the tip to the man's pale neck. "Settle down, scum! Or I'll slit your throat from ear to ear!" He called out, "Captain! We've caught a thief!"

Drugo the Red pulled his tent flap aside. He squinted in the morning light. "What is it, man? I have yet to eat my breakfast." Stepping out, he stood tall against the three men, his open robe revealing a barreled chest. A servant girl with long, raven-black hair peeked out behind him.

"We've caught a thief, m'lord," said his other lieutenant, Fulk. "Caught him with the silver locket lost by Otto's wife last week."

The tradesman's eyes widened in fear. "I took nothing, m'lord, I swear in the name of God!" The man was terrified, and rightly so. He had heard the fearsome, fireside stories about Drugo, about how the knight was once accused of theft by a lowly peasant and how, right then and there in front of everybody in Count Robert's court, he drew his sword and lopped off the man's head with a single blow.

The Count, enraged by his audacity, ordered him to do penance and seek remission for his sins, which is why he sent Drugo off to serve the Greek King, to whom he had promised fighting men and horses, ordering the unruly knight to atone for his evil ways by visiting holy places along the way. Drugo did as he was commanded but showed little remorse.

Drugo looked to his henchman. "This is a serious accusation, Fulk. Are you sure?"

"We are, m'lord. The locket was sighted in a bag among his possessions."

The tradesman squirmed. "I swear, Sir Drugo, I have no idea how it got there! You must believe me! I'm not a thief!"

"Then how do you explain its presence among your personal things?"

"M'lord, I cannot explain it, but I have never been near Otto's tent. I swear it!"

"So... I ask you once again... how did the locket come to be in your bag?" He glared at the man.

The tradesman squirmed under his piercing, blue eyes. "I don't know, m'lord."

"Who accompanies you, tradesman?"

"Well... my wife and daughter, m'lord—and fellow tradesmen."

"Perhaps your wife or your daughter took it?"

"Oh, no, no, m'lord." He struggled. "They are good, honest people!"

"Well then, it must have been one of your fellow tradesmen."

"Oh no, Sir. I... I can't imagine they would do such a thing."

A crease of irritation wrinkled Drugo's sunburned brow. "Then perhaps the fairies put it there in the middle of the night?" he mocked. His men chuckled. "You must think us fools, man! We have no place for thieves in our midst," he sneered. "You know the law... thieves will hang!"

"Please, m'lord! In the name of God's mercy!"

Drugo paused, glancing at the tradesman with feigned forbearance. "Thieves must be punished... I will not tolerate criminals among us. But I'm in no mood for a hanging first thing in the morning. You will see that I am not a cruel master, carpenter... I will let you live... with the lesser sentence." He turned to his men. "Cut off his hand. That is the law."

"Mercy, m'lord, I have done nothing wrong!"

"Take him away!" Drugo shouted with annoyance. He spun to his tent and the girl within. "Get my breakfast, woman!"

Soldiers dragged the pleading carpenter to an opening in the camp, tied his right arm to a large block of wood and stuffed his wailing mouth with a rag. Knights, servants, and slaves rushed in to watch, jostling and pushing for a better view. A line of soldiers held them at bay. They all fell silent. The only sound was the wail of the carpenter's wife.

A huge, broad-shouldered Norman wielding a wide battle-axe stepped up to the block. He hoisted the massive blade high above his head, focusing on the carpenter's wrist, poised to strike...

"Stop! Stop at once, in the Holy Name of God!" A booming voice rattled the air. The axe-man held his weapon. He staggered a little as he turned his head in the direction of the intruder. People jostled to see who it was and a hundred voices spoke at once.

Ramiro burst through the crowd like a wild bull, knocking people off their feet as he charged forward. His black ring of hair fluttered in the morning breeze and his black robe flapped behind him. He stormed forward in wide, strong strides, infused with the brazen courage of an ancient prophet, pushing right up to the axe-man, glaring defiantly into his big face. The towering executioner strained to keep the heavy blade above him. Ramiro stood firm, his dark eyes flashed, his face dripping sweat. "In the name of Christ, I demand to know the sin of this man!"

The executioner shouted down. "He's a stinking thief, monk! We caught him with a stolen locket. The Captain sentenced him!" Dark locks swung off his shoulders as he yelled. He steadied himself as his axe grew heavy.

Ramiro glowered. "You will let me speak with this man... and with the Captain!" The axe-man hesitated, stepping back as he lowered his blade. An audible sigh of disappointment rippled through the crowd.

Another soldier rushed up. "The evidence is clear, monk. The man is guilty," cried Otto, the blonde-haired lieutenant who owned the locket. "Do not meddle in our affairs."

Ramiro spun to face him. "Only God's mercy meddles in your affairs, Otto of Bremen. What makes you so sure this man is guilty? What evidence do you have?" He took three long strides, right up to Otto's thin, pallid face. "I must speak with your Captain... at once!"

Otto averted the monk's intent stare. His pale green eyes darted about fretfully as he looked for support from his men, but they were too afraid to interfere. Finally, he summoned courage, folding his arms and sticking his chin forward. "He's a rotten thief, monk! Are you here to protect sinners and shit like this? We should hang the bastard!" The crowd roared their approval.

Ramiro spun on the bloodthirsty crowd, facing soldiers and servants alike. "And who among you will throw the first stone?" he shouted. "Who is without sin?" He swung an accusing finger at the crowd, pointing to individuals in turn, who now backed away in dread, each in mortal fear of having their sins made public.

He turned again to Otto. "I'm here to save souls, soldier. You would do well to heed my request. Perhaps the Church should learn of your arrogance and disrespect!" He folded his arms across his broad chest and stood firm, glaring at Otto. The crowd remained quiet, some slipped away.

Otto began to fidget. He knew Ramiro was Benedictine, as was the Pope himself. Beads of perspiration flushed to his brow. He turned away suddenly, muttering a curse. "Have your way monk... I will summon the Captain. But he won't be pleased."

Before Ramiro could console the terrified carpenter, Drugo exploded onto the scene, still half-dressed in pants and a loose shirt but now wielding a bare sword. Red with rage, his big nose wrinkled in a hard sneer, he leapt forward like a wildcat to its prey, jabbing the point of his blade to Ramiro's neck. A cry of shock came from the crowd.

Ramiro stood his ground.

Drugo's deep voice blasted across the campground. "What is it, monk, that you defy my orders? I have heard the evidence and sentenced this man! That is enough!" The blade trembled in his outstretched arm, scraping the skin of Ramiro's throat.

Blood trickled down Ramiro's neck as he glared past Drugo's dull gray blade, straight into the eyes of the Captain. He broke the silence in a calm voice. "I am a man of God, Captain. Do you intend to kill me?"

Drugo shifted from one foot to the other, then back again. He said nothing.

"Would you kill a man of the Holy Church?"

Murmurs and whispers ran through the crowd. Drugo spun his head in one direction and then the other, glowering at the masses, who again fell silent. He withdrew his sword a hand's length to dally it in Ramiro's face. "Perhaps I would, monk!"

Ramiro appeared oblivious to Drugo's sword. "Have you forgotten the Peace of God, Captain?" He referred to the papal decree protecting commoners and clergy from the exploits of nobles and knights. "If you commit this nefarious deed, Drugo of Flanders, there can be little doubt you will lose all honor among men. You will be excommunicated from the Church of Christ."

Drugo hesitated. His scowl faded in a blink of alarm.

In a tense interlude, the only sound was Drugo's heavy breathing. Ramiro moved his left hand slowly, taking hold of his cross, pushing it forward as far as the chain would allow. The bloodstone sparkled. "Neither crusade nor pilgrimage will absolve your sin. Is this your destiny?"

Drugo's sword wavered as he gawked at the cross. Another breath of fear swept across his face before he lowered his blade, holding it stiffly at his side. "This is my command, monk!" he bellowed. "I am the law! You will not question it!" Spittle sprayed from his lips, blood vessels bulged.

"I follow God's command, Captain, not yours," Ramiro said forcefully before taking on a more conciliatory tone. "Let me speak with the accused, Sire. I know him. He is Louis the Carpenter... a good man. Can we judge him so quickly? Give me some time to know the true events."

Drugo fumed at the challenge, taking a long stride to the left, and then another to the right. His men shuffled out of the way, the crowd moved too. He struggled with his ire, turning again to glare at Ramiro. "Know you, monk, that I will cut off this man's head if it pleases me!" He looked around with an angry stare, daring anyone to defy him. Most dropped their eyes while others shuffled away.

Drugo seethed. *Why did I ever vow to protect this bastard monk? I should slit his fat throat and be done with it!* He straightened his shirt, composing himself before speaking again. "I can show mercy, monk! I will grant your request. You have till noon before I hear you again." He turned, stomping back to his tent. The crowd parted in a hurry, giving him wide berth.

The Carpenter's Daughter

Louis' wife was a plump woman who, despite the increasing heat, wrapped herself in a woolen shawl and headscarf. She rushed to her husband, pulling the rag from his mouth before embracing him. "Thank you, Dom Ramiro, God bless you!"

Louis, a short man with shaggy brown hair, a flat face and a big nose, looked up with a blank expression of shock as his plump wife fell on him. "Thank you, Dom Ramiro... uh, this is my wife, Mathilda." As he spoke, a young woman dashed out from the crowd, running to his side. He motioned to her with a nod of his head. "And my daughter... Adele."

Politely, Ramiro glanced at the girl. He was about to turn back to Louis, but he looked again, captivated by her hazel eyes and shapely lips, by her smooth face and its sheen of youth.

He nodded in greeting but, alarmed by his own enchantment, soon turned away in a rush of shame. Quickly, he knelt to comfort Mathilda, taking her hand. "We have not saved him yet, Mathilda. But God willing, we will solve this matter."

"My husband is an honest man, Dom. He would never steal a thing!" She pressed Louis' head to her bosom.

Louis pulled back in embarrassment. "Mathilda, please, let Dom Ramiro speak."

Ramiro lowered his voice. "Louis, you must tell me everything if I am to help you. Did you take the locket?"

"No, Dom, I swear, I don't know how it came to be in my bag."

Ramiro scratched at the night's stubble on his chin, staring absently at Louis. "Is there anyone who would want to do you harm?"

Louis lowered his head in thought, he seemed to forget he was still tied to the block. "What do you mean?" he asked, lifting his head again. "You think someone put it in my bag?"

Ramiro forced a smile. "If you did not steal it, Louis, then that is the only other explanation."

"Why would anyone do that?"

"Perhaps to see you hang... or lose your hand," Ramiro said with grave expression. "But for what purpose? That is the question." He frowned in thought. "Have you argued with anyone?"

Louis pondered a while. "Nothing more than the occasional quarrel, Dom."

"Who told Otto the locket was in your bag?"

"I don't know, Dom."

Ramiro rushed off, leaving Louis to Mathilda's bosom.

Lieutenant Otto sat near a small campfire just outside his tent, his long blonde hair draped across his clean-shaven face as he bent over to sharpen and polish his sword. Ramiro confronted him without pleasantries. "Who told you your wife's locket could be found in Louis' bag?"

Otto stood, slinging the sword into its sheath. "My wife's slave girl accused the man."

"And why was that?"

He lifted his long chin. "She said she saw Louis lurking about my tent the night before."

"Where is this slave, that I may speak with her?"

"That's her right over there. We call her Sara." He pointed to a young girl with short blonde hair who sat under the shade of a beech tree mending a garment.

Without further ado, Ramiro approached the girl. She noticed him coming and abruptly dropped her eyes.

Ramiro noticed her aversion. "Good morning, Sara."

She looked up again, fidgeting with her needle and thread. She spoke with a heavy, Slavic accent. "Oh, greeting Father. What... what I do for you?"

"You can tell me why you accused Louis of stealing the locket."

She blushed. "I saw him near mistress tent night before."

"Surely, there are many about your tent at all times of the day. Why did Louis attract your attention?"

"He look inside," she blurted. "Inside tent." She dropped her needle in the grass and groped for it in a distressed manner. "I... I must finish chore, Dom. Excuse." She got up suddenly and rushed away, clutching her sewing in both hands.

Ramiro followed after her but could not keep up. "I will know the truth, Sara!" he yelled after her. But she vanished like a ferret into a throng of animals, people, and tents.

"Pepin!" Ramiro yelled as he returned to his tent.

The boy rushed over. "Yes, Father."

Ramiro took the lad by the arm, holding his elbow in a firm grip while guiding him out of earshot. He spoke quietly. "Pepin, do you know the servants of Otto, the Captain's lieutenant?"

"Well, I... I know them a little, Father. We talk around the campfires." He squirmed, his guileless face grimacing in Ramiro's vice-like grip.

Ramiro leaned to his ear. "Discover what you can of Sara, his wife's handmaiden. Does she have any connection to any of the carpenters?" He looked straight into Pepin's eyes. The boy stiffened, returning a vacant, cautious stare. Ramiro waited, raising an eyebrow. "Have you gone daft, lad? Did you hear? A man's life is at stake!"

Pepin lowered his eyes, beginning to cry. "But Father... everyone knows."

Ramiro tipped his head, scowling. "And what do you mean by that, boy?" he asked in a harsh whisper. The boy's face reddened. Ramiro tightened his grip. "Well...? Out with it!"

Pepin winced again. "All the servants know she's Raul's mistress, Father." Tears streamed down his smooth cheeks. "Please, Father, my arm!"

Ramiro stood still, momentarily shocked. Slowly, he gained expression, releasing his grip. "Forgive me, son." He put a hand to his chin. "His mistress? Are you sure? The one they call Sara?"

Pepin wiped his face before rubbing his arm vigorously. "Yeh, the blonde girl, the one Otto bought from a Venetian trader. But Otto doesn't know."

"Is that so?" Ramiro smirked. "And where is Raul's tent?"

"Over to the east, by the carpenter's wagon under a large oak. Do you see it?" He pointed across a hundred tents to the distant tree.

Ramiro peered through the pluming camp smoke. "I see the oak." He dismissed the boy. "Not a word to anyone! Now go about your chores." Pepin rubbed his arm again before scampering off to feed the horses.

Ramiro rushed back to poor Louis, who was still tied to the chopping block. "Tell me more of Raul. Who is he and what does he do?"

Louis looked up at him. "He's one of the guild, Dom. A carpenter, as I said."

"Have you argued?"

Mathilda intervened. "Not really, but he did ask for Adele's hand in marriage. She refused."

"Why is that?"

"My daughter is a bull-headed woman," said Louis. "She spurned him despite my approval. Look at her, she will be an old maid if she does not marry soon."

Adele rose up from her father's side. She was eighteen. "I cannot marry him, Dom Ramiro," she flushed. "He's a cruel and deceitful man—I despise him!"

Ramiro smiled gently. Despite her emotion, she spoke with disarming poise. She was a striking young woman. Long auburn hair, half covered with a deep blue shawl, dangled in soft curls about her shoulders. She stood with a look of defiance, her hazel eyes flashing as she rested her hands on curved hips. Her shapely bosom, emphasized by a tunic of tight-knit wool, rose and fell with every breath. Ramiro was captivated by her rugged beauty.

"Dom Ramiro?" she asked again.

Ramiro's cheeks reddened in another rush of shame. He lowered his eyes. "Uh... tell me... tell me Adele," he asked, lifting his eyes carefully. "What did Raul do when you refused him?"

"He was very angry, Dom Ramiro," she said with a very serious look. "He rushed out and kicked some poor dogs standing in his way. He never said a word to me after that." She lowered her eyes briefly. "Forgive me for disobeying my father, but I cannot marry a man I detest!"

With effort, Ramiro pulled his gaze from her, turning back to Louis. "What would Raul gain with you out of the way?"

"I can guess," Mathilda interjected. "Myself and Adele would be alone in this strange land with no man to speak for us. She would have to marry then, or we would risk being indentured to another master."

"Then he'd inherit all I have," Louis blurted out as the truth dawned on him. "Including my position in the guild!" His face soured. "That bastard!"

"It's only a possibility, Louis. That's all." He avoided looking at Adele as he left. "Time is short, I must investigate."

Louis looked about helplessly. A grim soldier stood watch nearby.

Ramiro pushed his way past hundreds of tents, eventually arriving at the carpenter's quarters near a large oak. It did not take him long to find a man who matched Louis' description. He was tethering a horse. "Good day. Are you Raul the Carpenter?"

Raul, a short man with shoulder-length brown hair, turned to him. "Yes, Dom, I am Raul. What brings you to my tent?" He continued to tend to his horse.

Ramiro stepped up close. "Surely, you must be aware that Louis, the head of your guild, has been accused of theft and is about to lose his hand?"

Raul shrugged. "What can I do, Dom? He's been charged by the Captain."

Ramiro moved closer until he faced the man nose to nose. "Yes, but you know the charges are false, do you not?"

Raul backed away with a flash of alarm. "It's a terrible tragedy, Dom. A sad state of affairs." He turned back to his horse, avoiding Ramiro's glare. "I... I would never suspect Louis of theft," he said nervously. "But they found the locket in his possession. What can I do?"

Ramiro moved again to face him, pressing closer. Once again, Raul backed away. "I think you can do something, Raul. Is it not true that the Russian slave, Sara, is your mistress?"

Raul looked down, his crafty eyes shooting from side to side. "That is not your affair, monk!" he blurted with feigned indignation.

Ramiro studied the fear in Raul's eyes. "And did you not instruct her to accuse Louis of theft so that you could eventually take Adele's hand in marriage and inherit his wealth and position?"

Raul paled, blinking nervously.

"I know your scheme, Raul. You have committed a grievous sin."

Raul betrayed himself with a guilty look and a quavering voice. "I... I know nothing of this... this affair."

"You would send another to his death simply to satisfy your own greed and lust?"

Raul tried to speak but could form no words.

Ramiro made the sign of the cross. "May God have mercy on your pitiful soul." He paused for effect. "Now you will face many accusations... that of a thief, and now perjury and deception. You will surely hang."

In a fit of terror, Raul realized his ruse had failed. He dropped to his knees. "Forgive me, Dom. Forgive me! What am I to do?"

Ramiro looked down with a mix of contempt and compassion. "You can submit yourself to Saxon law, Raul... or take what you can carry and return to France as quickly as you can. There is nothing I can do for you." He turned away.

"But Dom, by myself? I will die on the road!"

Ramiro glanced back. "No, Raul, not by yourself, you must take Sara with you. The soldiers will drown her if you do not. Your choice is to lose your life here or face the road. Decide!"

Raul soon told Sara of Ramiro's threat and before a half hour had passed, they took Raul's only horse, a few supplies, and rode west at full gallop.

"Brother Aldebert! Wake up!" Ramiro hollered as he opened the tent flap. "How can you possibly sleep through all this commotion? Come, man, it's time to recite morning prayers and get a meal. Must I remind you that slothfulness is a sin?"

Aldebert, jarred from his dreams of Burgundy, bolted upright on his horse-hair mattress. He still wore his black habit, as Benedictines do when they sleep. It hung heavily from his shoulders, spotted with food and grease stains. A wooden cross dangled from a chain about his neck. For a long moment, he gazed up at Ramiro through bloodshot eyes, as if unsure where he was.

Aldebert was uncomfortable speaking openly to a fellow monk, especially to a dean, a superior. Monks were discouraged from idle talk in the monastery. But as they traveled farther and farther from the Abbey of Cluny, the rule became more and more untenable.

"Father Ramiro..." he mumbled, "good morning—and praise the Lord!" He rubbed the sleep from his eyes with dirt-stained hands. "What commotion?"

Ramiro stood at the entrance with his hands on his hips. "In all my thirty years, I have never encountered a man who could sleep through such a ruckus."

"What ruckus? What happened?"

Ramiro recounted the morning events. "I put the fear of the Lord into them, Aldebert," he said with a thin smile and a twinkle in his eye. "I'm giving them both time to flee before I approach Drugo again. We almost lost a good man— and a good carpenter, to the deception of that villain. Wretched man!" He shook his head, lowering his voice. "These damned Normans are a treacherous lot, Brother Aldebert."

Aldebert whispered back. "I thought they were Flemings."

"Flemings, Normans. What's the difference, Brother? They're all bastard sons of those barbarous Northmen. Their tongues differ somewhat but they are all the same—greed infects their bones and the sight of blood amuses them." He plopped down on his mattress with a huff of breath. "You should have seen them, Brother Aldebert, hooting for the blood of Louis the Carpenter... with little more than the accusation of a slave." In a restless maneuver, he began to roll up his mattress. "Come now, we'll take our mattresses outside to air in the sunlight. It's beginning to stink in here!" He could hardly tolerate the reek of the man.

"But Pepin just did our laundry."

"Just? That was over two weeks ago, Brother. Quickly now, we must prepare for morning prayers, the faithful rely on us to guide them to our Heavenly Father, to the praise of God."

In a large space, they set up a small altar, placing on it an icon of Christ and another of Mother Mary. The whole camp came to worship. Ramiro and Aldebert led them in prayer, knowing that few, if any, could read the scriptures.

"Lord open my lips," Aldebert chanted.

Ramiro responded, cuing the crowd to repeat his words.

> *And my mouth shall proclaim your praise.*
> *Glory be to the Father*
> *and to the Son*
> *and to the Holy Spirit...*

Drugo the Red prayed, too. He prayed for Divine Providence to favor him with many rewards and riches. After all, *I'm a soldier of the True Faith, sent to destroy the infidels who threaten the Holy Church and the Holy Land. Guide my sword, oh Lord, that it may pierce the black hearts of your enemies. Surely then, my sins will be forgiven...*

As noon approached, Ramiro sauntered up to Drugo to relate his story. "Raul the carpenter and Otto's slave girl have fled in fear, Captain, thus confirming their guilt."

Drugo spun to Otto. "See if this is true. Check the whole camp and return to me as fast as you can!"

Otto left with two other men before Ramiro spoke again. "It is also well to consider the merits of the tradesman, Captain. He's a master carpenter—few mechanics can repair a wagon wheel as Louis can. And he has considerable experience with catapults and other war machines. But he will be of little use to you with only one hand."

Cursed monk! Drugo thought. He sat on a stool outside his large tent, his long legs sprawled out in front of him as his black-haired servant girl combed his red locks and trimmed his beard. *But he's probably right, the carpenter could be useful when the time comes.*

Otto returned within the hour. "Captain! Raul and my servant girl have fled."

"Well go after them! Bring me their heads!"

"Yes, m'lord."

"And release that wretched carpenter! I've had enough of this business! Tomorrow we break camp and ride to Genoa. Leave me now!"

Without another word, Ramiro spun on his heels, hurrying back to the chopping block to untie Louis' arm. Mathilda gushed in tears, flinging herself on Ramiro in a forceful embrace. He stood firm, patting her back awkwardly.

As Mathilda loosened her grip, Adele stepped forward with a beaming smile. She reached out, taking Ramiro's hand. "Thank you, Dom, we are forever in your debt."

Her gentle touch sent a pleasant shock through his arm, and her adoring look fired a forbidden passion in his heart. For a long moment, it took his breath away. He felt his ears grow hot. Gently, he pulled his hand from hers. "It's, uh... it's my pleasure to serve God and His righteousness. I... I must go now to attend to my duties." He turned away quickly, stumbled on a stone, chuckled nervously, all the while muttering good-byes.

A warm gust blew the shawl from Adele's head, tossing her long, auburn hair about her shoulders. She traced Ramiro's departure with a keen look and some amusement before shaking her head in a slow reprimand. He's a monk, you fool. Go about your business.

By nightfall, Raul and Sara could not be found, and Otto had given up the chase.

Ramiro tossed and turned in the silence of a hot night. Try as he may, he could not sweep the carpenter's daughter from his mind. He thought dutifully of his vows and chided himself for his lack of continence, struggling again and again to redirect his unruly thoughts to prayer.

> *Lord in your kindness, we ask you to lighten*
> *the darkness of this night and grant that your*
> *servants may sleep in peace...*

But it was in vain. She appeared again, like a bewitching angel who had found a secret entrance to the back of his mind. Please forgive me, Father, for my licentious thoughts. Purge my soul of all wantonness that I may devote my mind only to Your Cause. For a while, he managed to distract his thoughts by concentrating on his mission and the upcoming ride to Genoa. It is in the hands of God he conceded as a fitful sleep finally overcame him.

GENOA

The merchant galleys at harbor in Genoa were larger than any vessel Ramiro had ever seen. Square sails of light-gray canvas draped from huge yardarms, and racks of oars perforated long, swooping hulls sitting high on the water.

Longshoremen rushed about the docks unloading cargo with rough-hewn cranes, stacking wooden boxes, barrels, and canvas bags filled with goods of all kinds and from every corner. Exports of grain from the Po Valley and precious ores from the Alps were stacked beside imports of silk, spices, and sugar from the East. And all of it made its way to rows of neat, square merchant houses set along the shoreline.

Genoa was a vibrant and wealthy city-state excelling in trade, shipbuilding, and banking, with hundreds of branches throughout the Aegean and as far afield as Byzantium. Its navigational instruments and cartographic skills, much of it borrowed from Greeks and Arabs, were among the best in the Western world. But as the power of Genoa increased, so did that of its arch-rival, the city-state of Pisa.

Like Genoa, Pisa exploited the seas and benefited from the plunder of Arab settlements. The two republics grabbed all they could, fighting over cities and regions fallen to their prey. But by the time their hostilities had ceased, Pisa ruled supreme in the Tyrrhenian Sea and Pope Urban awarded control of Corsica and Sardinia to the growing republic. He decreed that Pisan rules of navigation would establish the laws and customs of the sea.

JUST WAR

Beyond Pisa, Drugo's company turned east for Florence and, from there, headed south, traveling through Tuscany at a rapid pace to avoid the German troops stationed in Rome.

Ramiro pulled back the hood of his black robe, exposing a circle of matted hair to the warm sun creeping out of a thin cloud. He was exhausted and longed for the quiet comfort of his private room at the abbey. Rarely did he have a decent night's sleep in his flimsy tent, which was incapable of shielding his ears from the constant clacking and banging of the servants, or the bellicose bragging of drunken knights.

He thought again of his mother's letter, still not sure what it meant. Was she really dying or just heartbroken? God willing, I will soon see her in the Holy Land, where I shall walk the cobbled paths of blessed Jerusalem, the Holiest of Holy cities. He thought of his final pilgrimage to the Holy Sepulcher, an act of penance and thanksgiving that would bring him God's love and favor, as it did for all who took this sacred journey.

But his quiet reflections quickly vanished when two knights barged through the line, their steeds bumping and pushing at everything in their way. In the fray, Aldebert's horse stumbled to the edge of the road and Ramiro fought to steady his own mount.

"Mother of God!" He tugged at his reins. "Pull left, Brother Aldebert! Before you throw me into the brambles!"

Aldebert pulled the other way, colliding with a nearby wagon.

"Good Lord!" Ramiro chided in exasperation. "When will you learn to ride, Aldebert?" He steadied his mare. "And how long must I forebear these arrogant Northmen? I tell you Brother, their impertinence would test the patience of our beloved Saint Paul, may God bless his name!" He reined his horse back to the road, attempting to regain his composure.

Aldebert still struggled with his confused mare. "Were you not once a soldier yourself, Father Ramiro?"

"True enough, Brother Aldebert, but that was long ago. Since then, my life at the abbey has been a simple one, and I suppose I've grown unaccustomed to the brutish ways of a warrior. But these men are particularly crude and uncivilized," he snorted. "Never before have I been treated with such contempt!"

Aldebert was not aware the knights were crude and uncivilized but nodded anyway. "I heard you once fought in Spain, Father Ramiro. Is this true?"

"Yes, yes, when I was young," he said. "You see, I was the seventh of eight sons, Brother, so I had little hope of inheritance and sought my fortunes elsewhere. I came from a proud and noble family in the city of León, in the Kingdom of León, ruled by the great king, Alfonso. We served our king well."

"You fought the Moors?"

"That's right. But I was wounded outside Salamanca and captured." He grew quiet for a time. The horses clopped on, people chatted, pots and tools rattled and clanked. "I spent two years as a hostage in Cordoba before being released."

Aldebert shuffled in his saddle. "Did you return to fighting?"

"Oh, no, no. I could no longer bear the carnage of war. So I retired from Alfonso's service and went on a pilgrimage to Santiago de Compostela to pray for my sins and seek forgiveness."

Aldebert gushed. "Did you visit the tomb of Saint James the Moor Killer?"

Ramiro winced. "Yes, some call him that, while others would say Saint James the Great. I worshiped at his tomb day and night, praying for God's grace. I was troubled, Brother. I have killed, though the Commandments say, "you shall not kill." I have taken booty from the enemy, though we are told "you shall not steal." And I have struck in anger, though the Lord Jesus teaches us to turn the other cheek. How can I live the life of a soldier, I thought, and still follow the path of Our Savior?"

"But surely, what choice did you have, Father? The war against the heathen is a just war sanctified by the Mother Church. How could God not favor your actions, even if it means killing another?"

Ramiro shook his head slowly. "I could never completely reconcile the two notions, Brother."

Aldebert pulled an apple from his saddle bag, eating feverishly. He spoke through a sloshing mouthful. "Truly, God has touched you with His Grace, Father Ramiro."

Ramiro could not drag his gaze from Aldebert. The red sores on his face were as red as his nose. And when he talked, he spat the white flesh of the apple from blackened teeth and red lips. At the same time, he swallowed whole chunks, as if he had gone without food for weeks on end. The poor boy could use a bit of God's grace himself, he thought. So ugly, so uncultured... and deprived of all common sense.

NORMANS

Normans love to fight. After all, they are the sons and daughters of the fearsome Vikings who pillaged Europe as far afield as Russia and Byzantium. They were ruthless warriors, but it was not so much the bloodlust of battle that drove them as it was the rich booty of war.

The Lombards were the first to hire Norman mercenaries in Italy. But in less than thirty years, these clever freebooters began to conquer southern Italy for themselves, taking Arab strongholds to the south, defeating Lombard princes, and driving the Byzantines from the port of Bari in 1071. They were first led by the resolute William Iron Arm and, later, by an ambitious opportunist, Robert Guiscard, once a roving highwayman.

After securing southern Italy, the Normans invaded Sicily to the south and infringed on Papal lands to the north. The Pope pushed back and skirmishes broke out between Guiscard's knights and the Papal Guard.

But not long after, in 1084, King Henry of Germany also invaded the Papal lands, seizing Rome from Pope Gregory. The King was furious because the Pope had challenged his authority to appoint bishops and so he decided to install his own pope, a man by the name of Giberto of Ravenna, a bootlicker who called himself Pope Clement the Third.

By taking Rome, King Henry had now become the real enemy of the Pope, forcing Gregory to flee for safety among his former foes, the belligerent Normans. And after Gregory died, Pope Urban had to do the same, reluctantly siding with the cunning warlord, Robert Guiscard.

And so it was for the next five years, the possession of Rome and the Holy See alternated between the Germans, who backed Pope Clement, and the Normans, who now fought on behalf of Pope Urban.

Because the Germans held Rome at this time, Captain Drugo was careful to give the city a wide berth as they made their way southeast for the Norman stronghold at Melfi. But his large band of soldiers and horses attracted too much attention.

Drugo's scouts came charging back. "The Germans come! The Germans come! Hundreds of men!"

Drugo put a hand up to shield his eyes, peering forward. He saw the knights thundering toward them, stirring up a cloud of dust. "To the field!" he yelled. "Move to the field! Take high ground! Everyone! Form a circle!" Men and women hollered and shrieked, children screamed in the chaos.

Knights and squires were the first to get to the mound, taking their horses and wagons with them, leaving everyone else to fend for themselves. Aldebert rode off in terror, toppling people to the ground as he went. Women and children ran to catch up, tripping and scrambling into the field, abandoning carts, dropping bags. Pepin rushed away, leaving the laden donkey standing alone. His blonde hair twisted over his shoulders as he looked back. "Hurry Father! Hurry!"

Ramiro watched in disgust. He helped a few stragglers along before he caught sight of Louis' wagon stuck in a hollow, his Belgian workhorse struggling to get it free. Mathilda and Adele scampered around, picking up tools and supplies thrown to the ground.

"Leave it Louis!" he cried as he rode up. "Leave it! Go with the others!" He glanced down to Adele, who stopped what she was doing. Their eyes met and, despite the urgency, he felt a stir. "Adele..." He forced his words. "You must go now. Please go."

She hesitated, looking down at the mess. But when she looked up again, she had fire in her eyes. "Everything we have is here, Dom Ramiro! Should we leave it to these damn Germans?"

Louis rushed up, taking the tools from her hands. "Go! Do as Dom Ramiro asks."

"Come on everyone!" Ramiro shouted, and the stragglers ran across the field toward the circle of knights. They were just twenty paces from the others when the Germans charged down on them, stopping suddenly at arrow distance before fanning out to face them. Their archers ran to the front, kneeling on the dry ground.

Drugo's men huddled behind a wall of shields forming a large circle, their long lances jutting out between them—the horses, gold, women, and children put to the center. The infantry took positions to the outside, wet with sweat, breathing hard under a hot sun.

"God be praised!" Aldebert shouted as Ramiro joined them. "Help us tend the horses, Father Ramiro."

"Horses do not concern me, Brother Aldebert! What of the safety of these poor people you so quickly abandoned on the road? Would you save yourself first? Is this the way of a Benedictine?"

Aldebert bowed his head sheepishly. "Sorry, Father, I was only following the Captain's orders."

"You follow *my* orders, Brother Aldebert. Is that clear?"

"Yes, of course. Forgive me, Father, for I have sinned."

Ramiro turned to Pepin, slapping him on the back of the head. "And you, my boy, you made no attempt to lead the donkey. Do you wish to be known as a coward?"

Pepin flushed bright red, lowering his eyes. "No, Father Ramiro."

Ramiro left them without another word, pushing his way past hundreds of mounted knights who watched and waited for any signal, their steeds stomping and snorting. He reached the front of the line, just behind the shielded infantry, where he studied the gathering German army.

Drugo ordered his own archers to the front, relieved to see the enemy had no more men than he did. He opened up the back of the circle to face them in a wide arc, matching the German formation. He had no desire for battle, the Germans were strong fighters and there was no prospect of gold here.

A German knight with a peaked iron helmet rode out to parley. He was a weathered, husky man sporting thick brown hair and a goatee. High over his head, flapped the banner of the Holy Roman Empire, a double-headed, black eagle on a gold flag.

Drugo reached out to one of his men, grabbing the banner of the Count of Flanders, a black lion on a gold flag. He rode out slowly from the wall of shields. Ramiro followed him, pushing past the soldiers on the outer ring just as the German knight and Drugo stopped to face each other at shouting distance.

"Who leads you?" the German shouted in colloquial Latin.

Drugo's Latin was rusty, and what little he did know was in the vernacular of Flanders. "I leading men," he replied haltingly. "I Drugo of Flanders. Travel to Gr... Greek land."

"Who are you and what is your business here?" The German spoke quickly.

Drugo strained at his words. "Past Rome," he replied uncertainly.

"What do you mean?" The German asked, shaking his head. An army of idiots, he thought. He tried again, this time in German. "Who... are... you?" he enunciated slowly, as if speaking to a child.

"We Fl...," Drugo started but he could not remember the words.

Ramiro sprang to his side. "Perhaps I can help, Sir Drugo."

Drugo gawked at Ramiro. He glanced behind to see if any others had followed him out. But no, just this pestering monk. "If I need your help, monk, I'll ask for it," he hissed under his breath.

"Well," Ramiro said quietly, "unless your German is better than your Latin, Sir Drugo, I'd say we're in trouble."

"Well, monk?" the German shouted impatiently. "Perhaps you can say from whence you come and the nature of your business here."

Ramiro faced the knight with a broad smile, addressing him in fluent German. "Of course, sir. I am Ramiro of..." For good reason, he hesitated to mention Cluny because of its association with Pope Gregory. "I am Ramiro of León, good sir. I would be glad to speak on behalf of our noble Captain Drugo." He waved an arm in gesture before speaking again. "And to whom do I have the honor of speaking?"

The man held his chin high. "I am Frederick, Captain of the Papal Guard and Defender of the Holy See." He looked down at Ramiro. "And you are Benedictine I see," he scoffed. "Just like the false pope himself, the one you call Urban."

Ramiro shivered a little but kept smiling. "We are on our way to the Greek kingdom, Captain Frederick."

"You are Normans?" Frederick's horse raised its head with a snort.

"A few, yes. But most are Flemish."

"What is your business in Rome?"

"We have no business in Rome, sir. We are on our way to Melfi and then Bari."

"To join those bastard Normans," Frederick scoffed. "I cannot allow it. You must turn back."

"You will have no trouble with us, Captain. But we must continue."

"I cannot let you pass. I will direct you east, to Pescara on the coast."

"What did he say?" asked Drugo, who struggled to keep up.

"He wants us to take another route."

"We could do that," Drugo replied, eager to avoid any losses.

"But we must reach Melfi within the week to see the Holy Father. I have been ordered there."

Drugo sighed impatiently. "We will still arrive in time."

Ramiro ignored him, turning back to Frederick. "No," he said flatly.

"What do you say?" Frederick raised his voice, astounded.

Ramiro folded his arms in defiance. "We must go south to Melfi."

Frederick sputtered in disbelief. "You dare to defy me? I will not allow it!" he bellowed.

Ramiro mustered his courage. "You will let us pass. Or must we do battle to resolve our differences?"

The big German leaned forward, looking him straight in the eye. "You want a battle, monk? We do not fear your riffraff! I need only draw my sword to begin a fight! And your head will be my first trophy!" He put a hand to the pommel of his sword.

Drugo watched in alarm. "What's going on?"

Ramiro ignored him. "Riffraff... indeed, Captain Frederick. These men may look a little haggard from their long journey but mistake not, they are warriors born and bred. They consider it an honor to die with boots on."

Frederick drew his sword. Drugo quickly matched his movements, raising his blade. A great commotion stirred on both sides, knights fixed their lances for charge, archers readied their bows.

"What did you say to him?" Drugo shouted in dismay.

"I told him we're going south to Melfi whether he likes it or not. I told him we would stand and fight."

"You said what? You bloody idiot! We did not come all this way to fight Germans!"

Ramiro waved him down. "Quiet, Sir Drugo or he will think you weak. Hold your head high and be not afraid. God is with you. Look angry, look stern."

Drugo, unsure of himself, sat upright, looking straight at the German. Damned monk! Horses tossed their heads, stomping and snorting. Behind them, the men waited anxiously for any signal. An eerie quiet settled on the field, broken only by the odd neigh of a horse or a cough from the men.

Frederick weighed his chances, glancing over Drugo's well-armed men. He studied the look in Drugo's eyes before his gaze fell to Ramiro. He felt a little unnerved by the monk's bold, unflinching stare. "You may go to Melfi," he relented, breaking the silence. "But we will escort you past Rome."

CASTLE OF MELFI

August 1089

The Castle of Melfi stood high on a hill, glowing the color of pure gold as the sun set below the mountains. It was a massive fortress with sheer granite walls guarded on all sides by tall, rectangular towers. This was the hub of Norman power in the Duchy of Apulia, ruled by Borsa and his half-brother Bohemond, the sons of the late Norman warlord, Robert Guiscard.

Bohemond was first-born, a giant of a man and a better warrior. But he was common-born of a Norman mother. Borsa, however, was high-born with Lombard blood and, through the intrigues of his wily mother and the intervention of Pope Urban, it was he who finally won the duchy.

And so it was that Duke Borsa presided over this eventful meeting taking place inside the cavernous hall of the Bishopric Palace. Pope Urban himself, along with seventy prominent bishops, attended the noisy affair, a meeting intended to establish new Church policy. Joining them, were dignitaries of the secular world, the warlords of Italy.

Duke Borsa was dominant, a quiet man with black hair hanging off his head like the shag of a dog. At a distance, sat Bohemond, his face shaved smooth, his yellow hair cropped short, Roman style. The fair countenance of his large, square head was set cold and hard, like the chiseled granite of the castle. He sat well away from Borsa, not because he feared him but, being recently dispossessed, he was sorely tempted to kill him.

Captain Drugo and Lieutenant Otto shuffled beside Ramiro, uneasy about giving up their weapons at the door. Drugo held his helmet under one arm and fiddled endlessly with his empty sword sheath. Otto looked more pale than usual and his thin, wiry hands hung limply at his side. They were both tired of the boring, endless talk of things they did not entirely understand and about which they could care less.

The bishops crowded around a long oak table, and they all seemed to be talking at once. Despite the noisy and lengthy proceedings, Ramiro was ecstatic. What a blessed day! The Holy Father himself!

Pope Urban stood at the front of the assembly hall, a red cape of damask silk draped from his shoulders and a white stole, decorated with gold crosses, wrapped about his neck. A red skull cap sat atop gray hair and a full beard jutted from his chin. He banged his staff on the granite floor. "Come to order!" he shouted in a croaking voice. In an instant, the hall fell silent. All eyes turned to the front. "How do you say?" he asked the bishops.

The Bishop of Apulia rose to his feet. "We have reached agreement, Your Holiness, and concur that the clergy should not marry, neither shall they abide concubines."

"Very well," said Urban. "I shall decree it so." A hubbub of chatter rose in the hall. He banged his staff again. "And what of simony? What have you decided?"

The bishop spoke again. "We agree also, Your Holiness, that no payment shall be received or paid for the appointment of any ecclesiastical office."

"As you say, this also shall be decreed," he replied solemnly. "And now, as the last matter before us, you have been asked to consider lifting the ban of excommunication against King Alexios, the Emperor of Byzantium. What have you decided?"

"It remains a difficult matter for us, Your Holiness," said the bishop. "The Greek patriarchs still refuse to accept the Church of Rome as the Mother Church of Christ. Nor will they agree to the filioque clause, among other things." He referred to the Latin belief that the Holy Spirit emanates from both the Father and the Son, rather than just the Father, as the Greeks believed. "But we have hope," the bishop continued, "that we will reach a compromise." The other bishops nodded in unison with a clamor of agreement. "Therefore," declared the bishop, "we agree to lift the ban of excommunication against the King of the Greeks."

"Praise be to God and His mercy," Urban cried loudly. "Today's outcome will help us unite the churches, free the clergy of vice, and bring us all closer to God."

He motioned to a servant, who came rushing up with a gilded box. Urban took hold of it with both hands, placing it on a small pulpit about ten paces from the table. He turned his eyes to the crowd. "And now I say to the lords of Italy, it is time to renew the Truce of God. Come forward and swear on the skull of Saint Peter that you will uphold the peace and remain loyal to the True Faith."

The richly attired men rose from their seats, some with reluctance, to approach Pope Urban in turn. The first of these was Duke Borsa, who put his hand to the holy relic, swearing his allegiance before kneeling to kiss the Pope's sacral ring. His brother, Bohemond, did the same, but only because he felt trapped by circumstance. All others followed suit.

After their vows, one of the bishops approached the Pope, whispering in his ear. Urban scanned the crowd. "Drugo of Flanders! Come forward!"

Drugo, aghast at the call of his name, slowly made his way through the throng. He did as he saw the others do, placing a nervous hand to the skull of Saint Peter before kneeling and swearing his allegiance to the Church of Rome.

"Rise to your feet, soldier of God."

Drugo stood awkwardly and the Pope continued. "See you all! Here is a valiant warrior who goes to fight for the True Faith! He hails from distant Flanders, serving the Count of Flanders. And he marches to the Greek Kingdom to scourge that land of the godless pagans and, for this, his sins will be forgiven and he will walk among the angels, as it will be for all who seek to free the blessed Holy Land from the blight of the heathen." He took a moment to scrutinize the lords of Italy, making it clear the words were meant for them. Then he motioned to a man standing nearby, the one suited in Roman armor.

"Drugo of Flanders," said Pope Urban. "Meet Commander Manuel, ambassador to the Roman Emperor."

Manuel stepped forward. A soft light reflected from the plate armor spread across his broad chest, half-covered by a red cloak. He was about thirty, a handsome man of average height who kept his chestnut-brown hair and short beard impeccably groomed. He nodded silently to Drugo, his aqua-blue eyes shimmering under a dark brow.

"Commander Manuel will escort you to Constantinople," said Urban. "You are fortunate to have such a distinguished Byzantine companion and I suggest you take advantage of his position. You both receive my blessing, may God go with you." He dismissed them before ending the synod with lengthy prayers.

Bohemond towered above the others as he milled about the hall deep in thought. *The Greek king wants fighting men. By God, there must be a way I can seize an opportunity here. But the bastard won't even speak to me.* He referred to Manuel. And he knew why he was being ignored. After all, only seven years ago, he had the audacity to invade Albania in the Greek kingdom, along with his scheming father, Robert Guiscard.

Meanwhile, Ramiro bowed his head in prayer, fingering his cross anxiously. *What about me? What of the letters?* And when a final chant of "amen" brought the prayers to a close and his name was not mentioned, he worked his way through the dispersing crowd, hurrying to make his way toward the Pope. But Papal guards stepped forward to stop him.

"What do you want?" asked the Pope's chamberlain, approaching from behind.

"Please, Your Grace, I am Ramiro of Cluny. I must speak with the Holy Father. I have urgent business. I have been sent by Abbot Hugh."

"Hugh of Cluny?"

"Yes, indeed. On a critical matter."

"Well then," he said with a comforting nod. "I believe I can arrange a brief meeting on the morrow. But for the moment, His Holiness is tired and needs his rest."

THE POPE'S LETTERS

Urban, once again draped in a red cape, slouched on his gilded, portable throne. A thick fragrance of incense hung in the air of his quarters in the Bishopric Palace. Attendees lined either side of the walkway, falling quiet when Ramiro approached to kiss the papal ring.

"Ramiro of Cluny," said Urban in a deep, tired voice. "I have been expecting you. I believe you have a letter for me."

"Yes, Holy Father, from Abbot Hugh of Cluny." He reached into his habit to draw out the creased envelope. "And I await your instructions, Your Holiness."

The room fell quiet. It was hot and humid, the air stifling. Urban opened the letter and read, nodding a little as if in approval. After a long while, he put it aside and signaled for Ramiro to rise from his knees. He looked at him squarely, his long nose looming over a thick beard. "And how fare my brethren at Cluny?"

"By God's Grace, all is well, Holy Father. And our work on the monastery continues apace."

"That is good. So you are the one who travels to the Greek Kingdom?"

"Yes, Holy Father."

"My chamberlain tells me you ride with Count Robert's men."

"That is true, Your Holiness."

"That is good," said Urban, raising a hand to a nearby page, who rushed up with three letters, each sealed with the papal insignia. "You will also ride with Manuel, the Byzantine ambassador. You will be well protected." He nodded to the page, who then turned to Ramiro, offering him the letters. "You are to deliver these letters personally. One you will see, I have addressed to the Greek King, Alexios. It introduces you as my legate and should serve you well. Another is addressed to the Patriarch of Constantinople, and the last to the Patriarch of Jerusalem. Do you swear on the blood of Christ to deliver these on behalf of the Mother Church?"

"Uh, yes, Holy Father, I do." He put his hand to his wooden cross, rubbing the bloodstone. "And I have the cross."

"The cross?"

"Yes, Holy Father, for the Patriarch of Jerusalem."

Urban nodded as if he understood. "It is good to bear gifts. You leave soon, I hear. May God speed your journey."

BARI

"So what was he like, Father Ramiro?" asked Aldebert as the mountains of Melfi gave way to the Murge Plateau of southern Italy, with its broad, dry plains and low-lying hills. In the distance, the Adriatic Sea glimmered under a blue sky.

"Who?" Ramiro asked, somewhat distracted by the vista.

"The Holy Father! What a blessing!"

Ramiro smiled, leaning forward to pat the neck of his mare. "He seemed a just and holy man." But his brief smile faded when he recalled mentioning the

Cluny cross. The Pope showed little interest in it. Did he know? The Abbot cautioned me to mention it to no one. Did he mean the Holy Father, too? And what of his talk of war? Popes had waged war in the past, it was true, but Urban... well... after all, he is Benedictine.

His thoughts soon dissipated when they reached the port of Bari. Despite the heat, it was a hive of activity. Hundreds of merchants, slaves, carts, horses, and donkeys thronged the paved streets. Wall-to-wall brick buildings, all topped in red tile roofs, lined the way to the docks.

Ramiro gazed over the blue-gray waves while they waited for official permission to enter the port. He felt a peculiar excitement, laced with some apprehension, as he tried to recall all he had learned about Byzantium from the library collection at Cluny. From this extraordinary collection of books, he believed he had gained some knowledge of the ways of the Greeks and Arabs. And his captivity in Spain had also introduced him to Arab culture and religion. But he was well aware that all this knowledge was fragmentary at best. And now, as they left the port of Bari, he knew he must prepare himself for an entirely new land—the home of Greeks and Arabs—and the mysterious Turks.

2 - BYZANTIUM

DYRRACHIUM

September 1089

Ramiro leaned on the starboard rail as the hull of the galley chopped against the rolling waves of the Adriatic Sea. He felt a wave of nausea and wished he had postponed his lunch of calzone. Seeking remedy, he held his head to the wind and, as the cool ocean mist brushed his face, he began to feel a little better.

Seagulls screeched above in a clear blue sky and the sound of the oarsman's drum beat below the deck. The oars, as long as twenty feet, swung in long arches, up and down to the rhythm of the drum, straining against the wind.

Knights and servants crammed together on the galley decks, along with horses and farm animals. And when the ship hit a swell and the bow lifted, people stumbled and horses staggered. More rushed to the rails.

"How are you feeling, Monk Ramiro?" someone asked using the Greek form of address.

Ramiro turned to see the Byzantine ambassador, Manuel, who stood steady on deck despite the heavy sway of the ship. "A little better, thank you, it's been many years since I rode the waves."

Manuel wore his helmet and full-plated armor as if ready for a battle at any moment. He joined Ramiro on the rail, his long, red cape slapping in the wind, his blue eyes sparkling with energy. "I'm sure you will soon regain your sea legs." He pointed eastward. "Look! You can just see the cliffs of Dyrrachium."

Ramiro peered forward. "Is that part of the Byzantine Empire?"

"Yes, it's our western bastion, although we've had some trouble holding it."

"What do you mean?"

"You have heard of Robert Guiscard?"

"I have heard mention. He was the father of Duke Borsa, was he not?"

"And the father of Bohemond," said Manuel with a smirk. "He was a very cunning Norman who believed he could conquer Byzantium."

"What did he do?"

"He and Bohemond assembled an army of many thousands and launched an attack by taking the same journey we take today. We fought some terrible battles with that cursed man and lost many good men. "The Weasel" we called him, damn him to Hades. But I have to admit, he was a good commander."

"What happened?"

"Fortunately, King Alexios, who is just as cunning himself, instigated a revolt in Italy, forcing Guiscard to run home to subdue it. After he left, we drove out the rest of them, including Bohemond."

"And that was the end of it?"

"Oh, no. Guiscard refused to give up, even though he was an old man by then. He gathered another huge army for yet another invasion. We were greatly outnumbered. But much to the joy of King Alexios, the Weasel died of a fever before it was launched."

"Your king sounds like quite a man," said Ramiro, feeling better with his mind off the waves.

"He has saved the Empire many times, Monk Ramiro." His voice filled with admiration. "You will meet him soon. Your Abbot must consider this to be an important assignment."

"He does," Ramiro nodded. "It is his hope to unite all Christians under one church."

"A noble task, Monk Ramiro, but is not the Latin Church itself divided?"

Ramiro thought of the anti-pope, Giberto, and nodded his head. "Alas, that is also true, Manuel. We can only pray King Henry realizes his folly."

ROME

Some weeks after Ramiro left the Castle of Melfi, trouble stirred in Rome. Deep within the walls of the Lateran Palace, which was now under the control of the Germans, Pope Clement's secretary rushed up a flight of stone steps clutching two letters. Huffing and puffing, he came to an arched doorway, where he banged the brass knocker. A voice cried from inside. He entered cautiously.

Giberto reclined on a sofa, his wild, black-gray eyebrows crossed in aggravation. "What is it?" he blurted with tired annoyance. "I asked not to be disturbed!"

Giberto, a thin, older man with a thin, angry face, was once the Archbishop of Ravenna, but he was vehemently opposed to the reforms of Pope Gregory and was excommunicated as a result. Shunned by the clergy of Rome, he turned to the German emperor, Henry, who was also opposed to Gregory. And Henry, in his spite, made good use of Giberto's conniving ways by forcefully declaring him to be the new pope, Pope Clement.

The secretary bowed low, his breathing labored by the long climb. "Your Holiness, please... please forgive me but I have just received important letters."

"Letters?" Giberto jumped to his feet. "From who?"

"The Po...," the secretary almost said 'Pope.' "... I mean Odo... Odo of Lagery." He glanced at the seal on the other letter. "And another from one of our emissaries."

Giberto snatched them from his hand. "That will be all," he said quietly, waving him away. The secretary bowed low as he backed out the door, shutting it quietly.

Giberto sauntered back to his desk, looking closely at the addresses on the envelopes. He picked one out, the one from that false pope, Odo. He flopped into his seat before breaking the wax seal recklessly, tugging out the parchment.

> To Giberto, Archbishop of Ravenna, from Pope Urban the Second, his bishops and cardinals, greetings in the name of Our Lord Jesus Christ.
>
> Know you, Giberto of Ravenna, that on March 12th in the year of our Lord 1088, I, Odo of Lagery, by the grace of God, was appointed the Bishop of Rome by the College of Cardinals. I am, therefore, the legitimate heir of Saint Paul and overseer of the Mother Church, in the name of Our Lord Jesus Christ.
>
> It saddens my heart to know that, in spite of these lawful proceedings, you continue to defy the Holy See by calling yourself Pope Clement. Know you that your appointment by Emperor Henry of Germany is not sanctioned by the Mother Church and is, therefore, illegitimate. I beseech you to forsake your false claims and return Rome and the Lateran Palace to its rightful occupants. Be warned that until such pretense is revoked, you will remain excommunicated from the Church of Christ. We pray for you, may God have mercy on your soul.
>
> August 26, in the year of our Lord 1089.

Giberto flushed red. "Damn you all!" he shouted to the empty room, flinging the letter to the floor. "You will never hold the Lateran! It's the King's God-given right to appoint the pope and his bishops. You will never control Rome!" He jumped to his feet, fuming as he paced. "And I will excommunicate you, Odo of Lagery!" He rushed back to his chair, grabbing hold of a quill. In angry strokes, he began to scratch a note to his secretary. But he paused in thought, glancing at the other letter. It was from William, his spy among Pope Urban's men. He ripped it open.

To Pope Clement the Third, by God's grace Lord of the Holy See, from William, your humble servant.

In as much as the protection of the Holy Church depends upon your care, Your Holiness, I must inform you of events that transpire in Melfi. Recently, Odo of Lagery, who claims to be Pope Urban, was visited by a large company of Northmen, about five hundred in all with some infantry as well as wives, children, and servants. These men are knights of Robert, the Count of Flanders, and are on their way to the Kingdom of the Greeks, where they have been hired as mercenaries.

What may be of concern to your Grace is that two monks from the Abbey of Cluny accompany these Northmen. One goes by the name of Ramiro, who holds the position of dean, the other is a novice. I know only that Ramiro held council with Odo at the synod in Melfi but, despite my best efforts, I have been unable to discern the reason for the visit. It is said they plan to sail from Bari with a Greek ambassador.

Forever at your service.

August 15, in the year of our Lord 1089.

The last line caught Giberto by surprise. August fifteenth? Why has it arrived so late? He jumped to his feet again, rushing over to the door to pull on the bell-rope. Moments later, his secretary huffed into the room.

"Tell me, why did this letter from William take so long to reach me?"

The secretary bowed. "What I have been told, Your Holiness," he heaved, "… is that the wretched Normans shot him off his horse as he rode out of Melfi. May God curse them!"

Giberto scowled. They had discovered his spy.

"The messenger's family found the letter weeks later when they went through his bags, Your Holiness. It was sewn into the lining. They sent it right away."

"Cursed Normans!" Giberto fumed. "Damn them to hell! They're the only reason Odo survives!" He grabbed the letters, leaving his private room in a silent rage. He stormed through the enormous halls of the Palace, ignoring the statues of Saint Peter and Saint Paul, charging past the German guards who stood erect, dwarfed by towering, marble pillars. With one hand, he held his white cap firmly to his graying head, his white cloak billowing behind him.

Coming to a large, oak door, he stopped suddenly. Papal guards stood on either side. Before entering, he spun to one of them. "Bring Captain Frederick to me! Right away!"

Captain Frederick swept into Giberto's office before the sun rose a quarter hand. Just in from patrols, he was still clad in mail armor. A sword hung from his left side. He tucked his helmet under one arm and bowed before Giberto. "Your Holiness, may the saints preserve you, my Lord." His graveled voice broke the cold silence of the stark room. He straightened, holding out his chin, his thick goatee jutting forward.

Giberto sat quivering behind an expansive, polished desk strewn with papers. Behind him, a fresco of a tortured Christ adorned the stone wall. He leaned forward over the desk, glaring maliciously, his clean-shaven face scowling in fury. "Tell me, Frederick, are you not the captain of my guard?"

A look of concern crossed Frederick's face. "Well, yes, my Lord, you know I am." He shuffled his feet uneasily, rustling his chain-link armor.

Giberto's eyes bulged. "And is it not your responsibility to keep me informed of all events?"

"Yes, Holy Father."

"But I am not informed!" he screamed. "I hear my news from petty peasants in the streets! From fish mongers! From idiot plebeians!" He rose from his chair with a start, stomping back and forth in the hollow room. "The Benedictine monks of Cluny plot against us! And you know nothing?"

"Forgive me, Your Holiness."

"You fail at your duties, Captain!" He put his hands on thin hips. "If I am to remain Pope, I must control Rome. I cannot crush these insidious plots if I know nothing of them!"

"What have you heard, Holy Father?"

"My steward tells me that a platoon of Normans managed to pass by Rome without a fight! Do you know anything of this?"

"Yes, of course, Your Holiness, but it was a formidable force and we discovered they were going straight to Melfi, so we let them pass."

"Idiot! Do you know why they go to Melfi?"

Frederick bowed. "Forgive me, Sire."

Giberto gestured madly to the papers laid out on his desk. "Those traitorous..." he sputtered at the thought, "... those cursed, conniving cardinals and this... this Odo work against us. A wretched Benedictine no less! Pope Urban indeed! He schemes against our King and plots to take the Lateran Palace for himself." He threw his hands in the air. "And now I fear he will gain support from the Greek Kingdom. He has already sent emissaries there!"

Frederick shrugged. "You should not be concerned, Holy Father, our forces will keep Odo out of the Lateran."

Giberto glared at him. "Well I *am* concerned, Captain Frederick. Odo meets secretly with the lords of Italy and France in order to turn them against us. And now the Greeks!"

"But what do the Greeks want with Rome, Your Holiness?"

Giberto fumed. "This Greek King... what's his name? He's not a fool, he manipulates events to suit his own evil plans and to strengthen his empire, may God curse him! He dreams of regaining the Holy Land from the infidels and he needs all the men he can get to drive them out." He glared again at Frederick. "And where do you think these mercenaries will come from?" He paused briefly before answering himself. "From the Normans! Do you not understand Frederick? The Greek King must recognize this Odo... this Urban... as the rightful pope in order to get help from the Normans."

"We will stop them, Your Holiness."

A sickly smile crossed Giberto's face. He waved the spy's letter in front of Frederick. "I hope so, Captain, for your sake. I have the name of one of these monks—Ramiro he's called. Apparently he's a dean from the Abbey of Cluny. He's the important one. Travels with a novice."

"What are your instructions, my Lord?"

"I want you to send three of your best men to discover all you can about this meeting in Melfi. And I want these monks stopped before they reach the Greek King. They left Melfi two weeks ago. Going to Bari, I would think."

"Two weeks ago, Holiness? It will be difficult to reach them in time."

"That's your problem, Captain. Just find them. They've probably left port by now."

"But Your Holiness, how will we get our men past the Normans at Bari?"

Urban shook his head in rebuke. "Think Captain! Think! Have you no good men familiar with their barbarian tongue?"

"Yes, of course, Holy Father," he said, although he was not sure. "And what shall we do with these monks once we catch them?"

Giberto put the letter down, resting his hands on the table before looking straight at Frederick. "In the name of God, you must finish them."

Frederick bowed. "As you wish, Your Holiness."

Giberto dismissed him bravely with a wave of his hand. But after the door shut, his angry face dissolved in worry and contrition. He sank into his armchair, dropping his head into his hands. "May God forgive me."

DYRRACHIUM

Cries of wonder burst from the galley deck. Ramiro wrapped his arms around the foremast, holding on with all his might. He was trying to keep his place as the crowd pushed and shoved for a better view of the cape and the castle fortress of Dyrrachium. This was the western bastion of the East Roman Empire on the Balkan Peninsula and, from its prominent position, it overlooked and guarded the Egnatia Way, a vital road heading directly east to the Byzantine capital, Constantinople, a distance of more than 700 Roman miles.

The shoreline below the fortress was a solid wall of crag, a long escarpment that jutted above the sea so suddenly there was hardly a strip of beach along its length. Its steep, rocky slope served as a natural defense for the fortress, which rose up on the southern point where the hills diminished, towering above the rock as if it were built by Hephaestus, the god of stone. The castle stood square, its walls rising the height of six men. They were so thick, said Manuel, that four horsemen could ride abreast on its battlement.

As they all stared in awe, the galley drifted to port with hardly a sound except for the soft splash of oars. The harbor docks looked unusually quiet for a common day of trade. The governor, John Doukas, had ordered all ships out of port and closed the markets. The streets were deserted and the townsfolk, forewarned, peeked out nervously from their small windows.

John peered out from the fortress watchtower. He bit his lip as he observed the four Venetian galleys curl their sails and row to port. *Am I ready for them? Over five hundred God-damned Kelts!* He brushed a lock of curly, black hair from his tanned forehead and rubbed the black stubble on his chin, shuddering as he recalled the vicious battles fought against Guiscard and Bohemond. He glanced down to his fleet of war-galleys and biremes, both of which flanked the Venetians around the point, then across to the waterfront where a large contingent of his infantry waited near the docks.

"Do you see Commander Manuel?" he asked his lieutenant.

"He just left the ship, my Lord."

"Bring him to me right away."

Ramiro took five awkward steps off the exit ramp. "Good God! Three days at sea and I must learn to walk again!"

Pepin laughed. "Look at all the soldiers," he said, pointing to hundreds of men lining the rise above the docks, all armed with sword, shield, and bow.

Ramiro looked around. "Yes, we have quite a reception."

"Are we being honored, Father?"

Ramiro scoffed, remembering Manuel's stories about the Normans. "I doubt that honor plays much of a role in this grim theater, Pepin."

"What do you mean?"

"Those men, my boy, stand guard not because they honor us, but because they fear us."

"Governor Doukas sends his greetings," said the Byzantine lieutenant to Drugo. "He welcomes you to Dyrrachium and is happy to provide food and drink or anything else you may require. However, he regrets to inform you there is little accommodation within the walls and offers his sincere apologies. But we have provided a suitable campground for you and..."

"How long are we expected to wait here?" Drugo interrupted.

"I do not know, my Lord."

"Is your Governor ever going to meet with me?"

"Yes, my Lord, if I may be permitted to continue."

Drugo nodded. "Get on with it, man."

"The governor invites you to sup at his table tomorrow afternoon. An escort will arrive at the ninth hour."

People came to Ramiro about many different things. Some came to ask for his blessing, others to confess their sins, even though he told them repeatedly he was not a priest. And many others, hearing of his healing skills, came to him for medical attention.

But he had never been as busy as he was on this particular morning, his tent crowded with sick Flemings of all ranks. Most suffered fits of vomiting and diarrhea. They spent hours burning incense in their tents, kneeling and praying, appealing to the saints for divine intervention. But none of it seemed to work so they came to Ramiro in hopeful assemblies, asking for his blessings and a sprinkle of holy water to cure their ills.

Ramiro did what he could, telling most to eat whole grains and drink lots of water before sending them away. He had set up his tent close to Louis the Carpenter and often glanced over to watch Adele as she went about her work. Carts of food and drink arrived from the fortress, and when she returned with an armload, he rushed to lend a hand.

"Thank you, Dom Ramiro. You are most kind." She smiled at him, a beautiful smile.

He fumbled with the bags, dropping one to the ground. "Oh dear. I guess I'm not much help really."

She stooped to pick it up. "I believe you are most helpful," she said demurely, rising up slowly before placing the bag back into his arms.

Ramiro nodded quickly before rushing away like a bashful child.

Six men occupied one end of a long table in the expansive but stark dining hall of the castle. Spread out before them was a meal of roasted pork and fowl, vegetables, and pastries, all served with copious amounts of Albanian wine. John sat at the head, and sitting to either side were Drugo and the Byzantine commander, Manuel.

Servants were a few paces away, waiting for any signal. Near the doors, stood a squad of soldiers. And wandering about the room, sniffing in every corner, were two large Dalmatian hounds, their hard nails clacking back and forth across the gray concrete floors.

John Doukas had been questioning Drugo for some time. "It sounds like you have had an interesting journey, Sir Drugo. I'm sure you will be well accommodated on the way to Constantinople. I have arranged for a platoon of my men to accompany your Kelts on behalf of the Emperor."

Drugo bristled. "Kelts? We're Flemings."

"Of course," said John. "No offense meant. We refer to all your countrymen as Kelts."

"And we need no protection," Drugo raised his voice. "Our company is strong enough to look after itself."

John grinned. "Perhaps your small army is considered large in the land of the Kelts, but here, and farther south, it is not unusual to encounter hostile armies of many thousands."

Drugo looked up from his plate. "I'm sure we can deal with the situation, if it arises."

John leaned forward, black curls dangling across his cheeks. "Let me tell you something, Sir Drugo. Only two years ago, the Emperor battled an army of ten thousand heathen Patzinaks in a region southeast of here. Have you ever seen an army that size? I doubt your troops would be much competition for them. We've lost a lot of good men to those pagan bastards!"

Drugo stiffened. "So who are these...Pasaks?"

"Patzinaks is what we call them. They're an abomination!" John vented as he tore off a chunk of bread, "A filthy pack of Turkoman barbarians who steal everything they can!"

Drugo shuffled uneasily. "Well, whoever they are, we'll make our own way."

John didn't really care if these stinking Kelts were fed to the wolves, but he had his orders. "I'm afraid you have no choice, Captain," he said curtly. "You will almost certainly be mistaken as hostile if not accompanied by a Byzantine guard." He eyed Drugo carefully as he swallowed a draft of wine from his pewter mug. He had no liking of Normans. And the reek! Like a herd of goats!

Drugo seethed at the rebuff. "As you wish," he muttered through a mouthful of pork fat.

John raised his arms, bringing his hands together in a resounding clap, jarring the room. Drugo jumped from his seat, dropping his meat to the floor. In an instant, the two hounds scrambled for it, snarling and nipping in vicious competition. Ramiro sprang to his feet, backing away from the dogs, knocking over his chair. Others quickly hoisted their feet from the floor.

John and Manuel laughed aloud.

"Fear not, my man," John grinned at Ramiro, "...they rarely eat monks." He laughed again. "Forgive me if I alarmed you. I was merely summoning my servant. What is your name, monk?"

Ramiro lifted his chair from the floor. "I am Ramiro of Cluny, Sir," he said as he sat back down with an embarrassed look.

"Welcome Ramiro of Cluny." John reached over the table with the wine bottle, filling Ramiro's cup. "I hear some of your countrymen have fallen ill."

Ramiro nodded, accepting the wine eagerly. "I'm sure it's just the travel, Sir. The people are weary."

"Well, you and your company are welcome to stay until you recuperate. I have a physician who can tend to your sick."

"Thank you, Governor John. And if possible, perhaps you could help us find some more opium for my medicine bag, and some spelt or wheat for the sick."

"Of course. We will help you any way we can."

Drugo leaned back in his chair, his long red hair draping behind him. "My astrologer says the illness occurs because Saturn is ascending in Aries." He looked smug with his knowledge. "That would explain it—but it will pass."

John eyed Drugo incredulously. "I believe I would put more faith in my physician, Sir Drugo," he remarked, trying not to smile.

Drugo's face reddened, he had an impetuous urge to kill this Greek... or Roman... or whatever cursed race he was. "I appreciate the offer, but our women folk know the ways of medicine." He turned to look at Ramiro. "All approved by the Church, of course."

"Well, of course," said John. "The decision is yours, but the physician is a good man, he can work wonders."

"How so? Is he a magician?" Drugo mocked.

"No, actually he's a Hebrew from Thessalonica. He's very good."

Drugo jumped up suddenly. "A Hebrew!" he sneered. "They're nothing but a pack of crooked traders and stinking moneylenders! What do they know of medicine?"

John pushed his chair back in an instant, reaching for his sword. His guards moved in. "I advise you to sit down, Sir Drugo! Before you are cut down!"

A servant rushed over to right his chair. Drugo sat down hard, glaring at John.

John pulled his chair forward, calming himself. "I'm not aware of events in the West, Captain. But in our lands, Hebrews are physicians, philosophers, and men of learning. You would be wise to enlist their services. They give us no trouble and we let them be."

What John said was true at the time, although he failed to mention that, many centuries before, the Romans had expelled all Jews from Jerusalem. Only after the Muslim conquest were they allowed to return.

"I'll have no polluted Hebrews among my men." Drugo fumed. "Any good Christian knows they're the scourge of Christ and unclean. They destroyed the Holy Sepulcher! Now they conspire against the people of Christ!" Otto and Fulk nodded in agreement.

Drugo turned to Ramiro for support. "You should know, monk. Wasn't it one of your own monks at Cluny who claimed this was so?"

Ramiro shuffled uneasily, he had heard the same. "Yes... but I..."

"So?" Drugo shouted at him. "Was this not the case? Can you not verify what I say?"

"Well," Ramiro muttered, "not all of us agreed, we..."

"It was not the Hebrews who destroyed the sepulcher," John interrupted loudly. "You speak of the mad Caliph of Egypt, a man by the name of Al-Hakim. And that was about eighty years ago, but he had no help from Hebrews. On the contrary, my dear Sir, the Caliph persecuted both Christian and Hebrew, demolished both church and synagogue. Everyone knew he was mad, but what could they do?"

"You can't trust them!" Drugo belted.

"You may think as you like, Sir!" John yelled back as he slammed his food down. He wiped his hands briskly with a cloth, cursing silently—bloody ignorant Kelts, or whatever detestable race they are!

ITALY

At the first light of day, three German assassins galloped out of Rome on the best of King Henry's stallions. Sent out by the antipope, Giberto, they rode hard for Bari, rising high in the stirrups, their long cloaks flapping madly in the wind. They traveled light, daggers and short swords their only weapons.

In the lead, rode a thin, wiry man with shoulder-length black hair, a big mustache, and a shaved chin. He went by the name of Wiker. Some say he was from Koln, but he didn't speak much and never talked about himself. His neighbors said he was polite and always paid his bills on time. But those who knew him well, knew him as Wiker the Blade, a relentless assassin who considered it a matter of professional pride to fulfill every assignment. And now he was on the hunt for two Benedictine monks.

DYRRACHIUM

Drugo the Red was glad to leave Dyrrachium. He rode quietly, still brooding over his confrontation with Governor John and deeply resenting Ramiro for not standing behind him when he cursed the Hebrews. Bloody monk! Nothing but God-damn trouble!

Knights and servants followed cheerfully. Those who had fallen ill had recovered and, as their health returned, so did a new-found sense of adventure. They spoke excitedly of the wonders and riches to come.

But others looked askance at the rough band of Bulgar and Romani mercenaries riding alongside. This was their Roman escort, led by Commander Manuel. They kept to the fore, flanking the head of Drugo's troops while sporting the gold banner of the East Roman Empire.

"I don't like this!" Drugo grumbled to Otto as he eyed the soldiers suspiciously. "We have come to serve the King of the Greeks and we are treated like his enemies!" His face reddened as he spoke. "Look at these miserable dogs! We could kill the damned heretics with a few strokes of the sword!"

Otto flung his blonde hair across one shoulder as he leaned over in the saddle, shifting his shield as he did. "No doubt, m'lord. I don't like the look of the bastards either, they're a strange lot. But there's little we can do about it. Besides, they're well equipped and may prove useful. Look... not only do they carry sword and lance, but the bow too."

Drugo looked around again. "All that gear is too much for a knight. All they need is a sword and lance. How can anyone shoot arrows from horseback and hope to hit anything?"

Wiker the Blade and his two accomplices disembarked in Dyrrachium. They rode at a trot by the light of the moon, attempting to catch up with their prey while avoiding the fortress and Byzantine troops. But as dawn approached, they picked up speed, keeping a steady gait along the Egnatia Way, pushing east through the Dinaric Alps and heading straight to the city of Thessalonica.

THESSALONICA

The Axios River rushed down from the Alps before it leveled off on a wide, marshy plain. At its mouth sat Thessalonica, a large port on the Gulf of Therma and second in size and riches only to Constantinople. Moored in harbor, were thousands of merchant galleys from far and wide. The nearby docks resounded with the clatter of merchandise and the loud bellows of hard-working men and women.

But Manuel was in no mood for sightseeing. He sent a small party to the markets to replenish essential supplies before heading east again. He was impatient with their slow pace and had to constantly hound Drugo to get his company moving, repeatedly warning him of the dangers on the road to Constantinople.

Gray clouds hung overhead and it rained the whole day. Ramiro and Aldebert covered themselves with oiled cloaks while Pepin held a sodden blanket over his head.

Ramiro often roamed through the long line of travelers with Aldebert at his heels. He offered greetings and support to the sick and weary, helping out whenever he could and, as the day drew to a close, he would wander back to join Louis the Carpenter at his wagon. He rode up front, sharing the bench with Louis while Mathilda and Adele sat in the back.

The road snaked along the foothills of the southern range. Snow-capped mountain peaks towered to the northeast, soaring almost two miles into the sky. Ramiro pointed up to the lofty crests where white, wispy clouds curled up from dark, green forests. "Look up there... at the mountains. The people here say those are the Rhodope, home of the Greek hero, Orpheus. They say, if you listen, the wind will carry the melodies of his lyre." He smiled.

"Louis has a lyre!" said the plump Mathilda. "And Adele plays it just beautiful. She sings too, Dom Ramiro. Like a songbird she does."

"Mother!" Adele snapped.

"Ah well," said Ramiro. "Then Adele truly is a follower of Orpheus, he is known as the 'father of songs.'

"My, my, Dom Ramiro," said Mathilda. "Where do you learn such strange things? Does this Or... Orphy still live there?"

"No, Mathilda," he laughed, "no he does not. It's an ancient legend of the Greeks. They have many legends."

Louis, lost in his own thoughts, rubbed absently at the bristle below his big nose. He held the reins loosely, allowing his Belgian workhorse to plod along at its own pace, its wide hooves squelching in the mud. And when a wagon wheel squealed in complaint, he raised an eyebrow. "Those wheels need grease again," he murmured.

"What do you use, Louis?"

"Hog fat. But you've gotta mix the right amount of lime with the fat. If too much, the grease gets thin and won't last long."

"Would you like a drink, Dom?" Mathilda interrupted. "I have some nice spring water from Thessa... Thessa... whatever it is."

"Thessalonica," Ramiro enunciated slowly. "And, yes, Mathilda, a cool drink would be nice."

She filled a cup. "Well, Dom, I'll let you worry about the names, it's too much for me. Doesn't anybody here speak Flemish or French?"

Ramiro laughed. "It's unlikely that you'll hear anybody but ourselves speak those tongues in this land. Best to learn Greek."

Adele peeked out from the wagon cover. "Dom Ramiro," she said softly, "I made some barley bread this morning. And there's a little cheese. Would you like some?" She leaned forward, offering it to him in a wooden bowl.

Ramiro grinned at the mention of food. He turned to face her. She looked as becoming as ever. "Yes... yes Adele, thank you." He took hold of the bowl, daring to look into her eyes.

Adele smiled. She had no idea why she was so fond of Dom Ramiro. But she could feel his warm, easy strength and his endless vitality. He seemed a little odd and was not particularly handsome, but there was something else about him... perhaps his kindness... his courage or.... She caught herself locked to his gaze and, in a timid blush, quickly lowered her eyes.

KOMOTINI

The fortress of Komotini protected the Egnatia Way, but it had fallen into disrepair and the Byzantine garrison had abandoned it. The people of the village learned to fend for themselves, so when they saw Drugo's small army approaching, flying the familiar gold standard of the Roman Empire, twenty armed riders came out to greet them.

"Greetings, we come in peace," Manuel assured them. "Do not be alarmed." He could see a scurry of frantic activity over the low village walls.

"Welcome... welcome to Komotini," stammered a thin man in a squeaky, nervous voice. "I'm the village headman." He approached uneasily on his small horse. "If you come in peace, why are you so heavily armed?" His small eyes darted about.

"The road is not safe, as you must know," said Manuel, scrutinizing the small party of men. "We are on our way to Constantinople to serve Emperor Alexios in his fight against the infidels. May God protect him."

The headman's stubbled face broke into a smile and he chuckled. "Well then, you could start right here, the Turkoman raid us from the north."

"They have come this far?" Manuel asked, trying not to sound surprised. He glanced up to the hills, fearing to see a horde of savages at the crest.

"We haven't seen them yet," said the man. "But people coming from the north and east say they have. No one is safe anymore. Where are the Emperor's men to protect us?"

"We are doing what we can," Manuel replied with a tone of sufferance. "Perhaps your men here would like to join us in the fight?"

"Uhm...," he mumbled, "well, they're not really fighting men, m'lord. We're just poor farmers." He nodded in deference. "But an enemy of the Turkoman is a friend of ours." He leaned to the side to look at Ramiro. The curious shaved heads and black robes of Benedictine monks were an unwelcome sight in these parts. He had dealt with Westerners before and did not trust them, and being a Greek Christian, he did not trust the Pope's men either. He was anxious to see them on their way. "May God speed you my good men," he said with a wry smile. "And when are you sending us another garrison?"

"That's not possible yet." Manuel prodded his horse forward. "We need all the fighting men we can muster if we're ever going to push the savages out of Thrace."

As they broke camp the next morning, dark clouds billowed to the south and a damp southerly wind beat at their tents. "We ride too slowly," Ramiro complained as he packed his gear. "We could reach Constantinople in half the time if we were all mounted. Look at all these women and children! God bless them, but they can be nothing but trouble. Why do the knights insist on bringing them to war?" He tied a belt around his waist and tucked a small dagger into it.

Aldebert watched him. "Why do you carry that knife, Father Ramiro? Are we not men of peace?"

Ramiro forced a smile. "A knife is useful for many things, Brother Aldebert. And, while I am a man of peace, many others are not. We are entering a strange land with many enemies and I'm afraid our black habits give us little safety."

"God will protect you, Father. You must have faith."

Ramiro glared at him. "Mind your tongue, Brother Aldebert!"

Aldebert flushed red.

For many hours, they rode without a word between them, following a narrow road winding through dark green forests. It seemed strangely quiet. Even the birds fell silent. The only sound was the clop of hooves and the unceasing cacophony of rattling armor and clanging pots. A cool breeze licked their faces as the gloomy gray clouds darkened by the hour.

"We must be careful along this stretch, Sir Drugo," Manuel warned. "We have little control here or to the north, where the Turkoman roam." He scoured the land. "We must be wary of ambush from forests and high ground."

Drugo picked at his red beard, his eyes darting across the rounded hills. "You mentioned Patzinaks and Turkoman, are they the same?"

"Yes, the Patzinaks are one tribe of Turkoman, but there are many others."

"So when you speak of Turks, do you mean Turkoman?"

"No, not really. When we speak of Turks, we speak of the men of the Seljuk Empire, the ones who took Persia, they are Muslim."

"What do you mean?"

"The Turkoman are not Muslim. They're godless pagans who worship stones and drink the blood of their enemies."

Drugo had spent most of his life fighting Normans and Flemings as they vied for control of the rich vales of Flanders. He was one of the Count's most valiant men. But here in this alien land, he felt a chill. Perhaps it was the strange landscape, the strange people, or the strange smells. These Patzinaks sounded unnatural. "Where are my damned scouts?" he bellowed.

An unusual silence fell upon the long procession of knights. The farther from France they rode, the more unnatural the countryside became; the land, the trees, the animals, the mountains—even the air was different, the people, the dress, the languages—all so unfamiliar. Knights fiddled with their weapons, archers inspected their quills.

The southern wind, once a gentle breeze, now blustered through the treetops, whipping back and forth. Twisters of dust danced along the road. People held tight to their capes while others ran after bags caught by the wind, yelling as they tumbled away. Whirlwinds of dust grew to thick billows, pushing north in long, rolling waves. The clouds darkened and broiled. Hours passed. The scouts did not return.

Ramiro covered his mouth and shielded his eyes to peer ahead, the dust too thick to see clearly. But he noticed a commotion at the front of the line, where Drugo and the Byzantines were in the lead. They were shouting at each other, trying to be heard over the howl of the wind.

Drugo suddenly held up his arm. "What's this?" he yelled. "By God's grace and mercy!" He backed away making the sign of the cross, something he rarely did. Curious knights rushed to look for themselves. They too, staggered back, crossing themselves.

Ramiro dismounted, dashing over. He barged through the knights and, as the haze cleared, he saw the grisly sight. There, on the side of the road, impaled on two rough poles, were the gaping heads of the scouts, still dripping fresh blood.

Before they could regain their senses, a rising chorus of long, piercing screams chilled the air. In a single motion, all heads turned to the shrill war cries sounding from the hilltop. Then they saw them, about one hundred paces up, the menacing silhouettes of armed horsemen.

Drugo felt his heart beat cold. He shouted above the commotion, "Are those your Patzinaks, Commander?"

Manuel looked up, shielding his eyes. "Sounds like them but it's difficult to see. I doubt they will charge, but we should get out of arrow range."

"We are well out of range, they're a hundred paces away."

"That's not enough!" Manuel shouted. "A hundred paces is not enough for a Turkoman arrow!"

Drugo, shaken by the sight of his dead scouts, grew increasingly alarmed. "Formations! Now!" he bellowed. "Keep it tight! Shields up!"

The uneasy knights jostled into position, preparing to meet the enemy, hearts pounding at the promise of battle. But before they could form a line of defense, a deadly hail of arrows rained down from the darkened sky.

Servants, women, and infantry, riddled with arrows, collapsed to the ground, writhing and screaming in pain and horror. All around them, arrows thudded into the dry earth while others glanced from armor or struck shields. Horses fell wounded, squealing and braying, tossing their riders to the ground.

Chaos followed and, in the commotion, Drugo feared they would be slaughtered like pigs in a pen. He held his shield high to protect his face. "Commander

Manuel! Take the rest of the company to the south, out of range!" he bellowed before riding off to challenge the Patzinaks.

Manuel motioned to him excitedly, shouting back. He was trying to warn him about something but the howl of the wind and Drugo's own shouts drowned him out.

"For the love of God, my men, take courage!" Drugo yelled, trotting behind the line of Flemish knights. "Fear not! Get ready for charge! Lances at the ready!" He waved his arm in a wide arc. "Archers to position! Shoot at will!"

The archers loosed their arrows, shooting five or six a minute. "God is at your right hand, my men! We will purge the earth of these pagan bastards! Chaaarge!" They bolted up the dry, rocky slope, hooting in bloodlust, the banner of Flanders flapping in the wind. They spurred their war-horses closer and closer to the heathen, the hooves churning the dry ground, creating a thick cloud of fine dust in their headlong charge.

The Turkoman held position, continuing to shoot their arrows. For days, they had watched the long party lumber eastward across the plain. What booty they would take! Horses and gold—and women! But as the galloping knights loomed closer and closer, they wavered. Their strategy relied on salvos of arrows to create havoc, causing the enemy to break rank. Then they would charge in to finish off their prey with lance and sword.

But the knights kept coming, and in their assault, fierce winds whipped the cloud of dust up the hill, blinding the Turkoman, who now faltered with their arrows. The unnerving sight of hundreds of strange horsemen charging relentlessly up the hill, and better armed than most on this lonely road, was enough to intimidate even the most courageous among them. They knew their shields of thick rawhide offered little defense against the heavy steel of a Norman sword. In an instant, they spun around, fleeing along a winding path leading north, higher into the mountains. They rode fast, unencumbered by heavy weapons or armor.

The Flemings charged onto the level crest of the hill, only to find the enemy had fled. Feeling vindicated, they galloped after them in mad pursuit, howling insults as they went, keen for the blood of revenge. But they had little hope of catching up. Their European mounts were slow and clumsy compared to the sleek ponies of the Eurasian steppes, and the weight of their armor slowed them even more. After a fruitless chase, the Patzinaks were nowhere to be seen.

Drugo called a halt to the charge, ordering his men to regroup. It was time to return to the company. But as he turned his steed near the summit, something caught his eye. He looked to the west, peering down the smooth slopes to the dark plain beyond. Then he saw them. "What's this?" he shouted to Otto. "Look!" He pointed. "There they are! On the plain below!"

"They're heading back to the main road!" Otto shouted. "They're going back to the camp!"

In a flash of dread, Drugo realized the ruse. He panicked, thinking of his gold and horses. "Ride like the devil!" he roared. "The sons of bitches are heading back to camp!" They galloped off in a frenzy, the line of charge no longer an ordered affair, every man riding as fast as he could, leaving the slow and the wounded behind.

In the initial attack, Ramiro's fighting instincts returned. He jumped off his horse, using it as a shield to escape the rain of arrows. As he took cover, an arrow pierced the hind quarter of his mare. It screamed, kicking its legs high in the air in a vain attempt to dislodge the barb. Ramiro fought hard to hold it steady, Pepin rushed over to help. Together, they tethered the frantic beast to a nearby tree. It screamed again as Ramiro pulled the arrow from its flesh.

"Come! Take this!" Ramiro shoved a wad of cloth into Pepin's hands. "Dress its wound. I'll tend to others!" In a moment of panic, he thought of his mission. Frantically, he groped under his robe. Ah! There it is. He felt a wave of relief as he fingered the pouch holding the Pope's letters.

The gust died down and the dust settled. The wounded came into view, sprawled along the road, writhing and wailing in agony. Ramiro's heart pounded. He sought desperately to regain his senses. "Where's my help when I need it?" he shouted to no one. "Where's Aldebert?" He ran closer to the woods. "Aldebert! Aldebert! Where are you, man? Come to help the wounded!" People began to creep out of their hiding, but no Aldebert.

He darted to and fro down the dusty road, looking about frantically, checking the wounded and dead sprawled in the dirt. Then he saw him, his black robe caked in a thick layer of yellow dust. "By all saints! Aldebert! Are you hurt?" He rushed over to crouch beside him.

Aldebert lay face down in the dirt, his arms and legs splayed out in a peculiar manner. Ramiro rolled him onto his back. "Dear Lord!" His face was cut and bruised, his mouth full of dirt. An arrow had pierced his left shoulder just above the heart. The shaft had snapped off in his fall and only a splinter of it protruded from his skin.

"Oh no! Dear God, no!" He pushed Aldebert onto his side, cleaning out his mouth with his fingers. He bent down, listening for breath. "Oh dear Lord. Thank you, Mother Mary, he lives!" He wiped Aldebert's face before propping his head on a flat stone, making sure he could breathe easily before rushing back to his horse, rummaging through the saddlebags to find his medicine bag.

When he got back to Aldebert, he knelt again, pulling the blood-stained robe off his shoulder. He took hold of the broken arrow shaft with a pair of iron pliers and, in a practiced maneuver, swayed it back and forth, dislodging the point from the bone. It came free and, to his relief, the barb came out too. Blood oozed from the wound. He let it bleed a little before wrapping his shoulder with a strip of linen.

An anguished scream jarred him from his work. He glanced over to a wounded woman writhing in the dirt far to his left, a Patzinak arrow protruding from her side. With a moan of worry, he left Aldebert, rushing over to her. The woman howled in torment, clutching at the arrow. "Help me monk... help me!"

Ramiro inspected the wound but said nothing. He had seen this kind of injury many times before and he knew the inevitable outcome. "Quiet, woman. I will do what I can." He could tell by her elegant dress that she was no servant girl, but the wife of a knight. She was small and slight, and her black hair, usually covered with a shawl as required by custom, was clumped and soiled from her fall. Ramiro attempted to stop the blood as it drained into the dust. "What's your name, and who do you accompany?"

"I... I'm Hellad, wife... wife of Arles," she sobbed and convulsed. Ramiro looked around for help. To his great relief, he saw Mathilda coming out from her hiding in the woods. Adele trailed behind. "Mathilda!" he shouted, "Come to help!"

The two women rushed to his side. "Dom Ramiro, what can we do?"

"One of you hold her still while I remove the arrow!" Mathilda hesitated at the sight of blood, staggering a little. "Quickly now!"

Adele hastened to take her mother's place, dropping to her knees beside the wounded woman. "Keep her arms down!" he shouted. She positioned herself at the woman's head. Ramiro glanced up at her as he worked. "How's Louis?"

Adele flipped her hair from her face with a toss of her head. "By God's mercy, Dom Ramiro, he is well."

"God be praised," he muttered as he placed a hand around the bloody wound and in a slow, steady movement, pulled the arrow from its lodging. Hellad screamed. More blood spurted from the wound, drenching her green linen dress in swathes of red. He halted the flow with a cloth and looked again at Adele, who had gone pale at the sight. "Quickly, wrap your scarf around the wound. We must stop the blood." Despite the severity of Hellad's wound, he was careful to keep her clothing in place. It was not acceptable for him to view her naked skin. "Get some help to move her to the woods. Tend to her there."

Adele nodded, looking up to Mathilda for help.

Ramiro muttered a prayer. "Please Father, take this poor woman's soul into your bosom." He made the sign of the cross. "May the Father of mercies, the God of all consolation, be with you." He had long studied medicine and surgical practices, and he was familiar with the works of Abu Al-Qasim, a resident of Cordoba considered the greatest surgeon of his time. But despite all his knowledge, it grieved him deeply to know there was nothing he could do for Hellad. The wound was fatal.

Manuel commandeered the rest of the men left behind when Drugo charged up the hill, including his Bulgarian mercenaries from Dyrrachium. He held his sword high, trotting his white steed through the disarray, barking orders into the chaotic crowd. "Move the bodies south. Take the wounded to the wood!" The Kelts were glad he had the courage to lead and they followed his directions willingly, even though he was not one of their own.

Manuel was worried. The knights had been gone too long. He was familiar with the tactics of these Turkoman and regretted not taking the time to discuss them with Drugo. He feared the pagans would return. "All who are armed and can fight, join me now!" The men rushed to arms. "Get everyone back into the woods," he shouted. "The wounded too! All of you with arrows will ring the outside! Those with lance and sword, stand ready for combat!"

Men and women rushed to do his bidding. But those at a distance failed to hear his warnings. A number of servants and infantry were far down the road collecting supplies and valuables dropped during the initial commotion.

The Turkoman appeared suddenly, thundering around the western foothills at full gallop. They came fast, startling the stragglers, who soon dropped their bags to flee. The Turkoman came faster still, hooting and yelling, their long, black cloaks whipping behind. One by one, they ran down the Flemings with lance and sword. Another leaned off his saddle, scooping up a young girl as she ran screaming. But the rest hardly slowed for the slaughter. They had their eyes on the wagons, the pack horses, and the women.

Wails of fear and desperate prayers howled from the woods. Anxious archers faced west, their strings half-drawn, waiting for a signal. Manuel watched the Patzinaks charge, gauging their distance. "Hold your arrows!"

The heathen approached fast. Still at full gallop, they steered their nimble steeds with their knees and, in a single motion, sheathed their bloodied swords to pull out their bows, their eyes fixed on chosen targets. At forty paces, they shot their first volley. A barrage of arrows pierced the woods. More screams.

"Loose your arrows!" shouted Manuel. The archers shot their own volley. At forty paces, even the Flemish arrow was deadly. The front row of galloping

Turkoman staggered, horses and riders toppled to the ground. Those charging behind leapt over the bodies or faltered, crashing into rocks and dirt. The rest galloped past to the right, where the Flemish aim was hindered. They shot as they rode. More shrieks pierced the air.

Manuel continued to bark orders and the archers hustled frantically to new positions. The raiders now approached the grove from the east but, just as they began their second charge, Drugo and his furious knights came charging down the low slopes. The Patzinaks realized they were out of time and grabbed what they could before turning to flee.

Drugo led the charge, attacking head on. While his steed was not swift, it was heavy and strong, trained to charge headfirst, kicking and biting the enemy. Fully armed and weighted with armor, he fell on the Turkoman with the ferocity of a Russian bear. Other knights rushed in with lances, stabbing at faces, legs, and chests. When their lances were spent, they drew out swords, axes, and maces, hacking at arms, legs, and heads in the crazed bloodlust of battle.

The Patzinaks, unprepared for the brute force of Norman savagery, tried again to outrun the killing frenzy, but Drugo's right flank closed in for the final kill. Only forty Turkoman managed to escape the pincer but the rest, outnumbered and outmaneuvered, were slaughtered to a man by the hooting knights, who hacked at flesh and bone long after they were dead, laughing in the relish of victory.

All fell quiet in the eerie aftermath. Ramiro ran from the woods to survey the battleground. The earth was wet with blood and the air thick with its smell. Gored bodies, strewn across the ground, mingled with hacked arms and legs. Saddles, swords, shields, and lances lay scattered between the corpses of men and horses. Five knights lay dead, thirty-one wounded. Infantry and servants fared worse, Ramiro counted over forty dead and a hundred wounded—men, women, and children.

Squires and archers ran in to finish off the wounded pagans. They wanted some booty of their own. But the knights drove them off with threats, rushing madly between the corpses, hoarding it all for themselves. They soon came to blows.

"I killed him!" shouted one. "His sword is mine! And so is his horse!" Two men stood defiantly, nose to nose.

"I killed him!" The other shouted. "Look—that's my lance!"

Drugo stepped in, shouting above the fray. "Quiet, you stupid bastards! Listen to me!" The squabbling subsided. "A man is entitled to anything he captures, regardless of rank! That is the law. If you have disagreements, then I will decide." The men grumbled and cursed, flashing greedy eyes at their luckier counterparts. They lay claim to weapons, horses, armor, and money. Only the shields were tossed aside, for who would display the colors of an enemy?

Archers pulled arrows from bodies and ran between the road and the hills collecting others that had missed their mark. Squires cut the throats of wounded horses and left them where they fell. Servants and infantry threw the dead Turkoman to the side of the road, where they rotted for three days before being burned by local peasants. Meanwhile, they buried their own with ceremony on the crest of the hill.

"Captain!" yelled Ramiro, tired and filthy. "I must speak with you."

Drugo was trotting around the bloody scene in an attempt to keep order among his troops. He turned with a scowl. "Yeh, monk, what is it?"

"Who is Arles? His wife is wounded."

"If you mean Arles of Ghent, he's over there, the big knight with dark hair, the one holding a black stallion." He pointed briefly before turning away.

Ramiro saw the man, who was waving his arms wildly while cursing a fellow knight. He recognized him. It was the tall executioner who had held his battle axe over Louis the Carpenter some weeks before.

"Are you Arles, husband of Hellad?" he asked, stepping up to the two quarreling men.

Arles, a giant of a man, looked down on him, frowning at the interruption. "Yeh, what of it? What do you want now, monk?

"I regret to tell you, Sir, that your wife is badly wounded."

"What?"

"An arrow struck her side, Sir. I'm very sorry but there is little I can do. May she rest in God's mercy."

"What do you mean, monk? She will recover, will she not?"

"It has pierced her bowels. I regret to say it is unlikely she will live the day."

"You lie! Stinking monk! Where is she! Tell me before I hack off your fat head and feed it to the crows!"

Ramiro stood his ground, although he knew rogue knights thought little of killing monks and robbing churches, as they had done so often in the past. "She's over by the grove with her servants."

Arles ran off without another word, ignoring the booty. He found Hellad in the throes of death, poisoned from her ruptured bowels, her face ashen white, dripping large beads of sweat. "Hellad! What's happened?" He fell to his knees beside her. "Don't die, my love! Promise me you won't die!"

Years before, Arles had forcibly taken Hellad from her home in the Welsh

Marches when he fought with Normans to seize that land. She had little choice and was betrothed to him as a payment of mercy, an effort by her family to avoid destruction. Nonetheless, she knew no other way and had become fond of the man, despite his blundering cruelty.

She could barely talk. "I... I can... cannot hold much longer, Arles. The monk tried to help, but the wound is too deep. He... Oh God..." she flinched. "... he has prayed for me." Another spasm gripped her and she wailed in agony.

In a fit of rage, Arles rose up, turning on his servants. "What are you doing you useless pigs? Have you dressed her wounds? Can you do nothing but stand there like idiots?"

A young girl braved a reply. "We have done all we can, m'lord. There is nothing more we can do for her now."

With a heavy hand, Arles struck the girl across the side of the head, sending her flying into a thicket where she lay unconscious.

"You stupid bastards!" he shouted through tears. "Go away! Go away! Before I slit your throats!" The rest ran for safety, leaving the poor girl in the bushes. He knelt again beside Hellad, the iron rings of his mail leggings digging into the flesh of his knees, but he did not notice. In his awkward way, he attempted to comfort her. Tears streamed through the grime on his cheeks. He threw off his helmet and sword to embrace her. And there, in a grove of hornbeam, he held her in his arms, swaying on his knees, still clinging to her long after she died.

Dark clouds burst in a torrent of heavy beads. Men and women, too exhausted and too shocked to resist, simply succumbed to the downpour, letting it wash away the dust, blood, and grime from their sunburned faces.

Aldebert lay on his back in the grass with the other wounded, rain pelting at his upturned face. Slowly, he began to regain consciousness, weeping silently from the gnawing pain in his shoulder. The rain stopped as suddenly as it began and he opened his eyes. Clouds dissipated and a few rays of afternoon sun swept across the people of Flanders.

Ramiro tended to the wounded all afternoon, returning to Aldebert's side before dusk. "Brother Aldebert, I see you remain alive and well." He pretended not to notice his tears. "Come now, I must finish dressing your wound." He knelt beside him, pulling back the wet, blood-stained robe to expose the gash in his shoulder.

Aldebert wailed. "Aaagh! O, my God... O my God. Blessed Mary have mercy on a pitiful sinner!" His lips curled in anguish and he heaved from the searing pain. "Father Ramiro, is this where I am to die… in this… in this God-forsaken land? Among these godless heathen? Aaagh! Careful, careful!"

Ramiro pulled the dressing from the open wound as gently as he could, but he still tore at the fresh scab cemented to the cotton wad. "God willing, Aldebert, you will live another day. You have no choice but to brave the pain as best you can." He took out a bloodied, curved needle from his kit, one he had used many times that day, squinting as he threaded it with linen string. "Pepin!" he shouted. "Pepin, come to help!"

Pepin left the horses, rushing to Ramiro's side to gawk in macabre fascination at Aldebert's open wound. The threat of death and the fray of war had brought him to new heights of awareness—his heart pounded.

"Come on, lad! Take that cotton and dab at the blood so I can see what I'm doing."

Aldebert began to pull away at the sight of the needle, but Ramiro put a heavy palm to his chest to flatten him back down. Aldebert resigned himself, eyeing the needle with terror, wailing like a child when it pierced his skin. He spun his head away, praying feverishly. "Our Father who is in Heaven, holy is Your name! Your kingdom come, Your will be done…"

"Come, come, Brother Aldebert, hold still." Ramiro's eyes strained to guide the needle. "You will never survive in this land if you cannot take a little pain. You wanted adventure, and now you have it. You wanted to come as my aide, well aid me now by lying still. I cannot do this work if you squirm like an eel." He lifted his head, nodding to his left. "Look at those soldiers over there, they sew their own wounds!"

"Father Ramiro! I never thought I'd have to be sewn back together! They told us the road to Jerusalem was safe! Now look at my sorry state! Blessed Mary!"

"Hold still! I'll give you something for the pain once I'm done." He finished tying the wound while Pepin sopped up the blood. After wiping his hands, he pulled out a pouch of crude pills from his bag. "Here, take one of these, it will ease your pain."

"What is it?"

"It's opium with a little mandrake. It'll dull the pain and help you sleep. Trust me, young man, the soldiers use it… and the Greeks say it's good for diarrhea, too." He smiled.

"But mandrake, Father? Isn't that what witches use to summon dark spirits?"

"Why would witches alarm a man of God?" He offered the pill. "If it gives you any peace of mind, my friend, it was uprooted at midnight with appropriate prayer and ritual. Take it… or live with the pain, the choice is yours."

Reluctantly, Aldebert took the pill, washing it down with a long draft from a water-skin. He continued to pray but, before the hour was up, he fell sound asleep with a rare look of contentment.

Nursing their wounds, the entire troupe struggled along for three more miles to remove themselves from the shadow of the hills and to find shelter. They carried the injured to a makeshift camp near a small, abandoned village. The inhabitants, hearing that alien warriors approached, had fled to the hills. Drugo and his men went about pillaging what they could from buildings and farms while Manuel and Ramiro tried to discourage them, but to no avail.

Aldebert woke to a flash of pain, sitting up suddenly, putting a hand to his shoulder. Ramiro was gone. His bed was packed. "Father—where are you?" he cried in near panic. "Father Ramiro! ... the torment... it's insufferable!" An excruciating pain seared through his shoulder when he yelled, and he soon fell silent. He tried to get up but fell back with a grimace. "O Blessed Virgin! Don't let me die in this heathen land!"

Within the hour, Ramiro flung open the skirt of the tent. "How do you fare this bright morning, Brother Aldebert?"

"I cannot move, Father Ramiro. The pain... it's so painful."

Ramiro smiled. "The pain is painful, you say. Well, well. I'll give you a little more opium."

This time, Aldebert took the medicine gladly and before long he was smiling quietly. He managed to get up with Ramiro's help. "I will ride today, Father. I feel fine now."

"You will not. Too much motion will break your wound. I talked to Captain Drugo and we decided to stay here for a few days before heading to Adrianople."

ADRIANOPLE

Not far past Komotini, the mountains gave way to the vast plains of eastern Thrace and, before long, Drugo's company left the Egnatia Way to follow the Maritsa River north to Adrianople, a fortress city guarding another major artery to Constantinople, the Via Militaris. The citadel of Adrianople sat on a hill, high above the plains and surrounded on all sides by merchant settlements and vast estates of rich farmland.

Ramiro was heartened by the promise of a good meal and another mug of red wine. After weeks of grueling travel, the prospect was as heavenly as meeting Saint Peter at the pearly gates. Maybe he would get a chance to sleep in a real bed! But when he turned to say something to Aldebert, his merriment vanished. His assistant rode bent in the saddle, his pale face whiter than usual. Ramiro had done all he could to tend his wound but it continued to fester. "How do you feel?" He raised his voice. "Brother Aldebert! Are you alright?"

Aldebert lifted his head lazily. "What?"

"We will rest soon. Not much farther now."

General Taticius

The small assembly hall in the citadel of Adrianople was stark and simple, lightly furnished with rough-hewn chairs and a plain wooden table marred with cuts and scratches. The men fidgeted awkwardly as General Taticius entered. They were not entirely sure why Manuel had diverted them north to this city.

As Taticius took his place at the table, the men stared at him with open mouths. Ramiro looked twice. Drugo and his men continued to gawk, not sure what they were seeing. Taticius was a short man with cropped, dark hair and olive skin, but these common characteristics are not what caught their attention. There was something else about him that was extremely peculiar—he had an iron nose. It was strapped to his face with a fine cord that crossed his cheekbones and wrapped above his ears. And while everyone gaped at this gray oddity, he stared back with fearless, resolute eyes. The spectacle unnerved them all, even more so when he spoke. His castrato voice belied his aggressive look and athletic build.

Taticius was a half-breed, his father an Arab and his mother a Greek slave. Taken as a young slave himself by the Byzantines, he was castrated and soon found himself employed in the royal household. But his intelligence and level-headed courage quickly earned him a name on the battlefield and, by the time he was twenty, he had become a lieutenant. But not long after, he fell in battle with the Turks, who cut off his nose, sending it to Byzantium along with a ransom note.

Taticius sat with his elbows resting on the tabletop, his fingers laced together in front of his iron nose. "I have heard of your troubles with the Turkoman, Sir Drugo."

"I lost five good men and several horses," Drugo said accusingly. "We had no idea the road was unsafe."

"My apologies," replied Taticius, opening his hands in a conciliatory gesture. "But this is a recent development. The Patzinaks have gained courage since defeating us in battle. Now they believe they can seize Constantinople too. The Emperor is doing all he can to crush them once and for all."

"I'll fight the bastards, General, but right now we need more supplies and medicines. Many of my men still suffer from their wounds."

Taticius nodded. "I will get you whatever you need, and I can send surgeons to your camp if you wish."

Drugo said nothing for a while, remembering his bitter argument with John Doukas over the Hebrew physician. He would not allow impure heathen among his men. It would curse them all. "Thanks for the offer, General, but we just need medicine and bandages."

For many hours, Drugo, Manuel, and Taticius huddled in discussion while Ramiro listened and translated. They talked about the food, the weather, and the land, and they talked about the Turks and the Patzinaks, about battles and strategies.

"You will be interested to know," said Taticius, "that I have quite a large detachment of Normans under my command. Some of them are here right now. After we settle in, I will introduce you."

After much wine, Drugo and his exhausted men stumbled to their tents while Ramiro dawdled behind. "General Taticius, may I speak with you?"

"Yes, Monk Ramiro, of course, what is it?"

"Is it possible, Sir," he asked quietly, "for one of your physicians to tend to my fellow monk? He was badly wounded in the attack and does not heal. He needs help, but I cannot afford to displease Captain Drugo, who is quite particular about who tends to his men, if you understand my meaning."

"Yes, of course, I will make the arrangements. Bring him here this evening. If it offends your Captain, tell him you go to the Church of Sophia to pray for his healing."

"Thank you, Sir. I will do as you say." He rushed away with hope in his heart.

A Physician

When Ramiro returned to his tent, he found Aldebert nearly unconscious. The air reeked of infection. "Come Brother Aldebert, we must leave now. I have found some help for you. Come on, get up. You will die if you lay here any longer."

Aldebert nodded in a stupor. "I cannot die here Father," he mumbled "... please Ramiro, ... take me home... I just want to go home..."

Ramiro took hold of his good arm, ignoring his pleas. "Come now, ease your weight on my shoulders and try to walk as best you can. We are going to pray." Aldebert made an effort to raise himself but fell back. Ramiro stooped to catch him, pulling him upright. They left in an awkward amble, heading for the city gates.

Taticius rose from his chair when they arrived. "Welcome, Ramiro of Cluny. Let me introduce you to my physician, Fawwaz Al-Baghdadi." He motioned to the man, who sat leisurely in the spacious guest room adorned with colorful rugs and blue ceramic tiles. Fawwaz wore a long white tunic and a white linen cap. He was a tall man with a round face, aquiline nose, and a full black beard.

Ramiro was a little surprised to see an Arab physician in the employ of a Byzantine, although he was starting to get accustomed to it. He nodded slowly. "Greetings, Sayyid Fawwaz. It was kind of you to come."

Fawwaz returned the greeting and motioned to his right. "Bring your fellow monk over to the couch so I may inspect his wound." He studied the two monks quietly and voiced several pleasantries before beginning his work. With Ramiro's help, he removed Aldebert's robe and carefully pulled back the old dressing. He reeled back in repulsion at the stench of the wound. Taking a deep breath, he leaned forward to examine it closely.

"Take the man's garments," he addressed the servants with some urgency. "Wash them in boiling water! And bring me a basin of hot water with salt and vinegar, and another kettle just boiled... and strips of clean cotton cloth, just washed and dried. Go, go!" After they scurried off, he picked up his medicine bag, opening it on a nearby table. Here, he laid out several instruments on a clean cotton cloth. "Who attended his wound?"

"I did," said Ramiro. "I have done this many times before and I know a little of medicine, but it refuses to heal. I even poured some vinegar on it."

"Your stitching is good, Ramiro of Cluny, but you have failed to clean the wound."

"But I let it bleed."

"Sometimes that is not enough. A man knows not to offer food with his left hand because it is unclean. So too, you should guard the wound against the foul matter the eyes cannot see. Come, you may assist me. Cover him with that blanket. What have you given him?"

"Just some opium for the pain, but I also have a sleeping potion."

"Good, give him some of that. Then we will wait a while."

After what seemed like an endless wait, Fawwaz sat on a small stool to begin his operation. With a small, razor-sharp knife, he cut away Ramiro's stitches and the wound immediately spurted pus and blood. He dabbed at the secretion with a small cloth before turning his head impatiently. "Where are those servants?"

Taticius, who was watching the affair with some fascination, rose from his chair, yelling down the hall to his chamberlain. "Get those servants in here… quickly!"

Fawwaz opened the wound as wide as possible, washing it in strong vinegar before examining it again. "As long as the infection is not in his blood, he may live," he said as he cleaned his knife and began to cut away dead flesh, washing out the wound periodically with a salt solution. When finished, he sewed the skin and dressed the wound with a poultice of linseed, mustard, and borax. "Wash the wound with vinegar and salt every day and use a similar dressing. I will give you the ingredients."

Ramiro beamed. "I cannot thank you enough, Doctor Fawwaz. You are a true Samaritan."

"Well, actually, I'm Sunni. But I understand what you say. I believe he will live. Give thanks to Allah."

"Yes, yes, of course. Praise God Almighty." He turned to Taticius. "May I stay with Aldebert tonight, General?"

"Yes, of course. The servants will arrange a bed for you."

Aldebert sat in a daze, staring absently at the plate in front of him, a breakfast of fruit, bread, and eggs.

Ramiro watched him anxiously. "Eat, Brother Aldebert!" But Aldebert stared glassy-eyed and did not respond. Ramiro slapped a hand on the table. Aldebert jumped. "If you will not eat, you will not heal! You will do as I say and finish your meal!"

Aldebert looked up, seemingly unaffected by Ramiro's ire. His left arm hung in a new sling. "I feel better, Father, thanks to our good Lord, but my shoulder still hurts terrible." He shuddered, pulling his robe tight around him before rubbing his dark-ringed eyes with his knuckles.

"Give it time, Brother, give it time. But God cannot help you if you do not eat!"

"It was good of those people to wash my robe," said Aldebert quietly. And my wound looks better. Who was the physician?" His hand shook as he reached for bread.

Ramiro looked into his bloodshot eyes and hesitated, he was not about to tell him the physician was a Muslim and that he had been given a bath. "He was a very good man, Brother Aldebert. Now please… finish your breakfast."

They left Taticius' house before midday, making their way to the church. "We must go to church, Brother, to pray and to thank God for healing your wound."

"But I have not healed yet."

"Nonetheless, we will thank God anyway." He had told Drugo he was taking Aldebert into the city to pray at the church, and that is what he would do.

"Do you have anymore opium, Father? I think my pain is getting worse."

"You've had enough for now. Let us pray."

Smoke rose in wispy spirals from Drugo's camp, where hundreds of canvas tents sprawled in chaotic clusters outside the south wall of Adrianople. Except for the constant shouting and clang of steel, the air was still, allowing the smoke to rise in thin columns before it flattened in a gray cloud high above. Weary servants rushed about to attend to the whims of their masters while knights and squires fought mock battles, trained horses and, as the day wore on, gambled and drank. Many arrived late to Vespers in a heady state of mind.

A huge crowd milled about Ramiro as he recited the last prayer.

> *May the peace of God, which passes all*
> *understanding,*
> *Be with us throughout this day*
> *And with all those we love.*
> *Amen*

After the crowd dispersed, Manuel arrived at Drugo's tent. "The bath houses are ready, Sir Drugo."

"Bath houses? What are you talking about?"

"For your presentation to the Emperor. We will arrive in Constantinople within the week and the baths in Adrianople are the only ones until we reach the capital."

Drugo laughed aloud. "You expect us to bathe?"

"Yes, Sir Drugo. You cannot arrive in the city like this."

"Like what?"

"Well... you... your men are filthy, Sir. They stink. We must make them presentable. The servants too, if you like."

"You jest, man." He quaffed the last of his beer.

"I jest not, Sir," said Manuel, becoming annoyed. "It is an order."

"An order?"

"Yes, Sir Drugo. You should remember that you and your men are now in the employ of the Roman Emperor and you will do as he bids."

Drugo reddened. "I have yet to make my oath to him."

Manuel could barely mask his contempt. His blue eyes flashed beneath his smooth, tanned brow. "If you are unwilling to follow simple instructions," he said with disdain, "you should turn back now."

"It is immoral!" Aldebert sputtered. "It is a sin in the eyes of God, Father. How can you condone such activity, let alone participate?"

"Why is it immoral, Brother Aldebert?" he asked, remembering the pleasures he had enjoyed while a prisoner of the Moors. "Where does it say in the Holy Scriptures that we shall not bathe?"

"Well... uh, well... what about Saint Benedict himself, Father? He says only the sick should bathe!" He had a smug look, feeling righteous in his quote.

Ramiro's tan cheeks widened in a broad smile. "If that is the case, it seems all the more reason for you to join in, Brother. And if you read his Rules carefully, he did not say we should never bathe, but to do it sparingly."

"But Father, our physicians say it removes protective films from the skin, letting in vile humors. They say it causes sickness ... even death!"

"Well, perhaps our physicians are wrong, Brother Aldebert. The Byzantines and the Muslims all bathe regularly and they seem healthy enough to me."

"How can you say such things, Father Ramiro? The Byzantine faith is blasphemous, and the Muslims are heathen!"

"You can deny their faith if you wish, Brother, but how can you deny their knowledge? Can you not admit they may know more of such things?"

"But even if you allow men in the baths," Aldebert fumed, "how can you justify exposing the women too? The thought is too much, Father Ramiro, for women to bathe openly in a public place!"

"The women bathe alone, Brother. Only women exposed to women. Even the slaves who tend them are women. How can a woman's body offend another woman?"

"Well, I think it is wicked, Father—wicked! I will say no more."

Ramiro rolled his eyes in exasperation. "Think what you like but you will bathe, even if I have to scrub you myself. I command it and the Emperor commands it."

Tears of fury welled in Aldebert's eyes. He stormed out of the tent.

Norman Expats

Captain Drugo and all his men gathered in the spacious mess hall, along with a number of other mercenaries and some Byzantine soldiers. A fireplace piled with logs blazed in one corner. And to one side, long tables held platters of roasted pork and venison, and several kegs of ale.

"Sir Drugo," said Taticius, his voice rising above the din, "Meet Captain Humberto, a Kelt who has served me well. I believe you may have some interests in common." With those words, he left them alone.

Drugo the Red studied the bulky, weather-worn man who approached him, a soldier dressed like the fighting men of Italy. He decided to try his feeble Greek, "Greeting Humberto."

Humberto strode up to him smiling, his green eyes glittering through a mass of reddish blonde hair and beard. "And greetings to you Drugo of Flanders." He replied in Norman French.

"You're a Norman?"

An uproarious laugh came from Humberto and his men. "Well, we've never been to Normandy, but we are of the Norman line." He filled Drugo's cup from a flask of ale he carried. "Come, we will sit at table to talk while we enjoy the best food the General has to offer."

Drugo had some trouble understanding Humberto. Like the Normans of Melfi, his French was anachronistic, using words and expressions that had long fallen out of use in the old country. "From where do you come?"

"We hail from Apulia in Italy. Come... we will sit here." They swung their legs over benches, sitting down to meat, bread, and beer.

"Apulia?"

Humberto nodded.

"We just came that way," said Drugo.

"Then you must have heard of Robert Guiscard?" He lifted his red-blonde eyebrows.

"Well... I've heard a little."

"He was not a very popular man in this region!" Humberto laughed aloud before wiping his mouth on a sleeve. "He was a cunning bastard... and ruthless. He got rich by marrying the daughter of a local prince. But that wasn't enough for him. He wanted power... so he murdered the prince!" The other men laughed. "Then the Pope made him a Duke!" They roared again.

Humberto took a long draft of ale and wiped his mouth again. "After that, he tried to seize the Byzantine crown for himself. Him and his bastard son,

Bohemond. And they almost did! So, as you can imagine, Normans are not always received kindly here."

Drugo nodded in understanding as he wiped his hands on his greasy pants. "I met Bohemond in Melfi. He's a big man."

"And he's just as cunning as his father," Humberto smirked. "Mark my words, we haven't seen the last of him yet."

"So tell me, Humberto. What brings you to the service of the Greeks?"

Humberto smiled wide. "Gold...," he laughed, "just gold."

"And to what house do you claim allegiance?"

"Well, I'm actually a nephew of Guiscard."

Drugo smirked. "You jest!"

Humberto laughed. "I'm quite serious. Alas, I'm not a very popular relative, other members of our house saw to that." He poured more ale. "They cut off my inheritance and I was forced to seek my fortunes elsewhere. So here I am. King Alexios pays well."

"Why would the King hire you if you're a Norman and a nephew of Guiscard?"

"They're happy to employ me as long as I swear allegiance to the Emperor." He smiled. "Besides, they need us to fight those devil Turks," he said, tearing at a loaf. "And what brings you to this far-away land?"

Drugo drained his cup. "I owe fealty to my Lord, the Count of Flanders," he divulged, not mentioning he was forced to come. "The one called Robert of Flanders. He made a pilgrimage to Jerusalem a few years ago and met with the Greek King. The King asked him for a few hundred fighting men and horses, so here we are. We were promised land and gold for our troubles."

Humberto chuckled. "Gold you will get, but the King wants all the land. I once made the mistake of turning against him. He took away my fief and everything I had and sent me away. I was lucky not to have my eyes burned out."

Drugo frowned. "And he took you back?"

"Yeh, after I renewed my oath of fealty to him. He'll hire just about any fighting man you can imagine," Humberto chuckled. He tilted his head toward Taticius, who stood at a distance conferring with some men. "You see our commander over there? We call him Iron Nose. He used to be a slave, captured as a boy by Alexios' father. They made him a eunuch."

"A eunuch? Why?"

"Because he was trained to be an officer of the king's household. Slaves are more trustworthy when their balls are cut off," he chortled. "He's done well.

Now he's a general... and a damned good one. The King likes to put him in charge of us Kelts."

"Why's that?"

"I'm not sure. Maybe because he understands men from the West. His Latin is fairly good too."

Drugo shook his head in disbelief. "From a slave to a general. I've never heard anything like it. And a eunuch!"

Humberto laughed again. "Let me tell you something, Sir Drugo, it would serve you well to learn the lay of the land and the customs of these Turks. They fight their battles differently and are not easily defeated, but I can tell you some things I've learned over the years."

"I've already learned a few lessons, Captain Humberto. But you must tell me all you know."

The Blade

Just beyond Komotini, Wiker the Blade and his fellow assassins came across a mound of corpses stacked high on the side of the road—the corpses of the Patzinak warriors—and they wondered if the savages had saved them the trouble of killing the monks.

They soon learned from local peasants that a small army had marched north to Adrianople some days ago. And so they followed the same route, arriving at the walls of the fortress the next morning. Wiker rode up front, passing through the Fleming camp just outside the city walls. He confronted a squire tending horses. "Where is your captain?" he asked softly.

The squire eyed the stranger warily, noting his accent. All three of the men were covered in road dust, but he could see they were Italian by their dress. "He stays with General Taticius, near the citadel," he said as he pointed.

"What's his name?"

"Captain Drugo, Drugo of Flanders."

"And what of the monks who accompany him?"

"The monks? Oh... yeh, I think they're staying inside too. Why do you ask?"

Wiker ignored him. He twirled his big black mustache in thought before spurring his mount toward the city gates.

"Have you seen a company of Flemings pass through?" he asked the weary gatekeeper.

The gatekeeper looked puzzled, he shook his head, replying in Greek.

Wiker enunciated slowly. "Flemings... Frenchmen. Where?"

The man shook his head again before summoning another man, the scribe who kept accounts. "Can you understand what this barbarian wants?"

The scribe turned to Wiker, speaking in halting Latin. "What you want?"

Wiker replied impatiently. "We seek the Frenchmen."

"Frenchmen? You mean Kelt like you?"

"Yes, Kelts. They were accompanied by two monks."

A look of recognition crossed the scribe's face. "Oh, yes, those Kelt. They come yesterday. Must be important. They dine with General."

Wiker swung a leg over his horse to dismount. "So where are these men now?" he asked, shaking the dust from his cloak.

The scribe looked annoyed. "Who you and what your business here?"

Wiker continued to dust himself. "We are soldiers of fortune. We come to serve the Empire. Where is your general now?"

"General Taticius stay in quarters outside citadel." Again, he pointed to the citadel, which towered above the other buildings. "Take this street. Turn north at market."

"And where is the leader of the Kelts? The one they call Drugo of Flanders."

The scribe checked his documents. "They in same place."

Wiker nodded, turning to pass through the gate. But two sentries stepped forward to block his way. "I not finished, Sir," said the scribe who followed behind. "What your names?"

Wiker hesitated. He thought of using aliases but realized the confusion this could create among his own men. Besides, no one knew them here. "I am Wiker," he answered, before offering the names of his accomplices.

"And where you from?"

"We hail from Italy."

The scribe's face soured. He didn't like Kelts from Italy. "You may enter. Leave weapon and horse at stable." He pointed to the stables.

"Our weapons? Is the city that safe?"

"Those the rule. Weapon and horse stay here."

Wiker stepped back to talk to his men. "Turn in your weapons to the gate keeper." He lowered his voice. "But hide a dagger in your boots."

Drugo's head throbbed from too much ale, his throat was as dry as dust, his stomach rumbled and groaned. He had already made two rushed visits to the public toilets and feared a third when he arrived at the door of the General's war-room.

Taticius was quick to notice his bloodshot eyes. "I trust you enjoyed yourself last night, Captain?"

"Yes, General."

He motioned to a chair. "Please, sit."

Drugo slumped into a chair, his head spinning.

Taticius, his hair and face impeccably groomed, wore a lamellar corselet over a long brown tunic. A freshly ironed blue cape covered his shoulders. "Can I get you something to eat or drink?"

Drugo nodded, trying not to stare at his iron nose. "Water please."

The General barked an order to one of the guards before turning back to Drugo. "I will get to the point, Captain. Soon, you will reach Constantinople. There, the Emperor will decide your course of action. I presume he will send you to Nicomedia, where I am often stationed. If I am correct, you will be joining forces with Captain Humberto and the other Kelts." He paused. "Do you have any questions?"

Drugo looked blankly at him. "No... no," he mumbled.

Taticius straightened in his chair. "How is your Greek coming along?"

"I try learn," he said in Greek as he rubbed his forehead.

"I will assign a tutor to you. All commanders must speak Greek."

Drugo shrugged casually.

Taticius was ruffled by his apparent indifference. He raised his voice. "I order it, Captain. Your life and the lives of your men depend on it."

A soldier returned with a large jug of water. Taticius motioned. "Please, Captain... drink."

Drugo drained his cup. He filled it again.

Taticius studied the man with growing revulsion—the reek of his breath, the yellow and black teeth, the stink of liquor exuding from his skin. May God help us, he thought before he spoke again. "Have you tried the baths, Captain?"

Drugo nodded.

"Ah, very good. I advise you to use them often."

Drugo glared at him.

"Furthermore," said the General, "it appears you could use a brush for your teeth. It can help rid them of those worms. I will arrange for you to see our dentist."

Drugo closed his lips unwittingly, running his tongue over his teeth. His ears reddened. God damned foreigners! Treat us like children!

Taticius did not wait for a reply. "On another matter, I have hired three more mercenaries. They came to see me yesterday. From Italy, they say. Not the most trustworthy credentials. I have put them under your command until they reach the city. The Emperor will decide their fate."

Taticius, unaware of the impending threat and eager for more fighting men, had hired Wiker the Blade and his two henchmen, who then joined Drugo's long procession as it left Adrianople.

"There they are." Wiker twirled his mustache as he nodded toward the monks near the front of the line. "We will introduce ourselves tonight. And remember... do nothing without my say." A soldier riding just ahead turned in his saddle when he heard them speaking German. Wiker greeted him in Latin. The soldier nodded before turning forward again. After that, they rode in silence.

TZURULOS

The setting sun was low in the sky when they arrived at the fortress of Tzurulos, a small stronghold resting on a rocky hill, from where it guarded the plains of Thrace. There was little room within the walls, so they rode around the foot of the hill seeking a place to raise their tents. Soldiers dismounted and the quest for tent space began.

Ramiro pointed to a spot. "We camp here. Quickly Pepin! Lay out the tent before one of these louts takes our place."

Wiker the Blade weaved through the crowd. "Over there," he said to his two henchmen as he nodded toward the foot of the hill. "Look for a space as close as possible to the monks. But not too close."

They spread out to search and, before long, one of his men began to signal above the crowd and the others soon converged on the spot. The monk's tent was about twenty paces away.

One of Wiker's men scoured the ground. "I can see why nobody jumped on this spot. Look at the rocks!"

Wiker looked around. "Do not concern yourself with rocks, Rolf. It is doubtful you'll have any sleep tonight." He kicked at the sharp stones. "Level it out as best you can and set up the tents."

After setting up camp, they huddled inside Wiker's tent to talk. "I will approach their tent and introduce myself," said Wiker. "That will give me a chance to study the campsite and learn their habits. The rest of you find some food and prepare for a fast ride. We meet back here at sunset."

Ramiro sat on a large stone outside his tent. He was busy cleaning dust from a figurine of Mother Mary when Wiker arrived. Hearing his approach, he looked up at the stranger. "Greetings, my son. What can I do for you?"

Wiker looked down on the stout monk and his bag of religious paraphernalia. "Tell me, Father, do you hold Vespers tonight?"

Ramiro smiled broadly. "Yes, yes, we do... every night, God willing. I hope you will join us." He looked around. "Have a seat if you like." He pointed. "There's a suitable stone. What's your name, Sir? You are new to us, are you not?"

Wiker studied the ground. He pulled up his pant legs as he sat. "I am Wiker and, yes, I joined up yesterday."

"Are you my neighbor here?"

"I'm camped over there." He pointed.

Ramiro smiled. "On that rocky ground?"

"Yes, well, there were few places left."

Ramiro looked around, seeing better ground not far off. "Where are you from?" he prodded as he studied the wiry man.

"From Venice," he said with a vacant look.

"A cavalryman from Venice? We don't see too many in our travels."

Wiker forced a smile. "And I see few monks from Cluny in mine."

Ramiro's eyes narrowed for an instant. He switched to the Latin dialect of the north. "It's a beautiful island, is it not?"

Wiker stiffened a little before replying in the same tongue. "Island?"

"Why, Venice, of course."

Wiker smirked. "Oh, yes, yes, it is truly beautiful. Are you traveling to Constantinople?"

"Yes, we are."

"What does a Benedictine monk do in that city? I hear they closed the Latin churches."

Ramiro shrugged. "Perhaps we can open them again, by the Grace of God."

Wiker hesitated. "Yes, yes, hopefully."

Ramiro put his things away. "Have you heard the news from Rome?"

Wiker shook his head. "What news is that?"

"Odo of Lagery was appointed Pope by the cardinals. He has been ordained Urban the Second and is now the legitimate heir of Saint Paul."

Wiker feigned a smile. "Yes... yes, I have heard—that was last year... but what of Pope Clement? Was he not appointed by the Holy Roman Emperor, His Highness Henry?"

"Ah, but as you must know, good Sir, there is much disagreement about who has the right to install popes and bishops. One side believes only servants of the True Church have that right, while the other claims that kings and queens have the right to choose."

Wiker shuffled uneasily, staring at him. "I can guess your position, Dom Ramiro."

"Yes, I agree with Pope Gregory's reforms, may God rest his soul."

"But what of the divine right of kings?" Wiker asked with a hint of annoyance. "Are they not ordained by God?"

Ramiro looked hard at the man. "No, I don't believe they are. They simply want to control the Church by controlling its people. Kings pay their bishops too well. They twist and pervert the truth to suit their own selfish designs."

Wiker stood up suddenly, flushing red. He hesitated, fighting for composure. "Forgive me, but I ache from my long travels. I... I will leave you now and take some rest."

Ramiro watched him leave. "It would appear some rest is in order, soldier. Farewell, Wiker of Venice. May God's peace be upon you."

Wiker climbed the nearby hill in long strides. You fool! He rebuked himself for losing his composure. The rebel monk is sharp—but he's a cursed Benedictine—a minion of that false pope who speaks blasphemy. He must be stopped! Halfway up the hill he paused, ostensibly to peruse the countryside. But he was more interested in the position of Ramiro's tent, which was adjacent to the hill. The area was crowded, and he knew their escape relied on getting to the main road as quickly as they could. He noted the best route before returning to his tent and his comrades.

"We wait until everyone is asleep," said Wiker. "Remember Rolf, to stab in the neck first so they make no sound." His beady eyes moved to the other man. "You take the horses. Tether them near the road. They must be fully saddled and ready to go." He leaned forward, speaking in hushed tones. "This is my plan..."

Campfires roared under a starlit sky and a festive mood pervaded the air. Constantinople was only a few days away and the Turkoman were behind them.

This was the day to celebrate Michaelmas, a day to rejoice in the Archangel Michael, the patron saint of horsemen. It was he who defeated Lucifer in the battle for the heavens and it was he who came to earth to protect us from the coming days of darkness.

Drugo revered Saint Michael, the heavenly warrior who stood against the Antichrist. He followed Ramiro's lead, reciting after him the Prayer of Saint Michael.

> *St. Michael the Archangel, defend us in battle; be*
> *our safeguard against the wickedness and snares*
> *of the Devil...*

The prayers ended and the dancing began. Servants and soldiers alike brought out flutes, horns, bells, and drums. Louis the Carpenter played his lyre while a small group of men and women danced a clumsy jig in the trembling firelight.

The night wore on, the music waned, and many stumbled to their tents. When all was quiet, Adele came into the circle with her father's lyre. Ramiro rushed out with a wooden box for her to sit, glowing like a candle when she thanked him with a smile.

She strummed the chords gently, testing the tune of the strings. Slowly, she struck up a melody, playing an old Keltic tune. She lifted her eyes to the stars and, much to Ramiro's surprise, she began to sing.

> *Alas, my love, you do me wrong,*
> *To cast me off discourteously.*
> *For I have loved you well and long,*
> *Delighting in your company.*

She had a sweet, melodious voice that sang the song of unrequited love with such feeling she managed to sway the crowd, charmed as they were by every lyric and chorus.

Ramiro could feel her singing to his own heart, to his own secret longings. It was a yearning he could not understand, yet it welled up in his chest in a flood of passion and sorrow. And when she finished, he wiped away his tears with a sleeve.

Adele seemed oblivious to the delight of the crowd. No sooner had she put down her lyre, when she got up to hand out bread to the remaining crowd. Ramiro followed her every move as she mingled cheerfully with soldier and peasant alike. She was so graceful, and yet feisty enough to hold back the greedy ones.

Ramiro followed her closely as she approached Wiker and his two friends. But the men noticed his hard look and averted their eyes. And every so often, one of them would look askance as they talked in hushed whispers. That's when he stopped thinking of Adele.

The festivities dwindled to silence, and the night darkened to its deepest pitch. A half-moon glowed dimly through a thin blanket of white cloud.

Wiker stepped out of his tent. Rolf followed. They heard a distant cough and the low rattle of snores. Treading carefully in the cold light, they slowly worked their way toward the monks' tent.

A flap rustled. They stopped, stooping to the ground. A man stumbled out of a nearby tent. They soon heard him pissing in the dirt. They waited, daggers in hand.

Wiker began to fret. We have been out too long, he thought. He stood up cautiously, looking around. There was a clink of armor. He stiffened, motioning to Rolf, waving him back down. After a long silence, he signaled again, and they slowly skulked forward to Ramiro's tent.

Clutching long daggers in tight fists, they primed for the kill. Still crouching, they took up positions at the entrance to Ramiro's tent, preparing for their deadly lunge. In a swift move, Wiker whipped open the flap. They burst in. Wiker dove to the right, Rolf to the left, stabbing and stabbing.

A loud clash of steel sounded across the campsite. People yelled in violent commotion.

Adele jumped from her bed. "What's going on, Papa?" she called out from the tent.

Louis stood outside brandishing an oak club. "I don't know, girl. There's a big ruckus over by the knight's quarter. I'll go take a look."

"I'm coming too!" she cried, pulling a cloak over her shoulders.

"No you're not!" spouted Mathilda. "You're hardly decent!"

"Mama! Please! I'll stay with Papa. I promise."

"Stupid girl! Well at least show some manners and cover your hair."

"Yes, Mama." She grabbed a headscarf, fitting it in haste.

"What's happened?" Louis asked a man coming from the direction of the uproar.

"The two monks have been attacked," the man said as he walked by. "Stabbed by German assassins."

Adele shrieked. She rushed out of the tent, running headlong into Louis. She stopped for a moment, staring at him with wide, terrified eyes. Suddenly, she raced away without a word, going straight for the knight's quarter. Mathilda came stumbling out behind her. "Wait for your father!"

"Adele!" Louis shouted. "Stop girl! Wait for me!"

Wiker the Blade was only a few paces out of Ramiro's tent when he ran straight into Arles of Ghent, the big man who had lost his wife to a Turkoman arrow. In an instant, Arles knocked the dagger from Wiker's hand with the haft of his axe. Then, taking hold of the man, he hoisted him high above his head like a sack of grain before throwing him down hard on the rocky ground. Wiker howled from the impact. Arles put a foot on his neck, his axe at the ready. Not far away, Drugo pressed the tip of his sword to Rolf's neck.

"Where's your other man?" Drugo shouted. They said nothing. Drugo pressed his sword hard into Rolf's neck. Blood poured from the cut. "Where is he?"

Rolf panicked, clutching at his neck. "He's down the road with the horses!"

Drugo lowered his blade, turning to Otto. "Take your men. Bring him alive if you can." The men rushed off, swords drawn.

Twenty paces away, an astonished Aldebert held his head in his hands. "How did you know, Father Ramiro? How did you know they were sent to kill you?"

Ramiro put a palm to his chin as he watched the scene unfold. "Well, there were several clues."

"Like what?"

He pointed to Wiker's tent. "Why would anyone camp on that rocky ground, Brother Aldebert? You remember, we looked at it earlier. That seemed odd to me."

Aldebert lifted his brow, eyes bulging. "That's it? The rocky ground?"

"No, no. There's more. When we talked, he knew we came from Cluny. Now, how would he know that after being with us for less than a day? He also said he was from Venice but clearly he was not fluent in the local tongue. Nor did he seem to know much of the city. Besides, how many mercenaries come from Venice? Venetians are merchant men or pirates. And look at his dress, hear his accent. He's a German. And so are his two friends. Now why is a German in Italy I ask you?…"

He paused. Aldebert shook his head. "Only to protect Henry's pope," Ramiro answered himself. "And then, when I challenged the king's right to choose bishops, well that was the final clue, that's when he stormed off in a rage."

"But Father, why would they want to murder you?"

"Murder *us*, Brother Aldebert. They were going to kill you too."

Aldebert moaned. "Blessed Saints! Devils and heathen! Now this! May the Lord protect us! What are we…"

"Dom Ramiro!" cried a girl's voice.

Ramiro spun around. It was Adele. She stood barefoot with her father's cloak wrapped tight about her shoulders. She was crying. "What's wrong!" he asked in alarm.

But she could not speak. She covered her face with her hands to mask her tears.

"Are you alright?"

She nodded with her hands still at her face.

"Is it your father? Your mother?"

She shook her head erratically and then, as suddenly as she had arrived, she spun away, running off without a word.

Ramiro leaned toward Aldebert. "Women are indeed the strangest creatures, Brother Aldebert. I doubt any man could live long enough to understand them."

"Really?"

"Oh yes, Brother, and this is why God, in his mercy, has given us love."

"Did you find the man with the horses?" Drugo shouted to Otto.

"He would not surrender, m'lord. We cut him down," Otto replied, still gripping his blood-stained sword. "We took their horses."

Drugo's men stripped Wiker and Rolf of their armor before tying them to a tree. Otto and Fulk held the points of their spears to their necks. The crowd milled closer, eager to watch in the torchlight.

Drugo bellowed at them. "Back to your tents! There's no business for you here. All is well. Back to your tents!" The people shuffled away reluctantly.

He looked down on Wiker. "Who sent you?" Wiker said nothing. He gave a nod to Otto, who jabbed his spear into Wiker's leg. Wiker clenched his teeth but made no sound.

Drugo turned to Rolf. "Who sent you?"

Rolf shuffled his legs uneasily. Blood still ran from the cut on his throat "I don't know. I only do as my Lord asks."

Drugo nodded to his other man, Fulk, who then jabbed his spear into Rolf's side. Rolf hollered in pain and Drugo asked again. "What's your mission?" Rolf moaned but said nothing more.

Drugo lost patience. "Kill him."

Without hesitation, Fulk heaved his spear through Rolf's throat. Blood spurted from the man's neck and he collapsed to the ground.

Drugo turned again to Wiker, glaring at him. He pressed his sword to the man's neck. "I will kill you next. Who sent you?"

"We are servants of Pope Clement," Wiker spouted in a defiant voice.

Drugo sneered. "So, you're bootlickers of the antipope. What business does that papal snake have with these monks?"

"I don't know." Wiker said as he eyed Drugo's sword. "I swear on Christ's name. I don't know. I was given a task, that's all!"

Again, Drugo pressed his sword into his neck, harder now. Wiker's eyes widened in fear. He tried to back away but Drugo pressed further.

"The monks betray the Holy Roman Emperor!" Wiker shouted suddenly.

Drugo kept his sword at his neck. "Filthy pig! Your master usurps the Holy Church. Pope Urban is its rightful heir."

Wiker spat into the dirt.

Drugo spat too, raising his sword in ire. "Heretic! I'll send you to hell!" But he hesitated mid-swing. *I'll discover nothing more from the man if he's dead.* He lowered his sword, turning away to cool his anger. He wanted to know more of the monk's mission and what it had to do with the Greek King but thought it best to conduct a private interrogation. The monks and others were too close and it was already late into the night. "Station a guard and leave him here till morning light. We will decide his fate at that time."

As he returned to his tent, he wondered again why these cursed monks were so important that Giberto would send assassins after them. *How could they possibly threaten the German king? Why do they travel to the Greek Kingdom?* It was pointless to ask that damn monk. He had asked him many times already but Ramiro would say nothing of any substance. Still, he had sworn to get them safely to the Greek King, and that is what he would do.

Fulk rushed to Drugo's tent just before dawn. "Captain, Captain! Wiker has escaped!"

Drugo rushed out of his tent, hurrying to the tree where Wiker was bound. The ropes were cut. He reddened in fury. "Who was watching him?"

One soldier offered a meek reply. "Sorry, m'lord. I fell asleep."

Drugo lunged at the man, striking him across the head with the flat of his sword. The soldier collapsed to the ground. "Find him!" he yelled to the others.

Otto dared to speak. "He has taken a horse, Sir Drugo."

"Then mount up and go after him!"

"Captain!" Manuel shouted as he rushed into the commotion. "We cannot delay any longer. Emperor Alexios awaits us. Besides, it's much too dangerous to turn back... or to wait here. Our scouts say the barbarians managed to repel the Roman army. So the Turkoman still roam the area and approach this village again. Wiker can do no harm now. It's unlikely he will reach Rome."

Drugo bristled. He stomped away, waving an arm in a wide circle. "Then we are done with this business! We leave now!"

Ramiro and Aldebert rushed to the scene. "He's escaped, Brother Ramiro! What shall we do? Holy Mother of God, what shall we do?"

Ramiro patted his shoulder. "Calm yourself, Brother Aldebert. We will trust in our good Lord and our own good judgment."

CONSTANTINOPLE

October 1089

The Egnatia Way skirted the sandy shores of the Propontis. A cool wind beat at the cobalt waters of the sea, churning up white crests on rolling waves before blasting against the cavalcade of knights and servants. Just off-shore, sun-burned fishermen pulled in their nets while gulls squawked overhead, waiting for them to clean their catch.

Ramiro reveled in the fresh, briny air. He seemed unperturbed that Wiker roamed free, although Aldebert kept glancing over his shoulder.

Rounding a bend, the massive walls of Constantinople appeared on the horizon. "Do you see the city in the distance?" asked Manuel.

"Yes, Commander, it looks magnificent. It's enormous." Ramiro was already thinking of a Byzantine banquet with vats of Albanian wine and, although he would never admit it to Aldebert, he looked forward to another hot bath.

"It is larger than Rome, Monk Ramiro, and the center of our world," he lifted his chin with pride. "It is the Queen of Cities. Merchants come from as far away as the Land of the Rus, the kingdoms of the Indus Valley, and farther still, the Land of the Sung."

Ramiro and Aldebert stared blankly. They had never heard of such places.

"Our city," said Manuel, unabashed, "has been a bastion of the Christian faith since Emperor Constantine made it the capital of Christendom seven hundred years ago. It is the seat of the Great Bishop, Patriarch Nikolas."

Aldebert pulled his horse closer, straining forward. "But surely, Commander, the ultimate authority of the Christian Church must be with Saint Paul and the Popes who inherit his seat at the Lateran. After all, was it not Saint Paul who first brought Christianity to Rome, and from there, by God's will, the Word came to Constantinople?"

Manuel pulled a water-skin from his bag, taking a long drink. He could sense Aldebert's ire. "I agree, Monk Aldebert, that Saint Paul introduced Christianity to Rome, but remember that he converted the Greeks of Antioch years before. They were the first to widely embrace the teachings of Christ. So you see, Christianity was well established here long before it reached Rome." He tried to be polite but was mildly annoyed. What arrogance! And now these Kelt upstarts want to rule the Holy Church!

Aldebert fumed too. Blood rushed to his head in hot waves, clouding his mind with fury. Unable to restrain himself, he gushed in anger. "Paul created the Christian Church! A position he inherited directly from Christ himself! The only true allegiance must be to Saint Paul and his successors!"

Both Manuel and Ramiro were taken aback by his ill-disposed outburst. But before they could respond, Aldebert continued to rant, the veins of his temple bulged. "The only true spiritual lineage of Christ is through the Pope...."

"That's enough, Brother Aldebert!" Ramiro snapped.

Aldebert stopped. In a rush of shame, he lowered his head. "I beg your leave," he muttered.

For the most part, Ramiro's views were similar, but a sliver of doubt pierced his thoughts. Manuel's grasp of Roman, Greek, and Christian history appeared much more comprehensive than his own. Could there be more to this? Surely, God ordained the Pope. Could the Patriarch also be ordained? Why would God create two earthly rulers for His Church? Are there any true rulers?

Manuel could barely conceal his contempt for Aldebert. The people of Constantinople had heard of the Abbey of Cluny and knew of its strong allegiance to the Pope. The infamous Pope Gregory was also a man of Cluny, a man who had betrayed them to that Norman bastard, Guiscard. Without another word, he swung his horse out of line and trotted away to join Drugo at the front.

"I told you, Father Ramiro," Aldebert hissed. "I told you we would have nothing but trouble with these Eastern heretics! Why did you not defend me? You know we are God's chosen people, the Pope said as much. It is we who carry the true message of Christ our Lord. Why do they not see that?" He flung his arms about as he talked, occasionally wincing from the pain in his shoulder.

Ramiro observed Aldebert's hard red sneer. "Are you going out of your mind, Brother Aldebert? If our mission is to be a success, then we must remain tactful and patient. We cannot afford to fail." He took a drink of water to clear his dry throat. "If you are going to engage yourself in hot-headed arguments all the way to Jerusalem, I will leave you in Constantinople and you can return to Cluny in your own time. Regardless of what you believe, I will not allow you to jeopardize this assignment with your personal prejudices. Do you understand?"

Aldebert fell silent, paling with anxiety. "Forgive me, Father Ramiro, for I have sinned." Then he looked askance at Ramiro while he fidgeted with his reins. "But how can we tolerate such vile thoughts?"

"Tolerate them you will, Brother Aldebert. And you will learn to control that bitter tongue of yours. It affords us nothing."

As they neared the walls of Constantinople, a platoon of Byzantine troops rode out from the city gates. Most had olive skin and high cheekbones, many had thin beards, and they all had their hair tied in long braids. "Who are these men?" Captain Drugo asked Manuel.

"They are Turks, going to fight the Turkomans we just left." Manuel raised his voice over the increasing din of the road, now thronged with shoppers, merchants, and farm animals. The scents and sounds of cattle, sheep, pigs, and crates of chickens filled the air.

"So how do we know which Turk is an enemy and which is not?"

"Just as you would anywhere else, Sir Drugo, ... by their banners. These Turks fly the Byzantine flag."

Drugo shook his head. "It's all very confusing."

"Not really. Some fight against us and some for us. Turks fight Turks, just as I'm sure Normans fight Normans under different banners. They are fierce fighters. Many have bought their freedom and now seek their fortunes in the booty of war... just as you do, my friend." He smiled. "The men you see here are called *mamluks*."

"What? Mam...look?"

"Mamluk are slave warriors, or they started out as slaves. These are the men you must learn to fight. Most of them are Turkoman taken from Iran and Khorasan when young, and then trained for a life of war. By the time they become men, they know of little else. They have no loyalty to other Turks. Besides, we reward them well for their services and they are often envied by those who seek their fortunes elsewhere."

"But why use slaves in the first place?" Drugo asked. "Are there no fighting men among the Turks or Arabs?"

"Of course, but the Arabs started using slaves as fighters because their religion forbids a Muslim to kill a Muslim. So when the Arab kings fight each other, they use the mamluks, who are pagans taken from the far north."

Drugo found it bewildering. True, they had mercenaries in Europe, but nearly all knights were the sons of the wealthy, they were men of rank and means. Few others could afford fine horses, armor, or weapons. Lesser men could become knights after gaining wealth, some through pillage, but they were seldom accepted as equals.

He stared in awe as the enormous walls of Constantinople towered over their approach. Such walls were a far cry from any he had seen in Italy, and there was nothing at all like them in France or Flanders where palisades were still made of wood. He knew of few places built of stone, although he had heard of the Tower of London, built by the Norman conqueror, William the Bastard. But never in his life had he seen walls like this.

The Greeks settled Constantinople six hundred years before the birth of Christ. They called it Byzantion. Its location was vital, guarding all sea traffic to and from the Black Sea and all land traffic from Anatolia to Europe. The Romans soon realized its strategic value and seized it from the Greeks four hundred

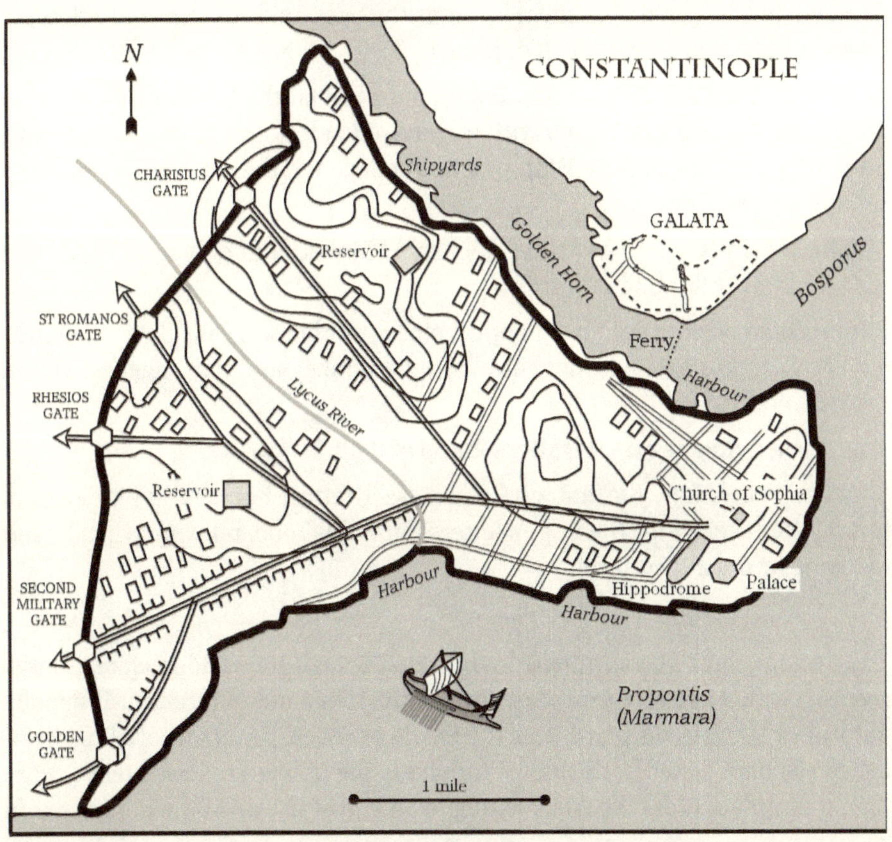

years later, calling it Byzantium. In the year 330, the Roman emperor, Constantine, made it his official capital, renaming the city after himself. And later still, when the Roman Empire split into East and West, it remained the capital of the East Roman Empire for more than one thousand years.

The ancient city sprawled out on a peninsula, shielded to the north by the Bosporus and the Golden Horn, and to the south, by the Propontis. Its walls stretched over twelve Roman miles, lining the shores and slicing across the western approach. The first line of defense to the landward side was a wide moat. Next, were three walls, a lower, middle, and inner, all spaced about fifty paces apart.

If the enemy managed to get past the moat and the first wall, they had to cross the space between to scale the second, which stood the height of five men. They would then have to contend with raining arrows and burning tar thrown down from the battlements and towers. If they managed to scale the second wall, they would be forced to climb the inner wall, the height of seven men, and face similar obstacles.

Built into these walls were ninety-six rectangular towers. Drugo could not see them all, but he could spot them as far as the eye could see. He could think of no army able to penetrate such defenses.

As Drugo's long line of men and horses approached the Golden Gate, a team of Byzantine slaves rushed out with wagons of food, clothing, and jugs of wine, even fodder for the horses. With practiced efficiency, they cleared ground and set up latrines.

"We have permission to enter the city," said Manuel. "But only ten knights and the monks are allowed in today."

Ramiro beamed with delight. "Pepin! Prepare our horses. Quickly now! Quickly! The Emperor awaits! Stay here with the donkey and our baggage. Guard them carefully."

"Yes, Father, don't worry. I'll sleep on top of it all."

"Just take care, boy. I'm not sure when we'll return but we'll try to keep in touch." He reached for the Pope's letters under his robe, relaxing when he felt the familiar crush of vellum.

Two rectangular towers funneled all traffic through the Golden Gate, a large archway with a massive iron-clad door as thick as a man's forearm. It opened onto an expansive courtyard near the Castle of Seven Towers where huge statues of elephants lined both sides. From here, the pillared road stretched more than four miles across the city, coming to an end at the tip of the peninsula. In this guarded location, sat the Imperial Palace, the Hippodrome, the Churches of Sofia and Irene, and the ancient Acropolis of the Greeks.

Manuel led them to a sprawling three-story building overlooking the Hippodrome and the sea. A wide flight of marble stairs took them to the third floor, where lavish rooms awaited their arrival.

Aldebert put down his bags, strolling over to the windows. He pointed down to the Hippodrome. "Why is it so big?" he asked Manuel.

"It's where we hold sporting events, chariot races, and ceremonies," Manuel replied.

"Look! What's that?" Aldebert noticed a large pile of ash near the center. Looks like there was a fire."

Manuel nodded solemnly. "An intentional fire, Monk Aldebert. I hear the Emperor sentenced a heretic to the flames."

Aldebert fell silent for some time, staring in shock. "You mean someone was... was burned alive?"

"Yes... that is the sentence for heretics."

The others rushed to the window for a look, staring in a stupor at the cold ash of the pyre. Terrifying visions of hot flames soon haunted their thoughts.

"I leave you now," said Manuel. "My mission is accomplished and I'm returning to my family for a few days of rest. From now on, you will be under the tutelage of the chamberlain, Little John."

He was no sooner out the door when Aldebert blurted. "Father Ramiro! They will burn us alive! God help us!"

"Control yourself," said Ramiro, thinking of Aldebert's recent outburst with Manuel. "I'm sure the Emperor will spare you as long as you keep your mouth shut."

Drugo and Otto grinned. It was one of the few times Ramiro had seen them smile. "They will burn you monks first," said Drugo with a nervous chuckle. "At least we are of some use to them."

"How can you laugh at the sight of this?" Aldebert cried. "Mother of Mary, I feel sick! We are in the hands of heretics who would burn *us* for being heretics!"

"Keep your head," Ramiro advised. "There is little we can do now but attempt to please the Emperor. We are at his mercy." But despite his outward calm, he felt a seed of fear.

As dusk approached, there was a knock at the door. Drugo opened it. A large man filled the doorway.,

"I am Little John, chamberlain to Emperor Alexios," said the man in a deep voice.

Little John was anything but little, standing a head taller than them all. He had a full head of black hair, a full beard, and a face laced with battle scars. In Byzantium, he was known as a warrior-monk. He wore the simple black robe of a monk, yet a long sword hung at his side, supported by a shoulder strap.

Drugo and his men, dwarfed by Little John's presence, remained silent, uneasy without their weapons.

"I have arranged for breakfast in your rooms. You must give your garments to the servants for cleaning. And please take advantage of our baths to refresh yourselves. Tomorrow you will meet the Emperor at the Palace. And, as you are all strangers to our Empire, let me give you instructions on Palace protocol."

Aldebert stood quietly at the edge of the large bath, his face red with shame. He felt conspicuously naked in a loincloth. But in fear of Ramiro's wrath, he said nothing. Reluctantly, he sat down at the rim of the pool, sticking his legs in the water.

"Come, come, Brother. Get in!" Ramiro splashed him with a handful of water.

Aldebert jolted. "Father Ramiro, please!"

"It's not going to kill you. Now get in!"

Frowning, Aldebert lowered himself into the pool, squatting carefully on a low bench under the water.

Ramiro handed him a bar of soap. "Now, rub that all over you. And you see this? Scrub yourself with it." He tossed over a strange object.

Aldebert picked up the sponge. It squashed in his fingers. "What is it?"

"Never mind, just scrub."

The sheer size of Constantinople, its grandeur, and its ostentatious riches overwhelmed the Flemings, as did the Imperial Palace rising up before them in elegance and opulence, a gigantic marble and stone structure spread out over acres of carefully manicured gardens replete with colorful flowers, exotic trees, and bubbling fountains.

In the palace anteroom, they waited hours for the Emperor's summons, resting awkwardly on luxurious red sofas lining the walls of the ornate room. Bowls of exotic fruit and vases of orange lilies decorated long marble tables.

Unused to such conspicuous luxury, Drugo wandered about aimlessly, pretending to inspect some corner of the room while habitually reaching for the hilt of his missing sword. To his great relief, Little John finally returned. "Follow me," was all he said.

Approaching the door to the royal court, Ramiro could feel his heart pound. Behind this door was the heart of the Roman Empire, the throne room of Alexios Komnenos, Imperial Emperor of the East.

THE KOMNENOS THRONE

The crowded hall fell quiet as they filed in. The only sound was the squawk of a brightly colored parrot fluttering high overhead in the dome of the ceiling. They were no sooner through the door when Drugo stopped suddenly, stepping back. Others stumbled into him. An African lion roared, restrained by a towering man with sapphire skin and rippling muscles, who held fast to the animal's chain.

"By God's mercy!" Aldebert shouted.

Little John smiled. "Come, my brave men. Follow me." The crowd tittered in amusement.

A wide, red carpet, lined with courtiers on either side, led them to an elaborate dais raised about two feet above the floor. On this dais, was the imperial throne, and on the gilded throne, was Emperor Alexios Komnenos. To his right, sat a man about the same age and height and, to his left, an older woman of graceful poise.

Little John approached and kneeled. "Your Majesty, may our Lord bless your reign. I present to you the Kelts sent by the Count of Flanders, as well as two monks, emissaries of the Latin Church." He rose, shifting to the side.

"Welcome to the Roman Empire, gentlemen." Alexios spoke in a soft tenor. "I trust you have been treated kindly?"

For a moment, the men were a little dumbfounded. The Emperor spoke fluent Latin. He had a ruddy complexion, was about thirty-five, and of medium height. Curly, dark-red hair hung to his broad shoulders while a trimmed beard tapered to a point from his chin. Lamellar armor covered his chest and a long, purple cape draped to the dais. His red leggings and scuffed riding boots were clearly visible. Indeed, apart from the cape, the only sign of royalty about him was a simple gold crown.

Drugo managed a reply. "Greetings, Your Highness. Yes, we have been well cared for."

Alexios smiled thinly. "You must forgive my dress," he said, as if guessing their thoughts. "I have just returned from another campaign against the Turkoman and have had little time to refresh myself." His green eyes sparkled in a menacing way, emphasized by elegant and expressive eyebrows. "I hear you've had your own troubles with these barbarians."

"Yes, Your Highness," Drugo answered, bowing stiffly.

Alexios twirled one end of his trimmed mustache. He waited and watched. The throne room fell silent. Drugo fidgeted. "And how fares your lord, the Count of Flanders?"

Drugo shuffled uneasily. "He fares well, Your Highness, and is glad to be of help to your Christian nation."

Alexios sat motionless, leaning on one arm. "And we are pleased that the Count has fulfilled his oath and has seen the wisdom of protecting the True Faith. We send our thanks to God on High that you have arrived safely. You will be well rewarded. I trust you are the commander of these troops?"

"Yes, Your Highness, I am Captain Drugo of Flanders," he replied eagerly as prospects of gold and glory danced through his head.

"Welcome Drugo of Flanders," said Alexios before motioning to the man sitting to his right. "This is my brother and trusted advisor, Isaak Komnenos." Isaak had similar red hair and beard but was thin and pale. The man acknowledged Drugo with a wan smile and a nod.

Alexios then gestured to his left. "And this is my mother, Anna Dalassene, also one of my most trusted advisors." Anna, a dignified woman in her fifties, nodded toward them with an expressionless face. A small gold diadem adorned her ashen-blonde hair, and a light application of eye shadow and lip paint highlighted her fine facial features. Despite her age, her graceful beauty equaled that of many a younger woman.

All of them bowed in turn as the royal members were introduced. "We are honored, Your Highness," said Drugo. "And I am pleased to announce that the Count of Flanders presents you with a gift of one hundred and fifty of our finest horses."

A loud murmur came from the courtiers. Alexios raised his long eyebrows. "That is extremely generous of the Count. I will send him a letter of appreciation. Your lord is one of the few men in the West who is aware of the present danger to Christendom, and we are grateful you have come to assist us in our divine cause."

Drugo bowed again, beaming in the attention of the Royal Court.

"And I am informed these two monks are representatives of your church," said the King as he peered beyond Drugo. "Step forward saintly people, that we may know you."

At the Emperor's call, Ramiro and Aldebert, who stood directly behind Drugo, momentarily hesitated. Ramiro had been studying the Emperor, who seemed an eloquent man, although he spoke with a slight lisp, especially when he sounded an "r." Summoning his courage, Ramiro stepped forward. Aldebert, petrified, staggered behind. "Greetings, your Serene Majesty, it is indeed an honor to be before you. I am Father Ramiro, Dean of the Abbey of Cluny." He motioned to Aldebert. "And this is my assistant, Brother Aldebert."

Alexios smiled. "Welcome, Father Ramiro of Cluny and Brother Aldebert. I am also honored that you have come so far in the interests of your faith." He examined the two monks for a long while. A green parrot squawked overhead before swooping over the silent courtiers. The lion growled. "I hear you have encountered some enemies on your journey. May I presume that some of your countrymen are not pleased with your mission here?"

Ramiro looked up. He was about to say they were Germans, not countrymen, but he was sadly aware that few in the Royal Court perceived any difference. "Yes, Your Majesty, it appears to be so."

"So tell me, Monk Ramiro, what brings you to our Empire?"

Ramiro did not expect such direct questioning in the presence of the court. He had hoped for a private audience with the King. "Well, Your Majesty, the venerable Pope Urban has charged me with the task of working toward the reunification of our churches. He is eager to have our differences reconciled."

Alexios raised an eyebrow. "Is this your sole objective?"

"Uh... yes, Your Majesty. I am here as liaison to His Holiness, Pope Urban the Second."

Alexios kept his intent gaze on Ramiro. "I believe you have something for me, Monk Ramiro."

Ramiro was taken off-guard. How could he know?

Alexios persisted. "You have a letter for me?"

"Yes, yes, Your Highness," he said, groping into his robe and drawing out a leather pouch. Thumbing inside, he selected one of the three letters which, like the others, bore the papal seal.

Alexios motioned. "Come forward, good monk."

Ramiro moved a few steps, placing the creased letter on a silver plate held out by a waiting page. "My letter of commendation, Your Highness."

The page offered the letter to Alexios, who passed it to his brother, Isaak, who held it unopened. "We will review this letter and speak to you afterwards."

"Yes, Your Highness," Ramiro was proud to offer credentials from the Pope himself. He stepped back.

Alexios leaned forward. "And you have another letter, I believe?"

"Well, uh, yes, Your Majesty," Ramiro replied, somewhat flustered. "But I was instructed to deliver it personally to Patriarch Nikolas."

Alexios returned a genuine smile. "Well here he is." He waved his arm to his right, where Nikolas stood a few paces to the side of the throne. A few chuckles came from the courtiers. Nikolas, a tall thin man, wore a draping white gown decorated in red crosses. Towering on his head was a black, conical hat with a red cross on the front. Dangling out of his hat was a mass of black hair, and a bushy beard almost covered his entire face. "I introduce you to Patriarch Nikolas, who is eager to discuss with you all things ecumenical." Nikolas bowed to the men and they bowed in return.

"You may give him the letter now," Alexios insisted.

This was not what Ramiro had expected. He had hoped for a face-to-face talk with the Patriarch before handing him the letter. "Yes... yes, Your Majesty."

Alexios waved a finger and the royal page rushed up to Ramiro, who reluctantly handed over the letter. The king sat leaning on one arm, staring at Ramiro for a long while.

Ramiro bowed again and began to back away.

Alexios raised his long eyebrows. "Monk Ramiro, you have a third letter, I believe."

Ramiro stammered in disbelief. "Uh... yes... but... but Your Highness, it...it is bound for Jerusalem."

"For the Patriarch of Jerusalem?"

"Well... yes," said Ramiro, flabbergasted. "It is for Patriarch Symeon, Your Majesty. But... I... I made a solemn vow to His Holiness, Pope Urban, that I would deliver it personally."

Alexios looked amused. "And how do you intend to do that, pray tell? A gauntlet of murderous Turks lines the road to Jerusalem. Just how long do you think two Latin monks would fare on that road?"

Ramiro flushed, seeing the direction of his thoughts. "Your Imperial Highness! How can I forsake my explicit duty to the Holy Church? I have given my oath!"

Alexios had a stern look. "And what was the nature of that oath?"

"As I said, Your Highness, it is to deliver this letter, as quickly as I can, to Patriarch Symeon of Jerusalem."

"Well then, would not your duties be fulfilled if you gave the letter to Patriarch Nikolas, who is of the same Church? Surely, you cannot believe that it would go undelivered?"

"Of... of course not, Your Highness. It was not my intention to suggest..."

Alexios smiled patiently. "I promise you it will reach Patriarch Symeon. And rest assured, he will receive it long before you could possibly arrive. Do you accept my pledge?"

The blood drained from Ramiro's face. "Yes, of course, Your Majesty."

"Then I accept your letter on behalf of Patriarch Symeon."

Ramiro's hands shook as he reached again into his purse to pull out the third letter. In a quavering, uneasy motion, he handed it over to the page. His heart beat heavily at the thought of betraying his Abbot and the Pope. After all, he had sworn on the blood of Christ. And he was supposed to show Abbot Hugh's cross to the Patriarch when he delivered the letter. Did Alexios know about that too?

Alexios nodded to him. "We have much to discuss, Monk Ramiro. I will summon you to council at a later date."

"Yes, Your Majesty." He bowed and stepped back.

The King returned his penetrating gaze to Drugo and, again, he paused for a while. "Drugo of Flanders, it is your custom, is it not, to swear fealty to your lord?"

Drugo brushed a lock of hair from his eyes. "Yes, Your Majesty."

Alexios looked hard at the man. "Then you will have no objection swearing your allegiance to me?"

Drugo hesitated. It meant he would serve no other master and that all lands and booty he seized would become the property of his lord. But he, too, felt trapped by circumstance. "I will swear my allegiance, my Lord, second only to my master, the Count of Flanders."

Alexios raised his brow. "The Count is a long distance from here, Drugo of Flanders. Did he not send you to serve the Roman Empire?"

"Well, yes, Your Highness."

Alexios looked down on Drugo, waiting in silence.

Drugo went cold under his relentless glare. "Of... of course, Your Highness, I will swear my allegiance to you."

"Then be so kind as to offer me a formal pledge."

Drugo flushed. "Now, Your Highness?"

Alexios nodded and smiled. "Yes, Sir Drugo, so that your oath is acknowledged in the eyes of God and witnessed by the whole court."

Drugo summoned his courage, speaking in a loud voice. "I swear, by the

Passion of Christ Our Savior, by His Invincible Cross, and by the Holy Gospels that I, Drugo of Flanders, will serve the Emperor as his vassal and I will arm myself against his enemies."

Alexios studied him, pausing momentarily. "And you swear to guard the Holy Sepulcher?"

"With my life, Your Highness." He bowed deeply.

Alexios nodded his approval before speaking with some gravity. "I accept you as my vassal, Drugo of Flanders. My scribes will draw up a contract to this effect and I trust you and all your men will put your names upon it."

"Yes, Your Highness, I will command it."

"Good. Then this matter is finished. I will assign you and your men to the stronghold of Nicomedia, east of the Propontis. The Turks are giving us much trouble there and we need strong fighting men like yourselves to whip them back. You will rest here for a time as we fear no attacks in the winter months. But by early spring, you will be stationed to your posts." He scrutinized each of Drugo's men as he spoke. They shuffled uneasily, averting his eyes. "I believe you have met Captain Humberto?"

Drugo raised his eyebrows. "Well... uh, yes, Your Highness, in Adrianople."

"Good. When you get to Nicomedia, you will join forces with him and follow the orders of General Taticius."

Drugo bowed. "Yes, Your Majesty."

Alexios stood up. "Thank you gentlemen, you are dismissed."

THE POPE'S LETTERS

A heavy rain lashed against the mullioned glass windows of the palace meeting room. Inside, Alexios and his advisors reposed in elegant armchairs, all huddled around a long table. The servants laid out Cretan wine, fruit, and honeycakes before slipping out the door.

Only after they left did Anna speak. "Alexi, do not keep us in suspense, my dear. What did the Pope say in his letter to you?"

Alexios glanced at Nikolas before turning back to Anna, grinning from ear to ear. He paused momentarily as the others leaned on his words. "Well, mother, I'm glad to report that Pope Urban has lifted his ban of excommunication against me." He handed her the letter.

Her eyes narrowed a little as she read, a wry smile crossing her thin, red lips. She said nothing.

"I don't see why it would make any difference to you, Alexi," Isaak blurted. "You are not of the Latin Church."

Anna put down her fork, turning to Isaak. "Because, my son, it now means the way is paved for communion between our two churches. With official communion, we are now in a much better position to negotiate terms of reconciliation. And hopefully, we'll be able to get some military assistance."

"And what do you think of this other letter to Nikolas?" asked Alexios.

She held the letter in one hand, reading it again as she brushed a lock of hair behind an ear. "For the most part, it looks as though the Pope is being quite conciliatory. There is much hope in this letter. However, there is no mention of providing troops."

"I also found the letter encouraging," said Nikolas through his bushy, black beard. "As I see it, Urban has only two main requests. First, that we reopen all Latin churches in the Empire and, second, that we return the Pope's name to the sacred rosters."

Alexios grinned. "By the Lord Jesus Christ! That is simple enough."

Anna frowned. "Please son, you must remain pious in order to receive God's favor."

"Yes, mother, sorry. But this is wonderful news! Reply at once that we agree with his requests."

Nikolas shook his head. "It is not that simple, Your Highness. We closed the Latin churches thirty years ago for a number of reasons. We cannot make any ecclesiastic changes without a synod—only the council of bishops can decide. Besides, the Latins continue with their abominable rituals—like using unleavened bread in Communion. This is not acceptable. And they insist on believing that the Holy Spirit emanates from the Son as well as from the Father. This is an absurd notion of the divine Trinity."

"Surely, these are not insurmountable problems, Nikolas. The Empire is at stake. Call a meeting of the bishops, we have no time to lose!"

Anna contemplated her somewhat impetuous son. "Use tact and diplomacy, Alexi. We also need to convince the Patriarchs in Jerusalem and Antioch."

"Yes, yes, and then we should draft a reply to the Pope," added Alexios, putting a hand to his forehead. "What about the letter to Symeon, Nikolas? What does it say?"

"I haven't opened it."

"Well, do so now. Our forgers will reseal it."

Nikolas broke the papal seal to unfold the letter. He read it before passing it on to Alexios. "You can see that Pope Urban reiterates the need to unite the Churches, which is encouraging. But there is something here not in our letters. Here, he argues for the primacy of the Pope, which means, of course, that

Urban himself would head this new church. This is nothing new," he scoffed. "But we can never agree to this demand... I will also send a letter to Symeon."

Alexios glanced at him. "Do not jeopardize this delicate balance, Nikolas. Tell the Patriarch anything that pleases him. And tell the other Patriarchs only what they need to know. We must manipulate the situation to our advantage—for the sake of the Empire!"

Isaak turned in his chair, his pale cheeks flushed. "Why bother with all this, Alexi! Why not recruit more men from the Bulgars or the Vlachs?"

Alexios paced the room. "We send our recruiters everywhere looking for mercenaries, brother, but there are few left. We need the Latins and their bloodthirsty men, whether we like it or not. The Patzinaks attack from the north, the Turks from the east, Bulgars and Serbs from the west. We have lost Asia, Syria, and Palestine ... even Antioch!" He paused, sincerely regretting the recent loss of such an important stronghold. "Our only relief is that, by the grace of God, that bastard Guiscard is dead, or we would have those black-hearted Normans on our doorstep as well!"

"This is my point, Alexi," said Isaak. "How can we trust these Latins? Lest we forget, it was not that long ago they tried to defeat the Empire. And they even had the blessing of Pope Gregory! And did not Gregory vow he would raise an army of the faithful and lead them personally to Jerusalem to recover the Holy Sepulcher? What if Pope Urban thinks the same? Do we really want him roaming our Empire with a vast Norman army?"

Alexios shuddered at the thought. He strode to the table, putting both hands down. His broad shoulders squared over them all. "Of course not, but it's unlikely that would happen."

"It seems sadly ironic," said Isaak, "that the Normans, who were so recently our mortal enemy, are now our potential allies."

Alexios smirked. "I suppose, but not all of them are Normans and we must do whatever possible to save the Empire. We fight God's war to preserve Christendom."

Anna leaned back in her chair, fingering prayer beads in one hand, moving them one by one. "So how will Urban raise an army to assist us if he cannot even hold the Lateran in Rome?"

Alexios dropped his head. "I don't know, mother, but what other hope have we? We need to find a solution that brings the Latins to our aid with the least cost. Somehow, Urban must put fire in the bellies of these Kelts. We need to give him a cause... a cause that appeals to these barbarians." He paused with a mischievous grin. "And I believe I know what it is."

"Alexi, darling, please dispense with the melodrama." She tapped her stylus on the table. "What's your idea?"

He became more animated. "The answer is the Holy Sepulcher, just as Pope Gregory suggested. On many occasions, I have heard how much these Kelts revere the Tomb of Christ. They come from the ends of the earth to worship it. John Doukas of Dyrrachium met with these men and he confirmed how they remember the misdeeds of Al-Hakim, the Egyptian king and how he destroyed the Sepulcher. They are indignant about this. There is a pent-up fury here. We can take advantage of it! Did you observe that Kelt in court today—that Drugo? When I asked him if he would defend the Holy Sepulcher, he said "to the death" without any hesitation. I sincerely doubt he would jeopardize his life for anything else... except perhaps a purse of gold."

Isaak looked up knowingly. "Gold is all these Kelts want. They would kill their own fathers to get it."

"I agree, we cannot trust them anymore than we can trust a Turk. We just have to remain one step ahead of them." He turned back to Anna. "But let me continue with my idea, mother. We will draft a letter to Urban telling him the Holy Sepulcher has fallen again to the hands of heathen Turks, who desecrate the place with their pagan filth."

"But Alexi, that's a lie!"

"Is it? The Turks govern Jerusalem and control all within it."

"But they leave the Christians alone. As long as they stay out of politics, they are neither threatened nor harmed."

"I know, I know, but the Latins know nothing of this. Let's take advantage of it." He took a sip of wine. "And it will be no lie to tell Pope Urban that Romans and Greeks, good Christians, now suffer in Asia. The Turks steal everything they own, ravage their crops, desecrate their churches, rape the women..."

"Yes, yes, that's enough, my son," said Anna with disgust. "We will consider sending another letter to Urban. Perhaps that monk could deliver it... what's his name?"

"Ramiro," said Nikolas. "Sounds like a Latin name, like those used in Andalusia." He glanced at her. "But I thought it puzzling that the Pope would give his letters to that monk. Why not give them to Commander Manuel or one of our other ambassadors when they were in Melfi?"

"Remember," said Anna as she wiped her hands with a napkin, "we have been informed that the Pope was once the grand prior at the Abbey of Cluny. He trusts few people but his own monks, which means he likely sent them as spies."

"I agree," replied Alexios. "We cannot afford to expose our weaknesses to these Kelts. We must be careful to control what they see and hear."

REPORT: ITALY AND BEYOND

The writing desk in the palace library was stuffed with the finest papers—made from cotton they say. And there was ample ink of the best quality and many fine quills. Ramiro dipped his pen to begin his first report to Abbot Hugh.

> *To my Lord, Reverend Father Hugh, Abbot of Cluny, from his humble and faithful servant, Ramiro in Constantinople, Empire of the Greeks, greetings full of peace and gladness in the Lord.*
>
> *By the Grace of Almighty God, we have reached the Greek city of Constantinople, although we encountered many difficulties and hardships along the way. I will attempt to recount to you, faithfully and truthfully, the nature of these events...*

He went on to tell the Abbot how the Genoese and Pisans had made tremendous strides in the Tyrrhenian Sea with their improved war galleys and seafaring skills, and how they had beat back the Arabs and took control of profitable merchant routes. And he told Hugh about the Normans and how they had taken Bari from the Greeks and southern Italy from the Arabs, and that they continued to fight against the pagans in Sicily.

He wrote, with mixed feelings, that the Normans were Pope Urban's only allies against the German king. Then he mentioned the synod in Melfi and the ecumenical council's canons on simony and chastity. He paused in his writing when a troubling image of Adele hovered in his mind. With effort, he dispelled it and went on to tell Hugh about the attack of the Patzinaks and how several men had died in fighting and that Brother Aldebert had been wounded. And he gave his first impressions of Byzantium, its amazing city, its king, its lords, its people, its sizable warships and its standing army of well-armed men of all races.

But he said nothing of the Pope's letters.

Wiker the Blade had managed to survive his escape from Drugo's men and, knowing their final destination, carefully made his way to a remote corner of Constantinople, where he rented a small room from a tinsmith.

He stared absently at his gleaming dagger, carefully honing its long blade with a fine whetstone. Satisfied with the razor edge, he took up a cloth of sheep-skin to polish it, all the while cursing two Benedictine monks and a mission unfulfilled.

Palace Intrigues

Ramiro paced back and forth like a caged animal. "This is intolerable! Intolerable, I say! We have been here three weeks... three weeks, Brother Aldebert! And still I have heard nothing from the Emperor! When will I meet with the Patriarch? What am I to do? Symeon's letter was my only excuse to get to Jerusalem, and now that is gone." He said nothing of the Cluny cross.

Aldebert leaned on a soft sofa, spooning a breakfast of yogurt, rice, and olives. "Let's go to Jerusalem by ourselves. We'll get Pepin to bring our horses to the city gate. I'm sure he'll be glad to get out of the King's stables."

They were now alone in their rooms overlooking the Hippodrome. On Alexios' orders, Drugo and his men were moved across the waters of the Golden Horn to the suburbs of Galata, far from the city walls. But Ramiro had no idea what happened to Pepin, or Louis and Adele and the others, who were camped outside the city walls for a time. Now the camp was gone. Did they also move to Galata?

Ramiro gazed out the window. "But we don't know where Pepin is, or how to contact him. Besides, you heard what the Emperor said. It's unlikely we'd survive on the road south, especially as monks. And anyway, how could Pepin bring us horses unnoticed?"

"Then let's go by sea. I hear they have boats sailing to Palestine."

"Yes, but it's very expensive. We have only a few coins between us. And how will we make any money here?" He sat down with a thump, letting out a heavy sigh. "We are so close to Jerusalem and the Holy Sepulcher. It would be a travesty to fail now. And how will I ever be able to face Abbot Hugh if the Pope's letter is not delivered as the King promised?" His thoughts drifted to his mother. What if she really was dying? I may never see her again. He fingered his cross, rubbing the bloodstone. And I've got to get this cross to the Patriarch! God give me strength!

From his sofa, Aldebert gazed over the waters of the Propontis. His wound had healed, his acne disappeared, and color returned to his cheeks. "We could take another walk around the city."

"I'm tired of sightseeing. Besides, everywhere we go that wretched guard follows us."

"Oh, that reminds me," Aldebert exclaimed, eyes bulging. "The guard said someone was asking about you."

"Who?"

"The man didn't give his name. He just asked if you lived here."

"That's odd. What did he look like?"

"Black hair and big mustache was all he could recall."

"Well that could be anybody. Did he say anything else?"

"No, except that he had a different accent and his Greek was poor."

"A foreigner then. Very odd."

"What's this?" Alexios asked.

Little John looked down on the envelope in his hand. "I got it from the post office, Your Highness. You said to intercept all mail from those Latin monks. One of them mailed this yesterday."

"Did you read it?"

"Yes, my Lord."

"And what does it say?"

"Nothing of any surprise or import. The monk tells his abbot about the Normans and reports on their skirmish with the Patzinaks?"

"Does he say anything about Byzantium?"

"Nothing of strategic value, my Lord. In fact, he complements you and the Empire."

"Very well, let it pass."

A hazy sun cast soft rays through the windows of the Palace morning-room, where Alexios sat at breakfast with his young wife, Irene.

"Tell me, Alexi, how went the call to synod?" she asked in a soft voice, her blue eyes sparkling as she wrapped her hands around a cup of lemon tea. "Did the bishops agree to your ideas?"

Alexios glanced across the long table. Irene's blonde curls whitened in the morning sun. He had married her when she was only fifteen, and he was still infatuated by her beauty. But it was a marriage hotly contested by his mother, Anna, who reviled the House of Doukas. It was one of the few times Alexios dared to defy his overbearing mother, even when she wailed and groaned in protest. He had married Irene not only because he was madly in love but also because he needed the Doukas family to keep him in power.

Now, Irene was twenty-three and looked more alluring than ever. "There is progress, my love. But the bishops can be difficult at times." He motioned to the servants and they left the room. "They just need to recognize the Pope."

"And how did they respond?" Irene asked, gazing out to sea.

Alexios stabbed at his breakfast with a fork. "They argue over clauses, unleavened bread and points of ritual. They say too much time has passed since the separation of our churches. But I disagree. That rift was less than forty years ago. Nonetheless, by God's mercy, we managed to reach a compromise. Pope Urban must send his profession of faith to Constantinople—and he must accept the holy canons adopted at the sixth ecumenical council."

Irene adjusted the shoulder of her blue silk dress. "So what was their response to the Pope's claim that only he can head the church?"

"I honestly doubt that will ever come to pass. Nonetheless, we can avoid that topic as long as necessary and let Urban believe what he likes. The most important thing is to get Norman and French troops to help us against the Turks."

"Alexi, you spend much time on the affairs of the Empire, but do not forget your children. They have not seen you for days."

Ramiro bathed and put on his freshly washed habit. King Alexios had finally summoned him. Aldebert helped him to shave his head and face, trimming his thin circle of hair.

Within the hour, an escort arrived, leading him through a maze of Palace hallways to a single door at ground level where two guards stood on either side. Ramiro went in alone.

"Come, Monk Ramiro, come in and sit," piped Alexios from his decorative armchair. His bright white tunic, embroidered in gold and belted at the hip with a golden tie, contrasted with his blood-red leggings and sandals.

The room was stacked with books and letters while maps were strewn about on several tables. At the back of the room, a small archway opened to a flowered garden, where golden orioles could be heard whistling from the branches of cherry trees.

"Good day, Your Majesty, may you receive God's grace." Ramiro bowed. He sauntered through the room, attempting to read some book titles before he sat.

"You are a man of letters," observed Alexios. "I can see your interest."

"I am, Your Majesty. Many things interest me." He sat stiffly.

"I hear you speak Arabic?"

"Uh yes, Your Highness," he answered, wondering how he knew.

"Perhaps you would like to see our library collection?"

"I would like that very much, Sire. And I thought I might take the time to learn Turkish as well."

"Turkish? Well, that could prove very useful indeed. If you like, I will deliver a Greek-Turkish dictionary to your room."

Ramiro smiled. "Thank you, Your Highness."

"So be it. Please, have some wine." He filled a glass goblet.

Ramiro picked it up gladly, taking a sip right away.

"Have you been treated well?" Alexios asked as he settled back.

"Oh, yes, indeed, Your Highness. Very well, thank you."

Alexios clasped his hands in his lap. "So Monk Ramiro, what brings you to our Empire?"

"As I mentioned in court, Your Majesty, Pope Urban has entrusted me to confer with the Patriarchs of your church in order to resolve our differences, hopefully to bring about the unification of the Christian church." He moved to the edge of his seat. "Consider, Your Majesty, the implications for the whole Christian community. Think of the strength of One Church, One Faith under One God."

Alexios stroked his dark-red beard. "But who shall rule this church? Is that not a concern to both parties?"

"Well, yes, I pray we can reach some agreement on that point."

"Perhaps this discussion is best left to the Patriarchs," said Alexios with a little impatience. "Now tell me, how does Pope Urban react to my requests for fighting men? Does he realize the gravity of the situation?"

Ramiro nodded. "I believe so, Sire. I met with him in Melfi, and he attempts to sway the lords of the West, although they see little profit in the enterprise. He understands that a greater purpose must be devised in order to provoke them to action."

"But there is much profit to be had," said Alexios. "Tell the Pope we have an opportunity to retake Jerusalem and the Holy Land, and in the name of Christendom, we have an opportunity to reclaim the Holy Sepulcher from the Muslim infidels. The soldiers will benefit from the booty of war. Think of the riches in Antioch, Aleppo, and Damascus."

"I will write to him of these things, Your Highness. How large an army do you require for this venture?"

"Many thousands are needed. We are terribly outnumbered. I beseech the Pope to send as many warriors as he can."

"I will mention this too." Ramiro paused before beginning his plea. "Your Majesty, I still hope to travel to Jerusalem. It is my desire to visit its holy shrines and especially to pray at the Holy Sepulcher." He was careful not to mention the Cluny cross, which seemed to be the only thing Alexios knew nothing about.

Alexios pondered the monk. He was thankful that his ambassador, Manuel, had kept him well-informed of the monk's doings. But he did not want the Pope's men meddling in Jerusalem where it was difficult for him to oversee their actions. "This is a bad time to travel that road, Monk Ramiro. Only when we reconquer Nikea and Antioch will there be much hope of safe travel to the south. The sooner we receive assistance, the sooner you may undertake your journey."

"But Abbot Hugh said you would arrange a ship to take me to Jaffa."

"Did he? Perhaps he is unaware of the long and dangerous journey by sea. We are plagued by Turk pirates on the Aegean, and by Egyptian war galleys farther south." He leaned on one arm. "Nonetheless, I will do my best to secure safe passage for you. In the meantime, I have another task for you."

Ramiro was hoping to avoid other duties. "But, Sire, getting to Jerusalem is my utmost priority."

"Ah, yes, of course." Alexios feigned concern. "There will be plenty of time for that. But if you wish to aid Christendom and help pilgrims to Jerusalem, there is no better way than to support our military. I need you as chaplain to the Latin soldiers in Nicomedia. There are many more Latins there. I trust you have met Humberto?""

Ramiro frowned. "Is there no one else to fulfill this duty?"

"As you must know, there are few Latin monks or priests in the Empire." Alexios smiled politely. "And your countrymen respond poorly to our Greek clergymen."

"But what could I possibly do there?" Ramiro blurted, somewhat perturbed.

"As all men of the cloth do for their soldiers, Monk Ramiro. Lead them to prayer, oversee their rites, urge them into battle in the name of God, rally them to fight for the True Faith, to destroy these vile heathen who attack the Churches of our Lord and threaten the Holy Sepulcher itself." He fingered his beard. "And if Pope Urban urges the faithful to wage war against the Turks, you will be doing a service to your men and to your faith."

Ramiro slumped in his chair. What does he mean... my men? he thought. Not those cursed Flemings! He tried to remain calm. "And for how long will my services be required, Your Highness?" he probed, fighting to control his mounting frustration.

"I'm not sure, perhaps six months or so. Think it over, Monk Ramiro. If this is not agreeable to you, I can arrange for your safe travel back to France."

His veiled threat did not elude Ramiro. "I will give it some thought, Your Highness. I foresee no problem serving with Drugo's men for a period of time. But you must realize that I cannot accept any permanent commission without the approval of the Abbot of Cluny."

"I will write to Pope Urban and relate to him the importance of your position here. Surely, he will relay the message to your Abbot?"

It was clear to Ramiro that the shrewd King was manipulating him. He felt a wave of despondency. "Yes, I'm sure he would, Your Majesty. And if the Abbot does agree, I hope that you will, after a term of service, facilitate my journey to Jerusalem."

"I will," promised Alexios, although his tone carried little conviction.

"Thank you, Your Highness. And on another matter, when am I scheduled to meet with the Patriarch?"

Alexios smiled. "I will make arrangements." He paused, changing the subject. "How are your funds?"

"Well, Sire, ... I did bring a purse, but it is not much. We were somewhat dependent on Sir Drugo. But now that he has moved to Galata..."

Alexios rose from his chair, going over to a large desk in one corner of the room. He dipped a quill and scribbled a note. "Take this to my treasurer, he will provide you with the monies you need."

Ramiro stood to accept it. "This is very kind of you, Your Majesty. May God bless your reign."

"And should you accept my offer to go to Nicomedia, I will provide you and your assistant with a monthly stipend." He gestured again to the chair. "Now, Monk Ramiro, please return to your seat and tell me all about your journey... and of events in Rome. How does Pope Urban fare against the forces of the German king?"

Ramiro related much of what he knew as Alexios prodded him with endless questions about the affairs of Europe. After hours of discussion, the King rose abruptly to signal the meeting was over. "I'm pleased we had this meeting and I look forward to your response."

Ramiro stood and nodded. "May God be with you," he said as he left the room.

Alexios was satisfied. *That should keep the damned monk occupied for a time. But we shall see, I may find a good use for him yet.* He opened the door to address the guard. "Send instructions to Commander Manuel," he ordered in a low voice. "The Latin monks are not to leave the city without my consent. Continue to intercept all messages."

Aldebert paled when Ramiro told him of his meeting with the King. "And where on God's earth is Nicomedia?" he asked wide-eyed.

"It's beyond the Propontis, near the battle line with the Turks."

"Blessed Mother Mary, Father Ramiro! We did not come to fight Turks. We are here on the Pope's business!"

"I know, Brother Aldebert, I know. But I am no longer sure what the Pope's business is. It's beginning to look like he condones this war against the Turks. Recall how he encouraged and blessed Drugo's soldiers as we left the castle at Melfi. It did seem overly zealous. I can only wonder at what he said in his letters..."

Aldebert slumped in a chair, rubbing the scar on his shoulder. "I have no desire to be a target for another Turk arrow. We should just return to France. We delivered the letters. Our mission is complete."

"No it is not, Aldebert."

Aldebert looked up with pleading eyes. "Perhaps you could make a pilgrimage to Jerusalem another time?"

"Brother Aldebert, I'm thirty. There is no other time. Besides, there is more to this journey than my desire to kiss the blessed Tomb of our Lord."

"What do you mean?"

Ramiro hesitated, biting his lip. He may have said too much and warned himself not to mention the Cluny cross or the nature of his mission, so he said the next thing in mind. "If you must know... my mother is in Jerusalem." This was the first time he had mentioned this to anyone but the Abbot.

"Your mother?"

"Yes, I received a letter from her when at the abbey. I was very surprised. I thought she was dead."

"By the cross! Then you really must get to Jerusalem!"

"Yes, and she promised me a holy relic. I hope to secure it for the abbey so that we may use it to venerate Our Lord and the Martyrs of the Faith." He crossed himself and prayed inwardly for God to forgive his mangling of the truth.

Aldebert jumped from his chair. "A holy relic! Perhaps a piece of the True Cross! A Holy Nail... or the bones of a saint! Some have found vials of the blood of John the Baptist!"

"Yes, yes, Brother, I have heard these stories."

"Do you really believe we could return with a holy relic, Father? We would become heroes at the abbey!"

Ramiro frowned. "Do not let vanity rule your thoughts, Brother Aldebert. It is our duty to the Church."

Aldebert lowered his head. "Yes, Father... may the Saints forgive me." But he soon looked up, his round eyes bulging. "We must get to Jerusalem! We just need some money!"

Ramiro dug into his purse. "That reminds me. The King gave me a note for the treasurer."

"Really? For how much?"

"I haven't looked." He pulled it out. "It's quite straightforward, the King has given us... let's see..." He squinted to read Alexios' scrawl, moving the paper back and forth. "No, wait, that cannot be."

"What is it?"

"Aldebert, brace yourself. The King has given us ten gold bezants and fifty electra, whatever they are."

Aldebert jumped about like a giddy child. "That's a fortune, Father Ramiro! That's enough to get us to Jerusalem and back!"

Ramiro sat down with a gloomy look. "But how can I betray the King with his own money? And how far would we get with that guard watching us all the time? And don't forget they check the names of all who come and go at the gates."

Aldebert's enthusiasm faded with a glum look. Again, he slumped into a chair. "We are prisoners of this King."

"Not entirely. He would have us escorted back to France, but as long as we stay here, we are subject to his whim and mercy."

"Do you intend to stay, then?"

"What choice do I have? I must get to Jerusalem. I will tell the King that we agree to go to Nicomedia."

"May God help us," Aldebert sighed.

A knock came from the door. They exchanged looks. "Well... go see who it is, Brother Aldebert."

Aldebert returned shortly, holding a book. "A guard delivered this."

Ramiro looked at the title. "It's the Turkish dictionary!"

Aldebert raised an eyebrow. "Turkish? I don't see how that's going to help."

Ramiro got up suddenly. "Come along, Brother. Now that we have a bit of money, let's do some shopping."

A JUG OF WINE

The markets of Constantinople were the finest Ramiro had ever seen. Lively shops huddled side by side in long, brick buildings lining cobblestone streets. Each had its own archway and a locking iron gate, the standard Roman style. Ramiro and Aldebert, flush with the King's money, occupied themselves by exploring the extensive collection of goods gathered from around the world. And in one dusty shop, they studied a wide selection of wines.

"This is our very best," said the wine merchant, pointing to one. "And the most popular."

"Is it spiced?" asked Ramiro.

"Yes, yes. With fresh anise."

Ramiro shook his head. "I'm not fond of it." He recalled its overwhelming licorice flavor.

The vintner picked up another bottle. "I've got posca if you prefer. It's a sour wine spiced with coriander."

"No thank you. It's too hard on my stomach."

"Aah," said the man. "Then you are a true connoisseur. I think you will like this." He went behind the shelf, pointing to another jug. "We import it from Mesopotamia. It's made from the finest black dates. "It's expensive but you must try it." He blew the dust from the jug before removing the stopper to pour a little into a cup.

Ramiro took a sip, rolling it on his tongue. "That is surprisingly good. I'll take the whole jug."

Aldebert struggled with the thick, ceramic jug as they went from shop to shop. "This is very heavy, Father Ramiro. Should we head back?"

"No, no, Brother. Now let's find the bookstores. I'm eager to see what they have."

Not far away, two men watched. One was the Byzantine guard who always followed at a short distance, and the other was Wiker the Blade, who stared out from the spice shop just across the street. He noticed the guard and felt for his dagger.

"We should go home," pleaded Aldebert, who was tired of carrying the burdensome jug of wine and looking at books. "It's getting dark and the markets are closing anyway."

"Yes, soon, Brother. Let's look at these books first. He perused the shelves with a keen eye. "Look at this, Brother Aldebert." He held up a book. "It's written by Saint Euthymius. *Barlaam and Josaphat* it's called."

The bookseller overheard. "A very interesting book," said the man, walking over.

"What's it about?"

"It's a story about a religious man from the Indus, far to the east. A man called Siddhartha the Buddha."

"That is interesting," said Ramiro, turning it in his hand. "I'll take it."

As they stepped into the dimming street, the bookseller closed shop behind them. "Where's the guard?" Aldebert asked, looking around.

Ramiro reached into his habit, stuffing the new book into a canvas bag hung from his neck. "Perhaps he got tired of watching us shop all day... but he's never left us before."

Wiker watched from a dark corner of the alleyway, wiping fresh blood from his dagger. The guard lay dead at his feet, a gaping slash across his throat.

Aldebert chewed on a lip while his eyes darted around nervously. The street was quiet and almost deserted. "Let's go home, Father. I can't carry this jug any longer."

"Yes, yes, Brother. It's time to go. Carry it a little farther and then I'll take over."

Aldebert heaved the jug up onto one shoulder and the two of them started home.

Wiker watched them approach, pulling back into the shadows, waiting for the right moment. He stooped low, and when the monks were only a few paces past him, he leapt out to strike from behind. But he faltered over the legs of the sprawling guard. And as he reached out to steady himself, his dagger clanked against the stone wall.

"What's that?" Aldebert asked, swinging around.

Ramiro turned too. He noticed a glint of steel and a dark figure. Suddenly alarmed, he pulled hard at Aldebert's sleeve. "Come quickly, Brother," he whispered. "Quickly!"

But before they could take another step, Wiker struck out again from the alleyway, this time as quick as an Armenian viper. Ramiro heard him coming and spun around to defend himself. Wiker backed away for an instant, but then lunged at him, plunging his dagger into Ramiro's chest. Before Wiker could pull the dagger out to strike again, Ramiro staggered back, the knife jutting from his sternum. Aldebert shrieked, falling back. Ramiro toppled to the cobblestones, writhing and grasping at the dagger.

Wiker reached under his cape for another blade. He jumped over Ramiro, ready to slash his throat. But before he could make the deadly cut, Aldebert regained his senses, rushing toward the two. Then, in an unusual show of strength and courage, he raised the weighty wine jug high above his head and, with all his might, smashed it down on Wiker's skull. The jug shattered and Wiker collapsed in a deluge of Mesopotamian wine.

The Sultan of Rome

Alexios paced back and forth behind a long table. His mother, Anna, and his brother, Isaak, sat to one side. All around sat his generals. Once he had their attention, he stepped up to a huge wall map, tapping a finger on Nikea, a rebel-held fortress on the eastern shore of the Propontis, located just south of the Byzantine stronghold of Nicomedia. He raised his voice. "And to the east, we have more trouble with Abul Kasim." Holding his finger on Nikea, he turned to look around the room, "the Sultan of Rome," he added sarcastically. They all laughed.

He continued in a more somber tone. "You all know Abul Kasim controls Nikea since the death of his master, Sulayman, and now extends his grip over our eastern provinces. He schemes to take Nicomedia from us, the very gateway to Constantinople."

Isaak moved forward in his chair. "Then we should send those new Kelts to reinforce General Taticius' position there."

"I agree," said Alexios. "The Normans are tough fighters and they may as well stay with their own kind. But we must control them!" He looked straight at Taticius. "I want you to put spies among them. Your informants will report directly to you... and you to me."

"Yes, Your Highness."

He looked down at his papers. "Very well, we will move the Kelts from Galata to Nicomedia immediately."

"I thought you were going to leave them in Galata until the spring," said Anna.

"I was, but apparently they create havoc there. I'm told they drink and fight almost every day. They've been in several drunken brawls with the Russians, the Italians, and even among themselves! Their rooms are pigsties. Our slaves are mistreated, some raped. The servants fear to enter their rooms."

Anna sneered in disgust. "They're all the same. Uncouth savages! They seem content only when inebriated into a stupor. Thank God we put them in Galata with the other pagans."

Isaak piped in. "We may as well move them to Nicomedia right away. At least they could vent themselves against our enemies and do some good."

"That's what I thought." Alexios grinned. "They should be able to keep that little bastard, Abul Kasim, at bay."

Anna looked worried. "Are you sure you can trust so many Kelts in one place?"

Alexios shook his head. "No, I'm not. But General Taticius has much experience with these Western barbarians. We must trust his abilities." He rapped a knuckle on the table. "We just need them to hold the walls of Nicomedia. And when the opportunity presents itself, we will send them on raiding parties to harass Abul Kasim's forces whenever they stray. They must learn how the Turks fight to be of any use to us."

"It's difficult to get Kelts to fight that way," said Taticius. "They just want to charge in and start hacking." The men chuckled.

Alexios nodded. "They're a hot-headed race, General, but you must train them. Our success depends on it." A shock of red hair dangled over his face. "We'll use that Latin monk to control them, the one called Ramiro."

"Did you hear what happened to him?" Commander Manuel asked.

Alexios shook his head. "No. What?"

"He was stabbed in the markets yesterday, apparently by the same man that attacked him in Tzurulos—the German assassin."

"Is that so?" Alexios pondered the monk's usefulness. "Is he dead?"

"Fortunately, no. The doctor said the killer's blade was slowed by a book he carried in a bag about his neck. Only a short length of blade managed to pierce his chest. By the grace of God, it missed his heart."

"What about the assassin?"

Manuel smiled. "The other monk hit him over the head with a large jug of wine. It split his skull open like a melon. He's quite dead."

"Are there any more assassins after this monk?"

"We don't believe so, Sire."

"So how long will it be before Monk Ramiro can travel?"

"The doctor thinks he'll be fine in a couple of weeks."

"Good," said Alexios. "So we can still send him off with the Kelts. Hopefully, he will assure them that the safety of the Holy Sepulcher depends on their success, or he can tell them they get no gold unless they follow our directions. Either way should work." The generals chuckled.

Anna smiled. "So the Latin monks have agreed to serve with the Kelts in Nicomedia?"

"Yes, with some convincing, mother. It will keep them busy until I find a better use for them. But Monk Ramiro wasn't happy about it."

"Why not?"

"He said he was very anxious to make a pilgrimage to Jerusalem."

"Good, keep him anxious," said Anna. "He may claim to be a man of God, but remember he is allied to Rome—not Byzantium. And the very fact that assassins are after him means he must be important."

"If he is a spy, I want to keep him away from the Holy Land," said Alexios. "We should make an effort to control all information going west, so we must keep him at a safe distance in Nicomedia. Then he can report as he pleases and it will make little strategic difference. Once I'm sure about his loyalties, I may find another use for him."

"How?"

"I'll think of something. He seems to have a gift for languages. I gave him a Turkish dictionary."

"If he could speak Turkish, he could be some help to us," said Anna. "Give him one of our best tutors to take with him to Nicomedia. Someone who can also keep an eye on him."

"Yes, yes! And I know just the man," said Alexios. He moved over to his secretary, speaking softly. He returned again to the map on the wall. "Now, my generals, let's finish our plans."

Report: Troubled Empire

Ramiro put a hand to the thick bandage wrapped around his chest as he thought about Wiker's attack. Secretly, he was relieved the assassin was dead. He scratched his head, trying to think of what to say to Abbot Hugh. He had no desire to tell him about the latest attempt on his life, nor how Brother Aldebert had killed the man with a wine jug. Poor Aldebert was beside himself for days.

But as far as the rest of it goes, he had been unable to discover much of Byzantine internal affairs. He knew what everyone knew, that pagan enemies surrounded the Empire on all sides and that the Emperor fought desperately to survive each onslaught. He wrote of the encroaching Turkomans from northern Bulgaria who raided and pillaged, leaving death and destruction in their wake. And he wrote about the Turks on the eastern frontier and how they had laid waste to Greek farms and continued to assault Greek cities. He mentioned how the Byzantines fought back with mercenary armies gathered from every corner of the Empire, even from the ranks of their enemies. And he emphasized King Alexios' desperate request for thousands more to fight the hordes.

He also told the Abbot how the Greek Church continued to defy the views of Rome on a number of issues. But alas, he was at a loss to suggest a compromise. And the Patriarch had made it clear he was unwilling to cede ecclesiastical power to the Pope. On this, he cited the decisions of the Council of Chalcedon and suggested, in his humble opinion, that perhaps both the Patriarch and the Pope could share power, just as the council had decided many years before.

TATRAN THE TURK

Aldebert dashed around the room in a frenzy. "God help us, Father Ramiro! Why are they rushing us off to the end of the world like this? I thought we were here for the winter. Now we're being ordered to Nico… Nico whatever."

"That's Nicomedia, Brother. It's the Emperor's last stronghold in the east. It can't be that bad," he said, secretly hoping to see Adele again. "I hear it has a magnificent palace and was once the capital of the Empire. Come now! We must go. The escorts are waiting and Pepin has our mounts ready."

There was a knock at the door.

"See who it is, Brother."

Aldebert scurried to the door and opened it a bit to peek out. A short man with a leathery face and long, braided hair stared back at him. "Who are you?" he asked the man.

"Greetings. I am Tatran. The Emperor sent me." His long braids dangled about his shoulders as he talked and his wide mustache bobbed below high cheekbones. He wore Roman armor and carried a sword.

Aldebert sputtered at the sight. "You… you teacher?" he replied in stammering Greek.

The man smiled. "Yes, I am Tatran, your tutor. Are you Master Ramiro?"

"No, no." He pointed. "He inside. Wait here."

Tatran nodded. "Yes, yes."

Aldebert slammed the door shut, sprinting back to Ramiro. "Father! Father! The tutor is here!"

"Ah! That's good… so why are you so flustered?"

"Father, he's a Turk!" Aldebert brushed a finger across his cheek. "He's got those strange eyes! And he's got a sword!" He motioned to an imaginary sword at his side.

"Calm down, Brother. He's my tutor. He's come to teach me Turkish. Why is it such a surprise that he's a Turk?"

"But he's got a sword, Father! And he carries a dirk in his belt!"

"So? Any man in his right mind would carry weapons to Nicomedia. He's loyal to the Emperor, Aldebert. We have nothing to fear. Now let's go."

"He's a heathen!" Aldebert hissed. "He could be another assassin! May God help us!" He made the sign of the cross before fumbling with his bag.

GALATA

Clean, gardened streets stretched for miles along the shores of the Golden Horn. Along each side, sat the luxurious mansions of privileged foreign merchants, such as the Genoese, Pisans, Venetians, and others who had assisted the Empire at one point or another. In gratitude, the Emperor rewarded them with the best markets of Asia. Their warehouses lay close at hand, clustered along the waterfront near the bustling shipyards. Less privileged merchants lived in Galata, just across the waters of the Bosporus strait, where Drugo and his men waited.

Ramiro and Aldebert followed Tatran to the busy docks, swarming with longshoremen, carpenters, traders, and travelers from afar. Carts and wagons of goods from all over the known world came and went. A large crane lifted logs from the hold of a Russian vessel, loading them onto long wagons pulled by teams of oxen. Other vessels carried crates of spices from distant Indus or copper from the mountains of Armenia.

Tatran raised his arm. "The ferry comes. Prepare to load!"

Reaching Galata, they found the knights rested. Their wounds had healed and they were, once again, greedy for battle and booty.

Ramiro glanced around the courtyard, his thoughts elsewhere. "Where are the women and tradesmen, Sir Drugo?"

"Only a few were allowed to come with us to Nicomedia," Drugo replied with a hint of regret. "We have our squires, archers, and a few servants. The others must stay in Galata. But the Emperor gave them all work."

Ramiro frowned, still looking over the crowd. "And what of Louis the Carpenter? Where is he?"

"Why are you concerned with carpenters?"

"Do you know where he is, Sir Drugo?"

"If you must know, the Emperor ordered them all to the shipyards. He's building a new fleet of war galleys."

Drugo appeared to have forgotten about Louis and the stolen locket. But Ramiro said no more of it. "And where are these shipyards?"

Drugo swung his arm north, rustling his chain link armor. "Along the coast of the Golden Horn, farther north. But you can't get in. They won't let anyone in or out. The tradesmen and their families must stay in the compound until the ships are finished." He climbed onto his horse. "We must leave." He turned, shouting to his men. "Move out, everyone, move out!"

Ramiro tried to hide his disappointment by directing his ire to Aldebert and Pepin. "Quick, mount up before we're all trampled!"

With a wide grin, Pepin leapt into the saddle of his new horse. He was happy to be back with Father Ramiro, eager for new adventure.

"Pepin!" Aldebert fumed with envy. "This horse does not excuse you from your duties. And put those weapons away!"

Pepin's smile faded. He covered his short sword and knife with his cloak.

"Father Ramiro, how can we allow him to carry these weapons? We are men of God!"

"Brother Aldebert, be practical. These are gifts from the Emperor himself. It would be rude for the boy to refuse them. Besides, it can do no harm for him to learn their use. We are entering a dangerous land."

Aldebert spread his arms wide and raised his voice. "Yea, though I walk through the valley of death..."

"I know the Psalms, Brother Aldebert!" Ramiro interrupted as he mounted his gray mare. "Nonetheless, I commend you on your faith. May God be with you." He felt for the knife beneath his robe. "We pray the next Turk arrow doesn't land between your eyes."

Pepin chuckled. Aldebert glared at the boy before swinging back to Ramiro. "You mock me, Father!"

Ramiro grinned a little. "Forgive me Brother Aldebert... but you would do well to keep your wits about you." He spurred his horse forward to hide his broadening smile.

They set out toward the rising sun, entering the vast and ancient land conquered over time by Hittites, Phrygians, Persians, Greeks, and Romans. The Arabs and Turks called it "The Land of the Romans." But to the Byzantines this land, reaching from the waters of the Propontis to the mountains of Armenia, was known as Anatolia or Asia— "The East."

3 - ANATOLIA

THE PROPONTIS

1090

East of Constantinople, thrived a vibrant world almost unknown to the people of Europe. Although they were aware of the Holy Land and believed it was "a land flowing with milk and honey" as described in the Bible, only a few weary pilgrims returning home had any idea of what it was really like. And even these few knew almost nothing of the triangle of power and intrigue encompassing the wider region.

In the northwest corner, sat the Byzantine Empire, a tired relic of the East Roman Empire, but now revitalized under the rule of the clever and ambitious Alexios Komnenos. To the northeast, was the young Turk Empire, built on the civilization of ancient Persia and now ruled by the Seljuk Turk, Malik Shah. And to the south, was timeless Egypt, forever a potent force in the affairs of the Mediterranean. Ruled in name only by the Caliph, real power rested in the hands of the vizier, Al-Afdal, commander of the armies.

At the time, the Byzantines were Orthodox Christian, the Turks were Sunni Muslim, and the Egyptians were Shia Muslim. Although they traded extensively, they harped on their differences more than their commonalities. And with some irony, the pathological hatred between the Sunni and the Shia was cause enough for the Egyptians to form a loose alliance with the Byzantine Christians. All three saw each other as evil heretics or misled pagans, creating a hostile milieu of ongoing animosity, fear, and distrust. Among themselves, they settled disputes with pacts and intrigues or, when diplomacy failed, with war. And the harsh, arid landscape of the Middle East was their bloodied battleground.

TURKS

Traveling out of Galata, the highway to Nicomedia headed directly southeast. It followed the northern shore of the Propontis, winding its way through rock and sand and thick forests of fir, pine, and beech. Above the trees, gray clouds rolled in from the Black Sea, billowing in thick waves across a brooding sky. White lightning laced through the clouds and the resounding thunder sent a shudder through Ramiro's chest. A freezing wind swirled about him and a hail of sleet pelted his face. With a grimace, he pulled his hood tight to his head and tucked his heavy cloak under his legs.

Tatran the Tutor seemed unperturbed by the cold forces of nature. He rode with his shoulders squared and his chin up, combing sleet from his long mustache with the fingers of one hand. A heavy cloak swathed his shoulders, covering a coat of armor, a long wool tunic, thick leggings, and fur-lined boots.

Ramiro pushed into the wind, pulling his horse alongside. "Tell me, Tatran, which country are you from?"

Tatran kept up a trot and Ramiro had to spur his horse on. "Yes, Master. I was raised in the mountains of Bulgaria," he said proudly. "I was a slave once—but I am a freeman now." His eyes gleamed. "Tatran of Oghuz at your service, your Excellency."

"Are you Christian?"

"Yes, yes, of course," he chuckled. "King Alexios insisted."

"So you really believe Jesus is our Savior?" Ramiro asked with a hint of skepticism.

Tatran squinted, forcing a smile. "Of course... he... uh... he was a great proph-et," he muttered before praying inwardly, 'may Allah forgive me.'

Ramiro nodded. "And what brought you to the service of the Emperor?"

"I'm a mercenary, Your Excellency... and the Emperor pays well."

Ramiro held up a hand. "Please, Tatran, do not address me for a station I do not occupy. You are my teacher. Just call me Ramiro."

"Very well, Master Ramiro." He said obligingly as he maneuvered a muddy turn in the road. "And if I am to teach you, let's begin now. From now on, we speak only Turkish."

"I am eager to learn your language, Tatran." He shivered in the cold, wet air. "But first you must tell me... who are the Turks?"

In a somber manner, Tatran related the story of how, in the time of the Tang Dynasty, Chinese armies persecuted his people, forcing them to flee from their ancient homeland near the Altai Mountains far to the north. That was many years ago and they long wandered in search of a new home, but as the Chinese Empire expanded, they were pushed farther and farther south until they finally settled into an uneasy existence in Khorasan, north of Iran.

He went on to say how, over the following years, they were raided and enslaved by the Arabs and Persians before one family of Turks, the Seljuks, managed to free themselves by fighting back. "Then, one fateful day, by the will of God," he said with increasing pride, "the grandsons of Seljuk defeated the King of Iran in a glorious battle. You have heard of the Battle of Dandanqan?"

Ramiro shook his head.

"No?" Tatran asked, astonished. "It was a famous battle... only fifty years ago."

"Forgive me Tatran, I know little about this part of God's world."

"Well it was an important day for the Turks." He brushed sleet from his brow. "Now the esteemed Seljuks rule a great empire. They are the masters of Iran, Khorasan, and Al-Iraq... they even hold Roman lands." There was a touch of arrogance in his voice, even though he worked for the Romans. He raised his voice. "And now it is all ruled by Malik Shah, the Great King, the Sultan of the World."

Ramiro frowned. "And he is a Seljuk?"

"Yes, yes, Master. The Great Sultan is the son of Arslan the Magnificent..." Tatran's long, black braids bobbed on his shoulders as he rode. "...the one who defeated the Romans at the Battle of Manzikert only a generation ago. The Seljuks have taken all Asia from the Romans. King Alexios is not pleased about this."

"I'm sure he's not," Ramiro agreed. "What of this Sultan of Rome? Is this the same man?"

"Aah! No, no. You speak of Abul Kasim. He claims the title because he now rules over some Roman land... although not easily. But he should not call himself sultan. This makes Malik Shah terribly angry. He's just an emir."

"An emir? Like a prince?"

"Possibly... or a military commander."

Ramiro nodded. "And have you met this Abul, the Sultan of Rome?"

"Yes, I've met him," he said with a sneer. "He is nothing. He is a little man who thinks he is a giant among men. He is a sly fox who rules only because his master, a true Seljuk, died in battle. But I tell you, the fox plays with the wolf. He plots to take Nicomedia from the Romans. He is the man King Alexios wants us to destroy."

NICOMEDIA

February 1090

Just before sunset, the tail of the storm abated and, as the skies cleared, Ramiro could see for miles along the flat road running east to Nicomedia. In the distance, the long walls of the city rose up from a low hill, from where it guarded the main roads leading west to Constantinople, east to Ankara in the heart of Anatolia, and south to Nikea and distant Antioch.

As they neared the city gates, a watchman signaled their approach with trumpet blasts, and the thick, iron-clad doors of the fortress opened to receive Drugo's small army.

General Taticius was there to greet them. Although he rarely smiled, perhaps because doing so would dislodge his iron nose, the arrival of more fighting men brought a gleam to his eyes. "Welcome, Sir Drugo!" he shouted over the clamor of men. "Welcome again to the service of the Emperor. I hope your quarters will be adequate. Tomorrow, we will discuss strategies."

Drugo nodded. "Yes, General," he replied in faltering Greek.

"Ah, Captain, you understand what I say. Your Greek is improving."

"I learning," he smirked. "Women help me."

A loud hoot came from above. Humberto was on the battlement. His big belly shook as he shouted down. "Hail, Sir Drugo!" A loud cheer filled the air and the men raised their fists.

Ramiro could not share their joviality. His quick smile of greeting faded to a look of profound disenchantment. The place was nothing like Constantinople. His heart sank at the sight of the decayed and austere surroundings. Moss and grass crawled between stones and bricks, paint and plaster peeled from the walls, no color, no design. Crumbling buildings lined the cobbled roads, doors hung askew from their hinges and smashed roof tiles littered the pathways. The filthy streets, the litter, and the stink of raw sewage made him nauseous. He shivered, folding his arms for warmth. *Blessed Virgin, what have we come to?*

From his room in the dilapidated Palace of Diocletian, Ramiro enjoyed a commanding view of the Gulf of Astacus and the Propontis beyond. And as the sun rose above the horizon, the mountains of Bulgaria glowed in the distance. "If nothing else, Brother Aldebert, we do have a beautiful vista. Although I cannot say much for the city below us."

Aldebert looked up from his meal, juice running down his chin as he talked with a mouthful. "They say this was once a home of..." he paused to chew, "... a home of Emperors. There's a theater and a large market. And many old temples... though to pagan gods."

"So they say," said Ramiro. "But these buildings are falling down. And the people who live here appear no better than beggars. Look at their filthy tunics and worn boots! There is no color... no joy among them."

Aldebert wiped his face with his sleeve. "They should embrace the True Faith, Father. That would cheer them."

Ramiro looked at him in dismay. "I believe there is more to it than that, Brother Aldebert. These Greeks are on the front lines against the Turkoman. Their fields are raided and their orchards plundered."

Aldebert didn't seem to hear. "What are we to do here, Father Ramiro?"

"Honestly, I have no idea. The King wants us to lend spiritual and moral support to the troops, the "Latin" troops as he calls them. Apparently, I've become little more than a chaplain. Drugo could easily do without us. And we didn't receive much of a welcome from the citizens. They seem to despise our presence."

"Have we not come to help them?" Aldebert poked at his food. "Why are they so cold?"

"Perhaps they tire of the constant warfare. Perhaps they just hate Kelts. I don't know."

Aldebert moved to the window, staring out. "How long must we stay here? When will we ever get to Jerusalem?"

Ramiro let out a long sigh. He moved his hand to his cross, thinking of his mother and his mission. "I don't know, Brother. The King has sent us here and we are at his mercy... for the moment."

RAIDERS

"Good morning, Captains," Taticius greeted his men loudly while rubbing his hands in the cold room. "I call you here so we can discuss some tactics to use against Abul Kasim, who now holds Nikea just south of here." He unfolded a map, placing it on the table. "Our primary mission is to stop him from advancing any farther north while the Emperor attempts to out-maneuver the Patzinaks in the west. Abul Kasim imagines himself as the new Emperor of Rome and we must foil his wretched plans as best we can."

Drugo looked down on the map. His long, red hair draped across his face as he traced the coast of the Propontis with a finger, finally tapping it on Nicomedia. "What's the distance from Nicomedia to Nikea?"

"About forty miles by road," answered Taticius. "Nikea lies at the eastern end of Lake Askanius." He pointed it out on the map. "We must pass through the mountains to reach it. Almost impossible in the winter." He moved a finger along the south coast of the Propontis. "From Nikea, Abul Kasim plans to conquer this region. He has taken the towns on the eastern shore of the Propontis. You see Civetot? Just west of the lake."

"I see it," said Drugo, staring in fascination, amazed at the quality and detail of Byzantine maps.

"For Kasim's plan to work," Taticius put a finger on the map, "he must take Nicomedia. Our job is to stop him."

"So when do we attack the heathen bastard?"

"We will let him come to us. We have too few men for a frontal assault on Nikea. When we travel beyond the city walls, it will be only to harass his forces whenever they stray. Our tactic must be to attack and retreat, attack and

retreat." He brushed a hand across his short, black hair and adjusted his iron nose. "Abul Kasim will wait for spring. He cannot do much in the rain and mud. In the meantime, we'll scout the coast and take care of any resistance we find."

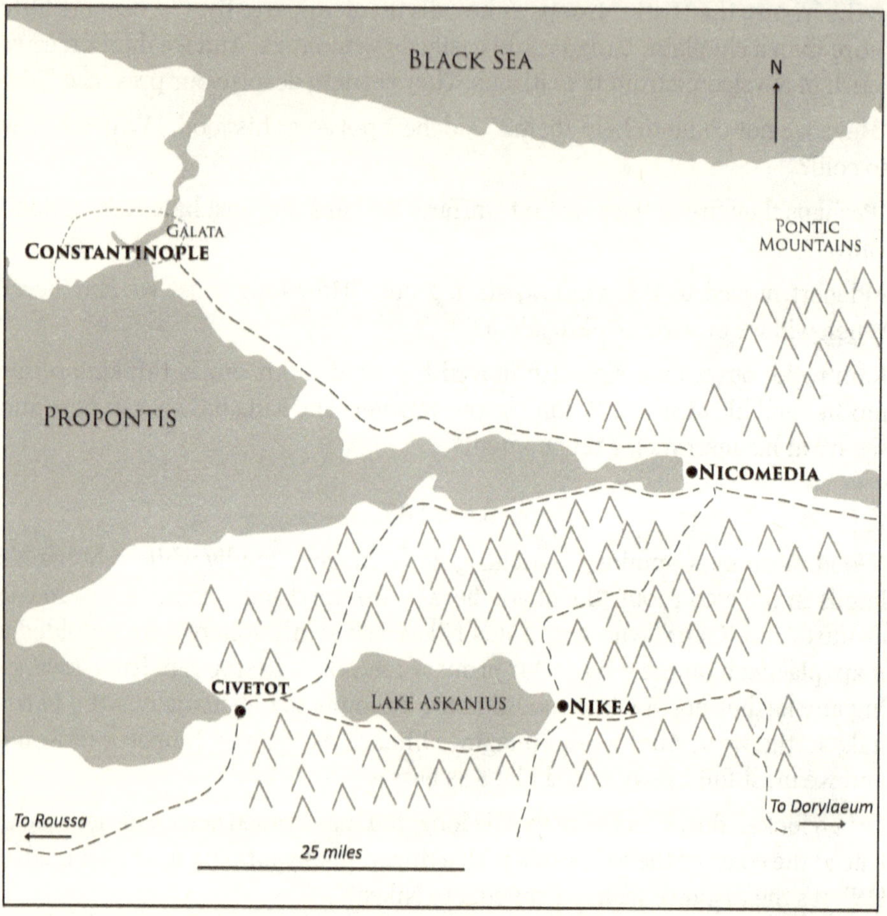

Drugo put a hand to his sword.

Taticius noticed. "Has it been a long winter, Sir Drugo?"

"Too long, General," he grinned.

A large fire blazed in one corner of the expansive assembly hall, its loud crackle competing with the boisterous laughter and rowdy voices of the knights.

Arles the Executioner swaggered as he recounted their recent raids on Turk settlements. "You should have seen that little shit try to run!" he hollered. "Ha, ha. I took his head off with one cut—but he still ran another ten paces!" The men roared, slapping each other's backs.

Taticius came into the hall, addressing them all in a loud voice. "My men, you fought bravely against the Turks today. But do not let these minor victories swell your heads. I have told you all before, you must strike and retreat, strike and retreat. This is the only strategy that will endure when we have so few men."

Mutters and curses arose from the men. "Must we fight like cowards?" asked the big Arles. "Where's the honor in that?"

"There is no honor in defeat, Arles of Ghent. I'm telling you, unless you understand the ways of the Turks, you will not win the day."

They continued to curse as they turned around to warm themselves by the fire.

"And where are the prisoners I need?" Taticius shouted. "I need captives for interrogation. It's not to our advantage to kill everyone!"

April 1090

Ramiro tried to focus on his book of Turkish grammar. He stomped his feet on the cold, stone floor. "Where's Pepin?"

Aldebert shook his head. "I think he's at the stables."

"Well, when he returns, send him right back out for more charcoal. It's freezing in here. The forty days of Lent have long passed and still this winter is upon us. Will it never end?" He slammed the book shut. "May God give me strength, Brother Aldebert. I will go mad here—completely mad! Three months! And still we have nothing to do and nowhere to go. It's a prison!"

Aldebert crouched in a corner of the room. He was mumbling a Psalm as he looked up from his Bible. "But Father Ramiro, are we not doing God's work here? Our men fight to destroy the heathen Turks and free good Christians from their evil grasp." He quoted a line from his book. "He subdues peoples under us and nations under our feet."

"You quote out of context, Brother," said Ramiro with a pedantic tone. "You must be careful not to twist God's word to suit your own designs." He let out a heavy sigh. "Anyway it could take years to defeat the Turks... if ever. I don't have the time to wait. I must get to Jerusalem!"

"But how, Father?"

"I wish I knew Brother. We're prisoners in a strange land. We know almost nothing of its customs, nor can we speak Turkish."

Aldebert rose to his feet. "At least you're learning it from Tatran, although it's too much for me, I'm still struggling with Greek."

"Well," Ramiro grumbled, snatching up his book again. "I suppose we may as well prepare ourselves in the meantime."

"Surely you please God by holding mass for the soldiers, Father?"

"Perhaps, but I am completely ostracized by the Greek clergy. They will have nothing to do with me after our uh... our debates over doctrine. All I tried to do was express my views on the nature of the Trinity. But they became quite upset. Now I fear to enter their churches, such is the degree of their hostility. And there are no Latin churches."

Aldebert sneered. "They're ignorant fools!" He glowered out the window. "Maybe we should try to leave, Father. There must be a way to get to Jerusalem."

Ramiro shook his head. "Brother Aldebert, even the soldiers dare not take the road south. How long would we last? I told you about Taticius' briefings. He said the Turk emir, Abul Kasim, controls Nikea and beyond. And bands of roving Turkoman dominate the roads farther south, even down the Aegean coast."

"But Father, some of the Greek priests say that pilgrims take those routes every year. And many arrive safely."

"Perhaps... perhaps it's not as dangerous as we are led to believe. But in all truth, our black robes and shaved heads would attract unwanted attention."

An icy rain lashed the walls of Nicomedia. Taticius shivered. His thick tunic, wool cloak, and wool leggings failed to keep him warm. He rubbed his legs, thinking briefly about donning the fur-lined trousers worn by the Kelts. He had to admit they seemed more practical, especially in this weather.

Torches burned in two corners of the war room, sending flickering shadows across the plastered walls. His men seemed ill at ease in the dim light. Among them, servants stoked coals in braziers, while others served pastries and wine. But soon, Taticius dismissed them with a wave of his hand.

He leaned back in his chair before addressing his captains and lieutenants. "You have done well over the last few months," he praised. "Now our forces have some mobility on the coast." He put his hands together, fingers meshed. "But it seems Abul Kasim is determined to stop us and we must prepare for the worst."

"What do you mean?" asked Drugo.

"Our spies say he plots a spring advance. His forces are much larger now. The Turks who once raided the countryside now flock to him on promises of gold and booty. Somehow, he has managed to convince them Nicomedia will fall easily and that Constantinople will follow. We must begin preparations for an assault!"

RAIN & FIRE

Overcast skies and a thick fog hid the Pontic Mountains from view. Ramiro had never seen so much rain. It rained all night and all day for weeks on end. Rivers of rain surged down from nearby mountains, flooding the sprawling lowlands and spilling through the streets of Nicomedia. Moss and mold gained new life, crawling along cracks of stone in streaks of green and black. Wagons bogged down in thick mud and peasants sloughed through mire.

But the Byzantines pressed on. Anyone who could walk was sent out to collect stones of all sizes and wood of any kind. Tradesman and soldier alike worked in the armories or reinforced sections of wall. Women and children made leather coats and water-skins or collected wood and feathers to make arrow shafts.

Ramiro and Aldebert, soaking wet, returned to their rooms as night fell. "Quickly Pepin, stoke those braziers!" Ramiro bellowed. "We must warm ourselves or risk falling ill." He shuddered as he removed his thick cloak, heavy with rainwater. "Brother Aldebert, tie up some ropes so we can hang these to dry."

There was a sudden, loud knock at the door. Ramiro opened it a little to peek out. A small man with a flat, round face and a big nose stood in the doorway, his leather cloak dripping rainwater into small pools at his feet.

"Greetings, Dom Ramiro," said the man.

Ramiro gawked, swinging the door open wide.

"Who is it, Father?" quizzed Aldebert.

"Brother Aldebert, it is our old friend, Louis the Carpenter!"

Louis' big cheeks cracked into a broad smile. "Dom Ramiro... God bless you! It's good to see you're fit and well."

"And you look good too, Louis, by God's Grace. Come in, come in. You must dry yourself, poor man."

Aldebert rushed over to clasp hands. "What brings you to Nicomedia?"

"Let the man sit first, Brother!" Ramiro clapped his hands in glee. "Pepin! Take Louis' cloak and hang it to dry. Then prepare some warm wine for our guest." He motioned to a stool. "Please, Louis, sit."

Louis pulled off his cloak before he sat down. "I'm here, Brother, because the Emperor ordered me here, along with several other tradesmen."

"And what of your wife, Mathilda?" Ramiro asked. "And, uh... your daughter, Adele?"

Louis took a cup of wine from Pepin. "They are well, Dom Ramiro, but were told to stay in Galata. They'll join me at a later date."

"Oh... oh, that is good news indeed!" he blurted with too much enthusiasm. His ears grew hot.

Aldebert shuffled in excitement. "What will you do here, Louis?"

"They want me to make catapults. General Taticius says he wants ten of 'em."

Aldebert scratched his long nose. "Catapults? What for?"

"For war, Brother Aldebert," Ramiro interjected. He turned back to Louis. "What else is said, my friend?"

"They don't tell us much, Dom Ramiro. But we've been building ships, one after the other, in the yards along the Golden Horn. And all kinds of siege engines..."

"What's a siege engine?" young Pepin asked, pouring more wine.

Louis opened his hands as he spoke. "Catapults are one type, Pepin, my boy. Some of 'em big enough to throw a horse. And then there are battering rams to smash through the gates, and big drills and towers."

"Drills?"

"Yes, boy, big bow-drills. Miners get up to the base of the wall and drill through the mortar to loosen the stones, then they dig down 'neath the wall and build fires to make it collapse." He looked around the room, squirming in his chair before lowering his voice. "Dom Ramiro, the Byzantines have a terrible weapon."

"What kind of weapon?" Ramiro whispered back.

"It's a special fire, a liquid fire of sorts."

"What do you mean?"

"Uh, well... I don't know much about it. I saw it once. It's a thick, black gooey stuff—smells like rotten eggs but shimmers like it's got silver in it. Burns anywhere, they say. Sometimes they shoot it out of brass tubes, or they put it in small pots, and then sling 'em with catapults or crossbows."

"So?" Ramiro asked. "Why not use flaming arrows instead—or burning tar?"

"Yes, that's what I thought at first, Dom, but this is quite a different fire. The flame cannot be put out. It'll even burn under water!"

"Under water?" Ramiro shook his head. "How in the name of heaven is that possible?" He finished his wine and motioned Pepin to fill their cups again.

"I don't know. They mix together certain ingredients. It's all secret. Some say the Arabs and Turks have copied it, but the Greeks say it's not the same stuff."

Aldebert sat back, his heart pounding. "It sounds like the Devil's work to me, Father."

Ramiro ignored him. "So when can we expect an assault?"

Louis shook his head. "I've no idea, Dom. They tell me little. As soon as it dries out, I'd think."

The rains stopped by the end of April and the roads hardened by May. The weeks passed, but Abul Kasim did not come. Sentries strolled the battlements of Nicomedia, always with an eye to the mountains in the south. Most were distracted by the monotony of their task but, on this day, one young man was more vigilant. He strained into the distance, peering down to the mountain pass to Nikea, shading his eyes from the bright sky. There, just out of the low foothills, a thin ribbon of dust wandered across the flatlands. "To the south! Rider approaching!"

Taticius and Drugo heard the cry and rushed to the battlement.

"It's a messenger!" the sentry shouted.

"What banner does he carry?" asked Drugo.

"I can't see it yet!"

A crowd of men joined them. They all peered to the hills. "Yes! It's yellow! It's our banner!" cried one. "He rides at full gallop!" The dust cleared for a moment and he shouted again. "Look! He's being chased!"

They could see them now. There, about two hundred paces behind the messenger, and in hot pursuit, rode a band of mamluks.

Taticius recognized them. "Those are Abul's men! Ready the gates! Put twenty men out right away!"

Before the messenger had galloped another mile, the south gate opened for Arles and nineteen others, who charged out to challenge the band of Turks. But when Abul Kasim's men spotted the heavily armed infidels bearing down on them, they hesitated and reined to a stop. One barked an order and they pulled their steeds around to flee back to Nikea.

The messenger sped past Arles, charging through the city gates. "They're coming!" he shouted. "They're coming!"

A full day passed before they spotted Abul Kasim's army. The Turkoman poured through the foothills by the thousands, amassing on the wide plains below. Farmers and villagers had long since fled, rushing for the safety of Nicomedia, leaving the countryside abandoned.

Taticius watched from a window of the citadel as the army approached. "Look! They bring sections of a tower and catapults!"

"I see that, General," said Humberto, "we are prepared."

Taticius paced. "Do not allow any miners near the walls. Put men on the battlements to drop stones, get the women and children if needs be!"

He watched helplessly as the Turks assembled their tower far beyond arrow range. Soldiers stalked around the base of the hill, concentrating their forces on roadways and gates. "Captains, we are now under siege," he said, strolling the battlements with Drugo and Humberto. "And we can expect no help from Constantinople. The King is leading an army west to Roussa at the Hellespont. He has to stop the Patzinak invasion. We are alone."

Ramiro watched too. The Turks were building their war machines with amazing speed and alacrity. "It won't be long now, Brother Aldebert. They will advance."

Aldebert wrung his hands in a fit of frenzy. "Blessed Virgin, what are we to do?"

"We will do what we must to survive, Brother. If needs be, we will throw stones on their heads."

"But we are men of peace," pleaded Aldebert, who still prayed for God's forgiveness after killing Wiker the Blade. "What of the Rules of Saint Benedict?"

"Brother Aldebert, the rules concern only the manner of everyday life and prayer. They say nothing about self-defense. If we let these Turks within the walls then you may as well throw yourself from the battlements... because that is exactly what they will do with you."

Aldebert raised his nose in a huff. "Then I will pray for peace and place my life in the hands of Divine Providence."

Ramiro glared at him. "And you will throw stones if you must!"

ABUL KASIM

Abul Kasim of Nikea was a Turk. He was not an imposing figure, nor did he have the countenance of a king. Instead, he appeared an average man of plain features with brown eyes, dark hair, and a thin beard. Were it not for his gold-laced turban and the small rubies sewn into his vest, he might have looked like an ordinary man of time and place. But Abul Kasim was the governor of Nikea and now, since the death of his lord Sulayman, he dared to call himself the Sultan of Rome. And like all sultans, he had kingly ambitions.

Certain of victory, he sat tall, prancing his black stallion through long lines of Turkoman warriors. Sunlight glistened from his polished chain-link armor, barely visible under his rich vest. He made sure all was going to plan and, as he looked again to the walls of Nicomedia, he dreamed again of riches and power. I will conquer Nicomedia... then I will seize Constantinople. I will be the new Emperor of Rome... my enemies will fall to their knees to worship me!

Beside him rode his brother Bolkas, the eldest son of his father's second wife.

"You see, Bolkas, we have encountered no opposition. The Roman Empire is weak. The King is preoccupied with the Turkoman near Gallipoli. This is our best chance to take Nicomedia. Do you still disagree, brother?"

Bolkas bit his lip. He was a slim man with a long face and sullen eyes. "By the will of Allah, I agree it is wise to enlarge our territory, my Lord, but why dedicate so much time and effort to the Romans? Did not our lord Sulayman reach an accord with King Alexios?"

Abul Kasim raised his thin voice. "I am the Sultan now, my brother—not Sulayman!"

"But please reconsider, Effendi. Perhaps we should take control of the south and east. Already, some upstart pirate has seized Smyrna... a Turkoman warlord by the name of Chaka. How can we allow this? It seems to me that his forces along the Aegean are more of a threat than those of the Roman King!"

"All in good time, my brother. Think of the riches in Constantinople. Even a portion of that wealth will allow us great power!"

Bolkas rode a little closer, a long, yellow cloak draped from his shoulders. "I agree, but what about the great Sultan, Malik Shah, may Allah keep him. Does he not have a pact with the Romans? He is not pleased that you call yourself Sultan, or that you have taken matters into your own hands. You would be wise to pledge allegiance to him. Then we could rule in peace."

"What does the Shah know about these lands? What does he know about our troubles?" Abul sputtered. "All he wants is Syria and Palestine. All he wants is to destroy the Shia heretics of Egypt!" He slapped a small hand against the saddle. "I want Byzantium!" His stallion whinnied and stomped.

"And the Turkoman want Byzantium!" cried Bolkas. "And now the pirate Chaka wants Byzantium!"

Abul sneered. "What do I care about Chaka and the rest of those scum? Let them all weaken themselves in battle with the Roman King. The barbarians will take their loot and leave, as they always do. Then we will take care of this Chaka."

After a moment of silence, Abul spoke of another matter. "What of these new mercenaries of the Romans? I was told the eunuch, Taticius, leads these pale-faced men."

"That is true, Effendi. They call themselves Franj."

Abul shook his head. "I have heard of these Franj. The King has used them before. He's a fool. How can he trust those filthy pigs?"

"They are vulgar fools, my Lord, may Allah curse them all, but I hear they can be dangerous in close battle. And they become even more dangerous when their many gods are aroused."

"No matter," said Abul. "Let them pray to their heathen mother goddess. To-morrow we start the catapults."

BATTLE FOR NICOMEDIA

The sun was not yet over the horizon when the first boulder smashed into the walls of Nicomedia. Ramiro felt the building shudder. He jumped from his bed. "It begins! Aldebert! Pepin! Let's go!" Screams of panic and dread filled the morning air. Children wailed, women yelled, and men shouted amid a clash of steel as they all rushed to their posts.

Taticius watched from the battlements as Abul Kasim aimed his big catapult for the south gate. He shouted to his captains. "Humberto! Set our catapults against theirs. We have the advantage of height."

"With pleasure, General."

"And keep the archers ready! Allow no one to advance."

Louis the Carpenter ran about the battlements checking the condition of his catapults. His were lightweight, stood the height of a man, and could be operated by one or two men. The lower end of the throwing arm pivoted on an axle wound tight with rope. The upper arm held a sling pouch loaded with a single stone about as big as two hands could hold. One man could crank down the arm by winding the rope around a spindle. Once released, the arm would snap upright, slinging the stone upward in a long arc.

"Release!" Humberto barked. A sharp whacking noise accompanied each launch as the arm of the catapult reached its stop.

A cascade of stones came crashing down on the Turks, pummeling men to the ground while others ran for cover. In a mad rush, Abul's men erected wooden shields for defense while continuing their own volleys.

Before long, another boulder slammed into Nicomedia's battlements, smashing through the castellations, sweeping two archers to their deaths. With deadly fury, it tumbled on, crashing into the courtyard below, crushing all in its path before spinning to a stop against a stone building. Minutes later, it was followed by yet another boulder, which came soaring in their direction, scoring a direct hit on the south gate, breaking the beam. One gate burst open, twisted and gnarled. Humberto fell to his knees as the battlements shook.

A loud cheer rang out from the distant Turks. They raised their lances high in the air, all the while shouting taunts and insults.

Abul Kasim roared with delight. "We will soon take Nicomedia!" he gloated. "Prepare the tower! Get the men ready!"

The Turks fell into position; servants, archers, infantry, and horsemen, all preparing to follow behind the tower as it made its way to the south gate. Twenty men pulled it along with ropes while twenty more pushed from behind.

Humberto yelled. "They're moving the tower!"

Taticius, who was overseeing the gate repair, rushed back to the battlements. "Get the archers in position! And keep the catapults on the bastards!" He turned to the men at the gates. They had managed to close the broken door and replace the locking beam, but it was still cracked and weak. "Quick, my men! Put a pry beam up against it! Secure it with braces! Let's go! The heathen are upon us!" He turned to his lieutenant. "Get the fire ready!"

The road to the gate was a gentle incline, so the tower advanced slowly. Stones from Louis' catapults continued to smash against it while the archers of Nicomedia took careful aim at the men pushing it. The Turks shot back, aiming for the archers stationed at the gatehouse parapets as they heaved the tower closer to the damaged gate.

Taticius rushed more men to the gatehouse towers, where they continued their barrage of arrows and stones. The Turks responded with their own continuous salvos. The Byzantines were outnumbered.

Ramiro and Aldebert scrambled about grabbing stones from a large stockpile in the courtyard before rushing them to the base of the walls. From there, Pepin, along with other young men, carried them up a ladder to the parapets. Arrows thudded into the ground around them or ricocheted from stone walls.

The tower inched closer and closer, and it soon loomed over the wall.

"Where are the fire grenades?" Taticius yelled.

"They are coming, my Lord. They were not prepared."

"God damn them! If they don't arrive soon, our heads will be impaled along these walls!" The tower banged against the wall near the gate. Its door slammed down on the castellations. "Humberto! Drugo! Get your men ready to fight!"

A mob of Turkoman raged out, screaming war cries. Many fell dead or wounded in a hail of Roman arrows. But more and more clambered out behind them. And they kept coming. The archers could barely keep up and the Turks began to push them back along the walls. They soon fought their way into the main compound in a frantic sword fight.

The Kelts charged forward, throwing their spears before drawing swords and daggers. But the Turks were good fighters with good armor. More and more kept rushing in from the tower door.

Two soldiers ran up to Taticius. Each carried a modified crossbow in one hand and, in the other, a burning wick. A bag of fire grenades hung from their waists. Taticius rushed them to positions along the battlements close to the tower. "Move! Move! Shoot as soon as you can!"

The men ran to the corner turrets to attack the sides of the tower. "Cover those men!" Taticius shouted. But as one grenadier neared position, an arrow pierced his throat. He plummeted from the wall, taking the crossbow with him.

The dead soldier thumped to the ground right in front of Pepin, who stopped and stared at the sprawled, limp body. Smoke from the dead man's wick trailed into the air beside him. The crossbow lay at his feet. All but one of the grenades was broken, the black and silver contents oozing over the cobblestones.

Men on the battlements shouted in panic. "Bring it up, boy! Get the wick! Bring it up the ladder! Grab the grenades!"

Pepin dropped the stone he was carrying. He snatched up the crossbow, the wick, and the last grenade before he scurried up the ladder as quick as a squirrel.

Ramiro shouted after him. "No Pepin! Give it to a soldier! Come back!" He ran back and forth along the base of the wall, keeping an eye on the boy.

Pepin did not hear. The fighting raged around him as he reached the battlements. "How does it work?" he yelled at the men around him, but they did not hear him over the din of steel.

Not far away, Humberto watched anxiously. He shouted as loud as he could. "Load the crossbow, boy! Put the grenade on it. Light the fuse and pull the trigger!"

Pepin stopped. He studied the crossbow frantically, remembering he had seen one used before. He sat down, placing his feet on the inside of the bow. With considerable effort, he tried to pull the string back with both hands. But it was a strong bow and he could not pull hard enough. A mamluk ran up behind him, howling as he raised his sword to strike.

Humberto shouted a warning, fighting his way toward Pepin, rushing up behind the attacking mamluk. The Turk spun around to face him. But Humberto didn't stop for swordplay. The heavyset man put his shield up, barging right into the enemy, sending the man spiraling off the wall. He hurried over to Pepin and, with little effort, loaded the crossbow. He placed the grenade into the crux and put the wick to the oiled cover, blowing gently. It erupted in flame.

Something caught Pepin's eye. "Watch out!" he screamed.

Humberto turned to see more Turkoman running toward him. He handed the crossbow to Pepin. "Move toward the tower!" he yelled. "I'll hold them off!"

Pepin hesitated, holding the bow awkwardly.

Humberto gave him a push. "Now! Now! If that tar catches, we're all dead!" He spun around to fight.

Pepin looked down on the tower. An arrow whistled past his ear. He pointed the crossbow, placing a finger to the trigger.

Humberto shouted again, all the while clashing with the enemy. "Quick boy! Let it go before it blows your face off!"

Pepin steadied his wavering sight and, with a shaking hand, he squeezed the trigger. The crossbow recoiled sharply, slamming into his shoulder, throwing him off balance. With a loud cry, he toppled off the walkway, dropping flat onto the roof of a side building. Unconscious, he began to roll off.

Ramiro watched in horror. He rushed to the building, arriving just in time to catch the boy before he hit the ground. They both collapsed to the pavement.

Pepin scored a direct hit on the tower. The grenade exploded in its center, consuming everything in a strange, ravenous fire. It was a blazing white fire, like the white light of the sun, and it clung to all it hit, sizzling and crackling. Thick clouds of choking, white smoke engulfed all nearby. Soon, another blast of fire hit the tower from the rear. The Turks caught inside died a fiery, white death, their short-lived shrieks piercing through the clatter of battle. Burning men rushed out screaming before collapsing into flaming balls of flesh. The rest fell back in a mad panic, stumbling and trampling the soldiers behind them.

Taticius saw the advantage. "Quick! Move the tower away from the wall before it burns through the gate!"

Abul Kasim surveyed the battleground with mounting rage. He watched the flames shoot skyward from the tower and cursed aloud as his men retreated in terror. It was already dusk. The battle was lost. "May Allah damn them!" he screeched in a pitched voice.

Bolkas watched too. He saw the Kelts storming out the gate to push the remains of the tower down the road, where it continued to burn rapaciously. "And what do you propose to do now, my brother?" he asked in a measured voice.

Abul returned a furious look. "We will build another tower and pound them again with the catapults! We will kill them all!"

Abul Kasim continued his siege for another month. He tried many times to construct new war machines, but the Byzantines managed to thwart his every effort. And there was little wood available because Taticius had the foresight to collect it all for miles around.

Abul was soon pressed for time and money. The weather warmed and it would soon be the season to plant crops. The Turkoman would not work for free and they expected their salaries to be paid on time. Many simply rode away to seek better prospects elsewhere. And he had more trouble from another quarter. The rebel Danishmends to the east were attacking his cities. In a fit of desperation and fury, he abandoned his siege of Nicomedia, returning to his stronghold at Nikea.

REPORT: NICOMEDIA

Ramiro scribbled another report to the Abbot. He described in detail the attack of Abul Kasim and even provided some drawings of the war machines used on both sides. He mentioned the ferocity of the Turks and their skill at battle, especially with the bow. But he also gave credit to the Flemish knights, relating how they had routed Abul Kasim's forces along the coast of the Propontis and drove them from the walls of Nicomedia.

He wrote of the Greek tactics and their defenses, including the strange and terrifying Greek fire. He told the Abbot of young Pepin's heroism in battle and of their ultimate victory. But he also mentioned the sorry state of affairs at the frontier of the shrinking Roman empire. Greeks and Romans once prospered across all Asia, all the way to Armenia, wherever that is. But now they live in fear of their lives and no harvest was safe. The Turks blocked the roads south to Jerusalem and demanded protection money from merchants and pilgrims. The route was perilous and almost impassable.

He sealed the envelope and rushed it to the courier's office.

August 1090

A hot wind blasted through an open window of the Palace, blowing Drugo's map off the table. He cursed as he chased after it, grabbing it off the floor and slapping it back down on the table. Otto and Fulk smiled but dared not laugh. "Look at this," he said, placing candlesticks on the corners. "Do you see?" He tucked his long, red hair behind an ear.

"See what?" Otto asked, rising from his seat.

Drugo held a caliper in one hand, spreading it between Rome and Nikea. He lifted a point off Rome, swinging the caliper end toward Jerusalem. "The Holy Land is eight hundred miles from here. That's almost the same as the distance from here to Rome."

Otto leaned over his shoulder. "That's a great distance, Sir Drugo. And nothing but heathen Turks and Arabs along the way."

Fulk was not interested. "When does this damned fast end? I could eat a whole pig."

"The Dormition Fast lasts till mid-August," said Drugo. "You'll just have to put up with it."

"How long can a man go without meat, Captain? Not even milk or cheese. And no wine! Christ! It doesn't seem right."

"Don't worry. They plan a feast tonight."

"Another feast? What the hell is this one?"

Drugo smirked. "They call it the Great Feast of Transfiguration."

"Can we finally eat what we want?"

"No meat, just fish. But at least we can drink wine, by the mercy of Christ."

Ramiro could not take his eyes off the long tables stacked with wine and food; bluefish with leeks, mackerel in onion, grilled tuna, anchovy, mussels, shrimp, and lobster. It was time for the feast to begin and they all rose to their feet to sing praises to the Lord.

> *You were transfigured upon the mount, O Christ*
> *our God, and Your disciples, insofar as they could*
> *bear, beheld Your glory...*

And when the long prayers ended, they all delved in.

"You eat too much!" Aldebert snapped at Pepin, who was busy sampling every dish.

"Leave him be, Brother Aldebert," scolded Ramiro. "Can you not see he is growing into a man?" Indeed, Pepin had grown considerably since leaving Cluny. He seemed a foot taller and a stone heavier. His voice had deepened and fine, blonde hairs bristled on his chin. And now, since he had shot the fire grenade against the Turks, he enjoyed some fame among the men. They even talked of his improving skill with the sword.

"It's been a long time since I've had food this good," said Louis the Carpenter. "Although the fare in Byzantium was pretty good too." He wiped his face with his sleeve before reaching for more shrimp.

"So tell me, Louis," Ramiro asked with as much indifference as he could muster, "when do you expect your wife to join you?"

"I was hoping she'd come soon, Dom, but she sent a letter. She's got a fever and wants to wait till next spring. Suits me fine. At least I know Nicomedia will be safe when they get here."

"I will pray for her health, Louis. And uh... your daughter, Adele? Will she come soon or... or has she found a husband?"

Louis shook his head in frustration. "No, she's not married yet. Too stubborn and fussy, I'd say. Stupid girl. She'll be an old maid soon."

A little elation fluttered deep within Ramiro's chest, but he pretended not to notice. "Yes, Louis, she should marry soon. She's a beautiful girl." He paused a while. "Did you say she's coming too?"

"Yes. It will be good to see them again. I hope they have a safe journey."

For a moment, Ramiro felt enraptured, thinking of Adele's smiling face. Then, realizing his thoughts, he blushed with contrition. "Yes, I too pray they will arrive safely."

CONSTANTINOPLE

December 1090

Winter closed in on Constantinople. A freezing wind swept down from the Black Sea, lashing against the city's stone walls. For the first time in living memory, the waters of the Golden Horn and the Bosporus were thick with ice. Snow fell for weeks on end, covering the trembling city in a thick, white blanket.

Icy blasts pelted those brave enough to venture out to market, where shivering vendors waited painfully, hoping to earn a few copper coins. Commoners wrapped themselves in heavy woolen capes, rushing home to huddle through the night in one small room of their brick houses where mattresses, cushions, and blankets lined the floors and walls. Charcoal braziers of rough iron were the only source of heat.

But in the Emperor's palace, and in the ornate mansions of the wealthy, sweating slaves in busy basements stoked furnaces with wood and coal to heat thick, marble floors. And hundreds of obedient servants rushed about to meet the capricious whims of their masters.

An expansive map of the Empire, past and present, draped from the plastered wall of the war room. Sconce oil lamps flickered lightly in cool drafts while servants scurried about with trays of bread, cheese, and warm mead, leaving as quickly as they came.

Alexios sat at the head of the table, greeting his advisors and generals as they sat. Satisfied all were present, his warm smile changed to a look of consternation. He furrowed his red brow, tapping a wand on the tabletop to get their attention. "This is a dangerous time, gentlemen," he said in all seriousness. He stood abruptly. "I need your undivided attention." The generals fell silent. "As you know, we have had some success keeping Abul Kasim from the walls of Nicomedia and we continue to harass his forces whenever possible. He is subdued for the time being and licks his wounds in Nikea."

He turned and pointed to the map, swinging his wand along the Aegean coast of the Asian provinces, to the region south of Constantinople. Then he pointed to the end of a deep harbor, just east of the island of Chios. "But we have more trouble elsewhere. A Turk pirate by the name of Chaka has taken Smyrna and our governor has fled. Now he controls the coastal road and builds ships to take the islands of Chios and Lesbos."

He swung his purple cape out of the way as he stepped to the other side of the map. His red slippers flashed below him and the gold trim on his belt glimmered in an orange light. He moved his pointer southwest to the Hellespont, a narrow strait that was the only access to the Propontis from the south, controlling all maritime traffic between the Mediterranean and the Black Sea. "And, to make matters worse, the Patzinaks have taken Roussa. They plan to strangle us at Gallipoli."

"What of the Patzinaks to the north?" asked John Doukas. "Are they not a greater threat?"

"They are a terrible threat, Governor. But we are short of men and are forced to make a decision on how to divide our armies." He swung his right arm back to the map. "Like John said, more Patzinaks, and now Kumans march again from the north. As most of you know, they have crossed the Danube and we've been unable to resist their advances. They are on their way to join their comrades already in Roussa." He paused, staring at the map. "We have lost too many good men to these barbarian hordes."

"There's more to it," said Isaak. "It's a three-pronged attack. This is a plot!" Some of the men chuckled.

Alexios frowned. "I believe Isaak is right. The Patzinaks in Roussa will attack from the west, Chaka from the south, and Abul Kasim from the east. Our spies say many messengers run between all three. Chaka is plotting with Abul Kasim as well as the Patzinak chiefs. They know we have to spread our forces too thin. Their plan is to lead a three-point, concerted assault on the Empire." He put his hands on the table. A serious look crossed his face. "We need a solution... and we need it now!"

"How long will it take the barbarians in the north to reach Roussa?" Isaak asked.

"Fortunately," said John, "it's a cold winter. Snow and ice trap them in the mountains of Bulgaria. They won't be able to move till late spring. And if we can find a small army to trouble their journey, we could possibly delay them until the spring of next year."

"That's a good plan," said Isaak. "But what of the pirate, Chaka? We cannot allow him to place an armada at the Hellespont... or to land thousands of barbarians on our shores."

Alexios nodded. "I would say Chaka and the Patzinaks at Roussa are the greatest threat right now. As soon as the ice melts, we will pit the full of our forces against them. We need to attack them both at the same time."

"I think we can do it," said John.

Alexios looked concerned. "Yes, but we will need every sword we can find. We must recall the Kelts from Nicomedia. We will use them against the Turkoman."

"But we cannot forget about Abul Kasim," Isaak interjected. "If he takes Nicomedia, we'll be cut off from the land route."

"That's the chance we will have to take. If we are to survive as a Christian nation, we will need everyone to fight the Turkoman."

NICOMEDIA

February 1091

A distant scream echoed from the dungeons of the old Palace. Taticius had caught a Turk spy. Ramiro winced when he heard the piercing cries of torture, bowing his head so it almost touched his desk. "Blessed Saint Benedict, guide me to the path of solitude with God and bring peace to my heart." He looked up from his desk, raising his eyes above the shelves of books to the ornate dome above the library. "It befuddles the mind, Brother Aldebert, that men could be so cruel and evil. It defies everything Christ teaches! It even defies all that Muhammad teaches!"

"Muhammad? How can you speak his name, Father Ramiro?"

"He is who he is, Brother Aldebert. One should know the ways of the Muslims and how they think. You would do well to study the Quran."

"I can't believe my ears, Father! It's the work of the Devil!"

"Really, Brother? How can you believe such nonsense? Do you see now why you are still a novice and why we restrict the books you may read?" He looked directly into Aldebert's astonished eyes. "Do not mistake me, there are many points on which I cannot agree and the Holy Testaments remain my guiding truth. But truth comes to us in many ways, Brother. From the word of a stranger, from a sentence in a manuscript, or from your own mind when it grasps new meaning. If you could read Arabic, you may see the Quran as I do, full of many ideas shared by Christian and Hebrew alike."

Aldebert flushed white, his thoughts stark and panicked. *Is Father Ramiro possessed by demons? And now he speaks well of Hebrews?* His heart pounded, fear clouded his mind and twisted his tongue, his breathing labored.

Another scream echoed through the cavernous halls. Ramiro stood abruptly. "How can any man of God condone such cruelty?"

Aldebert could not speak. His growing fear of losing Ramiro to the fires of Purgatory overwhelmed any reasonable thought, and the screams of torture only worsened his condition. The room began to spin. His eyes rolled in his head and he slumped off his chair, fainting onto the cold tiles.

Ramiro put his hands on his hips, looking down on the unconscious man. "You really are an idiot, Brother Aldebert!"

General Taticius waved a letter in an upraised hand as he addressed his captains and lieutenants. "The Empire is in serious trouble, my men. Another horde of Patzinaks marches south past Adrianople, threatening Thrace and the capital itself. They gather again near Roussa. Our spies report over forty thousand."

The men gasped. "Forty thousand!" Humberto bellowed. "How can we possibly gather enough men to fight them?"

"That's the problem, Captain," said Taticius as he waved the letter again. "That is why the Emperor himself has personally requested our services in Gallipoli. He needs as many good warriors as he can get." He put a hand to his face to adjust his iron nose. "But that's not all. A Turk pirate gives us trouble on the Aegean coast. Apparently, the man has built a whole fleet of warships and has already taken Chios."

"But what of Abul Kasim and Nicomedia?" asked Drugo.

"Abul Kasim will have to wait, as will this pirate," replied Taticius. "At this time, the King wants us to ride to Gallipoli to battle the barbarians."

Drugo and Humberto glanced at each other. They were tired of endless raids—but forty thousand heathen!

Ramiro was lost in his own thoughts, feeling a ray of hope. His determination to reach Jerusalem superseded all concerns of the Empire. *Maybe now I can finally get away.*

"Alas," said Taticius, "we must abandon Nicomedia for a time. We will leave a small garrison to guard the gates but, for the most part, the people will have to fend for themselves until we can return."

Ramiro's hopeful thoughts vanished as he remembered his talk with Louis—*what of Adele? Is she still planning to come to Nicomedia?*

"You're leaving?" asked Louis the Carpenter, who was obviously not pleased.

"I've been ordered to join the men going to Gallipoli," Ramiro replied gently. "I have little choice at this point."

"But I'm still waiting for Mathilda and Adele to arrive," said Louis. "And I haven't received any instructions. What am I to do?" He lowered his head in worry.

Ramiro regretted missing Adele again, although he would never admit it, even to himself. He put his hands on Louis' shoulders. "Don't stay here, Louis. It's no longer safe. As soon as your wife and daughter arrive, you must turn them around at once and head straight back to Constantinople. Promise me this."

"Of course, Dom Ramiro. I've no desire to stay here myself."

Aldebert was despondent. "So now we go into battle again, Father Ramiro? Am I to take up the sword too?"

"No, no, of course not. Nonetheless, we still have to accompany these Norman brutes. May God give me strength! Why does the Emperor send me galloping around the countryside like this? I have more important duties to attend to." He lowered his voice. "Brother, this may be our only chance to get to Jerusalem. Perhaps..." He looked about anxiously. "Perhaps we could sail there."

Aldebert looked askance at the door. "A dangerous journey, I'm sure," he replied, equally as nervous. "And we would defy the Emperor's orders."

Ramiro spoke in a harsh whisper. "I have the Abbot's orders, Brother. Whose shall I follow?"

"The Abbot of course, Father Ramiro. But the King has given us a large purse for our services. Should we use his money to flee to Jerusalem?"

"It is a moral problem, I must admit. But our loyalty to the Holy Church must precede all other loyalties."

"So what do you plan to do?"

Ramiro shook his head. "I'm not sure... but I must find a way. As I said, if the road is impassable, we should try sailing to Jaffa." He paused as another thought came to him. "And think of this, Brother, our robes would attract little attention on a sailing ship. And by the time we get to Jaffa... well, there must be many other monks in the Holy Land."

"Where do you think we could commission a ship, Father?"

"I don't know. But we ride to Gallipoli soon. That will give us access to the Mediterranean Sea. Hopefully, an opportunity will present itself." He got up, pacing the room as his thoughts raced. How much longer must I defer my arrival in Jerusalem? I must find a way to deliver this cross to Patriarch Symeon. What will I say to Abbot Hugh? Will I ever see my mother again? Overwhelmed by his thoughts, he slumped into a chair, dropping his head into his hands.

REPORT: MORE PAGANS

The dismal library of Nicomedia was always quiet. Times were tough on the frontier and most of the upper classes had fled for the safety of Constantinople. Those who remained had little time for books or letters. Ramiro could imagine it was once a grand institution of exquisite design, teeming with rare books and rolls from around the known world. But, like most buildings in this sad place, it had fallen into disrepair. Many shelves were empty, their contents moved to safer locations.

The place was freezing. The only heat came from a single brazier, over which huddled a lonely attendant, a middle-aged man who knew little about the collection and seemed to care less. Ramiro rubbed his legs for warmth before pulling his thick, wool cloak tight about his shoulders. Despite the cold, his eyes began to droop. He put his head down, resting it on an outspread arm. His report to the Abbot was already late but, until now, there was little to say that had not already been said.

He had told him that he was still posted to the eastern frontier, that he remained under the thumb of King Alexios but, because of serious trouble from the pagans, they would be moving on soon. Perhaps now, by the will of God, the way to Jerusalem would be open and attainable. He wrote again of the countless hordes of savages that repeatedly invaded the Greek Kingdom, raiding and pillaging, threatening the very existence of this good Christian nation.

THE HELLESPONT

Taticius' army of Kelts left Nicomedia on a cold April morning. Their combined forces proved over twenty-five hundred men, all on horseback. They rode hard along the south coast of the Propontis, passing through the port of Civetot, making short work of any resistance. But it did not take long for Abul Kasim's spies to discover their departure.

The sun sat low in the western sky when the small army arrived at the Hellespont two days later. Byzantine ships were scheduled to take them across the strait to Gallipoli and, from there, they would make the short ride to Roussa. But the ships had not yet arrived.

Pepin and Aldebert set up their tent in silence, both exhausted from the relentless ride. But Ramiro could not rest. "I'm going to take a stroll to the waterfront," he said quietly to Aldebert.

"At this time, Father? It's almost dark."

"We are out of time, Brother. This may be our only chance to escape the Emperor's bonds. Did you see the skiffs on shore? I'll have a chat with the fishermen. Perhaps we can start our journey right away. Otherwise, it may be too late by morning."

Aldebert chewed nervously on a filthy nail. "I wish we had more time... I'll come with you."

"No. You must stay to answer any questions and to divert suspicion."

"Then take Pepin, he's armed."

"No, I will go alone." He left before Aldebert could protest any further, sauntering down to the beach to greet the fishermen coming home from a day at sea. He mingled among them, most of them Greek, asking questions about their trade. They gawked at his odd appearance, smirking and whispering among themselves, but Ramiro gave no thought to his dress. He asked if any boats would be sailing for Palestine.

The fishermen laughed aloud. "None of our boats could make that journey," said one. "It is many leagues to Palestine. And the waters are dangerous."

Ramiro was desperate. "I can pay you well... in gold coin."

The men stopped laughing. "How much?"

Ramiro opened his hands. "Would five bezants be enough?"

The men whistled in disbelief. One of them shrugged his shoulders. "All the gold in the world will not get my small craft to Palestine."

Another man stepped forward. "I will take you," he said in accented Greek.

The fishermen laughed again. "Not in that little skiff of yours."

The man rebuked them. "I know this! But I can arrange passage on a larger vessel stationed south at Lesbos." He faced Ramiro. "I will take you there."

"How far south?"

"Not far. About seventy miles. If you like, come to my house in the village and we will make arrangements."

Ramiro hesitated. He wondered when Alexios' ships would arrive and how much time he had. "I need to leave very soon."

"Yes, yes, we can leave at first light."

"Very well, let's discuss your terms."

The other fishermen shook their heads as they went back to their work.

Ramiro followed the man to the nearby fishing village. It was getting dark and the way was not easy. He could see a few dim lights coming from the small windows of mudbrick houses up ahead. All seemed quiet.

They soon came to a gray, mud wall encircling the village, where they entered through a narrow gateway. After passing several buildings, they arrived at the door of a rundown house. Here, the man stopped and grinned. "Wait here, please. I must tell my wife to prepare for a guest."

Ramiro stood alone. He could hear excited conversation in the house. It sounded like Turkish.

After a short while, the door opened and the fisherman waved him in.

Ramiro walked in eagerly. But he was only two steps inside the door when he hesitated. The room was empty. "What's this? What...?" But he never had a chance to finish his question. In a flash, another man jumped out from behind the door, clubbing him across the back of the head. Ramiro collapsed to the floor.

"What have you done? You idiot! You've killed him." The fisherman looked down on the sprawling monk and the blood oozing from his head.

The young man stooped, the club still in his hand. He rolled the monk on his back and listened for breath. "He lives." He inspected the wound. "His skin is cut, that is all."

The fisherman dashed over to a small window, peering out anxiously. "Search him," he said without turning around.

The young man patted his way through Ramiro's black robe until he found a pocket inside. "Here it is." He pulled out a purse and opened it hastily. "Look! It's full of bezants."

The older man grinned. "Anything else?"

"Just a roll of paper. Looks like a letter."

"What does it say?"

The man shrugged. "I don't know. It's some strange tongue." He tossed it on the floor. "Oh now, look at this." He pulled out a short dagger.

The fisherman inspected the weapon. "It's just a cheap knife... poor steel. What's that about his neck?"

The young man tugged at the chain, pulling out the cross. "It's his cross. Look! It has a gem!"

"Give it to me... and the purse. Tie him up and gag him. Move quickly! The Roman army is on our doorstep."

The young man pulled some rope from his bag. He turned the monk over to tie his hands before stuffing a gag into his mouth. He tried to lift him up. "Ugh! He's as heavy as a mule. Help me carry him to the cart."

The older man grinned again. "What fortune! He's not too old. We'll get a decent price for this one. We'll take the mountain road to Nikea. Hurry!"

Aldebert was worried sick. The night was as black as tar and Ramiro had not returned. He waited for another hour, pacing outside the tent, chewing his lips, wringing his hands. *Would he leave without me?* He fretted for hours until, finally, in a desperate fit of anxiety, he dashed over to Taticius' tent. "General! I must speak with you!" he yelled outside.

A soldier stopped him. "The general has retired for the night."

"It's important!" Aldebert shouted, looking around the guard. "General! It's Aldebert! Father Ramiro is missing!"

Taticius poked his head out, still fitting his iron nose. He looked annoyed. "What is it, monk?"

"Father Ramiro went for a walk along the shore and he hasn't returned."

"How long has he been gone?"

"Since twilight. What could have happened to him?"

Taticius turned to his guard. "Send out five men with torches. Ask questions in the village."

They searched in futility. Several fishermen remembered seeing him. They said he went off with a Turk fisherman. But they thought that was odd because, as far as they knew, no Turks lived in the village.

Next morning, Taticius formed a large search party to scour the whole area. But no one had seen the monk since he left the fishermen on the shore, so Taticius ordered a full search of all houses.

The Kelts barged through the village, breaking down doors when not opened at their first shouts, oblivious to the fact that no one understood their tongue. They searched every room among screaming women and children who huddled in corners for safety. And they stole what they could.

Arles banged on a door. It was unlocked and flew open with the weight of his fist. The house was empty except for some debris strewn across the floor. He looked down, noticing a pool of blood near the threshold. Stooping, he put a finger to it. It was still soft. And there, not far away, he saw a letter. It was one of Ramiro's letters addressed to Abbot Hugh. "Captain! Captain! Over here!"

At the sight of fresh blood, Drugo dispatched ten men down every road and pathway. They stopped everyone they met, but Ramiro was not to be found.

Taticius became noticeably agitated. "Captain Drugo, we cannot send any men out now. Look! The Emperor's ships have arrived. We must leave immediately."

Aldebert was beside himself. "We cannot leave now! We must find Father Ramiro!"

"We have searched everywhere, Monk Aldebert. There is nothing more we can do. The very existence of the Empire is at stake! Thousands of barbarians are on our doorstep—and many thousands more are coming. We cannot delay."

Aldebert folded his arms in defiance. "Then I will stay until he returns."

"You will not! Look at you! A black robe and a shaved head in this land? You will not last the night."

Aldebert began to argue with him but Taticius interrupted. "And tell me, why did Monk Ramiro leave camp in the first place? The fishermen told us he asked about transport by sea."

"I... I don't know," Aldebert lied.

"It was a foolish thing to do. Now he'll have to make his own way back. Get your gear and come with us!"

In a dour state of melancholy, Aldebert plodded back to his tent. Tears welled in his eyes as he began collecting their things. But as he bent down to pick up Ramiro's book of Psalms, hot tears rushed down his cheeks, his shoulders heaved, and he collapsed to his knees with a wail of despair.

NIKEA

Abul Kasim tapped his calipers against an open palm as he leaned over to study a large map laid out on a wide table. He glanced over to Bolkas who sat reading recent reports coming in from scouts and spies. "Well, brother, what is news?"

Bolkas' sullen eyes looked down at the letters before him. "My brother, our scouts say the Romans have abandoned Nicomedia. They hasten to Gallipoli to stop the advance of the Turkoman, the ones they call Patzinaks. And that pirate Chaka has taken the island of Lesbos where he is building another fleet of ships. He prepares to sail against Constantinople."

Abul Kasim tapped a finger on the map. "Good, good... all is going to plan, dear Bolkas. Now that the Romans no longer harry us along the coast, we will start building our own ships on the Propontis." He pointed to the port of Civetot just west of Lake Askanius. "We will take Civetot, and we will send another force to Nicomedia. Let's take the city while the opportunity presents itself."

"But we have a pact with Chaka, Effendi. We are supposed to go after the Romans and stop them at the Hellespont."

"Forget Chaka. He has enough men. We must take Nicomedia."

"Brother, please, I urge you to reconsider. I have more reports from our spies in the east. The Sultan, Malik Shah, is sending more Seljuk troops to Edessa. He is angry because you do not pledge allegiance to him and now he plots to send an army against us. We cannot risk losing Nikea. By the will of Allah, we must make peace with the Shah."

Abul's face reddened. He flung his calipers against the wall. "To hell with the Shah! We are strong! Did we not drive those rebel Danishmends back to Malatya? Now we control all the land to Ankara and Kayseri! The Shah will have to cross mountains and desert to reach us. Our ramparts are high and thick, our reserves are good. We have nothing to fear!"

June 1091

The months passed and Abul Kasim continued his futile machinations to defeat Constantinople. Bolkas reproached him again, fearing the wrath of the Romans. But Abul dismissed him in another fit of rage.

Bolkas seethed as he stomped back to his quarters. My brother has gone mad! The idiot will destroy us all with his ridiculous schemes. He spoke harshly to the guards stationed at his doorway and chastised his second wife as she rushed to take his cloak. He slipped off his shoes before washing his hands in a brass basin. His wife, a slender woman with full lips and almond eyes, offered him a towel. He snatched it from her. "Where's that useless son of yours?"

She frowned. "*Our* son, my esteemed husband, makes good use of his time learning the arts of war."

"I'll be in the men's room," he snapped. "Bring me some hot lemon tea... and something to eat."

She turned in a swish of green silk, leaving without a word.

He called after her. "And tell your thick-headed son to meet me there!"

Hasan took off his sword and shoes before he stepped into the room. "Peace be upon you, father." He was the eldest son of Bolkas' second wife and, at nineteen, he was a good spy.

Bolkas looked up from his papers. "Sit down."

Hasan sat across from him, squatting on a large cushion. He was an attractive young man with a thin mustache, a smooth face, and full lips like his mother.

Bolkas sat back to sip tea from a small porcelain cup. "Now, tell me, what have you learned today?"

"Yes, esteemed father," he said dryly. "Caravan drivers from Samarkand report the Silk Road is open again. It seems the Sung still rule China. Many exotic goods and silks have arrived with the last caravan from Xi'an. We can buy these through the governor of Samarkand."

"So?" scoffed Bolkas. "The governor is greedy. We can still buy silks from Constantinople."

"Yes, father, but they are inferior. And the recent wars among the Romans have disrupted production. Prices are very high."

Bolkas rubbed his beard. "Very well, I will consider it." He wrote briefly on a memo pad before looking again at Hasan. "So, come on boy! What else did you hear?"

"As you probably know, my Lord, Nicomedia has now fallen into our hands without much of a fight. The governor had few troops left. We took some booty and some women slaves... and killed the rest."

"I know this," Bolkas said impatiently. "Tell me something new."

Hasan rubbed his cheek. "Well... we have hired many good tradesmen to build our ships on the Propontis."

Bolkas shook his head. "Why does your uncle persist with this fleet? With this... this mad craving for Constantinople? The Romans are strong again. And as unbelievable as it may be, King Alexios managed to defeat tens of thousands of Turkoman near Gallipoli. And once again, he has destroyed Chaka's fleet. Now Abul Kasim stands alone. We are wasting valuable resources."

"I agree, my father, the Roman King even now plots against us. He has built many new ships and plans an assault by land and sea."

Bolkas put his cup down. "So now we have the Romans attacking from the west and soon the Sultan's army will assail us from the east. We cannot hold both sides!" He paused. "What have you heard from the east—from Edessa?"

"There is little new, my Lord. No army marches against us at this time. The Shah has vowed to defeat the Danishmends at Malatya before besieging the walls of Nikea."

Bolkas stewed. My brother is a moron, he thought. He will be the demise of Nikea. Our heads will be impaled on the Shah's spikes and set in the market for all to see. I must convince the Great Sultan that I am loyal—that I want no part of my brother's reckless schemes.

Hasan cleared his throat, waiting on his father.

Bolkas turned to him. "Drink your tea. Your mother makes it with rose hips. It's good for you."

"Yes, Effendi."

"Anything else, boy?"

"Yes, I hear the Hashashin are causing more trouble for the Sultan."

"Those Shia Fanatics!" cried Bolkas, feeling a chill when he heard the name. "Murderers!"

"Some say they are crazed drug addicts."

Bolkas sneered. "Damned heretics! May Allah curse them." But he was truly worried, the Hashashin were not only Shia, they were deadly assassins. "Malik Shah is our only hope of peace, our only hope for a strong Turk empire."

Hasan shifted uneasily on his cushion.

"Is that all, my son?"

"One small thing, esteemed father. Apparently, there's a Christian monk in our slave-quarters. He's been there for three months and his captors request payment or release for ransom. They claim he is not a Roman monk but instead hails from the Far West, a strange land full of barbarians with strange customs."

Bolkas was about to take a sip of tea but put his cup down suddenly. "He must be one of those barbarians the Romans hired... the ones who call themselves Franj."

"Possibly, father. His captors wish to sell the monk. They believe the Emperor will pay a royal ransom for him." Hasan paused for a reply but none came. "What do you wish us to do with him, my Lord?"

Bolkas stared blankly before narrowing his eyes. "Buy him. Offer them the regular price. Then bring him to me."

"Now, my Lord?"

"Yes, now. Is that a problem?"

"I have seen the monk, Effendi. He is badly beaten and he stinks!" Hasan's face screwed in disgust as he recalled the reek of the slave quarters.

"Then deliver him to my chamberlain with instructions that he is to be bathed and fed, his wounds dressed. I will see him tomorrow. Find an interpreter. Go."

Hasan stood and bowed. "Yes, father. May Allah keep you."

Bolkas sat quietly, mulling over the latest events. *I must find a way...*

SLAVE QUARTERS

"Get up! Get up you filthy pigs or I'll cut off your balls and feed'em to the dogs!" The slave master cracked a heavy bull whip against the iron bars. Spittle sprayed into his black beard as he shouted. He was a man of girth. Long black hair, tied at the back, fell below his thick, leather helmet, and a black cape draped over his shoulders.

Ramiro clutched at the wall, pulling himself up. Like the other nine slaves in his cell, he moved to the back, avoiding the shit pail in the corner. The slaver opened a grate and other slaves working outside pushed in wooden buckets of barley gruel and water. As soon as the grate slammed shut, the captives moved forward to scoop food into their clay cups. This was the only meal they would get that day.

If Aldebert were present, he would not have recognized his master. Ramiro's robe was in filthy tatters. He had grown a full head of black hair and a small beard, both matted and greasy. His former bulk had dissipated, his face thinned, and visible sores laced across his head, hands, and feet.

Ramiro filled his cup with gruel. He sat down on the straw beside a young man who was thrown among them that morning. "Peace be upon you. I am Ramiro of Cluny," he said in much improved Turkish, albeit with a western accent.

The youth swept his long, black locks from his face but continued to stare forward. He had not eaten any gruel yet... but this was his first day. He replied politely. "And to you peace."

"I can see you are despondent, my friend. Tell me your story."

The man scowled. "I am not in the habit of discussing my life with strangers, especially foreigners."

Ramiro grinned weakly. "Perhaps not now, but the time will come. We can help each other. I can see by your hands that you are neither a servant nor a tradesman. And you still wear a fine tunic, even sandals."

"I'm a scribe," he responded flatly.

"A scribe and a Turk," said Ramiro looking into the young man's clear brown eyes. "How did you come to arrive in a place like this?"

"I... I was..." he bowed his head and fell silent.

Ramiro tried another approach. "May I have the honor of your name, Effendi?"

The young man held his head high. He was no more than seventeen. A whisper of a beard sprouted from his chin. "I am Ozan, son of Kubad, of the family Seljuk." An awkward silence ensued. Rats squealed along the rafters.

"You have an honorable name, Effendi," said one of the captives who overheard.

"Yes," said another. "How is it that a son of the great Seljuks becomes a slave?"

"Because it is the wish of Abul Kasim," he replied forlornly. "I was accused of the most licentious crimes, but I have done nothing wrong. May Allah be my judge."

The captives nodded. They understood.

Ramiro did not. "Please explain."

"He is of the Seljuk family," interjected one prisoner.

Ramiro shook his head.

"Do you not see, old man?" Ozan asked irritably. "I'm a nephew of Sulayman, the man who once ruled Nikea. Abul Kasim does not want Sulayman's relatives in the royal palace lest we seek to overthrow him and take the Roman lands for ourselves. So he drives us from power and position. We are exiled and enslaved."

"I pray to Allah that Kilich will return to rule," said one. Others nodded in agreement.

"Who is Kilich?" asked Ramiro.

"The eldest son of Sulayman, the rightful heir to Nikea. The Sultan keeps him in Isfahan."

"Where's that?"

The men stared at him, astonished, wondering if he was demented.

"Clearly, you are a foreigner," said Ozan. "Isfahan is a marvelous and wonderful city to the east, through the high mountains of Iran. It is the capital city of the great Seljuk Empire and the home of the Great Sultan, Malik Shah."

"Aah," Ramiro nodded in understanding. The prison cell fell quiet again. His mind wandered. He thought of Drugo and his Flemings. "Tell me, Ozan, have you heard any news of the Roman King and his battles with the Patzinaks?"

"Patzinaks?" Ozan looked around at the other men. They shook their heads. "Do you mean the Turkoman?"

"Yes, yes the Turkoman."

"I have heard the Roman King was victorious," Ozan replied.

Ramiro tried to hide his delight. "Really? But I thought he was greatly outnumbered."

"Yes, he was. But the King is a sly fox. Thousands of these Patzinaks came to do battle with the Romans and then many thousands of Kumans joined them. But the King, a truly deceitful man, managed to turn one tribe against the other. He convinced the Kumans to come over to his side and together they slaughtered these Patzinaks. Then the King turned against the Kuman, the very ones who had helped him, and drove them north, out of the land around Constantinople."

Ramiro was relieved at the news. "And what of your lord, Abul Kasim? Has he given up his fight against the Roman King?"

"No," Ozan whispered, looking around carefully. "May Allah curse him. He finally took Nicomedia and is now busy building warships on the Propontis."

Ramiro felt a chill. *Nicomedia has fallen? What of Louis and his wife? What of Adele? Oh, dear Jesus, I hope they managed to get back to Constantinople.*

A shout rang out through the prison cells. "Up, you sons of whores!" yelled the slave master. The captives backed against the wall as the slaver's whip cracked against the bars. "Which one of you is the Roman monk? Answer me!"

Ramiro stepped forward. "I am the monk."

The slaver opened the gate. "Come with me!" he shouted, grabbing Ramiro by the arm.

BOLKAS

With Hasan gripping his arm, Ramiro shuffled into the room, the ropes about his ankles impeding his steps. He was given a clean, brown tunic, and his hair and beard were freshly trimmed. But the red welts on his face were a testament to his treatment in the slave quarter.

Bolkas rose from his cushion, putting a hand to his heart. "Peace be upon you, holy man. Please, come and sit." He offered a seat before motioning to his guard. "Remove these ropes!"

Ramiro sat down with a thump, sticking his legs out for the guard. "And peace unto you, Lord Bolkas."

Bolkas was stunned. "You speak Turkish?" He turned to Hasan. "He speaks Turkish, you moron! Why do I need an interpreter?"

"Forgive me, Lord. I did not know." Hasan bowed his head.

Bolkas turned back to Ramiro. "Do you understand everything I say or did you just memorize a few pleasantries?"

Ramiro returned a thin smile. "I have memorized quite a number of pleasantries, Effendi."

Bolkas studied him for a long while. Suddenly, he waved his arm in dismissal. "The rest of you... out! I will speak with him alone."

"But, Master, are you sure...?"

"Out! Out!" he shouted, and they scurried out the door. The room fell quiet. Ramiro rubbed his ankles.

Bolkas offered him sage tea. "You have an accent but your grammar is fairly good. Have some tea."

"Thank you, Effendi." Ramiro was careful to accept it with his right hand. He fingered the blue and red floral designs on the small porcelain cup before taking a sip, then another. It tasted strange, but it was sweet and appealing. *Better than the slop I've endured for weeks,* he thought.

Bolkas then offered him khabis, a sweet made with dates and cream, and qubayta, a pastry stuffed with sugar, almonds, and pistachios. Ramiro stuffed his mouth. It was all he could do to restrain himself.

"What is your name, holy man?"

"I am Ramiro of Cluny," he mumbled through a mouthful of cake.

"And where is Cluny?"

"Far to the west, in a land called France."

Bolkas raised his eyebrows. "France? Never heard of it. You must be a long way from home. But you look a bit like an Arab. What brought you to our country?"

Ramiro took another sip of tea. Many insolent replies came to mind but he thought it best to hold his tongue. "My master sent me to the Roman King to discuss religious matters. I am here because I was captured at the Hellespont."

"So you have met with King Alexios?"

"Yes."

"Do you think he will pay for your release?"

"I don't know, but I certainly hope so."

"What do you know of the King's plans? Will he attack Nikea?"

Ramiro hesitated. "I only concern myself with religious matters, my Lord."

Bolkas forced a smile. "You were caught with his troops—surely you know something about his plans?"

"I know the troops were on their way to Gallipoli. That is all I know."

"How many men do you have? Who leads them?"

"I have no men, my Lord, but General Taticius leads about two thousand."

Bolkas squinted. "Are you trying to frustrate me, priest? Perhaps, you would prefer that I return you to the dungeon for interrogation."

Ramiro clenched his jaw, looking squarely into Bolkas' face. "What do you want with me, Effendi? I can tell you nothing you don't already know. Do you really think I am privy to the King's council?"

Bolkas leaned back on the cushions. The man had spunk. He let out a derisive snort, then chuckled. "I suppose not." He folded his arms and put a hand to his chin. How can I make use of this barbarian? Perhaps I should just sell him back to the Roman King. Suddenly, he had an idea. "Tell me, priest, what languages do you speak apart from Turkish?"

Ramiro rubbed the sores on his wrists. "I speak Arabic, Greek, Latin, French, Castilian, some German... some Flemish."

"Allah's blessing! Remarkable! But I have never heard of the latter tongues. Are they languages of the West?"

"Yes."

"Can you also write these languages?"

"I am still attempting to master Flemish."

A sly grin spread across Bolkas' narrow face. "You will leave now. I will give you a room for the remainder of your stay."

"Thank you, Effendi. May I return to Constantinople?"

"We shall see."

"And please, Effendi, what of my possessions?"

"Your what?"

"My money and my cross, Effendi. Especially the cross, it means much to me."

"Does it?" asked Bolkas with a dispassionate look. "Then I will see what I can do."

Hasan removed his boots before entering Bolkas' study. He felt uneasy. "Peace be upon you, esteemed father. I am at your service." He bowed.

Bolkas did not look up. He was rummaging through a stack of papers on his desk. "Do you remember getting a letter from the Shah's vizier?"

"You mean Nizam Al-Mulk?"

"Of course I mean Nizam! Who else would it be, you idiot!"

"We have several letters from Nizam, noble father."

"Well, where in Allah's name are they?"

"If you please, Effendi, they are filed over here." He walked over to an ornate cabinet embedded with mother-of-pearl designs. "Here they are," he said as he reached into a drawer.

Bolkas rushed over, snatching the folder from his hand. He flipped through the pages anxiously. "This is it!"

"This is what, my Lord?"

"It's a letter sent by Nizam's office to all the far western cities of the Empire. He requests translators and scribes for the Royal Library in Isfahan. Apparently, they have collected many western texts but have few who can translate them. This is just what I need, Hasan! Just what I need!"

"For what, Master?"

Bolkas hesitated, looking at Hasan with some reservation. "My son, I will put forth to you some of my ideas. These are never to be repeated to anyone. Do you understand? No one!"

"Yes, of course, father."

Bolkas went to the door and opened it slowly. He looked out briefly then shut it quietly before strolling to the window. "If one word of this gets out, our heads will roll and our families put to death."

A look of alarm flashed in Hasan's eyes.

Bolkas continued in hushed tones. "I believe your uncle, Abul Kasim, has gone mad. The Romans defeated the Turkoman in the west and Chaka to the south, yet he still plots against their Empire. Now he has taken Nicomedia and builds ships on the Propontis. He has learned nothing. Soon, the Roman King will send an army against us."

"And so will Malik Shah," piped Hasan.

"Do not interrupt me."

"Forgive me, esteemed father."

"We must find a way to appease the Shah. And we must do it before Abul Kasim destroys us all. We must find a way to return the rightful ruler, Kilich, Son of Sulayman, to the walls of Nikea."

"Kilich? He's just a boy," said Hasan before he leaned over to whisper. "Why not betray your brother and rule yourself?"

"It is not a position I aspire to, my son. Emirs have much wealth but rarely die in bed. I am content with my holdings in Cappadocia. Besides, the people will not follow me willingly. They yearn for the return of the Son of Sulayman. He is the only one who will unite us with strength."

"Excuse me, father. But why would Malik Shah allow Kilich to return? Was not his father a traitor to the Empire?"

"And Abul Kasim is a traitor," Bolkas sneered. "Malik Shah is angry and will probably send an army against us. But if he conquers this land, he will have trouble governing it at such a distance. We must convince him that Kilich is the best choice, and we must offer our profession of loyalty."

"So what is your plan, my Lord?"

"I will send a secret envoy to the Shah telling him all that passes. We will plead for the return of Kilich. And we will send him a gift."

"A gift? Of what?"

"A gift of a scribe, Hasan. We will send him the Christian priest."

"You do not wish to ransom him?"

"That would gain us nothing but a bit of gold. It is more important to curry the Shah's favor and save our heads."

"Yes, father, as you wish. And who would you like to send on this mission?"

"You will go. Prepare for a journey to Isfahan."

"Me? To Isfahan? My Lord—please! That's a one-month ride! Even more!"

"All the more reason for you to hurry, my son. The weather is good. You will take five men with you—all family."

"But we will be gone at least two months, my Lord. What will you tell Abul Kasim?"

"The Hajj is next month. I will tell him you went on pilgrimage to Mecca."

Hasan clenched his jaw in rage. His high cheeks reddened and he bowed quickly to hide his fury. "As you command, my father," he strained.

"I will give you a letter for the Shah to authenticate your mission and to explain events." He sat down at his desk and, in a neat hand, finished the letter and sealed it. "Oh, that reminds me," he said, handing the letter to Hasan. "The priest wants his money and his cross."

"There is no money," replied Hasan. "And what of this cross?"

"The cross that hung about his neck. You know how much these Christians like their talismans."

"But any cross will do, father. Why does he bother with this one?"

"Get it anyway. I need to appease this man for a while."

"Isfahan?" Ramiro was stunned.

"Yes, Isfahan," Hasan replied dryly.

"But I hear it is a great distance to the east, Effendi. Many months of travel."

"So it is, slave. But that is of no concern to you."

"May God have mercy on me! I beseech you, my Lord, please send me back to Constantinople. I promise you the Roman King will pay a generous ransom!"

"I cannot. My father ordered you to Isfahan. That is the end of it!" He fumed. Damned Christian barbarian! I must leave my fief and family to embark on this dangerous and ludicrous journey—all for a cursed Christian. Damn my father to hell!

"But why?" Ramiro asked. "What am I to do in Isfahan?"

"You will translate books for Nizam."

"Who?"

"Nizam Al-Mulk, the Sultan's vizier. Apart from the Great Sultan himself, he is the most powerful man in the Empire. It is an honor."

"An honor I can do without!" cried Ramiro.

"Do not presume upon my patience, slave. I would gladly slit your pagan throat and throw you to the dogs."

Ramiro's mind raced as he studied Hasan. He thought him a handsome man with a delicate nose and a strong chin, covered as it was by a thin, black beard. And like most Turkish men of the time, his braided black hair hung to his shoulders. He wore an expensive yellow cloak swathed over a new corselet of mail armor. Ramiro could sense his seething hostility and wished he had a friendlier companion.

"May I at least make one request, Lord Hasan?"

"What is it?"

"There is another slave who can read and write. I believe he would also be an asset to Malik Shah."

Hasan raised one eyebrow. "A scribe? What's his name?"

"He is Ozan, son of Kuban. I met him in the slave quarters."

Hasan looked shocked. "Ozan son of Kuban? Why in the name of Allah is a Seljuk in the dungeon?"

"Your master, Abul Kasim, condemned him. He was accused of consorting with his wives."

Hasan turned away, folding his arms. My father is right, he thought, my uncle has gone mad. If the Sultan hears that one of his kin suffers at the hands of Abul Kasim, he will have an even greater pretense to send his armies against us. But if I free him and take him with me, it may help my negotiations. He turned back. "I will see what I can do."

"Thank you, Effendi. And ah... just one other matter... did you find my things? I don't care about the money but I would like my cross."

"I know nothing of your money."

Ramiro sighed. "And what of the cross?"

Hasan dug into his pocket. "You mean this wretched thing?"

Ramiro looked down on the remains of his cross. It was in two pieces. The slavers had torn off the arm and pried the beautiful bloodstone from its setting, leaving splinters and a rough gouge. His heart leapt to his throat. The message! Was it removed? Was there a message? Slowly, he picked the two pieces from Hasan's hand, looking at them closely. But he could see no cavities. What will I say to the Patriarch when he sees this? Tears of frustration and grief welled in his eyes as he tried to refit the arm. He shook his head in disbelief. "It's mutilated!"

Hasan hissed. "Ignorant Christian! It's an icon... superstitious and idolatrous! Sinful in the eyes of Allah."

"I'm not ashamed to be a Christian, my Lord," Ramiro said with strong conviction. "My cross reminds me of my duty to God." He pointed to a small tubular amulet hanging from Hasan's neck. "Just as that amulet you wear reminds you of Allah. Can you deny me that?"

Hasan touched his amulet briefly. "What do you know of my amulet?"

"I know it contains chosen verses from the Quran. And that you believe it will protect you from the Evil Eye and other unseen perils."

Hasan smirked. "Impudent slave... you had better watch your tongue or it will be cut out!"

DORYLAEUM

To avoid Abul Kasim's attention, Hasan and his five men raced through the southern gate of Nikea in the cold light of a full moon. With Ramiro and Ozan in tow, they pushed east, making their way through the steep mountains east of Lake Askanius, riding fast until well out of sight of the city walls. Up and up they went, following tight winding trails through steep mountain valleys until, by evening, they came to the high and dry Plains of Dorylaeum set amid the rolling hills of the vast Anatolian Plateau.

Ramiro marveled at the horse he rode, a sleek and spirited gelding, faster than any he had ridden before. Lean, quick, and strong, the beast could keep a steady canter for miles at a stretch. And when prodded, it would run at terrifying speeds, even along thin mountain passes. And now on the open plain, it charged fast and smooth. His ears whistled in a hot wind.

He tried not to think of the rattling chain that bound his wrists and locked him to the saddle. And he tried not to think of Jerusalem and his mission. But he began to wonder if he would ever again return to the Abbey of Cluny, or if he would ever again see Aldebert, or Pepin or Louis or... Adele. Dear God, somehow I must escape!

He felt for the cross around his neck. He had taken the time to repair it by binding the arm with string, which he wrapped in a tight crisscross pattern. Hasan, of all people, told him to wear it conspicuously because, despite his scorn for it, he knew all Christians must wear one in Muslim lands.

Ozan rode alongside, but he was not encumbered by chains. He was Seljuk, so Hasan freed him as soon as they were out of the gates.

They camped near the ruins of a Roman trading post just as the sun began to dip below distant mountains. And here they washed in preparation for *salat*, the time of ritual prayer. Before sunset, Hasan cried "Allahu Akbar" aloud and they all knelt on the hard ground, prostrating themselves before God, facing the Kaaba Mosque in Mecca, far to the south.

Ramiro knelt too, praying in his own way.

> *Support me, O Lord, according to your word*
> *And I shall live*
> *Let me not be disappointed in my hope*
> *Glory be to the Father and to the Son and to the*
> *Holy Spirit...*

At morning light, Hasan gave strict orders to fill every water skin and canteen in preparation for the arduous, hot ride to Iconium farther south. They would stop at every watering hole to allow the horses a long drink. The dreaded sun was on the rise and soon it would torment them with its blistering heat.

Before long, the air was as hot as the blast of a kiln and the whole ground shimmered in heatwaves. The shadowless road snaked southeast as far as the eye could see, stretching through a vast wasteland. Whole villages lay abandoned, wells were blocked up, cisterns ruined, fields uncultivated, roads and bridges in a state of decay. This was the work of the Turkoman, who raided, pillaged, and scorched the earth, forcing Greek Christians to flee in their wake.

Ramiro covered his head with a scarf and, despite the heat, draped a thin, woolen cloak over his shoulders to hide the sun. Every beat of his heart pounded in his ears. He panted for breath, feeling dizzy.

Water ran short. The horses began to stumble, forcing the men to dismount. Nearly fainting from exhaustion and thirst, they eventually found relief at a small town nestled in the mountains, one of the few places spared by the Turks. Here they refreshed themselves, bought more supplies, and took a needed rest at a dilapidated inn.

Three days later, they reached the green valley of Meram, where the city of Iconium seemed like a veritable oasis. Rivers drained from mountains to the west, flowing across the valley to irrigate hundreds of fields, orchards, and vineyards before petering out in the endless, flat expanse of dry steppe.

"You see, slave?" Hasan waved his arm in a broad arc. "You see all this land to the north? This is Cappadocia—this is my land," he said with pride. "My father seized it from the Romans. One day, by the will of Allah, we will rule the whole Roman Empire and the Romans will be our slaves, just as you are."

While the long ride to Iconium had been torturous, the continuing journey farther south to Heraclea at the base of the Taurus mountains proved to be the most pressing of all. Hasan, informed of its impending dangers, purchased a mule to carry extra water.

Onward they trekked across the searing, waterless grassland, as flat as a board and not a shadow in sight. And so it was to everyone's great relief when they finally reached the green foothills, entering the cool reprieve of mountain forests, thick with fir and black pine.

Ozan and Ramiro sat together around a blazing campfire. They wrapped their cloaks tight to keep warm in the cool mountain air. Ozan felt he owed a debt of honor to Ramiro for saving him from Abul Kasim's dungeon and perhaps a tortured death. They talked often on this journey and came to like each other, though Ozan was careful to appear indifferent.

Ramiro was exhausted. "How much farther must we go?" he asked Hasan in a loud voice. Ozan tugged nervously at his sleeve, urging him to keep quiet.

Hasan glared at him. "How many times must I tell you, slave? You will not speak without permission!"

"Perhaps we should cut off a finger to remind him," threatened Sebuk, Hasan's brother.

Ramiro could abide Hasan, who was a devout man of some moral character. But he had come to detest Sebuk, a cold, heartless creature with a hateful, sneering face. "If you cut off my fingers, Effendi, what good will I be to the Sultan?"

Sebuk rose up in fury, belting him across the face. "Know your place, slave! Or I will gouge out your eyes and throw you to the jackals!"

Ramiro staggered from the blow, putting a hand to his cheek. "Then kill me now!" he shouted, red-faced, "so that I no longer have to endure your vile presence!"

Sebuk flushed, drawing his sword in a flash. "Stinking kafir!" He raised it to strike. "Son of pig shit!"

"Stop!" Hasan shouted. "That's enough!"

Sebuk slowly sheathed his sword before he sat down again, all the while glaring at Ramiro.

EDESSA

August 1091

Hasan pressed on to the Mediterranean coast, passing east through Mersin before leaving the lush Plain of Cilicia by way of the Nur Mountain pass, crossing through smooth, rolling hills where only a few black pine survived alongside cultivated groves of pistachio.

Off the mountain and down they rode reaching the rolling Plain of Haran, where a boat ferried them across the gray waters of the mythical Euphrates. From here, it was only a day's ride to Edessa, a city once conquered by a man known in these parts as Alexander the Infamous.

Edessa, the birthplace of King Nimrod, who built the Tower of Babylon, lies near the center of the Haran plain. Here, it is ringed on three sides by low limestone hills. Its high walls, built by the Romans centuries before, loom high above the flatlands. So protected, Edessa controlled the road running south into a vast alluvial lowland, a place called Mesopotamia by the Greeks, Al-Jazeera by the Arabs, and Al-Iraq among the Persians.

Edessa, rich in commerce and a powerful regional center, was the first city to embrace Christianity under Armenian rule. Once ruled by Arabs long before the coming of Muhammad, it passed between Armenians, Romans, and Persians before falling to the newly invigorated Muslim Arabs in 638. But it was now ruled by the Seljuk Turks under the Sultan, Malik Shah, who had seized it only four years before Ramiro arrived.

Inside Edessa's bath house, Ramiro wallowed in thick, billowing clouds of steam. He was naked except for his breeches and the mended cross hanging from his neck. His face and neck, burned red by the summer sun, contrasted with his pale skin. "How I love these Roman baths, Ozan! Can there be a more refreshing feeling?"

Ozan lay on his stomach while a servant scrubbed his back with a sponge. "We call them Turkish baths, Ramiro. And I agree, I cannot think of anything better at the moment. But if I have to ride another day, I fear there will be little left of my ass."

Ramiro chuckled. "Tell me, Ozan, if I am a slave, why am I allowed such treatment."

"Because you are a valuable slave, Ramiro. Hasan wants you in good condition before we reach the Sultan. Besides, we Turks are not barbarians. Slaves are given opportunities and can advance in rank." The servant poured cool water over him. Ozan shivered as the soap washed away, exposing his sleek copper skin.

Ramiro waited for the servant to leave. "Ozan, tell me, how far is Jerusalem?"

Ozan scoffed with a laugh. "For a man who can speak many languages and who claims to have read so much, you seem very stupid about many great places and people."

Ramiro blushed. "And what do you know of my land and people?"

"I know you come from a distant wilderness inhabited by crude barbarians. I have met many of your kind from the West. I admit, most are not like you—most are ignorant and vulgar and have not learned to wash."

"I could agree," replied Ramiro. "But what do you know of our famous people and places?"

"Why is that important? Is your civilization as great as that of the Romans? Are your backward villages as grand as the magnificent cities and wonders of the great Seljuk Empire?"

"Do you know what our cities are like?"

"Well, you must know. So tell me, are they as wonderful?"

Ramiro sighed in resignation. "No, they are not. So how far is Jerusalem?"

"It's about one hundred and fifty farsakhs." Ozan moved his fingers in thought. "Over six hundred of your Roman miles. That's at least ten day's ride from here."

"Just ten days!" Ramiro blurted a bit too loud. He lowered his voice, "I have told you that I must get to Jerusalem. Do you think there is any way to escape?"

Ozan's eyes widened in shock. He put a hand to Ramiro's lips and waved a finger of silence before getting up to inspect every corner of the steam room. Satisfied, he sat closer. "A very stupid idea, Ramiro. It's my job to watch you. Do you want me to lose my head too? Look at the robes you must wear, the cloth of a slave. And by your accent alone, people know you are not one of us. And where are your papers?"

"My papers?"

"Yes, man. People are known by the papers they carry, even slaves have them when they travel. Only the rebel Turkoman roam with impunity."

"I have no papers."

"That's my point. Any free man could seize you as a runaway slave. You have no family here, no tribe, there is no one to speak for you, no one to wield a sword for you. Say no more of this or we will be whipped and chained in our rooms."

"Can you show me one of these papers?"

"I can," he said cautiously. "Why?"

"Well, I've never seen one before," said Ramiro as he fingered his damaged cross. He had sanded it smooth but it still bore the rough gouge suffered when the bloodstone was pried out. Its original chain was gone, now replaced with a leather strap.

Ozan pointed at the cross. "Do you worship it?"

Ramiro glanced down. "No, I do not worship it. It only reminds me to worship God."

"Muslims have no idols. There is only one God... and He is so great, He cannot be portrayed with idols or pictures."

"I understand your words, Ozan. And, yes, many Christians revere sacred objects and let their minds fall from God's way. But to me, this cross is a symbol of love and courage. It..."

Heavy boots clapped on the tiles. It was Hasan. "Your bath is finished. Tomorrow we leave for Mosul."

RAMIRO'S RUN

Ramiro slipped from his bed in the dark of night. Fully dressed, he picked up a small bundle of things he had collected secretly. The room was quiet except for the sound of Ozan snoring. He peered out the window. The moonlit street one story below was empty. I must go now, he thought, creeping to the door in bare feet, holding his shoes and the bundle in one hand. He opened it a crack. By the dim light of an oil lamp, he could see one of the men slouched in his chair, breathing heavily. He watched for several minutes until he was certain he was sleeping. Then he opened the door a little more. The hinges creaked and the guard stirred. He held his breath. All was still. He stepped out slowly and, without a sound, tread lightly down the steps.

The hall was quiet and dark. He tried to see the front door but could not. Carefully, with an arm outstretched, he felt his way along the furniture. A faint moonlight coming through one window was his only reference. Just two more steps. But his foot hit the leg of a table with a thump. He froze in silence. All remained quiet and he continued to grope for the door. He ran a hand across the wall until he felt the door and the latch. He pulled gently and the door moved silently.

Outside, he put on boots and donned a long cloak. He tried to appear calm, walking casually down the cobblestone street, heading for the city gate. It was almost dawn. The gate was barred. Two sentries stood on guard.

"Where are you going at this hour?" one asked.

"Peace be upon you," said Ramiro. "I leave to join a caravan."

"Which caravan?"

"The one leaving for Jerusalem at first light."

"Show me your papers."

Ramiro reached into his bundle, bringing out a fresh sheet of paper. He gave it to the sentry and waited with trepidation. He had gone to the library yesterday after seeing Ozan's identification. He hoped his forgery would pass the guard's scrutiny in this dim light.

The guard looked it over casually. "Khoril Far? An Armenian. What was your business in Edessa?"

"Only to rest before I resume my journey."

The sentry returned his paper. "Very well, on your way."

Ramiro headed straight for the caravans parked outside the city walls. "May God forgive my deceit," he muttered. The sky brightened and he could see the caravan drivers preparing their mules and camels. He approached one. "Peace be upon you."

"And to you, peace," the driver replied.

"Do you travel to Jerusalem?"

The driver stood in a long green tunic, wearing a small turban of the same color. "No, we head north for Kayseri."

"Is anyone here going to Jerusalem?"

"Not that I know. You could see Mahmoud over there." He pointed to another caravan. "He heads for Aleppo."

"Thank you," said Ramiro as he made his way over.

"Aleppo?" replied the burly Iranian camel driver. "I will take you there, stranger. For one dinar."

Ramiro rummaged through his bag, pulling out several coins, which he showed to the driver. He had no idea what they were worth.

The Iranian scoffed at the coins in Ramiro's outstretched hand. "For this, I will take you one farsakh."

"Perhaps I could be of use?"

"Have you driven camels before?"

"No, but I speak many languages."

The Iranian laughed, holding up his whip. "The camels speak only one language."

A shout came from the city gates and the large doors began to creak open. Ramiro left the driver suddenly, rushing across a harvested field to a nearby village. He was halfway there when Hasan and three others rode out.

Hasan shouted to the caravan drivers. "Runaway slave! Runaway slave!" The Iranian driver pointed down the road to the village and Hasan rode off in pursuit.

Ramiro saw him coming. He cowered in the crevice of a wall. But a farmer waved his arms to catch Hasan's attention, pointing to his hiding spot. Ramiro took off again, running through the narrow streets looking for shelter. The peasants dodged him in fear, dashing into their small houses, slamming shut their doors.

Hasan charged into the village. He saw Ramiro bolting down a dirt lane and went after him.

Ramiro ran as fast as he could, gasping for breath. He sprinted out of the village, but there was nowhere to hide. He looked back to see Hasan bearing down on him, stumbled in a pothole, and crashed headfirst into the rocky ground.

MOSUL

A fresh welt burned on Ramiro's left cheek. He was cut, sore, and bruised from his fall, as well as the beating he received afterwards. Hasan put a rope around his neck and tied it to his saddle.

Ramiro hung his head, fighting against his deepening depression. *Every day, Jerusalem is farther and farther away. And what can I do? Now we travel east again. Always east. Always away from glorious Jerusalem. How many years will it take?* He looked up to the steep mountains and the snowy peaks beyond. *I wonder how Brother Aldebert is doing, poor lad. At least Pepin has some sense. I hope Adele is safe.*

They could soon see the walls of Mosul, miles in the distance. The city seemed to hover above the flat plain, its eerie mirage rippling in the hot, dry air. A steady stream of caravans, some from as far away as China, choked the road. And all around them, vast fields of ripened cotton rose and fell in an undulating sea of white bolls.

But after getting more supplies, Hasan had little time for Mosul. He headed straight to the ferry crossing the Tigris and, from there, they followed the foothills south to Kirkuk, skirting the Diyala Plain before heading east, up into the rugged Zagros Mountains of eastern Iran.

4 - Iran

Seljuk Empire

1091

Iran is a vast and rugged land with steep mountains, salt deserts, and rich river valleys. Few travelers can follow its meandering paths through thin forests of scrub oak and pistachio without sensing the great antiquity of the land, a land called Parsa by the Achaemenids, Persis by the Greeks, and Persia by the Latins. But for thousands of years, the people of this turbulent land have called themselves Aryans, and Iran is the Land of the Aryans.

It was here, in the time of the Biblical Abraham, that Zoroaster taught his people to worship the One God, Ahuramazda. It was here, in this harsh land, where the Medes built the first Iranian Empire over two thousand seven hundred years ago. And centuries later, under the rule of the Achaemenids, it became the largest and most powerful empire in the known world, stretching from the Mediterranean Sea to the mountains of China. These were the Persians, the chronic archenemies of Greeks and Romans.

But over time, this great empire weakened, eventually succumbing to the armies of Alexander the Macedonian in 330 BC. It was resurrected for a time by Sassanids and Parthians, only to fall once more to Muslim Arabs in the seventh century, and then to invading Seljuk Turks four hundred years later.

While King Alexios fought desperately to save the crumbling Byzantine Empire, the Turk Empire flowered under the powerful rule of Jalal Ad-Dawlah Malik Shah, the Great King, the Sultan of Iran. And from his throne in the luxurious capital of Isfahan in central Iran, he controlled a new empire spreading from the Aral Sea in the north to the Persian Gulf in the south, from Syria in the west to the foothills of the Himalayas in the east.

The Zagros

Campfire flames flickered and billowed in gusts of mountain wind, causing wispy silhouettes to dance like demons of the night across the canvas tents. Ramiro fidgeted with the rough hemp rope tied around his neck, trying to ease his pain. His skin bled from the chafe and every move of his head brought sharp grinds of agony. He glared across the fire at Hasan, who huddled in talk with his brother, Sebuk.

Ozan watched him. He leaned over, speaking in hushed tones. "You see, now you suffer for your foolishness. Hasan is very angry with you. And with me."

Ramiro sneered. "I don't give a damn what Hasan thinks."

Ozan spun away quickly, fearing Hasan might overhear.

But Ramiro cared no longer, he was desperate, furious, and ready to die. He stood up suddenly. "Ya, Hasan!" he yelled. A lull fell around the fire. Ozan pulled away, astonished that Ramiro would be so stupid.

Hasan rose up, putting a hand to his sword. "You dare to speak, slave?"

Ramiro pulled at the gritty rope about his neck. "Take this off!"

Sebuk snarled, bolting forward before Hasan had the chance. Seething, he drew his sword and rushed around the campfire, swinging his blade in a feint, stopping it just a finger away from Ramiro's neck. "Perhaps I should remove your ugly head, stinking kafir!" he shouted. "Then the rope will come off easily." The other men smirked.

"And just how will you explain my headless body to your father?" Ramiro asked derisively.

Sebuk went nose-to-nose with Ramiro, his gnarled face shouting with vengeance. "That is the fate of slaves who try to escape!"

"Better that fate," Ramiro shouted back, "than to be dragged around this God-forsaken land like a wild animal on a leash!"

Sebuk glared, his sword trembling in his hand. "Filthy heathen! Kafir dog! How dare you speak to me like this!" He grabbed Ramiro by the hair, pulling his head back, putting the blade across his throat.

"And what of the Vizier, Nizam?" Ramiro strained. "What will you tell him?"

Sebuk hesitated. He looked askance at Hasan before returning his glare to Ramiro. "What do you know of Nizam?"

"I know you should fear him."

Hasan stepped forward. "Hold your sword, brother. We must consider the consequences... and the importance of our journey."

Sebuk made no reply. He released Ramiro's hair before shoving him to the ground. But Ramiro rose up defiantly, staring at Sebuk in challenge. Sebuk slapped him across the head. Ramiro winced from the blow but soon steadied himself, running his fingers through his hair and straightening his tunic. "Is this how you want me to appear to Nizam? Will he see the bruises and cuts? Is this how you treat your scribes?"

Hasan brandished his sword, raising his voice. "We treated you well! But you tried to run!"

"You rescued me from one prison," Ramiro shouted back, "and threw me into another! What did you expect?" He made an effort to calm himself. "I beseech you, Effendi. Remove the rope about my neck and you have my solemn word I will not attempt another escape."

Hasan stood, glaring at him. "Swear it in the name of Allah!"

Ramiro looked around the campfire. All eyes were on him. He took time to look each man straight in the eye before turning again to face Hasan. "I swear in the name of Allah, the merciful and compassionate." The camp fell silent. It was more than expected from a Christian. Ramiro continued. "We are all slaves of Allah and, as you have all read in the Holy Quran... Allah is not unjust to his slaves. And does he not exhort us to treat our slaves with kindness?"

The men were surprised, never before had they heard the Quran cited by a kafir. Some began to squirm at the thought of Sebuk's injustice. Others just stared into the fire.

But Hasan showed neither regret nor admiration. He simply nodded. "Very well. Cut his ropes!" Then he dallied his sword at Ramiro in challenge. "But I swear to you, slave, I will skin you alive if you run again!"

ISFAHAN

September 1091

The cold, damp air of the high plateau began to warm as the men of Nikea descended to the valley floor below. The clouds cleared and their wet gear steamed under a dazzling sun. The farther down they rode, the hotter it became.

There, far below them, was the huge oasis of Isfahan, a green jewel bounded by steep, snow covered mountains to the west and the great Salt Desert to the east. The olive-green Zayandeh River, draining a watershed high in the Zagros Mountains, meandered through the lush oasis.

"You see! Isn't it beautiful!" shouted Ozan. "This is the magnificent home of the Great Shah, the most powerful man in the world—King of the East and the West!" He nudged his horse forward. "They say... if you have seen Isfahan, you have seen half the world!"

Ramiro said nothing.

"Look Ramiro!" said Ozan, hoping to cheer him. "This will be much better than Nikea!"

Ramiro scoffed. "Perhaps for you, young man, but I do not belong here. My home is far to the west."

Ozan leaned over in his saddle. "You must forget that, my friend. You must do the best with what Allah gives you. How many of your brethren have seen glorious Isfahan?"

Ramiro bit his tongue.

Forty days after leaving Nikea, they arrived at a checkpoint on the outskirts of Isfahan, where an old scribe in a guard house compared their names to a lengthy list of wanted men. He held the list close to his face, squinting as he read. Then he looked up to study Hasan carefully. "You say you come from Nikea in the land of the Romans? That is a long way. What is your business in Isfahan?"

Perspiration dripped from Hasan's smooth brow as he labored in the thick, balmy air of the valley. "We have come to see the Vizier."

The scribe smiled through a thin, gray beard. "To see the Vizier, eh? Are you a prince, Effendi?"

"I am Hasan, son of Bolkas, son of Mahmud of the Oghuz clan. Cousins of the Seljuk."

The scribe nodded. "There are many Seljuks in Iran, may Allah bless their name. What is your business here?"

"My father received a letter from the office of Nizam requesting translators and scribes for the new library. We have brought a scribe for this service."

"I know of this request," said the scribe. "Does your man have knowledge of the barbarian tongues?"

"Yes, Effendi."

The scribe wrote a brief note and handed it to Hasan. "Take this to the Vizier's secretary, a man by the name of Qubad." He motioned to the guards to let them through.

Extravagant mansions of wealthy landowners lined the road to Isfahan, sunlight glistening from their blue tile facades. On either side, towering elm trees, interspersed with willow and mulberry, swayed in a hot breeze. And spiraling above this lush, green canopy were the blue domes of mosques and the peaks of minarets.

Hasan found a respectable inn near the outer walls of the Shah's compound, the one called the Square of the Shah. They soon headed straight for the baths where they wallowed for hours in cool pools of clear water.

Ramiro climbed out of bed in the hazy, amber light of dawn. All was quiet except for the occasional chirp of a sparrow. He stepped out onto the small patio, looking down on gardened boulevards stretching out in all directions. Two stories below, three merchants squatted near the compound wall, washing their hands and feet in preparation for the call to prayer. He could hear their words echo from the stone walls.

bismi-llahi ar-rahmani ar-rahimi

He knew what it meant. "In the name of God, most gracious, most merciful." Soon, he heard the vibrant call to prayer from the minarets. The merchants below knelt on their prayer mats to face Mecca, prostrating themselves to God.

God is the greatest
I bear witness that there is no lord but God...

Truly, God is the greatest, Ramiro thought in a reflection of worship. He raised his head to the sky for a moment before lowering his gaze to the Square of the Shah, impressed by its magnificent beauty, the bubbling fountains, the manicured gardens, and the marbled pathways winding through colorful beds of bright flowers. To the north, the elaborate Friday Mosque rose majestically beside gushing fountains, to the south, stood the Mosque of Ali and, to the east, the Sultan's magnificent palace towered above them all.

Despite the disarming beauty of Isfahan, Ramiro could not dispel his overwhelming sense of gloom. Tears of frustration and despondency welled in his eyes. He fell to his knees as a crushing wave of melancholy swept over him. In a desperate effort to steady himself, he began to recite the twenty-third Psalm.

The Lord is my Shepherd; I shall not want.
Yea, though I walk through the valley of the
shadow of death, I will fear no evil, for You are
with me...

Ozan watched from his bed, listening to the strange words. "Ya! Ramiro!" he shouted. "What are you doing out there?"

Ramiro, jarred by his shout, wiped his face with a sleeve before rising up. "God is the greatest," he said quietly.

Ozan smiled. "Of that there is no doubt, my friend. But come, we must eat."

The Secretary

Ramiro squirmed on the cushion. He still had trouble crossing his legs on the floor for any length of time. He put his hands behind his waist, arching his back to relieve the pain. Ozan shuffled uncomfortably beside him, while Hasan leaned forward, resting his elbows on his knees. They had been waiting six hours for an audience with Nizam's secretary, Qubad.

When the call to sunset prayers reverberated from the stone walls, Hasan and Ozan rose from their cushions, kneeling on the central rug to pray, glad for a change of position. Ramiro knelt too, praying in his own way. Two grim looking askari, the elite guard, watched them in silence.

No sooner had the prayers ended when an aide opened the door. "Come!"

The secretary's expansive office was lavishly decorated in fine furniture made of imported rosewood embedded with mother-of-pearl. Here and there, exquisite vessels of bronze and silver decorated throughout. The best Khorasan carpets adorned the floors, and cushions of Samarkand silk were displayed in patches of vibrant color against mosaic walls.

Once inside, two askari took position behind them. There were no chairs and they were not invited to sit. The secretary sat behind a massive desk, writing busily. He did not look up for some time but, when he did, Ramiro saw he was not a Turk but an Iranian bureaucrat. He was neither young nor old, had a fine mustache, a keen look and square features. His tunic was of the finest cotton embroidered with silk and gold thread. Over it, he wore a purple vest hemmed in precious gems.

Qubad appeared comfortable with power. When he finally raised his eyes, he looked them over casually, as if judging cattle for slaughter. The men from Nikea lowered their eyes. "And who are you?" He directed his question to Hasan.

Hasan lifted his head. "Me, Effendi?"

"Yes, you!"

"Forgive me, my Lord, may Allah bless your name. I am Hasan of Cappadocia, son of Bolkas, son of Mahmud of the Oghuz clan."

"And this is the letter you brought?" he asked, holding up Bolkas' letter of introduction.

"Yes, my Lord."

"You are from Nikea in the Roman lands?"

"Yes, my Lord."

Qubad smirked. "You may be of the Oghuz clan," he said disparagingly, "but do not dare to ally yourself with the great family of Seljuk!" He raised his voice. "We have heard of your treason. Do you know what we do with traitors?"

Hasan shifted uneasily, he knew all too well. Cold perspiration dripped from his underarms. "Please, Effendi I can..."

Qubad held up his hand to silence him. "You conquer the Land of Rome in the name of the Great Shah and then you decide to keep it for yourselves! How do you reply?"

"My esteemed Lord," said Hasan, choosing his words carefully, "we are embarrassed by the follies of our lord Sulayman and wish to pledge allegiance only to the Great Shah, may Allah bless his name."

Qubad leaned forward, as if to emphasize his words. "If you wish to pledge allegiance, then why does your Emir call himself sultan? First, Sulayman dared to reject our ambassadors and now your cursed uncle, Abul Kasim, does the same. How do you reply?"

Hasan fidgeted. "My Lord, my father and I do not approve of Abul Kasim's actions. He is a fool and would destroy us all with his thoughtless schemes. The people of Nikea and those living in the Land of Rome want only peace. The Romans seek to destroy us and the Turkoman roam the countryside killing and pillaging. Our people would welcome the safety and stability of the Empire."

Qubad waved a hand of dismissal. "We are well aware of your difficulties, but they appear to be of your own making." He shook the letter. "And now you expect us to release Sulayman's son?"

"My esteemed Lord, the people humbly request that the Son of Sulayman be permitted to rule Nikea in the name of the Great Shah, may Allah keep him."

"The one named Kilich?"

"Yes, Effendi."

"He's just a boy," Qubad scoffed. "Besides, how can we trust the son if we could not trust the father?" He shook his head. "I think the Sultan, may Allah keep him, would rather give the rule of Nikea to an experienced man of his own choosing. Even now, our esteemed Shah leads an army to conquer the rebels in the west, and General Buzan of Edessa heads to Nikea with orders to depose this Abul Kasim."

Hasan looked askance at Qubad. The Great Sultan himself! he thought. My father was right!

Qubad noticed his alarm. "Is this not what you wanted, Hasan son of Bolkas?"

Hasan bowed a little. "Yes, yes, of course, my Lord."

"We will soon sweep away this mess," said Qubad. "Your uncle is weak. And this Roman King... this Alexios, now he sends an army of those Western barbarians against him. Fearsome fighters, we hear... like a pack of wild animals. They hail from the hills of Andalusia."

Ramiro piped in. "Actually, Effendi, most come from farther north."

Qubad's askari whipped out their swords with a ring of steel, lunging at Ramiro, ready to run him through. They watched Qubad for a signal.

"Enough!" Qubad shouted, holding up his hand. "He is a stupid foreigner. We must excuse his bad manners... for now." The guards sheathed their swords slowly, returning to position. "If you wish to keep your head, foreigner, you will hold your tongue." He faced Hasan. "Is this your scribe?"

"Yes, my Lord."

"And how do you name yourself, scribe?"

"I am Ramiro of Cluny, my esteemed Lord."

Qubad smiled. He studied Ramiro for some time. "Your Turkish is very good for a foreigner," he said with amusement, as if a monkey had learned to talk. "You are Christian?"

"Yes, Lord."

"Can you read and write Turkish?"

"Yes, Effendi."

"Do you know anything of mathematics or philosophy?"

"Yes, my Lord, I have read several manuscripts on these topics."

"Then perhaps you would like to meet one of our honored academics?" Qubad smiled condescendingly. "Surely, you have heard of Omar Khayyam?"

Ramiro looked puzzled. "Excuse me, Lord, I know not of this man."

Qubad raised his eyebrows in a feigned look of surprise. "You have never heard of Omar Khayyam, the greatest mathematician of our time?" He spoke with a measure of contempt. "Theories of cubic equations? Euclidean geometry? No? Well, well... perhaps we cannot expect Western barbarians to possess the intellect required to understand such complicated topics."

Ramiro bowed but made no reply.

Qubad nodded to Ozan. "And who is this?"

"Ozan of Nikea, my Lord," Hasan replied. "Another scribe we have brought to the service of the Sultan, may Allah bless him."

"And as a price for these scribes, you expect us to release Sulayman's son?" Qubad asked, curling his lips on one corner.

Hasan bowed. "As my Lord pleases."

"We will consider your request. You may leave."

THE LIBRARY

The months passed in monotonous procession. Ramiro thought again of escape, he always thought of escape. But what's the point? It was not as though they had him penned in a dingy dungeon, albeit his small room in the basement of the library was windowless, dark, and depressing. But strangely enough, he was free to go almost anywhere in the city as long as he showed up for work on time.

At first, this new-found freedom seemed to present a good opportunity for escape. But on reflection, the task seemed almost impossible. To get through the city gates, he needed official papers. And once outside, he needed money. Besides, he had a foreign accent and wore the dress of a slave. Even if he did get out, where would he go? Who could he trust? He recalled the peasants of Edessa who were so keen to turn him over to Hasan when he last tried to escape.

It's been almost three years since my mother wrote to me, he thought. Does she still live? And what of the Patriarch of Jerusalem? How can I approach the man and say that I have allowed the cross to be desecrated, that I have failed in my mission? What will the Abbot think? What perils have I brought to the True Faith?

More doubt and regret swirled through his mind as he leaned over his desk to study the book handed to him by the library administrator. He brushed the dust from its leather binding and opened it to the title page. It was a copy of Aristotle's *Politica*. "May the saints preserve me," he muttered in French.

"No talking!" scowled the librarian, a lean man with a sour look who glared out from an ornate desk at the head of the room.

Ramiro nodded. "Forgive me, Effendi."

"Do you know what you should be doing?"

"Yes, Effendi. I must submit a synopsis of the text to you."

"Then get on with it!"

"Yes, Effendi." He turned to the first page and began to read, taking notes as he went. He was astounded by Aristotle's frank discussion about the character of royalty and aristocracy, and of his theories on constitutional government. Ramiro had always accepted his kings and lords blindly, almost religiously, as if they were part of the natural order of things. But Aristotle challenged the whole concept. He found himself captivated and the hours passed unnoticed as he read through the day.

"Give me what you have," ordered the librarian when afternoon prayers ended.

Ramiro stood up, shuffling his notes together in an orderly fashion before handing them over.

The librarian stood by his desk as he read. "Your Turkish needs work. Obviously, you have not mastered all verb conjugations." He read for a long time before he tossed Ramiro's notes back. "That is enough. Give me the book."

"But I have not finished, Effendi."

"And you will not finish. This book is inappropriate."

"Inappropriate? Why?"

"The Great Shah, may Allah bless his name, does not want his loyal subjects to learn dangerous political ideas. What is this nonsense about democracy?

The people rule together? It can only lead to anarchy and chaos. Everyone for themselves... how can it work? Do you have this kind of government in your country?"

"Well... no."

"And men creating laws! Even a foreigner should know by now that God has written all laws. These are put down in the Sharia. This is what you should read." He shook his head in disgust. "Give me the book, it is finished. I will get another."

NIKEA

June 1092

Far to the west of Isfahan, in distant Nikea, Abul Kasim wrung his hands in distress. A bead of sweat dripped from his brow as he peered through a citadel port, watching General Buzan's army amass in the distance. Bolkas stood behind him and a messenger waited by his side.

"By order of the Great Shah, General Buzan requests your surrender, my Lord," said his brother Bolkas. "What is your reply?"

With increasing dread, Abul Kasim studied the size of Buzan's army—it was huge, ten thousand strong. But can it breach the walls of Nikea? Maybe they'll starve us out. Maybe I should surrender? What if another army comes? What a fool I've been! Bolkas tried to warn me. He turned to face the messenger and, in an act of desperate bravado, he waved him away. "Return to General Buzan and tell him I wish to negotiate."

Abul waited many long, tortuous hours, but General Buzan did not bother to reply. Instead, his whole army turned around to ride east, in the direction of Ankara. Abul Kasim watched in mounting trepidation and confusion. He was greatly relieved to see them go but secretly he knew this affair was far from over.

"You see?" he piped in a shaking voice as he watched the army fade into the distance. "General Buzan is no threat to us."

Bolkas could barely conceal his contempt. "More are coming, my brother, of that you can be sure. Another army fights the Danishmends in the east, and it is led by Malik Shah himself."

"By the Sultan?" Abul's eyes went wide. "Here?"

"He's camped near Malatya. Soon he will come this way. He is determined to take firm hold of the Roman lands."

Abul Kasim felt the blood drain from his head. He stumbled to some cushions, falling to his knees. "I... I offered to negotiate. Why did he not accept?"

"The answer is obvious!" Bolkas sneered in fury. "They want us dead!"

Abul Kasim shuddered. "I have done what I can, Bolkas."

"You have done nothing but endanger us all!" Bolkas shouted, emboldened by Abul's growing weakness. "The Sultan will slaughter us—our sons, wives, brothers, our cousins! And what have you done? You waste your time fighting the Romans! You let the Roman king deceive you. You thought you were smarter than him—but instead he has led you astray with vain promises of gold! Now we are weak on the western frontier while the Sultan's armies march from the east. If you do not make peace with him soon, we will all lose our heads!"

Abul Kasim tossed and turned. He could not sleep. Fear rattled his thoughts. *Bolkas was right, I must appease the Sultan.* He rose early, going straight for the treasury. Before noon, he had fifteen donkeys laden with gold. He was sure he could satisfy the Shah by pledging his allegiance and offering tribute.

Bolkas watched him leave the city gate. *What an idiot! Now he depletes our treasury and the Sultan will probably take our heads anyway.*

Abul Kasim set off with a train of servants and a squadron of his men. He was heading to Ankara to see General Buzan, to plead for mercy. His journey was uneventful for five days when, just outside of Ankara, a surly band of Buzan's askari thundered toward them, lances out.

"I am Abul Kasim of Nikea!" he shouted desperately. "I have come to speak with General Buzan! I have tribute!"

The askari kept coming, charging into Abul's men, running them through with hardly a fight.

Abul Kasim cringed in terror atop his mount. "I come in peace!" he squawked.

The askari dismounted in silence. Rushing over, they dragged Abul from his horse.

"What are you doing?" Abul wailed. "I come with gold for General Buzan!"

"General Buzan thanks you for the gold, traitor!" said one as he forced Abul Kasim to his knees. Before the horrified emir could utter another word, one askari whipped a garrote around his neck, pulling hard. Abul's eyes bulged in terror as he writhed and struggled in vain. And there, on the dusty road to Ankara, he died a silent, groping death. The askari hacked off his head as a trophy for Buzan, leaving Abul's bloodied corpse for the hungry vultures circling high above the dry steppe of the Anatolian Plain.

CONSTANTINOPLE

"Ramiro's alive?" Aldebert cried, jumping out of his chair, knocking it over. "He's a slave?"

"He was captured by the Turks," said Manuel, the Byzantine commander. "The Emperor's spies say he was kept prisoner at Nikea."

"Then we must pay the ransom!"

Manuel shook his well-groomed head. "I'm afraid the situation is more complex than that, Monk Aldebert. We hear that the Shah's men murdered Abul Kasim and have placed his brother, Bolkas, to rule Nikea. I made further inquiries but got little cooperation. Apparently, Ramiro is no longer there. Rumor has it they sent him to Isfahan."

"Isfahan? Where on God's earth is that?"

"Far to the east. It's the capital city of the Turk Empire."

"But how can we be sure he's there?"

"It would be very difficult," Manuel admitted. "We have no spies there."

"Why not just ask them? Ask the Shah."

"We could try but it may lead to nothing. How do we know the Shah is even aware of him? We would have to include something in the letter that would not only pique his interest in Ramiro but also prove to us that he's there."

Aldebert fell into a sullen mood. He righted his chair and slumped back into it. "Dear Jesus! What can we do?"

Manuel put a hand to his shoulder. "I'm sorry Monk Aldebert. I wish we could think of something, but you must realize the Emperor is very preoccupied with other serious matters."

In a rare flash of insight, Aldebert sprang to his feet again, his eyes lighting up. "I know what to do!"

ISFAHAN

July 1092

Hasan knew nothing of Abul Kasim's death, nor of the recent events transpiring in Nikea. He still lobbied Qubad for the release of Kilich, Son of Sulayman. But the secretary did not summon him, so he reluctantly stayed in Isfahan for the winter. He planned to return to Nikea in the spring, when the mountains were free of ice and snow.

But winter passed and his repeated requests for an audience with the secretary were summarily dismissed, as were his petitions to visit young Kilich. So he waited through the next summer, hoping for the best, but he gradually became more and more anxious as the months wore on. And then, much to his relief, he was once again summoned to Qubad's office.

He stood alone, daring not to speak.

"Hasan of Cappadocia," said Qubad with feigned interest. "You have come to make a request?"

"Yes, Effendi, for the release of Kilich, Son of Sulayman."

The rubies on Qubad's turban sparkled as he laughed. "I deny your request. But perhaps you would like to join him?"

Hasan frowned a little. "I do not understand, my Lord."

Qubad had a sinister look. "We have news that should be of great interest to you." He rose from his chair, motioning to the guards, who then grabbed Hasan by the arms.

"What's going on, Effendi?" Hasan panicked as the guards held tight, his black hair falling over his eyes.

Qubad smiled. "The good news, Hasan, son of Bolkas, is that Abul Kasim is dead."

"Abul Kasim, my Lord?"

"Yes. It seems he disappointed the Sultan, so General Buzan had him strangled. Now your father has taken control of Nikea." He paused. "Do you know what that means?"

Hasan understood. "That means my father Bolkas now rules the Roman lands."

"Yes," Qubad laughed again. "And so now you have become a hostage of Malik Shah, may Allah keep him. We must have some influence over your father, and unless he does as he is told, we will deliver your head to him. Let's see how well he negotiates under the circumstances." His thin smile changed to a glower. "Take him away!"

There was a furious knock on the door. "Who is it?" Ramiro bellowed.

"It's me! It's Ozan. Let me in!"

Ramiro rushed to the door. "By all saints!" he said, swinging it open. "Come in, come in. What is it?"

"It's Hasan, Ramiro! They've put him in prison! His brother, Sebuk too!"

"But why?"

"Because they are sons of Bolkas."

Ramiro shook his head. "You will have to tell me more than that, my boy."

"The Sultan has taken Nikea. Abul Kasim is dead. They strangled him."

Ramiro let out a low whistle.

"Yes, and now Bolkas rules—and he has pledged allegiance to the Sultan."

"Then why do they keep his sons?"

"To keep him an honest man, of course."

"Yes, yes, of course. And what about the other men who rode with us?"

"They were released. They ride back to tell Bolkas the fate of his sons."

"Come in, sit. I just made some tea." He put out two cups. "What about the Sultan? Is he still on campaign?" He leaned over the table, pouring the tea.

"Yes," Ozan replied, taking a cup. "He aims to subdue all Asia."

"And what about you? What will you do?"

"I could return to Nikea but I want to wait until it's safe. Besides, I have a good position here."

Ramiro thought again of Adele. "Any more news of Nicomedia? Does Bolkas rule it too?"

"I don't know. No one here cares about Nicomedia."

September 1092

Once again, Hasan stood in Qubad's office, escorted by a single guard. Despite his incarceration in the Sultan's jail for political prisoners, he looked healthy enough as he stood in a clean tunic, his long hair freshly braided and his beard clipped short.

"And so we meet again, Hasan, son of Bolkas." Qubad sounded oddly courteous.

Hasan bowed. "Peace be upon you, Effendi."

"I trust you have enjoyed your stay in Isfahan?" he said, his eyes twinkling with malice.

"Yes, Effendi."

"And you have had much time to chat with young Kilich, I presume?"

"Yes, Effendi."

"That is good." He picked up a letter from his desk, holding it between two long fingers, showing his manicured nails and gold rings. "Now we shall turn to another matter. I have received this letter from the Roman King—a very strange letter, indeed. It vexes me." He motioned to a guard. "I want you to have a look at it." The guard handed it over to Hasan. "Tell me what it says."

Hasan studied the strange words. "I do not know, Effendi. The letters are Roman but I have never seen these words before."

Qubad twirled an end of his mustache. "What about that barbarian scribe of yours? Perhaps it is one of his tongues?"

"Yes... yes, perhaps, my Lord."

"Then I will summon him." Qubad leaned back, resting an elbow on his chair. He gestured, opening his hands. "So? Do you have any further issues or concerns you wish to address?"

Hasan felt disarmed by Qubad's apparent kindness. "Forgive me, Effendi, may Allah bless your name, I have only one."

"And what may that be, son of Bolkas?"

"Will we be released soon, Effendi?"

Qubad laughed, like the chortle of a hyena. His face hardened. "Take him away!"

Two askari barged into Ramiro's room, pulling him from bed in the early hours. He hardly had time to get dressed before they rushed him to Qubad's office. And now he stood in front of the secretary, hair disheveled, face stubbled, barely able to hide his scorn.

Qubad looked tired too. He covered his night dress with a decorated cape. "Welcome, scribe," he scowled.

"Peace be upon you, Effendi," Ramiro replied cautiously.

"Look at this letter," Qubad demanded with no further ado. A guard passed it over.

Ramiro studied the single page, not knowing what to expect. But a look of astonishment soon flashed across his face. "By the love of Mary!" he exclaimed in French.

"Aha! You can read it. You must tell me exactly what it says—exactly, do you understand?"

"Uh, yes... yes, my Lord," he stammered in distraction as he read. The letter was written in Provencal, but King Alexios had signed it in Greek. He recognized Brother Aldebert's handwriting and was greatly relieved to know he had survived the Patzinaks at Roussa. He smiled after he read it through.

Qubad frowned. "You smile? What can be so funny? Is this a joke of some sort?"

"Forgive me, my esteemed Effendi. No, it is no joke. This letter is from the Roman Emperor, Alexios Komnenos, and is addressed to the Great Sultan, may Allah keep him. It is for his eyes only."

Qubad rose suddenly from his chair. "Why does the Emperor use this strange tongue? Read it to me!"

Ramiro shook his head. "I will not, my Lord."

Qubad glared at him in disbelief. "You will not? Is that what you said?" The guards drew their swords.

Ramiro glanced at the guards before turning back to Qubad. "My apologies, Effendi, but this letter clearly states it is for Malik Shah... for his eyes only."

Qubad paled. His ruthless uncle, the Vizier Nizam, had given him the letter with the critical task of translating it. "I will have you skinned alive! Read it to me!" he shouted.

"But my Lord, it is for the Sultan."

Qubad clenched his jaw, rippling the muscles in his square cheeks. He spun around, taking a moment to compose himself. He turned again to face Ramiro. "The Sultan," he said in a controlled tone, "is still on campaign in the Roman Lands. He has yet to return."

Ramiro shrugged. "Then we must wait, Effendi."

"You will tell me now!" Qubad screamed with a reddened face. Spittle flew from his lips.

"Forgive me, my Lord. I cannot."

"Ah, but you must, infidel. And you will." He drew his jeweled dagger, leaning into Ramiro's face while the guards still brandished their swords. "Or I will carve out your eyes! And, if that fails to induce you—I will slice off your manhood! Do you understand?"

Ramiro looked defiantly into Qubad's frothing face. "When I meet the Great Shah, I will be sure to inform him of your hospitality."

Qubad glowered at him, the dirk trembling in his hands. He turned away for a moment and then, in a sudden rage, he spun on his heels, slapping Ramiro hard across the face. "Take him to the dungeon!"

THE ISMAILI

Black rats rustled and squeaked as they scurried between prison cells. Ramiro sat idly on a few strands of straw, trying to avoid the filth around him while he rested his back against the cool stone wall. Five other men sat cross-legged around him, staring at him intently but saying nothing. He closed his eyes and prayed silently. By habit, he reached for his cross, but it was not there. Qubad took all he had, not that it was much.

After some time, a gaunt young man with a full, black beard spoke to him. "Who are you? Why are you here?"

Ramiro was in no mood to explain himself.

The man raised his voice. "You're a spy for Nizam!"

"Do you really believe I'm a Turk spy?" Ramiro asked with irritation.

"You're a foreigner!" The man blurted. "I can tell from your speech. Why are you here?"

"Because I am a slave who refuses to cooperate."

The thin man laughed, a cackling laugh. "If that were true, you'd be dead."

Ramiro smiled. "I suppose. Perhaps Allah has intervened."

The prisoner put his hands together. "Praise be to Allah."

"And why are you here?" Ramiro asked.

"Because I am Shia," he smirked.

"Because you are Shia? Is that all?"

"No, it's because I am both Shia and Ismaili."

"Ismaili?... the Hashashin?"

The man scoffed. "Do you even know what that means, foreigner?"

"I was told you are hash eaters and that you kill people when crazed by the drug."

All of the men laughed aloud. One started to cough and hack.

"That's what they want you to believe." The gaunt man chuckled. "It's all propaganda... filthy lies spread by the accursed Seljuks! Those Turk bastards."

Another man waved him down, warning him to lower his voice.

"What do I care?" said the man. "Tomorrow I die."

"Tomorrow?"

"Yes, I am to be executed."

"For what?"

"For complaining," he said despondently. "I complain about the mistreatment of Iranians... about the land the Turks have stolen from us. They take everything and give us misery and poverty in return. Ignorant barbarians!" He lowered his voice. "This is why I joined the Ismailis. Don't you see? Iranians have followed the wrong path, only the Shia know the truth, only the Ismailis have the courage to fight back against these evil Sunni, may Allah curse them!"

"But I was told that *you* are the fanatics," said Ramiro.

"Of course you were. These Turks believe they rule by the will of Allah. The Sultan and his vizier Nizam seek to destroy all Shia. Our people hide in the hills to escape their persecutions. But now we have a savior."

Ramiro saw the other men look askance at the iron door. He could see the fear in their eyes. "So who is this savior?" he asked softly.

The man leaned forward. "Why, Hassan i-Sabbah, of course," he whispered. "Leader of the Ismaili. The holy one who seized the mountain fortress at Alamut. He will free us from Turk shackles. He is not afraid to kill those who kill us. Even now he gains power. Then Iranians will rule Iran once again... and it will be Shia."

THE VIZIER

The only sound in the lush courtyard of Vizier Nizam's mansion was the nasal trill of a trumpeter finch as it flitted between the branches of an orange tree. Nizam reclined lazily under a huge umbrella while a slave cooled him with a wide fan of peacock feathers. Secretary Qubad sat nearby. More servants stood at a distance.

Nizam was Iranian, a strong-looking man even in his seventies, with a prominent nose, a heavy brow, and a gray beard that bobbed up and down as he chewed on purple grapes. Large emeralds glistened from his red silk turban whenever he spat the seeds onto a napkin spread out over his tunic of fine, red brocade. He held up the letter from King Alexios, staring at the strange, indecipherable words. "So you say the infidel will not translate this for us?"

Qubad squirmed in his chair. "He refuses, my Lord, despite my best attempt to persuade him."

A look of concern crossed Nizam's face. "I hope you have not harmed him."

"Not where visible, my Lord."

Nizam's bushy brows furrowed. "He had better be in the best of health by tomorrow, nephew. Or you will find yourself stationed on the Russian frontier. Is that clear?"

"I will obey your command, Oh Lord," he said, lowering his eyes.

"You will offer this barbarian the hospitality of the Sultan, as Allah demands it. Have you forgotten the ways of a good Muslim?"

"No, my Lord. I will obey."

"Bring him to me tomorrow. I want to know what this letter contains. There is little sense presenting it to the Sultan if it is merely trivial." He forced a thin smile. "Don't you agree?"

"Yes, Master, of course."

"And give me this Christian cross he wants so badly."

"Yes, Master." He handed it to a servant who delivered it to Nizam.

Nizam waved a hand. "Leave me now."

"May Allah exalt you, my uncle."

Nizam held Ramiro's roughly mended cross in one hand, twirling it between his fingers. He was visibly frustrated. "All we want to know is the gist of this letter, man. Will you not at least tell us that?"

Ramiro stood at a distance, neatly groomed in a clean white tunic, although his legs still burned and bled from the jailer's whips. He was glad to be out of the dark, stinking dungeon. He bowed low. "Please forgive me, my Lord, but I must obey Emperor Alexios. This letter is to be delivered only to your king, Malik Shah, may Allah keep him."

Nizam fumed. "How dare you! I am the Sultan's vizier! What impertinence!" Impulsively, he started from his chair but he caught himself and settled back down. The guards leaned forward, fingering their swords. He raised a hand to stop them.

"Forgive me, exalted Lord." Ramiro bowed again. "I have no intent to belittle your station. You must understand... I am a man of honor, great Vizier, and cannot, therefore, oblige your request."

Nizam tapped the wooden cross on a low table. "Do you realize your life is in my hands?"

Ramiro bowed slightly. "Yes, esteemed Vizier."

Nizam took note of Ramiro's demeanor. He could detect no fear in his eyes. None at all. How unusual. What should he do? He did not like it when only the Sultan was privy to news. How could he prepare for exigencies? Knowledge was the foundation of his power. Yet killing or torturing this cursed infidel would accomplish nothing, and the letter could be important. He stewed for a moment before he relented. "Very well. I will arrange an audience with the Sultan, who will soon return from his campaign in the west. My chamberlain will advise you on court protocol."

"Thank you, great Vizier. And, if it pleases my Lord, may I have my cross?"

Nizam glanced down at the wooden cross, its center wrapped tight with string. "I understand these crosses carry much weight for Christians. This one looks badly damaged. Why is it so important to you?"

"I have owned it for some time, my Lord."

"Then it has sentimental value?"

"Yes, my Lord."

"Muslims do not worship idols of wood or gold. They worship only God."

"As do I, my Lord. My cross is only a symbol that inspires me to do the will of God."

Nizam, despite his power and wealth, was a devout and deeply religious man. He examined Ramiro with interest. "Do you consider yourself a servant of Allah?"

"I serve God whenever I can, Effendi."

"Forgive me, Ramiro of Cluny, but your religion seems quite grotesque to me. Is it not true that you have rituals in which you feign to drink the blood of your prophet, Jesus, and to eat his flesh?"

"Yes, Effendi, but the ritual is only symbolic. By doing so, we imbibe the spirit of Jesus and of his wholehearted commitment to do the will of God."

"But do you not also pray to the bones and blood of your holy men? It sounds barbaric."

"Yes, my Lord, many believe the saints offer divine intervention."

Nizam shook his head. "Christians have many strange beliefs. Why do you worship this Jesus? Muslims worship only God."

"As do Christians, Effendi. But some Christians revere Jesus just as some Muslims revere Muhammad. At times, my Lord, it seems the messenger is mistaken for the One who sent him."

Nizam smiled. "You speak well, scribe. I can see you are a true servant of Allah."

"You are most kind. Uh... my cross, great Vizier?"

Nizam paused to look at the cross again. "I will return it to you when I am satisfied. In the meantime, you will obtain another cross and wear it about your neck."

Ramiro bowed. "Yes, my Lord."

Nizam waved him away.

THE SULTAN

Shortly after the Sultan, Malik Shah, returned from his summer campaign in Asia, two askari came for Ramiro. They rushed him from his room and, without a word, pointed and prodded him along gardened pathways leading to the Royal Palace.

Ramiro was familiar with the splendors of Constantinople, but the ostentatious grandeur of the Shah's Palace was equally impressive. In the vast courtyard, a glimmering pool reflected a clear blue sky, and trailing along its edges were crimson flowers of weeping ironwood. Cobbled pathways meandered through colorful beds of tulips, roses, and zinnias.

The palace was immense, its archways and pillars fashioned from an exquisite cream marble quarried from the steep mountains of Fars province. Gold and magenta tiles set in floral designs adorned its magnificent facade of arched windows and styled doorways.

Inside, the resplendence continued with high vaulted ceilings, marble colonnades, piers and arches, all laid out in rhythmic, radiating patterns. And high above, a brilliant light radiated through stained glass windows, splashing about the halls in showers of blue, gold, and teal.

But Ramiro's wonderment was soon shattered by the heavy hands of the Sultan's guards, who frisked him from head to toe, looking for hidden weapons and poisons. Satisfied, they escorted him to the enormous throne room.

The Great Sultan of Khorasan sat on a small throne of solid gold, crossing his legs on a gilded footstool. A loose, purple tunic with a red sash draped from his square shoulders. He was about thirty-five, a handsome man with fine features. Large, almond-shaped eyes swept up to the corners of his wide face, accentuated by thin, black eyebrows converging above his small nose. A neatly barbered beard ran along his jaw line. And towering from his head, was a domed hat with a gold rim and a brush of peacock feathers.

As Ramiro stepped forward, the vizier, Nizam Al-Mulk, joined him below the stepped dais. They both stooped slightly, careful to keep their heads lower than the Sultan's. Sitting on a dais one level below the Shah, was his eldest son, Berkyaruk, a glowering young man with long, black hair, a thin mustache, and ruthless eyes.

The Sultan dismissed everyone but his son, two pages, and four heavily armed askari. He did not waste time with pleasantries. "I hear you must be either a fool or a man of strong conviction to defy the orders of my Vizier," he said forcefully. "Tell us your name."

Ramiro bowed. "O Great Shah, I am Ramiro of Cluny. May God keep you."

"My Vizier tells me you are a man of God. A Christian. Is this true?"

"Yes, my Shah."

"Tell me, how did you come to Isfahan?"

"It is a long story, Your Highness."

"I have the time," said the Sultan smiling, as if amused by a child. "Please continue."

For the next hour, Ramiro summarized his journey, careful not to say too much, and careful not to speak ill of Turks.

"So you have spent time at the court of the Roman King?"

"Yes, my Shah."

The Sultan folded his arms. "We must talk more of this at another time." He paused, noticing a bruise on Ramiro's cheek. "How have you been treated?"

Ramiro hesitated. "I am thankful for your hospitality, my Shah, may God keep you."

With a frown, the Sultan looked askance at Nizam, who bowed his head in deference. "And now, Ramiro of Cluny, would you be so kind as to read this letter for me?" A page offered it to Ramiro.

Ramiro first read it through in silence. The only sound interrupting the quiet was the chirp of a caged goldfinch. The waiting scribe dipped his quill in readiness. Ramiro cleared his throat and began to read aloud. He read slowly, translating into Turkish.

> From Emperor Alexios Komnenos of the Roman Empire, greetings.
>
> To my Servant, Ramiro of Cluny, may God protect you. You are ordered to deliver this message to no one but the Great Sultan, Malik Shah.
>
> ———————
>
> To Jalal Al-Dawlah Malik Shah, the Great Sultan of Persia, Lord of the Turks.
>
> I have received your letter in which you make a generous offer to return the cities of Nikea and Antioch to my possession in exchange for my daughter's hand in marriage to your eldest son, Berkyaruk. I am presently considering your generous proposal.
>
> I have composed this letter in the tongue of the French because it has come to my attention that you are in possession of one scribe and holy man by the name of Ramiro of Cluny. Should you choose to reply to this letter, then I will know that he lives and remains safe in your care.
>
> I can verify that Ramiro is a monk and a man of peace who walks the path of God. He has come to you only because he was captured in Gallipoli while serving as a spiritual leader to my men.
>
> As a sign of good intention, I beseech you, in the name of God, to release the holy man so that he may return to his rightful home in the West. Upon his release, if it is your wish that peace be negotiated, I will dispatch an envoy to seek terms.
>
> Alexios Komnenos
>
> August 10, in the year of our Lord 1092.

Ramiro finished, standing quietly. The throne room remained silent except for the ongoing scratch of the scribe's quill. Malik Shah had concentrated on every word and continued to stare at him, not with distraction but with amused interest. Berkyaruk watched him too, but with an outward expression of malice and disdain.

"This letter," said the Sultan, "speaks very highly of you, Ramiro of Cluny. But how do we know you have translated it correctly?"

Ramiro bowed. "On that matter, Great Lord, I can offer no proof. I would merely suggest you send the letter to Antioch for verification. I hear some Western foreigners live there."

"He's a spy!" Berkyaruk blurted. "A spy for the Romans!"

Malik Shah quieted his son with a piercing glare before turning back to Ramiro. "If this letter is as you say, then there are two things of which we can be sure." He held up two fingers and touched one with his other hand. "One is that the Roman King has his spies everywhere." He paused while studying Ramiro. Then he touched his other finger. "And two, is that you must be a valuable man, Ramiro of Cluny," he smirked. "It seems you have both a king and Allah appealing for your release."

Ramiro looked down but said nothing.

"I am not familiar with your Christian calendar," said the Shah. "Can you convert the date of this letter to the Hijra calendar?"

"Please forgive me, Great King, but I do not know how."

The Sultan murmured something to a page who rushed out of the room. While he was gone, Ramiro cringed under the hostile glare of Berkyaruk, who seemed ready to run him through at the slightest provocation.

After a long and uncomfortable wait, the page returned with a sheet of paper which he presented to the Sultan. "Ah! The fourth day of Rajab. That's six weeks ago." He remained in thought for some time before looking down on Ramiro. "You may leave now."

Ramiro hesitated, he wanted his cross.

Berkyaruk stood abruptly. "You heard the Sultan!" the young man shouted. He glowered with a look of utter hatred, causing Ramiro to shiver as he backed away.

Malik Shah sat elevated at the head of a long, low table, his legs folded under him. "We had a successful campaign in Asia," he announced to his generals. "And we have eliminated that troublemaker, Abul Kasim. But we must be careful to keep King Alexios at bay. If we can bring his daughter as wife to my son, we may gain some hold over his decisions. But the only correspondence I have received from the King is a strange letter written in a barbarian tongue. In it, he requests that we return a holy man, one called Ramiro, who is now in our possession. He looked around the table. "What is your advice, General Buzan?"

Buzan had just returned from the western campaign along with the Shah. He was a slender man, his smooth facial features interrupted by a gnarled arrow scar on one cheek. "Return him, my King. It is a token offering, a small price to pay. And we gain the advantage of time."

"But what if he is a spy?" Berkyaruk challenged in a loud voice. He was only seventeen but already thickset, wide shouldered, and a head taller than most. If he lived, he would be the next Sultan.

"Has he been here long enough to learn anything of import?" asked General Buzan.

"If he has traveled this far," Berkyaruk argued, "he would know many things of interest to our enemies. Take no chances. Execute him!"

"Patience, my son," said the Shah. "Things are never that simple. This holy man may prove useful to us." He took several sips of mint tea before he spoke again. "On another matter, my secretary informs me that, last year, I received an envoy from Nikea with a request to return the Son of Sulayman to rule." He looked around the room for a reaction. "Do you think it wise to return the young man, Vizier Nizam?"

Nizam sat to his right, his hands folded in his lap. "There is little doubt the people in Asia would follow Kilich, my Shah. And there is nothing to be gained by keeping him any longer. But will he remain loyal to the Empire? Or become a traitor like his father, Sulayman?"

Malik Shah nodded. "That is the question. I will consider it. We have time." He paused to look down on his notes before speaking again. "And now let's move on to a more important matter—what of these Shia heretics— these Hashash-in? May Allah curse their sons! We know their depraved leader, Hassan i-Sab-bah, is a vile agent for the Egyptian Fatimids. He spreads their filthy propaganda everywhere and seeks to weaken the Seljuk Empire. Recently, he seized the Castle of Alamut, which you all know is a fortress in the mountains to the north, only two weeks ride from Isfahan! They grow stronger in our midst! What are we going to do about it?"

"Forgive me, my Lord," said General Buzan. "But we need more men. We already have one army besieging Kohistan in the east, while another is still fighting the Danishmend in the Roman lands, and our men in Syria are far away and have their own troubles."

"My Shah," interrupted Nizam. "May I suggest we use the Caliph's army in

Baghdad. We know the Caliph is becoming an embarrassment with his political meddling. We should exile him to Basra, put one of our generals in his place, and use his army to attack the Hashashin stronghold." The other generals nodded in agreement.

The Sultan rubbed his chin for a while. And then he nodded. "Yes, that is a clever idea, my Vizier. I believe the Caliph has become an irritant to the Empire." He paused for a moment. "You will go to Baghdad to make the necessary arrangements."

"Me?" Nizam asked, astonished. "To Baghdad, my Shah?"

"Yes," the Shah replied firmly. "You are the only one with the necessary credentials. He is the Caliph, after all."

October 1092

"Ramiro! Ramiro!" Ozan yelled as the door flew open with a bang.

Ramiro jolted up in bed and instinctively felt for his knife, but it was not there. "By the love of Mary, Ozan! Are you trying to stop my heart? What's the matter now?"

Ozan ran up to Ramiro's bed, falling to his knees. "You will not believe this! The whole palace... no, the whole city... no, even the whole country wails in grief!"

"You had better tell me soon, boy, or I will wring your neck! Out with it!"

"Vizier Nizam is dead, Ramiro! Murdered by the Hashashin on the road to Baghdad!"

Ramiro jumped out of bed. "The Vizier?" he cried in disbelief.

"Yes, yes!"

"When?"

"Two days ago!" He flung his arms out. "What will happen now, Ramiro?"

Ramiro drifted to the window. He looked down onto the teeming streets where everyone seemed to be talking in high voices. "How did it happen?"

"Two wicked men..." Ozan choked, "The Hashashin. May Allah damn them to hell! Just two men, Ramiro... when there were hundreds of the Shah's askari all about! They came to Nizam's litter in the guise of Sufis presenting gifts—then they stabbed him with poisoned knives! The askari soon hacked the bastards to pieces... but it was too late for Nizam!"

Ramiro stayed by the window. He shook his head in dismay, reaching for his wooden cross, but it was not there. In its stead was a gray iron cross, the only one he had managed to find. "This is a sad day for the Turks," he said sincerely. "Nizam was a great man who did much for the empire." He thought about the Vizier's influential manuscript, the *Book of Government*, which he came across in the library. And he thought about his great accomplishments—the distinguished schools of academia and the many hospitals with the best physicians in the world. He bowed his head in sorrow. "What now, Ozan? Who will take his place? Hopefully not that wretched man, Secretary Qubad." He turned from the window. "And how will I ever get my cross back?"

Ozan pointed at his cross. "But you have another cross."

"I want my own cross," said Ramiro.

"The one you wear is beautiful. Why do you want that broken old thing?"

"I must have it, Ozan. I will say no more."

RESURRECTION

Ramiro tidied himself frantically. Two weeks after Nizam's murder at the hands of the Hashashin, he was summoned again to the Royal Court. Noon prayers ended and it was time for his audience. Have I got everything? What do I need? Nothing. I need nothing.

The Sultan sat as before, flanked by his personal bodyguards and two servants while a squad of soldiers stood near the door. He looked tired, his complexion pallid, and when he spoke, it was with a hint of melancholy. Ramiro offered lengthy greetings but the Sultan, in his usual fashion, wasted little time with pleasantries.

"My son, Berkyaruk, would have you executed," he stated in a straightforward manner. "But I have decided to release you to King Alexios instead. Times have changed and I must find a way to appease the king and secure my western frontier while I attend to more serious matters at home." He waved an arm out slowly, as if to encompass his kingdom. "And it is time for the Feast of Eid, a day to forgive and forget our differences, a day to make amends."

Ramiro could barely contain his glee. He had to lower his head to suppress a smile. But he said nothing.

The Sultan looked at him kindly. "You have served me well. My librarian tells me you have done the work of three scholars." He paused for a while, drifting off in thought. And then, as if realizing where he was, he spoke again. "I will arrange an escort to take you to Nikea. From there, you may continue to Constantinople. I want you to deliver a letter to the Roman King."

"As you command, Great Shah." Ramiro was elated.

"For your troubles," said the Sultan, "you will be richly rewarded." He nodded to a page standing nearby. The boy held a silver platter covered with a napkin of red silk. He walked over to Ramiro, holding the platter before him. With finesse, the boy pinched one corner of the napkin, drawing it back.

Ramiro gawked at the object on the plate. It was a cross. A golden cross with a golden chain. He reached out slowly, picking it up carefully, as if it were a strange creature from another world. "It is beautiful, O Shah."

The Sultan nodded and smiled. "Look closely."

The cross was not made of solid gold. Instead, it was constructed using a thin framework of gold and silver. And encased within that frame, was a simple wooden cross.

Slowly, the truth dawned on Ramiro. My... my cross? Yes, yes, it's my cross! By all saints! It had been resurrected in new form. Each arm splayed out slightly, like the tail of a fish, and these were embellished with fine, floral designs. In the center, the frame artfully covered the gouge where the bloodstone had been, but left slots of exposed wood for the post and arms. The old, frayed wood was polished smooth and varnished, glistening next to the gold. He had never seen anything like it. "Thank you, Great Shah, may Allah keep you." He held the cross to his chest. Tears welled in his eyes as he choked back a sob.

"I tried to find the bloodstone you spoke of," said the Sultan in a calm voice, "but, alas, to no avail. Nevertheless, it may be of some comfort to you to know these modifications were made by a Christian, an Armenian jeweler. He is exceptionally good. You see—the gold and silver alloy gives it strength."

Ramiro nodded. "It is beautiful, my Shah, thank you."

The Sultan signaled to a page. "And for your journey home, I present you with another gift." The page came forward with a bulging bag of coins, offering it to Ramiro. It was heavy.

"Thank you, Great Shah, you are very, very generous. May Allah and the Prophet be praised!"

The Sultan motioned to another page. He too, stepped forward with a silver platter. On it was a piece of paper. "This document grants you full privileges in any part of my empire. You will find it useful." He straightened his back. "You will be provided with two horses and all supplies. Is there anything else you require for your journey, Ramiro of Cluny?"

"May Allah bless your sons, my Shah." Ramiro paused. "I have only one inquiry, Great Lord... what of my associates, will they also be released?"

The Sultan shook his head. "Who is this?"

"Hasan of Cappadocia and his brother. They brought me here from Nikea and were detained by the Vizier, may Allah's mercy rest upon his soul. Will these men accompany my return?"

"You mean the envoys who are kin to Abul Kasim?"

"Yes, my Shah."

The Sultan nodded with distraction. "I will consider the matter."

"And if it pleases the Shah, will Kilich also be permitted to return home to Nikea?"

"The Son of Sulayman?"

"Yes, my Shah."

"I will consider that matter also," he said with a hint of annoyance. "We are finished."

SON OF SULAYMAN

Kilich, son of Sulayman, wiled away his time in the Shah's detention compound along with several other political prisoners who were lucky enough to have some future value. It was a golden cage, quite unlike the fetid dungeons visited by Ramiro. Its inmates enjoyed baths, servants, and lavish meals while they studied Islam, the arts, science, and literature. Even shopping excursions were allowed under escort. It was here that Kilich had spent most of his young life, and it was here where two of Bolkas' sons, Hasan and Sebuk, were now detained.

Kilich soon became friends with Hasan and Sebuk, who were distant cousins. On this day, the three of them sat under the shade of an apricot tree while talking of local affairs. The courtyard was quiet except for the din of the market in the distance and the chirps of reedlings in the branches. Pleasing aromas of barbecued lamb and garlic hung in the air, while servants laid out bowls of oranges, dates, and almonds.

The three were deeply embroiled in discussions of political intrigue. They talked about what had come to pass in Nikea, the execution of Abul Kasim, and the appointment of Hasan's father, Bolkas, to take his place. Then the topic turned to the new-found strength of the Roman King after his defeat of the barbarians and, of course, they wondered what would happen in the Seljuk Empire now that Vizier Nizam was dead.

Kilich fingered dates from one of the bowls. His braided, black hair hung over one shoulder. A simple white tunic, belted with a blue sash was all he wore. He looked healthy and fit, his skin glowing with the flush of youth. At fourteen, he already stood the height of a man.

The boy stared into the distance, his big brown eyes unfocused, his thin, black eyebrows furrowed in thought. "Tell me Hasan, do you think the Sultan will release me now that Abul Kasim is dead?"

"Soon we hope. The servants told me that Ramiro met with the Shah to plead our case. Perhaps he will release you too." Kilich's maturity impressed Hasan, despite the fact that the young man had yet to grow a beard. In all things, he acted with composure and carried himself confidently. He was well read, gifted in the arts of war, and thoroughly indoctrinated in Sunni Islam. "One thing is sure," said Hasan, "the people of Nikea would welcome you gladly."

Kilich smiled. "I would like to meet this Ramiro, he sounds like an able man."

"He is very talented, but difficult to subdue." Hasan recalled Ramiro's flight in Edessa and his fearless confrontation with him around the campfire in the Zagros Mountains.

"Do you remember much of Nikea?" asked Sebuk.

Kilich shook his head. "Not really. I have only the memories of a child. But I have learned all I can of the Roman sultanate and of my father's life, may Allah have mercy on his soul. And I know it is my rightful inheritance, by the will of Allah."

"Praise be to Allah," the others chanted in unison.

Feast of Eid

Ramiro felt privileged—for an emancipated slave. Since his meeting with the Sultan, he had been moved from his small, spider-infested room to a compound right next to the library. His new rooms were spacious and furnished, and a small balcony overlooked a common courtyard beautifully adorned with a circular fountain at its center. And wrapping around this fountain, were gleaming marble benches interspersed with leafy green lemon trees.

The courtyard was unusually busy. It was the end of the month of Ramadan and great preparations were being made for the Feast of Eid, which marked the end to fasting. He looked down on the tables of delicious delicacies, smacking his lips. But, alas, he was Christian and could not attend.

"Look at this, Ramiro!" said young Ozan as he shuffled through the rooms. "You live like a king now!"

Ramiro pulled his eyes away from the tables of food, facing Ozan with a cheerless smile. "For a while, my friend. It will be better for a while." Inwardly, he was thrilled to be leaving, but many disparate thoughts tugged at his heart. What should I do? Should I head straight for Jerusalem? But I promised the Shah I would deliver his letter to King Alexios, a letter already in my possession. And I accepted gifts with this promise. But do I have the time? So much time wasted! I must get to Jerusalem!

"Ramiro!" pressed Ozan with a frown. "Did you hear me?"

Ramiro shook his head, dispelling his thoughts. "I'm sorry, Ozan. What did you say?"

"I asked—when are you leaving?" Ozan had matured somewhat since they left Nikea. His beard had filled in a little, as had his shoulders which he now swathed in a copper-brown cloak. He wrapped his long hair in a small turban and wore leather sandals. He looked like a true scholar.

"In the spring, I would think," said Ramiro after a lengthy pause. "I cannot imagine traveling through those steep mountains in the winter."

Ozan nodded as if he should have known. No route west could avoid the mountain snows until late spring. "Take me with you," he begged. "You have to go past Nikea anyway."

Ramiro moved from the balcony and gestured for Ozan to sit. "Can you get away?" he asked, moving two large pillows for a seat.

"I see no problem. I am free and I am Seljuk."

"What of Nikea? Will you be welcome there?"

"Abul Kasim was my only enemy, Ramiro."

"I suppose," he muttered as his thoughts drifted again. *Could I send Ozan to Alexios on my behalf? That would leave me free to pursue Jerusalem.* He said nothing to Ozan about the Sultan's letter, deciding to keep it to himself, unless the moment demanded otherwise.

"Ramiro?"

"Uh... yes, Ozan."

"Will you take me along? It would be my honor to escort you."

"Yes. Yes, I think that would be wise."

BLACK NOVEMBER

1092

Five months seemed like a long time to Ramiro, a long time before the end of winter. But the bag of gold he received from the Sultan eased his boredom and anxieties. He went on a shopping spree, buying new clothes for his journey— a cotton cloak for summer, a fur-lined leather cloak for winter, a money belt, boots and bags, even a new turban. No longer would he have the dress of a slave. He was a freeman now and had official papers stamped with the seal of the Shah himself.

But otherwise it was difficult to pass the time. He tired of his studies, although he still helped out at the library. He found little to do around the house as maids and servants now attended to all chores. So this particular morning, he occupied his time stuffing his money belt with the Sultan's gold coins. He felt some apprehension about traveling with so much gold. But then again, he should be safe enough riding with a band of the Sultan's mamluks. After filling his money belt, he put five coins in his purse.

As yet, nothing had been said to him about the release of Hasan and Sebuk. Nonetheless, he was feeling lively, if not giddy. Perhaps he would get to Jerusalem after all. He tingled with new-found excitement. "Thank you, Father in heaven!" he cried aloud. "I will say a hundred Hail Marys!"

He leaned over to pick up his reworked cross, again admiring the workmanship of its gold and silver framework. He was pleased to get it back, although it was a far cry from the original and much too ostentatious for a Benedictine monk. Would the Jerusalem patriarch even recognize it? And could he keep it safe? Any highwayman would slit his throat for it. Indeed, even the pious would be so tempted. So he wrapped it in a soft cloth and kept it in his vest pocket, leaving the iron cross about his neck.

When all was done, he sat on his bed to reminisce. He thought kindly of Brother Aldebert and Pepin and prayed they fared well. He wondered about Drugo and his Flemings and whether they survived their battles with the Turkoman. And what of Adele? Did she ever arrive in Nicomedia? And if she did, did she manage to escape before Abul Kasim seized the place? *Mother Mary, saint of all women, I pray you watch over her.*

But Ramiro's quiet meditations were soon shattered. In the distance he could hear the rising timbre of a woman wailing in the distance. He recognized it as the wail and ululation of death. Other voices soon joined in, and the cries grew in intensity, louder and louder, until the whole palace compound choked with screams and howls. "What in the name of God?"

He rushed to the balcony. In the twilight of dawn, he could see a great commotion on the streets. People scurried back and forth like a mass of rats. *Something is very wrong,* he thought. He ran to the door. The hall was empty. He rushed into the main library, but not a soul was there. The whole place was deserted. He hurried outside onto the busy street. All eyes wept and all hearts wailed in grief.

"What's happened?" he asked a man in the street, but the man brushed him away with a stark look of despair and fear, big tears coursing his cheeks. He spotted the librarian dashing back into the building and went after him. "Effendi, Effendi, tell me what has happened!"

The librarian was crying too, his eyes red, his cheeks wet with tears. "Allah has cursed us! It is a terrible day! A terrible day indeed, Ramiro. What will happen now? What will happen to the Empire?"

Ramiro shuddered. He gripped the librarian by the shoulders. "Effendi, what has happened?"

The librarian began to sob so heavily he had to squat on the steps. He was barely intelligible. "The Great Shah is dead!" he blurted.

"Malik Shah is dead?" Ramiro echoed in disbelief.

The librarian nodded his head.

"How? How could this happen?"

The librarian shrugged. "They say he was poisoned. They blame the Hashashin!"

Ramiro's heart began to pound. *May God protect us. Now what? Who will be the next Sultan? The Shah's vicious son, Berkyaruk, soon came to mind and he shuddered as he recalled his encounter with the malevolent young man, the one who would have him executed. Anything can happen. Now everything is different. Now Berkyaruk takes the throne. Will the Sultan's escort still come for me in the spring? Will Berkyaruk let me go... or will he slice off my head?* He soon realized what he had to do. Once again, he took the sobbing librarian by the shoulders. "Where's the Shah's detention compound? Where is it?"

The librarian pointed southeast. "On the Street of Flowers."

Ramiro rushed back to his room, grabbing his bag and money belt. *Ozan! Where's Ozan?* He ran through the building. "Ozan!" he yelled. "Ozan!" When he got to his door, he flung it open. Ozan cringed on the floor, swaying back and forth. He was crying too.

Ramiro rushed over to him. "Ozan! Come man! We must go!"

"Haven't you heard, Ramiro?" he sobbed, wiping his cheeks with his fingers. "The Great Shah—he's been murdered!"

"I have heard, Ozan. And now is a dangerous time. Come. Get your things. We're leaving Isfahan!"

"Now? What about..."

"Get your things, Ozan!" he yelled. "Trust me! We have to go!"

With all their baggage in tow, they rushed through the wailing crowds to the Street of Flowers and the Sultan's prisoner compound. There was only one nervous guard remaining at the gate when they arrived.

"What do you want?" threatened the young man as he put a hand to his sword.

"I... I want you to release some prisoners," Ramiro panted.

"On whose authority? Where are your papers?"

Ramiro hesitated, but soon remembered the Sultan's document. He pulled it from his belt, handing it to the guard.

The guard nodded approval and handed it back. "And where is your release form?"

Ramiro glared at him. "The Sultan is dead! The Vizier is dead! The Empire is in chaos! The men I want can do no harm now."

The guard looked around anxiously, his eyes darting from the street to Ramiro and then to the gate. He was flustered. "How much?"

"How much?" Ramiro repeated. "Oh! Yes, yes, of course. He dug into his purse for a gold dinar and handed it to the guard. It was a small fortune.

The guard studied the coin, glancing suspiciously at Ramiro before relenting. "Who do you want released?"

Ramiro told him.

"Kilich too?"

"Yes."

The guard opened the gate. "Hurry! Go into the courtyard to summon them. You must return the same way. I will not wait long."

Ramiro rushed through, running down an arched walkway leading to the courtyard. "Hasan! Sebuk! Where are you?" he bellowed.

The men dashed out of their rooms. The other prisoners joined them. "What are you doing here? What's going on? What's all the noise about?" shouted Hasan.

"The Sultan is dead! Poisoned in the night." Ramiro shouted for all to hear.

The men fell mute, returning blank stares of disbelief. "Malik Shah?"

"Yes, yes, there's no time to explain. I just bribed the jailer and we must go— now! Come! Forget your things! Come!" He headed for the exit. The men hastened behind. They rushed through the gate. The other prisoners did the same. The guard was gone.

"First we need weapons," said Hasan when they reached the streets. "Then we need horses."

"I have two horses!" Ramiro shouted as he remembered the Sultan's gifts.

"You have horses? But you are a slave," said Sebuk derisively.

"Not anymore, Sebuk. But I will explain it all later. We must go."

"Two horses are not enough!" said young Kilich. "We'll need two more! And we need arms—at least a sword."

"I know a place," said Ramiro, remembering his walks around the shops. But when they arrived, the shop was barred shut. Sebuk banged on the thick, wooden door. "Open up! Open up! Or we will smash the door in!"

A worried old man opened the door a little. Sebuk pushed it hard and it flung open, sending the poor man sprawling to the floor. They all moved into the shop.

"We mean you no harm, old man," said Ramiro. "But we need weapons. Your best swords, knives, and shields. And we need bows."

"I have no bows, Effendi. I'm a blacksmith."

"Then show us what you have." Ramiro dug into his money belt and paid the man handsomely.

Weapons in hand, they rushed to a nearby stable, offering the groom twice the price for good horses and saddles. But he refused. "These are not my horses!" he shouted. "You can't take them!"

Sebuk whipped out his newly acquired knife, slashing the man across the face. The shocked groom screeched in pain, slapping a hand to his bloodied cheek. "But we will take them anyway," he sneered. Hasan and Kilich drew their swords and the groom backed away. They took saddles and mounted up.

Before they rode off, Ramiro threw two dinar to the terrified groom. "Forgive me, son," he muttered under his breath.

They were no sooner on the streets when Ramiro shouted. "We need food and warm clothes to get through the Zagros!" The men agreed and they went in search of provisions.

Before the sun rose another hand, Ramiro retrieved his two horses from the Sultan's stable and met the other three men at the city gates. The guards stopped them. "Show your papers!"

Hasan and Sebuk kept their hands on their swords. Ramiro sensed trouble and took the lead. He handed them his pass. The guards were impressed. "My friends have no papers, Effendi, but we will gladly pay the fine." He threw them a dinar each. The guards hesitated momentarily, exchanging glances before rushing them through the gates.

Hordes of terrified citizens and slaves fled Isfahan, expecting more trouble. The road was choked with horses and carts. People prayed aloud, wailed in grief, cursing the Hashashin. The four men barged their way through the chaotic throng until they reached the open road. They rode hard, heading west to cross the cold Zagros mountains in the dead of winter.

AL-IRAQ

Ramiro, chilled to the bone, wrapped his damp cloak tight about his chest and adjusted his turban to keep the freezing rain and sleet off his neck. The four men plodded mile after mile through thick mud and wet snow, always looking for something to feed the horses in the cold, barren mountains of Iran.

Just south of Qom, they turned west for Daskerah to camp in the warmer valley. Ramiro helped to put up a canvas tarp, their only shelter from the sleet and snow. He shook his head sadly as they huddled around a small fire. "Who would murder the Sultan?" he asked the men. "Who could commit such an odious deed? Was it really these Hashashin?"

Ozan rubbed his hands close to the flames. "They murdered the Vizier didn't they? —why not the Sultan?"

"Perhaps the family of the Vizier plotted his death," said Kilich with a serious look on his boyish face. "I overheard some who blamed the Sultan for his death. They say he was the one who ordered him to Baghdad."

Ramiro was not convinced. "Why would the Sultan plot to kill his own Vizier?"

"Maybe because he was a very powerful man and an Iranian. The Sultan may have worried about this," he nodded his head as he spoke.

"More likely it was his half-brother, Tutush," said Hasan. "There were rumors that he met with the Hashashin to plot his assassination."

Ramiro frowned. "Why would he do that?"

"Tutush is angry because the Sultan sent his army to Syria and took control of the Roman lands—lands that he wanted for himself. To this day, Tutush covets those cities for his own and now he will want to be the next Sultan."

"Maybe," interrupted Sebuk. "But I overheard some in the markets who blame the Caliph in Baghdad. They say Malik Shah was going to depose him and appoint his grandson in his place."

"So what do you think will happen?" Ramiro asked.

"There will be war," said Sebuk, who stood near the fire drying his cape. His attitude toward Ramiro had changed considerably since their escape. "Tutush will claim the Empire, as is his right. But it is also the right of the Shah's son, Berkyaruk." He slung his cape across his shoulders before squatting near the fire. "Oh yes, there will be war. But the timing is good for you, Lord Kilich. You may claim Nikea with little opposition."

Kilich nodded. "I believe you are right, Sebuk. But what will happen to the Seljuk Empire?"

They rode west, passing through the deep, cold valleys of the Zagros before charging down the western slope, down to the Diyala River and onto the vast, warm plain of Al-Iraq. It was here, and only here, that Ramiro began to feel a new freedom. And as they headed northwest to Kirkuk and Mosul, a twinkle of hope returned to his eyes.

"What will you do, Ramiro, after you return to Constantinople?" Ozan asked.

"I'm not sure," he replied honestly as he felt for the Shah's letter. Should he fulfill his obligation to deliver it? Or did it really matter now that the Sultan was dead? "Perhaps I will return to Constantinople," he said, thinking of Aldebert, "and then continue to Jerusalem." Yet doubt plagued him. *What if Alexios holds me prisoner or appoints me to some other God-forsaken, heathen land?*

RAMIRO'S MALADY

Ramiro felt his first spasm of pain just past Mosul. He buckled over in the saddle and his reins fell free. With no direction, his horse slowed to a halt. Ramiro tried to dismount. Grimacing, he swayed in the saddle, losing his balance.

Ozan soon noticed and yelled to the others. He jumped from his mount, rushing to Ramiro's side, catching him just before he slid to the ground. "Ramiro! What's wrong?" he asked, kneeling down beside him.

Ramiro lay flat on his back at the side of the road, trying not to scream from the excruciating pain in his guts.

"Are you alright?" Hasan asked as he rode up and dismounted.

Ramiro waved a hand. "Yes, yes. I just need a little rest." He slapped a hand on Ozan's shoulders. "Help me to the bushes before I vacate in my breeches."

Ramiro thought he was feeling better after a night's sleep but the pain soon returned. It started in his stomach with flutters of nausea before it gripped his bowels. Then came more diarrhea and vomiting. It seemed they had to stop every farsakh so he could relieve himself.

"Bad water," said Sebuk. "I've seen it before." He took Ramiro's water skin and threw it away. "You can no longer use it."

Ramiro sat on the ground, hunched over from the sharp, searing cramps, oblivious to his surroundings.

"We must get to Edessa," said Hasan. "To the hospital." He put a hand on Ramiro's shoulder. "Can you make it to Edessa?"

Ramiro nodded weakly. He started to get up but faltered. Hasan took him by the arm. But Ramiro was no sooner erect when he fainted, crumbling to the ground.

Hasan turned him over onto his back. "We'll have to get a horse and cart. He cannot ride like this."

"We have no money for a horse and cart," said Sebuk.

"No, but he does," said Hasan. "And the money will be used to save his life!" He dug into Ramiro's money belt.

"Take a little for us," Sebuk urged. "We'll need it for the journey."

Hasan hesitated. "We can leave a note. And if he returns to Nikea, we will compensate him."

Sebuk nodded impatiently. "Yes, yes, brother, do it."

Hasan took out two gold dinar. "This is more than enough."

Sebuk crouched beside him. "Take more."

Hasan scowled. "Have we become common thieves, my brother? Have you no honor? This man saved your life."

The cart rattled and bounced along the rough road, jarring Ramiro to consciousness. With effort, he lifted his head from a soft bundle to see Ozan driving. He reached for the cross tucked in his vest, feeling relieved when he felt its form. He thought of a prayer and tried to speak but no words would come. His mouth was as dry as summer dust and his tongue swollen. The thick, fur blanket that covered him seemed to offer no respite from the cold. He shivered violently.

Ozan turned around to see he was awake. "How do you feel, old friend? You look terrible."

Ramiro looked at him but could not form the words, although he managed to raise a trembling hand in greeting.

"We will be in Edessa soon, my friend." Ozan tried to sound cheerful but spun his head away to hide his fear and sorrow. He rapped the horse's rump with his wand. "Yella! Yella!" he shouted.

Ramiro closed his eyes, falling into a thick fog of fleeting images and distant dreams.

Edessa

"Will he live?" Hasan asked.

The physician folded his hands across his bright, white tunic. He had a broad face and a long, flat nose that tapered up to his forehead, disappearing into a dazzling white skull cap. Shocks of black hair dangled about his ears and his long black beard bobbed as he spoke. "Probably not. The man is in shock and severely dehydrated. His pulse is slow and weak and his eyes rheumy. We have put him in quarantine and have begun treatment. We should know in four to five days. But only Allah knows if he will live or die, by his mercy."

"By the will of Allah," replied Hasan. His brow furrowed. "Does he talk?"

"Once in a while. He keeps muttering about someone. Does the name 'Adele' mean anything to you?"

Hasan shook his head.

"And several times he mentioned the Shah, at least I think he did, and something about a letter. I thought he was delirious at first, until I found a letter in his money belt."

"A letter?"

"Yes. It bears the seal of Malik Shah and is addressed to the Roman King, Alexios. Do you think it important now that the Sultan is dead?"

Hasan shrugged a little. "Perhaps not. Whatever arrangement they had is bound to be moot."

"Are you willing to deliver this letter?"

"Me? To Constantinople?"

"You can send it on from Nikea, can you not?"

"I suppose." said Hasan with hesitation. "Very well, give it to me." He reached out.

The physician looked at him warily. "Will you swear to deliver this letter?"

"I will do it," said Hasan with a hint of impatience.

"You swear in the name of Allah?"

"In the name of Allah, I swear, by the will of Allah."

The physician reached into his tunic. "Here it is."

Hasan looked at it briefly before putting it in a pouch about his waist. "Is his money safe?"

"Of course it is. The guards allow no one in."

Hasan nodded. "Is there anything we can do for Ramiro?"

"Not at this time. I will prescribe lots of water, a dose of lobelia, raw lemons, and simple soups. And, of course, he is in much need of rest. Then we wait. Allah will decide."

Sebuk paced the room. "But we cannot wait any longer, my brother. We must return Kilich to Nikea as soon as possible. Already, General Buzan plans to take Malatya—and the Danishmends still attack Kayseri from the north. If Buzan discovers the Son of Sulayman in his midst, he will have him in chains—or even executed.”

“You are right, Sebuk,” said Hasan. “Even if Ramiro does recover, he will be in no condition to travel for some time.”

“I should stay to look after him,” said Ozan.

“No,” said Kilich. “You are my cousin. I will need you by my side.”

Ozan wavered for a moment, he felt deeply obliged to stay with Ramiro—and yet returning to Nikea with Kilich would be a great honor and a privilege. He would share in his power and wealth. He had to go back. “But we must do something for him, Effendi, by the mercy of Allah.” Tears welled in his eyes.

“Perhaps we could use some of Ramiro’s money to buy a slave,” suggested Sebuk. “Then he would have someone to look after him... if he lives.”

“That’s a good idea,” replied Hasan. “We’ll talk to the physician about this.” He rubbed his chin in thought. “We cannot wait for him to recover. We will see the physician now and then ride for Nikea at first light.”

CONSTANTINOPLE

December 1092

Emperor Alexios was stunned. “Unbelievable! Are you absolutely sure?”

“Yes, my Lord,” replied the envoy, still caked in a thick film of road dust. “There is no doubt, Malik Shah is dead. The Turk Empire is in chaos. His son, Berkyaruk, claims the throne, as does his brother, Prince Tutush.” He reached into a small leather bag. “I return your letter, my Lord.”

Alexios took the letter, one which he had given to the envoy to deliver personally to the Sultan. This one followed the earlier letter he had sent in French to appease Monk Aldebert. But now this. He slouched low in his gilded chair, his thoughts raced. Now there is no need for us to make a pact with the Sultan. And my daughter will be pleased to know she no longer has to marry the Sultan’s son. He smiled. The Sultan is dead. Praise be to God! Now we have an opportunity to regain an Empire. He composed himself, speaking again to the envoy.

“Who is responsible for the Shah’s death?”

“There are many rumors, my King. Some say the Ismailis...”

“I’ve heard of them. You mean the Hashashin?”

“Yes, my Lord. And others say his brother, Tutush, plotted his death, or that Nizam’s family sought revenge. But others claim the Caliph ordered his death.”

Alexios stood up. “What else? You said you had three messages.”

The envoy looked into the king's ruddy face. "I have news of Nikea, my King. Our spies report that the Son of Sulayman has returned."

"Kilich? But he's just a boy! Who will be his military advisor?"

"He's fourteen, my Lord. But I hear that General Al-Khanes will be his atabek. They say the people cheered him home, and Bolkas, the brother of the late Abul Kasim, handed over the city without argument. Now Sulayman's family is once more in control."

Alexios cursed under his breath. Al-Khanes is a cunning military strategist. I should have seized the damn place when I had the chance. He put his hand to his chin. "How did he get to Nikea so quickly?"

"I heard he escaped the day after the Sultan's murder, O King. They say his jailer was bribed."

Alexios grew impatient. "And the last news?"

The envoy reached into his pouch. "I have a letter from the Sultan."

"From Malik Shah?"

"Yes, my King." He handed it over.

"How did you get it?"

On my return, sire, I stopped at Nikea. This happened to be just after the Son of Sulayman returned. One of Bolkas' sons, a man by the name of Hasan, he recognized my Roman dress and approached me. He begged me to take it and gave me a dinar for my troubles."

Alexios' face brightened. "So this letter must be the response to the one we sent on behalf of that Latin monk. Do you remember? We heard rumor he was captured by Turks and, only God knows how, he ended up in the Sultan's court. I agreed to test the rumor by sending a letter in his own tongue. I was merely amusing his fellow monk, or so I thought."

The envoy looked puzzled, shaking his head.

"Perhaps you know nothing of it. It was a favor I did to appease the monk's rather temperamental associate." He brushed a lock of red hair from his eyes. "Any word of him?"

"Who, my Lord?"

"Of the Latin monk. The Kelt with a ring of dark hair." He twirled one finger over his head.

The envoy looked puzzled. "I heard nothing of a monk, my Lord."

"The man who gave you the letter, did he mention any names?"

"Oh, yes, yes. He said he got it from a man called Ramirah..."

"Ramiro," Alexios corrected, further intrigued. "What did he say?"

"He said they left the man for dead, my King. That he probably died of dysentery in Edessa."

Alexios shook his head. "Most unfortunate," he muttered. "Most unfortunate, indeed." He opened the letter. It was written in Turkish. He handed it back to the envoy. "What does it say?"

The man read slowly. "He says he received your letter written in a... strange tongue on behalf of the holy man. He is... glad you are considering the... betrothal of your daughter to his son, Berkyaruk. And he says he will allow the monk to return as a sign of good faith."

"So the monk really was alive in Isfahan. How in hell's blazes did he get there? And how did he get out? And how did he end up in Edessa?"

The envoy shook his head. "I have no idea, my Lord."

Aldebert collapsed in tears. "Ramiro's dead?" he choked. "No! No! I will not believe it! May God have mercy!"

Commander Manuel tried to comfort him. "Well... we are not entirely sure, but it seems likely."

Aldebert lifted his head out of his hands, his long face wet with tears. "You're not sure? You mean he may still live?"

"We have no firm word, as yet."

"When did he fall ill?"

"I don't know. He was last seen near death in the hospital at Edessa."

Aldebert stood suddenly, brushing tears from his face. "Then I will go to Edessa. I will find him. Alive or not!"

Manuel shook his head. "It's a very dangerous journey. And worse if you travel as a monk. The Turk Empire is in chaos, warlords and Turkoman plunder with impunity. No city is safe anymore."

"To hell with the God-damned Turks!"

"Please, Monk Aldebert, you can barely wield a sword."

Aldebert stuck out his chin. "I'll take Pepin," he said defiantly. "He's learned to use a sword."

"Please," Manuel sighed in exasperation. "We have many experienced men at our disposal. Let me send a messenger to Edessa to find the truth."

"Who will go?"

"I will ask for Tatran, Ramiro's old tutor. He speaks several languages. And he's a good soldier. He can take a homing pigeon."

"But Edessa is hundreds of miles away!"

"No matter. The pigeon will return... unless it is shot down."

"And what can the pigeon tell us if it does return?"

"We will tie a marking to its leg. If it is white, Ramiro lives. But if black..."

Aldebert waved his hand—he didn't want to hear. "How soon can Tatran leave?"

"With the Emperor's permission, I will send him off tomorrow."

Spring 1093

King Alexios paced in fury. "That pirate Chaka has betrayed us again! Any treaty with that man is worthless!"

"And for the third time he builds more ships to attack our ports," said John Doukas.

"We must destroy him once and for all!" Isaak ranted. "We should send an army to Smyrna to capture the coast."

"We can send only one division, brother," Alexios moaned. "Even though we have managed to defeat the Patzinaks, we are still threatened by a Kuman horde approaching from the north and will need most of our men to drive them back. We must think of another way to dissuade Chaka."

John stood up, leaning with his fingers on the table. "And already Chaka has betrothed his daughter to Kilich, son of Sulayman. We can only assume he has made a pact with him to surround our eastern shores."

Alexios raised his hands in the air as he paced the room. "How can Kilich trust that treacherous fox? Damn him to Hades!"

Anna lifted her head with a concerned look, creasing her small, pale forehead. "Please, Alexi, do not curse. How can our Lord God be with you when you entertain such vile thoughts?"

"Sorry, mother," he said ruefully. "But this man drives me to rage."

She tapped a finger on a pad of paper. "Remember, there's no use wasting the lives of good men when other means present themselves. We should send young Kilich a letter. Something that would lead him to distrust Chaka... we need to turn these infidels against each other, like dogs over meat. That would save us much trouble. We might even be able to persuade Kilich to ally with us."

"But now Chaka is his father-in-law," replied Alexios with annoyance.

"My dear Alexi, you should know by now that any notion of kinship will dissolve like salt in water when it comes to money and power."

"Yes... yes," he mumbled. He thought for a moment and then smiled. "Let's tell Kilich that Chaka plans to conquer his sultanate—not Byzantium, which is probably true anyway."

"It's worth a try," said Isaak.

"I will gladly compose the letter," said Anna with a sly grin.

NIKEA

Kilich dressed himself in the fine raiments of a sultan. Now fifteen, he was a little taller and, with a growth of stubble on his chin, looked more of a man. He read the letter from Alexios aloud to his advisors. He then turned to Ozan. "Do you believe this letter, cousin? Do you think Chaka will betray us?"

"I do, my Sultan," replied Ozan. "Chaka cannot possibly win the Roman throne. And why else would he assemble an army and build a fleet in Smyrna? If we allow him to come up the coast with his ships, he could attack us from land and sea."

Kilich paused for a moment, looking at his men. "But can we trust King Alexios?" He caught the eye of his atabek, a rough-looking, battle-hardened mamluk who had previously advised Kilich's father about military matters. "What do you think, Al-Khanes?"

"I don't trust Chaka any more than the Roman King," Al-Khanes replied in a deep, graveled voice. He was a big man with long braids, a scarred face, and a gnarled nose, smashed by a war hammer years before. "May Allah curse them both. But the king's words ring true, my Prince. If we allow Chaka to strengthen, he will be a threat. We must do all we can to bring the Aegean coast under our control. For now, I say we ally with the Romans to defeat him."

Kilich nodded. "Then so be it!" he shouted with the eager naiveté of youth. "We will join the Romans on this venture. Assemble an army!"

SMYRNA

Chaka the Pirate looked over the walls of Smyrna, his stronghold on the Aegean coast. He was worried when he heard that a Byzantine army rode down the coast. But he was truly alarmed when he later learned that his new son-in-law, Kilich, had joined them. So when both armies reached Smyrna to camp outside his walls, he sent a messenger to the Son of Sulayman, seeking terms.

The messenger returned with good news and, much to Chaka's surprise, he was warmly received in Kilich's large tent, where he was subsequently plied with food and fine wine. Chaka's guards stood outside while inside, six mamluks guarded Prince Kilich, as did Ozan and Al-Khanes. They all exchanged pleasantries and began to feast.

Chaka put on his finest robe for the occasion. His hair was cut short, Roman style, his face rough, scarred by war and adversity. As was custom, he talked at length about the weather, about the crops, and about their sons before approaching the matter at hand. Finally, he could wait no longer.

"I am your father-in-law, Prince Kilich. Why do you side with these scheming Romans?" he complained through thick lips. "You cannot trust them. You know they will betray you. And if you drive me out, the sons of bitches will attack you next. Join me and we will rule the Roman lands together." He downed a mug of wine in one swill before wiping his face on a sleeve. He reached out, grabbing a handful of olives from the bowl, stuffing them all into his mouth, chewing loudly.

Kilich, who was well accustomed to the fine arts of Persian culture, eyed the crude man with disgust. A vulgar barbarian! He stinks, and eats like a pig. He leaned forward, reaching for the wine jug. "And how do you foresee this arrangement?" he asked with barely disguised hostility. "If I join you to defeat the Romans, how will the spoils be divided?" He filled Chaka's mug.

Chaka took another long draft. "Well... you can take all land west of Nikea, as far as the Propontis. I will hold Byzantium and the Roman lands west of the sea, and I'll keep the Aegean coast."

Al-Khanes leaned over, his long braids sweeping the low table, his dark eyes glaring over his gnarled nose. "It sounds like you will get the lion's share, Lord Chaka."

Kilich scowled. "My atabek speaks well. How do you reply? What of our position?" He dreaded the thought of being surrounded by Chaka's forces. "If you lay claim to the Roman lands, I want Smyrna and the Aegean coast."

Chaka looked at him with glassy eyes, the wine was taking its toll. "I have paid the price for Smyrna," he scoffed, "while you have done little. Why should I cede it to you?"

"Because you offer me nothing I do not already have," said Kilich. "You must concede more if you want my help."

Chaka, losing his composure, banged his mug onto the low table. "Don't you forget—you're nothing but an arrogant, young upstart. Do not think you can defeat me!" He took another drink before raising his voice. "My armies could easily overrun Nikea and the Roman lands!" He smirked. "I don't need you!"

For a long moment, Kilich glared at Chaka with wide eyes. Suddenly, he jumped to his feet. "The Roman King speaks the truth!" he shouted. "You plot against us!" In an impetuous flash of rage, he pulled out his sword. "Conniving old bastard! May Allah curse you!" And, to the amazement and shock of all, he thrust his blade right through Chaka's ribs before the startled man could utter another word. Everyone in the tent fell dead quiet, horrified by the sudden turn of events.

Chaka stared up at Kilich, his eyes bulging in total disbelief. He tried to speak but the only sound was the gurgle of his own blood. And after Kilich withdrew his bloodied sword, Chaka's eyes flickered briefly before he collapsed headfirst into a bowl of cold hummus.

5 - Syria

Land of Dreams

1093

Syria was not always dry and inhospitable. An Egyptian account from the Middle Kingdom describes the land as "afflicted with water, difficult from many trees, the ways thereof painful because of the mountains." Another says it is "overgrown with cypresses and oaks and cedars which reach the heavens," where "lions are more numerous than leopards or hyenas."

It was here, in this once salubrious land, where one of the world's oldest civilizations flourished—the Kingdom of Ebla—with its vast trading network reaching as far as Egypt, Iran, and Persia. The kingdom eventually succumbed to Sargon of Akkad, who united the land in a great Semitic empire, the motherland of Arab and Jew. But over the centuries, as empires rose and fell, Syria became a perpetual battleground, overrun successively by Hittites, Assyrians, and Persians, to name a few.

The people of the time believed Syria would always be a land of plenty. But over the years, they destroyed their forests and decimated the wildlife. To make things worse, the winds shifted and the climate dried out, transforming much of the arable land into a useless shrub steppe or a barren desert. Robbed of its natural resources and the wealth of its agriculture, the bright flower of empire withered and died.

Rather than a center of domination, Syria soon became dominated, remaining strategic only because it was a vital crossroads for the armies and caravans of Egypt, Greece, Rome, and Persia. Even so, much of its ancient culture persisted—its arts, literature, and science continued to flourish in the midst of conflict and turmoil. And to this day, Syria is the land of a thousand nights, the land of a thousand dreams.

Edessa

Ramiro gaped at the two angels. They appeared to shiver in a bright blue light, and yet he could see them plainly.

"What do you seek, Ramiro?" one asked.

"I seek Jerusalem, O Holy One."

"Why Jerusalem?" asked the other.

"Why... why because it is the Holy City of God, the most sacred place on earth."

He had no sooner spoken these words when a vivid and grotesque image appeared before him—a huge stone cube oozing blood from its top, a thick blood drenching all sides in scarlet swaths. "Blessed Mary!" Ramiro jolted. "Is this the Holy Sepulcher? What does this mean?" In an instant, the vision disappeared.

"And you have a cross?" the angels asked, unfazed by the spectacle.

"Uh, yes, yes, I do, for the Patriarch. I promised to deliver it to the Patriarch."

"And you seek a woman, one close to your heart," one asked.

"Yes, Spirit, my mother."

"But you think of another."

"Uh... yes, yes," he felt himself blush. "I... I pray for her safety." The angels did not respond, but he felt they were amused.

"Do you believe you will find God in Jerusalem?" both angels chorused.

"I believe the power of God is greater in Jerusalem," Ramiro answered sincerely.

"But do not your scriptures tell you the kingdom of God is within?" They asked wistfully. "Have you not learned that God lives in your heart and mind? And there, he waits patiently to guide you... if you would only listen and obey."

"Yes, I do believe that, Blessed Spirits. But is not the Holy Sepulcher a sacred place? The center of the earth?"

"There is no sacred place. Only a sacred life of service."

"I lead a pious life," Ramiro said defensively. "What more can I do?"

"You lead a troubled life, Ramiro of Cluny, your heart is torn with doubt, your mind clouded by tradition, your actions impeded by ritual. How is it possible to serve God in such confusion?"

"But I... I believe I have devoted my life to God."

"So you say."

Ramiro felt a rush of remorse. "Please, Holy Ones, what must I do?"

"Prepare yourself," was all they said.

Ramiro's young slave stood in the doorway of the doctor's office. He wrung his hands in a fuss, biting a lip. He could hardly contain his excitement as he waited for the physician to acknowledge him.

"What is it, Jameel?" the doctor finally asked in annoyance.

"Sayyid! I saw him move!" The young man's brown hair fell into his eyes.

"You saw Ramiro move?"

"Yes, Sayyid, I saw his eyelids flutter and his body twitch."

The physician rose from his cushion. "Well then, he is either dying or recovering." He rushed to the room, bending over Ramiro's limp figure to smell his breath and listen to its labor. He took his thin arm and felt his pulse. "I see no movement but I detect a slight quickening of his pulse. By the will of Allah, I believe he will recover." He made an entry in his notebook and prepared to leave. "Stay with him, boy. Keep that brazier burning to keep him warm. When he awakes, you must give him hot soup. If he doesn't eat soon, he will surely die."

Aleppo

As Ramiro showed signs of recovery in Edessa, other fateful events transpired in the city of Aleppo, a two-day ride to the south, where a Turk mamluk and a slave-girl would soon challenge his Benedictine vows.

Aleppo was a trading mecca. Merchant ships from as far away as India and China sailed thousands of miles across the South China Sea and the Indian Ocean to reach distant ports on the Persian Gulf. From here, exotic goods made their way up the Euphrates to Aleppo before being further dispersed to the lucrative markets of Byzantium and Europe. And even more merchandise arrived overland via camel trains trudging the long Silk Road from central China—including slaves from Samarkand.

Khuda the Mamluk

The sun was high overhead by the time Khuda the Mamluk neared the Red Gate of Aleppo. Within the city walls and soaring high above him was an enormous hill of solid limestone rising up one hundred and sixty feet, dominating the view for miles around. On the flat summit of the mound sat the enormous citadel encircled by stone walls and tall towers, and large enough to house a garrison of thousands.

"Toros! Son of camel shit!" Khuda yelled, his long braids swinging across broad shoulders "Easy with that whip or I'll hack off your feet and leave the vultures to pick your miserable bones!" He shouted loud enough to carry his threat to the back of the caravan train, a procession of six pack camels, seven armed horsemen, fifteen Turkoman horses, and a string of Samarkand slaves. The slaves, twelve barefoot children roped together at the waist, were dragged along by the strong pull of a sand-colored dromedary.

Khuda, a brawny Turk with a battle-scarred face, scratched his scruffy, black beard in vexation. They had traveled the road from Baghdad, following the Euphrates to Raqqa. From there, they crossed the Syrian Desert, a flat wasteland of rock and gravel. The slaves suffered on this last leg and he knew it would concern his employer, Harun the Slaver.

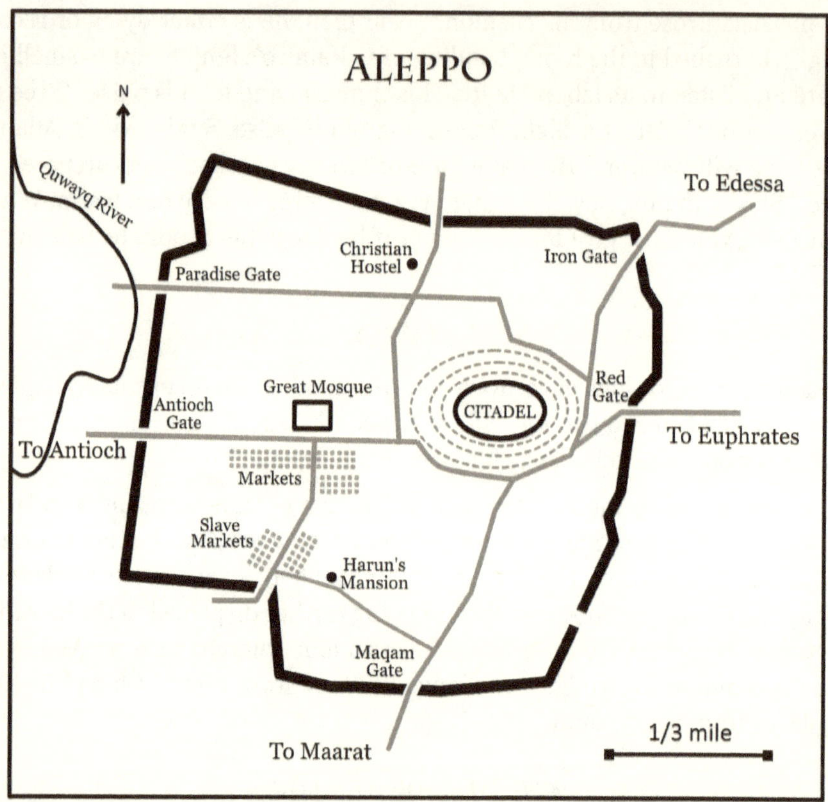

Passing through the gateway, they could soon hear the raucous cries of peddlers hawking their wares. Gray pigeons fluttered overhead, cooing from nests set along thick wooden beams. Not far in, Khuda stopped for the tax collector. He dismounted with effort, shifting the scabbard of his sword as he swung a leg over his mount, grunting as he hit the ground. Too many days in the saddle had made him stiff and sore. He offered greetings to the collector, an Arab employee of the Turk Emir.

The tax man glanced up at Khuda, all the while combing his fingers through his black beard. He did not return the greeting. In front of him, lay rolls of paper neatly stacked on a wooden table. He spread one sheet in front of him before dipping his quill in a pot of India ink. "How many slaves do you bring? And what do you carry on the camels?" He sat erect, swatting slowly at the flies circling the scroll.

This idiot has no manners, Khuda thought before he reached into his belt, pulling out a tattered piece of paper. He tossed it on the table. "Here's my list."

The collector looked askance in disgust. He smoothed out the list before reading it aloud. "Fifteen horses, twelve child slaves, one talent of silk, two talents of silver dishes, a talent of pepper, one of cinnamon, and four talents of sugar."

He transcribed the tally at his desk, making the entries on the scroll before ordering one of his assistants to check the cargo. The man rushed out while Khuda waited in the stifling heat.

When the servant finally returned to confirm the accounting, the tax man finished his calculations. "You owe the Emir, may Allah keep him, a tax of twenty-two dirham."

"Twenty-two dirham?" Khuda growled, perhaps a bit too loudly. He gritted his teeth, trying to remain calm. "That is more than I have ever paid for similar merchandise. Are you sure?"

The collector looked directly at him for the first time. "That is the fee, trader. Or would you like me to advise the Emir of your discontent?"

Khuda paused. "No, no. That will not be necessary. I will pay your fee," he fumed, knowing the amount was exorbitant.

Just as the tax collector handed Khuda his receipt, Harun the Slaver arrived at the gate. He rode up on a heavy Barqah mare, a working breed from North Africa known for its big head and thick legs. It was not a beautiful horse but it was the only breed capable of supporting Harun's excessive weight. He was eager to inspect his new merchandise. "Ya, Khuda!" he shouted in an excited, gasping voice.

Khuda looked up from the table. "Peace be upon you, Harun. May you receive Allah's blessing."

Harun, a huge man, dismounted with considerable difficulty. He grasped the horn of his saddle, twisting the harness and causing his poor horse to neigh in protest. A muscular slave dashed to his aid, but he could barely cope with the slaver's weight. "Get away you stupid oaf," Harun shouted at him, raising a kerchief to dab at the sweat pouring from his chubby face.

He waddled over to inspect the young slaves, who were filthy and teetering from exhaustion after weeks of travel under a blazing sun. "Khuda!" he yelled. "Are you trying to put me out of business? These waifs are barely alive! Get them to the house before they all die on me!" His shrill voice managed to rise above the deafening din of hawkers and hucksters who lined the narrow, teeming streets.

Khuda clenched his teeth. *You fat pig! What do you know of the trouble and misery we endure just to fatten your purse and belly?* He turned a piercing glance to Toros, an Armenian slave with light brown hair and green eyes who also worked for Harun.

Toros immediately sensed trouble and rushed to get the slaves in line, eight girls and four boys, some sobbing from fatigue, others silently morose. "Let's go! Let's go!" he yelled, cracking his whip. He turned on a crying boy, a frail lad of nine with thick, black hair, belting him across the head with the palm of his hand. The boy screamed as he fell. Toros glared at the cowering lad. "Shut up! You miserable dog! Who will buy you in such a sorry state! We'll sell you to the whorehouse! Quiet! Get up and clean your ugly face!"

Toros' shouts did not escape the attention of Ibrahim Al-Mufti, a clergyman standing in the doorway of the bakery across the street. He counted out a few copper coins for his hot flatbread before storming over to Toros.

"You, … slave-driver!" he shouted in a throaty voice that belied his tall, slender frame. So powerful was its resonance that the people around the bakery fell silent or turned to whispers. Many in the gathering crowd recognized his dress, a white turban and a long black tunic with long sleeves. Ibrahim was a mufti, a legal scholar and a Sunni Muslim known and respected for his knowledge of the laws and traditions contained in the Sharia and the Hadiths. Those who knew him told others and the word spread quickly throughout the crowd of shoppers and merchants.

Toros recognized Ibrahim's dress and tried to move away as fast as he could. Meanwhile, Harun turned awkwardly to see why such a hush had descended on the boisterous street. That's when he saw the mufti striding toward Toros.

"You!" Ibrahim shouted at Toros in indignation. "In the name of Allah, must you beat these slaves for no reason? Is your heart so devoid of compassion that you would treat these poor wretches with such malice?" He scowled at the young man.

"No Mufti," Toros replied fearfully, briefly meeting Ibrahim's fiery look before lowering his eyes.

Harun waddled back with servants in tow. Sweat ran freely down his pale, round face. "O Noble One," he gasped before Toros could say another word. "Praise Allah for your presence among us!" He bowed lightly. "I am Harun. How may I assist you today, O Great Mufti?" He took another deep breath. "Has my unworthy boy dared to offend you?

Ibrahim's face curled in a sneer of disgust. "You offend God, Harun, son of slavers, with your vile language and cruelty!" he said, laying Toros' sins on his head. The crowd closed in. "Do you not obey the Sharia, the Holy Law of Islam?"

"By all means, Great One," Harun flushed, his heart pounding. "We are simply on our way to market to sell these Turkomans, Holy One. We meant no harm or offense, they are merely infidels," his voice labored.

Ibrahim persisted in the same strong voice. "And how does the Sharia instruct us in these matters, Slaver?"

"Well…" Harun struggled for words, not really sure what to say. "It is the right way, Sayyid, the law...the way a good Muslim lives," he stammered. He grasped for ways to escape the mufti, but his brain fogged in the stifling heat. The crowd smirked at his difficulty.

Ibrahim raised his voice for the edification of all. "The Sharia is our guiding principle," he instructed with righteous indignation, "it specifies the laws and moral principles by which every good Muslim should abide." He paused to give his words effect. "Remember, in the words of the Prophet, you should give slaves the same food you eat, the same clothes you wear, you must burden them lightly and torment them not."

"Yes, Mufti," Harun quickly agreed as his small eyes shifted down the street toward the gathering crowd and the slave market. "Your wisdom precedes you ... and your knowledge of Islam is unmatched. May Allah and the Prophet be praised! I go now to obtain good homes and admirable occupations for these poor waifs. May Allah preserve them, by the will of Allah." And he began to turn away. The young slaves stared wide-eyed at the tall mufti, who showed such courage in the face of cruel slavers.

Ibrahim could see them inching away... without his leave. "Go, then, and do not forget your prayers!" he cried aloud in an effort to save face. He hesitated to press the issue, but he had done all he could. He knew he could not prevent the mistreatment of slaves despite the laws and admonitions of Islam. And it was foolish to think slaves would eat and dress as their masters. Indeed, they were marked by their dress and grooming.

But further protest was unwise. There were many wealthy people in the dispersing crowd, Christians, Muslims, Jews, and Zoroastrians alike, who all relied on slave labor to work their homes and businesses. And the ruling Turks needed slaves to fight their battles. Captives came from near and far; the infidel Turkoman of the north, the Armenians of the Caucasus, the Slavs of the Dnieper, and even the Greeks of Byzantium. And here they all mingled on the bustling streets of Aleppo.

Free of the mufti, Harun's procession continued to carve its way through the narrow streets, dodging an endless stream of people, horses, donkeys, camels, and carts. Thick odors of human sweat, animals, and dung hung in the air, occasionally interspersed with more pleasing aromas of grilled lamb and roasting camel.

Harun came to a stop at the walls of his luxurious mansion, a two-story stone building cornering the market at Slave Alley. "Get the slaves inside." he cried to his chamberlain. "They need food and drink... And bathe them!" He wheezed. "I will take my meal as soon as I wash and dress. Go! Go! Go!"

The chamberlain scurried off. "Come Khuda," Harun muttered, "You must brief me on recent events. We will bathe and dine."

Pear and orange trees wrapped around a marble fountain in Harun's courtyard. The place was quiet except for the tinkle of water. Even the birds fell silent in the heat. "So tell me Khuda, what news have you heard?" Harun prodded as they emerged from the baths. He plumped down on a bench while a slave served orange juice.

Khuda shook his head. "Trouble is brewing since the death of the Shah, Master. Everywhere, local emirs fight among themselves, trying to grab more land and cities. Raiders and thieves haunt the roads. It's too dangerous to return to Baghdad. Berkyaruk still fights for the Sultan's throne. His uncle, Tutush is challenging him. I hear he leads an army to Isfahan."

"Apparently not," said Harun. "He abandoned the campaign and returned to Damascus."

"Why? What happened?" asked Khuda as he dried his long hair with a towel.

"Not enough men. The Emirs of Aleppo and Edessa failed to follow him into battle as they had promised. Now he schemes to destroy them in revenge."

Khuda nodded in understanding. "And what of Antioch? Do you think Tutush will besiege it too?"

Harun shook his head. "It's unlikely that even Tutush could breach the walls of Antioch."

"I suppose that's true. And what of the West? What of the Roman lands?"

Harun smiled, lifting his puffy cheeks. "Oh yes, there is trouble there too. Did you hear that the Son of Sulayman escaped Isfahan after the death of the Shah and has returned to rule Nikea?"

"No, I did not." replied Khuda. "This should prove interesting."

Harun nodded. "Yes, and I just purchased some fine young women captured when they seized Nicomedia some months ago. Greeks and Romans. Even a few of those Western barbarians. Some with red and blonde hair. I'll get a good price for them."

While Harun and Khuda sat down to a meal of roasted lamb, the slaves in the cells below ate bowls of cold barley gruel. The basement of Harun's expansive mansion served as a slave-quarter, divided into dim cells separated by stone walls. The boy slaves were thrown into one and the girls in another. Four other cells held more. One held black slaves, another Turkoman women, while another held eight white women, the Roman slaves.

In a nearby chamber, Toros the Armenian and Dmitri the Slav sat on goat-hair cushions to enjoy a meal of dates, cheese, and flatbread. Dmitri, a blonde boy of twelve, was captured in the upper reaches of the Dnieper by the Rus, descendants of Viking raiders and the fathers of Russia. His white-blonde hair, blue eyes, and tanned skin made him a rare sight. Harun thought he was pretty and purchased him in the markets of Baghdad.

"Did you see Harun's face when the mufti scolded him," Dmitri smirked.

"I thought his beady eyes would burst out of his fat head!" Toros sputtered through a piece of flatbread and they both laughed aloud. "Careful—be quiet, we don't want that bitch, Huda, to hear us."

"Toros, let's go to the market today. I want to buy a knife from the old armorer." He stuffed a date into his mouth.

Toros yawned. "I'm too tired to go anywhere. Besides, you stink of camel shit."

Dmitri smiled. "And you talk like an old man."

Above them, an iron door squealed on its hinges before slamming shut. "Huda comes!" Toros whispered. They cleaned up their meal in a hurry and sat waiting.

Harun's corpulent wife, Huda, huffed down the stone stairway. Two slave girls accompanied her, one carrying stacks of rough linen robes and the other stooping from the weight of two buckets of steaming water. "Toros!" Huda shrieked. "You Armenian bastard! Come and help us before I sell you for dog meat!"

Toros rushed to the base of the staircase. Dmitri followed. "Yes, Mistress. Your wish is my command."

She thumped to the floor, panting heavily. "It's a wonder you didn't kill them all, you stupid infidels. Look at their condition! I should have you both whipped!" Her heavy jowls fluttered and her thick lips sputtered.

Toros eyed her pale face, distracted by the thin, black hairs growing out of her chin. Her big head bobbed as she heaved her words. You ugly old hag! But he lowered his eyes lest they betray his thoughts. "Welcome, Sayyidah, your kindness and mercy precede you."

Huda clicked her tongue in disapproval before turning on the girls carrying the buckets of water. "Prepare our new arrivals for a washing. The physician comes to tend their wounds." She plodded over to the cell holding the Roman women. "And make sure one of you takes care of these white girls. I want them fed and cleaned. And I want their hair brushed."

She looked over the eight women in the cell. Some were sobbing while others stared vacantly. Only one of them showed any spirit, the one with red hair, the one who spoke a strange barbarian tongue. She was a beautiful woman, thought Huda, but too old for the best price. "Well, well my pretty ones," she screeched. "Soon you will have the pleasure of a prince's harem."

The red-head snarled at her, screaming in a language no one understood. Huda stepped back in alarm, then laughed nervously. "Come on Toros!" she shouted. "Unlock these doors so my girls can get to work. We have one month to transform these heathen bitches into precious dolls. Then we take them to market."

EDESSA

June 1093

Ramiro had another dream. He soared like a bird over the rolling hills and lush valleys of Burgundy. There, far below, was Cluny and the monastery and the vast farmlands spread out around it. A small hamlet caught his eye and down he came, slowly, slowly, until he found himself in a garden of bright flowers. Adele was there, she held a babe in her arms.

He opened his eyes with a start, staring at the ceiling for some time. It was white. He looked down to the walls. They were white. The door was white. Where am I? Is this heaven?

With effort, he tried to get up but could not. He managed to rock to his side, propping himself on an elbow, but he had no strength and flopped back. He tried again and, this time, managed to balance. He looked around, soon realizing he was in a small room, all plastered white. A window opened behind him and he could hear the twitter of birds.

He lay back down for some time, trying to collect his thoughts. Suddenly, the door swung open. He jolted, turning his head to a young man standing in the doorway. Ramiro tried to speak but only a dry squawk emerged and he fell to coughing.

The smiling boy ran to his side, grabbing a jug of water from a nearby table and, with shaking hands, poured a cup, spilling over the table. He tipped Ramiro's head up, giving him a sip.

"Are you a... an angel?" Ramiro croaked in French.

Jameel shook his head, confused. He replied in Arabic. "What are you trying to say, Master?"

Ramiro stared vacantly for some time.

"Master, can you hear me?"

Ramiro heard the words, like someone calling from far above. Slowly, he began to pull himself into the present, inch by inch, as if clawing out of a deep well. Soon, he recalled the tongue of the land and repeated the phrase in rasping Arabic.

The boy looked astonished, then smiled broadly. "No, Master, I am Jameel. I am the one your right hand owns."

"What?"

"Your friends purchased me for you, Master."

"My friends? What do you mean?" His voice a harsh whisper.

Jameel stood by the bed looking demur. "I am your slave, Master."

"My slave?"

"Yes, Master. Your friends bought me to care for you."

As Ramiro studied the boy, a flood of memories returned, washing away his lingering dreams. "Where are my friends?"

"They left fifteen days ago. They left for Nikea."

Ramiro rolled to his side. I'm still alive, he thought, and a wide smile cracked his dry lips.

"Please, Master," Jameel pleaded. "You must eat."

Ramiro again tried to pry himself up but fell back. "Come on, then," he said softly. "Make yourself useful, my boy. Help me sit up."

Jameel lifted him to a sitting position, stuffing a pillow behind his back. The boy was about fourteen and, except for a few minor blemishes, was strikingly attractive, with chestnut brown hair, blue eyes, and a small nose.

So young and beautiful, Ramiro thought—just as the slavers like them. He raised a weak hand to scratch an itch on his chin and was startled by a growth of beard—and his hair, it hung over his ears. "Blessed saints!" he grated. "I need a barber."

Jameel laughed. "You look like a holy man, Master. I was told you are a holy man."

"Where am I?" Ramiro asked.

"Why, you are in hospital, Sayyid."

"Which hospital?"

"The hospital in Edessa, Master." Jameel began to wonder if his new master was addled.

Ramiro's eyes widened with a sudden thought. "Where's my cross?"

"Your cross? Oh, yes, the Christian cross. Not to worry, Master, it is in the cabinet with all your possessions. Now I will get some soup for you." He ran out the door.

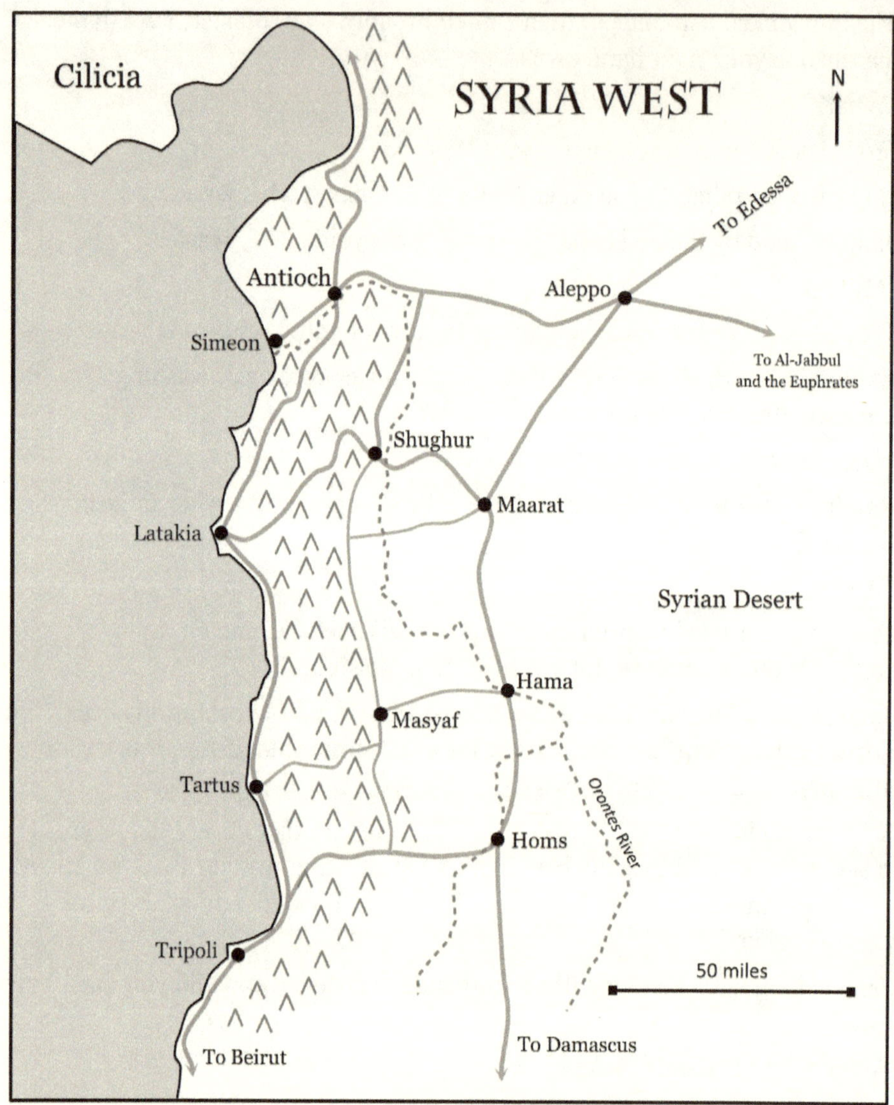

SYRIA WEST

"This is not a good time to ride, Master," Jameel protested. "It's too cold and wet. And you are still weak." He followed Ramiro along the winding path of the hospital garden. Dark clouds threatened in the distance and the air cooled, giving strength to his words.

Grudgingly, Ramiro knew the boy was right. He had lost weight and strength and, after weeks of recovery, was still in no shape to travel. "But that's not what I asked you, I want to know the best route to Jerusalem," he said with a touch of irritation.

"Yes, Sayyid, forgive me." Jameel was right on his heels, like a friendly shadow. "First you must go south to Aleppo, then keep going south on the road to Homs and Damascus. I'm not sure how to get to Jerusalem from there. But I think you will have to travel down the Jordan River."

Ramiro studied the slight young man, beautiful but poorly educated... and he was not a warrior. "How do you know these things?" he asked skeptically.

Jameel smiled. "Everyone knows this, Master."

"Is this the only route?" Ramiro asked as he ran his fingers through his trimmed beard, his hair clipped just below the ears, the current fashion.

"Oh, no. You can also travel the coast from Aleppo to Latakia, from there to Beirut. After that, I'm not sure."

It started to rain. They took cover in a small shrine at the riverside. Here they sat and watched as it poured in heavy beads. "So which route is the best?"

"It all depends, Master. The road to Homs and Damascus is flat but it's hot. You can follow the river south all the way to Homs."

"Which river?"

"Why... the mighty Orontes, Master." Jameel said proudly, happy to demonstrate his knowledge.

"And the coast road?"

"Many more Christians live along the coast road, Master. But there are still problems."

"Such as?" Ramiro asked, rolling a hand to urge him on.

"Well, there are many hills to climb and ... and farther south, the Egyptians wait to enslave us."

"Why would they enslave us?"

"Because we are not Shia, Effendi."

"Are these the Ismailis... the Hashashin?"

"No, no, Master." Jameel laughed. "Not all Shia are Ismailis. The Egyptians are Fatimid Shia."

"And which are you Jameel, Shia or Sunni?"

"Oh, no, neither Sayyid, they tell me I was born a Christian."

"So are you a member of the Greek church?"

"No, no, Sayyid. My last master said I was a stinking Maronite. But I'm not sure what a Maronite is... and I've never been in church."

Ramiro brought out his gold cross. "You have seen this?"

"Yes, Master, it is very beautiful."

"Where is your cross?"

"I was not allowed to have one," Jameel said sadly.

"I thought all Christians had to wear one?"

"Slaves are slaves, Master. There are no Muslim slaves."

"Well, now you will have one. We will go to the markets."

"You are good to me, Master," he beamed. "I will serve you well."

"You do not need to serve me, Jameel, I set you free."

"Free, Master?" Jameel's eyes went wide, his voice filled with apprehension. "But what will I do, Master? I have no money, no family... no position."

"I will give you some money."

"Please, Master, let me come with you. I have nothing here."

Ramiro pondered the young man and wondered if it was wise to bring him along. After a long moment in thought, he smiled a little. "Very well, you may come." He stood up. "In the meantime, we will continue with your reading lessons. And then we will prepare for Aleppo. I want you to find us two horses."

"Horses, Master?"

"Yes, horses. We will soon ride to Aleppo."

"But Master, Christians are not allowed to have horses."

"What do you mean? I rode a horse all the way to Isfahan!"

"Yes, Master. Please excuse me, but you said you traveled as a slave of the Muslims. South of here, you may not own a horse or a weapon. It is the law."

"What about a donkey?"

"Yes, or a mule. But you must dismount when passing important Muslims."

REPORT: EDESSA

Ramiro tried to focus on a long overdue account to Abbot Hugh. He first told him of his capture by the Turks, his escape, his illness and subsequent brush with death. Then he went on to describe the Turk Empire and its vast extent, its power and civilization, its hospitals and universities, its literature, mathematics, architecture and art. And with genuine sadness, he wrote of the assassination of the Great Sultan and his Vizier and how their deaths had caused the empire to spiral into a state of chaos. He told Hugh about the lay of the land, its deserts and mountains, and he told him about the cities of Isfahan, Mosul, Edessa, and Antioch.

But he said nothing of the cross. He had promised Hugh he would deliver it intact. How could he tell him it had been broken and its bloodstone torn out? And how could he tell him it had been remodeled in gold by heretics?

He put his pen down, rubbing his chin. I have said enough. Now I must send a letter to Aldebert. He must be back in Constantinople by now.

THE MESSENGER

Some weeks later, a Byzantine messenger arrived at the Edessa hospital. "May Allah keep you. I am Tatran of Oghuz," he said to the physician. "I'm looking for a man by the name of Ramiro of Cluny."

"He was here for some time," the physician replied. "But he left for Aleppo over a week ago."

Tatran smiled. Ramiro was alive. "Did he say any more about his destination?"

The physician eyed him suspiciously. Whoever this man is, he thought, he is clearly a Turk. "And what is your business, Sayyid?"

"I've been sent by the Roman Emperor to find this man, Ramiro." He dug into his vest. "Here are my papers."

"The Emperor?" the physician asked skeptically as he perused the document, written in Greek. It looked authentic. He raised his eyes. "Ramiro gave me an envelope," he said, looking Tatran square in the face. "He addressed it to a man by the name of Aldebert of Cluny, now residing in Constantinople. Do you know this man?"

"Well, yes, I know him well."

The physician turned to a cabinet next to his desk, retrieving a large envelope made of thick, Baghdadi paper. He put it on the table. "Ramiro asked me to send this on with the next courier going to Constantinople. Perhaps you could deliver it? Otherwise, considering the turmoil these days, it may be some time before I can send it off."

"Of course, Sayyid, I would be glad to."

He handed it over. "Ramiro told us he was going to Aleppo, but he often talked of Jerusalem. His friends from Isfahan have returned to Nikea. That is all I know."

"His friends from Isfahan?" asked Tatran. "What friends are these?"

"Three men from Nikea who, like himself, were imprisoned in Isfahan by the Sultan, may Allah's mercy rest upon his soul. One of them was the Son of Sulayman."

"You mean the boy called Kilich?"

"That's right... that's his name."

Tatran returned to his room. What was Ramiro doing with the Son of Sulayman? How did he get to Isfahan? He paced the floor, he could make no sense of it. Finally, he sat down to scribble words on a small piece of parchment. He waited patiently for the ink to dry before taking hold of the pigeon cramped inside a small cage. It flapped weakly as he tied the note to its leg with a white band. Gently, he placed it on the windowsill, where it fluttered for a while before spreading its wings and venturing off. At first, it flew erratically, and then, with renewed confidence, it soared high into a clear blue sky, heading west for the city of Byzantium.

ALEPPO

The muezzins of Aleppo sounded the call to evening prayer just as Ramiro and Jameel arrived at the northeast Iron Gate with their mule in tow. Ramiro enjoyed the mesmerizing resonance of the *adhan*, its chant instilled in him a sense of mystery and awe. They dismounted and knelt to pray at the side of the road, as did many others. They prayed to the same God and faced the same direction as the Muslims, but in their hearts they turned to Jerusalem.

Prayers ended and the crowd milled through the Iron Gate of Aleppo. The colossal mound of the citadel loomed above them. "Where are your papers?" asked a guard.

Ramiro groped into his bag. "I have them here," he said, bringing out the certificate given to him by the Sultan.

The gatekeeper perused the document, then he looked at Ramiro with some suspicion. "You are Christians?"

"Yes, Sayyid."

"Where are your crosses?"

Jameel reached inside his tunic to bring out his new cross. Ramiro showed him the iron cross he purchased in Isfahan while keeping his golden cross tucked safely inside his vest. He offered apologies.

"Christians must always show their crosses so we know who you are," he scolded. "And you must wear a yellow sash too. Get them at the market."

Ramiro bowed lightly. "Yes, Sayyid," he said, turning away.

The guard held up a hand to stop them. "Wait! I need to see your tax receipt!"

"Tax receipt?"

"The poll tax. Don't play dumb with me."

Jameel tugged at Ramiro's arm. "All Christians must pay tribute to the Emir, Master. Once a year."

Ramiro forced a smile. "Of course, Sayyid. Please excuse me, I am an ignorant traveler."

The man pointed. "Give your names and your money to the scribe. He will issue your certificates."

Ramiro stormed out of the building in long, heavy strides. "A dinar each! That's outrageous!"

"All who are not Muslim must pay, Master," Jameel puffed as he struggled to keep up.

In the Christian quarter of Aleppo, gray brick buildings hemmed the narrow, cobbled streets. There were no windows at ground level and there was nothing to see but stone and brick and flat iron doors. The only exception was the occasional flash of color from bright buds of jasmine and rose blooming in windowpots one story up. Throughout it all, a delightful fragrance of orange blossom wafted in from nearby orchards, dominating the stale air of city life.

The only thing that identified the Christian hostel was a small, brass plate inscribed in Arabic and Greek. The innkeeper was a talkative man and Ramiro had little trouble extracting information from him.

"Oh, no." The innkeeper waved a finger and shook his head. "Do not travel to Jerusalem by way of Damascus. It's too dangerous now. Tutush, brother of the Great Sultan, is taking revenge on all those disloyal to him. Even now, I hear, he prepares an army to ride north against us here at Aleppo."

"Why?" Ramiro asked.

The man raised an eyebrow. "Haven't you heard? Tutush went to Iran to claim the Sultan's throne but returned in disgrace. The emirs of Aleppo and Edessa did not follow him as planned. Instead, they showed their loyalty to the Sultan's son, Berkyaruk."

Ramiro felt a chill as he recalled the angry young prince, Berkyaruk. The last thing he wanted was more trouble. He had to move south, and fast. "I should pay more attention to politics, my friend. So, what route do you suggest?"

"Go south to Maarat before Tutush rides to war. It's the fastest road. Then continue south to Hama and then Homs. From there, you head west through the Homs Gap to avoid Damascus. That will bring you to the coast road where you head down to Tripoli, then Jaffa."

"And from Jaffa, one travels east for Jerusalem." Ramiro interjected, pleased that he knew a little geography.

"That's right. It's a short journey from there." He offered more tea.

Ramiro held up his cup. "I hear the Egyptians might be a problem."

The innkeeper shook his head. "Not yet. They haven't had much say on the coast for some time, except farther south. But not long ago, they ruled the whole seaboard right up to Antioch. They even seized Aleppo for a while." He leaned forward, resting his elbows on the desk. "I think Jaffa may still be ruled by the Egyptians—but not to worry, the Romans still do a lot of business there."

"So you would feel safe on that route?"

"Only God knows what will happen," he shrugged. "Nowhere is safe since the Sultan died. Now everyone fights for themselves, taking what spoils they can."

"And what of Jerusalem? Is it safe?"

"Oh, yes, usually, anyway. The governors change from time to time. Now Tutush rules it, but he prefers to live in Damascus and he's left some cousins to govern... can't remember their names. Idiots, really." He shook his head again. "But I'll bet those Egyptians are just waiting for a chance to seize Jerusalem again."

A SLAVE GIRL

Ramiro strapped on his money belt. The hospital in Edessa had kept all his possessions safe and he was startled when they refused to take any money for his treatment. But in true thankfulness, he insisted on making a generous donation before he left.

"Come, Jameel," Ramiro said cheerfully. "Let's return to the markets for supplies." He donned an expensive new tunic, a blue turban, leggings, and a wool coat before wrapping a yellow sash about his waist. The iron cross hung from his neck with a leather lace. He turned from side to side, admiring himself in the mirror, chuckling at his new appearance. "Then we'll take the road to Maarat." he said loudly. "I talked to the innkeeper yesterday and he said this is a good time to travel that route." He unconsciously put a hand to his money belt. He still had about half the gold given to him by the Sultan, Malik Shah. It all seemed so long ago now.

"Yes, Sayyid, I'm ready," said Jameel, standing behind Ramiro. He was pleased with his new clothes. No longer did he dress in the rough cloth of a slave.

The Aleppo markets sprawled for blocks just south of the Great Mosque. Hundreds of small booths spread throughout the plaza in neat rows. Along the perimeter, more enduring shops of brick and stone offered the finest cloths, silks and satins, wools and cottons, fine leatherworks, bronze and silver dishes, ornate candlesticks, and spices from the Far East.

But little of this merchandise occupied Ramiro's thoughts. He could think only of supplies for his journey south to Jerusalem. Finally, he would be able to complete his mission and see his mother.

"That will be five fals, Sayyid," said the storekeeper.

"Oh, yes, of course." Ramiro studied the coins in his hand. He paid the merchant before handing a few more coins to Jameel. "Here, take this and buy some nuts and cheese for our journey. I need to find some medicines. I'll meet you later at the inn." Jameel ran off, happy to have an important errand.

"Where can I find an apothecary?" he asked the storekeeper as he paid him.

The man pointed past throngs of shoppers and noisy hawkers. "Go to the end of this street. It's near the women's corridor."

Ramiro wandered for some time but could see nothing that looked like an apothecary. And he wasn't entirely sure what the storekeeper meant by "women's corridor." The narrow street wound endlessly through the city but no one he asked seemed to know the way. I must have passed it, he thought.

Coming to an intersection, he stopped, not sure which way to go. The crowds of shoppers had trickled to just a few. He looked around for shops or signs but there were none to be seen. He soon noticed two men watching him from a doorway, so he strode over. "Peace be upon you, Effendi. Tell me please, where is the women's corridor?"

Toros the Armenian looked puzzled but returned a sly smile. "This is it," he said, waving a hand to the door. He looked at Ramiro's fine clothes. "Come inside."

Ramiro stepped into the hallway of a poorly lit stone building teeming with activity and echoing with loud voices. The hallway led to a vast room with a pillared open space. Men and women attired in plain brown tunics sat in groups on the floor while guards with whips strolled between them. He lifted his eyes to one corner of the room. On a raised platform, two men held a naked woman by the arms as she squirmed under the prodding fingers of a well-dressed man, who stuck one finger in her mouth to check her teeth, and then he felt her breasts and inspected her thighs.

Ramiro paled, turning away. Oh, blessed Saints, what have I come to? This is a slave market!

Khuda the Mamluk looked at him suspiciously. "Over there," he growled, pointing to an area where several richly attired men sat on plush cushions. "Please, sit."

Feeling momentarily trapped, Ramiro joined the slave merchants, some of whom nodded in greeting. One of them was a huge, corpulent man sitting on several large cushions while assisted by two muscular slaves.

He moved sheepishly to an outer seat. Red with shame, he turned his eyes from the naked woman to look over the sad lot of dejected slaves waiting to be sold. Most were young men and women. Nearly all were white, a few black. Shameful! Father in heaven, deliver me from this vile place of misery! He bit his lip to stem tears of pity.

He remained quiet as the bartering continued, thinking about how he could excuse himself and leave politely. But it would be bad manners to leave right away so he endured the auction of three slaves before he looked around to see his way out. He was about to get up when something in the crowd of captives caught his eye. In one group, he spotted several women with light hair, some blonde, another red, an uncommon sight in these parts. He looked at the redhead, watching her for a moment or two, curious to see if she was Greek or Latin. The woman turned her head toward him, as if she sensed his presence. She looked straight into his eyes.

Ramiro gawked in disbelief. The blood drained from his head and he began to swoon. No! It can't be! He blinked several times before wiping his eyes and looking again. His heart pounded. Oh dear God! It *is* her! How can this be? Oblivious to his surroundings, he fixed on the woman sitting on the floor. It's Adele! It's Adele!

He bolted up from his cushion. "Adele, it's me!" he yelled out in French. The slave market fell silent, all eyes went to Ramiro.

The woman jolted at the sound of her name, a name she had not heard for some time. She stared at the man shouting at her but did not recognize him. He had a full head of hair and a beard and dressed as a man of leisure.

"Adele! It's Dom Ramiro!"

She knew the voice. She looked into his eyes, those dark, twinkling eyes. In a flood of recognition and distress, she wailed a plea. "Dom Ramiro! In the name of God! Help me!"

Khuda moved up behind her, lashing out with his whip. "Shut up, wench!"

Adele flinched before turning on him in anger, grabbing at the whip. Khuda took hold of her hand and twisted it. She cried in pain and he slapped the back of her head. Then he turned to Ramiro with a snarl. "And you, foreigner! You have no business talking to the slaves!"

"I will buy her!" Ramiro shouted impetuously. "I will pay twice her value!"

Khuda hung his whip near Adele's face. "The bitch is sold already. You are too late."

Ramiro turned to the buyers. "Who bought her? I will double the sum!"

The men shook their heads in disgust. What terrible manners. Cursed foreigners!

Harun the Slaver was outraged. He even forced himself to rise, balancing his bulbous body with the help of his slaves. "May Allah curse you." he cried with flapping jowls. "How dare you! I will have you whipped and thrown into the streets! This woman goes to Antioch—to the House of the Emir, may Allah keep him." His voice grew hoarse. "Your money means nothing to him! Desist!" He fell to coughing.

"Please, Sayyid," Ramiro pleaded. "I will come to any agreement."

Harun waved a pudgy hand in repulsion. "Throw him out!"

Toros marched toward him, resting one hand on his dagger. Khuda came too and they both grabbed Ramiro by the arms, hustling him to the doorway. The buyers laughed as he struggled in vain. Adele slapped her hands to her mouth to stifle a scream.

"No, no, please! We must talk!" Ramiro shouted. More laughter.

The two men opened the door and together they heaved him onto the street. Ramiro spun, tumbling onto the dark cobblestones. Khuda yelled from the doorway. "Don't show your face again, kafir... or we'll gut you like a dog!"

Ramiro barged into his room at the hostel. He was disheveled in every way and his new tunic soiled. Jameel dropped an apple he was eating and backed away.

"Come Jameel! We leave now! Go to the stables to get our mule. We're going to Antioch."

"Antioch, Master? What of Jerusalem? What has happened?"

"Jerusalem will have to wait. I have important business to attend to. I'll explain it all later." He studied the skinny, defenseless Jameel, comparing him to the gnarled slave-driver, Khuda. Secretly, he wished he had a more aggressive companion. "Move now! Pack our bags!"

KHUDA SCHEMES

Harun the Slaver glowered at Khuda. He was flabbergasted. "What? What do you mean you will not renew your contract? Have you been offered a better price? We could renegotiate. I have been good to you all these years. Does that mean nothing to you?"

"Forgive me, Master," said Khuda, "but I tire of slave trading and seek my fortunes elsewhere." He spoke with no hint of regret.

"But what will you do?"

"I leave to join Yaghi Siyan, the Emir of Antioch. He is hiring and pays well."

"You will take up the sword again?" Harun stuffed his wide mouth with baklava, washing it down with a gulp of red wine.

"I always have my sword, Effendi. I am mamluk," he bristled, straightening his shoulders. His short beard had been clipped, his hair washed and braided into four tails, two down the front and two at the back. "The Emir hired me as one of his personal askari. I might even get a diwan."

"A diwan? For how much?"

"Half a percent of taxes."

"Who offered you this?" Harun asked as he picked at his teeth with a little finger.

"Yaghi Siyan's buyer. At the market."

"He's just a buyer," Harun scoffed. "You cannot take his word."

Khuda stiffened. "He's an emissary as well. He came to talk to the Emir of Aleppo about uniting against Tutush."

"Against Tutush?" Harun shook his head slowly. "That sounds like more trouble than three wives."

"My business is trouble, Effendi." Khuda paused to sip his wine. "The emissary hired me to escort his new slaves to Antioch."

"Including that red-haired bitch?" Harun chuckled.

Khuda smiled. "Yes. Who was that madman at the market today?"

"An accursed Christian, I hear. He sure wanted that woman."

"Terrible manners," growled Khuda as he reached for a cake. "And do you remember the mufti? The one who stopped to berate us in the market?"

Harun nodded. "Yes, the one called Ibrahim. Damned clerics. Ranting and raving. Why do they make our lives so difficult? So what about him?"

"The emissary wants me to escort him to Antioch as well," said Khuda. "He says the mufti fears to travel the road unguarded. Those murderous Hashashin have gained much confidence since the death of the Sultan."

Harun snorted. "Well, good riddance to the mufti. That will be another thorn from our side."

There was a long moment of silence before Khuda spoke again.

"And I have another matter to discuss, Sayyid."

"What is it?"

"Toros asked me to approach you. He has served you well and can now pay for his freedom." He paused, watching Harun.

Harun's beady eyes narrowed as he flushed red. "What! What? No! This is too much, Khuda. You are leaving, and now Toros—one of my best drivers! I will not allow it!"

"You have many drivers... besides, it is the custom, noble Harun."

"I curse the custom! Nobody enforces it. Toros stays!"

Khuda lifted his head, tossing a braid over his shoulder. "I am willing to add to Toros' purse. I will pay you more than his value."

Harun shook his head, his jowls flapped. "No, no, I cannot."

Khuda's voice grew cold. "I could take the matter to the judge... or to the Emir himself."

Harun glared at him. "Are you threatening me?"

Khuda glared back. "Maybe the Emir would like to hear about your trading activities outside the city walls?"

Harun turned his head away from Khuda's malicious stare, fear gripping his loins. If the Emir discovered his tax evasion, he would be skinned alive and his bloodied corpse hung in the square for all to see. He felt betrayed. "May Allah damn you! Go! Leave me!"

"We'll camp here." Ramiro gestured to the campsite near a spring of cool water.

Jameel pulled the mule to a stop. "But Master, we are only a few hours from Antioch."

"Nonetheless," said Ramiro. "we will camp here so I can watch the road."

"You look for your lady friend?"

"Yes, Jameel. By the grace of God, they will have to go by eventually. I know we left before they did."

"But what will you do, Master? How will you recognize her? She is sure to be covered and veiled. And even if you do see her, you cannot seize her. They will kill you. And once she's in the Emir's harem, how will you get her out? It's heavily guarded."

"I don't know yet," Ramiro sighed. "I don't know. I will just have to put my faith in God."

"Praise God," Jameel said softly.

"Here they come!" Ramiro whispered.

Jameel rose from his stone seat, rubbing his buttocks. "Praise the Lord, Master.

Finally! It's been two days." He shivered as he looked down the road. "How do you know it's her?"

Ramiro nodded toward the small party. "See the two men riding in front? They're the ones who threw me out of the slave market." He took cover behind a hawthorn. "You stay there."

Khuda the Mamluk and Toros the Armenian, along with Mufti Ibrahim and three more of the Emir's men, escorted a procession of horses on which the slaves rode. Ramiro watched them go by. He could see the women were covered as Jameel had said and he was disappointed, he hoped they would stop at the spring, as many did on this route, although he had no idea what he would do if they did. He stood up. "Let's go. We'll stay a hundred paces behind."

CONSTANTINOPLE

"He lives!" shouted Aldebert. "He lives! Oh, Blessed Mary, Mother of God. He lives!" Tears rolled down his cheeks as he fought to catch his breath.

Commander Manuel put a hand on his shoulder to comfort him. "We will find him. Tatran sent a brief note along with the pigeon. It says Ramiro went to Aleppo and he has gone to follow."

"Aleppo?" asked Aldebert through another sob. "Why?"

"We are not sure," said Manuel, running his fingers through his neatly trimmed beard. "Apparently he heads for Jerusalem."

Aldebert jumped to his feet. "I will go to Jerusalem too!"

"Now wait before you do anything rash," Manuel advised patiently. "He also mentioned that Ramiro had sent on an envelope."

"An envelope?"

"Yes, he entrusted it with one of our caravans heading this way. It should arrive in a week or so."

August 1093

Aldebert studied the large envelope for some time. It vibrated in his trembling hands. Ramiro had written the address in three tongues, Latin, Greek, and Arabic to "Aldebert of Cluny at the Court of Constantinople." He bit his lip to summon his frail courage and, with sudden daring, as if he were about to hurl himself off a cliff, he tore it open. It ripped in half and two sealed letters fell to the floor. "Mother Mary!" he squawked, falling to his knees to pick them up. Only one was for him. The other, much thicker, was addressed to Abbot Hugh of Cluny.

His hands continued to shake as he held Ramiro's letter in front of him. He wanted to open it—but was afraid to. He stared out the window of his small room. The bells of the Church of Sophia pealed in the distance. Can I finally leave? In a fit of anxiety, he fell into a chair before attempting to break the wax seal carefully, but he tore the paper with shaking hands. "Dear, oh dear," he muttered as he unfolded the letter.

> *From Ramiro, Dean of Cluny, to Aldebert of Cluny, greetings in the name of Our Lord Jesus Christ.*
>
> *My dear Brother Aldebert, I pray you have not worried much for my well-being. I have survived these last years as a captive of the Turks and managed to secure my freedom only when the Great Sultan died. At the moment, I reside in Edessa, where I had fallen ill some months ago. By God's grace, I was renewed of spirit and spared to live again in the world of men.*
>
> *Do not seek me out, my friend. It is much too dangerous to travel these roads. I head again for Jerusalem and when I arrive, God willing, you can join me there. When the time comes, you must arrange passage on a Genoese or Byzantine vessel and sail to Jaffa on the coast of Palestine. From thence, travel east to Jerusalem and seek out the Christian area.*
>
> *But if you do not hear from me within the year, you must return to Rome to give a full account of all you have seen and heard to His Holiness, Pope Urban the Second, may God bless his name. Then it is your duty to return to the Abbey to explain events to our Reverend Father. I leave you the vital task of forwarding to him the enclosed letter. This must be done with immediate haste.*
>
> *I pray for your safety.*
>
> *June 12, in the year of Our Lord 1093*

Aldebert jumped around the room like a schoolboy, laughing and crying at the same time. "I'm going to Jerusalem!"

ANTIOCH

Leaving the west gate of Aleppo, Ramiro and Jameel followed the road to Antioch. It skirted the basalt foothills just north of the Syrian Desert, pushing through the mountain pass called Bab Al-Hawa before eventually opening onto the wide Plain of Antioch. To the north, was Lake Antioch, a body of water

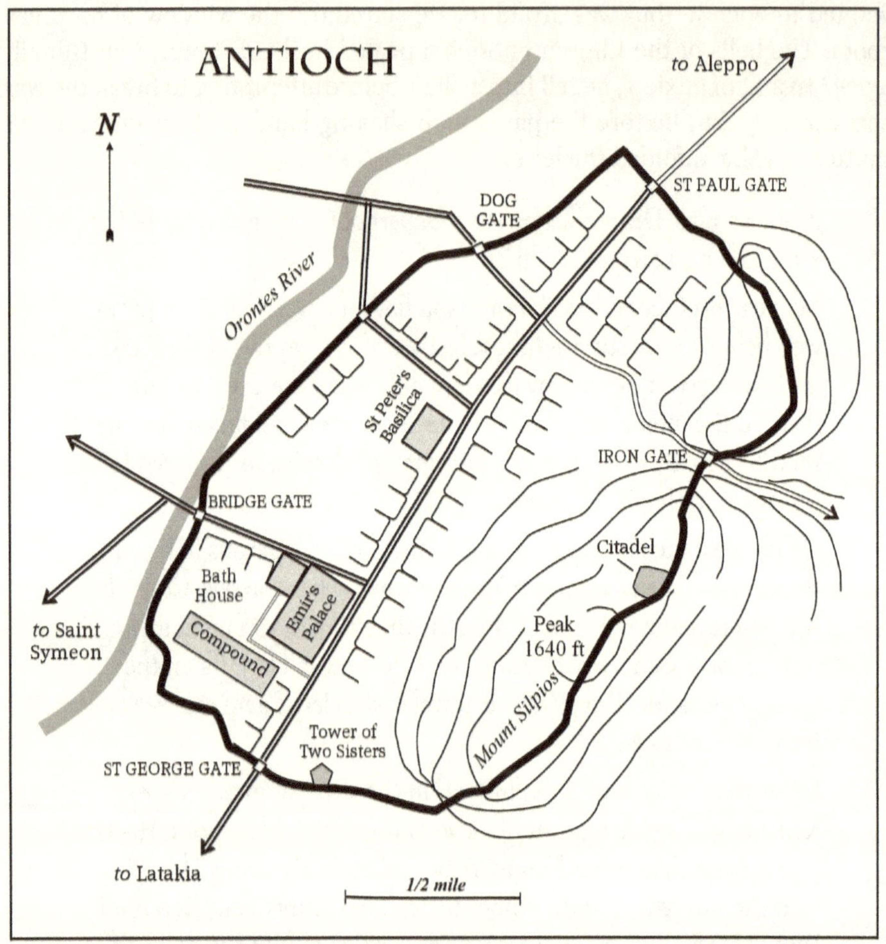

twenty miles wide, glittering like topaz between the mountain ranges. And straight ahead, the Nur Mountains towered more than a mile above the plain.

They pressed ahead, following the Orontes River into the wide gap that ran all the way to the port of Saint Simeon on the Mediterranean coast. And there, at the mouth of this gap, the fortified city of Antioch nestled between the waters of the Orontes and the foothills of Mount Silpios, spreading out onto the flats of the river bend. From this vantage point, it dominated all northern traffic from the Mediterranean Sea to inner Syria.

Since the time of Saint Paul, the city had been Christian. But it fell to the Arabs in 637, was recaptured by the Romans in 969, only to be lost again to the Seljuk Turks nine years before Ramiro arrived. Although long past its moment of Roman glory, it remained a wonder of the ancient world, the cosmopolitan home to hundreds of thousands, most of whom were Greek Christians, even when the Turks ruled.

The commander of Antioch was the fierce Emir, Yaghi Siyan, a Seljuk Turk appointed by the late Malik Shah. He was a wily, seasoned warrior and, by his firm hand, the city enjoyed a period of prosperity and peace.

A HAREM

The enormous walls of Antioch shadowed Ramiro as he made his way through the Gate of Saint Paul. Massive towers studded the fortification walls every hundred paces. Indeed, only the walls of Constantinople could begin to rival their height and extent.

To the east, the battlements climbed up the steep ridge of Mount Silpios, rising sixteen hundred feet above the plain. Along this stretch, at a dip in the mountain crest, there was only one gate, the Iron Gate. From here, the walls continued along the ridge for almost two miles before dropping down the mountain to cross the valley floor at the Gate of Saint George.

Ramiro's thoughts, distracted by the grandeur of Antioch, soon returned to the streets, where noisy shoppers haggled with merchants and boisterous hawkers peddled their wares in Greek, Arabic, and Aramaic. Through it all, he kept a keen eye on the slave procession just ahead, occasionally looking behind to make sure Jameel had not lost his way in the chaotic crowd.

Halfway down the main street, stood the majestic Basilica of Saint Peter, the official residence of the Patriarch of Antioch and one of the few Christian churches not converted to a mosque by the conquering Turks. Ramiro longed to enter its doors but pressed ahead, keeping up with Khuda and the slaves.

Farther south, the opulent Palace of the Emir came into view and, just past the palace, Khuda turned right, heading toward the river. Ramiro rushed to keep up, coming to the corner just in time to see him turn again, wrapping around the palace grounds on a narrow street. And there, the procession came to a sudden halt.

Ramiro dismounted, taking note of his surroundings. The street was eerily quiet compared to the din of the markets. One side opened onto a treed parkway and a bathhouse. On the other side, was the palace, its walls rising up three stories. The slaves dismounted, passing through the palace gate. Two guards slammed it shut behind them.

To avoid scrutiny, Ramiro strolled across the street to the park. Jameel followed. There they sat watching as innocently as they could. "Get out some food, Jameel, and we will have a picnic." Hours passed but they saw no more signs of activity.

Ramiro spotted a patron leaving the bathhouse, the man wore a cross. "Peace be upon you," he said to him. "Can you tell me, Sayyid, what is that building over there?"

"That one?" He nodded discreetly toward the Palace. "That's a wing of the Emir's residence... I think it's his harem. Listen. You can just hear the women in the courtyard. Usually after sunset prayers."

"Thank you, and tell me, where can a Christian rent a room?"

The man pointed north. "In the area around the cathedral."

With careful discretion, Ramiro asked many questions about the Emir and his palace. But exhausted from his daily excursions, he returned to the inn to rest. "It's hopeless, Jameel. It's as though she's disappeared from the face of the earth."

"It's a harem, Master. It's got more guards than the treasury. You will probably never see her again."

"I cannot accept that, my friend. I must find a way."

JOHN THE OXITE

Soft rays of red, blue, and yellow streamed through the stained-glass windows of Saint Peter's Basilica, bathing the smooth tile floors where Ramiro knelt in prayer. He faced the altar, nestled between two massive pillars, and looked up to a life-sized image of a crucified Christ towering above him. After a long wait, he heard someone approach. Rising to his feet, he turned to see the Patriarch, John the Oxite.

A black cylindrical hat rose high on the Patriarch's head and his simple black robe draped loosely to the floor. In one hand, he held a long, black staff capped in gold, while a yellow-gold pendant hung from a thin chain about his neck.

John spoke softly through a long, blonde-gray beard. "Forgive me for interrupting your prayers, my son, but my time is short. Do you seek an audience with me?"

Ramiro bowed. "Yes, Your Eminence, may all the saints keep you. I am Ramiro of Cluny."

"Cluny? That sounds familiar."

"I hail from the Abbey of Cluny in France and, despite my dress and appearance, Your Eminence, which... which I can explain, I am a disciple of Saint Benedict."

The Patriarch raised his chin. "Do you mean to tell me you are a Cluny monk?"

"Yes, Your Grace."

"Well, well." John took some time to look him over. He appeared skeptical. "I would agree, your dress is certainly not that of a monk. Where is your robe?"

Ramiro smiled apologetically. "I would gladly tell you my story, but it would take many hours to relate."

"No matter," John replied impatiently. "Your new Pope is a man of Cluny. Is that not correct?"

"Ah, yes, Your Eminence."

"And tell me, what is the Pope's name?" John tested.

"Why... it is Pope Urban the Second, Your Eminence, born Odo of Lagery and formerly the Bishop of Ostia."

John nodded gently, the top of his tall hat swayed. "So what is it you want from me, Ramiro of Cluny?"

"Well, Your Eminence, to be honest, I... I hope to save a woman from a life of slavery."

"To save a woman? A very odd request, indeed. Perhaps I can take a few moments to hear your story. Come to my office."

John shifted uneasily in his chair. "That is quite a tale, Monk Ramiro." He opened his hands in a despairing gesture. "But you must understand, there is little I can do for you. Our church remains unmolested by the Turk authorities only because so many Christians live and trade here. But make no mistake, the Emir sees us as allies of Byzantium and thus a potential threat. If I begin to meddle in his affairs, it will cause much trouble for all of us. I hope you understand." He rose from his chair. "But please come to worship with us any time you like."

Ramiro stood up, clutching his turban. "Surely, there must be something I can do?" he pleaded in frustration.

"You could ask the Emir for an audience. Though it may take some time. Christians are not often heard at court. It may be best to approach a mufti on the matter."

"A mufti?"

"Yes, a Muslim lawyer. Some of them can be very effective. Once they hear your case, they may present the matter to a qadi, the judges who enforce the Sharia. The Emir has the ultimate say, of course, but his actions are constrained somewhat by the religious courts."

Ramiro nodded politely. "Thank you, Your Eminence. So where can I find a good mufti?"

IBRAHIM AL MUFTI

Ibrahim, the stern-looking mufti who had berated Harun the Slaver on the streets of Aleppo some months before, squatted behind a low table on a slightly raised platform. His big ears stuck out below a white turban, and a gray-black beard almost covered his face. His dark eyes had a fierce look.

Behind him, sat a scribe with a chalk board spread across his knees. Another servant rushed in with lemonade before moving quietly to the side.

"You say you wish to free a female slave owned by the Emir, Yaghi Siyan?" Ibrahim asked in a throaty voice, somewhat taken aback by the odd request.

"Yes, Mufti," Ramiro replied, shifting uncomfortably on his cushion.

Ibrahim worked his fingers through his long beard. "The Emir is a powerful man, this could be very difficult."

Ramiro leaned forward, putting his hands to his knees. "I am willing to pay all I have."

Ibrahim looked him over warily. "Is this woman kin of yours?"

"No, Mufti, but she is the daughter of a dear friend."

Ibrahim tipped his head, wondering if he should probe further into this delicate matter. "Money cannot be the sole issue when it comes to dealing with a wealthy and eminent man like the Emir," he said, staring at the tabletop, "even when the most tactful negotiations are employed." He looked up. "You say the woman is Christian?"

"Yes. Is that a problem?"

"Not really. More lemonade?" He paused to refill Ramiro's cup before he spoke again. "Islam discourages the enslavement of the People of the Book—Christians and Hebrews. This may work in our favor, although the tenet is largely ignored. Tell me, how was she captured?"

"As far as I know, she was taken when the late Abul Kasim seized Nicomedia."

"And I presume this was a holy war?"

Ramiro shook his head. "I don't know. Why?"

"If it was not a holy war, then her capture is illegal."

"How can you tell if it was a holy war?"

"If it was a war against unbelievers, it was a holy war. Who held Nicomedia at the time?"

"The Romans."

"Then holy war could be justified."

Ramiro leaned forward to press a point. "But the Roman King had a pact with the Sultan, and Nicomedia was to remain unharmed and intact."

"Really? Are you sure? Can you verify this?"

Ramiro looked down, slowly shaking his head. "I'm not sure. But it may be impossible to get any verification from Isfahan at this time because of the civil war."

The mufti regarded him with deep, sympathetic eyes. "Then what can I do?"

"Well," said Ramiro with a hint of desperation, "you say that, as a Christian, she may be freed?"

"Ideally this is the case... but it is not always practiced. It is considered an act of great benevolence to free a slave, but most masters demand a good reason. Although..." he paused in thought, "freeing a slave is also seen as a way to expiate sins."

This caught Ramiro's attention, the forgiveness of sins was a Christian specialty. "What sins in particular?"

"Usually murder, or perjury before the courts."

Ramiro sighed heavily. The chances of a Christian bringing serious charges against the Emir were slim at best. "Can we simply ask for her release with an offer of compensation?"

"We can try, but it will take time."

"How long?"

"Maybe a year."

A VISITOR

Ramiro sat in his room reading a copy of the Quran. The lyrical beauty of Arabic always moved him in strange ways—but this copy was written in a fanciful script and he struggled with the elaborate letters. Once in a while, he scribbled a note on thick, hemp paper, which he sorted into piles related to different topics. He pondered on a phrase about slavery and was so absorbed with its meaning that he failed to hear a light tap at his door. The tapping got louder, finally breaking into his thoughts. Book in hand, he wandered to the door, opening it a little. A short man with long, braided hair and a drooping, black mustache stood outside.

"Excuse me, Sayyid," said the man in Turkish. "I am looking for Ramiro of Cluny."

Ramiro beamed. "I am that man, Tatran! My tutor!" He swung the door open and rushed to clasp his hand.

Tatran backed off suddenly, putting a hand to his sword.

Ramiro stopped. "It's me! It's Ramiro!"

Tatran gawked. "Master Ramiro? Is it really you?"

"Yes, yes," Ramiro laughed. "Come in, my tutor. Please, come in."

Tatran entered cautiously, never taking his eyes off Ramiro. "You look so different, like a Christian merchant, Master. I can hardly believe my eyes. And your Turkish is really good."

Ramiro laughed again. "You look well too, Tatran. Please sit. How did you find me?"

"I met your innkeeper in Aleppo. He seemed to know all about you."

"Oh, him. Yes, a talkative fellow. Would you like some wine?"

"Please, Master."

Are you still a warrior for King Alexios?" he asked as he filled a cup.

"Not really. I'm rarely on the front lines anymore. I spend most of my time in negotiations or running errands for the King." He looked down, nodding toward Ramiro's hand. "And you are reading the Quran? May Allah be praised!"

Ramiro smiled a little. "I thought you were a Christian?"

Tatran blushed. "Christian... Muslim. Both praise God, do they not?"

"Yes, they do," he smiled.

"You look fit, Ramiro, although a little thin. We all feared you dead. The Emperor sent me to find you at Aldebert's request."

"Brother Aldebert? Is he well?"

"Oh yes," he nodded. "But he worries very much. He waits like a nervous schoolboy for you to summon him to Jerusalem."

"And what of my servant, Pepin. Is he still with Aldebert in Constantinople?"

"He is still there, but not with Aldebert. They had many disagreements."

"I can imagine."

"Yes. Now he is a horseman for the King."

Ramiro lifted a brow. "Is he now? Perhaps he has found his calling." He motioned to a cushion. "Please sit, Tatran. You must be exhausted from your journey. I'm eager to hear all that has come to pass." He brought out a bottle of red wine and they sat down for a long talk. Tatran briefed him on recent affairs while Ramiro told him of his adventures in the east and of his sickness in Edessa. "So, did you get my letter?"

"Yes, Master, and I sent it forward with reliable men."

"So why do you seek me out, Tatran?"

"Why... to see that you are well, Master Ramiro. To see if you need help. Nothing more. We all feared for your safety." He took a sip of wine. "I thought you may have traveled to Antioch to board a vessel for Palestine, or that you took the road south to Jerusalem."

"No, there is more to it, my friend," he said with a shake of his head. "Although my heart is still set on Jerusalem." He leaned back on the cushions, folding his legs. "Do you remember Louis the Carpenter?"

Tatran shrugged. "I don't think so."

"He was the man who built the catapults at Nicomedia."

Tatran nodded. "Yes... yes, now I do. He was a good man. It was very sad."

Ramiro scowled. "What was sad?"

"Well, Master, you remember when we all abandoned Nicomedia to fight the Patzinaks with General Taticius and your French barbarians?"

"Yes, of course."

"Well, Abul Kasim knew we had left and later that year, he came back with another army. But we had too few men to fight him off, everyone fled. Those who stayed were killed."

"This is old news, Tatran. But are you sure everyone was killed? You never saw Louis again?"

"No Ramiro, not even in Byzantium."

Ramiro was stunned, taking a moment to gather his thoughts. "May God have mercy on his poor soul."

"Yes," said Tatran, shaking his head sadly. "They killed all the men and the old women. The rest they took for slaves."

Ramiro stood up, stepping over to the window. He bowed his head as he thought of Louis and Mathilda. "So that explains how Adele ended up in Aleppo."

"What? Who is Adele?"

"She's the daughter of Louis the Carpenter." Ramiro told him what happened in Aleppo and how he had followed the slaves to Antioch.

Tatran leaned over and put a hand to his shoulder. "You can do nothing now, Master Ramiro. Leave her. I will ride with you to Jerusalem."

"No, no, Tatran, I must rescue the girl. I cannot bear the thought of her suffering as a slave. And it's the least I can do for Louis."

Tatran shook his head. "But what can you do? It's an impossible situation."

"I must free her. Dear God, somehow I must free her. Will you help me?"

Tatran sighed heavily. "So where is she now?"

Ramiro pointed to the western wall of Yaghi Siyan's palace. "That's where she went in," he explained to Tatran. "Somehow we must get her out." He pulled his cloak tight to his chest to fight off a soft drizzle falling in the cool morning air. A dim light signaled the approaching dawn and the call to prayer reverberated through the moist air.

The palace wall sided the narrow street, ending abruptly at the gates, the entrance for servants and goods. Behind the gate, sat two guards.

"So where's the courtyard?" Tatran asked, his narrow eyes darting about.

"Why is that important?"

"The courtyard. The women must have an outside area."

"Well, I don't know," said Ramiro. "And how can we tell?" He looked up. The walls were the height of four men.

"I will climb that tree, Master," Jameel piped in, pointing to a tall oak tree across the street. "Then I can see over the walls."

Ramiro looked up at the billowing tree, which stood majestically near the entrance to the park. "Very well, Jameel. Climb quickly when I give you a signal." They crossed the street and waited until the guards were preoccupied and all was clear. "Now! Go, go! Keep out of sight. You must tell us all you see. Come down when I whistle."

"Yes, Master." He scrambled up a branch.

Ramiro and Tatran sat on a bench under the tree, trying to look like tourists. Within a few minutes, Jameel had reached the upper branches. He stayed there for a long time. The sky cleared.

Finally, they heard women's voices and laughter coming over the walls. At the same time, the two guards came out of the gate to march around the palace perimeter. Sometime later, they passed by again. One of them stared over suspiciously.

"We cannot stay much longer," said Ramiro as he turned his head away.

"I agree. We'll be skinned alive if caught."

The guards talked for a moment, then strolled away to continue their rounds. Ramiro looked up, whistling softly.

Jameel rustled through the leaves and jumped to the ground. Ramiro rose from the bench. "Come! We must leave."

"So, tell us everything you saw, young man," ordered Ramiro after they returned to their small, dim rooms. He lit two candles, placing them on the table. "Ah! Better still..." He grabbed a pad of paper and a charcoal stylus, handing them to the boy.

"But Master! I don't know how to write very well."

"I want you to draw, Jameel. Draw everything you saw."

Jameel held the stylus awkwardly. "Well... um...let's see..."

Ramiro rolled a hand. "Get on with it, boy! Draw the road to start."

Jameel drew two straight lines across the page. Then, wall by wall, in a jittery hand, he drew the western outline of the Emir's Palace.

Tatran could make no sense of it. "Tell us what you are drawing, Jameel."

"Yes, yes," he said in an eager voice. "Here is the building. This is the door where the slaves were taken in. Now, right beside it... to the right..." he pointed, "is part of the grand entrance to the palace. It is very nice, there are many beautiful fountains and wild animals, Master. Just running around."

"Very good, Jameel," Ramiro said impatiently. "But what about the women's courtyard? Could you see it?"

"Oh yes, it is here... on the other side. Did you hear the women laughing?"

Tatran nodded. "That was just after sunrise prayers. It's likely they will come out again after sunset prayers."

"I think you're right, Tatran. The first time Jameel and I were there, it was dusk and we heard them. Do you think we can assume the courtyard is used every day in the same fashion?"

"Probably, except perhaps on Friday, the holy day. These things are generally routine."

"The courtyard is very big, Master Ramiro," said Jameel. "Its wall goes to the end of the street... where you see the gates."

"Can we get around the end of the wall without going through the gates?" asked Tatran.

"Yes," Ramiro replied. "The buildings do not adjoin. There is a passageway lined with mulberry trees." He put a hand on Jameel's shoulder. "What did you see inside the walls, boy?"

Jameel moved his pen to the right. "In the center is a fountain and a small pool, and there are four kiosks around the pool where the women drink and eat."

Tatran scratched his head. "Where are the guards?"

"They are at this end, beside the door to the courtyard. And there are many eunuchs to serve the women."

"Did you see any women with colored hair?"

"Their hair is mostly covered, Master, but I think I glimpsed one or two."

Tatran tapped on the drawing. "The far wall is best—we have the cover of the mulberry trees."

Ramiro threw his hands up. "Then what? How do we know Adele will be there?"

"If she belongs to Yaghi Siyan, it is very likely she will be there," said Tatran.

Ramiro glanced down at Jameel. "Somehow... we must inform her of our plan. Tell me, boy, how old are these eunuchs?"

"They are about my age, Master."

Ramiro smiled. Tatran looked at him, then he smiled too.

Jameel watched them both before his eyes went wide. "Me? You want me to be a eunuch? No, no. That is very dangerous, Master Ramiro, yes, very dangerous. If they catch me they will burn out my eyes with hot irons! Then they will skin me alive! Chop me into pieces!" He went to his knees.

"Get up foolish boy! I will give you a gold dinar."

Jameel's pretty face broadened in a wide smile and he jumped back to his feet.

"Now tell us, what did the eunuchs wear? You must remember exactly."

"Yes, I remember."

"We could give her a letter," suggested Tatran as he swung a braid of hair over his shoulder.

"A good idea, Tatran, but it's unlikely she can read, although she may speak some Turkish or Arabic by now. And Jameel cannot speak French."

"We could draw pictures," offered Jameel.

Ramiro huddled up to the table. "That's also a good idea. We will do just that. And Tatran, you must get another fast horse. This is what we will do..."

HARAM

Ramiro waited for the guards to begin their morning rounds before dodging past the palace gate. Tatran and Jameel quickly followed, and when they reached the corner of the wall, they all darted into the tall mulberry trees growing along its edge.

Without a word, Tatran stooped while Jameel climbed onto his back. Jameel, now dressed like a royal eunuch in billowing striped pants and tunic, put his feet on Tatran's shoulders. He bent down to grab a rope from Ramiro before straining upwards for the top of the wall. He could not quite reach, so Tatran took hold of his feet, raising him up with his arms.

Meanwhile, Ramiro tied one end of the rope to a stiff branch, disguising it as best he could. Then he moved slowly back to the corner of the wall to check the gate and the street, cautiously looking around to see if the guards had returned. He looked back just as Jameel scurried over the top.

They waited in what seemed like an endless wait before Jameel gave the rope a tug, letting them know he was down on the other side. Ramiro peeked around the wall again. All looked clear and he entered the quiet street with Tatran. But they were just around the corner when they heard a shout.

"Stop! Stop and identify yourselves!" Two guards rushed across the street. "Where are you going at this hour?"

"Peace be upon you," said Ramiro. "We enjoy a morning walk before prayers, Sayyid. Nothing more."

"Let me see some identification," he ordered.

Tatran reached into his tunic, bringing out a worn document. He handed it to the guard, who squinted in the morning light as he read.

"You work for the Romans?"

"Yes, Effendi, I come to trade."

The guard looked at him suspiciously, then he turned to Ramiro, noticing his cross. "And yours?"

Ramiro handed him the document given to him by the late Sultan. Then he gave the guard his poll tax receipt.

The guard studied the documents. A surprised look crossed his face. He gave Ramiro a sheepish glance before handing them back. "My apologies, Effendi, but it is my job to check everyone around these gates."

Ramiro smiled. "You do your job well, guard, now go about your business."

Tatran looked at Ramiro in amazement after the guards left. "What is that document you have? It must be of great authority."

"It was a gift from Malik Shah."

"The Sultan himself?" Tatran gawked, tripping over his own feet.

Jameel hid behind a cluster of rose bushes at the far end of the courtyard. He could feel his heart pound against his ribs and began to regret that he agreed to Ramiro's scheme. The courtyard was empty, the air cool. And when he heard the chant of morning prayers, he looked to the sky, praying in Aramaic. "Please, God," he whispered. "Help me now. I will go to church every day."

As the sun rose a hand above the horizon, he heard loud voices. It was the women flowing into the courtyard with the eunuchs trailing behind. For a few moments, he watched them stroll about the fountain while the eunuchs spread out bowls of fruit, hummus, and hot flat bread in the kiosks.

Jameel recalled Ramiro's description of the girl—long auburn hair, hazel eyes, slim, fine features. He studied the women closely, looking for the color of their eyes and hair.

"What are you doing there? You stupid boy." A young woman startled him.

"I'm so sorry, Sayyidah," said Jameel. "I am looking for a brooch lost by another." He pretended to search behind the roses.

"Whose brooch?" she asked.

"Uh... uh... I think her name is Adele, Sayyidah. I am new here."

"You do look unfamiliar," she said, observing him with a puzzled look.

Jameel avoided her eyes. "Adele, Sayyidah, the lady with red hair and hazel eyes."

"Oh, Adelah." She nodded. "The rebellious one."

"Yes, Adelah, where is she now?"

The young lady pointed. "She's sitting in that kiosk, the brooding one. Never says much. Speaks a strange tongue."

"Oh yes, I see her now. Thank you, Sayyidah." He brushed off his pants and tried to relax as he strolled toward the kiosk. He was almost by Adele's side when a concubine sitting near the fountain raised her voice to him. "Boy! Bring me some bread."

"Yes, Sayyidah." He stepped into the kiosk where Adele sat alone. She had a vacant look and did not seem to notice him. He leaned toward her as he picked up one of the plates of bread. "Ramiro," was all he said.

Adele turned, looking at him in surprise. "What?" she said in Arabic.

Jameel held a finger to his lips before he rushed off with the bread. He returned a moment later. "Ramiro," he nodded, saying the name again. Carefully, he reached into his tunic and took out a small sheet of folded paper. He placed it discreetly on the table, putting a plate over it.

Adele looked around nervously. One of the guards seemed to be staring in their direction, so she waited. But when he turned his back, she tilted the plate and snatched the paper, stuffing it into her bosom.

With a nod of his head, Jameel made a slight gesture to the north wall before walking in that direction with a plate of fruit. A while later, Adele followed, pretending to stroll. She wandered to the wall while Jameel offered fruit to others nearby. He caught her eye and motioned with his head to a spot at the top of the wall. She walked under the trees but saw nothing. She glanced back at Jameel with a puzzled look. He motioned upward again with his eyes. She looked up once more, this time spotting the rope before quickly diverting her eyes in fear. Jameel ignored her, continuing to serve the ladies.

Their time ended and the Harem Master called out in a high voice. The ladies of the court rose slowly, keeping their poise as they strolled in procession to the main door. The eunuchs followed, but Jameel held back, slipping into the bushes as the crowd dispersed. When the courtyard emptied, he went over to the rope to pull himself up and over the wall. He lowered himself to the ground with a thump, tore off the eunuch's clothing and slipped on a plain tunic he had left in the bushes.

Adele rushed to her room. She was alone. With shaking hands, she pulled out the paper to have a look before her roommates returned. What will I do? "Oh, dear God. I can't read." The small page quivered in her hands. She looked at it for a time, flipped it upside down and looked again. Then, with another quarter turn, she understood. There was the wall. And Ramiro, dressed as a monk, stood on the far side. She smiled a little when she thought of him. God bless the man! And on the far right of the paper, was a familiar depiction of the sun. Sunset! Tonight! She slapped a hand to her mouth. Mother Mary, give me courage, I beseech you. She heard women laughing and hastily stuffed the note between her breasts.

"You're sure it was her?" Ramiro asked.

Jameel smiled. "Yes, Master. It was her."

"And you gave her the note?"

"Yes, yes, as I said."

Ramiro worried. "I just hope she understands it."

The call to sunset prayers sounded from the minarets. Ramiro knelt on the ground. He said a prayer for Adele and then for Jameel and Tatran. The guards prayed too. Soon they would change shifts.

Prayers ended. Ramiro waited on the bench under the tall oak tree that Jameel had climbed the previous day. Tatran sat on the grass some paces behind him, and Jameel stayed with the horses at the end of the street.

The time had come. The guards walked away and their replacements had not yet arrived. Ramiro crossed the street in brisk strides, coming to the wall where he soon fell in behind the mulberry trees. He heard the women in the courtyard and waited. All fell quiet. Despite the cool night, he dripped with sweat.

There was a tug at the rope. The branch shook and he rushed to hold it still, taking the weight in his hands. He could hear Adele grunting softly as the rope pulled at his arms. She appeared atop the wall and he motioned to her frantically.

A yell came out from the courtyard. "Stop! Stop in the name of the Emir!"

Adele looked behind her, then she looked down in terror. It was a long drop.

"Jump!" Ramiro hissed in French. "For the love of God, woman. Jump!"

"Stop at once!" came another shout.

Ramiro heard the guard's footfalls as he ran across the courtyard. From the gate, another guard cried out. "Who goes there?"

Adele looked behind her again before looking back at Ramiro. In a panic, she opened her arms and leapt from the wall. He caught her fall and they both collapsed flat to the ground. Her long hair fell over his face and he caught the scent of rose. He rolled her off and got to his feet. "Are you alright?" he whispered.

"Yes, Dom Ramiro. What do we do now?" she whispered frantically.

"Come! We must go!" He took her hand and they ran to the street.

Tatran waited nervously by the oak tree. He ran toward them just as two guards came out of the gate. "Take her!" Ramiro shouted. "Take her to Jaffa!"

"I will fight!" Tatran bellowed.

"No! Take her now!"

Tatran hesitated, then he grabbed Adele by the hand and they ran toward Jameel and the waiting horses. Ramiro turned on the two guards, who now drew their swords, shouting to their comrades. He pulled out a knife to threaten them both. They stopped and began to parry with their swords. Tatran reached the horses and Ramiro could hear them gallop away.

Ramiro swung his knife back and forth, trying to fall back toward his mount but the guards noticed and blocked his path. Six more guards ran out from the gate, surrounding him. He held up his knife in surrender before dropping it to the ground. Four guards seized him, beating him down and tying his hands. The other guards ran to the end of the street, but the culprits had disappeared. "Get the horses! Search the streets! Check the gates!"

The Reckoning

Ramiro had committed a grave offense. The harem was sacrosanct, a forbidden place. Apart from the master of the house, the only men allowed into these inviolable quarters were eunuchs, and they were there only to protect and serve. For all others who dared to enter, the penalty was death.

Ramiro clawed at the wall of the cell as he tried to get up. It was pitch black, small and stark. Only a few rays of light pierced through the cracks of a poorly fitted door. He sat on the cold stone floor, rubbing his shoulder, bruised from the fall he suffered when the soldiers hurled him inside. He heard a commotion and soon two of the Emir's askari barged through the creaking door. He looked up. One carried a torch, the other held a whip.

The one with the whip spoke with a snarl. "Before you die, kafir, you will tell us all you know."

Ramiro recognized him, it was the slaver from Aleppo. The one who threw him out of the slave market and onto the street. He said nothing.

Khuda the Mamluk put his whip aside to draw his knife. He grabbed Ramiro by the hair, holding the point to his face. He was about to spit more curses at him when a look of amazement crossed his face. "It's you! The infidel from Aleppo!" He smiled in derision. "The man who wanted the red-haired slave girl," he sneered. "Where is she, you stinking kafir? Where has she gone?"

Ramiro did not respond and Khuda pressed the point of his knife under an eye. "First I will gut you," he smiled with pleasure. The light of the torch flickered across his scarred face. "Then I will peel off your skin, one strip at a time. Do you hear me! You mound of dog shit! Speak now and enjoy a quick death!"

"I... I wish to see the Emir," Ramiro strained to talk.

Khuda looked at his companion. He grinned and the two askari roared in cruel amusement. Then the one with the torch made a fist, striking Ramiro across the head, sending him reeling to the floor. "You arrogant pig!" Spittle flew from his lips. "The Emir does not waste time with thieving infidels." He drew his sword and poked it into Ramiro's side. "Where is she? Who are your friends? Speak!"

Ramiro got to his knees, putting a hand to the side of his head. Blood ran between his fingers. He fumbled into a pocket and brought out the Sultan's document, holding it up for Khuda with a shaking hand. But as he did, the golden cross fell out his vest pocket. He picked it up in a snap and shoved it back into his vest. But the guards noticed.

Khuda grabbed the paper. He held it up to the light of the torch. There was a long moment of silence. "Where did you get this?"

"From the hands of the Great Sultan," Ramiro grunted. "From Malik Shah, may Allah's mercy rest upon his soul."

"Search him," Khuda said to the other askari, who pulled Ramiro to his feet and took all he had, drawing out the golden cross with a low whistle.

"Give it to me," Khuda ordered. The guard handed it over, looking at him suspiciously.

"And look at this," said the guard as he ogled the gold coins in Ramiro's money belt.

"Those are mine," said Ramiro, rubbing the side of his head. "You have no right to take them! I will report your theft."

Khuda wavered, looking again at the paper and then back to Ramiro. He had an angry look, like that of a man deprived of certain pleasures. He had hoped to hack off this man's head, but the document in his hand appeared official and he was loathe to commit some grave offense that may cost him his own head. He motioned to the other askari and they both left the cell with Ramiro's money and his cross. Outside, Khuda barked an order. "Move him to the prisoner's quarter. We will let the Qadi decide his fate."

No one entered or left Antioch without being checked at the gates. And now, with all the trouble after the death of the Shah, security had been tightened even more. The guards at the Gate of Saint George were busy inspecting papers as Tatran and Adele waited in a long line of people, donkeys, and handcarts. A merchant at the front of the line fumbled for his papers and tax receipts. Tatran tried to remain calm, he had his papers ready. He glanced ahead to Jameel. *The boy has his papers too. But what do I do about the girl?*

Adele sat behind him on the horse, covered head to toe in a long, black hijab that Jameel had brought for her. A black veil covered her face, hiding her pale fear. *Where's Dom Ramiro?* she thought anxiously, looking behind. But the veil obscured her vision. *Dear God, where is he?*

Jameel glanced back to Tatran while he toyed with the certificate that Ramiro paid for in Aleppo. He tried to assure himself that all was going well, but he feared for Ramiro. He brought out his tax receipt and put a hand to his cross.

Tatran watched as Jameel showed his papers. Everything seemed fine. There! There he goes through the gate. The boy is safe.

"Papers! Receipts!" a guard shouted.

Tatran handed him his papers.

"And her?" the guard pointed to Adele. He had just been ordered to check all women leaving the city.

"She is my wife, Effendi," he replied in a calm voice.

"Then show me your marriage certificate," said the guard.

Tatran opened his hands in apology. "I did not bring it, Effendi. I was not aware I would need it."

The guard eyed him suspiciously. "What was your business in Antioch? You carry nothing."

"I... I am looking for work, Effendi."

Tatran had hesitated too long. The guard waved his arm and five more guards joined him. "Your wife must remove her veil for identification. We have orders from the Emir. She must dismount."

"How dare you!" Tatran shouted, but he was not very convincing and the guard remained unmoved.

"Remove your veil!"

Tatran studied his surroundings carefully before shrugging his shoulders a little and, with a toss of his head, he ordered Adele to get down. He knew the guards would kill him on the spot once they discovered the truth.

Adele's heart beat in her throat and she felt faint. In shaking movements, she worked her way off the saddle.

No sooner was she on the ground and out of the way, when Tatran jabbed his heels into his stallion's ribs, pulling on the reins at the same time. The horse reared up, flailing its hooves at the guards—a trick he learned from the Normans. The guards fell back and he charged forward, straight through the crowd around the gate. People screamed. Carts crashed to the side.

"Stop him!" the guards yelled. "Stop him!"

The soldiers at the gate began to close in. Tatran barreled towards them, swinging his sword. And then, suddenly, with a signal from his knees, the stallion lurched into the air, vaulting over them all. He landed in another crowd, scattering people in all directions. The guards, blocked by the fracas, could do nothing. And Tatran galloped south as fast as his steed would take him.

"After him! After him!" a guard yelled. Ten askari rushed to mount up and soon thundered out the gate. More people scattered to the sides. They rode hard and fast but Tatran was already out of sight.

Adele kicked and thrashed the guards, trying to escape, but she did not get far. They grabbed her by the arms and she kicked some more. "Let me go!" she screamed. "Filthy pigs! Bastards! God curse you!" The men laughed at her futile struggle and her strange tongue. They tied her hands before dragging her back to Yaghi Siyan's palace.

Jameel, who had been waiting down the road, jumped up when he saw Tatran coming fast. The girl was gone. He sensed trouble, and when Tatran swung his arm in a frantic motion for him to stay behind, he moved into the crowd of traffic to hide. Moments later, the askari flew past in determined pursuit.

Jameel waited anxiously near the road for two days, sleeping at a campsite. But Ramiro never came. I will wait for them in Latakia, he thought tearfully. They will have to pass through sooner or later. But doubt gnawed at him. Will I ever see him again?

ANTIOCH

Spring 1094

Yaghi Siyan gazed out the eastern portal of the Antioch citadel, sitting high on Mount Silpios. Gray clouds billowed in the distance, hovering over the dry hills and wide plains of Aleppo. Deep in thought, he momentarily disregarded the nervous messenger who stood waiting, as he did the council of advisors who sat patiently in the stark war room.

The long creases in Yaghi's aging face seemed deeper than usual and his white hair and beard made him appear old by warrior standards. But his age did not hinder his ambition. He turned to the messenger. "Are you sure about this?"

"Yes, Beyfendi."

"Does Prince Tutush plan to besiege Antioch as well?" He stroked his long beard as he spoke.

"We... we are not sure, Beyfendi, but we think not. He has his eye on the Sultan's throne. He wants to lead an army back to Iran and has no time to waste besieging Antioch."

"Then why did he attack Aleppo and Edessa?" he asked, although he already guessed the answer.

"Because the Emirs betrayed him, my Lord. They did not follow him into battle when he marched to Isfahan last year."

"And they were both executed?"

"Yes, Master, as I reported." The messenger fidgeted. "And now that Tutush has conquered, he claims the loyalty of their men. He will increase the size of his army and march again to Iran, where Berkyaruk stands ready to defend the throne."

Yaghi waved the man away. He turned to his advisors after the messenger left. "May Allah curse him! How long will it be before Tutush takes our heads, too?"

"Some say he made a pact with the Hashashin to kill the Great Shah," said one of Yaghi's sons. "May Allah bring death to their families!" The councilors shuddered at the mention of the Hashashin.

Yaghi Siyan fell quiet for some time. The whole room fell quiet. "All we can do is wait," he said absently, still staring out the window. "We will prepare our defenses and wait. We will see how Tutush fares against Berkyaruk." He looked to his secretary. "What else do you have?" The secretary bowed before handing him a letter. Yaghi pretended to read but his sight failed him. He handed it back. "Read it to me."

The secretary cleared his throat. "It is a letter from the Qadi, my Lord. In this particular case, he has failed to reach a verdict and refers the matter to your judgment, for your personal pleasure."

"What matter is this?"

"It is to do with the trouble we had in the harem, with the one that your right hand owns."

"The red-haired one?"

"Yes, Beyfendi. One of the men was caught and remains in prison."

"That was many months ago. He should have been executed by now."

"Yes, my Lord," the chubby secretary began to tremble, his voice squawked. "But the man possesses authentic papers delivered and sealed by Allah's Chosen, the Great Sultan, may Allah's mercy rest with him. The Qadi cannot determine if the late Shah's document is still valid, Beyfendi. At least, not until a new Sultan takes the throne."

Yaghi frowned a little. "What document?"

"The Christian was a scribe for the Sultan, Beyfendi. This document gives him all the rights of a freeman and says specifically that he is not to be harmed in any way."

"A Christian scribe? Favored in the courts of Isfahan?"

"Yes, my Lord."

Yaghi Siyan returned the Qadi's letter to the secretary. "This may prove amusing. Bring him before us. And bring the Qadi too. The council will decide his fate."

"Please, sit," said Yaghi from the head of the table.

Khuda shoved Ramiro to his knees before the council. After suffering months in the Antioch dungeon, he was pale and thin, his hair and beard disheveled, his movements stiff, his fine clothes in tatters.

Yaghi waved a hand and Khuda stepped back to the wall. A servant offered Ramiro a cup of apple cider, lightly fermented, and he took it with both hands. There was a scent of lemon. He drained the cup and the servant refilled it.

"What... is... your... name?" Yaghi asked slowly in Turkish.

Ramiro cleared his throat. "I am Ramiro of Cluny, my Lord," he replied fluently.

Yaghi had seen Ramiro's iron cross and was surprised when he spoke Turkish. "You have been charged with abducting one of my girls, have you not?"

"Yes, Beyfendi."

Yaghi Siyan turned to his secretary. "Who arrested this man?"

"Why... why the askari Khuda did, my Lord," replied the secretary, pointing to the big soldier standing to the side.

Yaghi Siyan studied Ramiro's document before looking again at Khuda's report. More creases rippled his large face when he scowled. He looked directly at Khuda. "Is this your report?"

"Yes, Beyfendi," he replied in his graveled voice.

Yaghi looked again at the Shah's document. He held it at arm's length. "It states that he was an accomplished scribe in Isfahan and has been discharged with honor, given all the rights of a full citizen of the Empire."

Khuda kept his dark eyes lowered. "Yes, Beyfendi."

"And this is the man who attempted to abduct one of my girls?"

"Yes, my Lord. He plotted her escape from the courtyard." His eyes narrowed.

"Tell the council what you know of this man," interjected the Qadi, who had previously heard Khuda's tale.

Khuda related the story of his encounter with Ramiro in the Aleppo slave market. He told them about the infidel's outrageous behavior.

"Is he related to this woman?" Yaghi inquired.

"I do not know, Beyfendi, but he was desperate to buy the girl."

Yaghi adjusted his jeweled vest as he studied Ramiro. His thick lips curled under his broad, white mustache as he glared at the infidel. "Are you related to this woman?"

"No, Beyfendi."

Yaghi raised his voice. "Yet you dare to invade my harem! I should have you skinned and hung in the market!" He leaned over, rapping a knuckle on the low table for emphasis. "What do you say in your defense?"

Ramiro cleared his throat. "May Allah look kindly on your mercy, Great Emir," he said meekly before telling them briefly of his journey across the Balkans and how Adele had accompanied them to Constantinople as the daughter of a tradesman and a dear friend. He recounted that Abul Kasim had seized Nicomedia when the Romans left it undefended in order to fight the Patzinak barbarians. And that Abul had enslaved the women and children of Nicomedia. "I felt a moral obligation to free her, Beyfendi, despite the danger."

Yaghi scoffed. "You are a brave man, scribe. But you are more a fool. You accomplished nothing."

Ramiro had a rush of foreboding.

Yaghi Siyan smiled as if reading his thoughts. "I still have my girl. She was captured at the gates."

Ramiro lowered his head as the truth set in. He had failed. A crushing wave of disappointment swept over him. He could think of no reply.

"Is this all you have to say for yourself?" Yaghi taunted.

Ramiro had a sudden thought and forced himself to remember what he had read in the Quran as well as the conversations he had with the mufti, Ibrahim. He raised his head slowly. "If I may speak boldly, Beyfendi, I feel her capture and enslavement may be contested on two points."

"Go on," said Yaghi, somewhat amused.

Ramiro held out his hands in a gesture of appeasement. "Council members, I cannot profess to know the law as you do. I am a Christian, as is the woman now in our Lord's possession. But does not the Sunni faith discourage the enslavement of the People of the Book? Does not the Prophet, may Allah exalt him, show mercy for these people?" He paused for effect.

The council was astonished. They marveled at the barbarian's Turkish. But the Qadi, a corpulent man who covered his drooping shoulders and big belly with the most expensive silks, was not impressed. He shouted in anger. "Only if the infidels accept the domination of Islam!"

Yaghi waved him down. "And what is your second point?"

Ramiro glanced up at the long-bearded Qadi as he took more cider. "My second point, Beyfendi, is that the woman's capture cannot be justified by holy war. Abul Kasim's capture of Nicomedia was against the wishes of the Great Sultan, who was negotiating a pact with King Alexios at the time. Abul's foray was not a holy war and cannot, therefore, be used to legitimize the woman's enslavement."

The councilors chatted among themselves, some arguing loudly. Yaghi Siyan quieted them before turning back to Ramiro, smiling condescendingly. "You are indeed a man of letters, Ramiro of Cluny, and you defend your points with eloquence... for a Christian. I will consider leniency." Most of the councilors nodded in agreement.

But Ramiro was not finished. "If you accept my arguments, Great Emir, I wish to negotiate the girl's freedom."

There was a hubbub from the council. Yaghi sneered, taken aback. What impudence! But he took a moment to reflect on his personal experiences with the barbarian slave girl. What trouble she is! Wild and untamed! Like a feral cat! She brings nothing but grief to my household and refuses to submit, despite the lash of my whip. He pulled himself from his thoughts, studying Ramiro with some suspicion. "What makes you think you can buy her? I could save myself this trouble and take your head tomorrow."

"But my Lord," Ramiro pleaded. "Does not the Holy Quran say it is good to free slaves, as the Prophet himself did? That your sins will be forgiven?" He looked straight into Yaghi's eyes.

Yaghi stirred uncomfortably under Ramiro's dark gaze. Many sins filled his mind and he felt embarrassed, as if Ramiro had brought them into the room for all to see. A flicker of fear crossed his face before he composed himself.

Ramiro continued. "And does not Allah urge you to 'Force not your slave-girls to prostitution so that you may seek enjoyment of the life of the world, especially if they would preserve their chastity'?"

The men were aghast. Never before had they heard a dhimmi recite a passage from the Quran, especially in challenge to the Emir himself. All heads turned to Yaghi Siyan to see his reaction.

Yaghi found himself in an awkward position. At this point, to deny Ramiro's eloquent and just request would look miserly. He sought to gain face. "You cannot afford to buy her," was his response.

"But I can, Beyfendi, if you return my money."

"Your money?" He motioned to his secretary. The secretary shuffled his papers, pulling one out. It was an accounting of Ramiro's possessions. "How much?" Yaghi asked in amazement. The secretary showed him the figure and his eyes went wide.

Yaghi turned to his councilors. "It seems the man can indeed afford the girl. What is your opinion, my Councilors?"

"Let it be the will of Allah," said the Qadi, glad to have this case settled. "But an unwed Christian cannot own a female slave unless he marries her." The others nodded their agreement.

Ramiro sputtered. "Marry her? But Beyfendi ... no, no, I... I cannot!"

"You must," the Qadi huffed. "It is the only honorable thing to do."

"But I am a..."

"Enough!" Yaghi shouted, silencing the room. He was pleased to save face, get rid of the girl, and get his money back. "You will pay the price and marry the girl, or I will have you both executed before the sun sets!"

Ramiro bit his tongue and lowered his head. "As you command, my Emir." He paused for a moment. "And if it pleases my Lord, will you return my cross for the wedding?"

"What cross? You are wearing it."

"No, Beyfendi, the other one, the golden cross. It must be in the report."

The secretary read through the list again. He shook his head. Yaghi Siyan opened his hands apologetically. "There is no golden cross listed here."

Ramiro, taken aback, was stunned for a moment. Then he turned to look at Khuda, but the man did not look back. He pointed to him. "He has it, Beyfendi. He took it from me at the gate."

Khuda looked down, glaring at him, a piercing glare. His right hand twitched near his empty sword sheath and his lips curled in a snarl. He could barely contain his indignant fury and almost lurched at Ramiro before stopping himself.

Yaghi noticed, as did the others. "Is this true, Askari?" he asked Khuda.

Khuda shook his grizzled head. "No, Master. He must have dropped it outside the wall when he was about his thieving business."

"Liar!" Ramiro shouted.

The councilors gasped. Khuda lunged at Ramiro but several guards jumped in to hold him back.

"Enough!" Yaghi shouted to Khuda. "Leave! Now!"

Khuda's face turned to stone. "Yes, Beyfendi, may Allah bless your name." He bowed stiffly and turned to leave. As he did so, he hissed at Ramiro. "I will see you die a slow death, kafir!"

Yaghi fumed. "And you!" he pointed a finger at Ramiro. "You are in no position to call any Muslim a liar. You will show respect for your masters! Or you will not live another day to worship your vile mother goddess!" He turned to his guards. "Get him out of here!"

A RELUCTANT GROOM

Yaghi Siyan wasted little time. He arranged for the Patriarch himself to marry them in the Cathedral of Saint Peter.

Ramiro grappled with his faith. Marry her! In his heart, he knew this was what he had secretly wished for over the years. But I'm a disciple of Saint Benedict! I have taken sacred vows... a vow of chastity and obedience. He recalled the synod at Melfi, where Pope Urban and the bishops decreed that no clergy were to marry or take concubines. Blessed saints! But for the love of God, what choice do I have? Is it worth our lives?

Adele wore a full-length, white dress with long, draping sleeves. A white shawl and veil covered her head. Although Ramiro was a reluctant groom, he still wanted to please her, so he had it made especially for her, French style.

John the Oxite faced them both. "You will exchange your rings now."

Ramiro and Adele did so, giving each other a slim gold ring.

"Have you, Ramiro of Cluny, a good, free and unconstrained will and firm intention to take to wife this woman, Adele, daughter of Louis the Carpenter, who you see before you?"

"I have, Reverend Father," said Ramiro, his stomach churning.

"Have you promised yourself to any other woman?"

"I have not promised myself, Reverend Father."

No sooner did the ceremony end when Yaghi's men whisked them back to the Emir's compound, where they were given a spacious apartment and were expected to consummate their marriage.

Ramiro was visibly agitated. He wandered to the balcony while speaking to Adele in a loud, distant voice, as if she were a complete stranger. "The rooms are pleasant enough," he said with too much affectation. "And we have a nice view of the gardens from the balcony... and the baths are just down the hall... and... and we will have a servant assigned... and..."

"And we are alive, Dom Ramiro," she said kindly.

Hesitating, Ramiro turned around to face her. She tugged at her shawl. It slid from her head, leaving long, soft curls draping across her shoulders. At twenty-three, she was no longer the innocent, young girl he once knew, although her enchanting beauty still unnerved him. And she still had a determined fire in her eyes. "Please... please, Adele, just call me Ramiro."

Adele stepped towards him, taking his hands in hers. He stiffened and started to pull away, but he could not. Just the touch of her electrified his whole being with emotion and desire. She smiled. "I owe you my life, and for that I am truly grateful."

Ramiro caught the scent of bergamot orange. He could feel the warmth of her body, her face was so close. He tried to look into her eyes but could not find the courage, lowering his head as he spoke. "Thank you, Adele. And I am grateful that God brought your affliction to my attention." He raised his head again.

Adele smiled, raising thin red eyebrows, her hazel eyes sparkled. "Tis surely God's fate," she said. "And we should make the best of it."

"Yes, yes, of course." He gazed at her full lips. It was all he could do not to embrace her with a passionate kiss. But he lowered his head.

"Am I that ugly that you cannot look at me, Ramiro?"

He raised his head, his eyes went wide. "No, no, not at all, Adele. Forgive me, I think you are a... a beautiful woman. But I am unused to a woman's presence, especially one so near."

Adele, still holding his hand, led him to the cushions lining one wall and motioned for him to sit. "Well, you better get used to me, at least for a while," she said as a matter of fact. "And we can't go on not looking at each other when we speak." Her small nose wrinkled with a light-hearted smile.

He dared to glance into her eyes. "Of course." He looked away, then he looked back again. "Just give me some time to get used to it."

She looked at him sympathetically before rising to her feet and swinging out onto the floor, gliding in a slow pirouette, her white dress billowing in front of him. "I'm going to change my clothes," she said, stopping suddenly in her turn. "And you, my husband, should call the servants for some food and drink."

"Uh... yes... very well." She looked like an angel.

"And then you must think of a way to get us out of here."

Yaghi Siyan summoned Ramiro to his war room. Only his atabek was with him. "Sit down," he ordered.

Ramiro squatted on a cushion.

"You spent some time in the courts of Isfahan. Is that correct?"

"Yes, Beyfendi."

"Tell me what you know. What of Berkyaruk? Do you think he will take the throne?"

"He is young, strong, and ruthless, my Lord. And many men flock to his call."

"Do you think Tutush will defeat him?"

"I don't know. But the mamluks of Isfahan will not harken to Tutush. He is seen as a rebel and a troublemaker." Ramiro went on to discuss matters of court, the murder of Nizam by the Ismailis, and then the death of the Shah under mysterious circumstances.

Ramiro's mention of the Hashashin again sent a nervous shiver through Yaghi Siyan. He was all too aware that these fanatical assassins had a stronghold just to the south of him, in the hills of Lebanon. "Now tell us what you know about the Romans.... will they attack Antioch?"

"I have heard little, Beyfendi. I know only that the Roman King looks to hire mercenaries from the West."

Yaghi Siyan asked him many more questions. When he could think of no more, he ended the discussion abruptly.

"My Lord," said Ramiro as he stood up. "I have received my money but not my cross. Will it be returned soon?"

Yaghi waved a hand of dismissal. "You were told it was not on the list. I will hear no more of this. Leave me."

Ramiro bowed and left.

The door closed. Yaghi fumed. "I do not trust him," he said to his atabek.

"But the Great Shah trusted this man, Beyfendi," said the man.

"And the Great Shah is dead! This man knows too much. What if he returns to the Romans?" He stroked his long beard. "We will keep him here for a while until things settle down."

"As you command, Beyfendi. And what of the Romans? What will we do?"

"You heard the infidel. The Roman King plots against us. I know it!" He stood to gaze out the window. "Send more spies to Constantinople! Damned Christians! May Allah curse them all!"

Months passed and Ramiro waited patiently for Yaghi Siyan to release them, but no word came. He asked time and again for an audience, but his pleas were ignored. They were prisoners, that much was clear. But it was not an unpleasant prison, their rooms were luxurious, servants cooked and cleaned for them, and almost anything they desired could be had by sending one to the markets.

Their rooms formed part of a large compound situated across from the palace.

It housed favored prisoners, servants, and staff, as well as the askari of the Emir. It had only one entrance, which was heavily guarded. But they were free to roam the lush courtyard with its gardens and fountains and here they soon discovered many others in the same predicament, people of position who had fallen out of favor with Yaghi Siyan.

At first, Ramiro and Adele settled into an awkward existence. He slept on a mattress on the floor of another room while she took the bedchamber. He managed to acquire some books and stationery and occupied his time reading and writing. Adele went about collecting a new wardrobe and dedicated much of her time to sewing and embellishment. In the evenings, Ramiro would try to teach her to read and write, but she was not an eager student of letters.

Adele was glad to be out of the harem but she was not entirely happy. Ramiro showed little interest in her and kept his conversations formal and aloof. Nonetheless, she could sense his eyes on her on many occasions and wondered about his affections. Sure, he was a monk, but now they were legally married. What now? Years ago, she had grown fond of him and she thought he felt the same. And why had he gone through so much trouble and danger to rescue her if only to disregard her now in such a lukewarm manner? She was still attract-ed to him, even more so as she came to know him intimately. He was kind and strong, a resolute spirit who showed no fear of life's travails. How she longed for his love and attention—just one embrace.

Ramiro was obsessed with her. Every time she swished and swayed past him, he could barely refrain from reaching out to pull her into his arms. Her lit-tle movements and quaint mannerisms were a rhapsody to his heart. But he could not reconcile his faith and turned to his books for comfort and distrac-tion. With considerable effort, he dismissed the seductive demons harassing his troubled mind and constantly reminded himself of his sacred vows, taken in the sight of God. He thought of the Abbot and the Pope. They had trusted him. How could he betray them and all that he had vowed? But now he had made another vow, a vow to Adele.

With a distracted look, Adele picked away at a salad of banana, mango, and watermelon. She gazed over the balcony, across to the verdant gardens of the Palace. "Why is life so full of horror and fear, Ramiro?" she asked without mov-ing her head.

Ramiro looked up from his writings. So far, he had learned that Adele and her parents fled Nicomedia only to be caught by a band of highwaymen who put Louis and Mathilda to the sword before carrying her off into slavery. She was held at Nikea for more than two years before being traded off to Harun in Alep-po. Ramiro could not begin to imagine the treatment she had endured at the hands of her captors and she showed little inclination to discuss it. He tried to think of something heartfelt to say but felt constrained. "Because men refuse to accept the peace of God," he said after some thought. "Not to mention greed and selfishness."

Adele shook her head sadly. "How can so many men profess to follow God in word but not in deed? How can they be party to such atrocities?"

"Weak minds lack the courage and conviction to live righteous lives," he said softly. "They justify their actions to suit their own evil plans. These are the worst of men." He put down his pen to stretch his back.

She gazed into her fruit bowl. "Do you think Yaghi Siyan will ever let us go?"

"We can only pray. Somehow, I must get to Jerusalem. But first I need that cross." He looked down to his desk, askew with books and papers, books to translate, letters to write. But the Emir allowed no letters out and he thought of the futility of it all. And God knows, the Abbot must think him dead by now.

ROME

October 1094

Aldebert waited anxiously in Constantinople, hoping to receive Ramiro's promised letter from Jerusalem. But it never came. In his previous letter, which Aldebert had received over a year ago, Ramiro instructed him to leave for Rome in a year if he heard no further word from him. Now he began to fear the worst.

Did Ramiro mean to wait a year from July when he wrote it? Or from the date I received the letter, three months later? He convinced himself it must be the latter and used this excuse to wait until October. But now that time had come and he could wait no longer, winter was upon them and this was his last chance to sail to Italy until next spring.

And so, with a heavy heart, he returned to Rome to tell the Pope all that had transpired in the Greek kingdom, just as Ramiro had asked him to do. But after this, he did not return to Cluny as instructed. He knew that, if he did, Abbot Hugh would never allow him to leave the monastery again. So he dallied in Rome for a time, given the task of helping the bishops re-establish themselves in the Lateran, which was now in the hands of Pope Urban. It was here that he encountered the Bishop of Apulia, the same bishop he had met years ago at Melfi.

"You cannot stay here indefinitely, Brother Aldebert," said the Bishop. "And you cannot go to Jerusalem. You are Benedictine and you must receive permission from your Abbot."

"Yes, Your Grace," said Aldebert plaintively. "But it is my heart's desire to go. I know Father Ramiro will send another letter."

"You have said this many times. How do you know he's still alive?"

"I feel it in my bones, Your Grace."

"Well, I sincerely doubt that such an argument will hold sway with Abbot Hugh. And my duties here are fulfilled. I must return to Bari and my diocese."

"Please, Your Grace, help me to compose a letter to the Abbot. If I cannot go to Jerusalem, perhaps he will let me stay to serve you in Bari?"

"That is unlikely, Brother Aldebert," he sighed. "But he may be satisfied to let you join the Allsaints Abbey at Valenzano. It is Benedictine and is just a few miles from Bari.

"Thank you, Your Grace," Aldebert beamed. "Thank you."

"And since you seem to know more about affairs in the East than many of us, I will let the Abbot know how indispensable you are to me as an advisor. But if he declines, you must return to Cluny. Is that understood?"

Aldebert bowed his head. "Yes, Your Grace."

Antioch

March 1095

There was a rap on the door. "Come in!" Ramiro shouted. A servant entered with a covered silver tray. "Your hot meals, Sayyid."

"Thank you, Boris."

Boris, a graceful man, swept through the room like a gentle breeze, placing the tray on a low table surrounded by four cushions. "You will enjoy this, Sayyid. It is a special Magyar recipe, just like I used to have at home."

"What is it?" Ramiro asked as he lifted the lid a little.

"Chicken and rice, very good."

"Boris... how can you claim this dish is Magyar? I've eaten chicken and rice from Constantinople to Isfahan."

Boris lifted his chin in defiance. "This is a special dish, Master," he said as if he had a personal hand in its creation. "With special Magyar spices."

Ramiro smirked. "My dear man, do you know that chicken and rice come from Hindustan, not Hungary?"

"Humph! You are so smart, Master Ramiro. Sometimes too smart." Boris turned to Adele, motioning to a cushion. "Please Sayyidah, please sit and try it." He lifted the lid. "It is the spices that are so special," He looked askance at Ramiro in mild defiance.

Adele smiled. "Thank you, Boris. It does smell good."

Ramiro ignored the meal. "Sit down, Boris," he commanded. "Tell me again all that you have seen and heard."

Boris put the lid aside and sat down uneasily. "I really should not be speaking with you about such things, Master."

"All I want is news, Boris," Ramiro smiled congenially. "Nothing more."

"Your supper will go cold, Sayyid." He squirmed on the cushion.

Ramiro smiled. "It is weeks since we have had a good chat, Boris. Tell me, has Prince Tutush won the throne in Persia?"

Boris glanced briefly into Ramiro's dark twinkling eyes. "Oh no, Master Ramiro, Tutush was killed by his nephew, Berkyaruk, who is now the new Sultan."

Ramiro whistled. "Tutush is dead? By all the saints! What now? Has any peace returned to Syria?"

Boris shook his head. "Oh no, Sayyid. It is worse. Now Berkyaruk is too busy fighting his brother to worry about us. There is no peace. They all fight."

Ramiro tasted his supper. "What will happen to Syria now that Berkyaruk rules the Turk Empire?"

"I don't know. Now that Tutush is dead, his sons squabble over his cities."

Ramiro shook his head slowly. "Can they not rule together?"

"That is not the custom, Sayyid. Two swords cannot fit in one sheath."

"My Lord! What a mess!"

Boris nodded. "Yes, and now Yaghi Siyan has formed an alliance with Damascus." He paused. "But Kerboga sides with Aleppo."

"Wait a minute, Boris. Who is Kerboga?"

"Kerboga rules Mosul."

Ramiro frowned. "It is all very confusing," he said quietly. "So... if I have understood you correctly... does this mean that Antioch and Damascus are allied against Aleppo and Mosul?"

"It seems that way for now, Sayyid... are you going to eat?"

"What of the coast? Is the route to Jerusalem safe?"

"No, no. The Egyptians have taken many cities on the water—they claim the entire coast south of Dog River. There is no peace." Slowly, Boris looked around the room, and then he whispered. "I have heard they were here."

"Who?"

"The Egyptians, the Fatimids. They came here to speak with Yaghi Siyan."

"Why?"

"He needs their help to defeat Aleppo. People are very nervous. Pilgrims fear to travel."

"This chaos bodes ill for Syria," said Ramiro. "The Turks fight among themselves. Everyone is weak. And the more they fight, the weaker they get. Soon, no house or road will be safe."

Boris nodded. "Yes, Sayyid. Even now, many flee their farms for the safety of city walls."

"Ramiro," said Adele as she dabbled with her food. "Eat. Leave poor Boris alone."

"Yes, love." He turned to Boris again. "And what of the West? Have you heard anything about the Romans?"

"I know they have taken ports along the Aegean coast since the death of the pirate Chaka. And they still hold Cyprus. So this too, has Yaghi worried. He fears a naval strike from Cyprus. He knows the Byzantines have built many ships, and the Genoese side with them."

Ramiro furrowed his brow. "What of Nikea?"

Boris pursed his lips, shaking his head. "I haven't heard much. Except that the Son of Sulayman still holds it."

"Thank you, Boris. Keep your eyes and ears open." He handed him a silver coin.

The Law

Mufti Ibrahim was unaccustomed to house visits, especially to the home of a Christian. But he found himself unable to turn down Ramiro's request since he had already been paid well for his advice and, furthermore, he knew Ramiro could not come to him.

"I have presented your case to the Qadi," said Ibrahim. "But you have made my pleas for clemency less forceful by interfering with another man's woman and violating sacred customs."

"I understand, Mufti," said Ramiro. "But now I have done all that is asked by the Emir. I have wed the woman and paid the fines. Am I not redeemed? On what charges can he still hold me prisoner?"

Ibrahim smiled politely as he brushed a crumb of almond cake from his white tunic. "The Emir needs no pretense to hold you, he can do as he pleases. The best we can hope to accomplish is to convince him you are no longer a threat."

"What threat can I possibly be to the Emir? I have no power, no position—the Christians here are Orthodox and will not follow my lead."

"The Emir, may Allah keep him, must see some advantage to your detention, although I must admit it is unclear to me."

"Is there nothing contained in Sharia or the Hadiths that could aid my case? Can I ransom myself?"

Ibrahim shook his head. "Only if your master agrees."

"What of the expatiation of sins? Surely the Emir has transgressed the laws of Islam at one point or another. Is there no way we could use this to our advantage?"

"I have tried to position your case in this way. But you must realize it puts me in a very delicate and possibly dangerous position. My pleas were dismissed. Nonetheless, I am impressed by your knowledge of the Quran. And this brings to mind something that may help your case considerably."

"Really?" asked Ramiro, pouring more tea. "And what is that?"

Ibrahim held up his cup. "You must become a Muslim," he said as a matter of fact.

Ramiro looked up suddenly, missing the cup and pouring hot tea on the table. "A... a Muslim?"

"There is no other way, Ramiro. Yaghi Siyan would be very pleased, and the Qadi too. It is the best way to ensure your release."

Ramiro shook his head as he lowered the teapot. "I value your advice, Mufti, but this is asking too much. I have taken solemn vows. I have dedicated my life to the teachings of Jesus."

Ibrahim opened his hands in appeal. "Understand that Muslims do not revile Jesus. We believe he was a great prophet. You are asked only to uphold the seven pillars of Islam. One of which is to assert that Muhammad was also God's prophet—his last prophet."

"With all due respect, Mufti, it does not appear that simple to me. There are many divisions in Islam, are there not? How am I to know what to believe?"

"And there are many divisions among Christians." Ibrahim retorted. "Does that dissuade you? Besides, there is only one True Faith in Islam—and that is Sunni."

"So you say, but I'm sure the Shia would not agree."

Ibrahim's cup shook in his hand and the muscles of his jaw drew taut. "Heretics!" he hissed. "Blasphemers!"

Ramiro held up a hand to calm him. "Of course, Mufti, of course. I was only pointing to the differences."

"Yaghi Siyan is Sunni," Ibrahim explained with condescension. "The Turks are

Sunni. Only becoming a Sunni will guarantee your release." He rose suddenly from his cushion. "That is my proposal. I must leave you now."

Ramiro followed him to the door. "I will consider your proposal, Mufti. In the meantime, can I count on your continued support?"

"We will see," he replied brusquely.

CONSTANTINOPLE

Emperor Alexios leaned over in his saddle, swinging hard. There was a resounding whack and the leather ball streaked between the goal posts. The crowd cheered and his teammates raised their polo mallets in victory. He pulled hard on the reins of his Palomino stallion. It whinnied, skidding to a halt on the dry grass before rearing its front legs high in the air. "A good game, Taticius!" he shouted. "Your team played well."

Taticius held his excited mount steady. He bowed his head slightly, sunlight winking from his iron nose. "Not as well as yours, my King... congratulations."

Alexios pulled his horse around, looking over to his wife, Irene, who smiled and waved back. A lock of blonde hair draped from her headscarf. He dismounted, walking over as the crowd began to disperse.

Irene rose from her chair, taking his hand. "You were wonderful, darling. I so seldom get to see you ride."

"He rides like a Turk," huffed Anna, who sat next to her.

Alexios smirked. "The Turks ride well, mother. We would win more battles if our men could do the same." The thought of the Turks brought Alexios' thoughts back to his struggling Empire.

Anna clicked her tongue in disapproval. "We must talk, Alexi."

"I have sent letter after letter to the Pope!" Alexios shouted in his war room. "I have pleaded for help. I have told him the heathen Turks hold Jerusalem and have desecrated the Holy Sepulcher. Indeed, that they have desecrated the Holy Land itself!"

"Patience, my son," Anna consoled. "Pope Urban has just regained the Lateran from the Germans. Give him more time. Even now, we hear, he gains support in the north of Italy."

"We are out of time, mother. Now is the time to strike. We have destroyed the Patzinaks and the Kumans. Thrace and Bulgaria are again in our hands. And we have rid ourselves of that pirate, Chaka." He smiled. "Murdered by the Son of Sulayman, his own son-in-law!" The men laughed.

Alexios continued with convincing force. "And now the Turks are weak. They fight among themselves." He swung his arm in a wide arc. "Now that we have regained the Aegean, we can afford to put some pressure on young Kilich. We must devise a way to occupy Nicomedia once more, and then take Nikea." He paused. "And then we will besiege Antioch." His men stirred in their seats.

"Antioch?" said Isaak. "How many Kelts did you ask for?"

"As many as I can get, brother. If we can find more men to fight like those barbarians, we could take Nikea and then head straight for Antioch."

John Doukas spoke up. "But you know the Kelts are trouble, my King. They are difficult to control."

"You're right, John. But they fight like a pack of dogs... and we have few good fighting men left."

Isaak shook his head. "You cannot trust them!" he hissed. "Have you already forgotten that weasel, that... that Norman bastard, Guiscard? They'll take your money with one hand and stab you in the back with the other. All the while claiming it is God's will!"

Anna raised her small chin, her ashen-blonde hair tied at the back. "I agree, Isaak. I believe they are the most deplorable race of men." She pointed at him with her quill. "But what do we do? Are we content to let the heathen Turks hold Nikea, only miles from Constantinople? Every day they harass us."

"But we don't need the Kelts to take Nikea." Isaak protested. "Kilich is not that strong. We should gather up all our fighting men and make an assault."

"Then what, dear brother?" Alexios joined in. "Once the new sultan strengthens his hold, he will return in force to retake Asia and all of Syria. We need to establish our positions now—and then begin to reinforce them. But to do that, we need more men. That's why we need the Kelts. That's why we must take this chance, a chance to regain the full extent of the Roman Empire. It is our God-given right!" He slapped the table with the palm of his hand. "We must attack now!"

John interrupted in a calm voice. "So what have you heard? Will these Kelts come?"

Alexios stroked his red beard. "Pope Urban is holding a council at Piacenza and I have sent representatives to plead again for help. I have made the atrocities of the Turks abundantly clear."

"What's this council all about?" John asked.

"The Pope is consolidating his power. Many important people will be there. Bishops and lords. Even the King of France will grovel on his knees to appeal his excommunication." Alexios placed his hands on the table. "Our envoys are there to seek military assistance wherever and whenever they can... and they are in a position to make generous offers."

"Whatever happened to those Latin monks who came years ago with letters from their Pope?" Anna asked. "Surely, they could speak well on our behalf."

"It's too late for that, mother. Only one survived and he returned to Rome last August."

"Which one?" John asked, remembering the two black-robed monks he had first met at the fortress of Dyrrachium some years before.

"The stupid one... Aldebert I think his name is. Lieutenant Tatran said the intelligent one was lost to the Turks at Antioch. All over a slave girl if you can believe it."

CLUNY

1095

With the help of the Normans, Pope Urban tightened his grip on Rome. Then, at a feverish pace, he set out to make personal visits to the lords and bishops of Lombardy to the north. If he was going to hold Rome against the Germans and reassert his papacy, he needed their staunch support.

In March of 1095, he held council in the small town of Piacenza. Two hundred bishops attended, as well as thousands of church officials and nearly all the lords of Italy. In all, nearly thirty-five thousand men gathered here to discuss religious reform, the antipope, heresy, and the marital problems of the King of France.

Also present was a delegation from King Alexios, who made emotional and elaborate pleas for military support in their battle against the accursed barbarians who had seized and desecrated the holy places of Christendom.

Pope Urban kept up a tireless campaign and, in the fall of 1095, he entered Burgundy to pay a visit to his old monastery, the Abbey of Cluny. The whole abbey rang with excitement. Monks fell to their knees, praising God for the safe arrival of His Holiness, whose very presence would bring God's blessing to their monastery.

"Do you have any more news from your spy in the East?" asked Pope Urban as he made himself comfortable in Abbot Hugh's private chambers.

"Alas, no, Your Holiness," said Hugh. "Not since the report we received last year from Edessa. We were quite surprised to get it because we heard nothing for a number of years and feared he was either dead or captured. As events turned out, he actually was captured by the pagans but, by the grace of God, managed to escape. Said he was heading for Jerusalem."

"And this came from your monk? The one I met in Melfi?"

"Yes, Holy Father. The one called Ramiro. Apparently, the Persians imprisoned and enslaved him, which accounts for the absence of his reports."

"Yes, I heard this from your other monk, the one now in Rome."

"Brother Aldebert?"

"Yes, that's him. He seems to know much about these Greeks and their affairs."

"He wrote to me recently," said Hugh, "requesting to be moved to a Benedictine monastery near Bari."

"That would serve us well," Urban nodded. "Many pilgrims and soldiers come and go from Bari. He can report on all he sees and hears."

Days ago, Hugh was angered when he read Aldebert's impudent request to go to Bari and was about to order him back to the monastery. But now he had a change of heart. "As you wish, Holy Father."

"Do me the favor, Abbot, of recounting these reports. I'm afraid my memory does not serve me well in old age."

"Of course, Your Holiness, would you like some refreshments?"

"Just some water, if you will."

Hugh poured a cup from the sideboard. "Well, it seems the Greeks are having much trouble holding against the Persians and have lost vast tracts of their Christian empire, especially in Asia. Good Christians are driven from their homes, tortured or enslaved. Holy places are defiled, churches profaned. Antioch, home of our blessed Saint Paul, is scourged and oppressed."

Urban shook his head in sadness and shame. "We cannot allow this to continue, it threatens the whole of Christendom."

"But there is some news in our favor," Hugh went on. "It seems the King of the Persians was murdered and the country has fallen into civil war. The princes of Syria fight among themselves, but few have any real power. So you see, Your Holiness, God has cleared a path for our Holy Crusade."

"Praise God!" said Urban. "Did you know the Greek King sent a delegation to our council in Placenza?"

"I heard rumor, Holy Father. What did they say?"

"No more than we have come to expect. That Holy Jerusalem itself suffers at the hands of these godless heathen, violated and polluted by their very presence, that the Tomb of Christ is corrupted and that the alms of pious Christians are pilfered from the Church of God. They persecute the devout, enslaving and massacring them by the thousands, their bodies left to rot in heaps. We can no longer tolerate this villainy and heresy!"

"I agree, Holy Father. We must destroy them."

"For many years," said Urban, "the Greek King has pleaded for the soldiers of Christ to come to his aid. The time has come to harken to his call, in the name of God."

"It has been too long, Holiness. We should have rallied forces years ago. But the lords of France continue to undermine themselves with their petty quarrels and internecine battles. We need to redirect their energies to a more noble and Godly cause."

Urban nodded. "I have been urging them to Byzantium for some time. Finally, they begin to listen. I talked to some of the lords and I believe Count Raymond of Toulouse is the best man to lead this Holy Crusade."

"I agree, Raymond is an excellent choice. He has the money and is devoted to our sacred cause. And surely, Holy Father, these men will receive God's grace and the remission of their sins for entering on the divine path to the Holy Sepulcher, for wresting the Holy Land from such an evil race."

"They will," said Urban. "And now it's time to rally the people to action. I plan to hold another council in France for this purpose, for a call to Holy War. Perhaps Cluny would be a suitable location for this undertaking."

"Here, Your Holiness? At the monastery?" Hugh was visibly unnerved.

"You think not, Abbot?"

"Forgive me, Holy Father, but is it a good idea to associate the Benedictine Order with war of any kind?"

"Perhaps not. What do you suggest?"

Hugh paused for a moment. "I suggest Claremont. It's about eighty miles to the southwest and closer to central France. Several important councils have been held there in the past and the new cathedral is splendid. It would serve our purposes."

"So be it, Abbot Hugh. We go to Claremont."

Antioch

Ibrahim the Mufti paid another visit to Ramiro. "I'm leaving for Jerusalem," he stated bluntly. "There is little more I can do for you here."

"Jerusalem?" Ramiro felt a flood of envy. "Why Jerusalem?"

"I have been asked to take up the position of Qadi there. It is a great honor and rare privilege. I must go."

"But what of my case?"

"Like I said, you should embrace Islam. This is your only hope of release."

"I cannot do that, Mufti."

"But your situation here is unlikely to improve, Ramiro."

Ramiro pursed his lips in frustration. "Dear oh dear, may God help us. If only I could go with you."

"I doubt that is possible."

Ramiro had an idea. "Perhaps you could do something for me?"

"And what is that?"

"Deliver a letter to the Patriarch."

"The Christian leader?" Ibrahim shook his head. "No, no, I dare not. If anyone should discover this, I would be accused of being a spy, a traitor."

"But I promise, Mufti, there will be nothing of vital military interest in the letter. It is only to explain my absence to the Patriarch. He must wonder what has happened to me. Please, I beg of you."

Ibrahim had a look of exasperation. "Very well, but I reserve the right to review and approve this letter. Do you have it?"

"One moment," he said, rushing to his desk. "It will only take one moment to write." He began to write in Latin before he realized that Ibrahim would not be able to read it. So he tore it up and wrote another in Greek. He briefly told the Patriarch what had transpired and beseeched him to forward his message to Abbot Hugh of Cluny. He blew on the ink to speed its drying before handing it over to Ibrahim for his approval.

Ibrahim looked it over. "Very well. God willing, I will deliver it. Although it is against my better judgment."

HOLY WAR

Weeks became months and months became years. Still, Yaghi Siyan would not hear their pleas for freedom. Ramiro refused to give up and continued to take notes for his reports to Abbot Hugh, reports that he could never send out. Month on end, he vainly kept up hope, but despair and doubt gnawed at him.

"Checkmate!" Boris yelled.

"For the love of Mary, Boris! There's no need to shout." Ramiro glared at the chessboard. "I don't understand," he confessed, unable to suppress his anger and frustration.

Adele could not stifle a smile as she added more charcoal to the brazier.

Boris was too eager to help. "You see, my castle attacks your king. But you cannot move because your only escape is here." He pointed to a square. "And my horseman covers this square. Your king is dead," he smirked.

"What of my vizier? Or my qadi? Can they do nothing?"

Boris was still smiling. "Oh yes, some moves ago. But you missed your opportunity."

Ramiro rubbed his hands as cold, winter drafts penetrated the room. "Enough, I'm tired."

"Do you want to play backgammon instead, Master Ramiro?"

"No, Boris. I've had enough of games." He leaned away from the table with a feeling of despair. *How much longer? How much longer must I waste my time playing games? Has Abbot Hugh forsaken me? God knows my mother must think the worst. If, indeed, she still lives.*

There was a knock at the door. "You have a visitor, Ramiro!" a guard shouted from behind the door.

"A visitor?" he asked, getting up. "But I have no appointments today."

The guard opened the door a little and motioned behind him with his eyes. "It is a very important visitor."

Ramiro gestured to Boris. "You had better leave."

Boris got up and swept out the door. The guard moved aside and John the Oxite stepped in, his black cape flowing behind him.

"Your Eminence! May God bless you. What a pleasure this is."

The Patriarch made an apologetic gesture as Boris slipped out. "Forgive me for appearing without notice. Until now, the Emir has been reluctant to let me see you."

Ramiro bowed. "Please, Your Eminence. Sit down."

Adele rose from her seat when John arrived. "Would you like some orange juice?" she asked.

John waved a hand of refusal as he sat on a sprawl of cushions. "No, no, dear woman. I won't be long."

Adele retired to her private room, as was customary when men talked. But she could still hear every word.

John looked tired. His eyes were heavy, his face pale and drawn, and his gray-blonde beard seemed a little grayer. He shuffled on the cushions. "How have you been, Monk Ramiro?"

Ramiro gave a little shrug. "As well as can be expected, given the circumstances."

John smiled briefly. "If you had followed my advice, you would not be here now. Why didn't you use the mufti, as I suggested?

"I was too impatient, Your Eminence. The mufti said it would take over a year for my case to be heard."

John opened his hands. "But now you have been held captive for an even longer time. So what have you gained?"

Ramiro raised his chin. "I saved the woman from an unthinkable fate, Your Eminence. That is reward enough."

Adele smiled when she overheard.

John raised one eyebrow. "You are indeed a strange man, Ramiro of Cluny, perhaps a foolish one. But I admire your resolve."

"I asked to see you many months ago, Your Eminence. But I heard nothing. And they do not allow me letters."

"I was never informed of this. But there are some events that may interest you. I have news from Italy." He leaned forward. "The Bishop of Rome has taken the Lateran Palace. The Germans have quit."

"You mean Pope Urban has finally taken his seat?"

"Yes, last year. Now he asserts his power throughout the West and calls for a Holy Crusade."

"What do you mean?"

"Urban called for a crusade to liberate the Holy Land from the infidels. He promised the men of Europe that God would forgive their sins if they took up the cross to fight a Holy War."

"And... and what was the response?"

"Very good, I hear. Even now, hordes of French and Germans rush to Constantinople. And many lords of the West prepare for a spring advance."

Ramiro rose suddenly from his cushion, stepping over to a side table to pour a glass of wine. He offered one to John, who shook his head. "This is incredible!" he said before draining his glass. "I thought Urban's mission was to unite the churches in peace. Now he goes to war?"

"He still hopes to rule Christendom." John scowled. "Mark my words, this war will be as much against the Greek Church as against the infidels."

"No, I cannot believe that, Your Eminence. Pope Urban would not wage war on Christians."

"But we are not of his church. And you know the deep enmity that exists between us. I pray for the best... but we shall see."

"What does King Alexios think of all this?"

John scoffed. "It was his plan, Monk Ramiro. He has plotted for years to get mercenaries from the West. Now he has succeeded. But I tell you he is asking for trouble. They are unpredictable."

Ramiro paced by the window. He thought of the brutal Drugo and his greedy men. "I agree, Your Eminence, they are an unruly lot. But do you really believe French armies can reach Jerusalem?"

"Why not? And if they do, they will surely pass through Antioch."

Despite John's dire predictions, Ramiro felt inwardly elated. "Well, at least it would mean my freedom. It would put Jerusalem in Christian hands and allow pilgrims a safe passage."

"But war is never a safe gambit," said John. "Surely you know that."

Requited Love

Ramiro and Adele knelt in prayer, as they did every morning and evening. Ramiro laid his iron cross in front of them before praying aloud.

> *O Holy Cross*
> *by which that Cross is brought to mind*
> *on which our Lord Jesus Christ*
> *through his own death*
> *raised us up from that eternal death...*

They prayed for family and friends, for the Pope and the Holy Church, and they prayed for their freedom. When all was said and done, Adele served two cups of sage tea before returning to her sewing at the table.

Ramiro sat across from her, picking through a book of poetry that Boris had smuggled in. The author was Abu Nuwas, a man scorned by some for his lewdness, while adored by others for his extensive learning. There were poems about the pleasures of the hunt, about his love of women, and about his love of boys. He read quietly.

> *O moon of the darkened bedroom*
> *I kissed him once, just once*
> *as he slept, half hoping half fearing*
> *he might wake up*
>
> *O silk soft moon*
> *his pajamas held such softness*
> *Ah how I'd like a real live kiss*

how I'd like to be offered
what's under the covers

In a flush of embarrassment, Ramiro slammed the book shut. "Blessed saints!"

"What's the matter?" Adele asked.

He shook his head in wonder. "I cannot believe that men write of such things!"

"What's it about?"

He flustered, too abashed to tell her. "It's... it's about love."

Adele looked up from her sewing, smiling in her charming way. "Are you so embarrassed by love, my husband?"

"Well, not really, as long as it remains within the moral bounds of the Church."

"Is our love within these bounds, Ramiro?"

He blushed, turning his eyes away. "Yes," he replied softly.

She put down her sewing, leaning across the table, taking his hand and squeezing it gently. Her affectionate move surprised him and he dared to gaze into her round, pleading eyes. "Ramiro," she said candidly, "... we've been living together almost two years. When will you come to my bed? I am your wife." She paused. "Don't you love me?"

Ramiro reddened in confusion and indecision. He thought about the first time he had noticed her on their journey through the Balkans. Her beauty had swayed him then... and it swayed him now. How he longed for her loving touch. "I... I do love you, Adele," he said with a touch of apology.

Adele smiled. She moved around the table to cuddle on the cushions beside him. "You really do love me?"

Ramiro nodded. "Yes, dear woman, I think I've loved you since I first set eyes on you."

She caressed his arm and whispered into his ear. "And now we have each other, dearest Ramiro." She pulled gently on his arm. "Come with me... come to my bed," she murmured in a low, seductive voice. "Love me." Her soft lips touched his ear.

Ramiro swooned, his loins stirring with a carnal craving he had not felt since the days of his youth. In an instant, a mounting wave of passion and desire swept away years of denial. Awkwardly, he put his arm over her shoulder, hesitating for a moment before pulling her gently into his chest until they were face to face. At first, their lips met in a timid, soft touch but, in a few precious moments, they pressed harder and harder in a bold, reckless embrace, releasing long, pent-up cravings in a frenzy of passionate love.

July 1096

Ramiro enjoyed his walks throughout the compound but preferred the court-yard where he was sure to avoid Khuda the Mamluk, who was stationed in the same place and still threatened him on occasion. Here, he could bask in bright sunshine, talk to fellow prisoners, and hear scraps of news from every corner.

He strolled to his favorite bench under a pear tree, but it was already occupied. "Good morning, Rabbi. What a lovely day!"

Rabbi David said nothing, his shoulders hunched, his demeanor morose.

"What is it, Rabbi?" asked Ramiro as he sat beside him. "Do these prison walls weigh heavily on your mind?"

David glanced up with large, sad eyes. "These walls always weigh on me, Ramiro. But today, terrible news has come my way."

Ramiro tipped his head. "And what is that, my friend?"

David reached over, putting a hand on Ramiro's arm. "You remember that your Pope called for Holy War against the infidels?"

"Yes, I do," he replied, feeling guilty. "But it does not sit well with me. What has happened?"

"Well, it seems it is first a war against the Hebrews." Tears welled in his eyes.

"What do you mean?"

"There have been terrible massacres, my friend. Hundreds of German brutes terrorize Jews in their towns. They have murdered hundreds, maybe thou-sands... they burn and pillage their homes." He wiped his eyes with a kerchief. "What have my people done to deserve this?"

"Are you sure, Rabbi? Where did this happen?"

"Yes, I'm sure," he said in a quaking voice. "My son just told me. In Mainz, Worms, and Cologne. Last year. Mobs of fanatics went on a rampage. Now these same mobs travel east to... to Constantinople."

"But why would they do this?"

"Who knows? Because we are both hated and envied. Hated because we are not Christian. Envied because a few of us have money. And our people are always blamed for the death of your messiah. All of this!"

"And now their armies march to Constantinople?"

"It's not much of an army, I hear. But more a band of murderers and thieves who profess to follow God. That God would be so cruel!"

"Who leads them, Rabbi?"

"Hermits and madmen is all I've heard."

6 - CRUSADERS

CONSTANTINOPLE

August 1096

King Alexios surveyed the grounds with dread. There, far beyond the city walls, gathered thousands upon thousands of zealous Christian peasants and ruffians who had made the long trek from Germany and France, divinely inspired as they were by the fiery oratory of Pope Urban the Second and his call to Holy War.

But this was not the mercenary army Alexios had hoped for. Only a few hundred had horses, swords, bows, or armor of any kind. Most carried only knives and sharpened stakes. Among them were thousands of women and children, even the elderly. They waved palms and wore rough crosses sewn onto their shoulders. Thousands more arrived every day and their numbers soon became unwieldy. But there was a ray of hope amid the gloom. He was informed that more formidable armies readied themselves for a Holy Crusade and should arrive in a few months.

"May God have mercy on us!" he shouted to his captain. "Don't let them inside the city walls. But keep them well-fed. And bring their leaders to me right away!"

The captain bowed as he backed away. "Yes, my King."

Peter the Hermit sat with drooping shoulders. Walter the Penniless sat beside him, both dressed in soiled wool shirts and pants. Peter was balding while Walter had shoulder-length, greasy hair. They appeared uncomfortable in the splendor of the palace and shuffled uneasily in elegant armchairs. For two hours, with the help of a translator, Alexios had tried to give them good advice, but his words of wisdom fell on deaf ears.

He first studied the short man with balding, blonde hair, his skin burnt from the sun and his beard matted with grease. He had heard much about Peter, who was renowned as a stirring orator capable of arousing the masses. But he was a stubborn man, too fanatical for his liking, although not as bad as Walter, who could do nothing but respond with thoughtless, dogmatic tirades. And the stink! Worse than a pig sty! He reached for a scented kerchief, pretending to wipe his nose. "So Peter, I hear you have been here before."

"Yes, Your Highness, I was captured and tortured by these heathen some years ago, may God curse them!" He scowled red-faced.

"Will you not wait as I ask?" Alexios pleaded. "I assure you, more capable armies are on their way. I hope you will follow my advice and tarry here until they arrive."

Peter opened his soiled hands in a gesture of resignation. "I have led the faithful here, Your Highness, but I cannot restrain them. They ignore my pleas and continue to plunder the countryside. They are the chosen of God, chosen for a Holy Crusade to Jerusalem. They are anxious to fight the heathen and will have their way."

Walter broke in loudly. "We've been sent by the Pope himself to regain the Holy Land!" Clotted hair swung across his filthy, round face as he ranted. "We will not be stopped!"

Alexios stood abruptly. "Then you leave me little choice. I will move your people across the Bosporus. You may stake yourselves along the shores of the Propontis at a fort called Civetot, which we recently recaptured from the Turks."

Alexios thought this best as it would not only relieve him of these troublesome peasants, but also because Civetot was not far from Nikea, where these so-called crusaders could prove to be an irritant to young Kilich, Son of Sulayman.

Peter and Walter eagerly set up camp at Civetot. It was on the coast and could be supplied easily across the Propontis. Shortly after they arrived, thousands set out from camp to pillage the countryside, believing they were doing God's work. Everyone they met was considered a godless, evil pagan who needed to be scourged from the face of the earth. They rampaged far and wide, killing Muslim and Christian alike, looting homes, mosques, and even Greek churches. They ridiculed, raped, and tortured their captives before burning them alive, screaming on pyres.

NIKEA

Kilich laughed aloud. His commanders laughed too. "So this is the great Franj army," he smirked. "This army of rabble that the Roman King prays will defeat the Turks." He laughed again.

Ozan smiled. "Yes, my Sultan. They occupy Civetot and the Roman King supplies them across the sea. They pillage every village and lay waste. They kill everyone—even the Christians!" The men chuckled.

"How well organized are they?" Kilich asked.

"Not very well, my Lord. There are different tribes with different tongues and they distrust each other. Nonetheless, some armed horsemen are among them. They are crude and violent men, my Lord. They ravage the countryside, destroying all in their path. They like to torture their victims before they kill them. The people say they slaughter infants and roast them on spits!"

Kilich turned away in disgust. "Animals! Barbarians! May Allah damn them to hellfire!" He looked back. "And now you say they plan to march here, to Nikea?"

"Yes, my Lord."

Kilich turned to his atabek, Al-Khanes. "Kill them all. Send a patrol to confront them."

"Yes, Master. But perhaps we should send a more sizable army to destroy them and then we can retake Civetot from the Romans."

Kilich smiled. "No, I do not believe that is necessary. We will show them how mamluks fight."

But Kilich was wrong. His patrol of mamluks was killed to a man, overwhelmed by the sheer number of fanatical, would-be Crusaders.

"You were right, Al-Khanes," Kilich admitted, shaking his head in shame and regret. "What should we do now?"

"Watch and wait, my Lord," the big warrior crackled. "They advance toward us. We should lure them away, lure them into a trap."

"And what do you propose?"

"Use the fortress at Xerigordos, my Prince."

Young Kilich frowned. "What do you mean?"

"Xerigordos is only a few miles from here. Remove our troops from the fortress and send a spy into the barbarian camp. He will tell them we have fled in fear and that it is free for the taking. Since these barbarians are so stupid and greedy, they will not be able to refuse the offer."

Kilich brightened. "And then we will besiege them!"

October 1096

These barbarians are so predictable thought Al-Khanes as his troops surrounded Xerigordos. And they are so stupid. Could they not see that the well sits outside the fortress walls? Now they have suffered eight days without water and will not last much longer, not in this heat. My spies say they drink the blood of their mounts, and others drink their own piss. He smiled. May Allah curse them with a slow death!

A messenger ran up to him. "They wish to surrender, Commander."

Al-Khanes hardened. "Did you tell them they will live only if they renounce their faith and embrace Islam?"

"Yes, Commander."

"Very well. When they open the gates, enslave the converts and slaughter the rest."

Prince Kilich was emboldened by his success at Xerigordos. "Filthy kuffar! May Allah curse their ancestors! We will kill them all and rid the earth of this heathen scum! We ride to Civetot!"

"But, Master, they will be prepared. And the Emperor supplies them by sea," Al-Khanes protested.

"Then what do you advise, my atabek?"

Al-Khanes rubbed his bushy beard before scratching at an old scar running down his cheek. "Send a spy to Civetot. He will tell the Christians that their comrades have managed to take Nikea and now share in its rich spoils. They will come running—like greedy rats to a carcass. Then we lay an ambush in the valley just east of Civetot."

"You are a wise atabek, Al-Khanes," Kilich smiled. "We will do as you say. But we must do it quickly before the pagan devils discover the truth."

Walter the Penniless danced with joy when he heard Nikea had fallen to their comrades. "By the grace of God we have conquered!" The whole camp at Civetot screamed with delight. Thousands gushed in tears, falling to their knees to thank God for their divine victory over the wicked heathen. But they soon forgot their prayers of thanksgiving and began to shout with envy. What of the rich booty from Nikea? They wanted their share and began a mad rush to join the victors.

"What of Peter?" asked Walter. "We should wait for him to return from Constantinople before we head out."

But their greed soon overcame all common sense and they stormed out of the gates, heading for Nikea with Walter in the lead. They had no sooner left the gate when a lone survivor of Xerigordos came stumbling back to camp. He tried to stop them. He warned them that their comrades did not take Nikea, but instead, were either slaughtered or enslaved.

Walter ranted and cursed when he heard the terrible news. But he was so enraged by the slaughter of fellow Christians that, rather than heeding good advice, he worked the crowd into a frenzy of revenge and they rushed forward in an angry mob. This time, they vowed, they would reach Nikea and they would destroy it.

The Turks lay in ambush in a narrow, wooded valley not far from Civetot. As soon as the mass of Christian zealots entered the mouth of the valley, Kilich sent horsemen to face them. But Walter egged his peasants forward, reminding them of their first easy victory over the mamluks. They rushed against the Turks, confident that God would favor them. But these wayward souls soon died screaming in a deadly hail of Turk arrows.

Walter the Penniless, riddled by seven, died before he hit the ground. The rest fell back in a stampede of fear, storming out of the valley the way they had come. But now, Turk infantry had taken a round-about route and blocked the way. With nowhere to flee, terrified French and German paupers died by the thousands on this bloody battleground. And in the gory aftermath, surviving slaves were forced to pile their bloodied corpses in great mounds, where they were left to rot in the burning sun of the valley. Before long, hundreds of jackals, hyenas, and vultures picked their bones clean.

But Kilich did not stop there. He charged right into the camp at Civetot, over-running the remaining few with brutal suppression, killing everyone, sparing only a few pretty boys and girls for the slave markets of Aleppo.

Kilich felt the throb of victory in his veins. "Now we must fight the Danishmend to the east! They have grown too bold since the death of the Great Shah. We must ride against them to regain Malatya!"

"But what of the Franj, my Lord?" asked Ozan. "We hear that many more march from the far West."

Kilich scoffed. "You cannot be serious, Ozan. You saw what they were like. Why should we fear these rag-tag warriors?" He took on a more serious tone. "It's the Danishmend who are the real threat to our domains."

"But my Lord,' said Al-Khanes in his crackling voice. "We have heard these new infidel armies are better equipped and are personally led by their chiefs."

Kilich shook his head. "No. We will not sit here worrying about a thousand more peasants from the West. But you can be sure the Danishmend will continue their raids until they have taken all our cities. We need those cities! We need the revenues. We must ride to Malatya!"

CONSTANTINOPLE

May 1097

Alexios shook his head when he heard of the massacre at Civetot. He had tried to warn them but they would not listen. His hopes were revived only when more formidable French armies began to arrive in Constantinople.

At first, he expected small groups of soldiers who could be easily managed.

However, like the band of peasants who died at Civetot, the newly arriving armies were much larger than he anticipated, and they continued to arrive by the thousands. Not just men of war but, once again, thousands of women, children, servants, and slaves. They were camped outside the city walls, a mass of filthy zealots who yelled and screamed and sang and danced in the thick choking smoke of a thousand campfires.

Prominent among the men was Raymond of Toulouse, a dominant lord of Provence and a favorite of the Pope. With him, was Bishop Adhemar, the appointed spiritual leader of the Holy Crusade.

Robert of Flanders also came, the son of the man who sent Drugo the Red to fight for the Greek King. And traveling with him, was the rich and powerful Norman, Godfrey of Bouillon.

Raymond and Adhemar were keen to maintain détente with the Byzantine king. In their wisdom, they realized they would have to rely on him for vital supplies and military intelligence. They readily swore allegiance to Alexios. But Godfrey refused, citing his distrust of the Byzantine King.

Alexios responded by cutting off his food supplies—and that's when the pillaging began. Godfrey's men went on a looting rampage, setting fire to a number of buildings. Alexios sent out the full force of his troops, putting down the rebellion.

But given time, flattery, and some generous gifts, Godfrey eventually yielded to Alexios and swore an oath of fealty to him. So the King moved them all across the Bosporus to Pelekanon, a camp on the plains west of Nicomedia.

Then Bohemond arrived with a small army.

"Bohemond of Italy?" asked Isaak incredulously.

"Yes, along with his nephew, Tancred. But he has little money and only a small army," Alexios contended, as if it were some comfort.

"But we cannot trust him, my King. He is the son of Robert Guiscard. He invaded our lands with his father. He has only one intention—and that is to take Byzantium for his own!"

"He will take the oath of allegiance. For the moment, he is no threat. But like you say, Isaak, he cannot be trusted."

"It's too much, too fast, my son," said Anna with a sincere look of concern. "We must move them east as quickly as possible before they do any more damage. We are still recovering from Godfrey's rampage."

Alexios nodded. "I agree, mother. I have sent them all to Pelekanon from where they will soon retake Nicomedia. Once they have reaffirmed their oaths, we can make better use of their aggression by setting them against the Turks at Nikea."

Drugo the Red was elated at the news, as were his three hundred or so remaining men, who were still housed in the military barracks at Galata. "Count Robert is here!" he shouted. "Our lord and master!"

The men cheered with great enthusiasm, drawing their swords, jabbing them into the air.

When the cheers subsided, Otto blurted out. "But we still serve the Greek king! How can we join Robert?"

General Taticius quelled them. "It's true, you still owe allegiance to King Alexios. But don't worry. You'll have your chance to fight alongside Robert. We will join them to besiege Nikea."

The men roared their pleasure. "Death to the heathen!" they howled. "God wills it!"

NIKEA

We need more men, Ozan thought with mounting trepidation. These new Franj armies are determined, not like the beggars who came before. Our spies say three thousand labor on the mountain road heading south from Nicomedia to Nikea, busy clearing hundreds of trees, pulling the stumps to widen the narrow road for their growing army. And there was no one to stop them. Kilich had left to fight the Danishmend to the east.

Thousands upon thousands of Crusaders camped near Nicomedia, preparing for their advance on Nikea. They encountered no resistance here. The Turks who had taken the city under Abul Kasim had long since fled for the safety of Nikea.

But the sheer size of the gathering army soon depleted all food supplies. So they split their massive army in two, taking different routes but both heading to Nikea. And days later, both armies began to converge on the outskirts of Lake Askanius, over thirty thousand men.

Ozan frantically wrote another letter to Kilich. He sent the first letter when he heard the Franj had returned in great numbers and were now camped at Pelekanon. But alas, his master was distracted by the Danishmend's siege of Malatya. His only response was to send a few detachments back to Nikea to appease his wife, who was pregnant and fretting.

Kilich must come, Ozan panicked. And he must come soon! He handed the letter to the messenger. "Ride as fast as you can. The Sultanate is under attack!"

MALATYA

Kilich sat in his war tent reading Ozan's letter. A deep frown wrinkled his boyish face. He summoned his atabek, Al-Khanes. "What should we do? If we return now, the Danishmend will take Malatya. But if we do not, Nikea will fall to the barbarians. Our families are there. Our treasury is there."

Al-Khanes took a moment to think, rubbing his gnarled nose with a finger. "Then you must make peace with Ghazi of the Danishmend."

"Peace?" Kilich shrugged. "How?"

"These Christian barbarians threaten all Muslims, Shia and Sunni alike. It makes no difference to them. They even kill the Christians of Byzantium. No one is safe."

Kilich saw the direction of his advice and felt encouraged. "Do you think we can convince Ghazi to join us in a holy war against these infidels?"

"Yes, my Lord. He hates Christians. I'm sure Hasan of Cappadocia will join us as well."

"Yes, yes." Kilich muttered, thinking of Hasan and his escape from Isfahan with Ramiro and how Hasan had helped him on the long journey back to Nikea. Hasan had proved to be a faithful ally since the death of his father, Bolkas. Now he ruled Cappadocia.

And so it was. Against all odds, Ghazi Danishmend, a fierce man of Islam, was convinced to reach a truce with Kilich and to join him against the heathen Christians. And Hasan came too, inflamed by his own seething hatred of invading Christians. Their combined armies rushed to Nikea. But by the time they arrived, tens of thousands of Crusaders had already surrounded the city walls, preparing for a long siege.

NIKEA

The walls and ramparts of Nikea were two and a half miles in circumference, and along these walls were one hundred towers and four gates. The western wall rose out of the waters of Lake Askanius where a water-gate allowed the passage of boats and supplies. The remainder of the wall, standing the height of six men, was surrounded by a moat full with the runoff from nearby streams. Nikea was almost impregnable. But it could never sustain an onslaught of this size and intensity. The Crusaders had enough men to surround the whole city and to attack every gate, except the one on the water.

In utter dismay, Kilich looked down on Nikea from a nearby hilltop. The enormous size of the infidel army shocked him. The real possibility of losing his family, his gold, and his beloved Nikea struck him as if a cold sword had pierced his heart.

"We are too late, Master," said Al-Khanes with little comfort. "There must be forty thousand. We cannot penetrate their lines. It is better to turn back now and save our men for another day of battle." Ghazi Danishmend and most of the commanders nodded in agreement.

"But there must be a way!" Kilich shouted in despair. "We cannot give up without a fight. Look! They are weak in the south. We will attack there! By the will of Allah!"

Reluctantly, Ghazi and Hasan agreed. They would attack at dawn with the sun at their backs. But Kilich's plan was soon foiled. The French captured and tortured two of his spies found among their ranks and discovered his plot. So when Kilich charged out, the Crusaders were ready for him. A fierce battle ensued and many fell on both sides. But when Bohemond joined the fray, Kilich saw that all was lost and retreated south. Never again would he return to Nikea.

Ozan watched the battle from the city walls. Tears streamed his cheeks. It was over. They had to surrender. But the Turk garrison of Nikea refused to give up, despite the overwhelming odds. They would not waver, even when the Crusaders cut off the heads of their comrades and catapulted them over the city walls.

Only when Commander Manuel and General Taticius arrived from Constantinople did things change. Unknown to the Crusaders, Alexios had arranged for several ships to be taken overland from the port of Civetot, transporting them overland ten miles from the shores of the Propontis all the way to the western end of Lake Askanius. They then sailed across the lake to approach the Nikea water-gate, where they hoped to convince the Turks to surrender.

When the Crusaders spotted the Byzantine ships on the lake, they rejoiced and gave glory to God, knowing victory was close at hand. But their raucous cheers did little for the morale of the Turks, who soon let Manuel and Taticius into the city, where they sued for peace.

At dawn on the following day, the Crusaders were somewhat startled to see Byzantine flags stationed along the walls of Nikea. They soon realized that Alexios had taken the city by stealth rather than by storm. And they were furious when they discovered that the King had let the pagan Turks run free. They knew of the massacre at Civetot and had seen the macabre remains of French and German peasants slaughtered by Turks ten months before.

They thought now of these stinking mounds of skulls and bones and the sun-dried flesh of good Christian folk, and were sorely disappointed to be denied their revenge. But they were even more enraged when they thought they had been deprived of the booty of war. So when Alexios asked them to repeat their pledges of allegiance, they refused. Only when the King promised them the treasury of Nikea, did they relent.

But Alexios gave them much more than gold. He offered them invaluable advice on the lay of the land and the state of political turmoil among the Turks and Arabs. He rehearsed the enemy's fighting habits, their strengths and weaknesses. He gave them maps and guides, appointing Taticius to serve as an experienced advisor. The King stressed the strategic importance of Antioch and he put fire in their bellies with exaggerated tales about the violations of holy places.

Feeling encouraged and heavy with Nikea's gold, tens of thousands of Crusaders headed south, deep into Turk-held territory. And once again, to avoid being unwieldy and inefficient, they divided their masses into two great armies.

Drugo the Red and his men now followed their lord, Count Robert. They were confident of victory and glad to be among their own kind again. But Drugo was wary. He had become accustomed to the fighting habits of these Turks. "I don't like this, Humberto. I feel we're being watched." He put a hand to his sword.

Humberto laughed. "Of that you can be sure, Sir Drugo."

DORYLAEUM

July 1097

"They ride south, Prince Kilich," said the scout. "There are many, many thousands but they have divided into two armies. The smaller one leads the way. They head for Iconium."

"Then they must cross the Plains of Dorylaeum," said Hasan of Cappadocia. "The road narrows through the valley beyond the ruins."

"And now we have almost thirty thousand men," said Ghazi of the Danishmend. "We are ready."

"Very well," said Kilich. "We attack at Dorylaeum."

The Crusaders traveled for several days without incident, although Turk scouts were spotted on the hilltops. But all of that changed when they reached the Plains of Dorylaeum. Here, as the plains opened up before them, they were shocked to see Turks amassing by the thousands in this low valley, hemmed in by mountains on all sides. They gathered on the plain, blocking the path of the Crusaders. Thousands more appeared on the crests of surrounding hills. Soon, they began to blow their trumpets and howl their piercing war cries.

Fear rippled through the Crusader ranks. And fear soon turned to terror when deadly hails of Turk arrows riddled their ranks in relentless volleys. But when the heathen hoard came screaming down the hills in full assault, terror turned to blind panic. Hundreds dropped all they had and began to flee.

Bohemond and Taticius knew that a frenzied flight was just what the Turks wanted, and that it would mean certain death. With level heads, they took control, barking commands to hold them in formation. Together, they managed to form an enormous, defensive circle, putting women, children, goods, and horses to the center while the best armored men stationed themselves to the outside. Fast messengers rode back to warn the other army, the one led by Godfrey.

Another cloud of arrows rained down on the army of God, then another, and another, killing hundreds with every volley. Horses, mules, and donkeys fell screaming to the ground. Thousands lay dead or dying. Terrified priests slinked through the crowd attempting to boost morale. "Stand fast together, trust in Christ and the Holy Cross. Stand fast. Stand fast. Trust in Christ and the Holy Cross."

As the priests chanted, Kilich came racing down the plain with all his men, charging into the circle head on. They broke through, piercing with lance, slashing with sword. But the harder they pressed, the harder the knights pushed back, closing the circle once more.

As the first day of bloody battle drew to a close, they huddled all night, dreading the rain of arrows they knew would come with the dawn. Where are the others? Bohemond agonized. Where is Godfrey? When will he come?

At first light, Kilich no sooner began his assault when a thin trail of dust appeared on the western horizon.

Bohemond shouted with relief. "Here they come!"

Kilich saw them too, shaken by the size of the approaching army. But the worst was yet to come. Just as he sighted Godfrey's army, another appeared behind their lines, trapping them in a pincer. Seeing that all was lost and in fear for his life, he fled with the other emirs, racing into the mountains at full gallop. The other horsemen followed, leaving the infantry abandoned and trapped. The Franj cut them to pieces, chasing and killing for hours. Only a few hundred young captives were spared for the slave markets of Byzantium.

Three thousand Turks died on that day. But it was a Pyrrhic victory for the Crusaders. Over four thousand perished, and thousands of their precious horses and pack animals had died in the relentless fusillades of Turk arrows.

But where the Turks failed, Mother Nature had more success. Leaving Dorylaeum in the dead heat of summer, the Crusaders took the road south, skirting the blistering, barren desert as they headed for distant Iconium. This was the same destitute route taken by Ramiro years before when Hasan dragged him as a slave to Isfahan.

Unfamiliar with the heavy demands of the barren land and the scorched-earth policy of the Turks, the Crusaders soon ran short of water. Even General Taticius was unprepared for the devastation they encountered; villages abandoned, wells poisoned or blocked, fields destroyed, animals slaughtered.

Thirst and hunger soon ravaged their ranks and thousands upon thousands suffered a lingering, miserable death along this lonely, ruthless path. The children and the old died first, even Godfrey's young son died from the heat. Many of the remaining horses succumbed and the army of knights quickly became an army of foot-soldiers. The pack animals died too, forcing them to leave much behind.

It took them three long months to cross Anatolia, a journey usually accomplished in a single month. By the time they reached drinkable water, nearly twenty thousand Christian corpses lined the desert route.

Taticius survived this journey, as did Drugo the Red, his lieutenant, Otto, and the executioner, Arles of Ghent. But the cheerful Humberto succumbed to the heat, along with Fulk and another twenty-four of Drugo's men, who all died with glazed eyes and gaping mouths.

ANTIOCH

The Crusader deaths barely made the news, but the defeat of the Son of Sulayman at Nikea, then again at Dorylaeum, sent waves of panic throughout the world of Islam. Already shaken by the death of the illustrious Malik Shah, the latest news was even more distressing. A Christian army had defeated the once-indomitable Seljuk Turks. Muslims everywhere quaked in dread and shame, many abandoning cities and towns lying in the path of the advancing barbarians.

As all this transpired, Yaghi Siyan of Antioch was occupied elsewhere, leading an army south to help defend his ally in Damascus. But he was only half-way there when he heard the news.

"They took Nikea?" He questioned in disbelief.

"Yes, Beyfendi," said the messenger, wringing his hands. "And Kilich, Son of Sulayman, lost a great battle at Dorylaeum. No one can stop these barbarians, my Lord. Prince Kilich runs with his tail between his legs. He hides in the hills."

"By the Mercy of Allah! And you say these foreigners head for Antioch?"

"Yes, my Lord. With an army of many, many thousands."

A cold fear gripped Yaghi Siyan. He could no longer afford to engage in these local disputes. The Byzantine threat was too close and too dangerous to ignore. "Damascus will have to wait!" he yelled as he turned his army around, riding in furious haste back to the walls of Antioch.

Egypt

Al-Afdal

Not all Muslims wept at the fall of Nikea. The Egyptian vizier, a man by the name of Al-Afdal, laughed aloud when he heard the news. Al-Afdal was an Armenian Muslim, a fighting mamluk and the son of a mamluk. His father was vizier to the Caliph and, after the old man died, Al-Afdal inherited his position. But he had no sooner taken the post, when the Caliph himself died suddenly under mysterious circumstances and all power fell into his hands. To make sure it stayed that way, Al-Afdal appointed a mere child as the new Caliph.

By the time he was thirty-five, Al-Afdal ruled a nation of seven million people and, with guile and ruthless perseverance, he continued to rule for the next twenty-four years. He was an ardent disciple of Fatimid Shia and a firm believer in the doctrine of the twelve Imams. As such, he hated the Seljuk Turks. He hated them because they were Sunni, he hated them because they defeated the Arabs, and he hated them simply because they were Turks.

For years, he had fought against the Seljuks in Syria and Palestine. Some even whispered that, despite his hatred of the Hashashin, he secretly supported their stronghold in northern Iran and their bloody efforts to defeat the Seljuks from within. As far as Al-Afdal was concerned, anyone or any army that stopped the advance of the Turks was an ally of his. So when the Byzantines and the Crusaders left Nikea and headed deep into Turk territory, he was jubilant.

"Send an envoy to King Alexios," he ordered his aide. "Let us see how we can assist this new army of his. And we must negotiate who gets what. I want everything south of Dog River, especially Jerusalem."

Antioch

Antioch was in chaos. Yaghi Siyan, filled with dread, began food rations and daily inspections of all fortifications. He laid plans for a long siege and sent his eldest son to Damascus, seeking help.

"The Christians have rebelled, my Lord," said his atabek. They besiege our outposts and our garrisons have fled. May Allah strike them dead!"

"We can't trust these damn Christians!" Yaghi shouted. His advisors nodded in agreement. He said nothing for a while, staring straight ahead, stroking his long, white beard with distraction. "That Greek priest, the one they call Patriarch. He plots against me! I'm sure of it. Bring him in for interrogation."

"What shall we do with the others, my Lord?" asked the atabek. "Most of the city is Christian. The merchants and our taxes will suffer."

Yaghi waved a hand in dismissal. "I'm worried about our heads, Atabek, not taxes. Devise a plan to get them out of the city. And do it soon."

The atabek nodded. "Your wish is my command, Great Emir."

Boris knocked on the door, opening it just enough to stick his head through. "Psst! Master! Master! I must speak with you." He tried to keep his voice down.

Ramiro woke with a start. He was taking a midday nap, as many do in the heat. He stumbled to the door. "Boris? What is it? Come in man."

"Sorry to wake you, Master. But I have just heard something you should know right away." He strode over to the cushions to sit.

Ramiro went over to a bronze basin. "Well? What is it?" he asked, dipping his hands to splash his face.

"The Roman army approaches Antioch," Boris huffed. "They have thousands of mercenaries! Barbarians from the West!"

"We have heard, Boris," he said, drying his face with a towel. "Do you think we are in danger?"

"Yes." Boris nodded fretfully. "Yaghi Siyan is furious, he blames all Christians. He says the Patriarch is a traitor! He hung the poor man from the walls of the Cathedral and beat his feet with iron rods! God have mercy!"

Ramiro stopped what he was doing. "By all Saints! John the Oxite?"

"Yes," said Boris, close to tears. "His Eminence himself. God help us! And the Cathedral, Ramiro, they have desecrated the Cathedral of Saint Peter! They smashed everything—and now bring in their horses to use it as a stable! May God curse them!"

Ramiro put a comforting hand to Boris' shoulder. "Yaghi Siyan fears the Christians will rebel."

"It's true, Master. Even now, they drive out anyone of prominence."

"Does he plot to kill us?"

"No, no, he is not that stupid. But he plans to cast out the clergy and every Christian man of fighting age."

"What do you mean? When?"

"Well, today he sent out a large corps of men, all Muslim, to dig trenches around the walls."

"Yes, I heard," said Ramiro, hanging the towel.

"Well, tomorrow he will send out another corps, but this time it will be all Christian."

Ramiro nodded. "So?"

"It's a ruse, Master, he plans to keep them out."

"Outside the walls?"

"Yes."

Ramiro rubbed his beard in thought. "I see. Will I be one of the chosen?"

"Probably. Yaghi Siyan fears you."

"Really? Why?"

"He thinks you could easily rally the Christians to your cause."

Ramiro shook his head. "I have no cause here, Boris. But now we may have a chance to escape Antioch and get to Jerusalem." He moved closer to Boris, sitting beside him. "This means that I have only today to retrieve my cross from Khuda. I know he has it. Do you remember the plan we spoke of."

Boris wrung his thin hands, speaking nervously. "Master, you cannot do this. He will kill you! He's a fearsome man."

Ramiro ignored his plea. "This is Friday, Boris! The perfect day!"

Boris looked confused for a moment, but soon a quick smile came and went from his drawn face. "Because today is the day his concubine shops!"

"And today is the day Khuda will be at the mosque," Ramiro added.

Adele sauntered into the room wearing a long, yellow tunic decorated at the hem with delicate mauve flowers.

"Did you hear what Boris said?"

"Most of it." She replied, tying her hair back. "So what's our plan?"

Adele's Venture

"No, you will not!" Ramiro shouted.

"Yes, I will!" Adele shouted back. "It doesn't make sense for you to go. His cleaning slave is a woman. How will you pass for a woman? Are you going to shave your beard and put on earrings?" She smiled.

"Adele, it's much too dangerous."

She ignored him. "And it'll be easier for me to go unnoticed. You'll never get past the guards."

Ramiro shook his head again. "Then we will forget the cross. It's a trinket and not worth a life."

"It was entrusted to you by the Abbot—and it's a gift from the Great Shah," said Adele, thinking of the gold. "It's worth the risk. Do you not trust me?"

"Of course I do."

"Am I not capable?"

"Yes, yes. That's not it."

"Then I'll go. And I better go soon!"

"You are an impossible woman!"

She smiled again.

Adele put on a simple, gray tunic with a plain sash before slipping on a pair of reed sandals, the dress of a slave. She carried an empty water pail and a mop, making her way along the cavernous hallway to the askari barracks on the other side of the compound, her footsteps echoing from the stone walls.

When she reached Khuda's door, she took out the key that Boris had made at great expense and turned it in the lock. To her great relief, the door opened. Picking up the pail and mop, she entered quickly, closing the door quietly. Once inside, she began a frenzied search for the Cluny cross, rummaging through drawers, clothing, and wooden trunks, careful not to disturb anything. It was not a big place. It must be here, somewhere.

Time passed but she could not find it. With tears of frustration, she sat on the floor, putting her head in her hands. The sound of footsteps echoed nearby and she tensed, but they soon passed. She leaned forward on her elbows, watching a tear splash on the mosaic tile. In distraction, she stuck a finger into it and swirled, following the design. The tile moved slightly.

The tiles! It's under a tile, you stupid girl! She picked at the one that moved. It lifted easily, but there was only mortar underneath. She crawled about the floor, testing every tile frantically. The first room revealed nothing. The second room, nothing. It was getting late. She went into a small, dark storage room. Here! Here's a loose one. Her heart pounded as she lifted it up, revealing a dark cavity. She reached in, grabbing a small canvas bag. This is it! It was heavy—full of gold and silver coins—and there's the cross!

She heard voices, women's voices echoing in the hallway, and they were getting closer. The concubine was returning. The tile clacked as she dropped it back into place with trembling hands. Rushing to the door, she tossed the bag into the empty pail before dashing outside with mop and pail in hand. The voices grew louder. Adele groped with the key to relock the door, but her hands shook so badly, she had trouble getting it in. Finally, she spun the tumbler before darting away in the opposite direction, walking as fast as she could.

The concubine did not see her come out the door, but she saw her rushing away. "Where did she come from?" she asked her escort. The escort shook her head. "You! cleaning-woman! What are you doing here?"

Adele made no reply. She kept walking, rounded a corner of the building, rushed to the other corner, then headed back the way she came. She could hear the woman yelling after her.

"You got it?" Ramiro was astounded, and greatly relieved. He slumped into a chair. "Praise the Lord, my dear! You are an amazing woman!"

"I thought you said I was impossible," she grinned.

"Then I hope you will forgive me for that. Let's see." He reached for the bag. Immediately, he felt the weight of it. "What's this?" He opened it, reached in and pulled out the golden cross. "Adele," he paused. "Adele, I am very grateful to have my cross back. I cannot thank you enough."

"I can think of a way," she cooed.

"I'm sure you can, my dear." He looked in the bag again and frowned. "But you should have left the money. We're not thieves, I just wanted my cross back."

"Sorry. But everything happened so fast... I wasn't thinking."

"Dear, oh dear," Ramiro lamented. "May God have mercy. Khuda will hunt us to the death for this."

"I'll take it back," she said hastily.

"You will not. It's much too late for that."

"Well... maybe we could leave it here with a note."

Ramiro gave her a despairing look. "And do you really believe he will get it?"

She stomped her foot. "Then to hell with the man! We'll just take it with us."

Ramiro shook his head. "I want nothing to do with it!"

Adele grabbed the bag from his hand. "Then I'll take it," she glared. "And I don't want to hear another word about it!"

Ramiro slept uneasily in the August heat. He awoke with a start, getting out of bed to check the door lock. He went to the window and looked out onto the courtyard. He checked the window latch.

Adele rose from bed, sauntering up behind him. "Do you think he knows already?"

Ramiro jumped at her voice. "By all Saints!" he caught his breath. "You frightened me out of my wits."

She took his arm. "You're awfully nervous."

"I admit, I'm very worried. When Khuda discovers his money is gone, he'll come to our door—no matter what the hour. He's a seasoned warrior. Our heads will roll. I just hope we can get out in time."

It was the day for the Christians to dig trenches.

"The guard will be here soon. We must hurry!" Ramiro fussed.

Adele scowled. "I'm going as fast as I can!"

"We can't take all of this, woman!" he gestured in frustration. "Do you really need all these bags of clothes?"

"I'll carry them myself!" she snapped. "You've no need to worry yourself to death."

He raised his eyes to heaven, praying inwardly. Dear Lord, give me strength...

"Come on, Ramiro!" Her auburn hair dangled in her face. "We don't want to be roaming the roads after dark!"

Ramiro prayed again. ...and especially with this mule-headed woman. He took a bag from her hand. "You don't need to carry all that."

"When can we leave?" she asked.

"I'm not sure. We must wait for the guard."

Khuda paled in shock and anger. His cache was gone. "Where is it?" he yelled at his concubine.

"I don't know, Master, I swear in the name of Allah!"

He slapped her face and she staggered back. "Where is it, you whore? I'll slit your throat right here!"

The woman cringed. "Please, Master! I know nothing of it. I didn't even know it was here." Tears streamed her face. "I swear it, my Lord." Khuda stepped forward to beat her again. She backed away. "It was the slave! The cleaning woman!"

He grabbed her by the arm. "What do you mean?"

She told him she saw the cleaning woman rushing away. "I thought little of it, Master. But that is all I saw, by the mercy of Allah!"

"Get up! Bring the slave to me!"

She got to her feet cautiously before scurrying out the door.

The cleaning woman screamed in terror. "It was not me, Effendi! I wasn't here!" Khuda beat her again with a stick. Blood ran from her head. "It was the Christian woman!"

"What woman?" he shouted, striking her again.

"The one... the one with red hair," she sniveled. "She paid me to stay away."

Khuda lowered his stick, glowering at her. He knew only one woman with red hair. "So how did she get in?"

The slave lowered her eyes to the floor, too frightened to speak.

"You gave her a key! Didn't you?" He hit her again.

Her eyes widened in fear. "I meant no harm, Master. Forgive me!"

Khuda lunged at her, grabbing her by the throat with his big hands. She lashed back with arms and legs—but she struggled in vain. He squeezed hard, watching her die.

September 1097

A guard banged on the door.

"What is it?" Ramiro asked as he peeked out.

"You will come with me!" he shouted. "The Emir has ordered you to the work party."

"Very well," he said, opening the door. "Give us a few minutes to get ready."

The guard looked in, seeing Adele standing ready with bags. "Just the men are ordered out," he said. "No women or children."

"But she must come," Ramiro countered.

The guard was unmoved. "Sorry, I have my orders."

Adele stood behind Ramiro. He knew her temper and could feel her push forward to confront the guard. He turned, putting a hand out to stop her while placing a finger to his lips. He turned back to the guard, scratching at his black beard and pursing his lips in thought. "Tell me," he asked the guard, "did not Muslim women draw water for the men working outside yesterday?"

The guard shuffled a little. "Uh, yes, I suppose."

"Well then, that is what this woman will do. A Christian woman to draw water for the Christian men. How can you deny her that?"

The young man hesitated, he appeared uneasy. "I'll have to check with the sergeant."

Ramiro put a hand into his pocket, pulling out a silver dirham. He gave it to the guard. "Thank you. Thank you very much. Please keep this for your troubles. We will wait here."

The guard walked away, staring at the coin in his hand. He had no sooner rounded a corner when Ramiro took a bag from Adele. "Let's go. This way. Quickly! We'll head for the Gate of Saint George." They rushed downstairs to join the others. The sheer number of Christians leaving the compound seemed to overwhelm the two guards checking papers at the exit. Ramiro and Adele pushed themselves into the middle, and no one stopped them.

Christian men clogged the streets, all heading out to dig trenches, but there was little order among them. Ramiro took Adele's arm with one hand and held his shoulder bag with the other. "We must head south and find an inn before dark."

She leaned into his ear, huffing from the weight of her bags. "We should go north to join the Christian army!"

"No, I will take no part in holy war. I'll take you to the port at Saint Simeon. You can get a ship to Byzantium."

"But I'll be safer with my own kind."

"The French? Do you really think you'll be safer with the French or the Germans?" he asked in a harsh whisper. "These people are not farmers, Adele. They are soldiers of fortune, filled with bloodlust and greed. Gold and glory are all they seek. You will become their slave!"

"The Turks are no better!" she snapped. "They killed my parents and put me into slavery!"

"Your parents died fighting a war, Adele. And everyone takes slaves in war. I sincerely doubt French masters would treat you any better than Arabs or Greeks." He continued to take long strides along the cobbled streets. "But you are free to make your own decisions. I do not hold you." He took a drink of water from his flask, trying to appear indifferent.

She rushed alongside him. "And what will you do, Ramiro?" She jutted her chin. "You would leave me alone?"

"I want you to be safe. I can find an escort for you... a Byzantine escort. But I must go to Jerusalem. Only God can stop me."

She dropped her bags and grabbed him by the arm, pulling him to a stop. "Then I'm going with you." she said with a tone of finality.

He shook his head. "No, you cannot. It will be an arduous and dangerous journey."

"Ramiro, my husband, every road is fraught with danger, like you always say."

"Blessed Saints, woman! I'm telling you it's too dangerous!"

Adele shook her head in disapproval. "Now, now, dear Ramiro. God would not be pleased with your hot temper."

He reddened, putting a hand to his iron cross while muttering a prayer. Then he bent down to take one of her bags. "Very well, have your way. But I'll hear no complaints." He looked into the sky. "We better go. It's almost noon. We'll head south for Latakia."

"Look!" She pointed. "There's the gate!"

Ramiro looked over to the Gate of Saint George and the long line of men and women waiting to pass through. Guards stood on either side. He took a minute to scan the crowd, but he stopped suddenly, spinning around. "It's Khuda!" He motioned for her to turn her face away. "He's watching at the gate!" He pulled her in the opposite direction. "We must head north—to the Gate of Saint Paul."

"That's too far," she said, pulling him back. "Let's go to Bridge Gate... it's closer and we can still head south to Latakia." She referred to the western gate that bridged the River Orontes.

"Good idea. Let's go, let's go."

They hurried up the main street heading north but had no sooner reached the intersection of the Bridge Gate Road when Ramiro stopped again. "Look," he said, tilting his head to the intersection. "That man on a horse. That's one of Khuda's men. I recognize him from the slave market in Aleppo—do you remember?"

Adele glanced toward the man. It was him—the man called Toros. "Yeh, yeh. I remember that one! He worked for the slaver," she said with bitterness. But she had no sooner uttered those words when Toros looked in their direction, catching her eye. She turned away quickly, but her quick turn exposed a lock of auburn hair from beneath her headscarf. "He saw me, Ramiro! He saw me!"

Ramiro glanced over. She was right. Toros was heading toward them. "Quick!

Down this alleyway! Come!" They took off, walking as fast as they could without drawing attention, delving into the alleyway.

Long stone fences, standing the height of a tall man, lined the alley on either side. Small wooden gates interspersed, each one leading to a private residence. They rushed along and Ramiro tried every one. But they were locked. He looked behind. No sign of Toros yet. He tried a few more gates. One was loose. The hooves of a horse clattered on the flagstones behind them. He put his shoulder to the gate and it flew open. "Quick! Inside." They slipped into a small courtyard, shut the gate, and ducked down behind the fence. The clatter of hooves grew louder. A rider went by. Then another... and another. He held a finger to his lips.

But just as the clatter of hooves faded away, someone screamed behind them. They turned with a start to see an old woman rushing out of the cottage wielding a broom. "Please, Sayyidah, please be quiet." Ramiro tried to speak gently. "We mean you no harm. I swear to Allah." Again, he put a finger to his lips.

The woman shrieked. "Get out! Get out!"

Ramiro was somewhat relieved at her cry. Even though he had spoken in Arabic, the woman yelled back in Greek. He held up his palms in surrender. "Please, mother, we are Christian," he answered in Greek before turning to Adele in French. "Adele, give her some money. Quick now. Before Khuda's men return."

Adele fumbled in her bag, taking out a silver coin. She offered it with outstretched arm.

The woman looked at her suspiciously. Then she squinted at the coin. "What have you got?" she asked in a shrill voice.

"It's a dirham for you," Ramiro said softly. "And I will give you more if you help us." The old woman hesitated, not taking the coin.

Just then, a young man rushed out the door of the cottage, raising a club against them. But the woman held out her arm. "Enough!" she shouted, stopping him in his tracks. "Take the money." A dirham was more money than her son could earn with three months' hard labor.

The young man stepped forward, still holding up the club. Cautiously, he took the coin from Adele's hand to inspect it. He looked back at his mother and nodded his approval.

Meanwhile, Toros had heard the old woman's yell and turned his mount around. He rode back standing in his stirrups to look over the fences. His men did the same.

They all heard the horses returning. "Inside!" the woman cried. "Inside!"

"You are safe for now," said the young man as he drew away from the window.

"How can we get out of the city?" Ramiro asked. "They're probably watching every gate."

The man sat down as his mother served mint tea. "Take the Iron Gate high up on Mount Silpios. You can bribe the guards there. The Turks expect you to try the south gates to head into Christian territory."

"Is that the gate by the citadel?" Adele asked. "The one near the crest of the mountain?"

The young man blushed, not used to being addressed by a strange woman. "That's the one," he replied without looking at her. "But you must stay off the main road. Use the alleyways."

"Guide us to the Iron Gate," Ramiro said. "And we will give you another dirham."

Ramiro let out a heavy sigh of relief. They had just stepped outside the Iron Gate to begin their journey down the rough, gullied road that headed east for Aleppo and, after a distance, south to the Orontes Valley.

"You gave him too much!" Adele complained.

"Blessed saints, Adele! I would have given him everything to get out of this wretched city. "We're free, Adele. Free! Come! We must head for Latakia. We'll have to take the long route around the mountains."

"We can still afford to sail," she said. "Perhaps we could get a ship back to Byzantium or Italy."

"I'm not going back to Byzantium until I've delivered the cross!" Ramiro retorted, somewhat vexed.

"Have it your way!" she huffed, turning away while lifting one of her heavy bags with a grunt. "But we'll need a donkey, Ramiro. We'll never get to Jerusalem on foot. And now you'll have to use Khuda's money after all!"

"The infidels have escaped, my Lord," said Khuda to Yaghi Siyan. "I ask permission to hunt them down." He was red with fury.

When Khuda became Yaghi Siyan's askari, he had given up his independence. The Emir, always worried about the loyalty of his men, kept all weapons and armor in the citadel, giving them out only when needed. Even the horses were confined to the Emir's stables.

Yaghi Siyan stared at him in disbelief. "How can you ask such a thing at a time like this? The barbarians ravage the countryside! The Christians massacre our garrisons!" His long, white beard wagged as he ranted. "And you come to me about your money—about a slave-girl! What do I care about a slave! I need all the men I can muster. You will stay!"

Khuda gritted his teeth and bowed his head. "Yes, Beyfendi. As you command."

SUGAR BRIDGE

Ramiro and Adele hurried east across the rough terrain of Mount Silpios before turning south to follow a wending path through miles of dark-green forests, thick with pine and cypress and teeming with wolves and wildcats. They escaped with few supplies, sleeping under a rough lean-to while keeping a small fire to ward off the beasts of the night. By next afternoon, they were off the mountain and the path dropped to the wide floor of the fertile Orontes Valley, where it passed through vast fields of sugarcane spread out in emerald blankets on either side of the Orontes river.

They soon came to the village of Jisr Ash-Shughur, a sugar farming community nestled between the northern foothills of the Coastal Mountains and the Orontes river. The villagers shied away, fearful of strangers. But Ramiro managed to rent a small room in a quiet tavern, the only tavern. The village seemed a peaceful place, ruled as it was by a petty Turk governor with a single garrison of troops.

Ramiro was elated to be out of Antioch. For over three years, they had been prisoners of Yaghi Siyan, and for over three years, they were forbidden to send out letters. Now they were free, free to go to Jerusalem and free to complete his mission. If, indeed, there was any mission left to complete. *Abbot Hugh must think me dead by now. I must get a report to him and ask what I should do. But what shall I say? There is so much to say. Where do I begin?*

He gazed north from the small veranda of his room in the tavern, surveying the road to Antioch as it meandered up the hill before disappearing in thin forests of Aleppo pine and Valonia oak. Clutching a quill in one hand, he tried to think of the right words, but his mind wandered to the boy, Jameel, and his old tutor, Tatran, and he wondered what happened to them after they fled Antioch. *He prayed they had escaped the clutches of Yaghi Siyan. His thoughts strayed to his mother and he feared he had broken her heart. And then he thought of the Patriarch and the meaning of his cross, if indeed there was any meaning. But soon he came to his senses thinking about how furious Khuda must be. A chill ran down his spine. Will he come after us?*

He felt for his golden cross, still pinned into his vest pocket. He was so relieved to have it back. Finally, there was some hope. "Please Lord," he prayed aloud. "Guide my feet to Jerusalem."

Adele yelled from inside. "Ramiro! Come! Lunch is ready!"

The innkeeper gesticulated wildly as he spoke. "The Western barbarians raid and pillage all the land, even to Aleppo," he said in a loud voice. "They are coming this way."

"Are you sure?" Ramiro asked.

"I'm quite sure, Sayyid. My cousin told me. He has seen them!"

Ramiro said nothing. His mind raced. Trouble was brewing. We must leave for Jerusalem, and we must leave now... before the rains come.

The next day, he loaded a mule and a donkey, bought with Khuda's money. "Where's the tent?" he shouted.

It's still upstairs," said Adele. "You get it."

"And where's my new medicine bag?"

"It's right there," she pointed. "You hung it from the saddle horn."

"Are you ready to go yet?" he fretted. "The sun is already a hand up and it's going to be a hot day."

Highwaymen

Ramiro struggled up the steep road heading west through the Coastal Mountains and beyond to Latakia on the Mediterranean coast. Adele plodded beside him, straining from the arduous climb in the heat of a hot autumn day. By the time the road flattened out, the sun settled behind high peaks and the air began to cool.

"We better camp here," he said. "It'll be dark soon."

A twig cracked and the bushes rustled, then another crack. Adele looked around cautiously. "What's that?"

Ramiro peered into the dimming light. "I don't know, an animal perhaps."

Another noise, and now he wished he had a weapon. Adele scoured the ground before grabbing a hefty stick of oak. They stood still and watched.

"There!" she whispered, pointing through a cluster of dry buckthorn.

Then Ramiro saw it move. "It's a dog—I think it's a dog."

"Strange dog," said Adele. "It's got black and white stripes."

He looked again. "It's a hyena. I've seen them before."

"Hyena? What's that?"

"It's like a dog... but more vicious and sly."

"Will it attack?"

"Probably not, but we should be vigilant."

"How can we sleep with that thing lurking about? You should start a fire."

Adele slept nervously, waking at every sound. She thought she heard another noise just as the faint light of dawn glowed against the tent. "Ramiro!" she whispered, jabbing him in the ribs. "Somebody or something's out there. I think I heard a horse... or maybe that hyena."

He lifted his tired head. "By God's mercy, woman! How will I get any sleep?"

She gave him a push. "Go look!"

He groaned loudly before he threw off the blanket and stumbled out. A thin trail of smoke still rose from the embers of their fire. He looked around. "I see nothing. You will make an old man of me with all this worry."

But then he heard it too. It was the pounding of hooves—and it was getting closer. "Quick! Get out of the tent!"

She rushed out. "What is it?"

"Someone comes. I'll get the mule. You grab the donkey. Move into the bushes!"

They were barely concealed when three riders came charging down the mountain road. They rode straight for the tent, where they came to a sudden stop. A cloud of dust followed their path, drifting through the bushes. Adele coughed.

The men jumped from their mounts, drew their swords and ran after them.

Ramiro saw them coming. He moved into full view, holding up his hands. "Peace be upon you, Sadah. We mean no harm."

The men wore black kafiyas, and black capes covered their long, white tunics. Three had mustaches, one a full beard. With sinister laughs, they surrounded the two. "Give us what you have!" said the bearded man. "Before we slit your throats!"

Ramiro and Adele stood in tunics alone. "We have nothing on us," said Ramiro, hoping they would leave.

"Search the tent!" said the man.

One of them scurried into the tent, throwing everything outside. He searched their clothes and bags. That's when they found the purse of coins in Adele's coat. And soon, he found the cross in Ramiro's vest. He held it up for the bearded one to see. "Look at this, Yaqut!"

Yaqut took it from his accomplice, turning it in his hand. Then he grabbed the purse and shook it. His cruel eyes twinkled as he smiled.

"Please," said Ramiro. "I must have the cross. Take the money and leave us."

Yaqut walked over to him and, without warning, belted him across the face. Ramiro dropped to his knees.

"I will take both your money and your gold cross, kafir!" Then he leered at Adele and smirked. "And I will take your woman too." He moved over to her, grabbed her arm and put a hand to her breasts. Adele slapped him. He slapped her back. Her head spun from the impact.

Ramiro knelt on the ground, holding a hand to his bruised face. But when he saw Yaqut slap Adele, an indignant fury boiled in his chest, soon exploding in blind rage. Without thinking, he charged forward like a mad bull, crashing head-on into the tall highwayman, lifting him right off his feet and dashing him to the rocky ground. Ramiro got on top of him with all his weight and began to pound his head with his fists. Yaqut, a big man himself, managed to heave him off and they rolled on the sharp stones, locked in a brutal duel. The money and the cross flew from Yaqut's hand, spewing onto the gravel. But neither man gave heed as they fought for their lives.

The other two highwaymen simply watched and laughed. They were confident Yaqut would prevail, and then they would have some good sport. They would torture and kill this troublesome kafir before having the pleasure of his woman.

But while the two men watched the fight, Adele moved behind them. She held the club of oak she had found the night before and readied it for the highwayman closest to her. Gripping it with both hands, she swung it as hard as she could—right against the back of the man's head. There was a loud, hollow whack, as if she had hit a tree trunk. The man flew forward without a sound, falling face first into the dirt. He lay motionless. The other highwayman turned, staring at his fallen comrade in disbelief. He spun his eyes to Adele, raised his sword, and went after her.

Ramiro's weight was to his advantage. He pinned Yaqut under him, putting a knee on his sword arm. Then again, he pounded his fists into the highwayman's face until the man stopped moving. He heard Adele scream for help. He looked up to see her dodging behind thin pines as one of the thieves tried to slash her. Ramiro pulled Yaqut's sword from its sheath. He rushed over, raising the blade as he ran and, with breathless fury, swung it hard against the robber's right side.

The blow severed the man's forearm and it fell twitching to the ground. The highwayman shrieked as blood spurted from the stump of his arm. He looked at Ramiro in astonishment and horror before falling to his knees, clutching uselessly at his bleeding stump. "Please, Sayyid!" he yelled. "Have mercy!"

But Ramiro was no more the pliant monk. In the tempest of battle, his soldier's instincts became acutely alive. His black eyes glowered, his heart pounded, and his chest heaved. The flush of battle was on his cheeks. He raised the sword again, ready for the fatal strike…

A loud whack! The highwayman's head flopped forward and he slumped to the dirt. Adele stood behind him, holding the bloodied club.

"Devil's bastard!" she yelled. She hit him again, even as he lay motionless. Then she kicked him, and kicked him again.

"Adele!" Ramiro shouted. "He's down. We're alright. Stop now."

A horse whinnied behind them. Yaqut had recovered from Ramiro's beating and, while they scuffled with the other highwayman, he managed to get back to his horse. Ramiro ran after him but Yaqut kicked in his heels and galloped away, heading down the road the way they had just come, down to Jisr Ash-Shughur.

"The cross!" Ramiro cried out. He rushed over to the spot where they had fought and searched the ground. "It's gone!" he wailed. "And the money too!" He picked up several coins dropped in the scuffle. "Quickly, we must go," he said, putting on his vest and coat.

Adele straightened her hair. "What about these men?"

"They're dead."

"Should we bury them?"

"We have no time. The hyenas will clean them up." He threw Yaqut's sword to the ground but took a dirk from one of the dead highwaymen and strapped it to his belt. He looked about. "Come now! Get the donkey."

"What about the money?" she asked. "What are we going to do now?"

"Did they get it all?"

"No," she sighed. "I put some of it in the saddle bag, but the bastard got most of it."

"It doesn't matter," Ramiro said dismissively. "We should still have enough to get to Jerusalem."

"So, what do you think?" Adele asked as she looked down the road. "Should we still head for Latakia?"

"We can't go to Latakia now. I must retrieve the cross."

She shook her head. "No, Ramiro. Let's get out of here while we can."

"No, I cannot," he said with a look of annoyance. "I cannot arrive in Jerusalem without it."

She put a hand to his arm. "I thought you wanted to avoid the trouble in Antioch? We can be in Jerusalem in two weeks."

The muscles of Ramiro's face tightened. "As I said, I cannot arrive without the cross."

"God's blood, man!" she shouted, her face crimson. "What about your mother?"

"Really, Adele, must you curse like a Provencal fishwife?" He took her hand. "Believe me, my dear woman, my heart yearns to see my mother again but I have serious obligations which I cannot ignore. I promised in the name of God I would deliver it."

She pulled her hand away. "Can the cross be that damned important?" she asked in a bitter voice. "Are you going to risk our lives over it?"

"No, I'll risk my own life—not yours."

"And what am I supposed to do? Travel by myself?"

"You can stay in Ash-Shughur until I retrieve it."

"God's blood!" she spat. "I think not!"

Jisr Ash-Shughur was as quiet as ever. Ramiro described the brigand to all he met. "Have you seen him?" he asked. "His face is badly beaten. The other bandits called him Yaqut." But no one had seen the man.

"You were robbed?" asked the innkeeper. "Where?"

Ramiro told him the story.

"You see? This is the trouble when there is no rule, no order." The innkeeper shook his head. "The Turks can no longer protect us."

"Which way would he go?" Ramiro asked.

"He could go south along the Orontes and travel to Homs. Or maybe he went east to Maarat An-Numan. Or north to Aleppo."

"I doubt he went north. The Christian army comes."

The innkeeper pointed east. "Go to the road leading south and ask returning travelers. Someone must have seen him. Then go to the Maarat road and do the same."

Ramiro asked everyone he met on the road to Homs. No one remembered the man. So they rushed to the road going east to Maarat and asked again.

"You've seen this man? His name is Yaqut."

"Yes, Sayyid," said the farmer. "He was very rude. Took our water without thanks. His face was swollen—like he was stung by bees. He's heading east for Maarat An-Numan."

"Go east? To where?" Adele asked as they rode away.

"To a place called Maarat. It's on the plateau we saw from the other side. It's not far—but we must hurry before the highwayman heads farther east."

"You'll never get to Jerusalem that way," she piped in a cold voice.

MAARAT

The vast, rolling steppe of Syria opened up before them when they reached the summit of the plateau—a dry and brittle grassland of low, rounded hills that stretched as far as the eye could see. The road to Maarat wound its way through it, disappearing into a hazy horizon.

Miles before the city, the grasslands turned to fields of wheat and barley where peasants worked the harvest. Grain was the gold of Maarat, and the city lay on a lucrative trade route. Ramiro and Adele approached from the west, but the main traffic through the city was by way of an ancient road running from Aleppo in the north, to Hama, Homs, and Damascus in the south. The Romans paved it all the way to Petra in the Transjordan and then west to Egypt. They called it the Via Nova. But the Arabs still thought of it by its old name, the King's Highway.

"We must find the cross as quickly as possible," Ramiro said as they approached the city gate. "Look at this traffic! Head for the stables first—then we'll go to the markets!"

"So what now?" Adele asked as they walked away from yet another storefront. "We've tried every jeweler and pawnbroker. It's not here."

"It's got to be here," said Ramiro.

She let out a long sigh of exasperation. "Let's get something to eat."

As they made their way across the market, winding past stalls and shoppers, a small group of armed men wandered nearby, led by a plump man in fine attire. Two thin scribes followed him closely, going from stall to stall. Adele eyed them suspiciously, avoiding their path.

"Not to worry," said Ramiro, noticing her aversion. "That's the Muhtasib, the market supervisor. He's just collecting taxes from the merchants."

A boy at a food stall rolled hot flatbread around a dollop of couscous and vegetables, handing them to Ramiro in paper napkins. They wandered about for a place to sit before taking a low bench recently abandoned by another couple.

Adele was half-way through her meal when she suddenly spat her food to the ground. "There he is!" She jabbed at Ramiro. "Look! Over there!" she pointed. "It's him! It's Yaqut!" And so it was. Yaqut the highwayman, his face badly swollen and bruised, was arguing with a merchant. He was no more than twenty paces away.

Ramiro saw that Yaqut had found another sword. He got up suddenly, leaving his meal on the bench before striding briskly toward the thief, feeling for the dirk he had recently acquired from the dead highwayman. "Yaqut!" he shouted.

Yaqut looked over in alarm. Someone knew his name. He saw Ramiro, then Adele following behind. He reached for his sword.

But Ramiro was on him, grabbing his sword arm. "I want my cross, thief!"

Yaqut broke free, jumping back while drawing his sword. The crowd around them gasped, shuffling out of the way. Ramiro pulled his knife, standing defensively, but he knew it was no match for a sword. The merchants yelled for help. Yaqut looked around warily. He started to back away. Suddenly, the crowd parted and four soldiers of the Muhtasib barged onto the scene, swords at the ready. Ramiro dropped his dirk, showing open palms. The soldiers turned to Yaqut.

Yaqut panicked. He was a known thief, he would be executed. He jumped at one of the soldiers, slashing his arm. The others backed away in shock, not expecting real trouble. Yaqut parried with another, stabbing him in the side. When the soldier kept advancing, he slashed his legs, making him stumble and fall. The other two called for help. Yaqut backed away before turning to barge through the crowd. People screamed and yelled as they fell out of his way. The soldiers went after him. More troops arrived, and they too rushed off in pursuit.

Ramiro put his hands down, he had been forgotten in the melee. The two fallen soldiers lay nearby, groaning and clutching at their wounds. He rushed over to one of them, who held a bloodied hand to his side. "I can help," he said to the soldier. "Let me see the wound." Yaqut's sword had missed vital organs. He would live if they could halt the bleeding. "Quick!" he shouted to the crowd. "Give me a scarf!" Someone offered and he wrapped it tight around the soldier's torso. The crowd offered more strips of cloth which he used to bind the cut to the man's leg and to stifle the bleeding of the other soldier's arm.

"What's your name?" someone asked boldly.

Ramiro looked up. It was the Muhtasib. "I am Ramiro of Cluny, Effendi."

The Muhtasib, a well-fed man with a full beard, folded his arms. A jewel sparkled from his red turban. Two soldiers, holding whips, stood beside him.

"Ramiro of Cluny," said the Muhtasib, "I see you are Christian. Don't you know it is forbidden for you to own a weapon?"

Ramiro stood and bowed lightly. "A thousand apologies, Effendi. But that man is a thief. He robbed us in the mountains and was going to kill us."

The Muhtasib ignored his entreaty. "You must also know it is forbidden for a Christian to attack a Muslim? I don't like this kind of trouble in my market."

"But the man drew his sword against me, Effendi. He's a thief. He took my cross."

"Your cross? You fight over a trifle?"

"It is a gold cross, Effendi, of some value."

"Aah," said the Muhtasib in understanding. "You will come with me. I want a full report."

Ramiro opened his hands in plea. "There is little else left to say, Effendi, it is simple theft."

The Muhtasib seemed not to hear. "You will come with me—or do my men have to drive you with their whips?"

Ramiro sat alone in the small holding cell. He told them all he would dare to tell. He said he was from Antioch but not that Yaghi Siyan held him as a prisoner. He told them of his cross but not that it may contain something for the Patriarch. After hours of questioning, they left him alone on a stone bench. Only after the muezzin sounded the call to sunset prayers, was he released without a word.

"Did they catch the thief?" asked Adele as she rubbed her arms in the cool evening air. She had been waiting outside for hours.

"They would not say," he said as he removed his cloak and threw it over her shoulders.

"Thank you." She pulled it tight around her. "And what about the cross?"

"They said they would look for it. I gave them a quick sketch."

"What do we do now?"

"We wait. Come, we will get a room for the night."

The Qadi of Maarat sat on a large, golden cushion raised on a dais. A long, white cloak draped from his shoulders, partially covering his red, silk tunic.

And a white turban sat atop his chiseled face. He stroked his gray beard in thought. "You say he is a physician?"

"Yes, Qadi," said the Muhtasib, bowing before him. "He attended to the soldiers and dressed their wounds in a most professional manner."

"We could use more physicians... even if he is a Christian."

"Yes, Qadi."

"Did you catch this thief?"

"We did, my Qadi. We cut him down at the north gate. He had a bag of coins and the cross was hidden in his tunic."

"Let me see this cross."

The chubby Muhtasib signaled to a servant who rushed to the Qadi's side with a wrapped object. He unfolded the wrap to reveal Ramiro's cross and offered it up with an open palm.

The Qadi picked it up, turning it in his hand. "A beautiful piece. But it seems a little beaten up. What happened to it?"

"The dhimmi said it was thrown to the ground during his scuffle with the thief."

"Is it really made of gold?"

"The smith said it is made of gold and silver, Qadi. The Christian is very keen to have it back."

"I'm sure he is," he said before falling silent for a long moment. "You will bring him to me."

Two fierce looking mamluks stood on either side of the seated Qadi, who was adjusting the shoulders of his white cloak. He gestured to another cushion beside the platform. "Sit," he ordered.

Ramiro sat down awkwardly. He said nothing.

"What brings you to Maarat An-Numan?" he asked with hands on folded knees.

"My wife and I are on our way to Jerusalem, Qadi. We were robbed on the road to Latakia."

The Qadi studied Ramiro, his eyes sweeping up and down. "Tell me, Ramiro of Cluny, how did such an expensive piece come into your hands?"

"I am just a courier, my Lord. I am bidden to deliver it to the Patriarch of Jerusalem."

"You are Roman?"

"No, Qadi, I come from a land farther west."

The Qadi nodded with disinterest. After a long pause, he spoke again. "You are a physician?"

"Well, Effendi, I know something of medicine and have studied the works of physicians and scholars, but I was never trained at your universities."

"The Muhtasib tells me you dressed the wounds of our men. I am in your debt. Is there anything I can do for you?"

"If it pleases my Lord, I desire only to retrieve what was taken from me so that I may continue my journey."

The Qadi's lips spread wide in a thin, contrived smile. "Then you will be pleased to know that we managed to retrieve your cross."

"Why, that is wonderful news, indeed!"

The Qadi held up a hand to silence him. "But it has come at a cost," he lied. "We had to buy it back from a merchant. It was extremely expensive."

Ramiro frowned. "How expensive?"

"Three gold dinar."

"But what of our purse? Did you not recover it as well?"

"Purse? No, only the cross," he lied again.

Ramiro groaned. It was an impossible sum. It would take months to collect that much. "I do not have the money, Effendi," he admitted.

"No matter. I'm sure we can come to some arrangement for you to work off the debt," said the Qadi in feigned sympathy.

Ramiro glanced at him suspiciously. "And what do you suggest, my Qadi?"

"I suggest you join the hospital," he said raising his bearded chin, "where you can attend to injury and illness. You will be well remunerated for your troubles."

"But Qadi, that could take some time."

The Qadi tried to look concerned. "Well, if you can think of any other way to obtain the money, that is up to you. But it is unlikely you will find a position with better pay."

Ramiro bowed in defeat, realizing he must play for time. "Yes, my Qadi. As you wish."

"So how long is this going to take?" Adele asked in mounting frustration.

"I'm not sure," said Ramiro as he squatted on the floor of the empty room. "But at least we know he has the cross. How much money do we have left?"

"Not much. It may add up to a silver dirham or two. How much are they paying you?"

"They didn't say and it didn't seem like the right time to ask."

Adele tossed her head back. "Blood of Christ!" She looked around their newly rented room and her small nose wrinkled in disgust. "Well, I'm not staying here. The place stinks! And the cockroaches are as big as mice!"

He waved a hand to settle her down. "Rest assured, my dear. There is no need to stay here. The Qadi has given us very nice quarters near the hospital."

Weeks passed in Maarat and, over time, Ramiro became popular at the hospital. His jovial manner, linguistic skills, and his first-rate knowledge of medicine quickly endeared him to the staff. He was in the laboratory making a tonic for dysentery when the horrendous news reached the hospital.

"The barbarians march on Antioch!"

REPORT: MAARAT

Ramiro squinted at the long, yellow flame of the oil lamp. He wondered if his reports to the Abbot were just a waste of time now that the French had begun their invasion. It had been four years since he posted his last report from Edessa and two years since he gave Ibrahim his letter for the Patriarch. Did he get it? If so, did he notify the Abbot? He put his pen down and stood to stretch. What else could he say to the Abbot? He told him all he knew of Antioch, of its impregnable walls and towers and how the city guards all traffic coming from the sea into northern Syria. And he mentioned that many Christians lived there and they were free to worship and engage in commerce.

He sat back down and dipped his quill to remind Hugh that the Great Emir of Syria, brother to the Sultan, had died in battle and that now his sons fought internecine wars, letting the country fall into a state of lawlessness where highwaymen roamed freely. Only the walled cities offered any safety, Jerusalem among them. While admitting much was hearsay, he told him the Egyptians fought for southern Palestine and controlled several port cities, including a place called Ascalon and maybe even the busy port of Jaffa.

But he said nothing of the cross, and he certainly could not tell the Abbot about Adele. He finished the report, putting it aside before taking up a fresh sheet of paper. He would send another letter to Aldebert to let him know he was safe and to explain his delay in reaching Jerusalem. Ramiro remembered that he had told Aldebert to return home if he did not hear from him after a year. So he must have gone back to the abbey by now.

ANTIOCH

"Tarsus has fallen, my Lord. And the whole of Cilicia. The barbarians took it with hardly a fight. The Armenians helped them. May Allah curse them!"

Yaghi Siyan wrung his hands as he paced back and forth in the citadel sitting high above the city of Antioch. These unholy barbarians seem unstoppable, despite their heavy losses, "Damned Christians! May Allah render them helpless. This is the work of the devil Roman King!" He was about to bark an order to his men when he heard a frenzied shout from the sentinel.

"They're here! They're here!"

Yaghi peered north over the parapets. There, across the broad Plain of Antioch, miles in the distance, rose a billowing cloud of dust. The barbarians had arrived. They swarmed out of the Hatay mountain pass, a writhing mass of flesh and steel spreading across the land like a darkening cloud of locusts.

A prolonged lull of trepidation weighed over the city as word of their arrival passed quickly from mouth to ear in hushed whispers. Men and women prayed in fear. The markets came to a standstill and an eerie silence gripped the air, broken only by a child wailing in the distance. A single warbler trilled from the parapet as if confused by the sudden quiet.

Yaghi Siyan shivered. Why do I worry? These wretched kuffar will never breach the walls of Antioch! Our water is inside. And we have months of food. Even with all their numbers, they cannot guard every gate. We will outlast these heathen dogs! Curse them to hellfire!

The Franj kept coming by the thousands in what seemed like an endless stream of knights and infantry. There were tens of thousands. They surged across the Orontes at the Iron Bridge and, in a rising din of shouts and clacking steel, took up their positions near the three northern gates. The siege of Antioch had begun.

Khuda the Mamluk stared out from the battlements. Thousands of other mamluk did the same, many of them spewing loud insults and vile curses to the stinking foreigners gathering near the gates. But Khuda said nothing. He lamented the loss of his money and the golden cross, brooding bitterly over Ramiro and the red-haired woman. Wrath and revenge burned in his mind. Dog-rutting Christians! They will die! They will take days to die!

Despite his fury, the scene beyond the walls filled him with a sense of overwhelming hopelessness. The barbarian army is huge, and they are everywhere. If I could just get through the Iron Gate. But I need weapons—and I need a horse. Curse the Emir!

Yaghi Siyan's mamluks attacked the Franj whenever they could, picking off strays, foragers, and squads of soldiers. But in every skirmish, they were turned back. Then the ruler of Damascus came up with a great army, declaring Holy War against the infidels. But, alas, to the bitterness and shame of Yaghi Siyan, the man turned away and fled after his first ill-fated battle against the barbarians.

The Crusaders pillaged the countryside for miles around, which forced the Emir of Aleppo, Yaghi Siyan's archenemy, to mount his own attack. The Emir had a strategic advantage at first but he underestimated the fanatical resolve and ferocity of these barbarians. He hoped to surround them but, when he tried, he made a tactical blunder and found his own forces cornered instead. The tables turned quickly and, in another fateful battle, a thousand men fell to the barbarian sword. Yet another campaign ended in disgrace.

"Heathen scum!" Drugo the Red shouted as he brought his sword down hard onto the neck of a Turk captive. But it was a poor cut and the head did not sever on the first blow. The Turk fell forward spurting blood, his head lobbed to the side. "Sarding pagan!" Drugo bellowed as he hacked again, cutting it free. He grabbed the bloodied skull by the hair and threw it onto a pile.

Otto and Arles helped load the large catapult with the grisly heads of the enemy, aiming it over the castellations of Antioch. Otto pulled the release and the bloody payload shot forward. The men around them laughed and jeered as they watched the mutilated heads fly through the air, some soaring over the walls, smashing into city streets, while others missed their mark, splattering against high stone walls.

Robert of Flanders observed from his mount. His flat-topped helmet almost covered his smooth, sloping brow, its nasal strip reaching down to the end of his long, hooked nose. He smiled with thin lips and there was a glint of approval in his blue eyes. He was pleased with the efforts of his men, as were Godfrey, Bohemond, and Raymond, who also watched from horseback. They hoped to drive holy terror into the Turks.

And it worked. The morale within Antioch faltered. Yaghi Siyan had trouble getting any more information about the invading Franj. His spies were terrified. The starving barbarians had captured one of them, torturing and killing the man in gruesome amusement before roasting him on a spit and, to Yaghi's horror, eating his flesh. Now, in heightened desperation, he appealed to the only man with an army large enough to save Antioch from the foreign horde, and that was Kerboga of Mosul, far to the east.

November 1097

The siege of Antioch went on for months. Cold, wet weather weakened the Crusader's resolve and they soon began to starve and die. And when an earthquake shook the mountains, their faith was severely tested. Some deserted in fear and panic, including Peter the Hermit and many others who thought the situation was hopeless. Others blamed the Byzantines for their troubles, so they forced out General Taticius and his men. Those who stayed behind endured weeks more of relentless, freezing rain. Illness and starvation compelled thousands to scrounge for food—any food—grass and nettles, even seeds picked from piles of horse dung.

In desperation, Bohemond and Robert led raiding parties south along the King's Highway but often had little to show for their efforts. Over the following weeks, they survived by slaughtering their pack animals and, eventually, they began to butcher their remaining horses. By winter's end, only seven hundred horses remained for twenty thousand knights.

MAARAT

January 1098

The foreign army dominated the news. But the people of Maarat were not overly concerned about the siege of Antioch. They were primarily Christian and Arab and they had no love for Turks. Nonetheless, it was an uneasy time. They heard rumors of barbarism, even of massacred Christians. And when Bohemond and Robert raided the countryside as far south as Albara, some fled farther south for the relative safety of Homs and Hama.

But Ramiro stayed. Their rooms near the hospital were not spacious but they were clean and well-furnished. He lay on his back on a slew of cushions spaced out on the floor. A wool blanket covered his legs from the cool air of winter. "How much money have we got?"

"Not enough to get the cross," Adele said sharply. "Not even one dinar. You should talk to the Qadi again."

"I agree. We can't stay here any longer. Only God knows what will happen next. And Khuda will come after us sooner or later. I must get the cross so we can move on to Jerusalem in the spring."

Adele studied her appearance with a small glass mirror. "Even if Khuda gets past the French lines, he won't travel easily."

"That's true, but he knows the ways of this land much better than they do. He will come. We have to get to Jerusalem! God help us!"

Adele brushed a lock of hair behind a small ear. "How do I look?"

Ramiro glanced up. A cream wool shawl covered her shoulders. She wore green, silk pajamas with long, embroidered sleeves, a prize she secured in Antioch. "You look as beautiful as ever," he said in all sincerity.

She smiled. "Would you like some more fattoush?"

He shook his head. "No, thank you, I've had enough. And if you keep feeding me like this, I'll soon be as fat as the King of France."

She giggled. "So what do you think?"

"About what?"

"Do you think the French will ever march for Jerusalem?"

"I doubt it. I hear they lost most of their men and horses. Many have deserted and the rest starve. And many more will surely die before they reach the Holy City... if they ever do."

"They've been at Antioch a long time," she said, brushing her hair slowly. "Why do they spend all this time and effort to capture it if they head for Jerusalem?"

Ramiro picked up his cup from the low table, draining the last bit of wine. He cleared his throat. "Without Antioch, their supplies from Byzantium and the West would soon be cut off. They must capture it... or die in the attempt."

"Would you like more wine?"

Ramiro held out a palm. "No thanks, I've had enough."

She didn't seem to hear and filled his cup anyway. "We have all we need to travel."

"All but the cross," Ramiro lamented. "The journey should be safe enough if we can leave soon." He stretched his arms out and yawned. "I'm going to bed," he muttered, but made no effort to get up.

Adele rose to her feet. Her hair hung loosely over her shoulders and her silk pajamas whispered as she moved toward him. She bent over to take his hand, giving it a tug. "And I'm going with you," she cooed with a coquettish grin.

"Are you now?"

She pulled at his hand until he rose to his feet. "Come along, dear husband. You have an important duty to perform."

Antioch

On a cool, sunny morning in February, three Egyptian war-galleys skimmed along the calm waters of the Mediterranean. They headed for the northern port of Saint Simeon, joined by a flotilla of Byzantine triremes sailing out from Cyprus. King Alexios had arranged for the Crusaders besieging Antioch to meet the Egyptian ambassadors sent by Al-Afdal and reminded them that Egypt was his ally against the Turks. On the King's recommendation, the ambassadors met with Raymond of Toulouse the following day. Raymond heard them out, noting their demands before calling a council of commanders.

Raymond greeted the commanders one by one as they filed into the large tent. He stood tall, with gray hair and beard, sporting a muscular build despite being in his sixties. A gray, leather patch covered the empty socket of his right eye, a wound suffered when battling the Moors of Spain.

Raymond was a deeply pious man who rushed to Pope Urban's call, believing he was doing God's work by fighting the heathen. Certainly, age did not hinder his vigor nor his ambition for he saw himself as the leader of the Holy Crusade and the future ruler of the Holy Land. But the wages of war and age were beginning to take their toll and he was often ill.

Bohemond of Taranto waited impatiently. He towered above them all. Born of brutish Norman blood, he was a gigantic man who stood a forearm's length above all others. A heavy brow jutted over his ruthless, light blue eyes. Short, yellow hair, cut Roman style, crowned his huge head. He was a muscular man with a narrow waist and broad shoulders. All this, along with his engaging charm, swayed many a young maiden to his bed. But wise men feared him, for under his smiling, clean-shaven face lurked the ambitious, crafty, and savage persona of his father, Robert Guiscard.

Bohemond had no love for Count Raymond. He knew the man wanted Antioch, but he wanted it too. "So, what did the Egyptians say?" he shouted at Raymond.

Raymond moved to the front, furrowing his eye-patch as he scowled at Bohemond. But he ignored him, remaining quiet until the hubbub of men subsided. Finally, he spoke. "The Lord of Egypt made a proposal. As we have learned, there is no love between the Egyptians and the Turks, even though they are both Muslim."

"Who cares?" yelled Godfrey of Bouillon, who also resented Raymond's command. "They're both whoring pagans!" Godfrey stood taller than most, but not as tall as Bohemond. He was a big man with long, blonde hair and beard, a barreled chest and thick arms. By the age of sixteen, he was an accomplished warrior whose weapon of choice was the crossbow. Now he was thirty-eight and a high nobleman of Lorraine.

Raymond fixed on Godfrey with a look of sufferance. "Thank you, Duke Godfrey, for your keen observations. Now, if you will allow me to continue…"

"Get on with it," said Bohemond.

Raymond raised his voice. "The proposal is this—the Egyptians will assist us in every manner by providing supplies to the ports of Syria and Palestine, giving military assistance whenever possible. In exchange for their cooperation, they request that all former Egyptian territory be returned to them and that all other lands jointly conquered will be divided equally."

"What do they mean by former territory?" asked Robert of Flanders. "Does it include Jerusalem?"

Raymond nodded. "Unfortunately, yes. It includes most of Palestine."

"Never!" Bishop Adhemar snapped. "The Egyptians ask us to forsake Jerusalem! The most blessed Tomb of Christ! What good is Syria to us? The devil can have it for all I care."

Raymond nodded in a gesture of peace. "Of course, I agree, Your Excellency."

"It goes against God's will!" continued the bishop with such conviction that all men felt obliged to nod in agreement.

"I already told the ambassadors as much," said Raymond. "But I present this to you so we may formulate an official response."

Bohemond spoke up. "It would not be wise to infuriate these Egyptians right now. We are in no position to acquire more enemies. And seeing what little help we get from the Greeks, we could use another ally."

"But we cannot agree to forgo Jerusalem!" Adhemar shouted vehemently.

"I know that," said Bohemond as he raised his palm. "But we can delay our response as much as possible. Anything to gain cooperation and time."

"What do you suggest?" asked Raymond grudgingly.

Bohemond stepped to the front. He turned to face the men, his giant build almost hiding Raymond from view. "We should keep them here as long as possible. When they return to Egypt, we will send our own ambassadors back with them."

"What good will that do?" asked Robert of Flanders.

"First," said Bohemond, "it will allow us further delay tactics by letting the Egyptians think we will eventually come to some agreement. And second, our men will have a chance to learn all they can about Egypt and Palestine."

"They will be our spies," said Robert.

"Exactly. We can make a pact with these pagans if it means our survival. Then... who knows? By the will of God, things change, do they not?"

The French ambassadors left for Egypt in March and, not long after their departure, an English fleet put in at Saint Simeon, carrying Italian pilgrims and a store of supplies and material from Constantinople—all destined for the siege of Antioch. With this desperately needed shipment, the Crusaders were able to tighten their blockade, as General Taticius had recommended to them long before.

THE EMIR'S FOLLY

June 1098

Yaghi Siyan paced in the palace. He rubbed at the sharp pain in his arm. His stomach churned. "When will Kerboga come from Mosul? He's three weeks late!"

"No one knows, my Lord," said the atabek. "We have trouble getting scouts past the barbarian lines. But we hear that one of them, a man called Baldwin, has seized Edessa from the Armenians. Perhaps he challenged Kerboga's army on the way." He spread his hands apologetically.

"He must come soon. We cannot hold much longer, we need more supplies." He pulled at his white beard. "By the mercy of Allah, when will he come?"

A dawn trumpet sounded. But it was not the horn of Antioch, it was the trumpet of the Franj. "My Lord, wake up! Wake up!" the chamberlain shouted. "The barbarians have taken the citadel!"

"The citadel?" Yaghi gasped. "Eight months of siege and now this! How?"

"We were betrayed, my Lord, by an accursed Armenian! May Allah strike him dead!"

The citadel was the last stronghold, the last hope. The news was more than Yaghi could bear. He staggered in fear. "Get my horse ready! At once!"

In dreaded haste, Yaghi Siyan abandoned his city, his family, and all his possessions. He fled Antioch with a small group of askari, Khuda among them. They charged through the Iron Gate, galloping east along the thin mountain road to Aleppo.

But Yaghi was no more than a few miles from the city when he succumbed to deep remorse. His flight had been frantic and reckless. In wailing grief, he collapsed from his mount, falling to the ground. The askari attempted to put him back in the saddle but he would not stay, slumping again, barely conscious. Fearing pursuit, they left him there to die, racing for the safety of Aleppo.

But after an hour's ride, Khuda left the others, turning south on another path. Now that Yaghi Siyan was deposed, he was free and had a chance to recover his gold. And he knew where that damned Christian was heading.

Yaghi Siyan's flight was foolhardy. If he had kept his head, he would have soon discovered that the Western barbarians did not take the citadel. Instead they had captured the Tower of Two Sisters on the south wall. If he had assembled his troops, he could have easily driven them off.

But now, in the confusion, the Franj managed to get inside the walls to unlock a city gate. The doors swung wide and the waiting barbarians stormed in by the thousands, swords drawn, hooting and yelling, rampaging through Antioch like a scourge from hell, hacking and stabbing, raping, pillaging, and burning, killing every man, woman, and child. Muslim, Christian, and Jew alike died in a frenzy of slaughter. The apocalyptic infidels, drenched red with blood from head to toe, howled above the terrified screams of their victims, "God wills it! God wills it!"

But Khuda gave little thought to the distant screams from Antioch. He raced south along the King's Highway, heading for Maarat. *They have been gone ten months... but I know where they went and I will find them. And by the will of Allah, I will kill them both!*

Maarat

Salim the physician could barely speak, his big brown eyes glistened, his lips quivered. "Have... have you heard what happened at Antioch?" he asked in a small voice.

"No," Ramiro replied as he filled in the forms for a new patient. "What is it?" He could see that Salim was highly agitated.

"It has fallen to the barbarians!" His voice cracked in grief. "They slaughtered everyone! They are worse than animals! May Allah damn them to hell!" He wiped a tear from his cheek.

Dumbfounded, Ramiro's quill stopped moving in mid-word. Ink began to smear across the paper in a slow crawl. "Everyone?" he asked quietly, staring ahead.

"Yes Ramiro, anyone within the walls. Women and children—everyone."

"Not the Christians?" he asked in disbelief. He recalled how Yaghi Siyan drove out thousands of Christian men from Antioch but kept their women and children as hostages.

"Everyone, my friend," Salim replied dolefully.

"Father of mercies! But why?"

"Allah has cursed them. Only Allah knows why."

"What about Kerboga of Mosul? Did he not come as promised?"

"He came too late."

Ramiro felt a gnawing, bitter ache in his chest. "This is unbelievable. Did no one escape?"

"Only a few, Ramiro, may Allah have mercy."

Ramiro thought of all the people he had come to know in Antioch, he thought of his servant Boris and his family, and he thought of the Rabbi and all the others he had befriended, many of them Arabs and Turks. He bowed his head and wept.

"May God protect us!" Ramiro lamented when he was alone with Adele. "This is their Holy War! Most of Antioch was Christian! I cannot believe the blessed Pope of Rome would sanction such cruelty and bloodshed. He is a man of Cluny!"

Adele took a sip of wine, lost in thought. She hated the Turks for taking her as a slave, but she had made many friends among the women of Antioch, Christian and Muslim alike. She tried not to think about how they had died.

"Not only are these so-called crusaders barbaric," said Ramiro in a voice of reason, "they're stupid! All those people—they provided food and services, they paid taxes. Where's their revenue now?"

Adele dabbed her lips with a napkin. "It's very sad, although there is one small comfort."

"What's that?"

"Khuda must be dead."

Ramiro looked around as if expecting the enraged Turk to come barging through their door. "I hope so, Adele. Nonetheless, the French will be coming south soon and that will be bad enough. We must get to Jerusalem so I can deliver the cross. I must plead with the Qadi to return it to me."

A SHADOW

It was the twenty-seventh day of Rajab, the time of Laylat Al-Miraj, and the neighborhood was unusually quiet. Muslim parents shuffled their children off to the mosques to hear the story of Muhammad's climb to heaven. There, they were taught to view the event as a symbol of their own soul's journey in the afterlife and to emphasize the need for prayer and piety.

Ramiro took advantage of the quiet to compose a letter to Abbot Hugh. But he was not sure if it would ever be delivered. The last one he sent to Tripoli before the French started raiding the countryside. Now most feared to travel, especially if they were Muslim. There was little to say. How could he explain that he had lost the cross? He wanted the Abbot to know that he planned to leave for Jerusalem as soon as he could, but he could not leave just yet.

"What did the Qadi say?" Adele shouted from the kitchen.

Ramiro put his quill down. "I offered him a dinar and a half for it but he was unwilling to let it go. We've got to find a way to get more money."

She came out of the kitchen drying her hands on a towel. "Perhaps I could find a job. You know I'm good with leather work."

"No, no. I won't have it, Adele. Besides, your Arabic is terrible. I must give you more lessons." He rose from his low table to settle back on the cushions.

"Wait!" she said to him as he picked up a book. "Before you make yourself comfortable, go to the market before it closes. I need some sage."

"Is it absolutely necessary?"

She stuck out her chin. "Yes it is, old man. Or you can eat your meal without seasoning."

He smiled. "Very well," he said, rising up slowly. "Besides, I could use a little walk."

"Well, don't be gone too long. And stay away from the tavern," she said with a stern look, "...or it'll all be cold when you get back."

Ramiro stuffed a small bag of sage into his pocket. He paid the merchant and continued his stroll home, passing through the quiet marketplace. He caught a scent of rose and took a deep breath. *How I love this time of year.*

His path led him past the door of the tavern and he could hear the boisterous voices of the patrons inside. He hesitated by the door. It was the best place for any news... and they had an incredibly good wine made from the black dates of southern Iraq. *I wonder if there is any more news of Antioch and the French.* He was about to open the door when he heard a voice behind him.

"Good evening, Ramiro," a man said. "Peace be upon you."

Ramiro turned, feeling a little startled and a little guilty. It was Salim the physician.

"Are you going to the tavern?" he asked with some surprise.

Ramiro reddened a little. "Oh no, of course not. I'm just taking a stroll. And you?"

"I'm going to the market before it closes."

"Well, I'm on my way home. I'll walk with you a while."

They had no sooner turned to leave when an angry roar erupted inside the tavern, followed by a crash against the door. A deep, gravelly voice shouted from within. "Mind your own damned business! You ask too many questions!"

Ramiro felt a chill in his bones. He knew that voice.

Another voice squawked from behind the door. "Forgive me, Effendi, I was just trying to make conversation!"

"Get out of the way!" the voice shouted again.

Ramiro grabbed Salim by the sleeve, pulling him aside. "Let's go," he said. "Quick, follow me."

"What's going on?" Salim asked, just as the tavern door began to open.

Ramiro kept pulling. "Quiet. Follow me." He pulled Salim along at a frenzied pace just as an armed mamluk came out the door.

"Don't look back, Salim. Just keep walking." Ramiro led him down the street, turning a corner. "Alright, we can stop here for a while."

"What is it Ramiro? What's all the fuss?"

Ramiro put a finger to his lips. He peeked around the corner. It was him. It was Khuda. "May God protect us!"

"He's still alive? Oh Lord! Blessed Mary!" Adele cried. "What are we going to do? How did he escape Antioch?"

"I don't know, but don't worry, he's gone for now. Salim sent his younger brother to keep an eye on him. The boy said he mounted up this morning and rode south."

"So? What are we going to do? We can't stay here."

"Khuda has no idea we're here. He's heading south, probably to Jerusalem. Or maybe he's just looking for a new employer in Damascus."

She wrapped her arms around him. "Do you think he's forgotten us?" she asked, resting her head on his shoulder.

"After all this time? I'm sure he has," he said with little conviction. "Not to worry."

ANTIOCH

The corpses of Antioch rose in macabre pyramids outside the city gates. Muslim slaves, beaten and bruised, their heads bowed in shame and defeat, trudged to and fro, pulling carts stacked with the bodies and limbs of the men, woman, and children massacred within the walls.

For the Crusaders, the plunder of Antioch was disappointing. The siege had gone on for so long, there was little left to steal, not even much money. None-theless, they wasted little time grabbing all they could. By their rules of war, they owned all they seized.

Bohemond wasted little time claiming control of the city and was quick to fly his banner from atop the citadel, high on the crest of Mount Silpios. Count Ray-mond was furious. He resented Bohemond's claim and wanted the city handed over to King Alexios as they had promised. So he thwarted Bohemond's efforts by holding the Emir's Palace and the Bridge Gate, which controlled the road leading west to the port of Saint Simeon, a vital supply route.

After the frenzied bloodlust of battle had subsided, the Crusaders gathered at the now-vacant Cathedral of Saint Peter, falling to their knees on the blood-stained tiles to give thanks to God for their glorious victory.

It was here that a young servant by the name of Peter Bartholomew approached Bishop Adhemar and Count Raymond to tell them of his divine revelation. He claimed that Saint Andrew the Apostle had come to him in a vision, command-ing him to retrieve a holy lance buried beneath the floor of the cathedral. He was to give it to Raymond as a sacred standard in battle.

Adhemar was not impressed. He resented any attempt to usurp his heavenly power. Besides, Peter had no station, he was just a servant. But Raymond, in his arrogance, found Peter's predilection compelling and became greatly excit-ed at the prospect of obtaining one of the most holy relics in all Christendom.

So the men tore up the floor tiles and began to dig, shoveling furiously for hours until a great pit had formed. But no lance was found. In a frenzy, Peter jumped into the hole, fell to his knees, and began to pray fervidly. He prayed that God would return Christ's lance to His Holy Crusaders, thereby bringing strength and victory to His chosen people. Moments later, lo and behold, Peter discovered the point of the lance sticking out of the earth. All the men crowding about the deep pit fell to their knees, wailing with tears of exaltation. Before long, cries of great joy and celebration rocked the desolate, blood-soaked city.

July 1098

But their euphoria did not last long. One month after the occupation of An-tioch, typhus raged through their filthy ranks. Thousands of men, weakened by months of hunger, quickly succumbed to high fevers and failing hearts. The leaders and the wealthy stationed themselves outside the city, leaving the men to fend for themselves. Only Bohemond and Bishop Adhemar remained, the former feared for his precious Antioch and the latter for his people. But Adhe-mar, weak and pale, died by the end of the month.

The men were shocked at his death. They could not understand why God had taken the Papal Legate from their midst in such a cruel and undignified manner. Was he not divinely protected? What sins had they committed to deserve such a harsh penalty?

Bohemond towered above his nephew, Tancred. He lifted one leg to let out a long fart. "I shit on Raymond of Toulouse," he bellowed. "Antioch is mine! I'm the one who broke the gates. I'm the one who seized the citadel!"

Tancred, a slim man in his early twenties, backed away from his uncle Bohemond, whose very presence he found intimidating. "We can't control the city until Raymond gives up the Palace and the Bridge Gate," he advised. "We should force him out."

Bohemond shook his close-cropped head. "No, we must be tactful," he said in a rattling baritone. "Raymond has taken possession of the Holy Lance and uses it to draw men to his cause. If we start fighting among ourselves, we accomplish nothing. We must lay plans."

Tancred brushed a lock of long, brown hair from his hard-set eyes. "What can we do? We lost three thousand men to the plague. God punishes us! Even Bishop Adhemar has died. And many more are sick and weak. If God does not protect the bishop, what hope have we?"

Bohemond ignored him. He had no interest in theological debates. He put a hand to his chin before strolling to a northern portal of the citadel, where he looked north across the sea to the rich plain of Cilicia and beyond to the rough peaks of the Taurus Mountains. "We will wait. Like you say, the plague has killed many of our men—but it shows signs of abating. As for Count Raymond, well... he cannot hold for long. He's a self-possessed, deluded old man with one eye. We will push him out. But first things first, my dear Tancred. We must make sure the Greeks do not get Antioch."

"So you will not hand over the city as we agreed?"

Bohemond flushed red. He slammed a thick hand on the table, the noise echoing from stone walls. "What have they done to capture Antioch?" he bellowed. Tancred flinched. "We starved and froze for months outside the walls and they did nothing! Nothing! Only after we conquered did they send an army. And when they heard Kerboga was coming, they turned back like a pack of cowering dogs! God curse them! They do not deserve Antioch!"

"How will you stop them? What if they amass an army?"

"We will secure Cilicia. It is our northern frontier. If we can do that, the Greeks will have no chance to advance on us."

"But I already control Cilicia."

"You have too few men. I will send more."

Tancred eyed him suspiciously. He feared his uncle, knowing he was making a sly attempt to usurp his control of the region. But he was outranked. What could he do? And what spoils would be left for him? "What of Jerusalem?" he asked, trying to divert the subject. "And what of the Egyptians? They claim the Holy City too."

Bohemond laughed. His crafty blue eyes gleamed. "I'm not concerned about the Egyptians or Jerusalem. We'll let Godfrey and Raymond go to Palestine to fight them. I want Antioch. From here, I will control all Syria."

EGYPT

Although the Egyptian vizier, Al-Afdal, had rejoiced when the Roman army of barbarians first defeated the Turks at Nikea, and then again at Antioch, he was now a troubled man. He had met with the Franj ambassadors from Antioch, and he had heard their demands. So he went to pray. He faced the *mihrab*, indicating the direction of Mecca, and prostrated himself in the hall of the exquisite Al-Azhar Mosque of Cairo. He begged Allah to lift the terrible plague that racked the people of Egypt, and now he prayed for the death of these fanatics, these Roman mercenaries from the West.

Events were not unfolding quite as he had hoped. The Franj were obstinate. He felt he made a generous concession on one issue of his proposed alliance; instead of dividing all conquered lands equally, he told the ambassadors they could have all of Syria and any other lands they conquer, all except for Palestine, which he believed belonged to Egypt. He assured them they would have no trouble visiting the holy sites of Jerusalem.

But they flatly refused. They wanted Jerusalem and would hear no compromise. This was not the bargain he had made with King Alexios and he could not understand why these men were so inflexible. He had an alliance with the Romans. Is this not what the King wanted? To regain the cities of Anatolia and Syria from the Turks? Why do they insist on marching to Jerusalem? And what will I do if they enter Palestine?

He rose from his prayers, leaving for his office in the stronghold of Fustat. A long entourage of servants and soldiers followed after him. Along the way, he summoned his atabek.

"Prepare an army for a spring advance into Palestine. I cannot trust the Romans or these barbarians. We must seize Jerusalem before they do."

"Yes, my Lord."

"And send a delegation to the Roman King," he fumed. "I want to know why his army refuses to negotiate with us, I want to know his intentions, and I want to know the status of our alliance."

CONSTANTINOPLE

Emperor Alexios had made a grave mistake—a mistake that cost him Antioch. He could barely contain his anger and frustration. "I should never have listened to those wretched Kelts!" he shouted at the roomful of generals, admirals, and lieutenants. They squirmed in their seats.

"Who?" asked his brother Isaak.

"The deserters. They're the ones who told me all was lost at Antioch. They're the ones who said two Turk armies marched on the city. Armies of thirty thousand! That's the only reason I turned back!" He paced the room, his uncombed red hair dangling over his shoulders. "No doubt, the French at Antioch now think me a coward! And worse still—against all odds, those bumbling morons have managed to take the city! Unbelievable!"

John Doukas tried to console him. "They signed a pact, my king. They must relinquish Antioch into your hands."

"But can we trust them?" he asked in all seriousness. "I offered to send another army—but they refused! They had the gall to refuse me! And now—now I fear they will use my retreat as an excuse to claim Antioch for themselves. They will say I have broken my vow." He took a gulp of water before looking at the men seated around the table. "Who can we trust?"

"I don't trust any of them," said Anna with the inherent authority of a dowager. "They are the most arrogant and fanatical of men. I have to say, I am quite worried about having thousands of marauding Kelts in our midst. I'm sure you all remember the trouble they cause. Foolhardy barbarians! Their souls twisted by avarice. I fear for the empire."

"You are right, mother, of course," Alexios said. "But this is the gambit we took in an effort to regain our empire. We must be careful, I know. We certainly cannot trust Godfrey and especially not Bohemond. Those two will make use of any argument to hold Antioch."

General Taticius rose to his feet. A dull glint reflecting from his iron nose. "Bohemond forced me out," he complained. "And then he told the others I deserted, that I was a coward. He's just a scheming, crooked Norman, like all the rest."

"What should we do now?" Isaak asked.

Alexios threw his arms in the air. "Now we wait. And we negotiate. A plague has fallen on Antioch. Probably typhus. They say thousands are ill, many have died. Even their so-called spiritual leader has succumbed—what's his name?"

"Bishop Adhemar, my Lord," answered Patriarch Nikolas. "He seemed reasonable enough, although some of his views were too fanatical for me. Saw himself as the new Pope of the East."

"This is an unfortunate development," said Alexios. "Like you say, Your Grace, he was one of the most reasonable of these self-proclaimed crusaders. I had hoped he would sway others to our cause."

Anna held up a finger. "There is another matter that needs our immediate attention."

"And what is that?"

She ruffled through her stack of correspondence. "We just received a letter from the Egyptian Vizier and a messenger is waiting for your response."

"Go on."

"The Vizier is upset. He wants to know why the leaders of your army in Antioch have refused to negotiate. He says they refuse to compromise on Jerusalem, which leaves him no alternative but to send an army across the Sinai. He wants you to clarify your intentions. And he wants to know if we still have an alliance."

"Perhaps we should tell him we have no control over these savages," suggested John Doukas.

"No, not yet," said Alexios, rubbing his forehead. "We must delay. We may still need their help. Tell Al-Afdal whatever he wants to hear. We know the Kelts are intent on Jerusalem but whether they will ever make it remains to be seen. Many have died and now the plague ravages their ranks. Who will be left to march to Jerusalem?"

"Then I will tell him we still have an alliance," said Anna, "and that our intentions are to concentrate our efforts on north Syria. After that, we can only hope the Kelts will abandon Antioch and then we will be in a better position to reclaim it."

Patriarch Nikolas raised his voice. "I would not be so sure of that, my Lady. Now the barbarians say they have found the Holy Lance in Antioch, the very spearhead used to pierce the body of Christ at his crucifixion. It was supposedly buried in the Basilica of Saint Peter. They claim this is a sign from God—that Divine Providence favors them to rule Antioch."

Alexios laughed bitterly, shaking his head. "This is a preposterous claim! Another lie put forward by one of their sham priests! How can they believe such a ridiculous account? Everyone knows that we alone possess the Holy Lance. It is stored in our own Church of Sophia." The men nodded their agreement.

Nikolas rose from his chair. "The Latins will do and say anything to further their cause! Barbarian heretics!"

Alexios waved him down and the Patriarch returned to his seat, red-faced.

Tatran of Oghuz fiddled nervously with one of his long braids. He stood up suddenly. "My King, is there any word of Ramiro of Cluny?" he asked with an undercurrent of guilt and remorse. It had been four years since he had made his harrowing escape from Antioch, leaving Ramiro and Adele to the pitiless whims of Yaghi Siyan.

Alexios looked bewildered. "Who?"

"The Latin monk, my Lord," Tatran reminded him, "... the one captured by the Turks some years ago. Was he found at Antioch?" His broad mustache rose and fell as he spoke.

"Oh, yes—him. The one who escaped from the Sultan's prison. An interesting man." He paused with a hand to his chin. "I don't know, Lieutenant. We have little information from inside the walls." He glanced at the others. "Does anyone know the whereabouts of this man?"

The men shook their heads, mumbling nays.

"It's unlikely he lived," said Alexios. "We hear the savages killed everyone." He shook his head in dismay, "...even the Christians."

MAARAT

A young woman ran through the entrance of the Maarat hospital, shrieking and wailing. "Help me! By the mercy of Allah! Help me!" In her arms, she clutched her two-year old son. The young boy squirmed madly, hacking and wheezing, struggling to breathe.

At the sound of her frantic cries, Ramiro and Salim rushed out from the infirmary. They made a brief inspection of the boy. "Quickly," said Ramiro as he took the child from his mother's arms, "we'll put him in room number three."

He rested him on a table, his small arms flailing in his struggle to breathe. With effort, he managed to stick a tongue depressor into the child's mouth. "His throat is inflamed and badly swollen."

"Is it croup?" asked Salim?

"I'm not sure yet. But if it gets worse, he will suffocate."

The boy's mother burst into tears at Ramiro's words while Salim made an awkward attempt to console her.

Ramiro rushed to his medicine cabinet, searching furtively. "Here it is!" he exclaimed, reaching for a concoction of hyssop, licorice, and opium. Dashing back, he tried to force it down the boy's throat, but the child could not swallow. His small chest heaved as he spat it out, straining for air.

Ramiro lifted him to a sitting position, slapping him on the back, but to no avail. "We must do a tracheotomy!" he shouted. "Or the boy will die!"

"A tracheotomy!" Salim had a worried look. "But I have never seen one done, Doctor Ramiro. Have you ever performed such an operation?"

"No, I confess I have not," he replied, moving the boy in various positions, trying to make it easier for him to breathe. "But unless something is done soon, he will suffocate." The child's mother moaned aloud, covering her face with her hands to hide her tears.

"Go get Al-Zahrawi's manual!" he shouted to Salim. "You know the one, *The Method of Medicine*. I'm sure he describes the procedure."

Salim ran off while Ramiro tried to clear the boy's airway by depressing the back of his tongue. Long minutes later, Salim rushed back with the book in hand.

Ramiro flipped through the pages. "Here! Look! Here it is. We make the incision at the sternal notch." He looked at the boy, who was now unconscious. "I'll get the scalpel. Find a speculum."

When all was in hand, the mother and Salim held the child on his back. Ramiro bent over him with the scalpel, making a slow puncture of the throat. Blood poured from the cut. The mother staggered. "Hold him still!" he barked. He pushed the thin knife deeper and deeper until, suddenly, a spray of blood blew from the cut, splattering into his face. He wiped his eyes with his sleeve before grabbing the speculum, a rounded glass tube used for internal inspection. He pushed it into the incision, curving it down into the boy's windpipe. Air hissed through it as the child gulped for breath. In a moment, his breathing steadied and, slowly, color returned to his cheeks. "He will live," Ramiro smiled.

Dawud the Silk Merchant was no sooner through the door when he fell to his knees, prostrating himself in front of Ramiro. "May Allah bless you!" he wept. "May your sons become princes! May you live for a thousand moons! I am forever in your debt, Sayyid."

"Get up, man!" cried Ramiro, somewhat flabbergasted. "It is only by God's grace that the boy survived. Give thanks to God and say no more of it."

Adele peeked into the hallway. She quickly fitted a headscarf and moved behind Ramiro.

Dawud was a plump Arab merchant who had become wealthy trading Byzantine silks. He rose to his feet with effort, putting his right hand to his heart. "Praise be to Allah," he cried sincerely. "Please Sayyid," he continued. "If there is anything in my power I can do for you, only say the words and it will be done."

Ramiro put a hand on the man's shoulder. "I am thankful the boy lived, Dawud. That is enough."

Adele jabbed a finger into his back. Startled, he turned around.

"The cross!" she whispered. "Get the cross."

"Oh, yes... yes, of course," he whispered back. He turned back to Dawud. "Well, actually there is one thing..."

Ramiro studied his golden cross. Dawud had paid off the Qadi and it was his again. He rubbed it meticulously with a soft cloth until it began to shine, although some marring remained. He let out a heavy sigh. "Well, it may be a little damaged," he said to Adele, "but at least we can get on our way to Jerusalem."

Adele was busy sewing coins into the hems of their blankets and clothes. "Thank God," she said without looking up. "When do we leave?"

"Soon. I just have a few things to finish at the hospital and then..."

Sudden trumpet blasts drowned out Ramiro's words. A great commotion arose from the streets below. He moved to the patio to have a look. Adele followed. From their room on the second floor, they could see all the way down the street to the city walls and the main gate.

"What's going on?" she asked.

"That was a warning trumpet," he said. "A call to arms. Look! The garrison is mounted and waiting by the gate. We must be under attack!"

In the distance, a small Crusader army gathered outside the walls of Maarat, no more than a thousand men in all. Since the fall of Antioch, the French and Normans had gained courage and sought to expand their holdings. Raymond of Toulouse still vied with Bohemond for control of Antioch and his plan was to seize as many fiefdoms as possible to give his claim more weight, so he sent out a small army to conquer towns and villages to the south. Maarat An-Numan seemed like a profitable target.

Ramiro dashed down the stairs, rushing to the market square. "What's going on?" he asked the tinker, who seemed to be the best source of information apart from the tavern.

"The barbarians come!" said the wizened old man with bushy, gray eyebrows. Just as he spoke, a gust of wind blew against his stall. Brass pots hanging from a crossbar clanged together, making an ominous chime. The old man put out a hand to steady them before turning back to Ramiro. "They will kill us all! May Allah strike them dead!"

Ramiro felt cold, despite the dry heat. "Do you know what they're doing outside the walls?"

"They prepare for siege, Sayyid."

"So what is the garrison going to do? They are at the gates."

"They will attack. They cannot afford a siege. But if they lose, we will all die by the sword... just as they did at Antioch."

The tinker no sooner spoke when the gates flew open and the full garrison of angry mamluks charged out against the Crusaders, catching them off guard. The intruders were too busy making ladders and a battering ram and were barely fit for battle. With fierce determination, the mamluks drove straight into their camp, hooting and hollering and stabbing with lances. They had heard of the massacre at Antioch and decided they would rather die in battle, meeting the devil face to face, than to be slaughtered in their beds.

The knights mounted up in a mad frenzy but had little opportunity to organize any proper defense. A wild and fierce battle ensued. The French were routed, suffering heavy losses, and the battered survivors fled back to Antioch.

Ramiro and Adele made hasty preparations to leave. He gathered all supplies while she took the time to sew their remaining coins into the hems of cloaks and blankets.

"Quick! We must go. We'll head back to the River Orontes!" he yelled, mounting the mule. He reached out a hand to Adele, who was fumbling, trying to get her foot into the stirrup. "Come on, Adele! Are you sure you know how to ride?"

She frowned as she lifted herself into the saddle, sitting behind him. "Never you mind! I'll be just fine."

He smirked. "We'll take the road that follows the river south. Then we'll head for Tripoli. It's not safe to stay on the King's Highway."

"Ya, Ramiro," a voice yelled. It was Dawud the silk merchant. He held the reins of another mule, complete with saddle and bags.

"Peace be upon you, Dawud."

"And you, Ramiro of Cluny," Dawud huffed as he approached. "I hear you leave us for Jerusalem."

"Yes, and we must go soon."

"But you cannot travel on a single mule, Doctor Ramiro. Please take this one as a gift of thanks. I would have given you a horse if it was allowed. And here is a purse to fund your journey."

Ramiro held up a palm of refusal. "You have done enough, Dawud. We will take no more from you." Adele jabbed him in the back.

"Please, Doctor, I insist. The Prophet tells us 'whoever does you a favor, respond in kind...' The life of my son is a debt I can never repay. Please take my gifts and I will pray for you."

Ramiro nodded. "As you wish, Dawud. We pray God will provide you many sons."

When Khuda the Mamluk left Maarat weeks before, he galloped south for Jerusalem, riding across the vast grassland spreading from Hama to Homs, and he kept riding, passing through Damascus and onward south to the dry outskirts of Amman. From there, he headed west, crossing the cool Salt Mountains before making the steep descent into the blistering hot Jordan Valley. In a slow, steady gait he crossed the deep valley floor, took the bridge over the River Jordan, and headed up into the dry forests of the Judean Hills where the Holy City of Jerusalem sprawled out over its crown.

7 - Levant

Tripoli

Ramiro and Adele hurried south along the King's Highway, turning west at the Homs Gap to reach the Mediterranean coast. They had journeyed long and hard, hoping to avoid another encounter with highwaymen. And now, after reaching the relative safety of coastal communities, they began to relax a little. Indeed, the people here seemed indifferent to the troubles farther north and east.

Expansive orchards of oranges and lemons decorated the low foothills on the approach to Tripoli, an ancient Phoenician city situated on a green promontory jutting into the Mediterranean. Dominating the view was the colossal citadel sitting adjacent to the Abu Ali River, its massive walls and towers forming a huge octagon, rising five to six stories above the city's paved and gardened streets.

"Did I tell you this is where my father died?" Ramiro asked.

Adele reached out, taking his arm in a gesture of comfort. "No. What on earth was he doing here?"

"He was on his way to Jerusalem with my mother. But he fell ill and passed into God's care."

"Do you know where he's buried?"

"Alas, I do not. And I cannot imagine how I would ever know. At least, not until I talk to my mother. No matter, we have no time for excursions. I want to go to the armorer next."

"You plan to buy weapons?" she asked, somewhat surprised. "They can't sell to you."

"Maybe not, but I'll wager they can be persuaded with silver. I want a knife at least, and since you seem so adept with oak, a mace would be a good weapon for you." His eyes twinkled.

"That's not funny," she snorted.

"I'm quite sincere. It's easy to swing and more effective than a simple club."

"And where do you think I'm going to put it?"

"We'll get a leather belt. You can cover it with your cloak."

The docks of Tripoli were quiet. It was a Friday, the Muslim holy day. But a few Christian stores were still open. The office of the Byzantine shipper was among them, a small place nestled between the barrel-maker's shop and the currency exchange.

"Where are you going?" Adele asked.

"I've got to get this report off to the Abbot. Here's the place." They found the attendant sleeping at his desk.

"Hello!" Ramiro shouted.

The young man jumped up, straightening his tunic. "Yes, Sayyid," he said in accented Arabic. "Peace be upon you." He brushed back his shaggy brown hair with one hand.

"And to you," said Ramiro in Greek. "When does the next ship sail for Bari?"

"It should arrive next week," said the man. "It's coming up from Jaffa. Then it sails for Saint Simeon before heading to Bari."

"Good, good." Ramiro handed him the envelope. "How much to deliver this?"

The courier weighed the package. "Fifty fals."

Ramiro paid the man. "Is Jaffa safe?"

"Safe enough. The Egyptians have a garrison there."

"And what of Jerusalem?"

"The Turks still hold it."

DOG RIVER

Just north of Beirut, is the ancient divide called Dog River. With the passing of time, the river had carved its way through limestone mountains, creating a deep ravine that was virtually impassable for horses and carts until the kings of old built roads and bridges across it.

To control the pass at Dog River, was to control all north-south traffic along the coast, and much blood was spilled to possess it. Over the centuries, the victors included the kings of Egypt, Assyria, Babylon, and Rome, who boasted of their achievements and conquests by making inscriptions, by carving reliefs into the limestone cliffs, or by erecting stelae along the roadside.

Adele looked up at a weather-worn relief of a man wearing a tall hat and a short skirt. People living nearby said it was old Egyptian, but nobody knew it was the Pharaoh Ramses. Below the reliefs, the narrow road dropped to the bottom of a steep ravine where a stone bridge, built by the Romans centuries before, took them across Dog River.

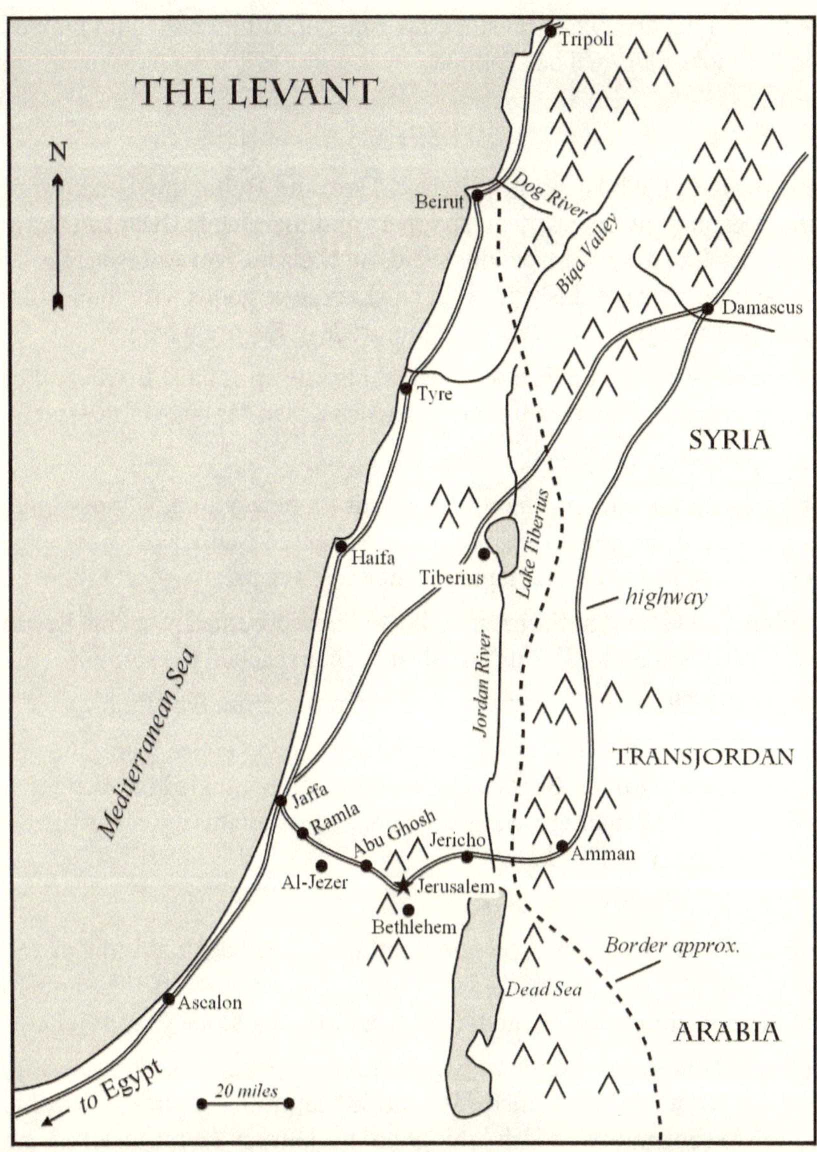

Ramiro scanned the area cautiously before descending to the riverside, where he knelt to refill their water-skins. He pushed one under and air bubbled out. "Let's go for a swim."

"Here? Now?" she asked, looking around.

"Yes, here, now."

"We can't go naked."

"We'll wear what we have on. A good opportunity to do our laundry and have a bath at the same time. Come. We'll move upriver, away from the bridge."

Adele hugged his arm when he stood up. She pulled him close and nibbled at his ear. "It looks like we'll be all alone."

JAFFA

Passing through the busy ports of Beirut, Tyre, and Haifa, they finally arrived in Jaffa. Despite the August heat, shoppers and merchants thronged the bustling streets. On either side, peddlers laid out their meager wares across worn carpets spread over the dusty ground, hawking their goods with loud bellows. And milling through the crowds were hundreds of Egyptian troops.

Ramiro, undeterred by the masses, pushed his way up Jaffa Hill, where the ruins of nine thousand years of human existence rested far below their feet.

"Let's stop now!" Adele yelled, exhausted.

Ramiro was far ahead, striding up the hill like a new man, his bones tingling with expectation. Jerusalem was so near. He shouted back. "No! I want to go to the top. We'll stop there!" He tugged at the mule's reins.

A crumbling citadel sat at the crest of the hill, now occupied by a lone Egyptian garrison. "Did you notice?" Ramiro asked as they reached the summit.

"Notice what? The magnificent view?" Adele huffed from the climb.

"Well, yes that too. But look at all these different people. See there," he pointed. "I think those two are Genoese or Venetians." He nodded to his right. She looked over to see a man attired in a formed, knee-length tunic. His tight, red hose climbed far above his knees.

"It seems such odd dress now, doesn't it?"

"I always thought it was odd," he said, tipping his head again. "And look there. Those are probably Egyptians. And over there," his eyes moved. "The local folk, Philistines and Hebrews." He motioned to a large, flat stone. "Let's sit here."

Adele looked out to sea, taking in the magnificent panorama with a slow turn of her head. "Ramiro," she smiled. "It really is beautiful. Despite so many hardships, we've seen many wonderful things on this journey." As she spoke, a swallowtail butterfly flapped past their noses, its bright yellow wings in stark contrast to the gray stone around them. She chuckled, watching it for a moment before it swooped down the hill.

"Yes, indeed, my dear," he replied, not mentioning his long imprisonments and beatings. He pointed out to sea. "Look. From here, you can see every ship for miles around. And look along the coast. Whether south or north, you have a clear view of the roads."

Adele nodded. "Then you are telling me it's a strategic beauty."

Ramiro looked at her, furrowing his brow. "You jest."

She chuckled, pointing to the docks below. "Look at all the different ships. And flags of every nation!"

Ramiro pointed too. "There's the Byzantine banner. Now's your chance to go back... back to the safety of France."

She frowned. "Are you trying to get rid of me again?"

"I'm only thinking of your safety, my love. Soon, the Egyptians will march on Jerusalem... and then maybe the French. No doubt, there will be more trouble."

"I'll be safe with you," she said, taking his arm. "Besides, a child should be with his father." She beamed.

Ramiro stared at her, dumbfounded. Her words did not quite register. He tipped his head, wondering if she was jesting again. "What... what do you mean?"

"I'm with child, my husband."

"With child... with child?" His eyes went wide. "You... you mean... that we...?"

Adele nodded, still smiling.

He forced a thin smile. "Are you serious? You're sure?"

A wisp of disappointment trailed across Adele's face. Her smile faded quickly. "I'm quite serious," she said in a steely voice.

Ramiro said nothing for a long while. One part of his mind was elated with the prospect of fatherhood, while another was greatly disturbed. He had broken his Benedictine vows, and the child would be proof of that. He could never return to the Abbey of Cluny. But all these thoughts were swept aside with a new-found fear—the safety of Adele and the child.

"I see you are not pleased," said Adele, her voice breaking.

Ramiro turned to see tears streaming down her cheeks. He took her in his arms and she quickly clung to him. "Forgive me, my love. Yes, I'm very happy. But you must understand, I'm also very worried. More than ever, I want you to return to Constantinople. For your safety and for the child's."

She wept quietly on his shoulder. "I... I can't leave you, Ramiro. Where will I go? I have no one left. I would rather die by your side than roam France without you."

Ramiro's resolve soon vanished in her flood of tears. It was more than his heart could bear, and he fully realized at that moment that he was deeply in love with Adele, more so than he ever thought possible. And now that she bore his child, he felt an immeasurable bond that surpassed all doubt. He could never leave her.

In that same moment, he also realized he would never return to the Abbey.

"Then you will stay," he said as he took her hand and pulled her to her feet. He turned to face the east, putting an arm out toward the Judean Hills. "And thence lies Jerusalem, my love. Soon, we will worship at the Holy Sepulcher and give our thanks to the Lord." He squeezed her hand lightly. "Come. We will find an inn and get some rest."

JERUSALEM

For weeks, Khuda the Mamluk wandered the streets of Jerusalem, visiting every market, tavern, inn, and hostel, even the churches. "I'm looking for a man named Ramiro," he said to the innkeeper. "He's about this tall." He held out a hand. "And he's heavyset. He's got black eyes, like the Devil himself. Speaks with an accent. Travels with a red-haired woman."

The innkeeper looked at Khuda with suspicion. The man was clearly a Turk. "There was no one here like that," he replied. "And what interest do you have in these people?"

"My interests are none of your business." Khuda snarled. "Did you see a red-haired woman or not?"

"I have seen several red-headed women in my time," he replied sarcastically.

Khuda reached across the desk, grabbing the man by his vest, yanking him forward, right off his feet. "I'll ask once more before I slit your throat!" He whipped his knife from his belt, sticking it to the man's neck.

The innkeeper yelped. "No, Effendi, I swear. I have not seen them!"

Khuda threw the man to the floor before rushing outside. They must be in Jaffa. But what if the Egyptians come?

RAMLA

The road from Jaffa to Jerusalem was wide and well-traveled. For miles it followed the flat, coastal plain, eventually coming to the rugged, low hills of Filastin and the city of Ramla, the capital city of Palestine.

A call to prayer sounded just as they reached the city gates. "Come," Ramiro urged. "Where there is a mosque, there is a market."

"Let's get a room at the inn first," Adele pleaded. "I'm exhausted."

The old innkeeper turned them away with a shake of his head. "This is a Muslim hostel. This is a Muslim city. You must go to the Christian church in the outskirts... or to the Christians at Ludd."

"How far is that?" Ramiro asked.

"About an hour's ride north," he replied brusquely.

Ramiro was about to get more detailed directions when suddenly, Adele, tired and irritable, lurched forward, flushing red. "Need rest! Need room!" she yelled in strained Arabic, her auburn hair dangling from her headscarf.

The shocked innkeeper made no reply to her. Instead, he turned to Ramiro. "You see? You Christians cannot control your women," he admonished in anger. "Any man of honor would beat her. You are not welcome here. Imshee!"

Ramiro scowled as they left the inn. "Are you daft?" he snapped. "How can you accomplish anything acting like that?"

"I'm tired!" Adele spat. "And I can speak my mind if I wish!" She rushed ahead with her mule.

He hurried to keep up. "Words can be foolish or wise," he said in a tempered voice. "A wise man first measures the weight of his words."

She said nothing and kept walking away, pulling her mule behind her.

"Don't you see, Adele? You must adopt the customs of the land. Do you really expect a whole nation to change just for you?"

She said nothing.

He turned toward the mosque. "Come. We must go to the market, we need supplies. Then we'll ride for Ludd."

She followed in simmering silence.

The pale, marble walls of the White Mosque glowed with a tint of rose, colored by the setting sun. A square minaret towered above the grounds and its long shadow crept across the courtyard like a giant sundial.

They found a water-seller near the mosque where a muscular young man drew fresh water from an underground cistern. Ramiro paid the attendant, asking him a few questions before turning to leave.

Adele broke her silence. "Are we going to Ludd now?" She asked curtly while pulling her headscarf tight around her head.

"I've reconsidered," said Ramiro tugging at the mule. "I don't like the idea of going to Ludd, it would mean going back. I would rather continue east. The water-man said there's a campsite at a place called Al-Jezer. It's only five miles east."

Khuda eyed the travelers coming and going, always on the lookout for Ramiro and the red-headed woman. He left Jerusalem that morning, taking the road to Jaffa. He tried to remain inconspicuous by changing his dress to that of a merchant, stuffing his long hair under a turban and packing his mail armor and sword in his saddlebags. He was careful to speak only Arabic. But he could not hide his face, he looked like a Turk.

After the death of the Great Sultan, and then of Prince Tutush, Seljuk power in Palestine declined rapidly. The Egyptians took advantage of the situation, helped by their dubious allies, the Byzantines and Italians. And now, east and south of Jerusalem, Turks were not welcome. So when the Egyptians advanced into southern Palestine, poorly equipped Turk soldiers abandoned their garrisons in fear, making hasty retreats to Jerusalem or Damascus. They had no greater enemy than the Fatimid Egyptians.

Khuda stopped in Abu Ghosh, a small town between Jerusalem and Jaffa. Once again, he asked at every inn, although he was much more polite here. But no one had seen the pair. He went to the markets to scrutinize the crowd, and then rode down every street. They're not here, he thought. Maybe Ramla or Jaffa? Can't go to Jaffa, too many cursed Fatimids. And soon, the heretics will march on Jerusalem. May Allah curse them! He rode out of Abu Ghosh, heading for Ramla just as Ramiro and Adele turned off the main road, traveling to Al-Jezer.

AL-JEZER

Just above the village of Al-Jezer was a flat-topped hill that was often used as a campsite for travelers on the Jaffa to Jerusalem road. When Ramiro and Adele arrived, they found it almost deserted except for one man squatting under a simple lean-to on the far side.

Adele pointed to a mass of huge stones jutting from the earth. "Look at these ruins."

Ramiro nodded. "An abandoned city no doubt, robbed of its stone." He spread his arm toward the coast. "But I can see why the place was once important. Look at the commanding view of the coastal plain, the valley, and the road to Jerusalem."

Adele was unimpressed. She strolled along the grassy platform, glancing warily in the direction of the squatter. "Here's a good spot for the tent."

The stranger called over to them. "Peace be upon you!"

"And to you, peace!" Ramiro shouted back. He tied the mules to one of the stones before strolling over to introduce himself.

The young man said he was traveling to Jaffa to work for an uncle in the construction business. But he was worried about the Egyptians, who had taken the coast and, as rumor had it, would soon arrive at the gates of Jerusalem.

"Can we still get into the city?" Ramiro asked.

"Maybe. But the Turk Emir is suspicious of everyone right now. I see you are Christian. You will need papers. Do you have any?"

Ramiro thought of his letter from the late Turk Sultan. It may still prove useful. "Yes, I do."

After more talk of politics and economic affairs, Ramiro said polite good-byes. "It seems the Egyptians will soon lay siege to Jerusalem," he said to Adele. "This is a dangerous time. We could rush and make an attempt to get in before the army arrives. But if the Turks lose the battle, will we be safe? It may be best to return to Jaffa."

She did not look pleased. "Our child will need a home soon, Ramiro. We can't keep wandering the countryside."

"We will get to Jerusalem, my love. We have plenty of time." He took her hand, raised it to his lips and kissed it. "It's not a long journey from Jaffa to Jerusalem."

"But what about Khuda?"

He shrugged. "Either he's dead or the Blessed Virgin has been watching over us."

She looked around again, as if danger lurked behind the bushes. "Let's set up the tent so I can wash my hair without our neighbor watching."

Ramiro lay flat on his back. A small fire flickered nearby, heating a pot of water. It was a dark, moonless night and the stars were brilliant. He pointed to the heavens. "The Romans call it the Milky Way. And look there—the constellations of Pegasus, Pisces, and there's Aquarius."

Adele knelt beside him, drying her hair. She smiled. "You could be an astrologer or a soothsayer."

Ramiro smiled back in the dim light of the fire. "And secure a position in the royal court of France?" They laughed.

"What do the stars tell you, Ramiro?" She yawned. "Is this a good time to go to Jerusalem?"

He looked at her with fondness, brushing a lock of hair from her face with his thick fingers. "For that, my love, we will put our trust in God."

The bushes rustled nearby. Adele tensed. "What's that?"

Ramiro felt for the dagger he bought in Tripoli. Was it just the wind? They heard it again. A rustle, a cough. Ramiro threw off the blanket, drew his dagger and crouched low. With a finger to his lips, he motioned to Adele to keep quiet. He peered into the blackness for any sign of life. The mules whinnied.

He looked hard in their direction. He thought he saw something move, a low dark figure. He rose up a little, taking a cautious step forward, then another.

First he heard thumps on the dry ground, and then a piercing scream just as a black shape rushed straight at him, smashing into his knees, sending him reeling to the ground. It came at him again, squealing as it charged. "It's a boar!" he shouted. The beast charged again and again, trying hard to gore him with its short, sharp tusks.

Thwack! The boar staggered. Thwack! Adele hit it again and, with a terrifying squeal, it fled back into the dark, rustling the bushes as it went. She stood alone, the bloodied mace in her hand.

Ramiro sat on the ground, rubbing the cuts on his knees. "It must have young ones nearby." He looked up at Adele and smiled. "You see? I knew that mace would be a good weapon for you."

A distant rumble brought Ramiro out of a fretful sleep. He rolled off his mattress, crawling outside to start a fire. Warily, he scanned the countryside and there, far in the distance, in the red haze of dawn, he sighted a cloud of dust. And soon after, he spotted the first of a long procession of troops. They were marching to Jerusalem.

Their fellow camper was also awake and watching. He shouted over. "It's the Egyptian army! Look, Al-Afdal leads them. I see his white banner."

Ramiro strained to see the banner but could not.

Adele peeped out. "They've come already? Now what do we do?"

He studied the marching army. "Now we wait. They will not take Jerusalem in a day. We must return to Jaffa."

"I don't want to go back to Jaffa," she scowled. "Why don't we simply follow the army to Jerusalem? We can always find a place nearby."

He shrugged. "I suppose there's no harm in that."

She began to dress. "Then we better get going."

RAMLA

"Oh, yes, I remember those two, alright," said the innkeeper at Ramla. "Christians with no manners at all. Yes, the raving witch had red hair. I sent them away."

"Which way did they go?" Khuda asked, excited by the news.

The innkeeper shrugged and opened his hands. "I don't know. I sent them to the Christians at Ludd. But who knows where they went."

"When?"

"Just yesterday." He shrugged again. "Maybe they went to Jaffa, maybe Jerusalem. But it's unlikely they'll get into Jerusalem. The Egyptian army passed by this morning. Surely you saw them?"

Khuda nodded. He had hid in his room until they left. He was beginning to feel uneasy. Soon, no place in Palestine would be safe for him. He thanked the callous innkeeper before returning to his mount. A menacing grin crossed his dark, weathered face. I know where they are going, he thought. I must return to Jerusalem. By the will of Allah, I will steal my way into the city, even under siege.

By noon, the Egyptian army had disappeared into the Judean Hills, following the mountain road winding its way up to Jerusalem. Ramiro and Adele followed some hours behind. They were just leaving the wide expanse of the Ayalon Valley to head into the limestone hills, when Ramiro pointed to a hilltop where a few soldiers stood watch. "Egyptians," he said. "Just be calm, Adele. We are ignorant pilgrims and nothing more." He reached into his tunic for a few coins. "We will pay their toll and move on."

But no one rode out to stop them. So they forged ahead and, before the sun set, they took a worn path off the main road where they found a place to camp in a sparse grove of oak and pistachio.

An hour later, Khuda spied the same soldiers. He could see their dark silhouettes against the waning light of dusk. He felt for the dagger about his waist, drawing his cloak to hide it. He thought too of his sword, now stored under his saddlebags so that its pommel was barely exposed. He hoped the soldiers would ignore him, but he unwittingly gave himself away. His spirited charger and his graceful movements proved he was proficient in the saddle. Even from a distance, the soldiers suspected he was mamluk. Two rode down the hill to intercept him.

"Identify yourself!" one cried as he rode up.

"Salaam alaykum," replied Khuda. "I am Mahmoud of the Shikara family and a merchant of Jerusalem."

"You look like a Turk," one of them challenged. "Where's your merchandise? Where are your donkeys?"

Khuda studied the two soldiers carefully. They were lightly armed. He glanced up the hill for a brief moment. The other soldiers remained on the crest, but they were watching. "I have just returned from business in Jaffa, and now make my way home to Jerusalem." He forced a thin smile.

"Dismount and show us your papers."

"Of course," Sayyid. They are in my bags." He swung a leg over his horse, hitting the ground lightly.

One soldier dismounted. "Let's see what you carry in your bags."

"As you wish," said Khuda, knowing the soldier would soon discover his arms and mail coat. Without any warning, he grabbed the hilt of his concealed sword, drawing it out. There was a dull flash of steel and a shout. "Curse your mothers! Shia bastards!"

Before the stunned soldier could respond, Khuda plunged the blade through his neck and, just as quickly, withdrew the bloodied sword as the man collapsed to the ground. By this time, the other soldier had regained his senses, drawing his own blade to fight. Meanwhile, the other horsemen on the crest saw the commotion, shouting loudly as they charged down the path toward them.

Khuda jumped to the left side of the mounted soldier, who tried to turn his horse to regain advantage with his sword arm. Khuda was faster. He swung his sword in a backswing, striking the soldier's left leg, cutting it off below the knee and slicing into the ribs of the horse. The horse screamed and bolted. The man howled, tumbling from his saddle in shock. Khuda jumped back onto his horse, riding off at full gallop. Arrows flew past his ears as four Egyptian horsemen thundered onto the road in dogged pursuit.

Ramiro contemplated the heavens as Adele slept beside him. It was another black, moonless night and the stars glimmered like jewels. He was searching the southern sky for the constellation of Libra when he heard the snap of a dry twig. He immediately thought of the boar and felt the pain of his fresh wounds. He thought, too, of brigands and Egyptian soldiers. As a measure of caution, he had forgone a campfire, insisting they set up their tent at a spot nestled against the hills.

Another snap, closer now. He reached under his mattress for his dagger. He listened; the crunch of dry grass, the snort of a horse. Soldiers? Travelers? He rose to his knees, crouching on the ground, peering into the blackness. He saw nothing. More noise... then nothing. A long moment passed. He heard a snore, a human snore. He relaxed a little. Another traveler.

~ ~ ~

Before the break of dawn, Ramiro was fully dressed. He sat facing the direction of the night noise, gripping his dagger. The morning light waxed slowly between the oaks. There he is! One man, one horse.

The man stirred, as though he could sense someone's gaze. In an instant, he jumped to his feet, rolled up his mattress and began to pack his bags. That's when Ramiro noticed his long braids. He's a Turk! He's armed!

The man was busy stuffing his braids under his turban when he noticed Ramiro staring at him from a distance. For one brief moment, their eyes met.

Ramiro could feel the blood drain from his head. It's Khuda!

For a moment, Khuda feared Ramiro was an Egyptian soldier, but when he saw his dress, he relaxed. Still… there was something about the man that made him hesitate. He looked back again but Ramiro had turned his face away and seemed to be laying back down. He scanned the area around him for other signs of life. There were none.

Ramiro rolled to one side. He poked Adele gently. Her eyelids flickered and she woke with a start. He was about to whisper a warning to her when she blurted out. "What is it? You want some breakfast?" He could not put his hand over her mouth fast enough.

Khuda had already mounted and was about to ride away when he heard the woman's voice. It was not Arabic, nor was it Turkish. It was the tongue of those Western barbarians. And those eyes! How could I mistake those eyes! The eyes of the Devil. It's the barbarian priest and that red-headed witch! Those thieving kuffar! A wicked grin crossed his face. He jumped off his horse, drawing his sword in a flash. By the will of Allah, I will have my revenge!

Ramiro watched him dismount with his sword out. "It's Khuda!" he gushed. "He knows! He's coming this way!"

Adele tore his hand from her mouth, reaching frantically for her mace. "That bastard won't kill me without a fight!"

He gave her a despairing look. She had spirit—but both of them together were no match for Khuda, a battle-hardened mamluk. Now here he was, stalking through the trees toward them, sword in hand. They would surely die. He looked around urgently. The spot he had chosen, which he assumed was safe, now proved otherwise. The hill hemmed them in and they had no way of escape. "Quick! Pull down the tent!"

"What?" she whispered. "The tent? Are you mad? He's coming!"

"Do it now!" he replied in a chilling voice, yanking out the pegs. "Now grab a corner! We'll use it as a net!" Khuda was only a few strides away. "If he goes my way—try to wrap around him! I'll do the same. Keep your mace ready and hit him whenever you can!" He put his dagger in his belt, holding the tent corner with one hand and scooping up a handful of dirt with the other.

"I have come to send you to hell, Christian dog!" Khuda yelled as he raised his sword to strike.

Ramiro surprised him by stepping forward, throwing the dirt straight into his eyes. Khuda's sword faltered in mid-swing and he staggered, groping at his eyes. Ramiro and Adele fell on him with the tent. But Khuda was too strong and agile and, even with their combined weight, they had trouble bringing him down. Adele hammered him with her mace but he fought back like a wild bear. Ramiro was about to drive in his dagger when Khuda's sword burst through the canvas, slicing across his right arm. Ramiro clutched at the wound, dropping his knife.

Khuda felt the weight shift and threw them both off. Getting free of the tent, he flung out his left arm, belting Adele across the head. She tumbled to the ground. Ramiro rushed to pick up the dagger with his left hand, blood flowing down his arm. Khuda rubbed his eyes again, still red and watering. Ramiro moved to strike but Khuda heard the noise and jumped at him, swinging his sword wildly. Ramiro held up his dagger, but Khuda's swing sent it flying out of his hand. And before he could respond, Khuda gained some sight and, too close for a sword thrust, punched out with the pommel, striking Ramiro in the throat.

Ramiro collapsed onto the rough ground, choking and gasping. Khuda put a foot on his wounded arm, pressing the point of his sword into his neck. "Where's my money, kafir thief?" He pushed down with the point. "Tell me now and you will have a quick death," he smiled.

Ramiro grunted in pain, he could hardly speak. "It's... it's on the mule," he croaked. "In the blankets."

Khuda's face twisted in a cold smile. He bent down to search Ramiro, finding the package in his vest. He cut the string and opened it. The gold and silver cross flashed in a ray of morning sun. "Ha, ha. You see, kafir? What good has this talisman brought you?" he sneered. "You will have no need of it now, barbarian! May Allah damn your soul!"

Adele opened her eyes, looking around carefully. She was behind Khuda. She rose slowly, reaching for her mace lying on the ground a short distance away. Getting a firm grip on it, she rushed at Khuda's back. But Khuda noticed a flicker in Ramiro's eye and spun around as fast as a panther. He swung his sword arm out to strike her, but Adele had already landed her mace squarely between his shoulder blades. He crumbled for a moment, but regained his stance before she could hit him again. He turned, belting her across the head. She fell again, blood pouring from her nose.

"You bitch!" he shouted, raising his sword to run her through. Ramiro reached out, grabbing his legs with his good arm. Khuda stumbled. Adele rose to her knees, swinging the mace as hard as she could. Khuda howled as it crashed into a kneecap. He fell to the ground, groping for his sword. Adele swung at him again. But he saw the blow coming, dodged and punched her right between the eyes. She toppled over, unconscious.

That's when Ramiro heard the soldiers yelling some paces away. Khuda heard them too. He cursed aloud, hobbling back to his horse as fast as he could. He mounted with difficulty, grabbing the reins of the mules too. Ramiro tried to stop him but was held back by the swing of his blade.

"I'll kill you later, kafir dog!" he snapped as he rode away into the hills with their mules in tow.

No sooner had he disappeared from view, when two Egyptian horsemen rode into the campsite. Ramiro clutched at his bleeding arm while pointing the way, and the men rode off in pursuit.

Ramiro winced as the needle pierced his skin. "Hold still!" Adele shouted as she pushed it through. "You are fortunate, it's a clean cut."

He dabbed at the sweat on his brow. "I would hardly call that fortunate, my dear," he moaned. "In two days, I've been gored by a wild boar and pierced by a mamluk sword. The only good fortune is that my medicine bag was left behind." He turned his head to inspect her work. "Keep it clean," he ordered, remembering the advice of Fawwaz, the doctor from Adrianople who had saved Brother Aldebert's life.

Adele scowled, her face badly bruised and cut from Khuda's blows. She strained to see through blackened and swollen eyes. "Never you mind!" she snapped. "It's clean!" She put a hand to his chin, turning his head away. "I know what to do!"

"Khuda took everything," he lamented. "I thought, at last, I could fulfill my pledge and deliver the cross to Jerusalem." He dabbed at his brow again. The shade of a thin pistachio tree failed to shield them from the torrid heat of day. "I must get it back."

Adele glared at him. "You don't mean you're going after Khuda?"

"I must."

Adele drove the needle in hard. "Bloody fool!"

"Aaagh! Careful! Are you going to stab me to death with that thing?"

"Forget the cross, Ramiro. We're lucky to be alive!"

"I cannot. Khuda's probably gone to Jerusalem anyway. It would be the best place to sell it."

Adele heaved a sigh of frustration. "Well, at least you will soon get to see your mother." She wiped the wound clean and wrapped it tightly in the cleanest cloth she could find.

He nodded. It had been a while since he thought of his mother, even though they approached Jerusalem by the day. "And, by the Grace of God, the Patriarch too."

"And, praise Mary," said Adele. "...we still have the tent and some gear. And we have some money." She reached for the hem of Ramiro's cloak and shook it. "Remember the coins I sewed into our clothes." She began to roll up the tent. "But we can't stay here long. We'll have to walk to the next town." She winced from a sharp spasm, putting a hand to her stomach.

Ramiro noticed her waver. She looked terrible. "What's wrong?"

Adele tried to steady herself. "Nothing... nothing's wrong. Help me to bundle these... these..." But she could not finish her words. Her eyes rolled in her head, her knees gave way and she collapsed to the ground.

Khuda was lucky. He found a grotto carved into the hills and darted in with his horse and mules. The Egyptians spotted him in their search and rushed in, swords drawn. But it was a trap. And they were no match for Khuda, even with a wounded knee.

When he eventually arrived at the outskirts of Jerusalem, he spotted the Egyptian forces besieging the Jaffa Gate as well as the Damascus Gate. But there were not enough soldiers to cover all gates. So, in the cover of night, he took a long route around the city to approach the poorly guarded Josaphat Gate near the Temple Mount, where the Turk guards gladly let him in.

JERUSALEM

Madteos the Jeweler studied the cross carefully, holding a magnifying glass in one hand and scratching the golden metal with a thin, sharp needle. His liver-spotted brow furrowed beneath a frayed, yellow cap. "What do you want for it?"

Khuda looked down on the jeweler's wide desk, covered with Christian crosses and figurines. "What's it worth, old man?" he growled.

Madteos shrugged his thin shoulders. "I'll give you one dinar," he muttered through a wide mustache.

Khuda leaned forward, grabbing the cross from his hand. "You insult me! I'll take it to another jeweler—one who knows the true value of gold art."

Madteos shrugged again. He could see Khuda was a Turk. "I might pay a little more. How did you obtain this cross?" he asked warily. "I don't want any trouble. Are you Christian?"

Khuda flushed red. He barged past the desk, grabbing Madteos by his vest, lifting the thin, old man off his feet before slamming him against a wall. Pendants and idols fell to the floor. "What do you think? Do I look Christian? Stupid kafir! May Allah curse you! How dare you speak to me like this! I'll knock every tooth from your withered head and gouge out your eyes!"

"Forgive me, Effendi!" Madteos squawked. "Forgive my bad manners! Of... of course it's worth more." He forced a smile. "I will give you two dinar—yes, two dinar."

Khuda released him slowly. "Give it to me now! I cannot abide the filth of this place."

Money in hand, Khuda limped back to his horse. He felt unclean and headed for the baths.

I have done well, he thought as the hot steam enveloped him. I got a decent price for the mules and found some coins sewn into the blankets, though it's not much compared to what I had. Damn them! Then he smiled a little with a pleasing sense of revenge. At least I got two dinar for that satanic cross. But his pleasure vanished in a flash as a jarring pain shot through his wounded knee. He leaned forward, rubbing at the tight bandages. May Allah curse that demon woman! I should have killed her right away. The priest too!

He moved to a low massage table, letting the masseuse rub rose oil into his scarred skin, squeezing the tension from his roped muscles. His head tilted to the side and his long braids almost reached the floor. He spoke in a low voice. "What have you heard about these Egyptians? Will the heretics take the city?"

The masseuse hesitated. "Uh, maybe, Effendi. We all worry." He could see Khuda's many scars and guessed he was mamluk. "Will you join the Turks to defend the city?"

Khuda grunted. "Perhaps I will. Nothing would give me more pleasure than to drive my sword through a stinking Fatimid."

ABU GHOSH

Ramiro couldn't stop crying. He wiped his cheeks with a kerchief already damp with tears. He paid no attention to the burning pain in his arm, now bandaged with a poultice. His precious cross was gone—but that didn't seem to matter any more. Jerusalem, the holiest of cities, where his mother waited, was just a walk away—but he gave no thought to it. "Adele," he choked in a whisper. "Adele."

When Adele collapsed, he panicked. He held her in his arms to brush the dirt from her swollen face. He saw the blood, there was so much blood, and he felt her pulse weaken. He remembered ripping open the hem of his robe for the coins and running out to the Jerusalem road for help. He rushed to a farmer pulling a handcart full of vegetables, thrusting a silver dirham into the surprised man's hands before taking the cart from his hands.

In a frenzy, he dumped the vegetables on the side of the road and rushed back to Adele. Her head lolled in his arms when he lifted her into the cart and, despite the wounds to his arms and legs, he pushed that cart at a near run—all the way to the hospital in Abu Ghosh.

He took her hand as she lay unconscious on the bed, her body as limp as bread dough. Khuda's blows had taken their toll, she looked like a corpse, the dark bruises around her eyes and cheeks stood in stark contrast to her cold, pallid skin.

The physician, a young man with jet-black hair, put his hand on Ramiro's shoulder. "Praise Allah she lives. She has lost a lot of blood from her miscarriage. When she awakes, by the will of Allah, you must feed her as much barley and chicken soup as she can swallow."

Ramiro raised his head. He put a hand to the physician's. "Thank you, Doctor," he strained through tears. "May Allah keep your children."

August 1098

The news rushed through the markets of Abu Ghosh. Everyone seemed to be talking at once. "Jerusalem falls to Egypt! The Turks have fled to Damascus!"

Adele sat by the window of their small room, unmoved by the news, staring vacantly at nothing in particular. The bruises and the swelling were almost gone, but her pallid complexion made her look weak and tired.

Ramiro lifted his head from his work. He was making a detailed ink drawing of the cross, which he planned to use in his search. He rose from a cushion. "Did you hear that? I'm going out to learn what I can. Can I get you something?"

She shook her head lethargically.

Ramiro walked over to her, kneeling to take her hand. "Adele, my love, you cannot go on like this. It wasn't your fault."

She pulled her hand away from his and wiped her eyes. "God punishes me for my sins. He has taken my child from me."

"God does not punish, Adele." He took her hand again and squeezed a little. "Khuda is the one to blame for our loss—not God."

But Ramiro's words fell flat. "Why didn't God save our child, Ramiro? Why? What have I done to bring this curse? What have *you* done?"

"We have done nothing, Adele. This is Khuda's doing. That's all."

She put her arms around his neck, resting her head on his shoulder. After a moment of silence, she lifted her eyes, putting the palm of her hand to his cheek. "Will we have another child, Ramiro?"

He kissed her forehead. "In God's time, my love. All in God's time."

ITALY

The Allsaints Abbey near Bari used to be a quiet place, but since the Holy War began two years ago, Aldebert rarely had a moment of peace. Would-be crusaders came to the abbey by the hundreds, usually to ask for something to eat or a place to sleep out of the weather. He spent much time with these people and helped many to continue on with their journey.

And two years ago, much to his surprise, Abbot Hugh had conceded to his request to remain in Italy, but only if he stayed at the Benedictine abbey. He was ordered to send Hugh monthly reports on all that was going on. And Abbot Martinus had instructions to let him roam the port where, ostensibly, he was to tend to pilgrims. During his escapades, he met several illustrious crusaders on their way to Dyrrachium and Constantinople.

As the months wore on, he heard of the Crusader's travails on their long march to Antioch, the very place where Saint Stephen was martyred. And he rejoiced when he was told that, after a long siege, they had finally conquered, cleaning the city of pagan filth, as was God's will. The news of victory gave others courage and they came from all corners of Europe to join up. Some were true warriors, well-armed with good horses, but most were common folk with no horses and few weapons of note. They were ill-equipped and poorly prepared for war, and they were the first to die.

Aldebert was older now, almost thirty, and his thin frame had filled somewhat. His face was heavier and his acne gone, leaving pale, pocked skin on his cheeks. He had waited, hoping beyond hope for Ramiro to summon him to Jerusalem. But the promised letter never came and he could not bear to think of what dreadful fate may have overtaken his fellow monk. Even now, years later, he had to fight back tears at the very mention of his name. So when a letter from Ramiro finally did arrive, he was beside himself.

He started to cry the moment he took it in his hands. It was the letter mailed from Maarat the year before. Ramiro had sent it to Cluny and the Abbot had been kind enough to forward it through. He tried to read it through his tears but could not and had to settle himself down, dabbing his eyes with an already damp kerchief before the words became clear.

> *From Ramiro of Cluny to Aldebert of Cluny, dearest greetings in the Name of Our Lord and Savior.*
>
> *I pray my letter finds you safe and well at the Abbey. Although I have much to tell, I will remain brief. With God's help, we will meet again in more auspicious times.*
>
> *I regret to inform you that I have yet to arrive in Jerusalem. Not long after I left Edessa, I was captured again by the Turks and held for three years as a prisoner in Antioch. By the Grace of Almighty God, I managed to escape to a lonely city in the heart of Syria. Lord willing, I will resume my journey to Jerusalem in the spring. But I must tell you, no place is safe to travel since the death of the Turk Sultan. I will write again when God, by His will, finally places my feet on the Holy Soil of Jerusalem.*
>
> *Maarat An-Numan, October 12, in the year of Our Lord 1097*

"Praise the Lord!" he blubbered. "Thank you, Jesus!" He continued to wipe the tears streaming from his pale cheeks. Then he had a sudden thought. "In the spring? But spring has passed. He must be there by now!" He imagined Ramiro in Jerusalem, threatened on all sides by evil, bloodthirsty, godless pagans. He jumped to his feet. "I'll join the Holy Crusade!"

JERUSALEM

Ramiro tugged at the donkey he purchased in Abu Ghosh, leading it along the winding road to Jerusalem, passing by orchards of olive and pistachio. Adele walked alongside, holding the donkey's harness with one hand. Color returned to her cheeks and vigor to her stride. But she still had a distant, detached look.

Ramiro had his head down as he walked. He was deep in thought. *Jerusalem is so near. After all these years, does my mother still live? And what do I say to Patriarch Symeon? What of the secret message sent by Abbot Hugh? Or was* it a message? Now the cross is gone, stolen again by that heathen Turk. How will I find it?

A yell came from up ahead. A long caravan of camels approached. The lead driver shouted to clear the way. Ramiro pulled the donkey closer to the side. The caravan passed and his thoughts returned again to his dilemma. Perhaps it is too late anyway. How long has it been? Eight... no nine, it's been over nine years since Abbot Hugh gave me the cross. He felt a rush of shame. Can its message still remain vital? The Abbot said the fate of Christendom hung on this message. How could that be? Perhaps its meaning is intrinsic. Perhaps the cross itself is the message. He lifted his head from his thoughts as they rounded a sharp corner of the road. And then he saw it... there it was.

There, across the deep Valley of Hinnon, the high walls of Jerusalem jutted above a rough limestone plateau as if they were a natural and timeless extension of the rock itself. They towered into a dark blue sky like the majestic walls of a mythical castle. High above, a thin cover of cloud, lit up by the morning sun as it crept over the Mount of Olives, glowed over the city like a golden halo. There stood the Biblical city of the Hebrews, of the prophets, and of Jesus.

Ramiro staggered at the sight. Blood drained from his head and he went faint, his legs weakened and he fell to his knees in the middle of the road. The years of delay, the perilous roads traveled, the long imprisonments, the disappointments, and the years of suffering—it all caught up to him in an overwhelming agony of spirit—a painful meld of anguish and ecstasy. His shoulders heaved and he began to sob openly, putting his hands to his knees to steady himself. "Oh Jerusalem," he choked aloud as a rush of tears streamed his cheeks. "Praise be to the Heavenly Father." He wiped his face with a sleeve, unable to stop the rush of hot tears.

"Ramiro!" Adele cried as she abandoned the donkey, rushing to his side. "Ramiro! Are you alright?" She rested a hand on his shoulder.

Her touch brought him to his senses. He turned to look at her and soon realized he was kneeling in the middle of the road. Some travelers stopped and stared, others cursed his obstruction. He wiped his face again. "Yes, yes, of course. I'm fine." He stood unsteadily before moving to the side of the road. "Come, let's get out of the way. I need to rest a while."

The walls of Jerusalem stand the height of eight men and are five paces thick. They wrap around a crest of limestone rock for two and a half miles, interspersed with six main gates and two fortresses. Below the walls, the deep valleys of Qidron, Josaphat, and Hinnon serve as a natural defense to the south, wrapping part way around the city like wide, craggy moats gouged from the

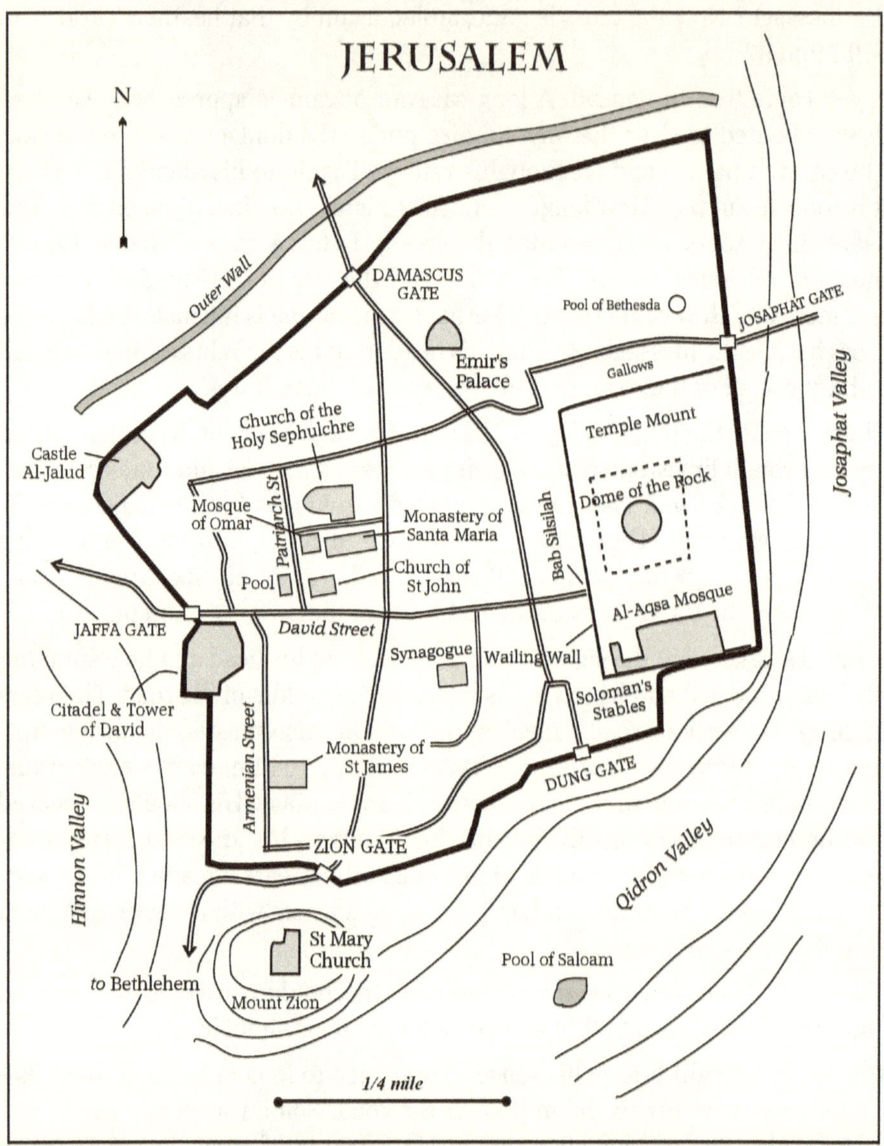

gray-white rock by the hand of God. Only to the north does flatter ground allow an easier approach, but here a second outer wall and a series of dry moats defend the main wall.

The Canaanites settled here four thousand years before, near a site that would later become known as the Temple Mount. They called it Jebus, after the name of their tribe. Nearby, was the spot where the High Priest Melchizedek later made a covenant with Abraham of Chaldea. It was called Salem. And the sweep of Jebus-Salem came to form the heart of emerging Jewish nations, the Kingdoms of Judah and Israel. But over the centuries, these struggling nations were conquered again and again by Assyrians, Babylonians, Persians, Greeks—and now the Romans, who had seized the land sixty-three years before the birth of Christ.

Later, in the year 70, Jewish zealots rose up in rebellion against their Roman masters. But they were soon crushed by the ruthless might of the Roman army and paid a terrible price. Over a million died and tens of thousands were crucified on Golgotha, the Hill of Skulls. In ongoing reprisals, the Romans flattened the city walls and demolished the Temple, just as the Persians had centuries before. And to satisfy their vengeance, they forever banned all Jews from the holy city.

Only after the Muslim conquest, almost six hundred years later, when the Caliph, Umar Ibn Al-Khattab, seized Jerusalem in 638, were the Jews finally allowed to return to their ancestral city.

Not long after his conquest, the new Caliph cleared centuries of rubble and refuse that had accumulated over the decrepit ruins of the old Temple. There, he built a splendid shrine, the Dome of the Rock, which he fancifully envisioned as a place of worship for all faiths.

For Jews, Jerusalem is the holiest of cities, the place of the covenant between God and Abraham. For Muslims, it is the third holiest city after Mecca and Medina, being the place where Muhammad rose to heaven. And for Christians, it is the holy site where Jesus proclaimed his divinity in the Second Temple, the place where he was executed by the Romans, where he was entombed, and where he resurrected.

Christians of the day believed Jerusalem to be the sacred ground where heaven meets earth in a divine union of God and man. And the very point of that heavenly juncture was the Holy Sepulcher, the Tomb of Christ.

When Ramiro and Adele approached the Jaffa Gate, the white banner of the Egyptian Fatimids flapped high above the Tower of David. The conquering Vizier, Al-Afdal, allowed the ruling Turks to flee to Damascus, a popular gesture. But he was not so kind to their askari and others who defended the city, putting most to the sword. Then without ceremony, he installed his own governor, a brawny, ambitious man by the name of Iftikhar, who he left with a full detachment of Egyptian troops. Satisfied with his victory, Al-Afdal returned to his pressing affairs in Cairo, feeling confident he had put an end to the Franj invasion of Palestine.

The people and bureaucrats of Jerusalem wasted little time bowing in submission to their new overlords, and life in the city resumed its busy pace. No one really seemed to care whether the Turks or the Egyptians ruled as long as commerce was good. But Governor Iftikhar remained wary and ordered his guards at the gates to check everyone going in or out. The long line of arrivals inched slowly through the dim, narrow entrance of the gate.

"Where are you from?" a guard asked in Arabic as he perused their papers.

"From Maarat An-Numan, Sayyid," Ramiro responded in kind.

"And what is your business in Jerusalem?"

"We are Christian pilgrims, Sayyid. We have come to worship at the Holy Sepulcher."

"Hmmph," he huffed. He glanced at Adele's red hair, looking them over suspiciously. "Are you one of those Western barbarians? The devils who, even now, have taken Antioch?"

"Oh no, Sayyid." Ramiro gushed. "We have nothing to do with those barbarians. We have come only to worship."

"How long will you stay?"

Ramiro hesitated. "Uh, by your permission, Sayyid, until the Nativity Feast."

"What? This means nothing to me. How long is that?" he asked impatiently.

"Well," Ramiro thought for a moment, converting the date of Christmas. "That would be until the end of the month of Muharram, Sayyid."

The guard handed the papers back to him. "That's a long time. You must register. Give your names to the clerk." He pointed inside the gate before turning to the next in line.

"Ha, ha!" Ramiro laughed. "We've done it, my darling! We have reached Jerusalem!" He gave Adele a warm embrace. The donkey tugged at the reins, braying in the commotion.

"Ramiro!" She pushed him away. "Mind your manners. People are all around us." But she smiled too, the first broad smile he had seen in a long time. She tossed her head with a gleam in her eyes "Where do we go from here? Where's the Holy Sepulcher?"

"I have no idea," he said, shaking his head. "But we will soon know." He took long strides down David Street to ask the nearest vendor, a man selling hummus and flatbread.

"We continue down this street and then turn left on Patriarch Street. It leads north to the church. Come! I must know if my mother lives. And I must meet with the Patriarch as soon as possible."

"What of Khuda? What if he's in the city?"

He scanned the crowd. "I haven't seen a Turk yet. I'm sure they've all left." But he looked over his shoulder one more time.

HOLY SEPULCHER

In 325, the first Christian Emperor, Constantine, prodded on by his devout mother, Helena, demolished the Temple of Aphrodite—the Greek goddess of erotic love—in order to erect a new Christian church in Jerusalem. Helena supervised all construction and, in the course of excavations, claimed to have found the remains of the True Cross and the Tomb of Christ. And so she named it the Church of the Holy Sepulcher and it soon became the most holy site in all Christendom.

Under Muslim rule, the church survived until the mad Caliph of Egypt, Al-Hakim, razed it to the ground in 1009. The news of its destruction spread like an angry fire throughout the whole of Europe. But in their shock and ignorance, European Christians blamed Jews for the desecration.

In 1048, the Byzantine Emperor of the time, Constantine IX, rebuilt the church, but it was only a partial reconstruction. When Ramiro and Adele arrived, it was only fifty years old.

The market on Patriarch Street was crowded, teeming with shoppers who came from far and wide to procure the bountiful and often rare merchandise of Jerusalem. Bags and barrels of goods from every corner of the world lined both sides of the busy street.

Ramiro pushed through the masses with Adele in tow. When he reached Saint Helena Street, he turned down a path so narrow only a single file of pedestrians and donkeys could pass. Adele rushed to keep up. The path turned left, then right, before descending a flight of stone steps, where it eventually came to a dilapidated courtyard, the entrance to the Church of the Holy Sepulcher.

"This is it," said Ramiro.

"This?" Adele asked with some amazement. "But it's half a ruin!"

"So it seems," he muttered. He had finally reached the site of the Holy Sepulcher, a mysterious, sacred place that had eluded him for so many years. But he was disappointed—it was far from the magnificent structure he had imagined from his readings. Nothing remained of the ancient basilica or the atrium, and the once-covered courtyard now stood open to the sky. Here and there, the fractured base of old walls jutted from the rough ground and, in some places, the shattered remains of a once-beautiful mosaic floor peeked through the dirt.

Slowly, with a throng of others, they made their way through the dim entrance, which led straight to the wide floor of the rotunda. Dusty-white stone pillars, joined by arches, circled all around, and at the very center was a gray stone shrine, poorly lit by a pale-yellow daylight radiating from small windows high above in the domed ceiling. This was the aedicule, and within it, was the Tomb of Christ.

Ramiro knelt beside the shrine before reaching out to touch its stone. He prayed quietly with his eyes shut. For years, he had pined for this moment. For years, he had suffered to reach this holy place. It was here, at the very Tomb of Christ, where he had no doubt the Holy Spirit would wash away all his sins and he would be renewed, he would be sanctified. It was here, where he expected some divine revelation and a feeling of spiritual bliss. But he felt nothing. Instead, he fretted in anxious thoughts.

Adele fondled her prayer beads and prayed passionately to Mother Mary. Tears of bitter grief stained her cheeks, grief at the haunting images of her parents slain by the Turks, grief at being cruelly enslaved, and the unbearable grief of losing her first child. She prayed for mercy and she prayed for the remission of her sins. She lifted her eyes to the soft light overhead and, in a moment of divine worship, she felt a flood of ecstasy. The exhilaration of the moment lifted her soul to new heights and she felt released, finally released from the cold bitterness that caged her mind. She cried some more and praised the Mother of God for leading her to the most holy place on earth. Her senses returned only when impatient new arrivals nudged her away.

They moved away from the aedicule to stand between the pillars. "When will you know of your mother?" she asked, wiping her face.

"I have asked. We must wait here for the nun."

Time moved slowly. Clergy and pilgrims came and went and the prayers of the faithful echoed from the unadorned walls. Pilgrims arrived in all kinds of dress, coming from near and far, despite the constant danger.

Adele poked him and pointed. "I think that's her."

A slight woman approached wearing a long, white habit and a white headscarf. "Are you Ramiro of Cluny?" she asked.

"Yes, Sister. Do you have news of my mother, Isabella Agueda?"

The nun answered brusquely. "I'm sorry to say, Sister Isabella passed away four years ago."

Ramiro took a moment to absorb her words. And what he heard was not entirely unexpected. He had feared this outcome many times but came to believe he had hardened his mind to it, telling himself that he had done all he could to get here on time and that death was, after all, just an inevitable part of life. But when the plain truth sank to his heart, he felt a heave of remorse and grief. He clenched his jaw, struggling to restrain his emotions. "By... by God's mercy!" he choked. "May she rest in peace."

Adele took his arm, holding firm.

"Who is your mother's father?" the nun tested, oblivious to his pain.

Ramiro blinked through tears. "Why, it is Eustace of León."

She handed him an envelope. "You answered correctly. Sister Isabella asked me to give you this. By the grace of God, she rests in the bosom of Christ."

"Thank you, Sister, thank you," he said in a strained voice, taking the letter. The nun turned around to walk away.

"Wait, please, Sister," he called after her. "Would you be so kind as to direct me to the Patriarch?"

She turned. "You wish to see Patriarch Symeon?"

"Yes, if you please."

She shook her head. "He was exiled almost a year ago. They accused him of collaborating with the Greeks and the Western barbarians and he fled to the island of Cyprus."

"Cyprus? All the way to Cyprus?"

"Yes," she said. "If you must see His Eminence, you will have to return to Jaffa to board a vessel."

"Then tell me, who is in authority here?"

"Bishop Aliphas is our guide for the moment. Unless they throw him out too."

Isabella's Letter

Ramiro's thoughts wandered in all directions as he and Adele sat on a low, stone bench outside the Church of the Holy Sepulcher. He could not help but think, with some remorse, that he would have seen his mother in time if he had not gone after Adele in Antioch. And the Patriarch too, perhaps in enough time to complete some vital assignment. But it was too late now. And it did not matter.

He glanced at Adele as they shared a handful of olives. He knew in his heart he would have changed nothing, that he could never live with himself if he had left her to the fancies of the Turks. And now, after five years together, he could not imagine living without her.

He opened his mother's envelope, unfolding her letter carefully. It was four years old and the paper was yellowed. An object fell out onto the flagstones. "What's that?"

Adele bent over to pick it up. "Looks like a small pouch."

Ramiro took it from her fingers and opened it. "By all the saints! This must be the relic my mother mentioned in her first letter." He tipped the pouch into his hand and a small piece dropped out. "I think it's a thorn."

"A thorn? Well, what does she say in the letter?"

Ramiro held it at arm's length. "Again she writes in Castilian. But her hand is weak." He faced Adele and read softly.

> To my dear son, Ramiro, son of Sancho, greetings and God's blessing
> from your loving mother, Isabella.
>
> Alas, my beloved, if you read this then it is too late. I prayed to see
> you before my last days on earth but my prayers were not answered.
> Soon, I will pass over to Christ. I beseech you, pray for my soul.

His voice broke as he read and he took a moment to compose himself. Adele pressed against him to give him strength. He took a deep breath and read on.

> It has been six years since I sent to you my first letter. Since that
> time, my son, there have been many rumors within the confines of
> the Church. It is said the Christians of Rome and those of the West
> Countries plot with the Greeks to free Jerusalem from the grip of
> heathen. If this is so, my son, you must position yourself for the great
> Christian kingdom to come.
>
> Take the Thorn of Christ I give to you and become a Soldier for
> Christ. Restore the Holy Land to God-knowing people. This is my dy-
> ing wish. May God be with you always.
>
> August 19, in the year of Our Lord, 1094.

Adele's eyes opened wide. "Is it really from Christ's crown of thorns?" She reached out to touch it.

Ramiro lifted one cheek in a skeptical grin. "Honestly, I don't know what to believe. My mother, God bless her soul, she believed it. But have you looked in the Christian markets? There are enough thorns for sale to make a hundred crowns!"

"Maybe so, Ramiro, but keep it with you, just in case—for your own protection." She tapped on the letter impatiently. "And what does she mean by 'position yourself'?"

"It seems she wants me to take up the sword and seek high office in this new kingdom." He shook his head slowly as he looked down on the letter. "I believe mothers are much the same in this regard. They all want what they think is best for their children."

She picked the thorn from his hand and studied it on her palm. "Is this what you'll do?" she asked with some distraction.

"Heavens no! I have no desire to take part in war or politics, nor to govern Jerusalem. That is not my path. I'm afraid my mother, may God bless her soul, was a little more zealous than I anticipated."

Adele picked up an olive from the napkin on her lap. "Then are we going back to Jaffa to find the Patriarch?" she asked before putting it in her mouth. "Are we going to Cyprus?"

"No, no. What's the sense in that? I have nothing to give the Patriarch. The cross is lost. And how do I know if any of this is still important?"

"So what do you plan to do?"

"I must speak to this Bishop Aliphas." He squeezed his hands together as he talked. "And I must try to find the cross. How can I face Abbot Hugh if I do not at least try?"

"That was nine years ago," Adele contended. "I'm wondering if this cross is cursed."

"Nothing is cursed," Ramiro frowned. "People curse, that is all."

She took his hand. "Must you put your life at risk again, Ramiro? What if Khuda still has it?"

He shook his head. "He would have sold it by now. Or melted it down. It's not likely a Muslim would want to be seen carrying a Christian cross. I know it's not in Abu Ghosh... I checked everywhere. So he must have brought it to Jerusalem. This would be his best market for it."

"So where will we stay?"

"Abbot Hugh ordered me to the Benedictine monastery, the Monastery of Santa Maria."

"And where's that?"

Ramiro looked around and chuckled. "It's right there, across the street."

She looked up. "That's a mosque,"

"That building is, yes. That's the Mosque of Umar. But on either side and behind it is the Monastery. I saw the plaques earlier. It's more of a hospice really. Mainly to attend to sick and weary pilgrims."

Adele stared vacantly. She did not seem to hear. "What will you do, Ramiro?" she asked, squeezing his hand, her freckled brow furrowed.

"What do you mean?"

"Will you return to the Order of Benedict?"

"I can no longer return. Although married men are allowed to be monks, as long as they take a vow of chastity afterward." He could feel her grip tighten. "But usually their wives enter a monastery too."

She looked down for a moment before raising her head again. "Is this what you want me to do? Become a nun?"

He put a finger to her chin, lifting her face. Her eyes watered and he bit his tongue to stop his own tears. The noisy plaza seemed to grow quiet except for the pigeons that waddled past, pecking among the stones. Gently, he put his hand on top of hers. "No. That is not what I want."

BROTHER GERARD

A stone wall wrapped around the expansive grounds of the Monastery of Santa Maria Latina. Up against this wall and lining the streets, were rows of adjacent shops, all displaying their wares in a great clutter, obscuring the entrance to the monastery itself. "Here it is," Ramiro said, opening a small iron gate concealed behind a rug merchant. "Come on."

No one guarded the gate. The unkempt gardens and crumbling courtyard appeared abandoned. The only sound was the whistle of a bulbul flitting between a few withering almond bushes.

Not far in, a heavyset nun came out to greet them. "I'm Sister Agnes. What can I do for you?" She spoke with an air of authority.

"We are Christian pilgrims looking for accommodation," said Ramiro.

"We can give you a bed," she said plainly, waving her arm to one side. "This building here is the hospice for women." She waved in the other direction. "And that one for the men."

"May I speak to the Abbot, Sister?"

"The abbot is not here. He was expelled by the Egyptians. You must see the superior, Brother Gerard."

Adele poked Ramiro in the back. "I'm not staying here by myself," she whispered.

He ignored her. "Thank you, Sister. And where will I find Brother Gerard?"

She pointed. "Go through that door—but no women," she commanded as Adele began to follow him. "You can wait with me, my dear. Come inside."

Ramiro climbed the low, stone steps. The door was open and the hallway quiet. "Hello. Anyone here?"

A short monk wearing a black habit came out of a nearby room, his hair cut in a tonsure with days of rubble showing. "Please, come in," he said, rolling an arm. "What brings you to the hospice?"

The sight of a Benedictine monk sent Ramiro's thoughts racing back to Cluny and, in an odd way, filled him with a renewed determination to complete his mission. But he also felt some embarrassment, dressed as he was with a full head of hair and a beard. And he had a wife.

"Sayyid?" asked the monk after a long silence. "Does something trouble you?"

Ramiro emerged from his thoughts. "My apologies. I am Ramiro of Cluny. I was told to see Brother Gerard."

"He is busy in the infirmary. Is it important?"

"It is very important, Brother. I have come a long way and have a message for him."

"Very well," said the monk. "Go down to the end of the hall and turn left."

"How will I recognize him?"

"He's the bald one."

Ramiro heard the groans of pain long before he found the infirmary. Narrow beds lined either side of the open room, interspersed every so often with tall columns reaching to a high ceiling. Stained glass windows on one side added bright colors to the otherwise drab and dismal scene. Three monks tended to the patients, men of all ages.

He soon spotted the bald monk, who was not completely bald, a thin semicircle of hair stretched between his ears at the back. He had a prominent brow, a clean-shaven face and a distinct chin.

Ramiro approached him. "Brother Gerard?"

"Yes, I am he," he said, looking stern. "And who are you... and what are you doing in my infirmary?"

"I am Ramiro of Cluny, Brother. I apologize for disturbing your work, may God bless you for your devotion. But I come on an important errand."

"Do you?" he said, cleaning the stump of a severed leg. "Did you say you're from Cluny? Cluny in Burgundy?"

"Yes, Brother."

Gerard wrapped the patient's leg in clean cotton before glancing again at Ramiro. "You don't look like a monk."

"But I am, Brother. The Abbot of Cluny ordered me here. I'm out of habit only because of a long and difficult journey."

Gerard nodded as he left the bed and went to the next one. "Have you come to join us in God's work?"

Ramiro followed him. "I would be glad to help whenever I can, Brother."

"That is good," Gerard replied in a matter-of-fact tone. "God knows we could use more help. Is that why you've come?"

"Well, no. I came to ask if Abbot Hugh mentioned my name or if he said anything of my mission?"

Gerard looked up at him and smiled, almost laughed. "Your mission? No, I've never heard a word from Cluny—nor from the Pope for that matter. We've been asking for money and supplies for years, but it seems we have been abandoned." He stopped at the bed of a severely bruised young man who wore a cast of wooden slats about one leg. "Here," he gestured to Ramiro. "Help me lift him to the next bed."

"What happened to him?" Ramiro asked as he lifted the boy in his arms. The young lad groaned.

"He fell from his father's roof. Put him here. So tell me, Brother Ramiro, what is this mission of yours?"

"Abbot Hugh asked me to deliver a message to Patriarch Symeon."

"Well you're too late for that, he was exiled some time ago."

"So I've heard."

He motioned to a table. "Hand me those bandages. Do I dare ask what this message may be?"

Ramiro passed him a wad of cotton. "I'm really not sure. I was asked to deliver a cross to him."

Gerard frowned with a smile. "A cross? What's that all about?"

"The Abbot said it had something to do with uniting the Churches. I was hoping you would know more." He pulled out the ink drawing he had made in Abu Ghosh. "Unfortunately, it was stolen from me before I arrived. It looks like this. Have you seen it?"

Gerard lifted his head from his work, looking briefly at the drawing before turning back to his work. "No, it doesn't look familiar. As I said, no one spoke to me of it. When did you leave Cluny?"

Ramiro felt his ears redden. "Nine years ago."

"Nine years!" Gerard scoffed. "You are late!" he laughed. "I've only been here for five."

A loud moan came from one of the beds. Gerard moved over to an old man with spiked gray hair who stared out from the covers, his eyes clouded by cataracts. "So where have you been all this time?"

"As I said, it has been a difficult journey." He did not want to say too much. "I was captured by the Turks and held at Antioch."

Gerard nodded, looking pleased. "Antioch? Well, we can thank the soldiers of God for liberating the city and cleaning away the heathen. And the sooner these brave men take Jerusalem from these contemptible pagans, the better it will be for all of us. They treat us like slaves and hinder our good efforts."

"But what of the massacre at Antioch?" Ramiro frowned. "Does this not concern you?"

"Why should it? We are Christian."

"Yes, but I hear they killed Christians too."

"The Greeks, yes," Gerard said with some indifference. "But the French are of the same Church as us. It will indeed be a glorious day when they take Jerusalem too."

Ramiro stood dumbfounded. Gerard's simplistic view was deeply troubling. "But are not the Benedictine men of peace?"

"Yes, that's true, but what of Augustine's notion of a just war? Surely, this is what the Pope speaks of."

Ramiro was about to argue that Augustine's "just war" was justified only in the defense of innocents and should be used only to restore the peace. But he thought it unwise to pursue the matter any further, especially since the Pope himself had summoned this war.

"Perhaps you should see the new Greek bishop," said Gerard, "... what's his name?"

"I believe you refer to Bishop Aliphas," Ramiro replied. "I have an appointment with him on the morrow."

Bishop Aliphas

Ramiro bowed low in the opulent reception room of the Palace of the Patriarch. "Bless, Your Grace."

"May the Lord bless you," Bishop Aliphas responded dryly as he put his hand out.

Ramiro stooped to kiss his sacral ring.

Aliphas seemed impatient. "And who are you?" he asked in a gruff voice.

"Ramiro of Cluny, Your Grace." He was a little surprised that Aliphas was an Arab. He had a thick shag of black hair and a black beard and looked ill at ease.

He wore a stiff, embroidered red cape, over which hung a rectangular scarf decorated with multiple crosses.

"Please sit, Ramiro of Cluny."

"Thank you, Your Grace."

"Cluny?" he asked. "In the land of the French?"

"Why, yes, Your Grace."

"Are you Benedictine?"

"Yes, I am, but I do not wear my habit because I have been traveling through Muslim lands."

Aliphas nodded in understanding. "So you have come to work at the Latin monastery? In the hospital?"

"Perhaps, but that's not the reason I was sent here."

"Then why have you sought an audience with me. I must ask you to be brief, I'm a busy man."

Ramiro told the Bishop of his mission, how Abbot Hugh ordered him to Jerusalem with instructions to deliver to the Patriarch a certain cross which, he believed, held some message for him, a message the Abbot deemed essential to the survival of Christendom. Alas, he said, the cross had been stolen by a Turk but he suspected it was somewhere in the city.

Aliphas looked him over with a sympathetic but skeptical smile. He shook his head. "To be frank, that sounds a little preposterous, Monk Ramiro. Are you sure it wasn't for some other reason you were sent here?"

"I swear in the name of God, Your Grace. If there is another reason, I do not know it." He had a sudden thought, remembering the letter he had given to the mufti, Ibrahim. "I sent a letter to the Patriarch in which I told him I was the appointed legate of Abbot Hugh and that I was on my way with the cross. Did he mention this?"

"Not that I remember. Who delivered it?"

"A Muslim by the name of Ibrahim."

"Ibrahim? The Qadi?"

"Yes, that's right. He did mention he had taken the position of Qadi here."

"How long ago was this?"

"A year to the month, Your Grace."

"Well, there are two things you should know. First of all, the Turks exiled the Patriarch and he fled to Cyprus at about that time, so the two may never have met. And second, the Qadi has gone missing. He either fled to Damascus with the Turks or he's locked up—or he's dead."

"But why would they harm a Muslim scholar?"

"Do not forget, he is first a Sunni... and an important one. The Fatimids have already taken over all the mosques. Most of the Sunni clergy have fled."

"Is there any way to discover what happened to him?"

"You could ask the authorities... at your own risk. But why are you so concerned about a Muslim?"

"Well... he was an acquaintance, that is all."

"So, do you still report to your Abbot?"

"Yes, Your Grace, whenever I can. But for long periods I could not. I was either held prisoner or had no way of sending a letter out. I resumed my reports after escaping Antioch but have yet to receive any reply. I'm hoping Abbot Hugh will contact me here in Jerusalem."

The Bishop leaned over his desk, speaking quietly. "Do you know why Patriarch Symeon was exiled by the Turks?"

"I have heard rumor, Your Grace."

"He was accused of treason... they say he plotted to facilitate the invading armies from Byzantium and the West. I dare say your Pope and perhaps even your Abbot were complicit in this affair. Now the Muslims fear that the Christians in Jerusalem will revolt. Our activities are tightly controlled and we are watched by the askari, first by the Turks and now by the Egyptians."

Ramiro looked perplexed. He was not sure he understood. "You say the Abbot... the Abbot of Cluny was involved in this? How so?"

"Well, I'm not entirely sure," said Aliphas. "But Pope Urban and the French armies seem to be well informed about the lay of the land and the military capabilities of the Turks and the Arabs, even the Greeks. Rumor has it that much of this information came directly from the Abbey of Cluny. How? We do not know."

Military capabilities? Ramiro flushed, suddenly feeling ill. The abbey? His mind raced. Can this be so?

"What's wrong, Monk Ramiro?"

Ramiro waved a hand. "Oh, nothing, nothing, Your Grace. I'm a little tired that is all."

Aliphas continued. "So I don't know what to make of this cross of yours. If indeed, it holds a message, I would be glad to receive it on behalf of the Patriarch."

"Yes, Your Grace, of course. I will do my best to retrieve it."

"A word of warning, Brother Ramiro. Tread lightly—and beware the Egyptians."

IFTIKHAR

Governor Iftikhar, the new Egyptian governor of Jerusalem, leaned over a table in the great hall of Castle Al-Jalud, a fortress built in the north-west corner of the city, just north of the Jaffa Gate. It served as his headquarters and housed a large garrison of mamluks. He was studying plans to repair the city walls damaged in the recent battle with the Turks when one of his lieutenants, a burly Sudanese, came through the door with several sheets of paper.

"What's this?" Iftikhar asked.

"It is an order of execution, my Lord," replied the lieutenant in his booming voice.

Iftikhar sat cross-legged on a green cushion. An expensive red turban topped his big head, a matching red tunic covered his gleaming mail vest, and a long, green cloak draped across his broad shoulders. He was a handsome man with olive skin, a thin beard, high cheekbones and a small nose. But his handsome beauty could not conceal the determined ferocity in his oval eyes. Iftikhar was an ambitious and merciless military man. "And who are these people?"

The lieutenant pointed to the list. "These are Turk soldiers, my Lord. The ones that eluded us after we took the city." He pointed to one name in particular. He's a bad one, Sahib. We caught him at the gates dressed as a merchant. One of our wounded men identified him as hostile. He deserves to die, my Lord. He curses Fatimids in an unholy and foul manner. I cannot repeat what he says."

"And the others?" Iftikhar asked.

"Turk brigands and spies. They were caught hiding in the city."

Iftikhar read the names and their titles. "You have Sunni mullahs on your list. Do you think this wise?"

"Yes, Sahib, they plot against us. And we have returned all mosques to the True Faith as you instructed."

Iftikhar nodded. "That is good, but you will not harm the mullahs. They may be Sunni, but they are Muslim. And, as you know, this is the end of Ramadan and the first day of Shawwal, a time to show forgiveness and mercy. We will take their names off the list and send them packing to Damascus instead."

"But, Sahib," said the lieutenant pointing to another name. "This one is a spy and an agitator. He was the Qadi."

"Which one? This Ibrahim?"

"Yes, my Lord. He plots with the Christians against us."

"How do you know that?"

"We have confessions from the others, my Lord. They saw him with the Christian priest, the Patriarch. Even his own kind view him with suspicion."

Iftikhar pressed his lips. "You may be right, Lieutenant. I will think on this. Leave him in the dungeon for now."

"Your wish is my command, Sahib." He bowed. "And what of the Christians, can we trust them?"

Iftikhar paused in thought. "No, we cannot."

"We should drive them from the city, my Lord."

Iftikhar frowned, thinking about the great loss of revenues this would entail. The Christian merchants were rich and paid steep taxes, and the poll tax brought in more. "No, we will let them stay for now."

"But Sahib, we hear the Christians in the north rebelled and allied themselves with the barbarians who took Antioch."

"I know, Lieutenant, but there were many Christians in Antioch. The few Christians here present no real threat as yet." He recalled the letter he recently received from his master, the Vizier, Al-Afdal. "The Western barbarians are the ones to worry about. Christian fanatics, I hear. Call themselves Franj." He waved a finger at the lieutenant. "They are the ones to fear. Our Vizier offered them half of Syria if they would cede control of Palestine to us. But they scorned his offer."

"They are deluded, Sahib. They cannot defeat our Great Vizier, may Allah keep him. His invincible army will destroy them all. We will stop them."

"There may be no need for us to stop them," said Iftikhar. "Allah has cursed them. Praise be to the Most High God, the heathen are stalled in Antioch and have fallen to disease."

"Yes, my Lord, they are weak."

"That is good. By the will of Allah, they will all die there." He reached for a pen, crossed out the names of the Sunni mullahs and signed death warrants for the rest.

"So what does all this mean?" Adele asked before she picked up her glass of orange juice. "Does Bishop Aliphas know anything about the cross?"

Ramiro looked around the restaurant patio. "Apparently not," he said before taking a sip of red wine. "I admit, I'm confused." He put down his cup, staring into it. "Although I must say I'm beginning to doubt there is any meaning to the cross at all. I hate to think that I have been unwittingly used as a spy for the Abbot. I find that even more distressing."

"Why is that?" she challenged. "It seems the Pope himself organizes armies."

Ramiro groaned, shaking his head with incredulity. "Perhaps you are right, my love. How can I be so naive? Now I hesitate to send another report to Abbot Hugh. But he should at least know that I'm in Jerusalem. At least here I will be in a position to receive correspondence from him. I'll ask him what I should do." He took a bite of his meal. "And I'll send another letter to Brother Aldebert. I promised I would write as soon as I arrived. He must be back at Cluny by now... but just in case he gets any foolish notion about coming to Jerusalem, I'll let him know it's not safe."

"Brother Aldebert," Adele reflected. "I barely remember him."

"I'm sure he'll be very happy to hear that I've finally arrived in Jerusalem. I hope he's in good health."

"Do you think he'll come?"

"No, no, he would need permission from Abbot Hugh, and that is unlikely." He picked at his food, wondering if he would ever see the Abbot again. And what would he say to him? What would Aldebert think to see him dressed like this, his head unshaven?

"So, what are you going to do about that mufti? What's his name? Ibrahim?" Adele asked, oblivious to his thoughts.

"I'm not sure yet. I must be tactful." He thought kindly of Ibrahim, who had petitioned Yaghi Siyan on his behalf. He wanted to help. "I suspect that..."

Ramiro's words were soon drowned out by a rising commotion on the streets. The voices in the market grew louder and louder as an excited mob swarmed past the restaurant doors.

"What's all the ruckus about?" Ramiro raised his voice to be heard.

"Looks like they're heading for the Temple Mount. Something's happening. Let's have a look."

"But I haven't finished my wine."

"You've had enough wine. Come on."

He emptied his cup anyway and they soon joined the gathering crowd as it made its way east to the large square near the Al-Marwani Mosque.

"What's happening?" Ramiro asked a stranger.

"It's an execution," the man said. "Enemies of Iftikhar are about to lose their heads."

Ramiro hesitated. He pulled Adele's arm, putting his mouth to her ear. "This is grotesque. I don't want to see an execution."

Adele pulled her arm from his grasp. She had a look of macabre fascination. "Come on, I just want a quick look."

They pressed through the crowd, making their way to the edge of the square where a regiment of Iftikhar's askari stood watch over six battered and blood-ied men kneeling on the flagstones. Their hands were tied behind their backs and tied again to their ankles, their hair sheared short to allow the execution-er a clean cut with his heavy blade. They all bowed their heads in resignation.

All but one, who held his head up, bleeding and bruised. Red slashes from the jailer's whip crisscrossed his weathered face and blood oozed from his scarred nose. He cursed aloud in a deep, gravelly voice. "Damn you all to hell! Cursed Shia! I curse your mothers and your sons! Sons of whores!"

Ramiro gaped in shock. Gone were the long braids... but the voice... the voice was unmistakable. "It's Khuda!" he exclaimed a bit too loudly.

Khuda had made the fatal mistake of joining forces with the Turks of Jerusa-lem. He had surrendered with many others and, since he was not a regular, he may have been released to Damascus. But he had the misfortune of being rec-ognized by a former Egyptian soldier with only one leg, the same man he had attacked and injured on the road to Jerusalem. And when the soldier further revealed that this menacing Turk had killed three other Egyptian askari, Khu-da's fate was sealed.

As he kneeled, Khuda writhed from the pain of his shattered knee—the one Adele had smashed with her mace. But he had heard his name coming from the crowd. And the voice... it was a voice he knew. He stopped cursing and, in a long, slow motion, scanned the gathering multitude with a vicious scowl. He saw them. It was them! The stinking, thieving kuffar!

Ramiro shivered as he caught Khuda's cold, piercing glare. The Turk's face red-dened, clenched in a loathing snarl. Never before had Ramiro seen such a look of raw hatred.

"It's you!" Khuda shouted in an explosion of rage. He tried to get to his feet. "You! It's you... you son of shit! The Devil whores your mother!"

The crowd gasped at his profanity. Two soldiers rushed in, clubbing him back to his knees. And before Khuda could utter another vile blasphemy, the big ex-ecutioner swung his heavy sword down hard, severing his head with a single blow.

Blood spurted from the stump of his neck and his body slumped to the flag-stones. His head flew forward, leaving a bloodied trail in its wake. And, in what seemed like a last defiant act, it tumbled slowly across the flagstones, rolling into the crowd, where it rocked and shuddered to a stop—right at Adele's feet. Khuda's narrow, empty eyes glared up at her, his scowl frozen in death.

Adele screamed.

The crowd laughed.

Much to Adele's relief, Ramiro abandoned any thought of staying at the monastery and instead, they rented a small room near the Church of Saint John. It was pleasant enough and had a view of David Street, a narrow road stretching from Jaffa Gate to the Dome of the Rock.

"He was a bastard!" she crowed over dinner.

"Good gracious, Adele," Ramiro sighed. "There's no need to speak like that. He was a thief, I'll admit. But remember that we took his bag of money and he believed we were thieves too."

"I don't care," she said bluntly. "He killed my child. I'm glad he's dead."

Ramiro nodded gently. He said no more of it.

She tossed her hair over her shoulders. "At least we can be fairly certain of one thing."

"What's that?" he asked as he scooped a spoonful of fruit.

She put both elbows on the table, lacing her fingers together. "That your precious cross is somewhere in Jerusalem."

Ramiro lifted his head, narrowing his eyes. "Precious cross? What do you mean by that, Adele? Do you mock me?"

She felt a sudden chill. "Forgive me," she said as she reached for his hand. "But it's ruining our lives, Ramiro."

Ramiro pulled his hand away. "I gave my word, Adele. I made a solemn vow. Why is that so difficult for you to comprehend? Do you want your husband to be a man without honor?"

AN OLD FRIEND

"Have you seen a cross that looks like this?" Ramiro held up the ink drawing of his golden cross.

The jeweler shook his head as he took Ramiro by the arm. "No, no, but look at these! Are they not beautiful?" he held up an embellished cross. "I will make you an excellent deal on this one. It is the will of God. You look like a good Christian."

Ramiro shook his head, turning away. "No thank you, I'm looking for this particular cross."

The jeweler clicked his tongue, waving a hand in dismissal.

Ramiro's reception was much the same at the other jewelers, and there were many of them. Then he tried every other shop, even the barbers. And there were many of these. But no one had seen his cross. So he returned home, taking a route that led him past the Church of the Holy Sepulcher. On the other side of the street, was the Mosque of Umar, built in commemoration of the Caliph who had captured Jerusalem many years before. The sight reminded him of Ibrahim the Mufti.

The mosque was small compared to the monastery, but it was busy. Outside the door, a skinny old man stooped, sweeping the steps with a short-handled broom. Ramiro walked over to ask about Ibrahim.

"Poor Ibrahim," Ramiro said when he returned to Adele. "The old man at the mosque said they locked him in the dungeon at Castle Al-Jalud. I'd like very much to hear his tale."

Adele wagged her finger. "Now don't get into any more trouble. God knows we've had our share. Next thing, you'll be the one in that dungeon. Forget it! Let's just find the cross!"

He lifted his chest before letting out a long, slow sigh. "I've tried all the jewelers, even those of the Hebrews and Muslims. They thought I was completely mad, of course. Perhaps I am mad."

"Did you try all the churches?"

"Well... no. How would they get the cross? It's unlikely Khuda would visit them."

"I don't know, but what else can you do?"

With little warning, overcast skies burst in an autumn downpour, pelting Ramiro in a shower of heavy beads. He rushed into the foyer of the Church of Saint John the Baptist, where he shook the rainwater from his cloak. A priest came out from an anteroom.

"Have you come for Matins?" he asked.

"Uh, no Father. I seek your help. I'm looking for a particular cross."

"A cross?"

"Yes," said Ramiro as he reached into his pouch. "Have you seen this cross?"

The man looked at the drawing, turning it in his hands. Then he smiled.

"You have seen it!" Ramiro almost shouted.

The man frowned at him. "I have not. But it is unlikely you will find it in this part of the city."

"Why? What do you mean?"

"Your cross has an Armenian design. Try looking in the Armenian quarter."

The downpour stopped as quickly as it started and the sun began to peep through thinning clouds. Rainwater steamed on the warm pavement as Ramiro twisted his way south along Armenian Street, heading toward the southern walls and the Zion Gate. He stopped when he came to the Monastery of Saint James.

The monastery's gray walls fronted the street. A brass knocker in the shape of a cross hung from one of its iron doors. He banged it twice. The resounding clang was louder than he expected and the whole door seemed to reverberate. A narrow slat clacked open and he could see two eyes glaring back at him, two blue eyes.

"What can I do for you?" asked a smooth voice.

"I come in search of a cross," Ramiro answered.

"A cross?"

"Yes. Of a special design. If you let me come in, I will show you my drawing."

There was no reply. The eyes continued to stare.

"If you could help me please," Ramiro pleaded. "I just want to know if you have seen it."

The voice behind the door stuttered and choked. "Ma... Master? Master Ramiro? Is it really you?"

Ramiro drew back at the man's words. They sounded familiar. He looked closely into those blue eyes. "Yes, I am Ramiro of Cluny. Who are you?"

The latch of the door slammed back with a loud clack. The door swung open, squealing on dry hinges. A young man dressed in a full-length, black tunic stood in the foyer. Dark brown hair hung to his shoulders, a few curls draping over blue eyes and a small nose. His boyish face was clean-shaven. Ramiro gawked. "Jameel? Jameel is that really you?"

"Yes, yes, Master Ramiro. Praise be to God Almighty! I thought I would never see you again." He rushed forward to embrace him.

"Blessed saints!" Ramiro shouted with a smile, returning an awkward embrace. "How you have grown since I last saw you. You are a man now."

"Come in, Master, come in. You must tell me what happened at Antioch. Did Yaghi Siyan capture you? How did you get here?"

Ramiro sat down to recount his arrest and imprisonment as the young man busied himself serving sage tea and pastries. "And what did you do when you left Antioch? Did you travel with Tatran?"

"No, Master. Tatran rode right past me on that fateful day, chased by a regiment of askari. I have not seen him since. I waited for a year in Latakia, hoping you would come. Then I decided to go to Jerusalem. You always talked of Jerusalem and I thought perhaps you made it safely by some other route. I've been here ever since."

"What do you do here?" Ramiro asked as he looked around. "Isn't this an Armenian monastery?"

"And Maronite. It's shared. Some are monks, others are priests. I'm not a monk. They pay me to take care of the place and to keep unwanted visitors at bay. We are not well liked by the Muslims. They say the Maronites give them too much trouble in Lebanon—and now they all blame Armenians for the fall of Antioch." He sat down. "And what of that red-haired woman, Master? What happened to her?"

"She's here too, Jameel. Her name's Adele. I married her."

Jameel let out a long, low whistle. "You married her? It must be God's will, Master, after all the trouble you went through to rescue her."

"Well," Ramiro replied demurely, "... I hardly rescued her. It was only by the fickleness of fate that we escaped."

"It was God's will, Master. Praise the Lord."

"And what of you, Jameel? Have you found a wife?"

A broad smile crossed his face. "Yes, and I have a son," he said proudly. "And another on the way."

Ramiro felt an unexpected twinge of envy. He leaned over to give Jameel a slap on the shoulder. "Congratulations! You will make a good father."

"You must come to visit, Master Ramiro. You and your wife. Come tonight. My wife is an excellent cook."

Ramiro smiled. "We would like that very much Jameel, thank you."

"So what happened to your cross, Master?"

"Ah, yes." He pulled out his drawing. "It's a long story and I will tell you all about it when we meet tonight. In short, it was stolen by a Turk. I'm sure he sold it here in Jerusalem." He unfolded the drawing. "I know it's been some time since you've seen it. Hopefully, this will refresh your memory. A man at the Church of Saint John said the design was Armenian and sent me this way."

"Oh yes, I remember it," Jameel said as he glanced at the drawing. "It's very beautiful. And yes, I remember the design. Do you have any idea where it is?"

"Not yet."

Jameel rubbed his chin. "Hmm. Perhaps you should visit the jewelers. They have many crosses like this."

"I'm sure I've been to every jeweler in Jerusalem. I had no idea there were so many."

"Try the Armenian jewelers again," said Jameel. "One of them must have it."

MADTEOS THE JEWELER

Madteos looked up at the customer standing in front of him. He felt uneasy as he met Ramiro's dark eyes. "What can I do for you?"

Ramiro showed him the drawing. "Greetings, God bless you. I'm looking for this cross. It's made of gold and silver. Have you seen it?"

"I remember you," said Madteos. "I've already told you I haven't seen it."

"Please, Sayyid, look again."

Madteos looked at the drawing. At first, he held it at arm's length, then he drew it closer and closer to his long nose. He pursed his lips and shook his head before glancing at Ramiro suspiciously. "Who are you?"

"Ramiro of Cluny, from France, a land far to the west."

Madteos shook his head again. "Never heard of it. What do you want with this cross?"

"A cross like this was stolen from me some weeks ago. Stolen by a Turk."

Madteos leaned forward, pretending to study the drawing again.

Ramiro noticed his pretense. "Are you sure you haven't seen it?"

"No, no," Madteos said with a little agitation. "I've told you—I've never seen it." He handed the drawing back to Ramiro.

"I see you have many crosses. May I look?"

"You can look all you like. It's not here."

Ramiro scanned the collection slowly, keeping an eye on the jeweler as he pointed to a cross with a similar design. "It looks like this one," he said, stabbing with his finger. "But it has a center of wood."

"Doesn't sound familiar," Madteos lied, not bothering to look.

"I would be willing to pay handsomely for its return."

Madteos lifted his head from his work. "Perhaps I can find a cross like that," he said with feigned disinterest. "But if it is made of gold and silver, it would be very expensive."

"How expensive?"

Madteos opened his stained, dry hands in gesture. "Perhaps ten dinar."

"Ten dinar?" Ramiro scoffed.

Madteos nodded.

"You jest with me. The cross I speak of does not contain that much gold. Much less, in fact. But I would pay five dinar. That's more than it's worth." He paused and wondered how he could possibly obtain five dinar.

Madteos sneered with a motion of dismissal. "Others will pay more."

Ramiro drew close. He leaned over Madteos' desk, looking straight into his eyes. Madteos backed away, startled. "The cross is mine, and I want it back," said Ramiro firmly. "You know it's stolen." He raised his voice. "Perhaps I should report you to the authorities!"

Ramiro's fiery retort caught the attention of two young men sitting at the back of the shop. They were cousins of Madteos, hired to protect him after Khuda had thrown him against the wall. Rising to their feet, they approached Ramiro in a menacing way.

Madteos, emboldened by their presence, jumped from his chair. "I told you I haven't seen it! Why do you continue to waste my time?" His cousins stepped forward, scowling.

Ramiro backed away. "My apologies, Sayyid. God's peace be upon you."

The markets closed. Madteos collected his wares in two large cases before locking up the shop. He walked home at a brisk pace, escorted by his two cousins. Reaching his house, he unlocked a thick, wooden door and entered quickly. When the door slammed shut, his cousins went home.

"Madteos? Is that you?" asked a plump woman carrying a lamp.

"Of course it's me, stupid woman! Who else could open the door?"

She forced a smile. "Would you like some tea, my husband?"

"Not now, not now." He moved his cases to an inside door. "Give me the lamp." He snatched it from her hand, holding its dim light to the jingling keys, picking one from the ring. His hands shook as he turned it in the lock. "Go away!" he blurted.

In a dark corner of the small room, he knelt to the floor before pulling at a small strap protruding between the wall and the floor. A large, square tile at the base of the wall swung open to reveal a cavity no wider than a man's forearm.

There, inside, was a long, rectangular strongbox made of iron and secured with two locks. He dragged it out.

With another key, he unlocked the lid and, right on top of his hoard of gold and silver, was a small bundle wrapped in oilcloth. He unfolded it slowly. The cross glowed in the lamp light. He held it up as if it were a frail flower. It is so beautiful, he thought, ...even if it is a little scratched. The workmanship, the engravings—a masterpiece! But his delight turned to fretful thoughts when he recalled his encounter with Ramiro. What am I going to do about that damned foreigner! May God curse him!

"What about the cross?" Adele asked as she swept the floor of their small rooms. "Any luck?"

"As a matter of fact, yes." He told her about his encounter with Madteos. "I know he has it, he looked as guilty as a sinner at confession." He offered her a bowl of raisins but she ignored him, rushing into the kitchen. "And he was very defensive," he said loudly as he gazed out a small window. "But I looked around and I didn't see it there."

"How will we get it back?" she called out from the kitchen. "We don't have ten dinar. Do you think Bishop Aliphas will give you the money?"

"I asked him already but he said it was too much. I believe the Church is short of cash with all this trouble brewing. And Aliphas questions the importance of the cross."

"So how are we going to get it back?"

Ramiro frowned. "I'm not sure. But it was good to see Jameel alive and well. You must remember him from Antioch. He was the boy who dressed as a eunuch at the palace—to give you my message." He stroked his short beard. "About four years ago, I guess."

"I remember the incident, Ramiro. How could I forget that dreadful place? But I doubt I would recognize him."

"Well, you'll have your chance tonight. We've been invited for supper."

She rushed out of the kitchen, wiping her hands on her apron. "Tonight?"

"Yes. What's wrong?"

"Oh dear, Ramiro. I'm a mess," she fretted, pulling back her long hair with both hands. "I'll have to wash and dress."

"Not to worry, you have time."

When she came back into the room an hour later, she had on her favorite yellow dress. "Ramiro," she said softly, fiddling with her hair, "...you know I love you." She walked over and took his hand. "But time is passing so fast. Let's go home. Let's forget about all this and go back to France. Don't you miss it?"

He looked down, clenching his jaw.

She squeezed his hand. "I'm twenty-seven, Ramiro. Soon I'll be an old woman. God willing, we can still have another child."

He felt his temper flare but soon subdued it, his shoulders sagging in resignation. "Perhaps you're right," he said with some melancholy. "I see no way of fulfilling my mission now. In fact, I really don't know what my mission is anymore." He fell silent for a long moment before squeezing her hand gently. "Nonetheless... give me a little more time."

Jameel's wife, Layla, was a slight woman of Arab descent who covered her long, black hair with a patterned shawl. Like her husband, she had fine facial features and beautiful eyes. She was clearly pregnant beneath her loose tunic.

Her swaddling son squirmed in her arms. "Do you mind holding him while I make the hummus?" she asked Adele.

Adele reached out gingerly. "No, not at all, Layla." She took the child in her arms, cradling him on her knee, looking at him adoringly, caressing his small fingers and stroking his hair. But her faint smile soon faded to a look of sorrow. She clenched her teeth hard, fighting back a well of tears, but a single drop managed to trickle down her cheek. She brushed it away as quickly as she could.

Ramiro watched her, knowing how she felt. He felt the same empty pain and it was all he could do not to weep with her. He turned to Jameel. "You... you are a fortunate man, Jameel. I thank God you have done well. Do you plan to stay in Jerusalem?"

"We would like to stay, Master. But we are worried about the barbarian army. They say it's heading this way."

"Well, if they do come, Jameel, you and Layla must flee. Promise me, if but for a while."

"Yes, Master. Will you stay?"

"I will stay long enough to fulfill my promise, God willing. Hopefully, I can eventually retrieve the cross from Madteos and give it to Bishop Aliphas."

"What will you do in the meantime?"

"That's a good question. I suppose I could volunteer at the hospice, and I thought about setting up shop as a scribe."

"A good idea, Master. Jerusalem always needs knowledgeable scribes like you."

A MIRACLE

"Where are we going," Adele asked, rushing to keep up.

"To the Jewish quarter," said Ramiro. "To the paper merchant. They say he has the finest paper—made in Baghdad." He walked in long strides. "I will need good paper and inks if I'm to set up business."

Adele caught up to him. "We have little money left," she reminded him. "So just get what you need to start."

"I know, I know," he said with irritation. "But there are certain things I must have if we are to make any money at all."

"I suppose," she said, not wanting to press the matter.

The Dome of the Rock grew large as they made their way to the Western Wall. Ramiro pointed. "The place should be down this street. Come on, it's getting late."

"Don't you think it odd, Ramiro, that the streets are so quiet today?"

He looked around at the empty storefronts. "You're right, everything's closed. There's hardly a soul out."

"Except one," she said, pointing to an old beggar huddled in a corner of a gray building.

Ramiro walked over to him. "Peace be upon you, Sayyid."

The grizzled beggar returned a toothless smile and waved the stub of a malformed arm. "And to you," he said in a raspy voice. "Have you got a coin for an old man?"

Ramiro dug into his purse, handing him a few fals. "Tell me, why are the shops closed today?"

The man took the coins before looking askance, his small eyes clouded with cataracts. "You don't know what day it is?"

"Excuse me," Ramiro said as patiently as he could, "but I am new here."

"It's Yom Kippur," said the beggar. "All the men have gone to the synagogue."

Ramiro nodded in understanding. He thanked the man before turning away.

"What's Yom Kippur?" Adele asked as they walked away.

"It's a day of atonement for the Hebrews. It's a day when they seek forgiveness for wrongs against God and man." He began to walk away. "I should have known better but I've been too busy with other things."

"Ramiro wait! Let's walk around a little before we go home."

"Now? It's almost dark."

"But look at the coming moon. It's full and will soon be bright. And I want to see the Western Wall while we're here. It won't take long." She pulled at his sleeve.

The Western Wall, also known as the Wailing Wall, was the only section of the Second Temple not destroyed by the Romans many centuries before. The plaza in front of the wall was eerily vacant. Adele looked up and down, studying the stark section of somber-gray wall built of enormous blocks of limestone and rising up the height of ten men. In the background, the roof of the Dome of the Rock glowed softly in the last rays of the setting sun.

Sounds of men yelling in the distance broke the silence. Adele turned her head in the direction of the noise. "What's that all about?"

Ramiro turned in the same direction. "Sounds like it's coming from the synagogue."

"Let's have a look," she said, walking away.

"Careful, Adele," he warned, "women are not allowed anywhere on the synagogue precinct, especially gentile women." But she made no reply and continued on her way. Ramiro hurried to her side.

No sooner had the synagogue come into view when a great hubbub erupted on its steps. Bearded men crowded around one spot, many dressed in fine, white coats. Ramiro hurried forward while Adele held back.

"He's dead!" a man wailed. "He's dead!" Groans and cries of grief rose from the crowd.

Ramiro stood at the base of the low steps, peering through a group of huddled men. He glimpsed an old man with white hair and beard lying flat on his back. He was dressed in the robe of a rabbi. The group of men soon dispersed, leaving the body in full view. "What happened?" he asked one of them.

The man scowled at him. "The rabbi collapsed coming out of the synagogue. But it's no business for a gentile," he said with an air of intimidation.

"Is he dead?"

"Of course he's dead. Would we say he's dead if he were not?"

"Excuse me, Sayyid, I meant no offense, but I'm a physician. Perhaps I can help."

"You are a gentile and unclean," the man said with contempt. "We cannot permit it. We have our own physicians."

Ramiro inched closer to the dead rabbi, staring into his hard, chiseled face, a face of strength and sorrow. Bushy, gray eyebrows grew wild across a pronounced brow and a full gray beard reached down to his stomach. Ramiro was about to turn away when he noticed the flicker of an eyelid. Or was it the torchlight?

"Move away!" one of the men shouted at him.

But Ramiro did not hear. He studied the rabbi's face intently. There it was again. The flicker of an eyelid.

"He's alive!" Ramiro shouted. "He needs to breathe!"

"Move away you idiot!" the man shouted again.

But Ramiro paid no heed to the man's words. Instead, he jumped forward, spreading his knees across the rabbi's torso. He put his arms under his midriff and lifted. He could hear a slight draft of breath pass through the rabbi's mouth. Ramiro let him down before lifting again, and again.

The Jewish men did nothing at first, completely dumbfounded by Ramiro's effrontery and sacrilege. But soon, in an indignant rage, they took hold of him, forcibly dragging him off the rabbi. They beat him with their fists before throwing him down the steps. He tumbled onto the road.

Just then, the old rabbi took a long gasping breath.

"He lives!" one shouted. "He lives!"

"What are you doing?" Adele asked as she watched Ramiro tie a long rope around a small pillar in the bedroom.

"I'm making an escape route. If necessary, I'll throw the rope out the window and lower myself down to the street."

She frowned. "Is it safe?"

"I think so. We're only on the second story."

She moved to the window and looked down. "And is it really necessary?"

He waved his hands in frustration. "Of course it is! I can't get out the door without being crushed by a crowd. They all want to touch me. They rend my garments. They impede my path. They bring their sick to me for healing. What nonsense! Brother Gerard says hundreds more await me at the hospice, people of all faiths."

"You have become very popular," she tried to restrain a smile but could not. "They believe you can raise the dead." She laughed.

"Humph! But Rabbi Moshe wasn't dead—although he was close to it."

"What do you think was wrong with him?"

"He's old. He probably just fainted from lack of food and drink. Yom Kippur is a fasting period."

Adele tossed her hair over one shoulder. "Well, the word has spread to the Christians and the Muslims. You've become a holy man of Jerusalem."

Ramiro groaned. "I don't want all this attention. I would simply like to retrieve my cross. Then we can go back to France."

A broad smile stretched across Adele's face. She beamed. "Really? Do you mean it? Back to France!"

Ramiro nodded with a grin.

"Then we really must find that cross," she said with renewed enthusiasm. She pointed across the table to a small stack of letters. "But what of all these invitations! What are we to do?"

Rabbi Moshe had not fully recovered and was still confined to a chair, but he welcomed Ramiro with open arms, making him the guest of honor. The other men who milled about him were much more kindly than they had been a few weeks before on the synagogue steps. They talked at length of the weather, the crops, and the markets before finally asking Ramiro more pointed questions.

"So what of these Greek mercenaries?" asked the Rabbi in a hoarse voice. "They seem to be trouble for everyone. You know these people do you not?"

"I know *of* them, Rabbi, but I am not one of them. They are intent on capturing Jerusalem, although it has been over two years since they first arrived."

"We are very worried about these armies. We have heard of the massacres of Hebrews in the Western countries, and now at Antioch—the massacre of a whole city."

"It is a terrible, terrible thing Rabbi," said Ramiro with true sympathy. "If they do approach Jerusalem, I suggest that all of you take shelter elsewhere."

"Do you think that possible?" One of the men asked. "I hear they suffer from the plague and starvation. And their numbers shrink by the year."

"I really don't know," Ramiro conceded. "It's in the hands of God."

Adele threw herself on a row of cushions. "I'm already worn out with all these festivities. But what a nice group of people! Look at all these gifts! I don't even know what some of them are."

Ramiro smiled. "I thought you would enjoy it."

"What are we doing tomorrow night?" she asked, becoming somewhat exasperated by the attention.

Ramiro watched her as she lay on the cushions. How he loved this woman. It was a love he could never explain, even to himself. Sometimes, she was as obstinate as an old mule and impossible to reason... and what a temper! But at other times, she was a complete angel and he could literally feel her love radiate over him like warm sunlight. But either way, he adored her. Every move she made was a dance to his eyes.

He smiled again. "All this socializing has been good for you, Adele. And your Arabic is improving nicely." He picked up another letter from his desk. "Well, it seems Bishop Aliphas has invited us to a celebration of the birth of Mary. The actual name of the event is 'The Nativity of Our Most Holy Lady, Mother of God and Ever Virgin Mary'—quite a mouthful."

"I've never heard of it," she said.

"That's because you're from the West. The ideas embodied in this celebration do not agree with Catholic thinking."

"Why not?"

"Well, on one point, they do not agree that Mary transmitted original sin but rather that she was free of sin by the Grace of God."

Adele was quiet for a moment. "I like that idea. Maybe that's why the Greeks treat their women better. What do you think?"

"I'm not sure anymore. The older I get, the less sure I am about anything..." He stood up to stretch. "Nonetheless, it is presumed to be a happy occasion and we should take part."

Adele sat up suddenly. "Ramiro," she said with some frustration, "...we simply must find that cross."

Ramiro slumped into his chair. "I agree. But we need to make some money. I get paid nothing at the hospice, despite my labors. Fortunately, Jameel was kind enough to find us a shop to rent near that jeweler, Madteos, so we can keep an eye on him. And Rabbi Moshe promised to help with any supplies we may need."

ANTIOCH

November 1098

Drugo the Red was richer. Count Robert's men were among the first to storm the walls of Antioch and the first to kill and plunder. The mansion Drugo now occupied belonged to a prominent Muslim family, one he had personally slaughtered. The building was once beautifully adorned inside and out. But now it was ravaged. Magnificent sprawling gardens lay in ruins, destroyed by frenzied searches for buried treasure. Inside, smashed furniture and everyday garbage littered the hallways, anything of value stripped away.

Drugo occupied a single room in which he stashed his entire hoard. He sat on one of the few remaining chairs, hunching over a burning brazier in an effort to warm his cold hands. "Find some more wood or some charcoal," he said to Otto. "This will go out soon."

Otto of Bremen and Arles of Ghent, along with one hundred and fifty-six others, were all that was left of Drugo's original company of five hundred. Over one hundred were dead by the time they defeated the Patzinaks with King Alexios at Roussa. And, after joining Robert of Flanders in the Holy Crusade, Fulk succumbed to the heat of the Salt Desert, as did a score of others. More died at the Battle of Dorylaeum and some died of starvation during the long siege of Antioch. Now, after the final conquest, typhus ravaged the remainder.

"There's not much left, Sir Drugo. And there's no one to collect more." Otto looked frail and ill. The onset of typhus had drained him. But he lived.

"Blood of Christ!" Drugo shouted. "Is there nothing to eat? There must be something left. Check the cellars."

"I've looked, Sir. There's nothing left. There's no food in the city. There's nothing for miles around."

Antioch was almost deserted. Its citizens were either dead or enslaved and the vibrant, bustling life of the city, along with its commerce and wealth, died with them.

"God help us!" Drugo shouted again. "I thought the Greeks were going to send supplies."

"Apparently, the Greek King is angry because we haven't handed the city to him as promised."

"Nor should we! God damn him! We are the ones who died in its taking!" He rubbed his hands over the glowing embers. "Thank the good Lord that Count Robert rides to Maarat tomorrow. He plans to lay siege and we'll have a chance to gain more booty and get some food."

Maarat

Once again, the Crusaders gathered en masse outside the walls of Maarat An-Numan, this time led by Bohemond and Raymond. Their previous humiliating defeat some months before, when Ramiro and Adele had lived there, was still fresh in their minds and they were determined to set things right. Now emboldened by their success at Antioch, they set out to seize more of Syria—and to get revenge.

The Turks and Arabs of Maarat greeted them with loud curses, screaming obscenities and taunts from the battlements. For a while, the Christians ignored them, setting up their tents just out of arrow range. But before long, the Turks hung makeshift crosses from the top of the walls—and these they began to abuse by smashing some with hammers and setting fire to others. Then, in a bit of animated theater, one of them climbed up on a castellation and began to piss, directing his stream over one of the crosses.

The Christians went wild, screaming their own curses, the most vile they could conjure. The shrill voice of the mystic, Peter Bartholomew, rose above them all. "You will burn in hellfire! Filthy pagans!" he screamed while jabbing his Holy Lance in the air. "I will kill you with my bare hands!"

Inside Maarat, the people worked furiously to resist the siege. Salim the physician and other hospital staff set up emergency beds, preparing to tend the wounded. Even Dawud the Silk Merchant helped to carry bundles of arrows from the armory to the battlements or to collect stones and bricks, anything they could throw down on the attackers.

The Qadi watched from the citadel, barking orders to his lieutenants, who rushed back and forth coordinating efforts. This foreign army was much larger than the last one, too large for him to attack head-on as he had done before. In desperation, he sent a fast messenger to Aleppo, pleading for assistance, but the Emir there had lost courage since his last defeat outside the walls of Antioch. They were alone.

The Crusaders labored at a mad pace, cutting trees from the nearby woods to make longer, sturdier ladders as well as a formidable siege tower. Sappers rushed out to undermine the walls by chipping away the mortar of lower stones. The men of Maarat fought back furiously, hurling everything they had at them; stones, arrows, fire, lime, even beehives.

It took ten days to finish the tower. It was higher than the walls of the city, had four levels connected with ladders, and required fifty men to move it along on four wheels of solid wood. Waiting inside the tower were a hundred fighting men.

Drugo, Arles, and fifteen other men held the top story as it bumped and swayed along the rough ground. An arsenal of stones and spears lay beside them. As they advanced, one of the men blew a horn in loud, sharp blasts. Peter Bartholomew and the priests trailed behind, beseeching God in loud voices to defend his chosen people.

The Turks threw all they had at the advancing tower, but it soon loomed over the wall. Drugo took the advantage of height, grabbing stones with the others and hurling them down on the defenders, breaking their ranks. As they approached the wall, they threw out large grappling hooks to secure the battlements, dragging the tower tight to the wall. The tower door opened, slamming down on the parapets.

Drugo was among the first to jump out. Arles was right behind him. Arrows peppered their ranks and men collapsed around them. They rushed at the Turks with their lances and the enemy fell back. But the Turks and every other Muslim in Maarat, driven by the fear of certain death, rushed at them again with desperate ferocity. Drugo and his men fell back in a frenzy of sword fight, some of them jumping from the walls in terror. But just as the Muslims began to gain the upper hand, the sappers below scored a success. A section of wall collapsed.

At the same time, the French overran an opposing wall amid heavy fighting and hand-to-hand combat. When the Muslims saw the Christians coming from two directions, and now pouring through the breach in the wall, they fell back in terror, retreating to the safety of fortified buildings. The Christians stormed over the walls, hooting and yelling—and the slaughter began.

Next morning, Bohemond and all his men left the smoking ruins and rotting corpses of Maarat. He feared King Alexios would take advantage of his departure from Antioch by sending out a fleet of warships from Cyprus. Robert followed him, as did Godfrey, both abandoning the obsessive Raymond, who they began to despise.

With bitter resignation, Raymond realized he would never wrest Antioch from Bohemond. So he turned his attention once again to Jerusalem, gathering his men to march south alone. He was determined to be the glorious leader who would command the Holy Crusade to liberate Jerusalem from the shackles of unholy pagans.

But Raymond was worried. He was about to march into the unknown territory of an unknown enemy. And since his quarrelsome allies had abandoned him, his forces were perilously few. At most, he commanded four thousand able men.

But his concerns were without warrant. When the Muslims heard that the invincible, barbarian cannibals were marching down on them, they abandoned whole countrysides in abject terror. The Emir of Shayzar, worried about his head, sent an embassy, offering to send provisions and to sell them horses from the Shayzar market. Meanwhile, the Emir of Homs, also in a rush to save himself from the Christian scourge, sent Raymond horses and gold.

Raymond accepted these gifts gladly, taking advantage of the fear, and moved on to the coast where he besieged the fortress of Arqah in an effort to squeeze tribute from the Emir of Tripoli. He succeeded, and the Emir sent him fifteen thousand gold coins, horses, mules, and silk garments.

It did not take long for the news of Raymond's financial success to reach Antioch, where Bohemond and Godfrey heard about the amazing riches falling into his hands. And it did not take long for their greed and envy to overcome any animosity they harbored toward him. They set out to join his forces, now scattered across the Tripoli countryside.

But as Bohemond approached Latakia, he heard that King Alexios had recaptured much of the Aegean coast and was now threatening Cilicia with a fleet of war galleys. In fear of losing his precious stronghold, he soon abandoned Raymond and the Holy Crusade, turning his knights back to Antioch.

8 - JERUSALEM

January 1099

Ramiro curled over his small desk, huddling in a shop he rented from the Monastery of Saint James. A heavy cloak covered his shoulders, draping down to wool leggings and fur-lined boots, keeping him warm in the cool, damp winter of Jerusalem. He had picked this location because it sat across the street from Madteos the Jeweler, which allowed him to keep an eye on the sly Armenian while offering his services to the public as a scribe and translator.

Adele also bundled herself in thick robes. She sat at the back of the shop, keeping busy with leatherwork, making quivers and bags, as well as sheaths for sword and dagger, all of which she fronted to other vendors.

For Christians, this was the last day of the Nativity Holidays and, for Muslims, the week before the Prophet's birthday. Customers lined up for long waits in front of the shop. But many had little use for Ramiro's services, they simply wanted to meet the miracle healer who had saved the life of Rabbi Moshe.

Ramiro's desk straddled the front, where cushions and a chair were set out for his clients. A frail, old man squatted on one of the cushions across from him. Ramiro listened carefully to all the man said, writing it down verbatim in Arabic. When the man finished talking, Ramiro dated the letter according to the Hijra calendar. It was the tenth day of Safar in the year 492. He took a burning candle, dropping a blob of wax at the end of the document before urging the man to step forward.

The old man stood up uneasily. He approached the desk to press his signet ring into the warm wax. When all was finished, he took hold of Ramiro's hands in a firm grip, holding fast for some time, as if the touch alone would bring him good fortune and good health.

Ramiro did not resist. "Peace be upon you," he said gently. Tears welled in the man's gray eyes. He paid Ramiro for his services, all the while muttering Allah's blessings.

With a heavy sigh, Ramiro looked to the doorway for the next customer. He longed to lay down for a nap, so when he heard the muezzin's call to prayers resound from the minarets, he felt some relief.

Another customer was about to enter the store when, through loud cries of alarm, a thickset soldier barged through the line, forcing the customer back with a strong arm before pushing him outside. The bulk of the soldier filled the doorway. Ramiro recognized his dress—the helmet and armor of an Egyptian askari. He was Sudanese, a warrior of rank with weathered, black skin and thick lips. A thin mustache and beard covered his heavy jaw, too thin to hide the pale battle scars trailing across his cheeks like narrow lines of war paint.

Ramiro was tempted to blurt out something about his bad manners but, with considerable effort, he stifled his words with a hard clench of his jaw. He stood to greet the intruder. "Peace be with you. Please sit down. Would you like some water… juice?"

The man did not return the greeting. He looked down, hesitating a little before sitting awkwardly in the rough, wooden chair. His chain link armor rustled and his sword clacked. He waved a thick hand in a curt manner. "I want nothing," he said in a deep, resonating voice.

Ramiro squirmed behind his desk, on which rested neat piles of papers and a stack of envelopes held down with stone weights. Near at hand, were inks of assorted colors and pens of varied shapes. He placed a piece of paper in front of him before glancing up at the askari. "So, what can I do for you, Sayyid?"

"You are Christian?" asked the soldier, his wide nostrils flaring as he spoke.

Ramiro thought that was obvious, his iron cross hung about his neck in clear view. "Yes," he answered with some apprehension. "So what can I do for you, Sayyid?"

The askari glared with narrowed eyes. "I hear you look for a Christian talisman… a golden cross," he spat the words.

Ramiro's trepidation vanished in hopeful elation. "Yes, Sayyid," he gleamed. "Do you know of its whereabouts?"

The big man snorted in derision. "I know nothing of your diabolical cross—nor do I care." He leaned forward with a fierce look. "There is something else that is of more interest to me."

Ramiro said nothing, his worries returned.

The askari smirked as if reading his fear. "I hear you speak the language of the barbarians from the West. The language of these heathen kuffar. Perhaps you are one of them?"

"I… I know the language, Sayyid. But I am not one of them," he said, glossing the truth.

The askari reached into his cloak, pulling out a sheet of yellowed paper. He stood up, tossing it on the desk. "Tell me what this says!"

Obnoxious man! Ramiro thought as he picked it up. The first thing he noticed about the letter were the blood stains smeared across it. Carefully, he unfolded the page. He looked briefly at the askari, forcing a wan smile before putting his head down to read. He expected to see Greek or Latin but this was different, the characters were Roman but the words were not. Then it became clear.

Why! It's the script of Provencal. The language of Burgundy! He was momentarily stunned. He again glanced up at the askari, who now towered over him, moving his hand from his belt to his sword.

"What does it say?" the man asked even louder.

Ramiro studied the words again.

"What does it say, kafir! We know you understand this tongue. We know you are one of them! We have heard it from others. Translate it!"

Adele heard the roar and stopped what she was doing.

Ramiro felt a flash of dread. What does he mean by 'we'? He stared at the guard in indignation. "Of course I know this script! And yes, I do come from the same land. But that was many years ago. I know nothing of these new armies and I have no communication with them."

The askari studied him warily before speaking with irritation. "If you can read this letter... then tell me what it says."

Ramiro cleared his throat and began to translate.

> Sir Guicher to Eleanor, his dearest and most amiable wife, to his beloved children and to all his vassals of all ranks, his greetings and blessings.
>
> By God's grace, our time of suffering in Antioch is at an end. The sickness has lifted and we have come to a quick recovery. Soon we will march...

"Enough!" the askari yelled with some urgency. "Give it to me!" He held out his hand.

"It's just a letter to his wife," Ramiro said as he handed it back.

The askari barged around the desk, taking Ramiro's arm. "You will come with me!"

"What do you mean? ... Now?" he sputtered. "What about my customers? Where do you take me? On whose authority?"

"On the orders of Governor Iftikhar. Come peaceably or die."

Adele put her work down, rushing to Ramiro's side.

He patted her hand. "Close the shop. Can you carry all this home?"

"Of course, don't worry about that. I'll ask Jameel to help. But how will I know where you are?"

He shook his head as the big Sudanese dragged him away. "I don't know. In the Emir's castle I should think... or his dungeon!"

IFTIKHAR'S CONTEMPT

A band of sunlight cut across the smooth skin of Iftikhar's face as he peered through an arrow-slit in the wall of Castle Al-Jalud. His thin beard and his small nose gave him a boyish look, a characteristic that belied his ruthless ambition. He fingered a string of prayer beads made of pearl and did not speak for some time. When he finally turned from the portal to face Ramiro, he sounded annoyed. "I hear you have become a popular man in Jerusalem, that you raise rabbis from the dead."

"It was nothing, my Lord. I merely noticed he was still alive and attempted to give him breath."

Iftikhar studied him intently. "So you make no profession to be a divine healer?"

"I do not, my Emir."

"That is good," he said with narrowed eyes. "I do not like so-called holy men leading the people astray and disturbing the peace. Only Allah, by His will, can perform miracles. Do I make myself clear?"

"Quite clear, Sahib."

Iftikhar continued to focus on him as he nodded lightly. "Very well. Now on to other business. My askari tells me you know the tongue of these Christian barbarians who invade our land. Is that so?"

Ramiro glanced at the huge Sudanese askari straddling the doorway. "Yes, my Lord. But I have no association with these men."

Iftikhar handed him the French letter. "Read it to me."

Ramiro read the letter aloud.

"And can I take you at your word that your interpretation is correct?" Iftikhar asked, his voice echoing from the bare stone walls.

"I swear it, my Lord, just as I read it to you. It's a letter to his wife and all he states is that they are on their way from Antioch to destinations south. I believe he refers to Tripoli."

Iftikhar waved a hand in frustration. He looked down to his desk stacked with letters and reports. A lock of black hair dangled from his blue turban. "This is old news now," he sighed. "It tells me nothing." He motioned to a cushion. "Please sit. You must tell me all you know of these mercenaries, these Franj who fight for the Romans."

Ramiro shrugged his shoulders before he took his seat. "I hear what others hear, my Lord. About the battles at Nikea and Antioch... and recently Edessa."

"And now Maarat," said Iftikhar ruefully.

"Maarat An-Numan?"

"Yes, yes," he said quietly, his gaze vacant.

"What happened, my Lord?"

Iftikhar swallowed hard, turning his face away. When he turned back to Ramiro, he had a grim look. "I have no love for Turks. The more these barbarians kill, the better. But I cannot condone the wanton murder of Arabs and good Muslims—it was a massacre!" He raised his voice. "Stinking beasts! They are worse than animals!"

"But I was there last summer, my Lord. The Franj were turned back."

"Not this time," he said, sticking out his chin. "They came back with a larger force and took the walls." Once again, he fell quiet for a time.

Ramiro said nothing.

"Have you not heard?" Iftikhar raised his brow. "They slaughtered the whole city... over ten thousand people!" He drew a deep breath. "Muslim, Christian, Hebrew, it doesn't seem to matter to them. Roman, Arab or Turk—they kill them all!" He glared at Ramiro with ferocious eyes, as if he shared the guilt. "And then, by the will of Allah, the devil sons of shit starve because they have destroyed everything—they have nothing to eat."

Ramiro fell into shock, thinking of Salim and Dawud and all the good people he had come to know in Maarat, all the people he had toiled with at the hospital. He shook his head in disbelief, a hollow ache filled his chest.

Iftikhar started to say something else but choked on his words. He turned away quickly, feigning to look through the arrow-slit. A cool gust of wind tossed his hair back. When he turned back to Ramiro, his hands trembled and his voice was filled with revulsion. "Our spies watched these barbarians eat human flesh! They saw them dig up the bodies of the slain martyrs of Islam to strip their flesh with carving knives." His face screwed with disgust. "They eat Muslims as if they were cattle! Godless cannibals! May Allah curse them and their bastard sons!" He bit his lip as tears welled in his eyes.

Ramiro reddened, lowering his head. He did not doubt Iftikhar's words and felt a wave of hot shame for his countrymen, recalling similar atrocities at Civetot and Antioch. He lifted his head to look into Iftikhar's glare of hatred. "May Allah's peace be upon them," he said sincerely. "I lived in Maarat, my Lord, for almost a year. The people were my friends. I am as deeply grieved as you are."

"Can I believe you, Scribe? Can I trust you?" he asked, tipping his head. "How do I know you are not a spy?"

"I assure you, Sahib, I am a man of God." He put his right hand to his heart. "In no way do I condone any murder, Muslim or Christian or Hebrew. It is true,

I come from the West as do the Franj, but I have lived and worked among the people of Syria for the last nine years."

Iftikhar inched his prayer beads through his fingers. "You will tell me all you know." His oval eyes sharpened. "And you will tell me what you have been doing here for nine years."

Iftikhar smirked after Ramiro finished his story. "And so this is why you ask around about a golden cross. That is quite a tale, Ramirah of Cluny." He leaned back on a cushion, scowling a little. "But I find it sad and worrisome that you have no children. A man without sons is truly cursed."

Ramiro felt a pang of anguish at the Emir's words. He bowed his head a little. "Yes, Sahib, in a way. But I must put all my trust in the good works of God and go where He guides me."

"Of course," said Iftikhar with some condescension.

Ramiro leaned forward on the cushion, trying to ease the pain in his back. "May I be so bold, my Lord, to ask your assistance in retrieving my cross?"

Iftikhar waved a hand of disregard. "I do not engage myself in the disputes of Christians. However, if you can find one Muslim to verify your story, I will reconsider my stance."

Ramiro nodded. "Thank you, Sahib, thank you." Mufti Ibrahim came to mind— but that won't do, he thought, he's Sunni.

"So you say you have been deep inside Turk lands. This is also of interest to me. Tell me all you know about the Turks."

"Now, my Lord?" The evening call to prayer sounded from the minarets, as if to emphasize the time.

"Yes, now." He smiled faintly. "Would you like some tea?"

Adele sat by the window of their room near the Jaffa Gate. She glanced down on the empty streets below, a single tear rolling down her cheek. Ramiro had been gone all night. She raised her head, looking across the rooftops of Jerusalem into the night sky. The golden Dome on the Temple Mount seemed to glow in the soft light of a half-moon. She fingered her prayer beads silently.

> *Hail Mary,*
> *Full of Grace,*
> *The Lord is with thee.*
> *Blessed art thou among women...*

But no amount of prayer relieved her anxiety. Was he alright? What should I do? I can't run the shop by myself. I can't wander the streets without a man at my side. She put her head in her hands. Who can help? She thought of Bishop Aliphas and Jameel.

She slept in fits, waking at every sound, jumping to the window or the door. Is it him? No. Again she returned to her empty bed.

The sun was only a hand off the horizon when a heavy knock came to the door. She jolted from bed, her heart pounding. "Who is it?" she yelled.

"It's me!" Ramiro shouted.

BROTHER PAKRAD

Madteos the Jeweler lifted his eyes from the golden cross he was cleaning. "They murdered the Christians?"

"Even Armenians and Syrians, elder brother" said Pakrad. "No one was spared."

With a blank look, Madteos put down his work before wiping his hands on a rag. His brother was a priest, and priests always seemed to get the news first.

Pakrad wore a brown robe that draped loosely down to his sandals. He was short like Madteos and had the same curly brown hair but, younger by ten years, his was not yet grayed. The man was educated and collected, but Madteos always had trouble taking him seriously—he had the appearance of a bumbling fool. Big ears jutted out from his long head, his nose was short, almost upturned, and his over-sized eyes seemed to bulge from his head like those of a monkey.

Madteos glanced down at his work. "Unbelievable! Why would they kill the people? What good is a deserted city that pays no taxes?" He lifted his head. "So what do you think we should we do?"

"Nothing for now," said Pakrad. "But we may have to flee Jerusalem. I can always move quickly. Not like you, brother, with all your gold."

Madteos scoffed. "And don't forget whose gold provides for your family."

Pakrad blushed, changing the subject. "What will you do if the invaders reach Jerusalem?"

Madteos stared straight ahead. "I haven't given it much thought, brother. But now... now it is worrisome."

"You should be worried. They'll come for your gold."

Madteos picked up the golden cross and started to polish it again. "When the Emir is worried, I will go. Until then, I carry on business as usual."

Pakrad studied the cross in Madteos' hand. "That's beautiful," he said, walking behind him for a better view. "It looks familiar. I think I've seen it before."

Madteos pretended he was finished and quickly wrapped the cross in an oiled cloth.

"Yes, I remember!" said Pakrad. "That looks like the cross that Christian foreigner wants. You know—that man with an Andalusian accent who saved the Rabbi."

"How do you know what it looks like?" Madteos asked as he tied the wrapping.

"I saw his drawing. One of the attendants at the monastery passed it around."

Madteos got up from his stool with a start. "You will keep your mouth shut! He has no right to it. I paid for it. It's mine!"

Pakrad stepped back in astonishment. He seldom saw his brother flare into a rage. "Of course, elder brother. As you wish."

"There he is again," said Ramiro, looking out from his storefront. "The Armenian priest. That's the third time I've seen him in Madteos' shop."

"Perhaps he comes to perform some prayer service for Madteos," said Adele.

"That seems unlikely. But it's possible he sold my cross to the priest." He stepped outside and watched him walk away. He looked up at the sky before rushing back inside. "It's almost noon. Close the shop. I'm going to follow him."

He trailed Pakrad through the crowded streets. The priest headed south toward the Zion Gate, but he did not go far. In an instant, he turned and disappeared. Ramiro ran up to the spot. Praise God, he thought, looking up at the iron doors and the large cross above the door. The Monastery... it's the Monastery of Saint James. What fortune! I'll ask Jameel who he is.

The Emir's Palace

February

Iftikhar was dining alone in the Emir's Palace when the messenger arrived. He lifted his head from his meal. "You say they got past Homs and Shayzar?"

"Yes, my Lord," said the Sudanese askari standing at a distance. "The barbarian army now besieges Arqah outside Tripoli."

"Let them come," Iftikhar said, trying to conceal his worry. "Our Vizier, may Allah protect him, advised us to wait until they reach Palestine and head inland. Then they will be isolated, without food or water. That will be our chance to surround them and destroy them, by the will of Allah."

"Praise Allah," replied the askari.

"But I am still concerned, Lieutenant. Another plague racks Egypt. Thousands more have perished, including many good soldiers. If it continues unabated, we will be severely weakened."

"We all pray to Allah for forgiveness, Sahib. We pray He will remove this curse from our cities."

Iftikhar said nothing.

"And what of the Christians, Sahib? Do you wish to leave them be?"

"No. I want all their prominent men detained. The Hebrews too. But we must wait until they finish their Easter celebrations." He put down his meat, wiping his hands on a napkin. "There will be too many pilgrims in the city and any hostile actions now could create more trouble."

"We should ban all Christian celebrations, my Lord."

"We will wait. We will wait for the month of Jumada Al-Awwal, then we will impose our restrictions and deportations."

"Yes, Emir. And what do you want to do with that Christian priest from the West, my Lord? You cannot trust him."

"I know Lieutenant," Iftikhar said quietly. "And I have no need of Christian heroes at a time like this. I want him watched at all times. I want to know everything he does, everyone he meets, every letter he writes."

"Yes, my Lord, as you command. And what of the golden cross he desires? If he finds it, he may gain power over the Christian people."

"I thought the same. We will leave things as they are but, if by some chance he does get it back, you must tell me right away. In the meantime, I may think of some use for the man."

TRIPOLI

The Crusaders in Tripoli flocked to a tall mansion once occupied by a wealthy Muslim baron. Built of stone, it stood three stories high, had battened windows and arched doorways, all wrapped in a cobalt-blue facade. All around, apple and pear trees blossomed in thick sprays of white and pink. And farther out, rows of verdant vineyards and fields of emerald-green sugarcane sprawled for miles. Count Raymond now laid claim to this lush estate, making it his headquarters.

Within its cool brick interior, a council of men, all dressed for war, milled about in an expansive reception room, still intact with Chinese vases, pearl-embedded oak furniture, and the finest of Persian carpets. The air reverberated with loud and raucous boasts of daring feats, laments at the loss of friends, and vivid descriptions of the strange things they had seen.

Days before, Godfrey and many others left Antioch to join Raymond in Tripoli, hoping to share in the unbelievable riches he had amassed in Syria. And now, these bellicose commanders gathered around a wide table, each accompanied by their lieutenants and clergymen, who stood some paces away watching the proceedings. Drugo the Red stood among them.

Count Raymond adjusted his eye-patch before slamming his gavel down while shouting through his thick, gray beard. "Order! Come to order!" The room fell silent and he stood to speak. "As most of you know," he bellowed to be heard, "we recently received another emissary from King Alexios of the Greeks. I have his letter here." He waved it over his head for all to see while he scanned the crowd with his one eye. "He repeats his offer to join us in June with a sizable army. I say we should accept. With his help, nothing will stand in our way."

Duke Godfrey stood up suddenly, standing a head taller than most. His long, blonde hair swayed across his broad shoulders. "With his help?" he asked incredulously, his voice thundering in the hall. "Where in hell was he when we needed him?" Murmurs of agreement followed his words. "What about his whimpering men who abandoned us in our time of trial before the walls of Antioch? Abandoned us like mangy dogs running back to their master!"

Raymond scowled, slamming down his gavel again. "Let me tell you what happened, Duke Godfrey!" He spat his words. "Bohemond was the one who sent the Greeks packing because he wanted Antioch for himself!" His words trailed off as he fell to coughing.

"Better that," said Godfrey, "than letting it fall into the hands of the bloody Greeks. We're the ones who died for it!"

"By God's mercy!" said Raymond. "The king is a Christian!"

"He's a heretic! He's a damned Greek! He's not one of us. Half his men are heathen Muslims. How can we trust him?" He raised his voice to appeal to the council. "After all our sacrifices in the name of God, are we going to allow this conniving King of the Greeks to lay claim to our conquests?" Many men shook their heads and several 'nays' could be heard.

"If we need help," he went on, "we should look to our brethren in Genoa or Venice. They have no need of conquest as long as they profit from trade. Even now, they moor their ships at Latakia. I say we send them a purse of the Emir's gold. Tell them what supplies we need. Tell them we march for Jerusalem and ask for their help."

"And where will they put to port?" Raymond asked. "The Egyptians hold the southern coast and Jaffa. But the King's ships can help us to secure these ports."

"Will we rule the Holy Land?" Godfrey appealed to the men. "Or will we just hand it over to these heretics?" He paused for effect before glaring at Raymond.

"And we are wasting our time with your ongoing siege of Arqah!" he shouted. "The Emir has already paid you tribute. We are wasting good men! We can't afford this. We must leave now to conquer Jerusalem!"

Raymond glared. "I will decide when we leave, Commander!" he shouted in a hoarse voice. "And if we leave Arqah undefeated, the Muslims will think us weak." He looked around the room for support. He knew his argument was frail and he tried to look sure of himself, but feared he was losing his grip. If he could not take Arqah, could he take Jerusalem? Even his own men had started to grumble.

"And if we stay to fight your fruitless battle, we will soon be weak!" retorted Godfrey. "It's already spring. We are ready. Now is the time to march!"

There was much murmuring and many nodded their heads in agreement, including Drugo and his men. But not all agreed with Godfrey. A resounding "No!" roared out from the crowd pressing around the table.

The hall fell silent and all eyes turned to the raving mystic, Peter Bartholomew, who stomped forward, his boots slapping on the marble floor. His thin face flushed red as he placed his hands on his hips. "How dare you speak to our Lord in such a fashion!" he shouted at Godfrey, his voice trembling with emotion. "My Lord carries the Holy Lance." He waved a hand in the air. "God has ordained the Count to lead us to victory over the heathen!"

"That's enough, Peter!" Raymond shouted, only to be cut short by another deep, racking cough.

But Peter continued in righteous indignation, stepping closer to Godfrey, who still stood at the table. "We are the ones who marched south!" he ranted. "We are the ones who cleared the path to Jerusalem while you idled your time in Antioch." He leaned forward. "In debauchery, no doubt!"

Godfrey drew his sword so fast that few saw it come out of its sheath. Before Peter could utter another word, the tip was at his throat.

"Why you stinking mound of horse shit!" Godfrey shouted. Spittle flew from his thin lips and long, blonde hair dangled in front of fierce blue eyes. "I'll take your ugly head right here and now—and feed it to the pigs!" He feinted with a push of his sword. Peter's eyes grew wide. "Even your precious Holy Lance won't save you from my blade!"

Raymond banged his gavel—he banged it again. "Enough!" he shouted in a strained voice, and again he fell to coughing.

"And you, old man!" Godfrey shouted, turning on Raymond again. "You're too weak to lead us any farther. You spend half your days in bed!"

Raymond could hardly speak through his gasps and no one else stepped forward to defend him. Most of the men were at a loss. They respected the imposing and muscular Godfrey, who showed no fear and fought like the devil himself. But Raymond was of noble birth and Peter was his spiritual leader. Peter was the one who discovered the Holy Lance at Antioch. But Peter was arrogant and not well liked and, as the days wore on, many began to doubt this would-be prophet's story of the lance. And many more disagreed with Count Raymond's unprofitable siege of Arqah.

In the tension of the moment, another man ventured forward, stepping courageously before the council. He was short and thin. The pallid skin of his narrow face stood in sharp contrast to his greasy, black hair and darkened eye sockets. It was Arnulf Malecorne, chaplain to the Normans, highly respected by some because of his erudition and eloquence, but highly derided by others because of his drinking and womanizing. He held his hands high to still the crowd, his long nose wrinkled in a sneer. "Please men! I beg of you," he said through wet, red lips. "We must remain civil!"

With Peter humiliated, Arnulf saw opportunity. "There is little to be gained by this bickering," he said, trying not to sound too condescending. "We must all ask God for Divine Guidance." He held his hands together in prayer. "We must all bear the Cross of Christ to Jerusalem." The men nodded, eager to have this feud settled and pleased that Arnulf had the courage to do it.

Godfrey withdrew his sword but, after a moment of hesitation, turned back to smash a fist into Peter's chest, heaving the frail man to the tiled floor. Gasps and rumbles came from the councilmen. "One more insult," Godfrey shouted down as he gripped his sword, "... and I'll gut you where you stand!"

That evening, Count Robert of Flanders met with Godfrey in a nearby house he had commandeered for himself. Robert had once allied with the older Raymond but now, since abandoning him after the siege of Maarat, had warmed to Godfrey.

"What is it?" Godfrey asked, finding it hard to take his eyes off Robert's long, hawk-like nose.

"I just heard," said Robert. "Peter Bartholomew claims to have had another vision of Christ."

Godfrey shook his head. "Not another! Who the hell does he think he is? The Pope himself?"

Robert grinned, lifting his high cheeks. "And wait 'till you hear this one. He says the Lord in person told him there were many sinners among us and that he, himself, was to be the one to root them out."

Godfrey guffawed. "What impudence!"

"But more disturbing," Robert continued without smiling, "is that he claims God has instructed him to execute all those found wanting."

Again, Godfrey shook his big head in disbelief. Then abruptly, he laughed aloud. "Ha, ha! That stupid shit! Does he think he can get rid of me so easily? I should have rammed my sword through his guts!"

"The men are outraged," said Robert. "And terrified. Even Raymond's own men."

Robert always had a look of polite satisfaction or mild humor, even when he discussed the most dire of issues. Some say his down-turned eyes and elegant eyebrows gave this effect, but no matter what, he always had the same demeanor, even when he raised his sword against the heathen.

"It's a good thing they're outraged," said Godfrey. "It's about time someone put that vile peasant in his proper place. How could anyone believe his story anyway? That he so conveniently found this so-called holy lance. Horse shit!"

Robert returned a half smile. "Now listen to this. The chaplain, Arnulf, has challenged him and his story. And I fully support him."

"Arnulf... the preacher who looks like a raccoon?" Godfrey chuckled spitefully. "The one who likes young girls and copious amounts of wine, I hear."

"Yes," said Robert with some concern, "I admit he's not the ideal candidate but he may be useful."

Godfrey laughed again. "This may turn to our advantage, Count Robert," he said with a wry smile. "If Arnulf has publicly challenged Peter's story... as well as the veracity of his so-called Holy Lance, then he will be forced to prove himself by Saxon law."

"Yes," said Robert, not really understanding Godfrey's mirth. "But if he fails, Count Raymond could be discredited along with him."

Godfrey said nothing. He sat with an elbow on a knee and rested his head on a huge fist, biting his tongue to hide his glee.

GOOD FRIDAY

It was the morning of Good Friday. Peter Bartholomew stared aghast at the tall stacks of blazing olive branches. This was his ordeal. By Saxon law, he would prove himself true. He watched the flames rise high above the crackling stacks, one on either side. They stood the height of a man, were spaced two feet apart, and ran the length of five or six paces. The intense heat already seared his face.

Thousands of men circled around him, all pressing for a better view. Only the heat of the flames and Raymond's Provencal guards held them back. No one said a word.

I'll show them all, Peter thought as he readied himself for the fiery test. God is with me. Oh please God, be with me now. Please God, show these unbelievers that I am your Word, my Lord! He strode forward, his eyes nearly closed, then suddenly, with brazen courage, he rushed headlong into the flames. "God help us!" he screamed as the fire swallowed him.

The inferno roared, dry branches cracked and popped. Wide sheets of red flame and gray smoke shot skyward, driving hot waves of sparkling embers into a clear blue sky. Moments passed. Everyone watched, no one breathed.

"Where is he?" someone yelled. More silence.

"There he is!" shouted another. "There he is!"

Peter leapt out of the flames on the other side, his hair almost burned off his scalp, his skin cooked red, his tunic in charred remnants, still smoldering. "God help us!" he screamed, faltering as he went.

A delirious roar deafened the air. Hundreds of hysterical men rushed forward to touch him, all crying "God help us! God help us!" They tore at his burned tunic for a piece of it. They grabbed his singed hairs. They pressed in harder and harder, and Peter collapsed in the mad melee.

Peter died two weeks after his ordeal. Some say he died of his burns, others blame the mob that broke his bones and tore his charred skin in the ensuing crush. Whatever the cause, those who once idolized Peter soon came to believe that his death was a sign he had lost favor with God, and the once venerated Holy Lance soon became an object of ridicule.

Raymond was humiliated. For a year, he had used the lance as a relic of sacred power. But now it was defamed and his power to command waned in mockery.

Godfrey was overjoyed.

SMYRNA

Emperor Alexios leaned back in his chair, allowing the servant to fit his knee-high red boots. Outside, he could hear the rolling waves of the Aegean crash against the rocky promontory below the tall citadel of Smyrna. Since he had taken control of Nikea, and now Smyrna after the death of the pirate Chaka, he was pleased with his on-going campaign to wrest control of the west coast of Anatolia. But he knew he could never be entirely successful in this regard without possession of Antioch and, as time went by, he began to realize he may never have the opportunity. The Kelts had betrayed him, as he feared they would.

When he made an offer to join them in Tripoli, it was not so much to march to Jerusalem as it was a ploy for Antioch. He realized that any venture for the Holy City would spread his forces far too thin and he would have to contend with the might of the Egyptian empire, which he could ill afford to do. Instead, he hoped to establish himself at Tripoli in order to create a base. Perhaps then he would have a better chance to squeeze Antioch from the south and the north.

But the Kelts in Tripoli again refused his offer of help and made veiled threats should he try. At this point, Alexios realized he had lost all control over their movements and began to believe they had outlived their usefulness. Indeed, they were now a threat to his plans. They had taken Antioch and Maarat and now the territory around Tripoli, coming to believe God ordained their victories. Apparently, they no longer needed the help of the Byzantines, nor that of the Egyptians.

He motioned to a waiting scribe. "Send a letter to the Egyptian vizier. Tell him we no longer have any control over these Kelts. I wash my hands of the whole affair. They act alone."

BARI

When Aldebert received Ramiro's letter from Maarat last October, he vowed to join the Holy Crusade. But Abbot Martinus would not let him go. The Crusaders were still in Antioch at the time and Jerusalem remained in the hands of infidels. Martinus was fearful of him traveling alone and he could spare no one to travel with him. Aldebert argued that many pilgrims go to Jerusalem at all times of the year, but the Abbot would not bend to his pleas.

Two things changed the Abbot's mind. One was an important bit of information Aldebert gleaned at the docks—and the other was a letter—a letter from Ramiro. It came from Jerusalem, taking seven months to get to Aldebert in Bari. Once again, it had taken the circuitous route of going to the Abbey of Cluny before being forwarded to him by Abbot Hugh.

But it was not the only letter delivered from Cluny. Another was addressed to Ramiro from the Abbot himself. Ramiro's last letter to Hugh had explained the situation in Jerusalem, that the Egyptians ruled and that the Patriarch was exiled. He had pleaded for instructions—and this letter was Hugh's response.

Aldebert put it aside to pick up the letter addressed to him. In it, Ramiro warned him to stay away from Jerusalem because of all the troubles. But Aldebert bristled at his warning. He had met many pilgrims in Bari who thought little of heading to the Holy City for Easter celebrations, even while the Crusaders continued to march south.

Already, the Soldiers of God had reached Tripoli, making ready for the final assault to reclaim the Holy City for the True Faith. It was a glorious time indeed, Aldebert thought. And now, more fighting men were willing to make the dangerous voyage across the Mediterranean, hoping to join the Holy Crusade they had heard so much about. He yearned to go too.

Abbot Martinus was visibly annoyed. "Yes, yes, I am painfully aware that you want to go to Jerusalem, but the Army of God is still in Tripoli."

"Forgive me, Reverend Father, but those two letters you gave me yesterday—the one from Father Ramiro says he's safe in Jerusalem. He's at a Benedictine monastery. And the other letter is addressed to Ramiro, from Abbot Hugh himself."

"Yes, yes, I saw that," said the Abbot with a hint of forbearance. "I thought you could take it to the port—find a ship going to Jaffa and send it on."

"I could take it myself, Reverend Father. Let me tell you what I heard at the docks yesterday…"

That evening, Aldebert huddled in his cold cubicle within the Allsaints Abbey. He leaned over to dip his quill before resuming his letter to Abbot Hugh.

> To his Reverend Father Hugh, by God's grace, the Abbot of Cluny, Aldebert, his monk and humble servant, greetings.
>
> It is with great joy and many praises to Our Lord that I inform you, my Reverend Father, that on this day, I encountered on the docks of Bari, six vessels destined to the Holy Land to lend aid to the Soldiers of God who fight for the Holy Cause. Four are Genoese and the other two hail from distant Anglia. They are laden with foodstuffs, tools, and supplies of every kind and, while at port, are taking on even more. With them are tradesmen skilled in the machines of war, and more men join them from Italy, including many good fighting men.
>
> Unfortunately, there are no clergy among these good men, no one to carry before them the mantle of the True Faith. So I was asked to join them, to carry the Holy Word. They know not where they will make port but will follow the Holy Crusaders south until such time, by the Will of God, they will be given an opportunity to unload their precious cargo. Seeing their need, I asked Abbot Martinus for permission to sail with them and, by his grace, he allowed me leave. In the name of the Holy Mother Church, I will continue to inform you of events.
>
> May 4, in the year of Our Lord, 1099.

Jerusalem

Easter

On a cool Easter night, Ramiro and Adele made their way through the noisy throng of pilgrims gathered at the Church of the Holy Sepulcher. People came from far and wide to attend the Vesperal Liturgy of the Easter Mass.

From Byzantium, pilgrims sailed from Constantinople, stopping in Cyprus before sailing to Latakia and then continuing south on the Via Mari. From Europe, they traveled to Italy and headed for the port of Bari, just as Ramiro did years before. From here, they embarked on ships to Jaffa before journeying inland to Jerusalem. And joining these venturesome pilgrims, were hundreds of Christians traveling from all parts of Syria and Palestine, many of them Maronites, Jacobites, and Nestorians.

The jubilation and devotion of the pilgrims gave no hint to the political turmoil of the time. Few seemed to care whether Egyptians or Turks ruled Jerusalem, even though most were aware that a hostile Christian army marched through Syria and was on its way to the Holy Land.

Some pilgrims, on hearing rumors of the Crusader's success at Antioch, and now at Tripoli, armed themselves to fight for the cause of liberating Jerusalem. But the Egyptian forces at Jaffa quickly disarmed these misguided adventurers and confiscated their horses. Like the Syrians and Turks, the Egyptians forbade Christians to bear arms or ride a horse. But more zealous pilgrims, angered by these restrictions, concealed their knives and clubs under their cloaks before heading north to join the Crusaders in Tripoli.

Inside the Church of the Holy Sepulcher, torch lamps flickered in every corner, casting dark shadows among the thousands of pilgrims gathered inside and out. "There he is!" Ramiro whispered to Jameel as the presiding priest read aloud from the Book of Isaiah.

"Who?"

"The priest I mentioned. That's him!"

"You mean the one reading?" asked Jameel, who sat beside them with his pregnant wife and son.

"No, no. The one standing to the far right. I watched him go to your Church."

"Oh, yes, I know him. That's Pakrad, an Armenian priest. He's a pious man. Very kind. Why are you interested in him?"

"I've seen him often at Madteos' shop. Perhaps he knows something of my cross."

"I think he's a relative—a cousin or brother, I'm not sure. Why do you think he has your cross?"

"If he's a kinsman, maybe Madteos gave it to him. It does have an Armenian design."

"But the golden cross, Master. It is too precious for a priest to own."

The Liturgy ended and all torches were extinguished except for the dim perpetual flame of the altar. The whole church fell into utter darkness, the blackness so complete that those just a few steps away from the dull altar flame were unable to see. And here the crowd waited patiently until the stroke of midnight when the high priest lit his candle from the altar flame. From this one candle, thousands of others were lit and the whole congregation, candles in hand, moved outside to join the ritual procession around the church.

But Ramiro and Adele were no sooner out the door when the big Sudanese lieutenant stepped in front of them.

"You will come with me!" said the dark, burly man as he took Ramiro by the arm. "The Emir demands it!"

THE FRENCH AMBASSADORS

"I'm glad you could come, Sayyid Ramirah," said Iftikhar.

Ramiro was about to correct Iftikhar on the pronunciation of his name but bit his lip. "Apparently, Sahib, I had little choice in the matter," he replied sullenly, thinking with some apprehension about the many hours Iftikhar had detained him last time. "...although it is always good to see you again, my Lord. And... uh, if it pleases my Lord, what matter does my esteemed Emir find pressing at this late hour?"

Iftikhar did not invite him to sit. "I will get straight to the point, Ramirah. It seems your invading countrymen in Tripoli have sent emissaries to meet with me. These barbarians have already met with our Great Vizier in Egypt but they failed to reach any agreement with him. Now they approach me without the Vizier's consent. I believe their purpose is to discuss the fate of Jerusalem and I want you to join me when we meet."

"Me? But why, Sahib?"

"Because you are one of their countrymen, are you not?"

Ramiro shrugged. "Not really. At least no more than Egyptians would consider Syrians their countrymen."

Iftikhar returned a suspicious glance. "Nonetheless, you are one of them, you are Christian and you speak their language."

Ramiro sighed. "I cannot deny I am Christian, Sahib. So what is it you would have me do?"

Iftikhar moved a little closer to him, speaking softly. "These men have their own translators, but none of my people know their tongue. I want you to write down everything they say, even if it's a simple aside to a compatriot."

Ramiro nodded. "I can do that."

"But" said Iftikhar, "... you will not be introduced—and you will not speak to them. You will sit behind me. When I motion to you, you will give me all that you have written. Is that clear?"

Ramiro bowed his head. "Your wish is my glad duty, Emir. Will I be detained for long? My wife is waiting."

"That is of no concern. My men will watch over your wife."

Ramiro stiffened, looking hard into Iftikhar's eyes. "I'm sure she will be safe in your gentle care, Sahib."

Iftikhar looked down on the three men of Provence, who sat awkwardly on cushions set in front of the dais. They looked uncomfortable, one of them kept stretching his legs out under the table. The men were unarmed but well-attired in expensive vests and pantaloons, styles clearly adopted from local fashion. The man in the middle was about thirty, blonde, his round face reddened by the sun. He spoke Greek and did all the talking. An Arab interpreter knelt beside him.

Two of Iftikhar's advisors positioned themselves to either side of the French ambassadors. Ramiro sat inconspicuously behind Iftikhar while two burly askari straddled the door, one of them the big Sudanese.

Iftikhar thought about the letter he had just received from his master, Al-Afdal, who warned him that the Greek King no longer controlled these bloodthirsty barbarians. They acted alone and he would have to deal with them as he saw fit. Al-Afdal had also informed him that the once mighty Crusader army was now greatly diminished in size and their resources thin. Armed with this knowledge, Iftikhar took a firm stance.

After long pleasantries and introductions, the French ambassadors began to discuss the purpose of their visit, presenting their proposals at length.

"What did you say?" Iftikhar asked after a time. "You want me to surrender Jerusalem to you?" He sounded amused.

The fretful interpreter kept his head down. "Yes, Sahib, that is what they ask."

Iftikhar chuckled. He put his hands to his waist, his elbows jutting out of his billowing blue tunic. "That is a preposterous request! The Vizier, may Allah bless his name, has already presented to you a magnanimous offer." He waved a hand in the air. "Let me repeat this for you. If you stop where you are now, in Tripoli, we are willing to cede all Syrian territory to you without contest. In fact, we offer you an alliance against the Turks. We will aid and abet your efforts to conquer their cities." He leaned forward as if to accentuate his next words. "But we will continue to hold Palestine, including Jerusalem and all land west of the Jordan."

The translator spoke to the emissaries in a similar meek tone. When they heard Iftikhar's reply, one of them leaned over to the blonde man, speaking in the tongue of Provencal. "Tell this God-damned pagan their blood will drench the streets," he whispered in a venomous voice. "This is unacceptable. Do they not understand Jerusalem is ours? God wills it."

The blonde man put up a hand to dissuade him. "Don't be a fool. You will anger him and he will slit our throats where we sit. Be civil." He turned to Iftikhar, speaking in Greek. "I hear your offer, Governor, but you must understand that Jerusalem is the most holy city to a Christian. How can we come this far without free access to its most holy shrines?"

Inwardly, Iftikhar seethed at the effrontery of these arrogant pagans. They had no manners and smelled like wet dogs. But outwardly, he remained calm. "That is not a problem," he replied. "Every year, thousands of Christian pilgrims come to Jerusalem unhindered. You too are free to come and worship at any time. All we ask is that your visits are limited in number so we can more easily accommodate your needs."

Once again, the French conversed in their own tongue. "I don't trust him," one said. "It's a ruse of the devil to deflect God's holy plan."

"It is our duty," said the other, "to seize the Holy Sepulcher in the name of Our Lord."

The blonde man pursed his lips, shaking his head apologetically as he spoke to Iftikhar. "We cannot accept your offer. Jerusalem is our holy right."

Iftikhar rose up in stifled rage. He could no longer tolerate these ignorant, bull-headed infidels. "So be it! I believe our negotiations have ended! Be warned—the armies of Egypt will stand against you if you march farther south. We control the coast. We will strangle your supply lines."

The Frenchmen got to their feet, mumbling and cursing among themselves.

"My men will escort you back to your quarters," said Iftikhar. "Prepare to leave Jerusalem before noon." He turned to Ramiro, speaking quietly. "Give me what you have." After Ramiro handed him his notes, Iftikhar motioned toward the Provencals with a tip of his head. "Go with the escort. Tell me all they say."

"You mean… go with them now, Sahib?" asked Ramiro.

"Yes, yes, that is what I mean." He motioned again. "Go, go."

Iftikhar read over Ramiro's notes. "Look what they say!" he exclaimed in alarm. "They know about our troubles in Cairo—about the plague and the rebellions. This is not good. The Vizier must send an army soon. We are dealing with fanatics!" He scowled, handing the notes to his lieutenant.

"I agree, my Lord," said the lieutenant as he read them over. "We must destroy them now."

Iftikhar turned on him. "And what would you have me do, Lieutenant? Send our cavalry to Tripoli? We can barely hold Palestine."

"But, my Lord, this kafir priest… what's his name?"

"Ramirah."

"Yes, he says here he overheard talk of them seizing Jaffa and even Ascalon. If they do this, we cannot win."

"They cannot take Jaffa, half our navy is there. And the Roman ships will no longer assist these barbarians. The King has washed his hands of the whole affair and has nothing more to do with them." But despite his bold words, Iftikhar felt an inner dread. Fanatics are dangerous people and he well knew he should never underestimate an enemy willing to die for a cause—like the Hashashin.

"With respect, my Lord," said the lieutenant, "I would not trust the Roman King. He's a sly fox. And what about the Genoese fleets the kafir speaks of? And these Engleezi. What of their ships from the West?"

"We will ask our Vizier what we should do," said Iftikhar. He motioned to his secretary. "Compose a letter to Al-Afdal, may Allah keep him."

The secretary nodded. "As you command, my Lord."

"And we should expel the devil Christians," said the lieutenant. "Before it's too late."

"Not yet," said Iftikhar as his prayer beads rushed through his fingers. "Not yet… but make preparations." He was about to dismiss the man but hesitated for one last question. "What about this Ramirah? Did you find the cross he looks for?"

"No, my Lord. But we think an Armenian jeweler has it."

"Why is that?"

"Our man says this Ramirah watches the jeweler and all who come and go from his shop."

"Good. Then we will watch too."

"So now you're a spy for the heathen Muslims?" Adele asked with obvious scorn. "I don't understand you, Ramiro. Why are you so against your own people?"

"For the sake of Christ, Adele! Iftikhar threatened both of us. What would you have me do?" he asked as she glared at him. "And I'm not against my people, I'm against holy war. I'm against people who kill, steal, and rape in the name of God."

"So you don't believe Christians should rule the Holy City of Jerusalem? The very place where Our Lord is buried. Instead, you'd rather have these infidels and heretics by your side?"

"Why do they need to rule it?" he argued. "Christians are free to worship in Jerusalem. You know that. As are Hebrews and any other creed. Can you honestly say the same is true for Muslims or Jews in France or Germany?"

Adele stomped a foot, her hair dangling in front of her eyes. "It's not right! The priests say the Messiah will return when Zion is complete. What about that?"

"Adele, my love, how can I make you understand? The Messiah has already come to teach us brotherhood, love, and mercy—but still we reject his words. Can you really believe that the Son of God, whose message is of spiritual peace, will return in heavenly glory to vindicate these bloodthirsty men who stand victoriously over heaps of slaughtered Muslims? It's an abomination!"

"Oh, so now your own countrymen are bloodthirsty. Next you'll be calling them barbarians like the rest!"

"They are barbarians, Adele. Only barbarians slaughter for the sake of slaughter. Only barbarians dare to eat the flesh of the vanquished like a pack of ravenous dogs!"

"God's blood!" she shouted in anger, spinning away from him.

MADTEOS' OFFER

Madteos wrung his hands in worry. "Are you sure, Pakrad?"

"Yes, Madteos, the barbarians are now at Tripoli and will come this way. It's not worth the risk. They kill everyone. They steal everything." Pakrad's big eyes darted about in a worried manner, as if expecting trouble at any moment.

"Do you really believe Jerusalem will fall?" Madteos asked, staring at him with aging eyes. "What of Al-Afdal and the Egyptians? Surely, they can defeat these barbarians."

"They took Antioch, brother. Why not Jerusalem?"

Madteos reflected for a moment. "So what do you think we should do?"

Pakrad lowered his voice. "It's rumored that Governor Iftikhar will evict the Christians anyway. We are not safe here. You should go to Bethlehem. Go to your son's house. You can always return when the situation is calm."

Madteos shook his head. "But I've got too much to carry. I'd have to hire guards, it would attract too much attention."

"Then sell what you have. Sell it here and take the money."

"Peace be upon you, Sayyid," Madteos greeted.

Ramiro looked up from his writing. A thin, old man with a wrinkled face and a wide gray mustache stood in front of his desk. "And peace to you, Madteos," he said with a hint of surprise. "What brings you to my shop?"

Madteos opened his hands as he spoke. "And to you peace, Sayyid. I uh... I think I have found the cross you are looking for. Are you still interested?"

"Yes, yes, of course," Ramiro answered, happily astonished that Madteos was willing to approach him openly. "But I cannot afford your price."

"Well, Sayyid, you must understand that my first price was only an estimate. An estimate based on your flowery description of a beautiful masterpiece."

"Of course," Ramiro replied with wry amusement. "So what will it cost now that you realize its true value?"

A forced smile cracked across Madteos' bristled face. "Oh, it is quite reasonable. I believe that only five gold dinar will secure it for you."

"Five dinar? Really?"

Madteos nodded in high expectation. "Yes, yes."

Ramiro fell silent for a long moment. He watched Madteos squirm and wondered why the old man was willing to take much less than he originally asked.

Madteos wrung his hands as he waited for Ramiro's response. "So what do you say, Sayyid Ramiro? Do we have a deal?"

Ramiro squinted at him. "Why this sudden change of heart, Madteos? What has happened?"

"Oh... oh nothing of any import, Sayyid. Except that now I see you for the holy man that you truly are. I hope that, by this small gesture of mine, I will gain your blessing."

He's a poor liar, thought Ramiro as he looked directly into his cloudy eyes. "I will give you three dinar," he offered.

"Please, Sayyid. I make no profit on this. But because you are a man of God, I will give it to you for only four dinar. Do we have a deal?"

Ramiro nodded. "We have a deal."

Madteos seemed happy enough. His smile looked genuine. "I will get it for you right away," he said as he began to rush off.

"Wait!" Ramiro called after him. "I don't have the money here. I will collect it tonight and see you in the morning."

"Yes, yes, of course, Sayyid, of course. I am a foolish old man. I will meet you here in the morning, God willing."

Bishop Aliphas looked annoyed. "With respect, Ramiro of Cluny, I'm not sure that I share the same sense of value toward your cross."

"You must trust me, Your Excellency," Ramiro replied in earnest. "Abbot Hugh thought it was essential that I deliver the cross to Patriarch Symeon. I admit I do not know the true reason. But what I tell you is the truth."

"And do you expect me to send it on to Cyprus? The Patriarch is old and frail and has fallen ill. I'm not convinced he could do much in your favor."

"Then you must open it, Your Excellency. It may have an important message locked inside."

"And you still believe this message is vital?" Aliphas asked with a thin smile. "Like you say, it has been almost ten years since you were first given this cross."

Ramiro reddened in shame. It had taken too long, he knew that. But what could he do? He had made a promise to Abbot Hugh. "Your Excellency, if you find no importance attached to the cross, rest assured that it is well worth four dinar in gold and silver alone."

Bishop Aliphas smiled a little, giving a light nod. "Very well, Ramiro of Cluny. I will give you the four dinar and trust on your honor as a Christian and a Cluny monk that you will deliver this cross to me. My secretary will draw up an agreement for you to sign."

TRIPOLI

For several months, Count Raymond kept up his siege of Arqah, just to the north of Tripoli. But the fortress, sitting high on a steep hill, proved impregnable. His men died by the day in hails of arrows and cavalcades of stone. With mounting losses, his siege appeared the worst of folly, a useless waste of time and men and, to Raymond's growing dismay and fury, that bastard Godfrey was vindicated. Even his own men joined the chorus to march on Jerusalem.

And now, after his ambassadors returned with news of their futile meeting with Governor Iftikhar, he could wait no longer. They advised him to march soon, not only because Iftikhar refused to hand over Jerusalem but also because of what they had discovered—Egypt was weakened by disease and exhausted by civil strife. It was unprepared for prolonged battle. On hearing all this, Raymond finally relented, quitting Arqah.

While Raymond's influence diminished, Duke Godfrey's prestige grew. He had proven himself a capable leader, a cunning schemer, and a terrifying warrior. And now his frequent admonitions to march south to Jerusalem appeared to be shrewd advice. Men from all factions flocked to his side. Even Tancred, forever the opportunist, was no longer swayed by Raymond's gold.

Arnulf Malecorne, the sly Norman chaplain, lost no time stepping into the mystical void left by the inglorious death of Peter Bartholomew. He worked feverishly to maintain the peace among competing French, Norman, and German factions. To let tempers cool, he used his new-found power and prestige to declare a period of fasting, prayer, and almsgiving. And slowly, he further entrenched his position, all the while nudging closer to Godfrey's side.

Before they set out for Jerusalem, the Christians of Tripoli, using the Emir's gold, fashioned a golden crucifix for Arnulf. Having successfully discredited Raymond's Holy Lance, Arnulf felt the need to create a new holy icon around which to rally the faithful—his icon. With relentless determination, he forged a new following centered around his golden crucifix and convinced Godfrey to become its patron and protector, although not all were so persuaded.

JERUSALEM

The messenger's breath came in gasps. He raised a dusty sleeve to wipe the sweat from his brow. "The barbarians have left Tripoli, Sahib." He drew another breath. "They... they march to Ramla." Sweat poured down his face in the stuffy heat of the meeting room. The air outside the citadel hung silent and still, offering no reprieve from the scorching heat.

"Straight to Ramla?" Iftikhar asked.

"Yes, my Lord. And they make great haste."

"Did they make no attempt on Beirut, Tyre, or Haifa?"

"No, my Lord. And no one dares to come out in challenge. The emirs hide in fear behind their walls."

"Surely, they will need to take Jaffa. How else could they get any help by sea? Did any of our reinforcements arrive from Ascalon?"

"No, Sahib." The messenger looked down as if suddenly afraid to speak. "And Ramla... Ramla, my Lord, it is abandoned."

"What?"

"Yes, my Lord. The garrison has fled, everyone has fled. They run in fear of these flesh-eating barbarians! They left behind all they could not carry. The whole city is deserted, only ghosts remain."

Iftikhar flushed. "Cowards!" he belted. "May Allah damn them!" For a long while, he stood in seething silence with his face down and a hand to his chin.

In fear of his rage, the men in the room kept completely still, the silence interrupted only when the adhan sounded from the minarets of the Al-Aqsa Mosque, and they all knelt to pray.

"We have become too complacent," Iftikhar spouted after their prayers ended and all were seated. "The barbarians tarried so long in Antioch and then Tripoli, we came to believe we had ample time. Now it appears not. They rush south, not bothering to conquer cities along the way."

"It is a foolish move, Sahib," said the Sudanese lieutenant. "If they move inland without securing the coast, they will soon run out of supplies."

"I agree," said Iftikhar, dabbing the sweat from his face with a napkin. "It's difficult to believe they can be so brazen and careless."

"We should attack, Sahib. Cut them down at once!"

"That would be even more foolish, Lieutenant. Do you suggest we leave Jerusalem unguarded?"

"No, my Lord," he said, bowing his scarred head.

"Our Vizier promised to arrive with an army next month. He has been delayed by the plague and has more trouble with rebellions. We must do all we can to hold them off until he arrives. Then, by the will of Allah, we will destroy them all!"

"We must prepare for a long siege, Commander."

"Yes, at once. Gather all crops, all livestock—kill, destroy, or conceal anything we cannot use ourselves. Leave only dirt for them to eat!"

"Poison every well and every pool, Sahib," said the Sudanese. "All of them within a farsakh of the city. We'll see how long they can last before they choke on their own tongues!"

"But what of the Pool of Siloam?" asked another lieutenant. "Fresh water gushes from the spring every three days."

"How far away is it?"

"About two hundred paces from the south wall, Sahib. But low in the Valley of Qidron."

"Put two of our best archers on the wall," one said.

"And just to make sure, fill the pool with dead animals."

"What about materials, Sahib?" inquired another. "We should collect anything they can use against us."

"I agree. Collect and burn all timber we cannot put inside the walls. All of it! I don't want a scrap left. Not enough for a single arrow! Nails, rope, axes... anything that could aid these accursed Christians!

"What of the Christians in the city, my Lord?"

"Get them out, especially their priests. Close the churches and throw out anyone else with money or influence."

"As you command, my Lord."

Iftikhar lowered his eyes in thought. A burning slit of sunshine pierced through a portal, creeping across his face. He raised his elbow for shade. "And bring that damned Christian scribe to me! The one called Ramirah!"

Bang! Bang! Bang! The door rattled on its hinges. Ramiro and Adele jumped from bed, exchanging nervous glances. "Who is it?" Ramiro shouted.

"Askari of the Emir!" a man shouted back. "Open the door!"

"Again? God help us!" said Ramiro with hushed breath.

He rushed to put on a tunic. "Hold on!" he shouted again, "I'm getting dressed!" He turned to Adele in breathless apprehension. "Get dressed fast! Take the money from Bishop Aliphas! Go to Madteos and get the cross! Hurry!"

"How do I get out Ramiro? What if they take me too?"

He rushed to the window. "The rope!" he cried. "Use the rope! The one I tied to the pillar for an easy escape." He rushed over to the coil of rope, checked the knot at the pillar and threw it out the window.

Adele looked down, shaking her head. "I can't do that!"

Ramiro nudged her to the rope. "You must do it, Adele. All depends on you."

Bang! Bang! "Open the door!" came another angry shout. "Or forfeit your life!"

"One moment, please!" Ramiro shouted. "I'll be right there!"

Ramiro held Adele by the arms as she stuck her legs out the window. "Grab the rope!" he whispered.

"Blood in hell!" she gushed. "I've got the damn thing!" She started to lower herself but stopped. "My mace, Ramiro, hand me my mace!"

"Yes, yes," he reached for it near the bed. "Here it is. Go! Go!"

She stuffed it into her belt before beginning her descent. She stopped again. "My shawl. I need my shawl."

"For the love of God, woman!" he said looking around the room. "Ah! Here it is! Go!"

She started down again but her tunic got caught in the rope. "By the Cross!" she cursed.

Ramiro scowled as he reached down to set her free. "You shouldn't curse. It's most unbecoming."

She looked up, scowling. "Lunatic! Don't forget to untie the rope!" She slid down to the alley.

Ramiro looked down on her—he loved her spirit. *She's down! Release the rope!*

Crash! The door flew open. Three askari barged into the room, swords drawn. Ramiro rushed out to greet them, closing the bedroom blind behind him. "What are you doing?" he shouted with indignation. "I told you I was coming! There's no need for this! I'm a man of God!"

They ignored him, sheathing their swords before taking him by the arms. "You will come with us!" They looked around. "Where's your wife?"

"She's not here. She went to market," he lied.

One of the askari ripped the blind from the bedroom. He pulled away cushions, throwing them about the room. Then he went to the window and looked down.

Ramiro held his breath.

"Did you bring the dhimmi scribe to me?" Iftikhar asked.

"Yes, Sahib."

"And his wife too?"

"No, Sahib, she was not there."

"Where is she?"

"The dhimmi said she went to market."

"At this hour? You idiot! Send men out to find her—now!"

The lieutenant bowed. "Yes, my Lord, at once." He signaled to a nearby askari who nodded and left.

"Did you manage to get his cross?"

"No, Sahib," replied the wary lieutenant. "It was not in his room so we went to the jeweler's home this morning but found no one. He has left the city. We tore the house apart and found nothing."

Iftikhar scowled. "May Allah curse your sons! Moron! Get out! Get out before I remove your head!"

The lieutenant lowered his eyes, backing to the door in cautious steps.

Adele pulled her headscarf close about her fair face, keeping her head down. She worked her way across the street, remaining as inconspicuous as possible, heading for Madteos' shop. But the shop was closed and empty. She looked about in worry before hurrying to another jeweler nearby. "Peace be upon you," she said as demurely as she could.

"And to you, Sayyidah" the man replied. "What would you like?"

"The jeweler—Madteos—where is he today, Sayyid?"

"I don't know. He didn't show up. Very strange,"

"Please Sayyid, where does he live?"

"To the south, near the Zion Gate. Ask the rug merchant at the end of the street. He will show you."

When she reached Madteos' house, it seemed eerily quiet. The narrow street was devoid of traffic except for a lone boy leading a gray donkey. She brushed her tunic and adjusted her shawl before approaching the door. She knocked. The door was ajar and it opened a little. She looked around again before pushing it further, just enough to slide into the dim interior. "Ya Madteos!" she said loudly. "Are you here? Madteos! I have money for the cross!" Silence. She ventured another step. Broken glass and pottery crunched under her feet. In the waning light, she could see the place was a mess. Something was wrong.

The door slammed shut behind her. Her heart pounded. She swung around, straining into the darkness. "Who is it?" she cried. "Who's there?" She heard the grinding of another step. With shaking hands, she fumbled for her mace.

SIEGE OF JERUSALEM

June 7

Iftikhar stared out from the rooftop of the Tower of David. His long blue tunic billowed and slapped in gusts of warm wind.

"There they are!" cried the watchman. On the hill! Beside the Mosque of Prophet Samuel!"

He saw them. Rays of morning sun flashed from steel as clouds of dust mushroomed from their midst, spiraling into a hazy blue sky, only to be swept aside in an instant by an erratic wind. There they are, he thought. Ten thousand strong. An army of Christian fanatics! How is this possible? Will Al-Afdal come in time?

He heard the slap of footsteps. The Sudanese approached. "What is it, Lieutenant?"

"My Lord, they have already taken Bethlehem!"

The Crusaders pushed and shoved for their first sight of the Holy City, the Center of the Earth, the very place where Heaven and Earth unite in spiritual glory. After surviving three years of long marches, arid deserts, starvation, disease and the perils of war, they had reached their goal, the holiest site on earth, the Tomb of Christ. They fell to their knees and wept, just as Ramiro did months before, giving thanks to God in loud voices.

Arnulf Malecorne held his new standard high above his head. Perched atop, was the golden crucifix made in Triploi. He jabbed it into the air repeatedly, as if it were a sacred sword. "Praise be to God!" he screamed as loud as he could.

By late afternoon, thousands of French, German, and Norman troops had gathered to the north of Jerusalem. By this time, Godfrey had established himself as the chief warlord of the Christian army, and Arnulf was his crafty servant of God.

Godfrey and Robert's men camped between the Damascus Gate and the Castle Al-Jalud. Meanwhile, Raymond of Toulouse, because of the deepening rifts with the others and his rapidly declining popularity, took up position on the opposite side of the city, to the south, where he gathered his dwindling troops outside the Zion Gate. Even some of his long-time allies had abandoned him to join Godfrey at the north wall.

ANOTHER DUNGEON

On the orders of Iftikhar, Ramiro was thrown into the dungeon of Castle Al-Jalud. The only light in the gloomy cell came from a small opening near the ceiling, casting pallid rays over the stark interior. A carpet of straw covered the floor, crawling with camel spiders and weevils. Against the walls, several benches served as beds, allowing the prisoners to rise above the creeping haven. A simple latrine, a bucket in plain sight, occupied one corner, its heavy stench permeating the stifling, hot air.

The cell door slammed shut. Ramiro, who had been shoved to the floor, rose quickly to his feet, defiantly brushing straw from his cloak. He looked around, his eyes slowly adjusting to the dim light. He saw three other men. To his surprise, one of them was Mufti Ibrahim. "Mufti, I'm glad to see you well... even in these sad circumstances." The mufti was thin and disheveled, his face bruised and cut, his white tunic soiled. For a man usually so stern and proud, he had a look of defeat.

Ibrahim looked up, not sure who he was.

"I'm Ramiro of Cluny. Do you remember me from Antioch?"

Ibrahim began to nod ever so slightly. "The Christian," he said quietly as his memory returned. "The one looking for a red-haired woman."

"That's right," he nodded, feeling a shiver of fear when he thought of Adele's safety. Did she get the cross? Where would she go?

"How did you escape Antioch," asked Ibrahim. "And how did you end up here?"

Ramiro sat down to tell him his story, although he left out many details that he had no wish to share. One of the prisoners, a Christian, sat alone at the far end, scowling in their direction. The other man, a Muslim sitting closer to Ibrahim, remained silent and morose.

"Tell me, Mufti," Ramiro asked, "did you ever have the opportunity to deliver my letter?"

Ibrahim nodded sadly. "Yes, I did, and it caused me much grief as I feared it would. Especially when the siege of Antioch began. The Turks became nervous. That's when they exiled the Patriarch and many others. Some of them accused me of collaborating with Christians." He shook his head. "What nonsense."

"But it was the Egyptians who threw you in here, not the Turks," said Ramiro, feeling some guilt and regret.

"That's right—for the greatest crime of all."

"What's that?"

"Being a Sunni—an enemy of the Fatimids."

Ramiro nodded in understanding. "You must tell me, Mufti, did Patriarch Symeon recognize my name or say anything at all?"

"He had no idea who you were, although he knew of the Abbot you mentioned. He asked me if you had a certain cross to show him. But I didn't know what he was talking about."

Ramiro had a distant look as his thoughts ran. The Patriarch asked about the Cluny cross. What's going on? What does this cross mean? Does it really matter anymore?

They fell into silence but soon, in the distance, they could hear people shouting. Their voices grew louder and louder. Ramiro could feel the tension in the air, the sounds of rushing feet, clanging weapons, people yelling. "By all saints!

What is going on?" He strained to hear. Only when someone yelled, "May Allah curse your mothers, Christian dogs!" did it dawn on him.

"The Crusaders have arrived!" he cried aloud. "Blessed Mary! O Jesus! They're here!" He thought of the slaughter at Antioch and then at Maarat, and he thought of Adele. Please God, keep her safe!

He heard the rattle of keys. The cell door opened and a big man came in with two servants, one with a tray of bread and water, and the other to swap the chamber pot. They did it all with nary a word.

Ramiro rushed up to the jailer. "Please, Sayyid, let me speak to the Governor. There is no need to keep me here. I will leave the city." The man made no reply. "I beg of you!" Ramiro grabbed his arm. The big man turned, throwing him to the floor with a sweep of his arm.

THE CRUSADER CAMP

The Christian camp sprawled out beyond the long, outer wall of Jerusalem, well out of arrow range. Governor Iftikhar quickly moved his headquarters from the Tower of David to Castle Al-Jalud to keep a close eye on their movements. He stood at one of the castle's ports, studying the nearest camp.

"You see the big one?" he said to the Sudanese. "The one with long, yellow hair? He's their leader. See the way he commands his men?"

"I see him, Sahib."

Iftikhar was amused when he heard that a group of infidels, covering themselves with shields, rushed madly at the walls, smashing at stones with simple hammers, as if expecting them to collapse with a single blow. But they were easily dissuaded with boiling oil and boulders. He was relieved to see they had no siege machines and, apparently, no means to construct one. Praise Allah. Let them hammer all they like. We will cut them down one by one.

Reports from the Zion Gate were similar. An old man with one eye led the Christians gathered there and he was kept busy guarding the Church of Saint Mary on Mount Zion.

Iftikhar knew these stinking kuffar had discovered the poisoned wells because his sentries saw them coming from miles in the distance carrying fresh animal skins full of water. He heard that a desperate and parched crusader crawled over the decaying filth of dead animals clogging the Pool of Siloam to find fresh water at its source. Hundreds followed after him, pushing and shoving and brawling for a single drink. All the while, his archers peppered them with arrows shot on high from the nearest tower.

"It's unfortunate," said Iftikhar, "but the barbarians seem to have enough to eat."

"Yes, Sahib. They stripped Ramla of its grain and other food, and now Bethlehem supplies them with more."

"Have we sent out our spies?"

"Yes, my Lord, three men dressed as peasants."

The air was dry and dusty, filled with the stench of death. All around the walls lay the carcasses of horses, mules, cattle, and sheep. If not killed on the orders of Iftikhar, they died of thirst, rotting where they dropped.

Iftikhar turned from the window with a pleasing sense of accomplishment. *The Christians are unprepared for a siege. They will soon die of thirst and wither away.* He rubbed his chin, barely able to conceal a grin. "Bring that dhimmi scribe to me."

Ramiro had no sooner entered Iftikhar's chamber when he blurted out, "Where's my wife? What have you done with her?"

Right away, the big Sudanese struck him across the side of the head with a heavy hand, sending him staggering. "Mind your manners, kafir!"

Ramiro caught his balance, rubbing his ear. "Excuse me, peace be upon you, Sahib."

Iftikhar clenched his jaw. He had little tolerance for disrespect, especially from a cursed Christian. "You would do well to guard your head, Ramirah of Cluny. You may still lose it."

"Come with me," Iftikhar ordered. He strolled through a small archway leading to the battlements. The lieutenant shoved Ramiro along until they came out into the open air.

That is when Ramiro first saw them—thousands and thousands of Crusaders milling about in the distance. He reached out to steady himself against the castellations. The height of the wall, the open sky, the stench of death in the air, it all made his knees weak.

"You see?" said Iftikhar. "These are your countrymen." He waved his arm in a broad arc. "They have come all this way from a distant land. And for what? To touch the shrine of Jesus?" He smirked, as if he had some inside knowledge. "Peaceful pilgrimage to holy places, that I can understand. But these men come armed for war, ready to die. In some ways, I admire their resolve, but then again, I pity their foolishness. Look at them now. Now they die of thirst and attack our walls with little hammers."

Ramiro looked out on the hordes of men. Strangely, they did not appear familiar. Their helmets, their armor, their dress, even their horses, they all seemed to have a distinctive Muslim character. Were it not for the few crosses sewn onto shoulders, and perhaps some red and blonde hair, they would be difficult to distinguish from any other army in the region.

"Do you recognize these men?" Iftikhar asked.

"Not at all, my Lord."

"You see no one you know?"

"No, my Lord, but my eyes are not as good as they used to be."

"What about an old man with one eye, does he sound familiar?"

"No, I'm sorry, Sahib. As I said before, I have been away many years and have never seen these men before."

Iftikhar stood looking north, resting a hand on his sword. His black hair rippled under a blue turban. "Well, scribe, you are of little use to me at the moment. Go." He waved a hand.

"Please excuse me, my Lord, but I'm concerned about my wife. Do you know if she is safe?"

Iftikhar turned, looking at him with a deadpan face. "She is well cared for," he lied. "... as long as you cooperate."

FIRST ASSAULT

June 13

The first assault on Jerusalem was foolish and desperate. But the Crusaders were so convinced that God would deliver the holy city into their hands, they charged forward with one makeshift ladder, climbing over the curtain wall to attack the main wall. They steadied the ladder against a section of wall near the Damascus Gate, soon rushing to the top. A fierce onslaught ensued. The first man to reach the battlement lost an arm to a mamluk sword and fell to earth. Others followed, engaging in hand-to-hand combat, but they were quickly repelled by reinforcements. A few survivors fled back to camp.

With his men demoralized and staggering from thirst, Godfrey called a council to decide on a course of action. No more would they waste good fighting men with these futile assaults. They needed siege engines. But the nearest forests were thirty miles away and they had not a single axe or nail, nor was there a soul among them who knew how to build a decent catapult.

MORE PRISONERS

From the depths of the dungeon, Ramiro could hear the din of battle in the distance, a sound soon interrupted by the rattle of keys as the jailer approached. The cell door opened and four more men were shoved in. All of them dressed in the robes of a rabbi. One of them was an old man assisted by two others—it was Rabbi Moshe.

Ramiro rose to his feet. "Rabbi? Why are you here?"

Two assistants led Moshe by the arms, taking him to a bench and trying to make him comfortable. "It seems we are a threat to Iftikhar," he replied in a raspy voice. He still looked pale and sick, his gray face sagging in despair. "They are afraid we will aid the Christians. A preposterous claim! Why would we help them? They slaughter Hebrews."

"Iftikhar is probably afraid of any dissent at this time," said Ramiro, who was really not sure what to say. Moshe was right, of course, and he tried to comfort him in a clumsy way. The other rabbis remained sullen. They were clearly worried.

Some hours later, the cell door opened again and the guards pushed in six more men. One was Bishop Aliphas from the Greek church, and the other was Brother Gerard from the Latin monastery. The rest were Latin clergymen, some of whom he had met briefly. They were all badly beaten and Gerard looked terrible. Crude, blood-soaked bandages wrapped his hands and feet. He could hardly walk and had to be helped in.

"Brother Gerard!" Ramiro shouted. "What have they done to you?"

Red welts ran across Gerard's bald head, cut by the lash of whips. He spoke with difficulty through swollen cheeks and lips. "I've been charged as a traitor."

Bishop Aliphas interjected. "We were all sent to the battlements, Ramiro. Iftikhar ordered us to throw stones on the Christians. Most of us refused so they beat us. And then they caught Brother Gerard throwing them bread so they burned his hands and feet and beat him too, as you can see. Then they raided the monastery, taking everything of value."

"Ramiro!" said Gerard gritting his teeth. "What are you doing here?"

"Apparently, I'm a threat too," Ramiro replied as he inspected Gerard's bandages. "It seems that Iftikhar fears I will aid the Christians as you did. And those ridiculous rumors about me creating miracles didn't help." He waved his arm to a bench. "Come, Brother. You must lay down here. Let me have a look at your wounds."

The days passed and the men in the crowded dungeon soon found little to talk about. They waited for any word of events, but nothing came. Bishop Aliphas hardly spoke at all. In fact, he had said nothing for days. Most of the time, he knelt in prayer, letting the camel spiders scurry across his legs. It was difficult to know where he stood on any issue, whereas Brother Gerard was painfully clear in his support for the Crusaders.

Ramiro paced back and forth. He went to the cell door to push on it, hoping that, by the will of God, it would open for him. With growing despondency, he returned to the bench, sitting down hard. Adele, he thought, I hope she's alright. I hope she got the cross. She can't go home, not now. He rose to his feet to pace again. What if they caught her? Where would she be? I must talk to Iftikhar. What in God's name is going on? He sat down again, gnawing on the knuckle of one hand. God forgive me. I should never have brought her here. You idiot!

"You look worried, Brother Ramiro," said Gerard, his face no longer swollen, although long, thin scabs remained. Rough bandages still wrapped his hands and feet.

Ramiro pulled his knuckle from his mouth. "How long will we be detained here, Brother Gerard?"

"For as long as Iftikhar wishes," he said, rubbing at the searing itch of his burns.

Ramiro nodded, still thinking of Adele. "You said all Christians were driven out. Are you sure?"

"I'm sure most were, certainly the clergy. Why do you ask?"

Ramiro was still uncomfortable speaking of his wife with a fellow monk. "I... I have many friends in the city," he said, veiling his thoughts. "I pray they are safe."

"So do I, Brother. And I pray these good men will conquer soon and bring the Holy City to Christian care."

There was no privacy in the cell and all men overheard his remark. "Unfortunately," said Rabbi Moshe in his raspy voice, "not all of us share your view. Surely you have heard of the massacre at Antioch? They slaughtered Christians too!"

Gerard said nothing. He turned his head away, whispering aside to Ramiro. "Cursed Hebrews."

Ramiro reddened, standing quickly, as if to disassociate himself from the man.

"And what of Maarat?" asked Mufti Ibrahim, breaking his silence. "There is nothing left! They killed everyone. Is this what you want?"

Gerard avoided his eyes too. Instead, he stared straight ahead. "God's will be done."

Ibrahim rose to his feet in defiance. He addressed everyone, as if he were giving a sermon in the mosque. "When the great Caliph, Umar, conquered Jerusalem, he persecuted no one. He assured the Christians their holy places would go unmolested. And this still holds true today." He turned his sad eyes to the Rabbi. "And was it not the Caliph who allowed Hebrews to return to Jerusalem after six centuries of Roman persecution and exile? So tell me now, is it better the Muslim way or the barbarian way?" He sat down. "I will say no more."

JAFFA

Unknown to the Crusaders besieging Jerusalem, the Egyptians had abandoned the port of Jaffa. The Vizier, Al-Afdal, had been informed that the barbarians were gathering around the walls of Jerusalem, so he believed that Jaffa was safe enough left alone. Instead, he decided to gather his troops at Ascalon. So when a Genoese fleet cautiously approached Jaffa with loads of merchandise for the Crusaders, they were happily surprised to discover their good fortune.

The Crusader's plea for help, sent from Tripoli with bags of gold, had been safely delivered and the Genoese answered their call with six merchant galleys, four of their own and two English, bringing much needed supplies of all kinds: tools, ropes, hammers, nails, axes, mattocks and hatchets, as well as food and shelter. Also sailing on these ships, were many craftsmen skilled in the building of war machines. And there was one monk, a single Benedictine.

Brother Aldebert clung to the rail of a Genoese galley. Sea air lashed his face and rippled his black robe. He stared out, tears rolling down his cheeks. The Holy Land! he thought with mounting exhilaration. Praise be to God, I'm here, I'm finally here! He felt for the Abbot's letter, the one for Ramiro. Please, Saint Benedict, I pray he is safe.

"Look, Father Aldebert," said Louis the Carpenter. "The docks are deserted. The cranes sit idle. No one is here. And no damned heathen. God paves our way."

When Aldebert reached the port of Bari, he was shocked to find Louis, who he thought was killed in Nicomedia after it was overrun by Abul Kasim. Louis told him his story, how he and Mathilda had watched in helpless terror as a band of raiders snatched up Adele and tied her to a horse. And how the same cruel men came after them with their swords, how he watched in horror as they slaughtered poor Mathilda, and how her dying screams still haunted his dreams. He too, was pierced through and left for dead in a pool of his own blood. But shortly after the assault, a compassionate Greek farmer rescued him, nursing him back to health.

Since the loss of his wife and daughter, Louis was no longer the light-hearted, jovial man he used to be. He seldom smiled anymore and, every once in a while, his round, rough-shaven face clenched in a grimace, as if his old wounds had never healed.

"You're right, Louis," said Aldebert. "The place is deserted. I see no one, not even an animal."

"The bastards have fled in fear," said Louis with bitterness. "But the Captain says he won't venture to port until an armed escort arrives from Jerusalem. Look," he said, pointing down to a skiff leaving the ship. "There go the messengers now."

JERUSALEM

No sooner had Iftikhar finished his prayers at the Al-Aqsa Mosque, when his lieutenant rushed up the stairs of the Temple Mount to greet him.

"Commander!" he heaved. "Christian ships have arrived at Jaffa!"

Iftikhar stopped suddenly. Behind him, stood a servant carrying his prayer mat. He waved the man away. "How many?" he asked, as he continued down the steps.

"Six, my Lord," said the Sudanese, rushing after him. "And the Christian army already knows. We failed to stop their messengers."

"And where is our fleet?"

"The fleet awaits in Ascalon, Sahib, along with six hundred cavalry."

Iftikhar reached the plaza where a soldier waited with his horse. "Send them out!" he yelled as he mounted up. "Now!"

ATTACK ON EGYPTIANS

June 17

The Crusaders roared with delight when the Genoese messengers arrived with the good news. Godfrey at once dispatched a hundred knights and fifty infantry for the one-day journey to Jaffa, not realizing that six hundred crack Arab troops waited for them en route.

A vanguard of knights first sighted the Egyptians east of Ramla and, despite being vastly outnumbered, they charged forward, confident that God would lead them to victory. But they were almost wiped out to a man before the other knights, riding at a distance, received news of the battle and came galloping to their aid.

The Egyptians had heard the grisly tales about these invincible, bloodthirsty barbarians who ate human flesh, and they were nervous. At first, thinking there were only thirty of them who charged recklessly, they were confident in victory and fought with valor. But when they sighted a billowing cloud of dust on the horizon, they were certain it was an ambush and that thousands more of the murderous infidels were on their way.

In a thoughtless frenzy, the Egyptians turned and fled. But Godfrey's knights chased them down and, in the disarray, two hundred Arabs fell to the Crusader sword while the rest rushed back to the walls of Ascalon, leaving all their possessions behind. The knights took much plunder, including gold and horses, and spent some time dividing the spoils before moving on.

When they arrived at Jaffa, there was a great celebration on the ships. They spent the night in festive drinking and feasting, telling wild tales of their victories to the excited Genoese. But in the hazy mist of dawn, when they awoke with pounding heads, they found themselves almost surrounded by the Egyptian fleet from Ascalon.

In near panic, and before the Egyptians could amass their land forces, the Crusaders rushed to unload their cargo onto the docks, abandoning their ships to the enemy. They soon commandeered every pack animal they could find before rushing off to Jerusalem with their precious cargo.

With supplies at hand, a renewed vigor and cheerful confidence took root among the Crusaders. Local Christians told them where to find wood in the forests of Samaria, thirty miles away and, with the help of fifty Muslim slaves, they soon returned with a long train of timber-laden camels.

Iftikhar watched in dismay as the barbarians, with the help of Louis and other newly-arrived craftsmen, furiously constructed the finest war machines of the time—two huge towers, a massive battering ram with an iron-clad head, catapults, large crossbows, scaling ladders, and portable screens. To the northwest, he saw Godfrey's tower rise up slowly between the Jaffa Gate and Castle Al-Jalud while, to the south, Raymond's tower rose higher than the Zion Gate.

"Are the catapults ready?" he said, barely able to conceal his worry.

"Yes, my Lord. We have aimed five at the north tower and nine to the south."

Iftikhar was more concerned about the Zion Gate to the south than he was the north wall, where Godfrey was busy assembling his tower not far from Castle Al-Jalud. Iftikhar was confident that the walls and towers of Jerusalem were well fortified here. But there was no curtain wall to the south and he felt it was more vulnerable. "Are the walls prepared?" he asked again.

"Yes, Commander. We hung ropes and bags of straw to soften the blow of their missiles."

Iftikhar clenched his jaw. In the name of Allah and the Prophet, when will Al-Afdal arrive?

CRUSADER TAUNTS

Brother Aldebert scurried through the raucous crowds of fighting men milling outside the walls of Jerusalem. He recognized Robert of Flanders, who he had met in Bari, and was pleasantly surprised to find Drugo the Red still in his service. Drugo was now thirty-five, and still one of Robert's best warriors, although he was not as fast as he used to be. His hair was now cut short, more conducive for battle in the heat, and his ruddy face boasted many new scars and broken teeth.

"Have you seen Father Ramiro," Aldebert asked.

"No," said Drugo bluntly. "I haven't seen him since Gallipoli. Do you really think he's still alive?"

With a shudder, Aldebert remembered that fateful day when Turk slavers captured Ramiro near Gallipoli. "I believe he is, Sir Drugo. I received two letters from him. He must be in the city."

"I doubt that. Christians were ordered out."

"And where did they go?"

"Some joined the fight. Others to Bethlehem."

Aldebert felt a thrill. "Bethlehem! Maybe he's there—at the birthplace of Our Lord!" He looked around. "Uh... which way is Bethlehem?"

Godfrey and his men yelled and hooted from a safe distance outside the Jaffa Gate as they paraded a stumbling captive back and forth, a corpulent man dressed in the finest Dabiqi cloth. They had captured him on a foraging expedition near Bethlehem and thought he might prove useful.

Iftikhar recognized the man, it was the sheikh of Bayt Jala, who had come to him some months ago to pledge his allegiance. What were these barbarians shouting?

"Bring that foreign scribe to me!" he shouted to his lieutenant. "Quickly!"

Within minutes, Ramiro was dragged from his cell and shoved in front of Iftikhar, who pointed out from the battlement of the citadel. "Tell me what they say! What are they doing?"

The men laughed aloud as the fat sheikh stumbled and panted, his face bruised and swollen from a recent beating. Ramiro spotted two belligerent men screaming vile curses. One had red hair. The other was a giant of a man. Blessed Mary, Mother of God! "It's Drugo!" he shouted. "And there's Arles the Executioner!"

"That means nothing to me!" Iftikhar yelled. "Translate!"

Another man, one with long, black hair shrilled at the hostage. "Renounce your pagan faith before the walls of the Holy City! Accept the True Faith and live!" It was Arnulf Malecorne.

The sheikh shook his battered head. "I will not," he huffed. "May Allah and the Prophet be praised!"

"Then you die!" Arnulf screeched. Two men forced the man to his knees. Arnulf looked up at the Egyptians watching from the citadel. "Look! You pagan bastards!" he yelled to them. "Look and learn the fate of all who refuse to accept Christ as their savior!"

A tall squire raised his sword and with a single blow of his heavy blade, hacked off the sheikh's head. The men roared their approval, shouting more taunts and curses.

Ramiro watched in horror, interpreting all that he heard.

Iftikhar exploded in anger. "Get those cursed Christian priests! We will show them the fate of those who refuse Islam!"

Gerard and his fellow monks, six in all, were dragged limping to the battlement. Ramiro was shoved among them and they were made to stand exposed on the battlements, facing the invaders. Iftikhar's executioner stood behind them, holding his sword with both hands.

But few Crusaders noticed. They had finished their amusement and were dispersing, going back to work on their war machines. Drugo looked up to the citadel just as Iftikhar's swordsman sliced off the head of a monk and tossed it over the wall. "What in hell's blazes are they doing?" he asked Arles. "Are those monks?" He could see their dark robes, but these men had full heads of hair.

"Could be," said Arles. "But who gives a shit? Probably those Greek heretics!"

"Good riddance! It'll save us the trouble." Drugo said with a smirk and they turned away laughing.

Ramiro looked down. The slain monk's blood drained onto the smooth stones of the battlement where it pooled around his feet. He thought of Adele and worried how she would survive here alone. He heard the executioner step up behind him and he lifted his eyes to heaven, asking God to forgive his sins, to prepare his soul for life everlasting. But he heard the men laughing and looked down again. "Look Sahib!" he cried out just as the swordsman raised his blade to strike. "They walk away! It means nothing to them!"

Iftikhar raised his hand to stay the executioner's sword. "Do they care nothing for their fellow Christians?"

"Not for Roman Christians, Sahib!"

"What do you mean?"

"They think we are Romans, my Lord. Just as you hate the Sunni, these men hate the Romans."

Iftikhar nodded slowly, he understood the parallel. "Take them away!" he yelled to his guards. "And clean up this mess!"

A PROCESSION, JULY 8

Aldebert returned from Bethlehem in disappointment. For many days, he had visited the churches and dallied about the markets, hoping someone would have seen Ramiro. But no one remembered a dark-haired, heavyset Benedictine monk.

So he returned to the outskirts of Jerusalem feeling downcast. But before long, he was swept up in the righteous emotion of the moment. He heard that a French holy man had a vision of the dead Bishop Adhemar, in which the bishop had told them to purge themselves of uncleanliness and to turn away from their evil ways, to march around Jerusalem barefoot and, through the patronage of the saints, invoke the mercy of the Lord. And then, on the ninth day, he said, God would come to the aid of His servants and deliver them victory.

Aldebert believed it all. He eagerly joined the priests, monks, and bishops as they walked barefoot around the walls of Jerusalem. Arnulf Malecorne walked up front, raising his golden crucifix high above his head. The rest carried with them many crosses and relics of the saints, praying to Almighty God in high voices that He should not desert His chosen people in time of need. Behind them, a lengthy line of Christian warriors also trudged barefoot, carrying their standards high, piercing the air with trumpet blasts.

But of course, the Egyptians did not share the Crusader sentiments and shadowed the plodding procession as it made its way from the Damascus Gate, around the wall, and up to Mount Zion. They stood on the battlements blaring their own horns, screaming curses and mocking the Crusaders in every way. And, as at Maarat, they fixed makeshift crosses atop the walls in further mockery and abuse. They beat them with sticks and smashed them against the stone walls, some they spat on, others they pissed on while hurling the most vile insults. And when the Christians neared Mount Zion, which brought them closer to the city walls, they peppered them with arrows, killing some and wounding others.

Aldebert seethed in fury. *God-damned pagans! They will burn in hellfire for this! May God give us victory.* But as the procession climbed Mount Zion, his thoughts turned again to Father Ramiro. *Where is he? Do the heathen savages have him?* He shuddered at the thought.

The long line of fervent followers reached their destination at the Church of the

Blessed Mary, where Arnulf, seeking to reassure his loyal flock, raised his voice in sermon, reminding them that God would be merciful to all who followed Him, even to his grave.

In the dungeon, Ramiro and the other prisoners heard the trumpet blasts, the shouting and a loud commotion. "Does the battle begin?" he asked, frowning in worry.

No one replied, although some shrugged their shoulders before returning to their nervous prayers. Ibrahim prayed for a Muslim victory, even if it was to be a Shia one. Rabbi Moshe, who feared a slaughter, also prayed for the Arabs. But Aliphas, Gerard, and all the clergymen implored God for a Christian triumph.

GODFREY'S PLOY

July 14

The Egyptian army rushed across the Sinai Desert, led by Al-Afdal himself. Word of its approach soon reached the Crusaders and they knew they had to launch their attack on Jerusalem before it arrived.

For weeks, Iftikhar had watched Godfrey's men assemble their tall, wooden tower outside the western wall, near the Castle Al-Jalud. Now its black silhouette loomed higher than the wall itself. But he felt ready. The walls were strengthened and buffeted, his catapults and ammunition placed strategically, tar heated, firebrands dipped.

To the south, Raymond's tower was ready to advance toward the Zion Gate. Here too, Iftikhar's men watched and waited, ready with a massive store of stones, arrows and firebrands. And when they saw the Christians filling in the dry moat, they knew they were going to attack soon.

"Sahib! Sahib! Wake up!" shouted the Sudanese lieutenant.

Iftikhar jumped from his bed, rushing to the door.

"Sahib, they have moved a tower!"

"What do you mean?" Iftikhar asked in confusion. "They moved it to the wall?"

"No, Sahib. The barbarians have moved it east of the Damascus Gate!"

"The Damascus Gate? Impossible! That's almost a mile!"

The lieutenant bowed. "The impossible is done, my Lord. What shall we do?"

Iftikhar donned his armor, jumped on his mount, and galloped to the north wall. He had underestimated Godfrey's intelligence and resolve. Unknown to him, the Christian lord had built his tower in sections so that it could be easily taken down and reassembled. Its construction outside Castle Al-Jalud was a ruse. In the cover of night, the Crusaders had carried it piece by piece, using hundreds of men and slaves, to a site near the Damascus Gate where flatter ground sloped down toward the wall, favoring the tower's movement. Standing beside the tower was a huge battering ram and three giant catapults, all ready to provide cover fire.

"Move the catapults!" Iftikhar shouted frantically. "Move it all! Let's go! Let's go!" He cursed himself for his stupidity. The north section of wall east of the Damascus Gate was one of the weakest and had no towers nearby to defend it. Worse yet, the battlements were narrow and his catapults would be restricted in movement.

Raymond's tower at the Zion Gate did not share Godfrey's advantages. Even after filling in the dry moat so his tower could approach the wall, he still had rough ground to traverse, and it was all slightly uphill. He had no element of surprise and the Arabs had a vast arsenal waiting for him.

Godfrey knew he had the advantage, and the attack began. His enormous catapults began an incessant barrage of stones and fireballs against the wall and fortifications. Under cover, hundreds of men strained to move the massive battering ram, pushing it up to the curtain wall. Arrows rained down as they repeatedly pulled the heavy beam back before releasing it against the massive stones. By late afternoon, a section of wall collapsed, creating an enormous breach. As the ram smashed through, its own momentum drove it forward, rolling forward until it crashed into the main wall itself.

The Arabs drenched the ram in burning oil until it roared in flames and, in a desperate bid to save it, the French began to throw their precious water on it and tried to pull it out. But Godfrey stopped them.

The ram had created a breach but now it blocked that same breach and was jammed between the curtain wall and the city wall. Hence, it blocked the path of the tower, which was the whole purpose of the advance. Godfrey realized their best hope was to let the ram burn to ash in order to clear the way. So he ordered his men to save their water and add more fire to it instead.

It did not take long for Iftikhar to see their ploy and, in a bizarre reversal of tactics, he ordered his men to put the fire out and they started to throw buckets of water over it. But the flames were so intense by this time, the water had little effect.

Meanwhile at the Zion Gate, Raymond's men were under a deadly barrage of stones hurled from Iftikhar's catapults. And as they attempted to move the tower to the wall, thousands of arrows and firebrands fell on them like a hail from hell, pounding the tower relentlessly. The men scurried around it putting out fire after fire, but they faltered under the weight of the Arab assault and, before dusk, pulled the damaged tower back to safety. As the sky dimmed, the battle stopped, and both camps settled into an uneasy night of fear.

THE FALL OF JERUSALEM

July 15, 1099

In the smoky light of dawn, both towers began another advance against the walls. And the Arabs unleashed another deadly hail of arrows, firebrands, and stones against Raymond's tower. Men shouted in defiance amid screams of death as stones pounded against them in a savage, incessant barrage. Balls of fire exploded in their midst and the air choked with burning tar and pitch. Raymond's tower began to burn and fracture in the hellish din of battle, and then suddenly, it collapsed.

At the north wall, Godfrey kept up the bombardment with his catapults while his men sweated and heaved against the three-story tower, inching it toward the wall. Arrows riddled them and balls of fire burned them alive, their dying screams piercing the summer dawn. A thick, putrid smoke hung about like a black fog, stifling all breath. Inside the tower, hundreds of men waited, including Drugo, Otto, and Arles. Godfrey himself was on the top floor as the cumbersome structure swayed and rocked toward the city wall. Arnulf's golden crucifix glittered from the tower roof as the Arab catapults pounded the wattle-and-hide covers. A stone crashed straight through the wattle, smashing the skull of a man standing next to Godfrey.

As the tower edged closer to the wall, Iftikhar's catapults began to lose their effect. The tight confinement of the battlements made it impossible to adjust their range for close encounters. The tall structure steadily approached, soon looming high above the wall. Now Godfrey and his men used the advantage of height to pelt the defenders with their own firebrands and missiles.

Iftikhar's men fought back with a vengeance, throwing everything they had at the tower, now only a few paces from the wall. But the French firebrands had ignited the wooden infrastructure of the lower wall as well as nearby buildings and, in minutes, the choking smoke and searing flames drove the Arabs back. Godfrey's tower hit the wall, the side came down and his men stormed out.

Drugo, Otto, and Arles charged out screaming their war cries as a flurry of arrows peppered their ranks. Arles staggered back—an arrow stuck in his throat. He pulled at it madly, choking on his blood. In an instant, another struck him right between the eyes and the huge man tumbled off the battlements. But few noticed in the mad melee and more warriors continued to pour out of the tower by the hundreds, hooting and hollering.

The Muslims faltered, pulling back in hopeless terror. The Christians charged into them, hacking and chopping with fanatic fury, soon clearing the battlements of all resistance. Now heady with the scent of victory, they stormed through the city like a pack of wild dogs, thrusting and stabbing their way through the screaming streets.

To the south, Raymond kept up his attack with catapults and arrows but he had lost the advantage. Then, suddenly, the Arab defense stopped. The walls were abandoned. A heaving messenger ran up to him. "Godfrey breached the wall!" he shouted. "Attack!"

With shouts of joy, Raymond's men rushed forward with their tall ladders, scrambling over the Zion Gate.

Iftikhar saw all was lost. He jumped on his horse, racing through the city to the Tower of David along with his officers and guards. They locked themselves inside the citadel and waited for the worst. Meanwhile his valiant men rallied around the Dome of the Rock, putting up fierce resistance, but the Crusaders soon cut them down by the sheer weight of their numbers.

French, Germans, Normans, and Flemings raged down every street, killing everyone and everything in their path. They smashed down the doors of every building, slaughtering women and children, chopping and stabbing with knife and sword, seizing infants by their feet, splattering their skulls against stone walls. They spared no one. The blood of their victims drenched the narrow cobblestone streets and poured into the gutters.

The Jews ran for the safety of the synagogue, locking themselves inside, cowering in terror. They yelled out the windows, begging for mercy. But the Crusaders scoffed at their pleas, setting fire to the building, laughing aloud at the hellish screams of those burning alive.

Hours later, when the long trail of terrified shrieks and screams finally subsided, the Soldiers of God began to pillage, grabbing all they could. Men ran to and fro over the heaps of corpses, slitting open bellies and groping into guts for swallowed gold and coins.

No one in the dungeon spoke, but Ramiro still had to shout over the blood-curdling wails and screams of the victims. "It's a massacre!" he said, wringing his hands. He thought of Adele, sick with worry.

"The Protectors of the Faith have arrived and conquered," said Gerard with satisfaction.

"Protectors?" yelled one of the rabbis. "They are nothing but butchers! And for what? To gaze upon the sepulcher of your crucified bastard!"

Gerard lunged at the rabbi but the other rabbis stood as one to beat him off. "Scourge of Christ!" screamed Gerard as his monks held him back. "You will burn in hellfire!"

"Hell is all yours, you Gentile shit!"

"God bless the Pope of Rome!" Gerard taunted. "And his almighty victory over the pagans and the unclean!"

"God damn the Satan of Rome and his wicked ways!" the rabbis shouted back.

"Enough!" yelled Ramiro as he stepped between them. "Enough! Are we going to start killing each other too?" The men settled back, still seething. And as the clamor in the cell died down, so did the din of battle outside. He went to the cell door. "Guards! Guards!" But there was no answer. He returned to his seat, waiting in the frightening silence.

While Tancred took Castle Al-Jalud and Godfrey laid claim to the Temple Mount and the Emir's Palace, Raymond circled the Tower of David. He wanted to rule Jerusalem and was well aware of the strategic importance of the citadel. He sent a messenger to Iftikhar, who was still holed up inside with his guards, and asked him to relinquish the tower, promising him safe conduct out of the city.

"Can we trust the old man, Sahib?" asked the lieutenant.

Iftikhar smiled in pity. "Trust? No, there is no trust. But what choice do we have? We will surely die if we stay here, but we may live if we accept." So he agreed to Raymond's terms and surrendered the tower. Much to his surprise, the old one-eyed man lived up to his bargain, giving them safe passage to Ascalon.

Ramiro jumped to his feet when a group of bloodied knights rushed into the jailhouse. The stark-eyed warriors, panting from their slaughter and still brandishing swords, milled about the iron bars silently, staring into the cells, their clothes drenched in the fresh blood of their victims, their hair and beards dripping in heavy, red beads. "What goes here?" one asked. "Give us your gold!"

"Praise the Lord!" Gerard shouted at them. "Soldiers of God! Free us from these pagan bars! I am Brother Gerard of the Church of Saint Mary and these are my blessed monks," he said pointing to his men, still dressed in black robes.

Bishop Aliphas went to his knees, joining his hands in prayer, his large cross dangling from his fingers.

One of the soldiers went to the nearby guardroom to grab the keys. Eventually, he unlatched the door and opened it. "Give us your money!"

Gerard rushed toward him. "But we are prisoners, we have nothing." The soldier pushed him away and he stumbled backwards.

Four other men charged into the cell, eyeing the prisoners with a loathing sneer. "Look what we have here. A pack of sarding Hebrews!" But only Gerard and Ramiro understood his words.

Rabbi Moshe understood their gestures and opened his hands. "We have nothing," he said in Arabic. The soldier did not understand him, nor did he care. With no further provocation, he brought his sword down on the old rabbi's head, splitting his skull. Moshe slumped dead to the floor and the other soldiers moved forward for the kill. The remaining rabbis, now splattered in Moshe's blood, began to weep, bowing their heads in prayer.

"Stop!" yelled Ramiro as he rushed forward in shock. By habit, he had spoken in Arabic and the blood-drenched knight, thinking he was an Arab, swung his arm out hard, smashing him across the head. Ramiro flew back against the wall, bashing his skull on the rough-hewn stones. He collapsed unconscious, bleeding at the temple. The soldier raised his sword to run him through.

"Stop!" Gerard cried. "Don't you see his cross? He's one of us! He's a Christian!"

HOLY SEPULCHER

Before the sun set below the Judean Hills, the so-called soldiers of God gathered en masse at the Holy Sepulcher, the very place for which they had given so many lives and so many years. They surrounded the aedicule, their hair and beards matted with half-dried blood, their clothes crusted hard with it. In both hands, they carried hefty bags of loot, gripping them greedily, even as they fell to their knees rejoicing and weeping and giving thanks to God, victorious and triumphant.

Arnulf Malecorne and the priests raised their voices in a ringing song of exaltation and the soldiers joined in, rasping their praise as hot tears streaked through the blood and ash on their cheeks. Arnulf made loud offerings and supplications to the Lord. "This is the day which the Lord has made," he cried, "let us rejoice and be glad in it! This is a new day, a new joy, the Holy Sepulcher has been liberated!" The filthy soldiers howled in ecstasy and Brother Aldebert fell to his knees as the savage euphoria of the moment overwhelmed him.

When Aldebert had first rushed into Jerusalem after the slaughter, he was exhilarated by the glorious victory. But even his wildest joy did not prepare him for what he saw. He was not a soldier. In fact, he was still haunted by the death of Wiker the Blade some years before. So when he saw the mounds of bloodied corpses and had to step through the grisly heaps of hacked bodies and severed limbs to make his way through the city, his zealous sensibility was soon overcome. He fled back through the gate, heaving up his breakfast on the way.

But he soon heard from others about the gathering at the Church of the Holy Sepulcher. And so, with envy and fascination, he quickly summoned some fortitude, making his way through the gruesome, desolate city. Now, as great tears streamed down his thin face, he could hardly believe he was actually in the presence of the Tomb of Christ, the holiest place on earth. God had delivered them a great victory, as was His will. He lifted his tonsured head to the high ceiling of the rotunda and thanked all the saints, Mother Mary, the Most Highs, Jesus, and all the hosts of heaven.

9 - Aftermath

Jerusalem

July 16, 1099

Ramiro opened his eyes, staring up at the dismal, gray ceiling. All was quiet. He put a hand to his throbbing head, feeling a mass of dried blood stuck in his hair. Confused and trembling, he strained to his feet, putting his back against the wall to steady himself while rubbing his face with both hands, trying to compose his thoughts.

As he pulled his hands away, his vision cleared and he soon discerned the macabre scene sprawled out before him in the murky light. Moshe and the other rabbis were all dead, their bodies strewn across the floor, drenched red with blood. Two were beheaded and others chopped to pieces. Ibrahim was dead too, his belly sliced open. There was barely a part of him that was recognizable. But Bishop Aliphas, Gerard, and the other clergymen were not among them.

He turned his head away in a dry heave of revulsion, but there was nothing to come out. He stumbled to the open cell door, keeping steady against the wall, making his way to the stairs leading up to the lower chamber of Castle Al-Jalud. There was only one thing on his mind, and that was Adele. Iftikhar said she was safe. What did he mean? Was she here—in the castle?

It was strangely quiet except for a distant scream, quickly silenced. He made his way up the thin flight of stone steps, entering the lower hall. Mutilated bodies spread across the wide, blood-soaked floor; soldiers, clerks, servants, men and women. "By the blood of Christ!" he blurted out in disgust. But his eyes crept back reluctantly to the horrific scene. He had to know. Was she among them? He stepped between the corpses, looking at each one, searching every room. Bodies lay everywhere but, with a skewed sense of relief, she was not one of them.

He saw no sign of the invaders and wondered where they had gone. Did they lay in wait for victims? He grabbed a short sword from among the bodies and, from another, he took a thick vest of leather armor. His thoughts turned to his rooms on David Street. Maybe she was there. He ran out into the street.

But he was no sooner out the door when he tripped on a knee-high stack of corpses and fell face first into the slimy, gory remains. He jumped up in horror but slipped again on blood and guts. Slowly, he pulled himself up. The gruesome sight before him boggled his mind. Maimed and disfigured bodies were piled deep on every street. Mounds of torsos, heads, limbs, hands, feet and guts clogged his every move. The air reeked of burned flesh and a thick, acrid smoke choked his lungs. His head reeled. He staggered from shock.

Covered in blood from his fall among the corpses, he worked his way down the street brandishing the short sword. He passed the Church of the Holy Sepulcher, where he heard men singing inside. A few Crusaders milled about outside but paid him no heed. He made his way to the building on David Street and rushed up the stairs.

The rooms were a mess. His books and papers were scattered everywhere, the furniture smashed. "Adele!" he shouted in desperation, dashing into the bedroom. The mattress was slit open and their clothes thrown about. She was not here.

Stunned by the turn of events, he sat on the battered remains of his desk and lowered his head, trying to collect his thoughts. He looked down on his letters and books and stooped to the floor where, in trance-like movements, he began to pick them up, as if somehow they could help him piece his life back together. Cold tears rolled down his cheeks, streaking through the blood on his face.

In a moment of dread, Ramiro left the room, running to check on Jameel and his wife Layla. On his way, he saw that every door was smashed through, all the houses ransacked, the churches too. He found Jameel's building and dashed up the littered stairs to their rooms.

The door was open. He entered cautiously, the place had been plundered, everything smashed or overturned. He worked his way through the rooms and, to his horror, soon discovered their mutilated bodies in the bedroom, the baby too. He clenched his jaw, stumbling back out the door. "Oh dear Lord, they were supposed to leave!" he cried aloud in a strained voice. "I told them to leave!" He put his hands to his face. "A Christian family! How could this happen?" He tried to steady himself but sank to his knees, sobbing.

Slaves heaved corpses and limbs onto a growing mound of flesh and bone rising steadily in the valleys just outside the city walls. Then, with bowed heads, they slowly returned to the blood-caked streets to refill their carts with more wretched cargo.

Ramiro watched them work while he checked the corpses. He noticed a shock of red hair hanging from a cart and yelled out for them to stop. Now inured to grisly visions of the dead, he pulled on the hair, drawing out a severed head to wipe the face with a rag. It was not her.

All day, he rushed back and forth to inspect the pyramids of the dead, but it was too much. There were too many. For a full week, he kept up this gruesome task, returning to his barren and demolished room after sunset for a few hours of fitful sleep.

When the worst was over, Christians who had fled the city began to return. Ramiro stood watch by the Jaffa Gate hoping to see Adele or anyone else he knew. People streamed in by the hundreds, holding scarves to their faces to mask the putrid smoke of burning flesh billowing from raging pyres in the valley below.

He stopped a priest who was entering the gate. "From where do you come?"

"I stayed in Abu Ghosh," said the man.

"Is that where all the Christians went?"

"Not all. They spread out to surrounding villages, staying wherever they could. I believe most went to Bethlehem."

"Have you seen a red-haired woman? Pale complexion, some freckles. Speaks poor Arabic."

The priest shook his head. "I'm sorry. I've seen no one like that. But I haven't had much time to notice people."

"How far is Bethlehem?"

"About six miles south of the Zion Gate."

"Is it safe there?"

The man shrugged with a despondent sigh. "As safe as anywhere if you're a Christian. The Crusaders seized it. A young man by the name of Tancred rules the place."

The Advocate

Days after the slaughter, the Crusader nobility and clergymen met in the Al-Aqsa Mosque on the Temple Mount, a sacred place hastily remade into an opulent palace for Godfrey. It was a chaotic scene, nearly everyone was talking while others shouted to be heard.

The Bishop of Albara, an ally of Raymond of Toulouse, raised his voice above them all. "Count Raymond deserves to rule Jerusalem! He outranks you all. And he's the one who led us south to begin this Holy Crusade!"

Arnulf Malecorne, now Godfrey's chaplain, jumped to his feet. "But it was Godfrey who breached the walls of Jerusalem! It should be his right to rule!"

Another bishop spoke up, red-faced. "The holiest city on earth should have no secular king. It must be ruled by the Mother Church!" Most of the clergy agreed in loud voices.

Aldebert nodded his head but had no courage to speak.

Robert of Flanders stood up. "We need someone to command the military," he bellowed. "We should choose one of us and I say Duke Godfrey deserves the position." Many knights nodded their approval.

Count Raymond held a hand high to quiet the men. His long, gray hair hung loosely to his shoulders. He glared around the room with his one eye and the crowd fell silent. His gaze settled on Godfrey and he raised his voice in indignation. "Have you all forgotten that it is I who first met with the Pope himself to organize and lead this Crusade? And that I was chosen as Commander-in-chief?"

The men fell silent for a moment, some murmuring among themselves. They knew Pope Urban had never publicly proclaimed Raymond, as was custom. Furthermore, the Count had lost credibility since he failed at Arqah. And in the siege of Jerusalem, it was his tower that failed at Zion Gate.

But Raymond persisted. "I remind you all again that we will need the support of the Greek King if we are ever to persist in this endeavor. And I'm the one who established detente with the King while others sought nothing but to satisfy their selfish ambitions!" His look fell again to Godfrey.

Godfrey yelled back in a rage. "You are one to talk of selfish ambition! Ever since this crusade began, you have done nothing but attempt to covet territory for yourself! And what has the Greek King done for us? Our supplies were delivered by the Genoese and the English!"

"Yes!" Raymond bellowed. "But you know they sailed from Greek ports with Greek supplies!"

"Enough!" Arnulf intervened with new courage. "Let the men vote. They will decide."

"But no one will be king," said the Bishop of Albara. "Whoever we elect will serve only as Protector of the Holy City."

And so it was, much to the seething anger of Raymond, that Godfrey was elected to the newly created position of Advocate of the Holy Sepulcher, and he wasted little time consolidating his power.

BETHLEHEM

Ramiro washed away the blood and grime in a basin of water. He found some clean clothes among the rubble of Jerusalem and donned his leather armor once more. Buckling his sword with a shoulder strap, he headed off to Bethlehem on foot.

The road was eerily vacant except for a few Christians traveling back to Jerusalem. And once in a while, a work gang of Arab captives passed by, all bound together with ropes and whipped along by jeering soldiers.

When Ramiro arrived in Bethlehem, he saw Tancred's banner fluttering above the Church of Nativity. The young Crusader from Italy had made his headquarters here. Shunned by his uncle Bohemond in Antioch and knowing he would never rule Jerusalem, Tancred worked to lay claim to Bethlehem and the surrounding region.

Ramiro entered the church, wandering about between the marble pillars lining the apse, questioning all he met. Most were Christians exiled from Jerusalem before the assault. But many were leery to return. True, they were Christian, but they were still shocked and appalled by the slaughter of innocents and the unbelievable cruelty of these savage men from the West.

"Have you seen a red-haired woman?" Ramiro asked a new arrival. "She's French. About this tall."

"There's an old hag who lives near the well," said the man. "She has red hair."

Ramiro found the house and lingered near the door to draw courage. He knocked. An old woman answered. "What do you want?" she asked curtly. Red hair with gray streaks peeked out of her shawl. It was not Adele.

"Sorry to disturb you, Sayyidah, but I am looking for a French woman with red hair."

"Franj you say?"

"Yes, have you seen her?"

"There's a new one who stays at the house of Abel."

"A man?"

The old woman cackled. "Of course he's a man, you fool." She slammed the door shut.

Ramiro approached the door of Abel's house. His palms sweat and he felt short of breath. The closer he got to the door, the more his heart pounded. By the time he was ready to knock, he felt faint. The blood drained from his head and he reached out to steady himself against the door jam. He knocked.

A young man in a bright white tunic opened the door a crack. "Peace be upon you, Sayyid. What do you want?" he asked cautiously.

"Peace to you. I am Ramiro of Cluny and I'm looking for a red-haired woman. She's French, pale face. Goes by the name of Adele. Have you seen her?"

"You are Ramiro?" asked the man.

"Yes, yes! You have seen her?"

The man motioned to him. "I am Abel. Please, come in."

Ramiro stepped into the tidy room, colorfully decorated with silk cushions and rich carpets. "Where is she?" he asked impatiently.

"I think she returned to Jerusalem."

"Praise the Lord!" said Ramiro loudly, barely able to contain himself. "But how did she get here?"

"She came with my uncle, Pakrad."

"Pakrad? The Armenian priest?"

"Yes. Do you know him?"

"Yes, yes. When did she return to Jerusalem?"

"Just yesterday. She left by herself. I warned her of the dangers but she would not listen. She's very worried. She's looking for you."

JERUSALEM

Ramiro ran most of the way back to Jerusalem, stopping only when he was out of breath. He hurried through the gates, ran down David Street and rushed up the stairs to their rooms—but she was not there. He stood still, trying to think where she would be. "Pakrad!" he shouted aloud. "The Monastery of Saint James!" He flew down the stairs, heading for Armenian Street.

The empty streets had been stripped of corpses, leaving thick, dried pools of blood over the flagstones. The hot air stank of it. He arrived at the monastery gasping from his run, only to find the door locked. He banged on it with his fist. There was no answer. He banged again.

The door slat opened but he saw no face. "What do you want?" asked a man's voice.

"Is Adele here?" he choked, fighting back tears.

"You are Ramiro?"

"Yes, is she here?"

He could hear the latch fall. The door opened. "Come in. Quickly!"

He stepped into the cool interior. It was the same place where he had met Jameel many months ago and, once again, he felt a sharp pang of sorrow for the bright young man and his family so senselessly slaughtered. The place was dark. "Are you Pakrad?"

"Yes," said the man as he shut the door and latched it. His big ears poked out from a shag of brown hair and his eyes bulged in a disarming manner. "Come with me."

Ramiro followed him through the rubble cluttering the long hall. After descending a short flight of stairs, they came to the monk's cells. Pakrad knocked on one of the doors.

"Who is it?" asked a familiar voice.

Ramiro tried to reply but choked on his words.

"It's Pakrad. There is someone to see you."

The door opened a little. Adele held her oak mace in one hand and nodded to Pakrad before looking at Ramiro. At first, she was taken back, dressed as he was in a bloodied leather vest and carrying a sword at his side. But when she met his tearful eyes, she dropped the mace, slapped her hands to her face, and burst into a sob. Ramiro sprang forward to embrace her.

"Tell me what happened," said Ramiro when they were alone.

Adele kissed him again as he held her close. "When I went to Madteos shop, he was gone. So I went to his house and it was deserted. Everything was upturned or destroyed, it looked like it was looted. But Pakrad was there."

"What was he doing there?"

"I don't know. I think he was looking for something. Maybe the cross. He scared the wits out of me. He said that Iftikhar's askari had ransacked the place just before he arrived. He thought they were rogue soldiers looking for gold before the battle." She rested her head against his shoulder. "I told him who I was, that I had come for the cross. But he said he knew nothing about the bargain you made with Madteos. That's when we heard the soldiers coming back. He told me to run but I couldn't return to our rooms, so he took me to Bethlehem, to the safety of his nephew's house."

"Did you meet Madteos there?"

"Yes, briefly. He said he didn't have the cross. He said he barely had time to flee with the clothes on his back. But he told Pakrad where it was hidden in his house and said we could have it. He said it was evil, that it brought a curse on his house." She stroked the back of Ramiro's head. "Is it cursed, Ramiro?"

"No, my love, it is not cursed. It is merely a thing among accursed men. Did he say exactly where it is?"

"No. But perhaps we can go with Pakrad to get it."

"Should I bother?" He shook his head. "It doesn't matter. The whole affair has been a failure. And what meaning will the cross have now? Patriarch Symeon is dead, they say." He lowered his head in thought. "Do you still have the four dinar from Bishop Aliphas?"

"Yes," she said, reaching for a purse under her cloak.

Ramiro stopped her. "Keep it, but tell no one," he warned. "We should return it to the Bishop."

Adele drew back. "If he's still alive."

"If not, then it belongs to the Church."

"The Church?" Adele scoffed. "You've seen what happens to gold in the Church. It fills the bags of these thieves!" She had a fierce look, catching Ramiro by surprise. "And since the cross is so near," she remonstrated, "I say we should go to Pakrad's and retrieve it. We could exchange it for a house and a new life in France."

"It's not mine, Adele."

"Then whose is it?"

"Well, it belongs to the Patriarch."

"You mean the one who's dead?"

"Well," Ramiro sighed. "I suppose we should make one last effort to retrieve it, although we should return it to Abbot Hugh."

Adele cursed under her breath.

Quest for a Monk

Aldebert asked every Crusader he met, but no one had seen a Benedictine monk named Ramiro. He kept up his efforts, asking exiled Christians as they returned to the many churches and monasteries of Jerusalem. Someone told him the Monastery of Santa Maria was Benedictine and he happily made his way through the gate.

"May I see the Abbot?" Aldebert asked in the dim foyer after he had introduced himself.

"Not at this time, Brother Aldebert," said the monk. "He has just returned from exile and is not feeling well. Can I be of any assistance?"

"I am looking for a Cluny monk by the name of Ramiro. Have you heard of him?"

"Ramiro? Oh yes, everyone has heard of him."

Aldebert lit up. "Really? Do you know where he is?"

"I have no idea, Brother, but he was well-known for his healing skills. He came to work here often. Alas, I have not seen him since we were expelled."

"Is there anyone else I could ask?"

The monk scratched the back of his head. "You could ask Brother Gerard, he was the superior at the hospice."

"Is he here?"

"Oh, I'm afraid he is no longer with us. He had a falling out with the Abbot."

"You mean he renounced the order?"

The monk leaned closer, eager to share his gossip. "Yes. A scandalous affair, I fear. Brother Gerard tended to many of the sick and wounded after the battle. He became very popular with the French and they offered him many gifts and rewards. But when the Abbot asked him to donate it all to the monastery, as a monk should, he refused and left in a huff. Needless to say, the Abbot was quite upset."

"Where is Gerard now?"

"The French gave him a building next to the Church of Saint John. He started his own hospice with the money he received. He now calls himself a disciple of Saint Augustine."

"Thank you, Brother," said Aldebert as he backed to the door. "Thank you." He rushed out.

ARNULF'S OBSESSIONS

Arnulf Malecorne set up home in the Palace of the Patriarch, all the while relishing his new-found power. Just two weeks after the conquest, a council of bribed bishops appointed him the new Patriarch of Jerusalem. His friendship with Godfrey had paid off and he was vaulted over the heads of more senior clergy, who were infuriated because of his low birth and his seedy reputation as a drunkard and a womanizer.

Meanwhile others, especially the Provencals under Raymond, saw his nomination as a Norman plot in which Godfrey made sure his own men held the reins of power. And the few remaining Greek Orthodox were outraged that their own candidates were not even considered for the position, which they felt was their traditional right.

And so, by the time Arnulf was making himself comfortable in the Palace, he had few friends indeed. And not one to forget a slight easily, he seethed with resentment at the many rebuffs, secretly vowing revenge. In short time, he put his own acquaintances into positions of power and, thinking enthusiastically of the tremendous income from church tithes, plotted to usurp the long-held authority of the Greek Church. Even among his own flock, he began to tighten the screws of office. Soon, the lewd stories about his nightly capers, which were given so much currency on their long march, were quickly silenced.

Nonetheless, Arnulf realized in his scheming mind that he needed the support of his countrymen. But his golden crucifix, forged in Tripoli, had failed to rally the faithful and, because of its association with Raymond of Toulouse, he feared it would be discredited, just as the so-called holy lance was. He needed something else, something to bring him closer to the glory of God, something of great spiritual authority. He needed a powerful, holy relic.

"What have you found?" Arnulf asked in the privacy of his den.

"One of the men says he has a vial of the blood of Saint John," said Lothar, a cringing man with balding, blonde hair and a wrinkled face. "And another claims he took a vial of the milk of Mother Mary from one of the churches."

Arnulf shook his head in displeasure. "But can we verify these finds?" he asked painfully. "It's got to be something genuine. Something to which everyone will give credence."

"Some say the bones of Saint James are here, Your Eminence."

Arnulf's sallow eyes narrowed in thought. He tucked his greasy black hair behind one ear. "No, that won't do. Our men believe the bones of Saint James are kept at Santiago de Compostela. I need something no one will contest. What of this rumor about a cross?"

Lothar rubbed his rough, stubbled face. "I asked the Greeks but they won't say much. All I've heard is that a piece of the True Cross was hidden away when the pagans took the city years ago."

Arnulf's eyes sparkled. "Praise God! That's what I need! The True Cross! We must find it!"

"But no one seems to know its whereabouts," said Lothar.

"They know," Arnulf said ominously. "The heretics know where it is and we will find it. We will make them talk."

"It seems that someone else was looking for it too, Your Eminence. A holy man, a Christian."

"What do you mean?"

"That monk at the hospice—what's his name?"

"You mean the physician, Gerard? He was looking for it?"

"No, no, but I asked him if he knew of any relics. He doesn't seem to know any more than we do, except that he mentioned a holy man, a monk actually, who was in the city before the battle."

"So?"

"Well, he said the man was looking for a cross... a particular cross," said Lothar, shifting his eyes. "Said he had a drawing of it."

Arnulf sprung to his feet. "Where is this man?"

"I don't know, Your Eminence."

"Find him! And send Gerard to me first thing in the morning."

"Yes, Your Eminence."

Arnulf lowered his voice a little. "But before you go, bring one of those pagan girls to me... so that I may convert the wench to the True Faith."

Aldebert dashed over to meet Louis the Carpenter, who was busy overseeing repairs to the Zion Gate in the southern wall. He found him near an oxcart full of fresh beams of wood. The workers scurried back and forth, hammering, sawing, and mixing mortar.

"Louis! Louis!" Aldebert shouted as he ran toward him.

Louis held up his arm, stopping him in his tracks. He turned to yell to his workmen. "Put your backs into it, men! The bloody pagans will return and we don't want them getting in the same way we did!" He turned back to Aldebert, who seemed flustered, but he was often flustered. "What is it, Father Aldebert?"

"Father Ramiro is here!" he shouted.

Louis' stern face broke into a broad smile. "Praise the Lord! You have seen him?"

"Well... no. But I went to see Brother Gerard at the hospice and he said Ramiro was in the dungeon with him before the attack began. Said he left him unconscious but alive!"

"Is he alright? Where is he now?"

"No one has seen him since. But he must be alive because Gerard said he sent someone back to get him—but he was gone!" Aldebert squealed like a giddy child.

"By the grace of God," said Louis.

"Yes, yes!" said Aldebert bubbling with anticipation. "And I have more good news, Louis. Very good news!"

Louis' brow furrowed over his big nose. He managed a half smile. "And pray tell, what is that, Father?"

"Gerard said Ramiro was with a woman." He nodded as he spoke, licking his lips at the end of every sentence.

"Is this a good thing?" Louis asked.

Aldebert bobbed with his whole body. "And her name is Adele!"

Louis gawked, his face turning ashen white. "Do not jest with me, Aldebert," he said, glaring with such intensity that Aldebert took a step back.

Aldebert's smile faded. "I do not jest, Louis. That is what he said."

"Dear Jesus!" Louis blurted as he tried to steady himself against the wagon. But he fell to his knees anyway. "My daughter is alive! Blessed Mary, Mother of God!" He made the sign of the cross on his forehead and clasped his hands together. Tears welled in his eyes as he looked heavenward. "Thank you, Lord Jesus!" he shouted, springing to his feet again. "We've got to find them!"

"We will, Louis, we will. Brother Gerard gave me his address. Come with me!"

"Wait," said Louis. "I can't leave these men alone. But we'll be finished soon, it's almost dusk. Help me pick up the tools and we'll pack the carts."

"You have met this holy man?" asked Arnulf. "The one asking about a gold cross?"

"Yes, Your Eminence," said Brother Gerard, nodding his bald head. "Many times. He said he was a Benedictine monk from Cluny."

"From Cluny?"

"Yes, Your Eminence, but he dresses like a scribe."

"How can you be so sure he's a monk?"

"He seemed quite knowledgeable of Cluny and was a good medicina. And just yesterday a Benedictine monk from Bari came asking about him."

Arnulf began to feel anxious. "And you say he showed you a drawing of this cross?"

"Yes, but that was some time ago."

"Can you describe it?"

"I remember that he said it was made of wood but framed in gold."

Arnulf leaned forward, trying to control his mounting apprehension. "Made of wood? Is it a piece of the True Cross?"

"I do not know, Your Eminence, he did not say."

"Did the man ever find this cross?"

"I don't think so. At least not when I saw him last."

"I hear he was called a holy man. Why is this?"

Gerard told him about the incident with Rabbi Moshe and how he became popular with all faiths in the city.

Arnulf leaned back in his elaborate chair. He put a hand to his chin. "You saw him consort with these pagans?"

Gerard nodded. "He went to a number of their festivities during his time here."

"What's his name?"

"Ramiro, Your Eminence."

"Where does he live?"

"Why is a Cluny monk looking for a particular cross in Jerusalem?" Arnulf asked Lothar when they were alone.

"It does seem odd, Your Eminence."

Arnulf paced back and forth. "He knows something. But we must be careful about this. Abbot Hugh of Cluny is a powerful man ... and a cunning one. He likes to get his greedy fingers into every pie. I'm sure he would like nothing more than to have the True Cross for his abbey. We must find it first!"

"I sent two men to search for this Ramiro... and to scour his rooms for the drawing. But they have yet to return. If he doesn't have it as you say, Your Eminence, perhaps we should ask the Greek priests again."

"Yes, Lothar, but this time we will not be so polite. Bring that Greek bishop to me. The one they call Aliphas. We will squeeze him until he squeals like a pig."

Bishop Aliphas tried to be courageous, but the Crusaders had a lot of practice with torture and terror and they soon had him wailing like a child. "I know nothing of the True Cross!" he cried, sputtering blood. "I swear! There is nothing hidden!"

Lothar brought his knife up under Aliphas' nose. "I'm going to slice your nose off for lying, heretic!"

Aliphas' eyes were on the blade. "It's all rumor! I swear!"

"And what of this man called Ramiro?" asked Arnulf. "Did he come to you about this cross? Did he show you his drawing?"

"Yes, as I said, Your Excellency. When I last saw him he said he had found it and I gave him money to retrieve it. But... but then the battle began."

"Did he say who had it?"

"He said the man was an Armenian, that's all."

"Armenian? And where would I find a filthy Armenian in Jerusalem?"

"Most fled. But some returned to their positions at the Church of the Holy Sepulcher, Excellency. And others may be at the Monastery of Saint James."

Bishop Aliphas, badly beaten and bruised, was then ordered out of the Church of the Holy Sepulcher, as were all other Christians of the Greek, Armenian, Nestorian, or Jacobite followings. Arnulf not only loathed all those of other denominations, but he also feared them. And he was convinced the True Cross lay hidden among the stones of the Church. He wanted to make sure none of them retrieved it. So he interned them all and called them, one by one, for a brutal interrogation.

DAVID STREET

The building on David Street was strangely quiet as Ramiro and Adele climbed the stairs to their rooms. Gone were the sounds of children playing, of people laughing. Gone were the aromas of home cooking and potted flowers. Only bare rooms remained, despoiled, empty of life, stinking of rotten flesh and blood. Ramiro was about to open the door but it was already ajar. "What in heaven's name?"

"What's wrong?" asked Adele.

"Somebody has been here since I cleaned up." He swung the door open. "Blessed Mary! Not again!" The place had been ransacked and, once again, his books and papers were strewn across the floor, every drawer and every corner disturbed, loose bricks pried out.

"Whoever they were, they were looking for something. What the devil could it be?"

Adele went to the bedroom. "What a mess! Look at my clothes! They're filthy. Oh no, they're ruined."

"I saved what I could," he said.

"Do you think they were looking for the cross?" she asked, folding salvageable clothing into piles. "But how would they know?"

"I'm not sure," he replied after a pause. "But if that is the case, they must think me a fool to leave it behind. They must have wanted something else."

He wandered over to his broken desk, bending to pick up books and papers. He said nothing for a long while.

"What is it?" Adele wondered at his silence.

"Look at this. Every book has been opened and my letters and notes have been flung about. They were looking for something in particular."

"Perhaps a book is missing?"

He stacked the books one by one. "No, they are all here." He leafed through his papers, spreading them across the desk. "But my unfinished report to Abbot Hugh is missing. And where are all my travel papers?"

"Who in Jerusalem would be interested in your report?"

"That's a very good question." He continued to look about for any scraps.

Gathering it all, he examined every one. "And my drawing is gone, the one of the cross."

They looked at each other. "Somebody knows," she said. "One of the returning Christians, perhaps. Maybe Gerard."

"That was my first thought, but why would he want my correspondence with Cluny?" He picked up a soiled blanket to spread it over the floor. "Help me pack this up, it's no longer safe here. We'll take all we can, then we'll go back to the monastery."

"When is Pakrad going to get the cross?" she asked with growing anxiety.

"He said he would go to Madteos' home tonight." He knelt to the floor to retrieve a paper. "He had to be sure no soldiers were wandering about."

Ramiro and Adele were only a short distance away from the Monastery of Saint James where Pakrad lived, when they heard yelling and, up ahead, spotted several soldiers milling about the entrance.

Ramiro squeezed Adele's arm. "Come on, get off the street!" He pulled her into an alleyway.

"What's going on now?"

He peeked around the corner. "I'm not sure. Those are Godfrey's men. Wait. People are coming out. They have the priests and the monks. They're bound like slaves. Oh dear God, they've got Pakrad."

They waited, slipping into the monastery after the soldiers left. A few boys and some patients remained.

"They were taken on the orders of the Patriarch," said one of the boys.

"The Patriarch?" Ramiro looked puzzled. "You mean Bishop Aliphas?"

"No, Sayyid, the new Patriarch, one called Arnulf. One of Godfrey's men."

"Where can I find this Patriarch?"

The boy shrugged. "At his palace, I guess."

Adele stepped forward. "Did Father Pakrad take anything with him?"

"No, Sayyidah."

"He has something that belongs to us. May we look in his room?"

The boy shrugged again. "The soldiers grabbed anything of value."

"He doesn't have it," said Adele as they made their way outside. "We have to go to Madteos' house to look for it."

Ramiro shook his head. "Not now. What of Pakrad? Why have they taken these men? Perhaps we should go to the Patriarch and plead on his behalf. God knows what they will do to him. It's the least we can do."

"We can't go now," she said, pulling him south on Armenian Street. "It's too late. We'll go tomorrow first thing. Come on. Madteos' house is near the Zion Gate. This could be our last chance, Ramiro. Come on."

"But it's almost dark."

"All the better."

"Do you know where he hid it?"

"Not really. But it's got to be somewhere in the house."

"Very well," he relented. "But we must be careful."

REUNION

Signs of life began to return to the barren streets of Jerusalem as more of the exiled Christians returned. But they were a sullen lot. Most had returned only to find their homes plundered and vandalized. Many were penniless, although Godfrey's men demanded rent. So they found themselves forced into work gangs for their new overlords.

One of these gangs sauntered up a narrow street as Ramiro and Adele neared Madteos' house. At the front, was a black-robed monk and a carpenter.

"Out of the way, man!" yelled the monk as their oxcart rumbled over the cobblestones.

Ramiro was about to step to the side, but something stopped him. It was the monk's voice, he knew that voice. "Wait here," he said to Adele.

He rushed up to the monk, looking hard into his face. It *is* him, older now. But the features are unmistakable. "By the grace of God. Is it you Brother Aldebert?"

Aldebert scowled. "You will address me as Father Aldebert!"

Ramiro smiled wide. "Aldebert! It's me."

Aldebert studied the bothersome man blocking his way, a man with shoulder-length black hair and a full beard. He looked like one of the heathen wearing cheap armor and carrying a sword. "And who are you?" he asked indifferently.

Ramiro laughed aloud. "I am Ramiro of Cluny!" He laughed again.

The blood drained from Aldebert's face as he sagged in shock. "Father Ramiro? Is it really you?" The workmen kept walking to their homes but the tradesman at the oxcart stopped and waited.

Ramiro nodded. "Yes, Father Aldebert. Praise all the saints you are well."

Aldebert continued to gawk. "By the providence of God. But... but your hair," he stuttered. "Your beard, your... your dress."

"It is a long story. I promise to tell you all about it when we have time."

Aldebert turned around, gesturing wildly to the man standing near the cart. "Louis! Come! It's Father Ramiro!"

Louis rushed up, astonished. "Father Ramiro? Look at you! Aren't you a strange sight!"

Ramiro stared back, equally dumbfounded. "Louis the Carpenter? God bless you, man. We heard you were killed at Nicomedia."

Louis nodded. "It seems God has spared me for another purpose."

"Papa?" Adele croaked in a strained voice as she stepped up from behind.

Louis gazed at her for a long time, unable to speak. His eyes watered as years of suppressed grief swelled in his chest. "Adele?" he choked. "My darling, Adele. Look at you. You're a grown woman." Tears streamed down his round cheeks.

Adele sobbed too, flinging herself into his arms. "Papa... Papa... I thought you were... I saw..."

"Never mind, my love," he said patting her back. "I'm here."

"And Mama?"

Louis shook his head. "I'm sorry, my sweet."

She burst into tears again and they stood in a quiet embrace as dusk faded to nightfall.

"We should move on," said Ramiro.

"You must come to my house," said Louis, wiping his face. "Come. It seems we have much to talk about."

Adele glanced at Ramiro, her cheeks wet with tears. They thought of the Cluny cross. He nodded to her knowingly. "Of course. Thank you, Louis. We would be delighted."

Louis' house sat across the street from the Church of Saint John the Baptist, not far from David Street. It was claimed by one of Godfrey's men who had pillaged the place. Louis paid him a small sum for rent and moved in shortly after the assault. It took him two days to clean out the debris and scrub the bloodstains from the floor.

The night wore on with a few bottles of cheap wine and much banter. "What happened to our groom, Pepin?" Ramiro asked. "I hear he became a soldier for the Greek King."

Aldebert's face dropped in a sad look. "I told him to stay with God's work but he would have none of it." He shook his head. "Now he has paid the price."

"What do you mean?"

"I received a brief note from Commander Manuel. Do you remember him? The Byzantine?"

Ramiro nodded.

Aldebert lowered his voice. "He said that Pepin had fallen in battle."

"A very sad business, indeed," Ramiro lamented as he thought fondly of the energetic young lad.

After a moment of silence, Louis spoke with some anticipation. "You must tell us your story, Father Ramiro."

Louis and Aldebert listened in amazement as Ramiro recounted his journey, falling deep into events of the past ten years. And when he told them how he had found Adele in the slave markets of Aleppo, they were astounded.

"That's incredible!" said Louis. "Surely God guided your feet, Father Ramiro."

And then Ramiro went on to tell them about his failed rescue attempt in Antioch and how he was forced to marry Adele by the Emir of Antioch. They whistled in disbelief.

"Not to worry, Father Ramiro," said Aldebert. "If you were married in the Greek Church, we can have it annulled." He felt pleased that he was able to offer Ramiro some good advice.

Ramiro and Adele glanced at each other. He hesitated for a while before reaching out to take her hand. "No," he said, as if he had made his final decision in the presence of God. "She is my wife and I love her dearly."

Aldebert leaned back, somewhat shocked. "But what of your vows? You know we cannot take wives or concubines."

Ramiro nodded. "I am well aware of the consequences. I will speak to the Abbot when I return."

"The Abbot!" Aldebert cried. "I almost forgot!"

"What?"

"I have a letter for you—from the Abbot himself!"

"Really? Well, that should prove interesting. He has finally replied. Where is it?"

"It's in my room at the church. I'll bring it tomorrow."

Louis beamed with pleasure. His daughter was finally married. And to a respectable man. He got to his feet, stumbling from cheap wine. "A toast!" he cried. "A toast to my new son-in-law!" He raised his cup and they all followed suit, although Aldebert still appeared a little dazed.

In his telling, Ramiro never mentioned the cross, and Adele, sensing his discretion, also remained silent on the subject. Aldebert never knew that Ramiro's mission was to deliver the cross. He was always led to believe that Ramiro was going to see the Patriarch on some church business, and that he also wanted to see his mother and worship at the Tomb of Christ, or perhaps to take up an honored position at the monastery, or even at the Church of the Holy Sepulcher.

"Did you ever meet with the Greek Patriarch, what's his name?" Aldebert inquired as he slowly recovered.

"Symeon. No, he was exiled before I arrived."

"Then you must see the new Patriarch, Arnulf. I've been assigned to the Holy Church and I'm sure he would be glad to give you a position. Perhaps... perhaps as a scribe or something."

Ramiro thought only of Pakrad. He intended to plead on his behalf. "Yes, I plan to see the Patriarch soon."

"I'll go with you," said Aldebert, who was becoming a little worried about Ramiro's appearance and state of mind.

"Very well, but not tomorrow. Adele and I need to look for accommodations." He squeezed her hand, knowing it was a lie. "But perhaps you can tell me why he arrested the monks at Saint James?"

Aldebert shook his head. "I'm not sure. But I know he doesn't trust those Greek heretics."

The next day, Aldebert and Louis returned to their work, heads throbbing from green Jerusalem wine. Meanwhile, Ramiro and Adele rushed again to Madteos' house. But now, the place was nearly destroyed. Complete walls had been demolished, broken floor tiles were scattered everywhere and small piles of dirt lay beside hastily dug pits in the floor. They searched every corner and Adele, remembering how Khuda had hidden the cross beneath his floor, pried at every loose tile. But they found nothing.

"Does it look the same?" Ramiro asked as rubble and detritus crushed under their feet. "Does anything look different?"

"I don't know. It was dark when I arrived and I never got a chance to look around. But it seems worse than I remember."

"That's what I fear." He took her hand. "It is over," he said with resignation. "We will leave Jerusalem and forget this whole business."

A HOLY RELIC

Ramiro and Aldebert arrived early at the Palace of the Patriarch, where they waited for hours in an elaborate foyer.

"Have you got the Abbot's letter?" Ramiro asked.

Aldebert knocked his head with one hand. "No, I forgot, I'll go now."

"Not now. We could be summoned at any moment."

While they waited in the foyer, Lothar and a servant waited upstairs outside the door of Arnulf's bedchamber. When the door finally opened, a young girl rushed out, pulling the hood of her cloak tight about her face. But the hood could not hide her tears, nor her look of distress and disgust. The servant pulled her aside, leading her away.

Lothar continued to wait. Eventually, Arnulf came out, dressed in the long, black cloak and tall hat of the Patriarch. In one hand, he held the golden-tipped staff of office, and at his midriff was a large medallion hanging from a gold chain.

"Good morning, Lothar," he beamed with unusual cheer. "Is the procession prepared?"

"Yes, Your Eminence, it is all arranged. And all of the Latin clergy have been ordered to attend."

"And my Sacred Scepter?" He asked as they descended the wide, curved staircase. "Did the goldsmith finish it? Is it ready?"

"Yes, it is finished, Your Eminence, and ready for you to reveal to all those in the holy procession. We plan to depart from the palace at noon and then we will walk around the Church before finishing up at the Tomb of Our Lord."

"Excellent," said Arnulf with exuberance. He breathed deep, sensing his growing religious power with heady delight.

"Until that time, my Lord, there is someone here requesting an audience.

"Not now, Lothar, I'm much too busy."

"Yes, Your Eminence, but he says his name is Ramiro of León."

Arnulf stopped suddenly. "Of León? I thought Gerard said he called himself Ramiro of Cluny?"

"He did, my Lord, but not many go by the name of Ramiro, especially in Jerusalem."

"Give me an hour," said Arnulf, his dark eyes narrowed in a cunning look. "Then send him to me in the meeting hall."

"Yes, Your Eminence."

"And bring my Sacred Scepter to me."

Arnulf sat stiffly upright on the throne of the Patriarch, doing his best to appear regal. Behind him, stood the cowering Lothar and a number of hand-picked priests. One of them held a few rolled documents. Arnulf put his hand forward and Ramiro stepped up to kiss his sacral ring.

"You say you are Ramiro of León, once of Cluny?" Arnulf asked.

"That is correct, Your Eminence," he said as he stood and stepped back.

"Does this mean you have renounced your vows to the Mother Church?"

Aldebert, who stood behind Ramiro, lowered his head in heartfelt shame.

"Only one," Ramiro said calmly. "I can no longer remain obedient to the Benedictine Rule."

"So you prefer the ways of the Greek monks?"

"No, that is not..."

"And you are the so-called holy man of Jerusalem?"

"That is a name used by others."

"And you are still Christian?"

Ramiro scowled at him. "I have dedicated my life to the teachings of Jesus, Your Eminence."

"So why have you come to me, Ramiro of wherever."

Already, Ramiro was beginning to dislike this man. Clearly, by his manner and speech, he was low-born and, worse yet, he was condescending and rude. He fixed his gaze on the Patriarch's eyes. "I come to beg your leniency, Your Eminence."

Arnulf met his determined stare with a shudder. "Leniency? For who?"

"For the monks of Saint James Monastery, Your Eminence. I would like to say that I know them personally and would vouch for their integrity."

"You are a friend of these heretics?"

"I am a friend of all, particularly Christians."

Arnulf sneered. "And a friend of the pagan Muslims, I hear. Is it true you speak the language of the infidels?"

"Yes, Your Eminence, but please understand, I have been here ten years."

"And one who consorts with vile Hebrews?"

"I have met several Hebrews but I would not say..."

"You know what I think, Ramiro of wherever?" Arnulf said loudly. "I think you are a spy!" He raised a hand and a priest stepped forward with a document. Arnulf held it up for Ramiro to see. "This is the proof. I have your report and it clearly notes all of our defenses and the number of our men. You are a traitor!"

"That is not so, Your Eminence," said Ramiro, realizing that Arnulf held the report taken from his room. "I wrote this report before the assault. If you read it carefully, you will see those are the numbers of Egyptian troops, not the French. These documents are for the Abbot of Cluny, who ordered me here. The Pope himself, may God bless his name, was a monk of Cluny. How can you believe I am a traitor?"

Aldebert stepped forward. "He tells the truth, Your Eminence."

"Shut up!" Arnulf yelled. "You will speak when asked!"

Aldebert bowed silently before backing away.

"Is this the only reason you came to Jerusalem?" he asked in a calmer but suspicious voice.

"Father Aldebert and I were sent here to see Patriarch Symeon and to await his instructions."

"Is that so?" Arnulf smirked. "Now you tell me that the great Abbey of Cluny takes its orders from heretics?"

Ramiro scowled, making no reply.

Arnulf banged his staff to the floor in anger before speaking in a shrill voice. "Well since you have come to follow the Patriarch, it is only logical that you now serve me." He raised his hand again, signaling Lothar to come forward with his Sacred Scepter. "Come forward Ramiro of wherever to kiss my holy scepter and to vow your allegiance to the Church of the Holy Sepulcher." He braced it to the floor and motioned for Ramiro to step forward.

Ramiro surveyed Arnulf with barely concealed contempt before his eyes drifted to the Sacred Scepter, a long staff of gilded gold crowned with a golden cross. He stared at it long and hard before clenching his jaw in recognition. It was a cross of wood framed in gold. "That's my cross!" he blurted. "How did you get it?"

"Your Armenian priest told me." Arnulf smiled in perverse delight as he gazed on Ramiro's awestruck face. "Are you claiming that the True Cross is your cross?"

"It's from the Abbey of Cluny. I was told to deliver it to Patriarch Symeon."

"So you claim that you brought this cross with you to Jerusalem?" Arnulf asked, feeling a moment of panic. If this were true, it would be discredited.

"That is correct."

"Father Aldebert," spouted Arnulf. "Step forward!" Aldebert shuffled to the front. "Can you verify this story? Have you seen this cross before?"

Aldebert looked hard at the cross. He glanced back at Ramiro sheepishly before turning again to Arnulf. "Well... well no, Your Eminence. I do not remember this cross and I know nothing of it going to the Patriarch."

Arnulf felt a flood of relief.

"I can explain," said Ramiro. "It is my wooden cross you see at the center, Father Aldebert. Unfortunately, Turk slavers at Gallipoli pried out the bloodstone. And the Sultan of Persia added the gold frame. I can tell you the story, Your Eminence."

Arnulf chuckled. "Turk slavers? The Sultan of Persia?" The priests behind him chuckled too. "If indeed, what you say is true, then why were you searching for a cross you already had?"

"It was stolen by a Turk, Your Eminence, when I was captured in Antioch. I managed to retrieve it and hold it for a while, but the same man chased me down just before I arrived at Jerusalem. He sold it to an Armenian jeweler."

As outlandish as Ramiro's story sounded to the others, it began to dawn on Arnulf that there could be some truth to it. His men found the cross at the house of an Armenian jeweler. But he could not afford the truth. "A ridiculous fable!" he shouted. "I should have your tongue cut out for your lies! You wanted the gold!"

"No, Your Eminence. As I said, my original wood cross is at the center. I believe it may hold some important message, a message for the Patriarch. If you open it, it will probably verify my story."

Arnulf laughed loudly. "Now you want me to destroy the True Cross just to satisfy your ludicrous tale? I begin to believe you are mad."

"If you would ask Bishop Aliphas, he will verify my story."

Arnulf smirked. "Rest assured, we have had a long talk with Aliphas."

Ramiro braced at his tone. "What have you done with him?"

"You seem quite concerned about these heretics. We know he paid you to retrieve this cross. Is this not true?"

"Yes, but that money was to pay the jeweler."

"So even if we are to believe your hare-brained tale, you would have to admit the cross rightly belongs to the Patriarch of Jerusalem. Unless you wish to admit it was all a lie to steal money from the Church. In which case, you would leave me no choice but to hang you from the gallows."

Ramiro bowed his head. For the love of God, he thought, why do I bother? He raised his head. "Yes, Your Eminence, of course. I lay no claim to this cross."

Arnulf rose to his feet, glowing with satisfaction. "You are dismissed. Both of you will join my sacred procession around the Church so all can gaze upon the True Cross and see that it has been returned to the victorious—to the people chosen by God."

After Ramiro left, Arnulf sat back with a worried look. The man knows too much. What if he discredits my holy relic?

"The man is an idiot!" Ramiro spouted when they were safely outside. "I'll go see Duke Godfrey. Perhaps he will intervene for the Armenians."

"Oh no, no," Aldebert warned.

"What? Why?"

"Patriarch Arnulf has the favor of Godfrey. He won't help."

"Well, who should I see?"

"Uh, maybe Count Raymond. He doesn't like Godfrey or Arnulf."

"So where does Raymond stay?"

"You can't go to see him now, Father Ramiro. The procession begins. The Patriarch ordered us to attend."

"You go. I have no more time for this sordid business."

Count Raymond still held the Tower of David, refusing to hand it over to Godfrey. He brought in expensive furniture and tried to make a comfortable home in the stark, gray surroundings of the citadel. But he had little company. Most of the men, even some of his own, resented his selfish intransigence. They just wanted peace.

Ramiro had little trouble getting an audience with him. They met under the archways next to an open courtyard, sipping cool lemonade while the sun set over the Judean Hills. Servants scurried around, putting out bowls of fruit brought in from the Jordan Valley.

"From the Abbey of Cluny, you say?" Raymond asked as he dabbed at the sweat dripping from his brow, careful not to dislodge his eye patch. He was already in his mid-sixties, but the last few years of war and strife seemed to age him even more. His wrinkles ran deeper, and his weatherworn face, burned by the sun day after day, was pocked by old blisters.

"Yes, my Lord," said Ramiro, glad to finally meet one of the foremost leaders of the Crusade.

"I know your Abbot well," said Raymond. "He has been of considerable help to us in our Holy Crusade against the infidels. I admire his vast knowledge of events."

Raymond's words were a knife through Ramiro's heart. He was reminded of his many reports to the Abbot and feared once again that he had been used as an unwitting spy. A feeling of profound regret swept over him. "Yes, my Lord," he said, trying not to think of the senseless slaughter of countless innocents. "So what of this matter of the Armenian priests? Can you help to get them released?"

Raymond shook his head slowly, furrowing his gray brow. "No, I cannot help you, Sir," he said sadly. "It is out of my control. I have neither the ambition nor the men to help the Armenians." His eyes grew distant as he stared into the courtyard. "Cursed Normans!" he spat. "First that bastard Bohemond took Antioch and now Godfrey claims Jerusalem! And to make matters worse, he managed to get that greasy, wine-soaked womanizer appointed Patriarch—and he's a bloody Norman too! The bastards have betrayed the Church and the Pope!"

Ramiro said nothing.

"I'm sorry," said Raymond, smiling a little. "But let's not worry about these things. You must tell me more of your story."

Ramiro sighed in resignation as he leaned back in his chair to recount his tangled saga to Raymond. "Well, it all started when Abbot Hugh of Cluny sent me off on this mission to Jerusalem ..."

MORE EGYPTIANS

August 1099

Tancred, the nephew of Bohemond, came galloping up from Bethlehem with alarming news. The Egyptians had arrived, as they feared they would. The vizier, Al-Afdal, led an army of twenty thousand and they were now at Ascalon, less than fifty miles away.

"Twenty thousand?" Godfrey muttered with a grim look. He raised his voice to a bellow. "We cannot remain here to be besieged! The walls are not yet repaired. We should ride against them before they organize themselves!"

"Against an army of twenty thousand?" replied Raymond, astonished. "I think not. We would be fortunate to get ten thousand men together. I say we would do better within the walls."

"Like at Antioch?" Godfrey retorted with bitterness. "We'll be starved out in a month! The will of God is with us—I say attack."

"I'll go," said Tancred.

"And I," said Robert.

"I will reconsider," said Raymond, "when you can verify this tale."

As they sat down for supper, Ramiro told Adele and Louis of his encounter with Arnulf and what happened to the Cluny cross. "Wretched man. Claimed I was a traitor. After all I've done for the Church."

"And Raymond was no help?" asked Louis.

"I believe he would help us if he could," said Ramiro. "He feels the Mother Church has been betrayed."

Adele piped in. "How much longer will we stay here?"

"We must leave as soon as possible." He took a sip of thin, leek soup.

"But which way will you go?" asked Louis. "The Egyptians hold the coast. Jaffa is not safe."

"Then we will have to ride north, up the coast to Latakia."

Adele tore off a chunk of barley bread and handed it to him. "We will never find a horse. We'll be lucky to find a donkey."

"But I hear many of the men want to return to Europe soon," said Louis. "Perhaps an opportunity will arise."

"What of Aldebert?" asked Adele. "Will he stay?"

"I have no idea. I suspect he's beginning to think I've lost my mind."

Adele turned her head to the window. "What's that noise?"

They stopped to listen, hearing loud chanting in the distance. The sound steadily got louder and louder. Ramiro rose to his feet, strolling to the window to look down on David Street. Louis and Adele rushed up behind him.

A long, trudging procession made its way down the street. Leading them was Patriarch Arnulf walking barefoot. He clutched his new Sacred Scepter of the True Cross with both hands while shouting loud glories to the Lord. Behind him were several clergymen and, behind them, were hundreds of knights and thousands of foot-soldiers, all of them barefoot, carrying their boots in their hands.

"What's going on?" asked Adele.

"I'm not sure," said Ramiro. "But it looks like a procession before battle." He glanced down at several men leading the soldiers. "Tell me Louis, which one is Godfrey?"

"He's the big man with the long, blonde hair," said Louis. "The one on his left—the one with the big nose, that's Robert of Flanders. The younger one with brown hair is Tancred."

"Which one is Raymond of Toulouse?" asked Adele.

"You can't mistake him," answered Ramiro. "He's a gray, old man with an eye patch, but I don't see him. Him and Godfrey don't get along." He pointed down. "There's Father Aldebert."

"Where?"

"He's just behind the Patriarch."

Duke Godfrey felt invincible. But even his unwavering faith could not disguise the fact that he was greatly outnumbered. His scouts spotted Al-Afdal's enormous army after they arrived at Ramla, so he sent a fast messenger back to Raymond, telling him it was all true, the Egyptians had indeed arrived. Raymond finally relented under pressure from his own men and reluctantly left the city unguarded.

Still, due to the attrition of war, the Crusaders could amass no more than nine thousand infantry and a thousand knights. They were outnumbered two to one and, to make things worse, the Egyptian army had thousands of skilled cavalry. So Godfrey was forced to make a daring decision when his scouts spotted the enemy camp outside Ascalon. He decided on an age-old tactic—that of surprise.

Al-Afdal felt confident the barbarian rabble would remain huddled behind the walls of Jerusalem. He knew they had no allies within hundreds of miles. Tomorrow, they would besiege the holy city and wait them out. So when the bloodthirsty knights came charging down on their camp at the first light of dawn, they were stunned out of their beds. The sheer ferocity of the Crusader assault, fueled as it was by their sense of fanatical righteousness, quickly overwhelmed one of Egypt's finest armies and the doomed battle soon turned into an all-out rout.

The French hunted them down one by one, hacking them to pieces, even as they groveled on their knees for mercy. Only Al-Afdal and Iftikhar and a few others managed to escape to Ascalon with nothing more than their horses and the clothes on their backs. And they soon set sail for the safety of Cairo.

And so it was that the Crusaders returned victorious to the walls of Jerusalem, and Godfrey was again their invincible hero, blessed with God's Grace. They brought back a vast plunder of gold, jewels, arms, and horses captured from Al-Afdal's camp, a treasure so great that the returning men could not carry it all.

And then, in another grand procession, Patriarch Arnulf led the bloodied troops victorious through the streets of Jerusalem, holding his True Cross high above his head, jutting it into the air again and again. The people fell to their knees in awe of its sacred power.

The resolute Crusaders had conquered the Holy Land against all imaginable odds and there was not a single army left to oppose them. The Byzantines still wrestled for control of the Aegean and Anatolia and were more interested in regaining Antioch from Bohemond. The Turks were still embroiled in bitter civil wars since the death of Malik Shah and were no longer interested in the affairs of Palestine. And the Egyptians were decimated by war, disease, and internal strife. The ancient triangle of Middle East power had collapsed, and in its midst was a new barbarian kingdom.

A Traitor

Godfrey's soldiers arrived at Louis' house before dawn, banging on the door. Louis rubbed the sleep from his eyes, feeling for the door in the darkness. He opened it cautiously. "What do you want?" he asked.

"On the orders of the Patriarch," said Lothar gruffly, "we have come for Ramiro of León."

"On what charge?"

"That is not your business. Where is he?"

"I am here," said Ramiro as he came up behind Louis. "What does the blessed Patriarch want with me?"

Lothar unfurled a roll and strained to read by the flickering light of a torch. "By the order of His Eminence, the Patriarch of Jerusalem, it has been judged that Ramiro of León, formerly of Cluny, is a traitor to the Mother Church of God and to the Protectorate of Jerusalem."

"That's preposterous!" Ramiro blurted.

"You will come with us," demanded Lothar. Two soldiers grabbed him by the arms and dragged him away.

"Ramiro!" Adele screamed.

Lothar punched Ramiro on the back of the head before he shoved him to his knees. Arnulf held out his hand so Ramiro could kiss his ring. But Ramiro did not approach.

Lothar kicked him in the back. "Show respect to your superiors!"

Ramiro winced from the blow but remained still.

Arnulf turned away seething. He sat down hard on his throne. "You have come to me with lies!" he shrilled. "You are a spy for the heathen!"

"That's ridiculous!" Ramiro bellowed.

Lothar belted him across the head. "You will speak when asked!"

Arnulf clapped his hands, motioning to a waiting servant. The man rushed forward with several documents.

Arnulf waved them in front of Ramiro. "We have proof!" He held up one paper and rattled it in his hand. "This one is written in the heathen tongue. We had it translated. It seems you are a servant of the King of Persia. How do you answer?"

Ramiro briefly contemplated Arnulf's deceit. "As I alluded to previously, Your Eminence, I was in Persia, held as a slave. Those papers are merely a form of identification."

Arnulf glared. "So you say." He picked out another paper. "And I have another. Also from the pagans. It seems you work for the Egyptians as well."

"No, Your Eminence. That document is merely a tax receipt. It is mandatory for a Christian in Muslim lands."

"So you say, Ramiro of wherever, but the evidence is against you."

"All I have said is true, Your Eminence. I met with Pope Urban himself. He will verify my story."

"Pope Urban is dead," said Arnulf, smirking with satisfaction.

Ramiro studied him, not sure if it was the truth.

"Yes," said Arnulf, sensing his doubt. "We hear he passed into heavenly care just before we stormed the walls of Jerusalem—doing God's work as he bid us," he sneered. "While traitors to the Holy Cause plotted against us!"

Ramiro paused, thinking of the Pope. He had liked the man. "I speak the truth. Abbot Hugh of Cluny will attest to that."

"I don't believe you," said Arnulf who yet again, shook another sheet of paper at him. "You say you are a monk, but we found this. You know what it is?"

Ramiro strained to look. "Ah... yes, well I can explain that too, Your Eminence. It is a marriage certificate issued by the Greek Church."

"A marriage certificate," he said derisively. "Since when do Benedictine monks take wives?"

"I was forced to marry, Your Eminence, under threat of death by the Emir of Antioch."

Arnulf looked at him with disgust. "The Emir of Antioch!" He tossed his head back, cackling. Then his white face sneered in malice. "Enough of your lies! You are a traitor and a thief."

"I am neither, Your Eminence."

Lothar slapped him again.

"Well what of this?" Arnulf held a small pouch in front of him. "Do you recognize it?"

"Yes, Your Eminence. It contains a thorn. It was given to me by my mother."

"Your mother?"

"Yes, my Lord. She was a nun here at the blessed Church. She claimed it to be a holy relic and left it to me on her deathbed."

Arnulf cackled again. "An outrageous story!"

"It is true, my Lord. If you will check the Church records."

"There are no records, traitor. We know you stole it from the Mother Church of God."

"That is not..."

Arnulf jumped to his feet. "Take him out of my sight!"

ADELE'S VENTURE

"What did you discover," Adele asked, worried sick.

Aldebert pursed his lips, holding back tears. His face writhed in anguish as he bowed his head.

"Come on man!" she shouted at him. "Out with it!" She had little patience for Aldebert's stupidity.

He lifted his head. Tears ran freely from his red eyes. "The Patriarch has denounced him as a traitor and a thief. They..." he started to blubber. "They... oh dear God! They are going to execute him!"

Adele clenched her jaw, spinning away to hide her shock. Louis stepped up to take her hand, but she pulled away from him, confronting Aldebert again. "Can't you do something? Why don't you tell the Patriarch who he is?"

Aldebert squirmed, his face went pale. "What can I do? He won't listen to me."

She slapped him hard across the face. "You spineless bastard! Coward!"

Aldebert, eyes bulging, rubbed his cheek in shock. Louis stepped in to spread them apart. The room went quiet.

"How?" she asked softly.

"To be hanged... hanged from the gallows," said Aldebert meekly.

"Mother of God! When?"

Aldebert squatted to the floor, putting his head in his hands. "Tomorrow!" he wailed.

"We should all go to the Patriarch to plead on his behalf," said Louis anxiously.

"What good will that do!" she screamed. "He will pay us no heed! A tradesman and his daughter!" She gestured to Aldebert. "And a whimpering, idiot monk!"

As if to prove her right, Aldebert wailed again. "And I never did give him the letter," he sobbed.

"What did you say?" She stood over him putting her hands on her hips.

He looked up, his big cow-ears drooping from his head. "The letter," he said again.

"What letter, you fool?"

"From Abbot Hugh. I brought it with me from Bari."

"Give it to me!"

He cringed. "It's for Ramiro—from the Abbot himself."

"Give it to me!" she screamed, putting a hand to her mace. "Or by God's blood, I'll beat you to death!"

Louis hovered over him, lending weight to her threat.

Aldebert backed away on the floor. He rummaged in his pockets, bringing out an envelope with a trembling hand. "You can't open it! It's God's business!" he belted out as a last defense.

"I'll give you God's business!" she said, snatching it from his hand. "Just like your bloody knights do! Don't you realize how important this is? It proves Ramiro is a man of Cluny!"

"I... I never thought..."

"That's right. You don't think."

"Calm down, Adele," said Louis cautiously. He was taken aback by the determined strength of his daughter, a side of her he had never seen. "We must think of something. We must know someone who can help."

"Drugo the Red is here," Aldebert said quietly. "I saw him."

"He's a common soldier!" Adele snapped. "And a savage brute! Have you forgotten what he tried to do to Papa? To cut off his hand for a crime he did not commit? And he never liked Ramiro anyway."

She paced the room in a frenzy, rubbing the back of her neck with her head down. "There is only one man who can stop this wretched Patriarch. And that's Lord Godfrey." She left the room for an instant, coming back in with a cloak over her shoulders. "Come on!" she ordered. "We're going to see Godfrey."

"Me too?" Aldebert asked plaintively.

"Yes, you too!" she shouted. "Or I'll hang you myself!"

The rubbish and litter of war still cluttered the nearly deserted streets. Adele rushed past broken doorways and shattered shutters. Louis and Aldebert struggled to keep up. The smell of death hung in the air, mixed with the acrid smell of still-smoldering buildings. They passed the burned-out synagogue before coming to the plaza near the Wailing Wall, now empty of life. Up the stone steps they went, through the narrow path leading to the Temple Mount. But before they reached the building, two armed guards blocked their way.

"What do you want?" one challenged.

"We have come to see Lord Godfrey," said Adele.

The guard smiled, then he turned to Aldebert. "Does this woman speak for you?"

Aldebert blushed.

"I speak for myself, soldier," Adele said defiantly. "I demand to see Lord Godfrey. It is a matter of life and death."

The guards, greasy-haired, filthy men reeking of stale blood, smiled at her spunk. "You're a pretty one," said the other.

"She's my daughter, Sir," said Louis, stepping forward. "Will you give heed to her request?"

"Is she now?" one said. "Well never you mind, Duke Godfrey is not seeing anyone today. Go about your business."

"This is my business, soldier," said Adele as she barged past them. But one reached out grabbing her arm. She spun around and pushed him away. "Let me go!" she screamed.

The other guard held a sword to Louis. Aldebert stepped back, terrified.

Drugo the Red emerged from the archway, limping to the gate. "What's the trouble?" he shouted. His once smooth, freckled face was now scarred and creased by war and adversity. Several teeth were missing, his hair and beard bleached white by the sun, and heavy bandages wrapped one leg, covering a wound suffered in the attack on Ascalon.

"She demands to see Duke Godfrey, Captain. I tried to send her away."

"What's your business?" Drugo asked Louis.

"We come to save a life, Sir Drugo," said Louis. "I'm Louis the Carpenter and this is my daughter Adele. Do you remember us, Sir?"

Drugo looked them over. "I remember you," he said. "You're the man who makes catapults."

"That's right," said Adele. "And he served you well. Now we demand to see Godfrey."

Drugo returned a hostile glare. He was not used to a woman giving him orders. "That's *Lord* Godfrey to you. Who are you trying to save?"

"It's Father Ramiro," said Louis interrupting. "He's been sentenced to death by the Patriarch. He's a good Christian, Sir Drugo. We're hoping Lord Godfrey will put a stop to it."

"Father Ramiro?" Drugo chortled. "So that damn monk is still alive, is he? Yeh, well I remember that troublemaker. The Patriarch probably has his reasons. Good riddance, I say."

Adele rushed up to him, slapping his face. "You worthless mound of shit! You're not half the man he is!"

Startled, Drugo hesitated for a moment, putting a hand to his cheek. Then, in a sudden rage, he cuffed her with the back of his hand, sending her reeling. "Bloody bitch!" he cried rubbing his cheek again.

Adele recovered from his blow and tried to dash past him. But he reached out, grabbing her by the hair.

Louis leapt to her rescue but the guards pushed him back with the tips of their swords. Meanwhile, Aldebert staggered in fear, spun around, and fled back through the gate.

Drugo pulled hard on Adele's hair as he pushed her toward the gate.

"Let me go! You godless bastard! Rot in hell!" She kicked and punched. One kick landed squarely on his wounded knee.

Drugo cried out, releasing his grip. Then, in a mad fury, he drew his sword.

"What's going on here!" a voice yelled. It was Robert, the Count of Flanders. Unlike the other men, Robert kept himself clean and neatly trimmed, as if he had never fought a battle. His face remained handsome, smooth, and unscathed.

"Cursed troublemakers, m'lord," said Drugo, who limped even more.

"We are good Christians, m'lord," said Adele, straightening her hair. "We ask only to see Lord Godfrey on an important matter."

Robert smiled at her, bowing a little. "Enchanté, my lady. You must forgive these uncouth men. They are good soldiers but unfortunately they are uncultured and have no manners." He waved away Drugo and the guards with a stern look. "Come and sit. Tell me your story." He gestured to a number of chairs put out under an archway.

A few weeks after the conquest, the Christians stripped the Temple Mount plaza of all things Muslim and converted the Dome of the Rock into a church, which they called the Templum Domini, Temple of the Lords. At the same time, the nearby Al-Aqsa Mosque had been completely remodeled as a luxurious palace for Godfrey.

Robert took a seat across from Godfrey, who was eating his lunch. "The woman pleads for the life of her husband," he recounted the story. "It seems Patriarch Arnulf will have him executed tomorrow."

Godfrey looked up from his plate of meat and bread. "You should try this, Count Robert." He pointed to his plate with his knife. "It's mule meat—rare. Not that bad." His voice echoed in the vast nave of the former mosque, wherein two great colonnades of white Italian marble propped up whitewashed archways rising the height of eight men. Over one hundred stained glass windows reflected rainbows of light from elaborate designs set in mosaic walls.

But its original beauty was marred by vandalism. The place had been gutted. The sacred *mihrab* was destroyed, as was the *minbar*, their remains burned in a huge pyre set ablaze on the plaza of the Temple Mount, as was every Muslim book and artifact.

"No thanks, I'm not hungry," replied Robert, watching blood drip from Godfrey's blonde beard as he chewed on the barely cooked flesh. "So what should we do? It seems this man was a Benedictine monk. The woman claims she has correspondence from the Abbey of Cluny that would verify this. Perhaps the Patriarch has overstepped his bounds." He could not conceal his loathing of Arnulf, even if he was a Norman. And now, after usurping the power of the Jerusalem Church, Arnulf revealed himself as a greasy, common man, an opportunist who was merely Godfrey's puppet.

"You say he was a monk?" asked Godfrey before he took a long draft of green beer.

"Yes. Apparently, he left the abbey about ten years ago on some mission for the Abbot but has since renounced the Order. Has the attire of a scribe."

"What are the accusations?"

"The Patriarch says he's a traitor. That he works for the pagans."

"Perhaps it's true," said Godfrey. He put his knife down before leaning back in his chair, his long hair sweeping over his shoulders.

Robert scowled, lifting the nostrils of his long nose. "Are you going to allow Arnulf to start executing Christians?"

Godfrey leaned forward again, putting his elbows on the table. He picked up his knife, jabbing it at Robert as he spoke. "You must understand, Count Robert, that we have only recently established ourselves. And now Arnulf claims he has found the True Cross. It is a powerful relic and rallies the men. If I allow him to be discredited at this time, what will it say to the others? The whoring Greeks would like nothing more than to see us weakened. Besides, what is one more man in God's great scheme?"

Robert remained quiet for a time, seething at Godfrey's indifference. Finally, he opened his hands and spoke. "You should at least look at the evidence, Lord Godfrey."

"Evidence? I'll give you shit for evidence. It's the power that's important. We need to let the people know we are ruthless and will not be stopped. Let the matter drop, it costs us nothing."

Robert stood up angrily. "I cannot condone such practices."

"Think as you please," said Godfrey with a tone of finality. "But I will not interfere with Arnulf's designs at this time."

"What?" Adele yelled when Robert told her the bad news. "But this is madness! He's one of our own!"

"I'm truly sorry. You must believe me, I do not in any way agree with Lord Godfrey's assessment. But I am powerless to stop it."

"Unbelievable!" she shouted. "You're a pack of bloody barbarians! Just like Ramiro said."

"I'm sorry, m'lady, but you will have to leave."

Adele broke down in sobs as soon as they entered the house. Louis did his best to comfort her, but to no avail. "I'll kill that bastard patriarch myself," she said in a croaking voice.

"That is unlikely," said Louis. "And it will accomplish nothing."

She wiped her face with her sleeve before reaching into her pocket. "I'm going to open the Abbot's letter." She pulled it out. "What harm can that do now?" She ripped open the envelope, taking care to keep the letter intact. For a while, she stared at the page, stumbling over the words. She offered it to Louis. "What does it say, Papa?"

"It's Latin. We need someone to read it," he confessed. "We could ask Aldebert."

"No, Papa, he's useless. I don't trust him."

Louis brightened. "Then we'll take it to that Armenian priest that Ramiro mentioned. I hear he's back at the Monastery of Saint James. Arnulf released him after he found his precious cross."

THE ABBOT'S LETTER

Pakrad's face was still swollen and bruised from the beating he suffered at the hands of Lothar and his men. He felt guilty and ashamed. It was he who had broken down under torture, and it was he who had told them where to find the cross in Madteos' hidden cache. "I'm sorry for all the trouble, Sayyidah. I never thought it would come to this."

"Never mind, Pakrad," said Adele. "No man could have done any better. Just read this letter for me."

He opened the letter, clearing his throat before reading aloud.

> To my humble servant, Ramiro of Cluny, from Abbot Hugh of Cluny. Greetings in the name of Our Lord Jesus Christ.
>
> Be it known, good monk, that I have received several of your reports and letters and am happy to say that the Mother Church stands deeply in your debt for the great service you have rendered on behalf of Almighty God.
>
> As I write, the Soldiers of God now triumph in Tripoli and will soon head south to liberate the Holy City from the grasp of pagans. You are instructed to brace yourself for much trouble and I command you, for your own safety, to remove yourself from the city for fear of retaliation by the heathen. You will travel north to join your brethren in Tripoli where you will serve as my personal legate to the brave men who fight for the Holy Cause. Here, you will join with Raymond, the Count of Toulouse who, even now, leads these men to a great victory.
>
> I pray for your safe return, as do all your fellow monks at the Abbey.
>
> March 2, In the year Our Lord 1099.

Pakrad handed the letter back. "How is this going to help you?"

"Raymond of Toulouse?" queried Adele. "Where is he now?"

"I hear he left the city in a rage. Went to Jericho after they drove him out of the Tower of David. They say he hates Godfrey and his new patriarch."

"So I've heard," said Adele.

"Which way is Jericho?" asked Louis.

Pakrad pointed with a thin finger. "About fifteen miles to the east."

Adele stood, taking the letter from his hands. "Thank you, Pakrad. I'm going to Jericho."

"But Adele, how will you get there?" asked Louis. "Nobody's going to lend you a horse and even if we had the money, you're unlikely to find one for sale."

"I'll find one," she said forcefully. She pulled her cloak tight to her shoulders, fastened her mace to her belt, and stormed out. She still had Bishop Aliphas' money for the cross, but she had promised Ramiro she would mention it to no one.

Louis rushed after her. "Adele, be reasonable. We have no time for this."

"I'm sorry, Papa, there is nothing more we can do here. I refuse to stand by while Ramiro hangs from the gallows."

"Where are you going?"

"To the Josaphat Gate," she said, taking long strides. "I'm looking for a horse."

"But we don't have enough money."

She felt for her mace. "I don't need money."

"Adele, my sweet, you're starting to worry your poor father."

Adele and Louis hurried through the eerily quiet streets of Jerusalem, heading for the Josaphat Gate in the eastern wall, the one that led to Jericho. A few of Godfrey's men checked everybody coming and going, but the pair of them had no trouble getting through. Outside, a line of about twenty travelers waited, trying to get into the city.

Once beyond the city walls, Louis expected Adele to continue on the road to Jericho. How she was going to get a horse, he had no idea. She was mum to his inquiries. But as they walked past the line, nothing could prepare him for what she did next.

The last man in line held the reins of a thin-looking filly. And as she passed, she pulled out her mace. With no hesitation and grim determination, she struck the unsuspecting victim on the back of the head. He had no sooner collapsed to the ground when she jumped into the saddle. "May God forgive me, Papa." She straddled the horse like a man, pulling it out of line before anyone knew what was happening.

"I'll come with you!" Louis yelled.

"Sorry, Papa, too much weight. Do what you can for Ramiro!" She dug in her heels and the filly galloped away.

The Gallows

The sun had just begun to rise over the Mount of Olives when a small wagon, pulled by a single mule and led by one of Lothar's men, creaked and groaned its way toward the plaza near the Pool of Bethesda, a city reservoir not far from the Josaphat Gate. Ramiro sat cross-legged in the cart as it rattled along, his face blackened with bruises, his ribs broken, his hands tied behind his back.

The gallows was newly built of fresh timbers. But already, the bodies of two men hung from the beam, rotting in the sun. Arnulf stood nearby with Lothar and a few of his cronies.

With them was Aldebert, who sobbed uncontrollably. He had no desire to be there but Arnulf had coerced him, telling him he was a necessary witness. Louis stood by too. He came of his own accord, hoping he could do something to help. But Lothar's men were well-armed. He felt useless and despondent and, when he saw Ramiro's sad state, he was grievously shocked.

The wagon made its way under the gallows, coming to a stop below a single rope. Lothar jumped on to fit the noose around Ramiro's neck. "Consider yourself lucky, traitor," he whispered with venom." If I had my way, I'd slit you open like a pig and strangle you with your own guts." He pulled the noose tight.

Lothar read the long roll of charges against Ramiro before passing a sentence of death. Then Arnulf led his clergymen in a long ramble of prayers asking God to have mercy on this poor sinner's soul. Ramiro waited for them to pull the wagon away. He listened to Arnulf's last prayer.

> *In the name of the Father and of the Son and of the*
> *Holy Spirit, Amen*
> *May the grace and peace of Christ be with you...*

But before Arnulf could finish the last rites, a tremendous ruckus broke out at the nearby Josaphat Gate. There was much yelling and a clash of steel. Arnulf fell silent. His men ran out to check the gate. "It's Count Raymond riding from Jericho!" one shouted. "And all his men!" A roar of hooves beat on the flagstones as the knights charged through the narrow gate. The guards scattered.

Raymond galloped up the street, whipping his horse, his gray hair fluttering beneath his helmet. Arnulf saw him coming. But, determined to execute Ramiro, he ran to the wagon. "Ayyah!" he shouted at the mule, slapping its rear. The beast whinnied and heaved and the wagon moved out from under the gallows. Slowly, the rope went taut, pulling Ramiro off by the neck. And when his feet left the wagon, he swung just off the ground, strangled by the rope.

Aldebert's eyes rolled in his head. He fainted to the ground.

Raymond spotted the gallows, in plain view from the road. He saw a man swinging from a rope and charged onto the plaza, driving away Arnulf's men. Raising his sword, he slashed the rope and Ramiro collapsed in a heap.

Lothar and his men ran toward him, swords drawn. Raymond spun around to face them and, just as Lothar was about to strike, Raymond brought his sword down hard, splitting the man's skull in two. The others ran away when the rest of Raymond's men charged up. But Arnulf, feeling invincible, stood his ground.

Louis was already at Ramiro's side before Adele jumped off her horse. Ramiro lay motionless, his face puffed out, red and black. Blood dribbled from the side of his mouth. Louis worked desperately to loosen the noose. Finally, he got it free, throwing it off.

"Ramiro! Ramiro!" Adele wailed and wept. "Don't die on me now, dear God, not now!" She put her ear to his mouth, trying to detect his breath. Unsure, she beat on his chest with clenched fists. "Don't die!" she screamed, putting her eyes to heaven. "Mother Mary help me now!"

Meanwhile, Arnulf began to rant at Raymond. "Defiler of the sacred! God's curses on your head!"

Raymond jumped off his horse with the agility of a younger man. He stomped over, grabbing Arnulf by the throat, putting his bloodied sword to his neck. "You low-bred dog!" he cursed as he tightened his grip. Arnulf struggled and paled, unable to speak. "Get on your knees, you slimy bastard! And address me for my station. Or I'll cut you down where you stand!"

Arnulf's courage vanished in an instant. He groveled to his knees, cowering in terror. Raymond loosened his grip, sticking the point of his sword at Arnulf's throat, ready to ram it through.

Arnulf writhed in plea. "Please, honorable Count Raymond. In the name of God's mercy!"

"My Lord!" one of Raymond's men shouted. "Godfrey comes!"

Arnulf's fear turned to elation. He looked up at Raymond with a devilish grin.

Raymond hesitated, pulling his sword away. But on second thought, he pounded the pommel into Arnulf's head. The man slumped to the pavement. "Let's go! Everybody!"

One of the men held Ramiro's limp body in the saddle. Adele and Louis jumped on another horse. And before any of Godfrey's men could reach them, they all charged back through the Josaphat Gate, riding fast for Jericho.

LATAKIA

September 1099

The Crusader victory was complete and the exodus began. The soldiers, exhausted by war and bloodshed, went home with their bags of loot, returning to their waiting families in Europe. They left by the thousands, leaving Godfrey with only three hundred loyal knights and a thousand foot-soldiers to guard his new kingdom.

But they could not sail from Jaffa, the nearest port. Even though the Egyptian army had been defeated, their fleet still ruled the coast and no Christian vessel would dare approach. So the Crusaders rode north to Latakia, which was safely guarded by the Byzantines, Pisans, and Genoese.

Count Raymond's entire entourage of Provencals rode peaceably along the Via Maris. No one dared threaten them. And when they passed through Tripoli, they discovered the entire coast had fallen into the hands of Maronite Christians, who helped them along.

But when they arrived in Latakia, they found Bohemond besieging the place, attempting to wrestle control from the Greeks. Raymond, fed up with the likes of him and Godfrey, rallied his forces and drove him off.

Over one hundred Pisan vessels waited for them in Latakia. But Raymond refused to leave. He had vowed to die in the Holy Land and eventually he would set sail for Constantinople to see King Alexios once again, hoping to find further opportunities. The rest of them boarded ships sailing to Bari and Pisa. And over the succeeding days, Robert of Flanders arrived, along with Drugo the Red, Otto of Bremen and, trailing behind in a dark and dismal mood, was Brother Aldebert.

The large, square sails of the merchant galley unfurled in a stiff, warm wind and the oarsmen heaved to the beat of the drum. The heavy-laden ship pressed into the rolling waves.

"Over here, Papa!" shouted Adele. "This is our berth."

"How can we afford this?" Louis asked.

"Count Raymond paid for it," she said dryly. "And gave us more." She rattled the coins in her purse.

"Well, God bless the man! This is a long journey to stand on deck."

"He felt it was the least he could do. He was grateful to discover all that Ramiro had done for them." She motioned to a bench. "Put him down there."

Louis struggled to the bench, putting Ramiro down carefully, flat on his back.

Ramiro groaned as Adele knelt beside him. The swelling was almost gone from his face and the gash around his neck looked better, although many bones and cuts had yet to heal. He winced from the pain, unable to speak.

"God watches over him, lass," said Louis. "The fall was not enough to break his neck."

Adele put a hand to Ramiro's head, combing her fingers through his hair. "It's alright my love," she said softly and bent to kiss his cheek "We're going home."

Cluny

April 1100

Abbot Hugh would soon be seventy-six, but he still ruled Cluny with an iron hand. And since Pope Urban had passed on, he now worked diligently with the new pope, Paschal the Second.

The news of a Crusader victory raced like a whirlwind across Europe, giving rise to much celebration and a new-found sense of Christian power. Pope Paschal was so enthused by its success, he pushed for a new crusade, and many eager young men rushed to his call.

"I'm very sorry to hear you are leaving us, Brother Ramiro" said Hugh. "The Pope needs men like you. You could be of great help to our Holy Cause."

"Thank you, Abbot, but I have had enough. I doubt I could survive another journey. How is Brother Aldebert?"

"He appears in good health." He shook his head sadly. "But suffers in mind, I fear."

"We will all pray for him, Abbot."

"I was deeply saddened to hear that Pepin fell in battle," said Hugh looking down. "But he gave his life for God and I think we can rest assured that his soul has found a place in heaven."

Ramiro sighed heavily, making no reply.

Hugh looked up with a meek smile, showing a few remaining teeth. "While I regret you are leaving the Order, I understand your situation and I am sure God will forgive you. Needless to say, we are very grateful for all you have done for the Mother Church. I hear you purchased a plot of land not too far away."

"Yes, Abbot, thanks to the generosity of Count Raymond. And, if I have your permission, my Lord, I'm still willing to work in the library."

"Of course, I don't believe there is anyone here who could match your skill with languages."

"May God bless you, Reverend Father." He stood still, not sure how to ask his next question.

"Is that all?" asked Hugh.

"Uh, yes, just one more thing, dear Abbot."

"Well, out with it."

Ramiro looked at him hopefully. "What was in the cross?"

Hugh frowned and shook his head. "What do you mean?"

"Did it contain a message for the Patriarch?"

"There was no message, I thought I told you that."

"Then what was its purpose?"

"It was simply a means of identification for the Patriarch. Through our correspondence, we agreed that my official legate would be identified by an olive-wood cross with a bloodstone at its center."

Ramiro clenched his jaw as he stared at Hugh. "I don't understand," he said irritably. "Why not simply use a letter for that purpose?"

"Only because we believed the cross would be more durable and have a much better chance of surviving the arduous journey than would a frail piece of parchment. We presumed it would never leave your neck. What happened to it?"

Ramiro looked down to hide his rising ire. "It was lost in the fall of Jerusalem."

"Ah, well, not to worry. We accomplished our aim with God's help—and we achieved a mighty victory."

"And what was I supposed to do in Jerusalem?"

"Only what you did all along. To send me reports and coordinate our efforts with the Greeks. To aid in the Holy War."

Ramiro felt another rush of indignation, but he bit his lip to still his angry thoughts. When he raised his eyes, he could think of only one thing to say. "But Jesus called us to live in peace."

Abbot Hugh's thin smile faded in bewilderment.

Not far from the monastery, a small hamlet sat amid the verdant fields of Burgundy. All in all, there were eighteen cottages, one of which nestled in the midst of a bountiful garden of herbs and vibrant flowers.

"And did you tell him what happened to his cross?" Adele asked as she sat comfortably in a soft chair, coddling a babe in her arms.

"No," said Ramiro, gazing at the flames flickering in the fireplace. "I sincerely doubt he would have believed my story. And what does it matter, it won't change anything."

"Look at her, Ramiro, she's reaching for you and smiling."

Ramiro smiled too. He rose from his seat to kneel beside her. "She's got your eyes." He stroked the child's head.

"Your daughter still needs a name, my husband."

He pondered quietly. "Would you like to name her Mathilda after your mother? Or Isabella after mine?"

"No," she said, cuddling the babe to her breast. "I want to think of nothing but peace when I look upon her face."

He touched Adele's hand. "Then we should call her Irene."

"A Greek name," she nodded. "I like that."

He gazed at the child, stroking her soft cheek with the back of a finger. "Blessed are the peacemakers," he said quietly, "for they will be called the children of God."

Adele smiled on the babe adoringly, rocking her gently. She raised her chin and, in a soft voice, she began to sing.

EPILOGUE

In every Crusader encounter thereafter, the Latin patriarchs of the Kingdom of Jerusalem marched into battle carrying the "True Cross" before them. But eighty-seven years later, in 1187, it was seized at the Battle of Hattin by Salah Ad-Din, the Sultan of Egypt, who defeated the Christians and recaptured Jerusalem later that year. The cross was never seen again.

The major events described are of historical account. One exception may be Abul Kasim's assault on Nicomedia, placed in the spring of 1090. But the evidence suggests the Turks took the city around this time.

And while Arnulf Malecorne (Arnulf of Chocques) did find the "True Cross" in Jerusalem—its appearance roughly as described—its true origin remains a mystery.

ACKNOWLEDGMENTS

Thanks to the many researchers on whose work this story is based. In particular, Steven Runciman, Frederic Duncalf, Peter Charanis, Claude Cahen, Hilmar Krueger, Bernard Lewis, Thomas Asbridge, Adriaan Bredero, Francesco Gabrieli, Amin Maalouf, Michael Angold, John Haldon, Edward Peters and, last but not least, Anna Komnene.

And many thanks to Patricia Bentham, Debbie Bartman, and Tristan Wingham for their constructive comments on the original draft.

About the Author

Mark Blackham has a keen interest in the history of the Middle East, whether it be the Bronze Age, the Medieval Age, or the current state of affairs. He earned a graduate degree in archaeology from the University of Toronto and continues to delve deep into the past, fascinated by the parallels between contemporary events and the tales of ancient history.

LIST OF CHARACTERS
FICTIONAL

Adele	Daughter of Louis the Carpenter	Flanders
Aldebert	Ramiro's assistant monk	Cluny
Aliphas	Greek bishop at Church of Holy Sepulcher	Jerusalem
Arles	Arles of Ghent. The Executioner - one of Drugo's men	Flanders
Boris	Ramiro's Hungarian servant	Antioch
David	Rabbi held in prison compound with Ramiro	Antioch
Dawud	Silk merchant who redeemed cross after Ramiro saved his son	Maarat
Dmitri	Russian slave of Harun	Aleppo
Drugo the Red	Captain of the 500 Flemish knights	Flanders
Fawwaz	Surgeon who tended to Aldebert	Adrianople
Frederick	Captain of the Papal Guard, Rome	Italy
Fulk	One of Drugo's lieutenants	Flanders
Harun	Slave trader of Aleppo	Aleppo
Huda	Harun's wife	Aleppo
Ibrahim	Mufti in Antioch. Later the Qadi of Jerusalem	Aleppo
Jameel	Christian slave left to care for Ramiro in Edessa	Edessa
Khuda	Mamluk in Aleppo, later with Yaghi Siyan in Antioch	Aleppo
Lothar	Aide to Arnulf Malecorne in Jerusalem	Crusader
Louis	Carpenter traveling with Drugo's knights	Flanders
Madteos	Armenian jeweler of Jerusalem	Jerusalem
Mathilda	Wife of Louis the Carpenter	Flanders
Moshe	Rabbi in Jerusalem saved by Ramiro	Jerusalem
Otto	Otto of Bremen. One of Drugo's lieutenants	Flanders
Ozan	Turk scribe who traveled to Isfahan with Ramiro	Nikea
Pakrad	Armenian priest, brother of Madteos the Jeweler	Jerusalem
Pepin	Boy (groom) sent off with Ramiro and Aldebert	Cluny
Qubad	Secretary to Nizam al-Mulk in Isfahan	Iran
Ramiro	Benedictine monk of Cluny	Cluny
Raul	Carpenter and brooch thief at Monferrato, Italy	Monferrato
Rolf	Assassin sent with Wiker	Italy
Salim	A physician in Maarat	Maarat
Sebuk	Brother of Hasan of Cappadocia	Nikea
Toros	Armenian slave of Harun. Later with Khuda	Aleppo
Wiker	Assassin sent after Ramiro by Giberto in Rome	Italy
Yaqut	Highwayman who stole cross in Jisr Ash-Shughur	Maarat

LIST OF CHARACTERS
HISTORICAL

Abul Kasim	Emir of Nikea after death of Sulayman	Nikea
Adhemar	Bishop and Papal Legate of Crusade	Crusader
Al-Afdal	Vizier (ruler) of Egypt	Egypt
Alexios	Emperor of Byzantium	Byzantium
Al-Khanes	Atabek (advisor) and general of Kilich at Nikea	Nikea
Anna	Mother of Alexios. Royal dowager	Byzantium
Arnulf	Arnulf of Chocques. Chaplain to the Normans. Later, the Latin Patriarch of Jerusalem	Crusader
Bohemond	A leader of first Crusade. Son of Robert Guiscard	Crusader
Bolkas	Half-brother of Abul Kasim	Nikea
Borsa	Ruler of Apulia, Italy. Son of Robert Guiscard	Italy
Buzan	Emir of Edessa and Turk general	Turk Empire
Chaka	Turk pirate at Smyrna	Byzantium
Danishmends	Turkoman dynasty in northern Anatolia	Anatolia
Gerard	Monk in Jerusalem and founder of Knights Hospitaler	Jerusalem
Ghazi	Leader of the Danishmends	Anatolia
Godfrey	Of Bouillon. Norman leader of first Crusade	Crusader
Giberto	Archbishop installed as anti-pope by King Henry of Germany. Pope Clement	Italy
Gregory	Pope before Urban. A reformer	Italy
Hasan	Son of Bolkas. Escorted Ramiro to Isfahan	Nikea
Hashashin	Assassins of the Ismaili	Turk Empire
Hugh	The abbot at Cluny monastery	Cluny
Humberto	Norman nephew of Robert Guiscard. Byzantine mercenary, Adrianople, Nikea	Byzantium
Iftikhar	Egyptian emir of Jerusalem	Jerusalem
Isaak	Brother of Alexios	Byzantium
John Doukas	Governor of Dyrrachium. Alexios' brother-in-law	Byzantium
John the Oxite	Greek patriarch of Antioch	Antioch
Kerboga	Ruler of Mosul. Led final Turk assault on Antioch	Turk Empire
Kilich	Son of Sulayman. Jailed in Isfahan. Returns to Nikea	Turk Empire
Malik Shah	Sultan of Seljuk Turk Empire	Turk Empire
Manuel	Byzantine commander and envoy to Melfi, Italy	Byzantium
Nizam al-Mulk	Vizier to the Turk sultan, Malik Shah	Turk Empire
Peter Bartholomew	Young mystic who found Holy Lance at Antioch. Died by fiery ordeal	Crusader
Peter the Hermit	A leader of the Peasant's Crusade	Crusader
Raymond	Leader of first Crusade. Older man with one eye	Crusader

LIST OF CHARACTERS
HISTORICAL

Robert of Flanders	A leader of Crusade. Count of Flanders. His father (Robert) send the 500 knights to Byzantium	Crusader
Robert Guiscard	Leader of Normans in Apulia, Italy. Invaded Byzantium in 1085. Died 1085	Italy
Sulayman	Ruled Roman lands in Anatolia before Abul Kasim	Nikea
Symeon	Patriarch of Jerusalem	Jerusalem
Tancred	Leader of Crusade, nephew of Bohemond	Crusader
Taticius	Byzantine general who commanded the Kelts	Byzantium
Tatran	Byzantine lieutenant. Ramiro's Turkish tutor	Byzantium
Tutush	Prince of Syria. Half-brother of Malik Shah	Turk Empire
Urban	Pope. Formerly, Odo of Lagery	Italy
Walter the Penniless	A leader of the Peasant's Crusade	Crusader
Yaghi Siyan	Turk emir of Antioch	Antioch

PLACE NAMES

Past Name	Current Name	Location
Acre	'Akko or 'Akka	Israel
Adrianople	Edirne	Turkey
Aleppo	Halab	Syria
Anatolia	Turkey	
Ankara	Ankara	Turkey
Antep	Gaziantep	Turkey
Antioch	Antakya	Turkey
Antioch Lake	Lake Amik	Turkey
Apulia region	Puglia	Italy
Ascalon	Ashkelon, Asqalan	Israel
Ash-Shughur	Jisr Ash-Shughur	Syria
Anatolia	Turkey	
Askanius Lake	Lake Izmit	Turkey
Astacus Gulf	Gulf of Izmit	Turkey
Axios River	Vardar	Macedonia
Beirut	Bayrūt	Lebanon
Bethlehem	Bayt Lahm	Palestine
Bosporus	Istanbul Boghazi	Turkey
Byblos	Jubayl	Lebanon
Cairo	al-Qāhira	Egypt
Cilicia	Mersin province	Turkey
Civetot	Gemlik	Turkey
Constantinople	Istanbul	Turkey
Danube River	Ister	
Daskerah	Arak	Iran
Dog River	Nahr al-Kalb	Lebanon
Dorylaeum	Eskişehir	Turkey
Dyrrachium	Durres	Albania
Edessa	Sanliurfa	Turkey
Filastin	District of Hashefela	Israel
Gallipoli	Gelibolu	Turkey
Haifa	Hefa, Hayfa	Israel
Hebron	Al Khalīl or Hebron	Palestine
Hellespont	Çanakkale Boğazı (Dardanelles)	Turkey

PLACE NAMES

Past Name	Current Name	Location
Heraclea	Eregli	Turkey
Hierapolis	Manbij	Syria
Homs	Hims	Syria
Iconium	Konya	Turkey
Isfahan	Esfahan	Iran
Jaffa	Tel Aviv	Israel
Jerusalem	Al Quds Ash Sharif or Yerushalayim	
Kayseri	Caesarea	Turkey
Latakia	Al Ladhiqiyah	Syria
Ludd	Lod, Lydda	Israel
Maarat	Ma'arrat An Nu'man	Syria
Malatya	Melitene	Turkey
Mosul	al-Maw☐il☐	Syria
Nicomedia	Izmit	Turkey
Nikea	Iznik	Turkey
Orontes	'Asi River	Syria
Propontis	Sea of Marmara	Turkey
Ramla	Ramlah	Israel
Rus	Russia	
Smyrna	Izmir	Turkey
St. Simeon	Süveydiye	Turkey
Sung	China	
Tarsus	Tarsus	Turkey
Thessalonica	Thessaloniki	Greece
Tripoli	Tarābulus	Lebanon
Thrace	Rumelia	Turkey
Tyre	Sūr	Lebanon
Xerigordos	Unidentified, but near Nikea	Turkey

GLOSSARY

Adhan	The Islamic call to prayer
Askari	Royal or elite guard
Atabek	Military and political advisor
Beyfendi	Supreme lord or master (Turkish)
Dhimmi	Non-Muslim citizen
Dinar	Gold coin about the size of a silver dollar
Diwan	Fiefdom with per cent of revenue
Efendi	Sir, mister, or lord (Turkish)
Emir	Military commander
Farsakh	Parsang or farsang = 6.2 km or 4.8 miles
Hadiths	Oral traditions of Islam
Hashashin	Assassins, hash-eaters
Hour, ninth	About 3 pm
Hour, third	About 9 am
Kafir	Unbeliever, infidel (derogatory)
Kafiya	Traditional headscarf for men
Kuffar	Plural of kafir
Mamluk	Slave-warrior, often of Turkoman descent
Mufti	Muslim lawyer
Nativity Feast	Christmas
Qadi	Judge, often the ruler of a city
Roman mile	1.1 English miles (1.8 km)
Sadah	Plural of sayyid
Sayyid	Sir or mister (Arabic)
Sayyidah	Feminine form of sayyid
Sharia	Laws of Islam
Souk	Marketplace
Synod	Meeting of bishops to decide issues
Talent	Unit of weight, about 26 kg or 57 lb
Vizier	The top bureaucrat, ruler's right-hand man